MEOW-ZA

HERE'S WHAT PEOPLE AR
SAYING ABOUT MAX MEOW!

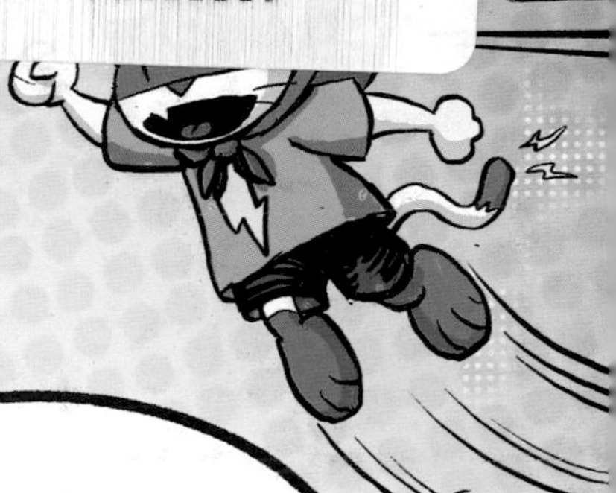

"Max Meow is a riot!"

—Jimmy Gownley, creator of the Amelia Rules! series

"I liked the part where he ate the giant meatball."

—Kevin, 1st grade

"Celebrates friendship, fun, and the fantastic, wrapped up in a ball of adventure readers of any age will pounce on!"

—Jamar Nicholas, creator of the Leon series

"My favorite character was Mindy because she kind of guides Max Meow."

—Santiago, 6th grade

"I give it 5★."

—Cole, 5th grade

"Super laughs on every page!"

—Norm Feuti, creator of the Hello, Hedgehog! series

"A super-fun romp for kids of all ages."

—Meryl Jaffe, PhD, author of *Raising a Reader! How Comics & Graphic Novels Can Help Your Kids Love to Read!*

"It's funny and amazing so you should read the book."

—Sorel, 6th grade

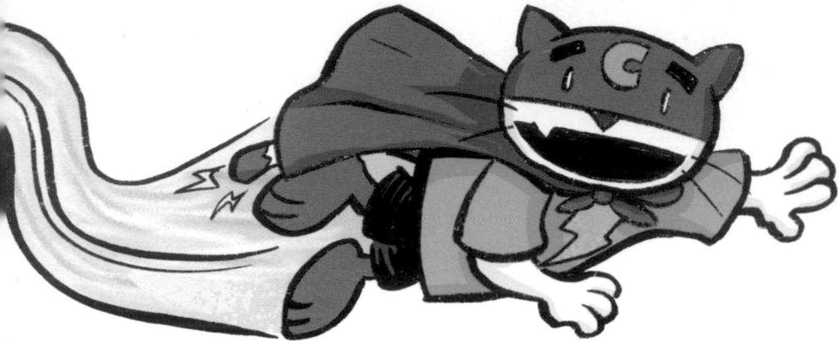

READ ALL OF MAX MEOW'S ADVENTURES!

Max Meow: Cat Crusader

Max Meow: Donuts and Danger

Max Meow: Pugs from Planet X

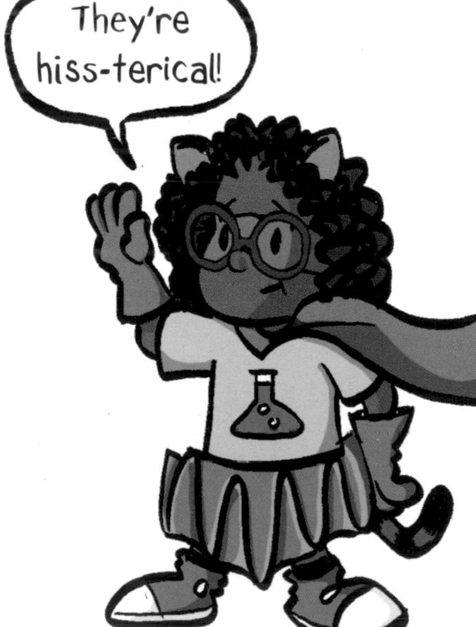
They're hiss-terical!

MAX MEOW
PUGS FROM PLANET X

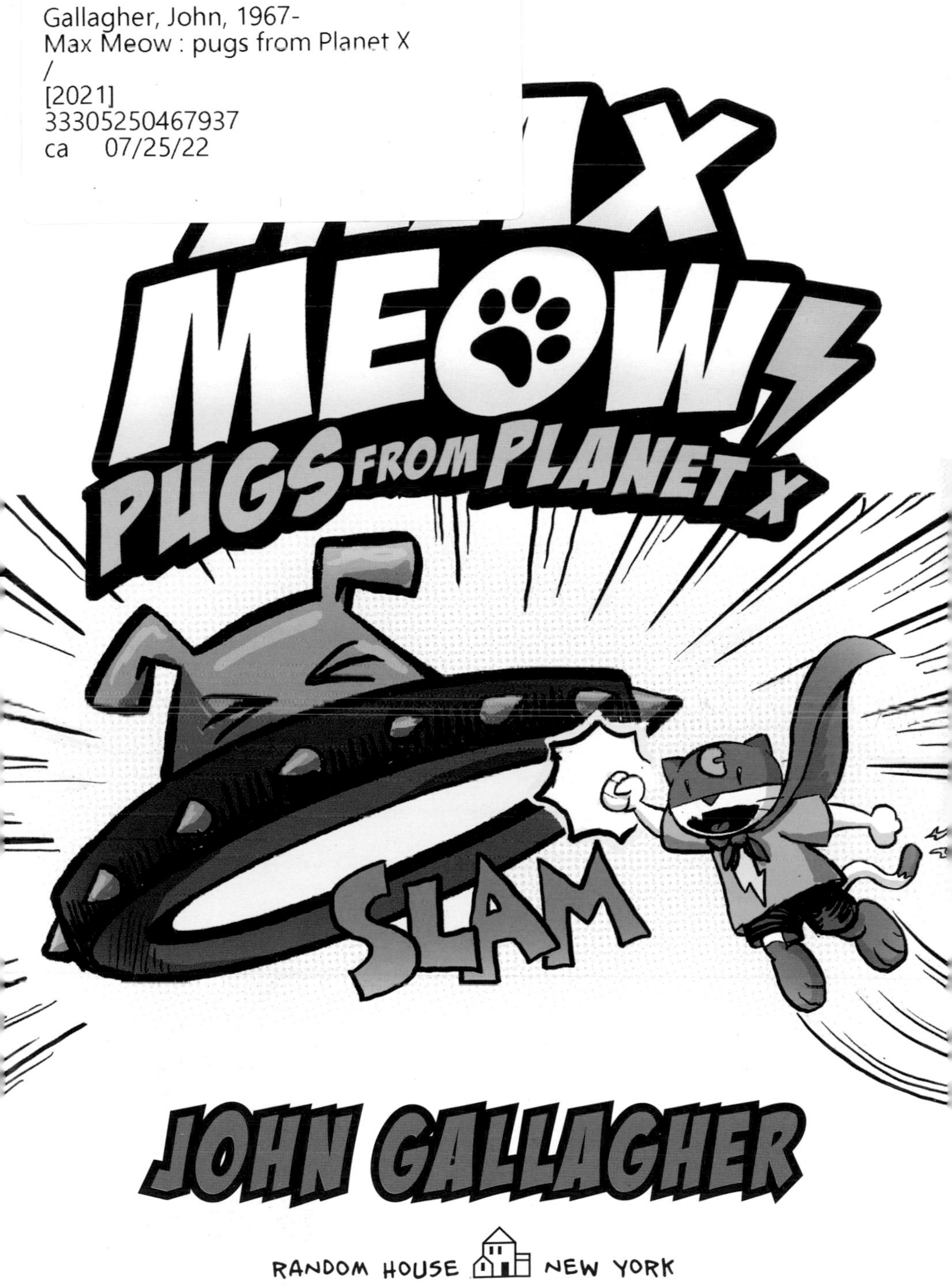
SLAM

JOHN GALLAGHER

RANDOM HOUSE NEW YORK

Copyright © 2021 by John Gallagher

All rights reserved. Published in the United States by Random House Children's Books,
a division of Penguin Random House LLC, New York.

Random House and the colophon are registered trademarks
of Penguin Random House LLC.

RH Graphic with the book design is a trademark of Penguin Random House LLC.

Visit us on the Web! rhcbooks.com

Educators and librarians, for a variety of teaching tools,
visit us at RHTeachersLibrarians.com

Library of Congress Cataloging-in-Publication Data
Names: Gallagher, John, author, illustrator.
Title: Max Meow: Pugs from Planet X / written and drawn by John Gallagher.
Other titles: Pugs from Planet X
Description: First edition. | New York: Random House Children's Books, [2021] | Series: Max Meow; #3
Summary: "Pugs from outer space want to steal the meatball that gave Max Meow his
superpowers, and it's up to Max and Mindy to stop them" —Provided by publisher.
Identifiers: LCCN 2020034909 | ISBN 978-0-593-12111-5 (hardcover) |
ISBN 978-0-593-12112-2 (lib. bdg.) | ISBN 978-0-593-12113-9 (ebook)
Subjects: LCSH: Graphic novels. | CYAC: Graphic novels. | Cats—Fiction. |
Superheroes—Fiction. | Pug—Fiction. | Dogs—Fiction. | Ability—Fiction.
Classification: LCC PZ7.7.G325 Mm 2021 | DDC 741.5/973—dc23

Book design by John Gallagher and April Ward

MANUFACTURED IN CHINA
10 9 8 7 6 5 4 3
First Edition

To my students,
past and present
(and future, too!)—
you have taught
me so much.

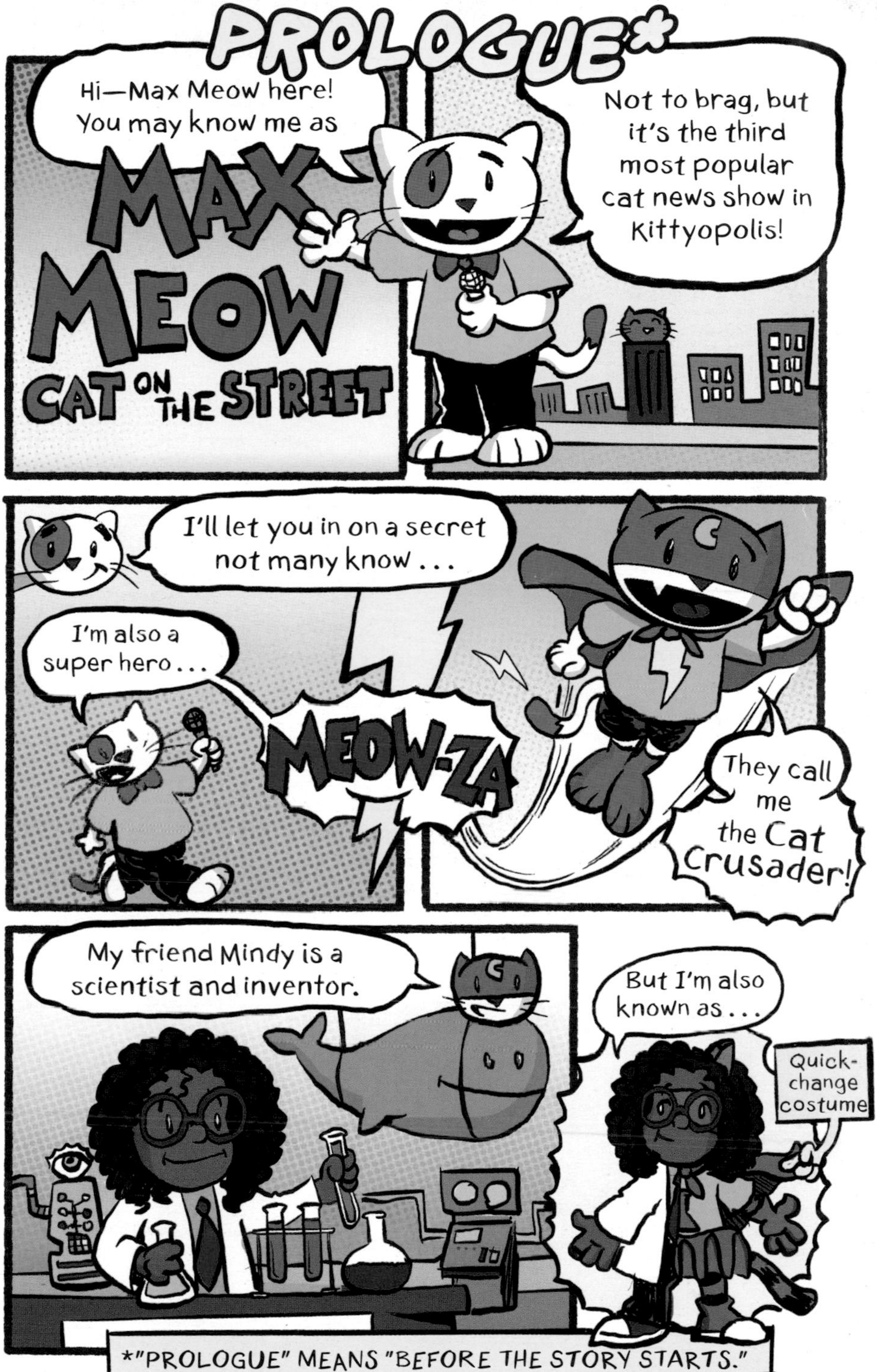
PROLOGUE*
Hi—Max Meow here! You may know me as
MAX MEOW CAT ON THE STREET
Not to brag, but it's the third most popular cat news show in Kittyopolis!
I'll let you in on a secret not many know . . .
I'm also a super hero . . .
MEOW-ZA
They call me the Cat Crusader!
My friend Mindy is a scientist and inventor.
But I'm also known as . . .
Quick-change costume
*"PROLOGUE" MEANS "BEFORE THE STORY STARTS."

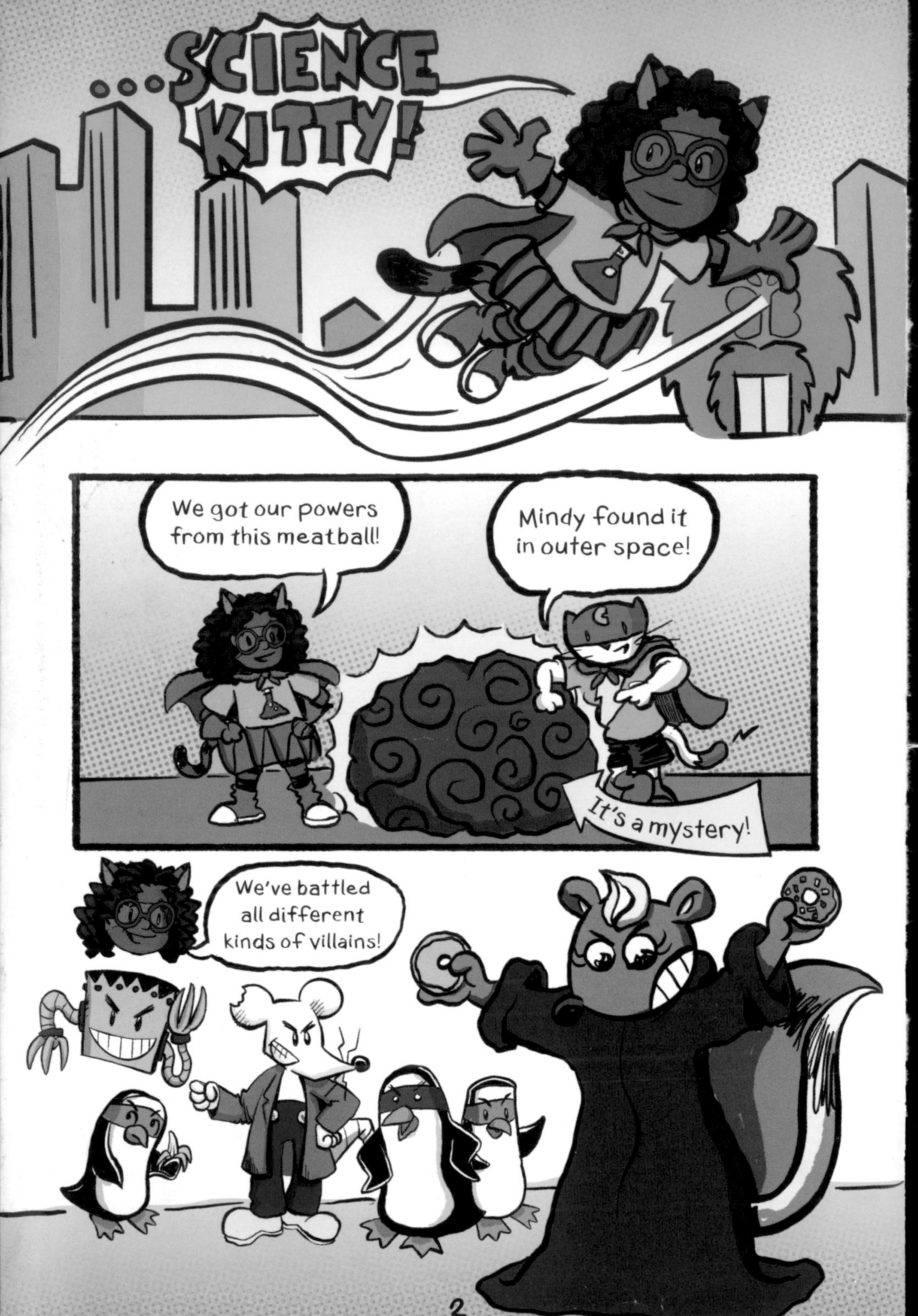
...SCIENCE KITTY!
We got our powers from this meatball!
Mindy found it in outer space!
It's a mystery!
We've battled all different kinds of villains!

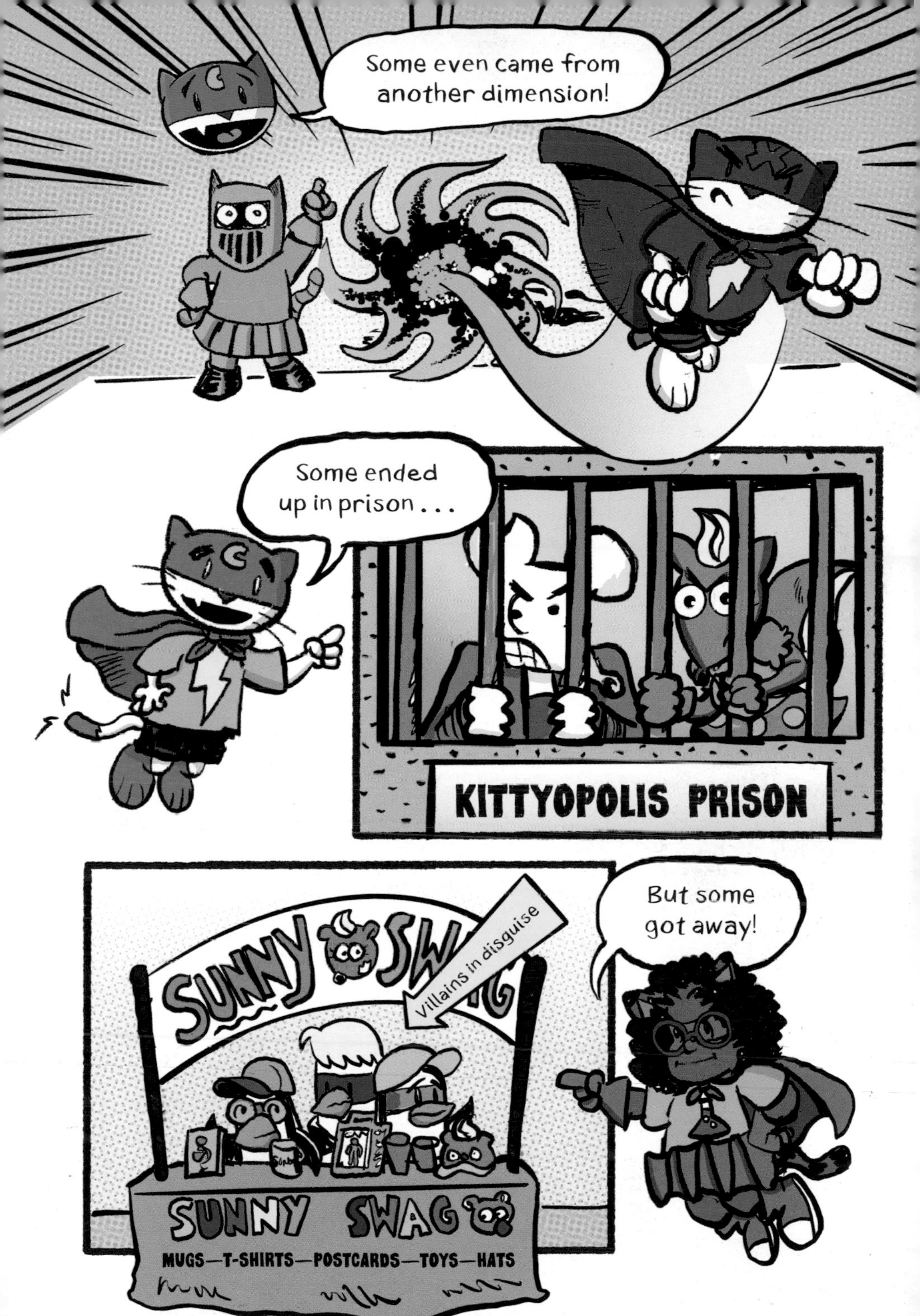
Some even came from another dimension!
Some ended up in prison . . .
KITTYOPOLIS PRISON
SUNNY SWAG
Villains in disguise
SUNNY SWAG
MUGS—T-SHIRTS—POSTCARDS—TOYS—HATS
But some got away!

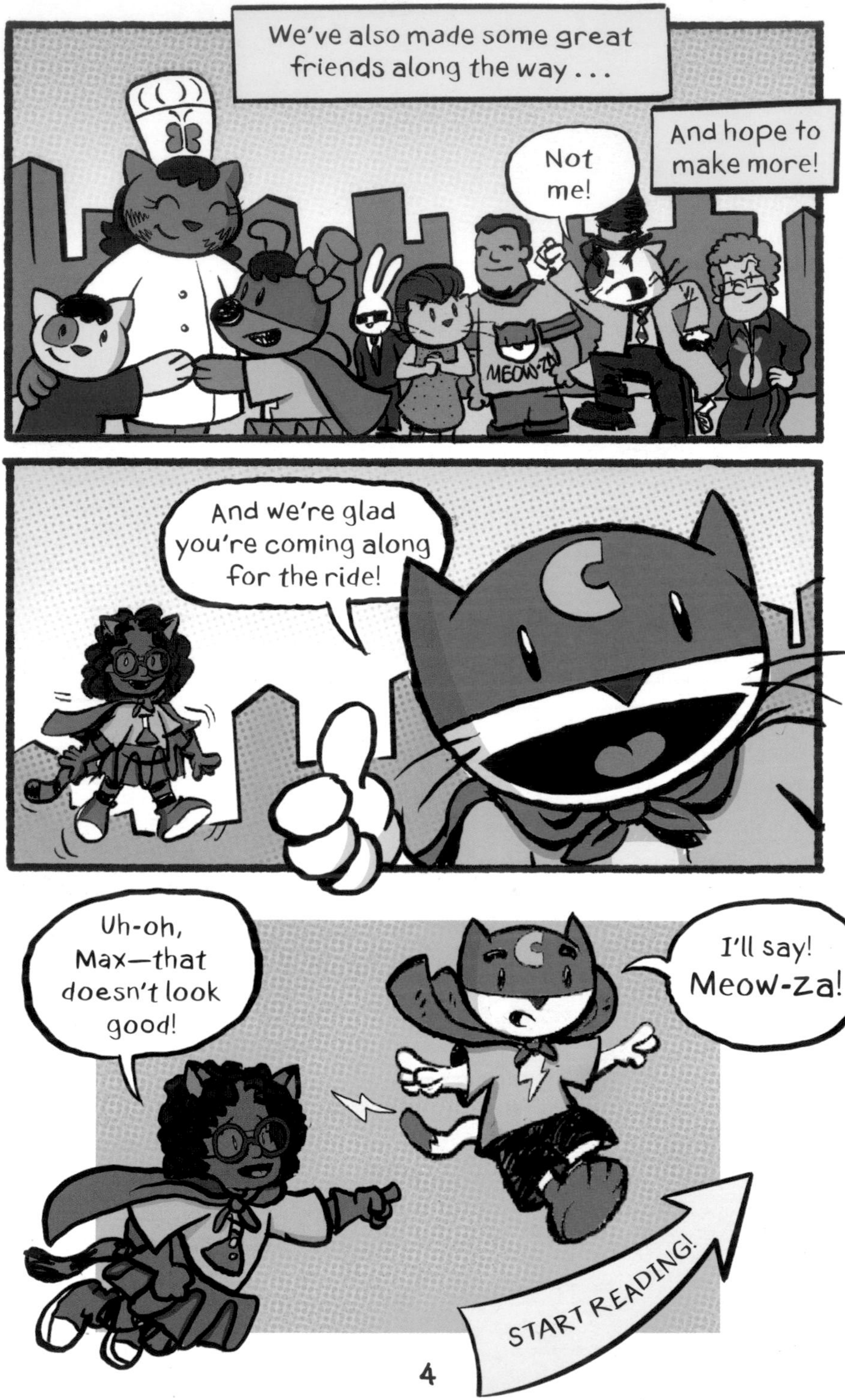
We've also made some great friends along the way . . .
Not me!
And hope to make more!
MEOW-ZA
And we're glad you're coming along for the ride!
Uh-oh, Max—that doesn't look good!
I'll say! Meow-za!
START READING!

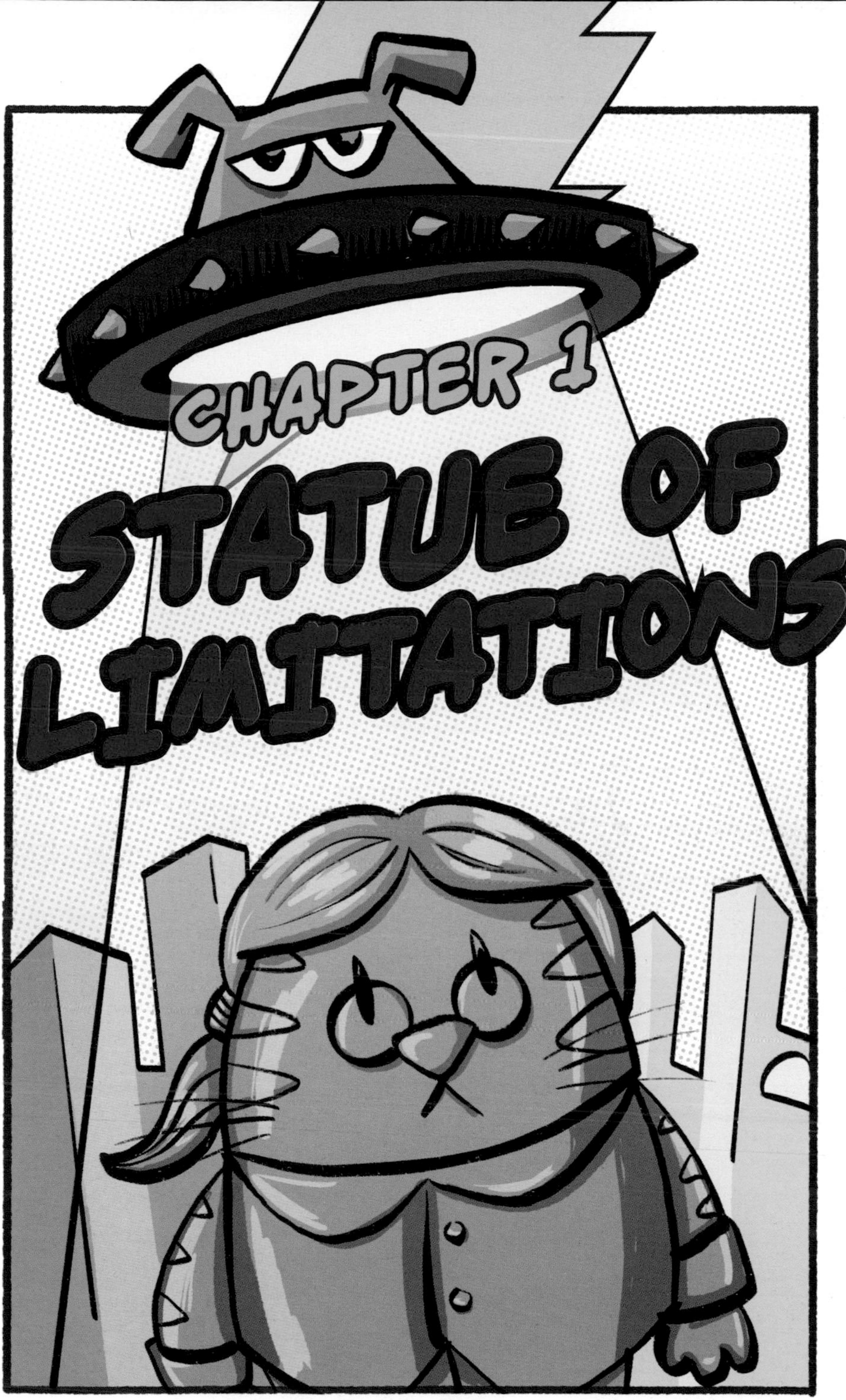
CHAPTER 1
STATUE OF LIMITATIONS

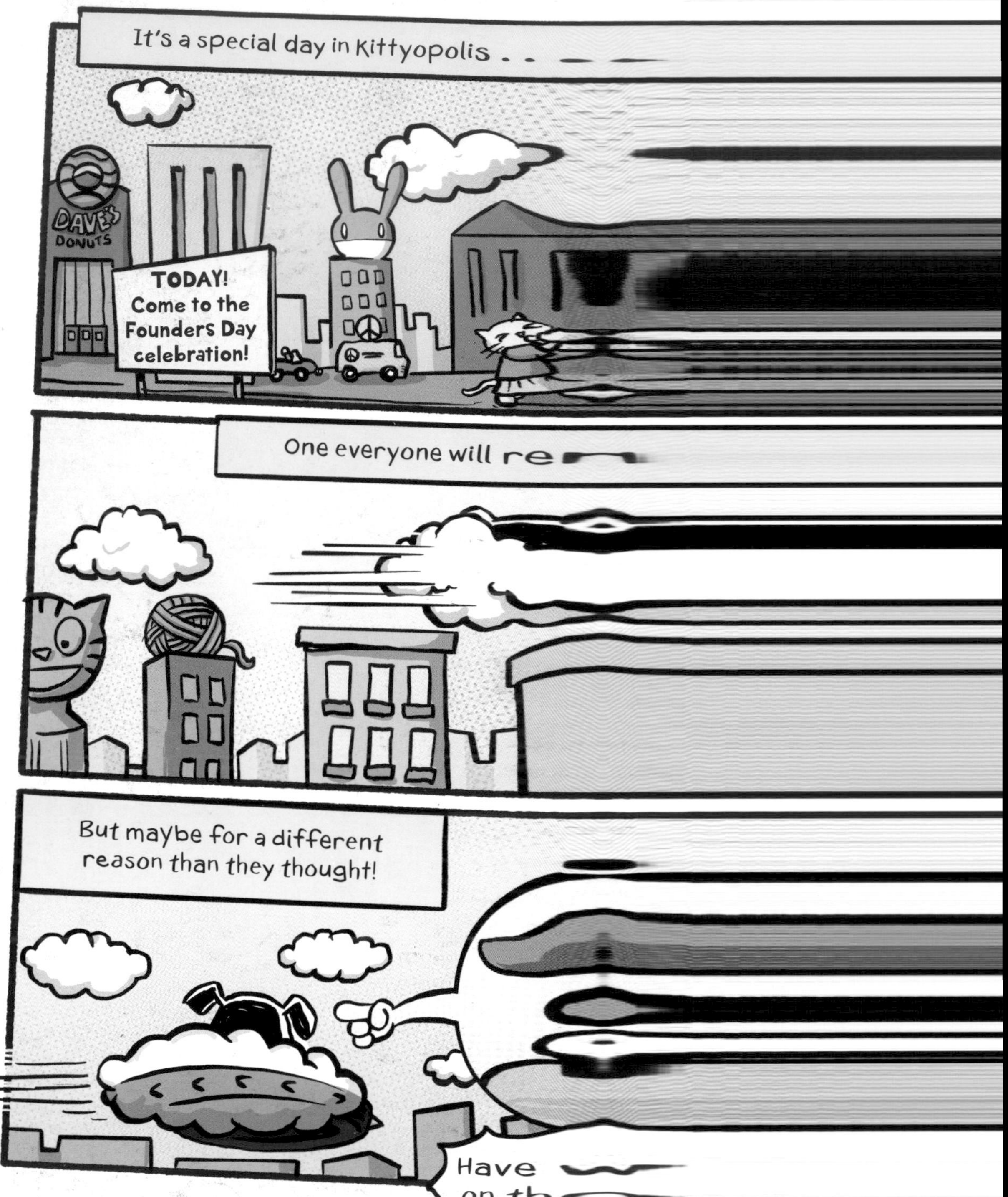
It's a special day in Kittyopolis . . .
DAVE'S DONUTS
TODAY! Come to the Founders Day celebration!
One everyone will re
But maybe for a different reason than they thought!
Have
on th

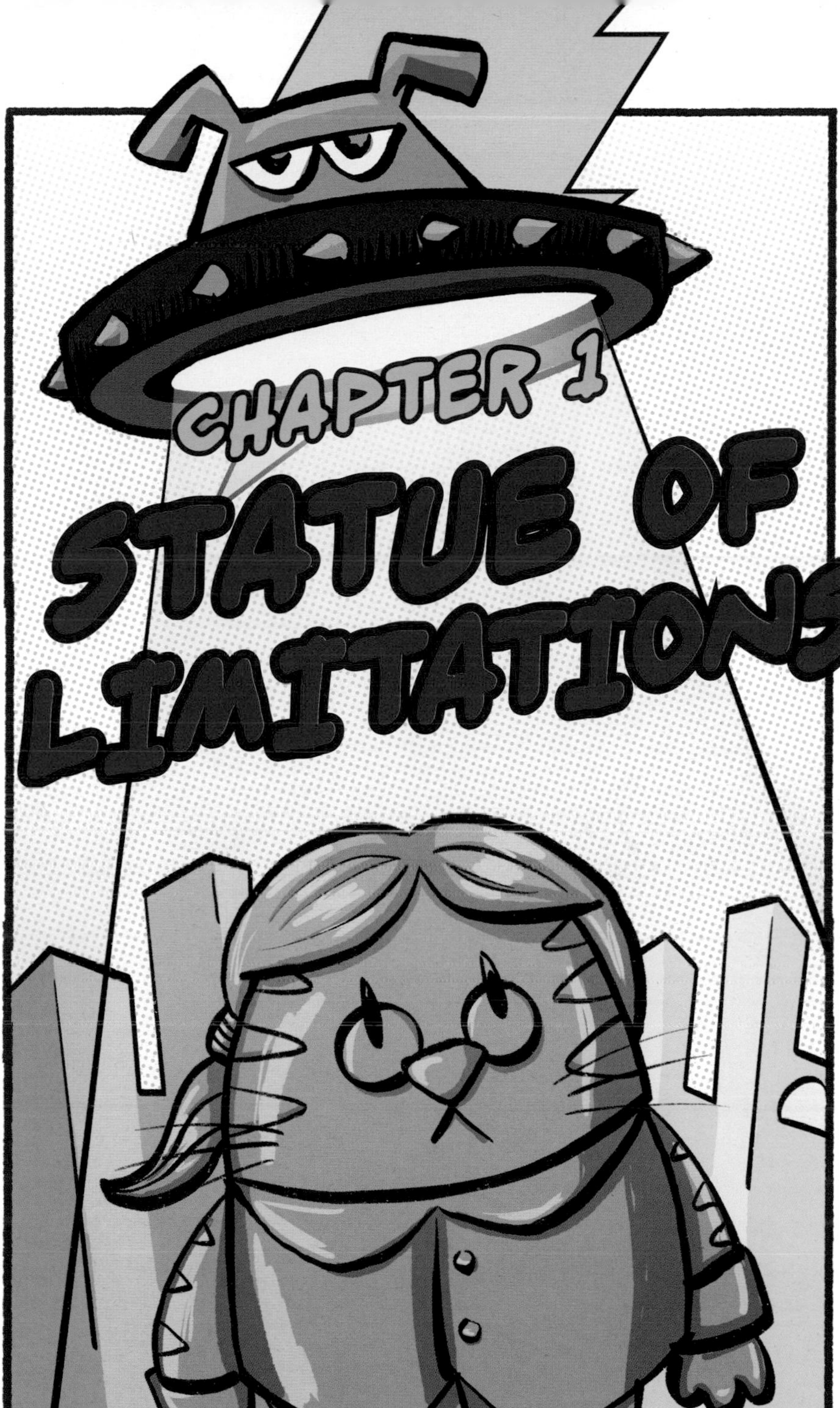
CHAPTER 1
STATUE OF LIMITATIONS

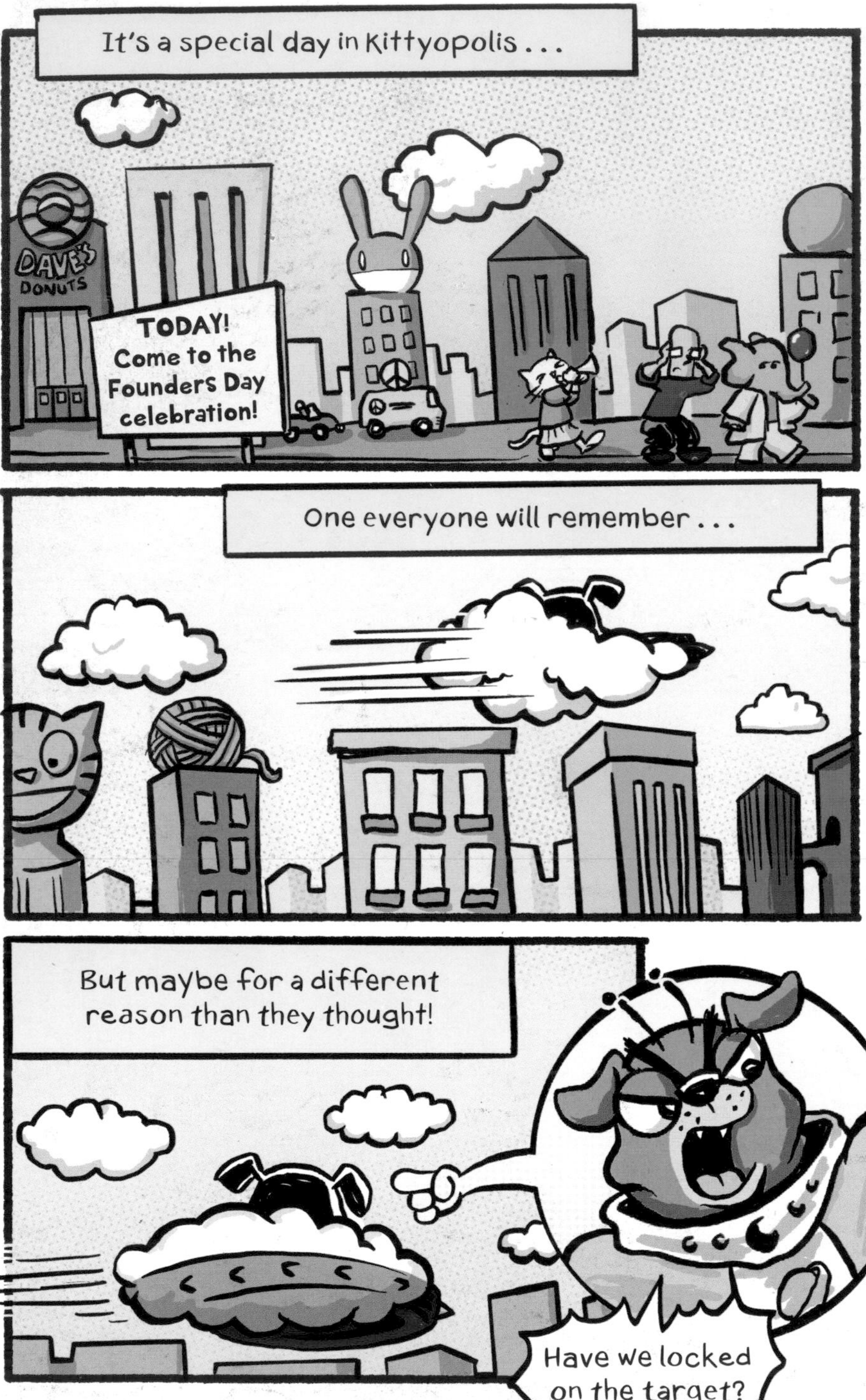
It's a special day in Kittyopolis . . .
DAVE'S DONUTS
TODAY! Come to the Founders Day celebration!
One everyone will remember . . .
But maybe for a different reason than they thought!
Have we locked on the target?

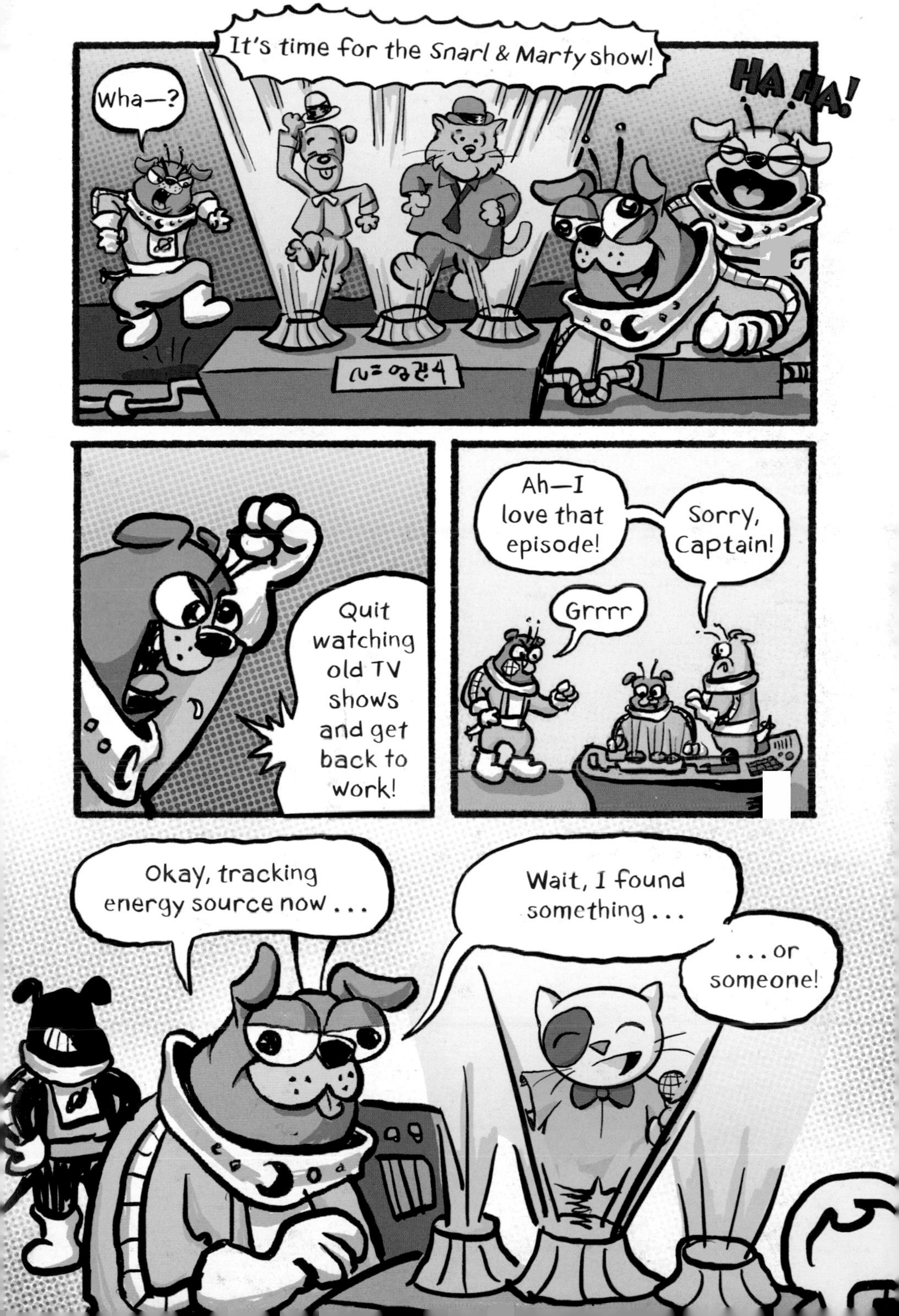

It's time for the *Snarl & Marty* show!
Wha—?
HA HA!
Quit watching old TV shows and get back to work!
Ah—I love that episode!
Sorry, Captain!
Grrrr
Okay, tracking energy source now . . .
Wait, I found something . . .
. . . or someone!

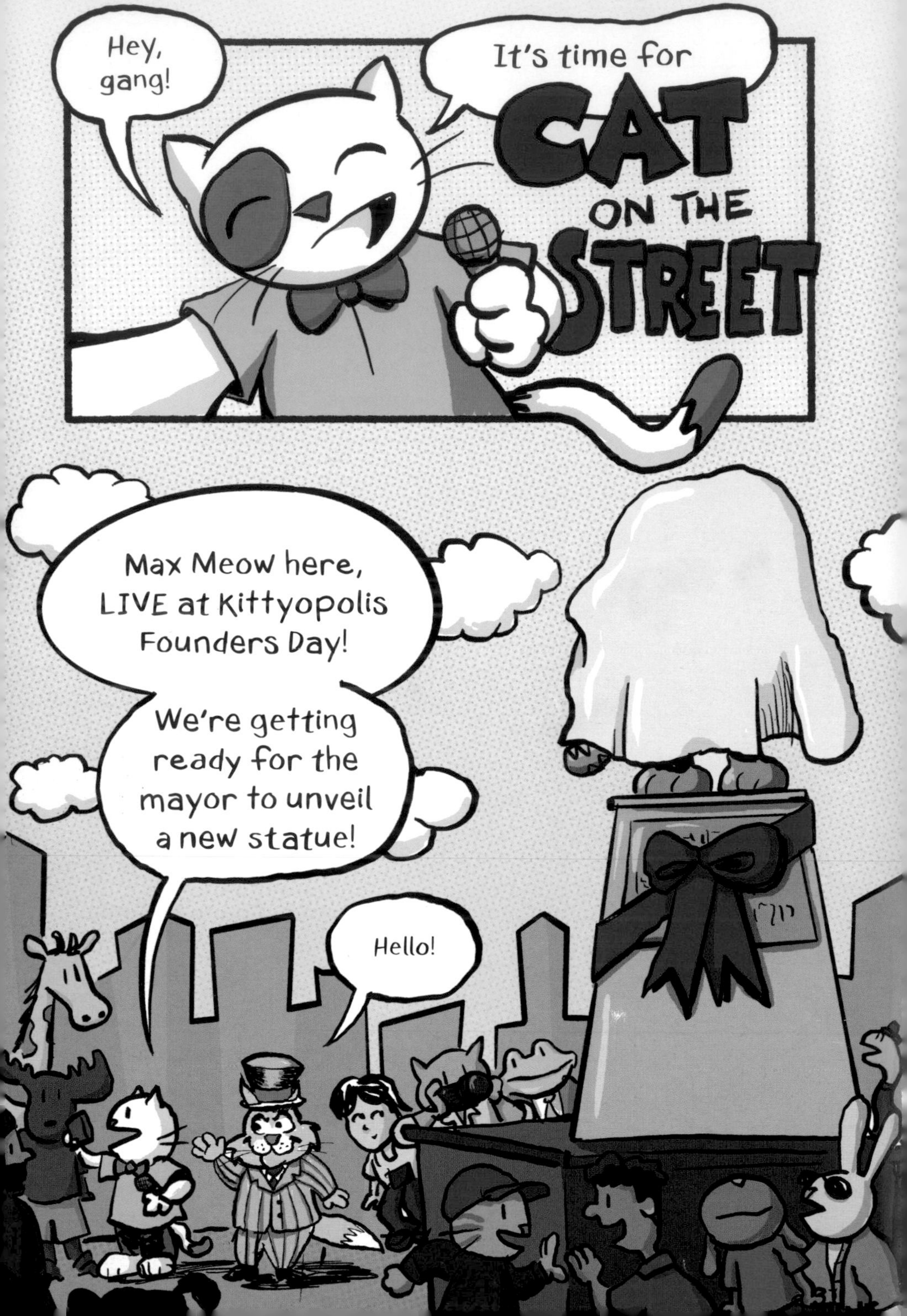
Hey, gang!
It's time for
CAT ON THE STREET
Max Meow here, LIVE at Kittyopolis Founders Day!
We're getting ready for the mayor to unveil a new statue!
Hello!

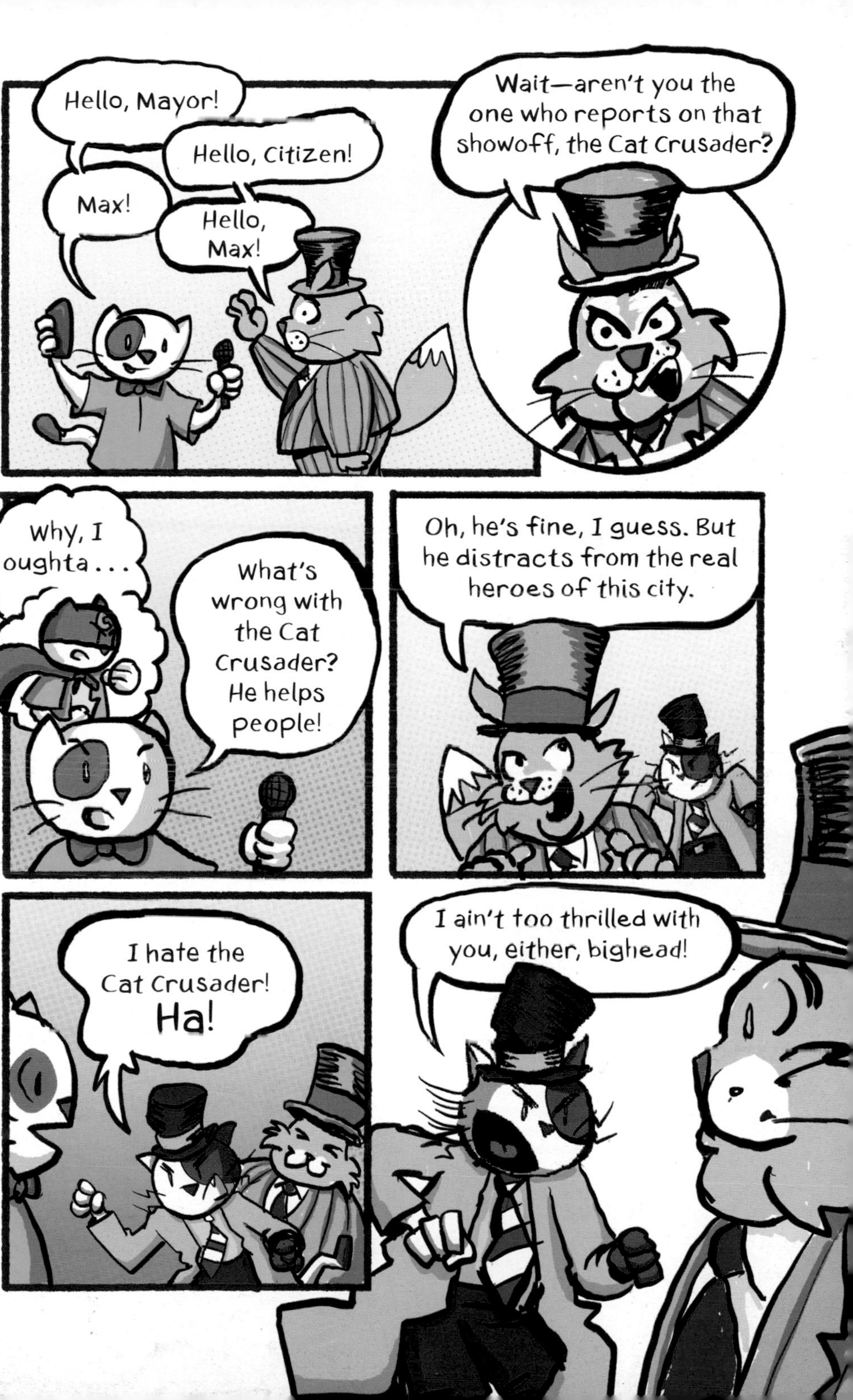
Hello, Mayor!
Hello, Citizen!
Max!
Hello, Max!
Wait—aren't you the one who reports on that showoff, the Cat Crusader?
Why, I oughta . . .
What's wrong with the Cat Crusader? He helps people!
Oh, he's fine, I guess. But he distracts from the real heroes of this city.
I hate the Cat Crusader! Ha!
I ain't too thrilled with you, either, bighead!

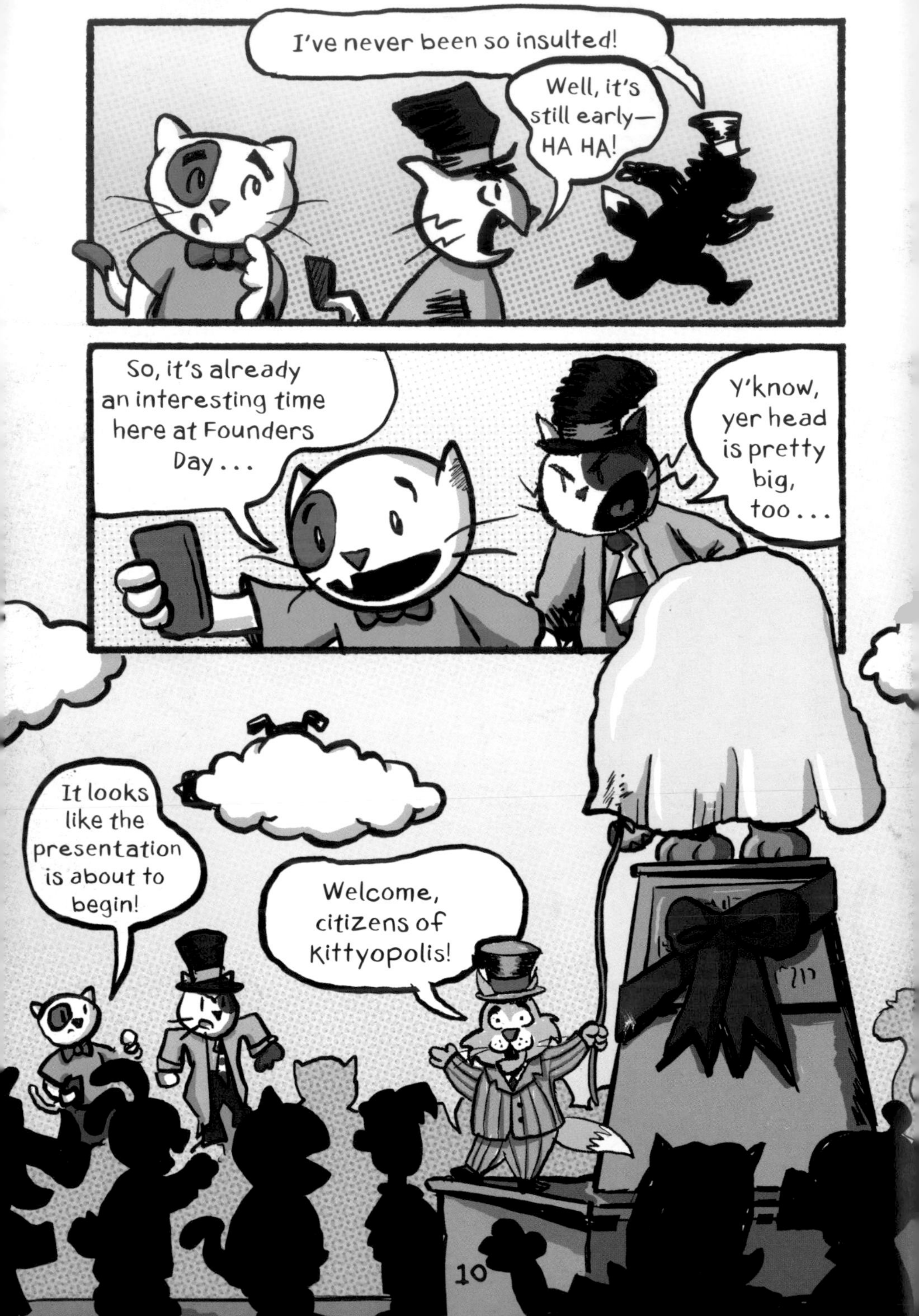
I've never been so insulted!
Well, it's still early— HA HA!
So, it's already an interesting time here at Founders Day . . .
Y'know, yer head is pretty big, too . . .
It looks like the presentation is about to begin!
Welcome, citizens of Kittyopolis!

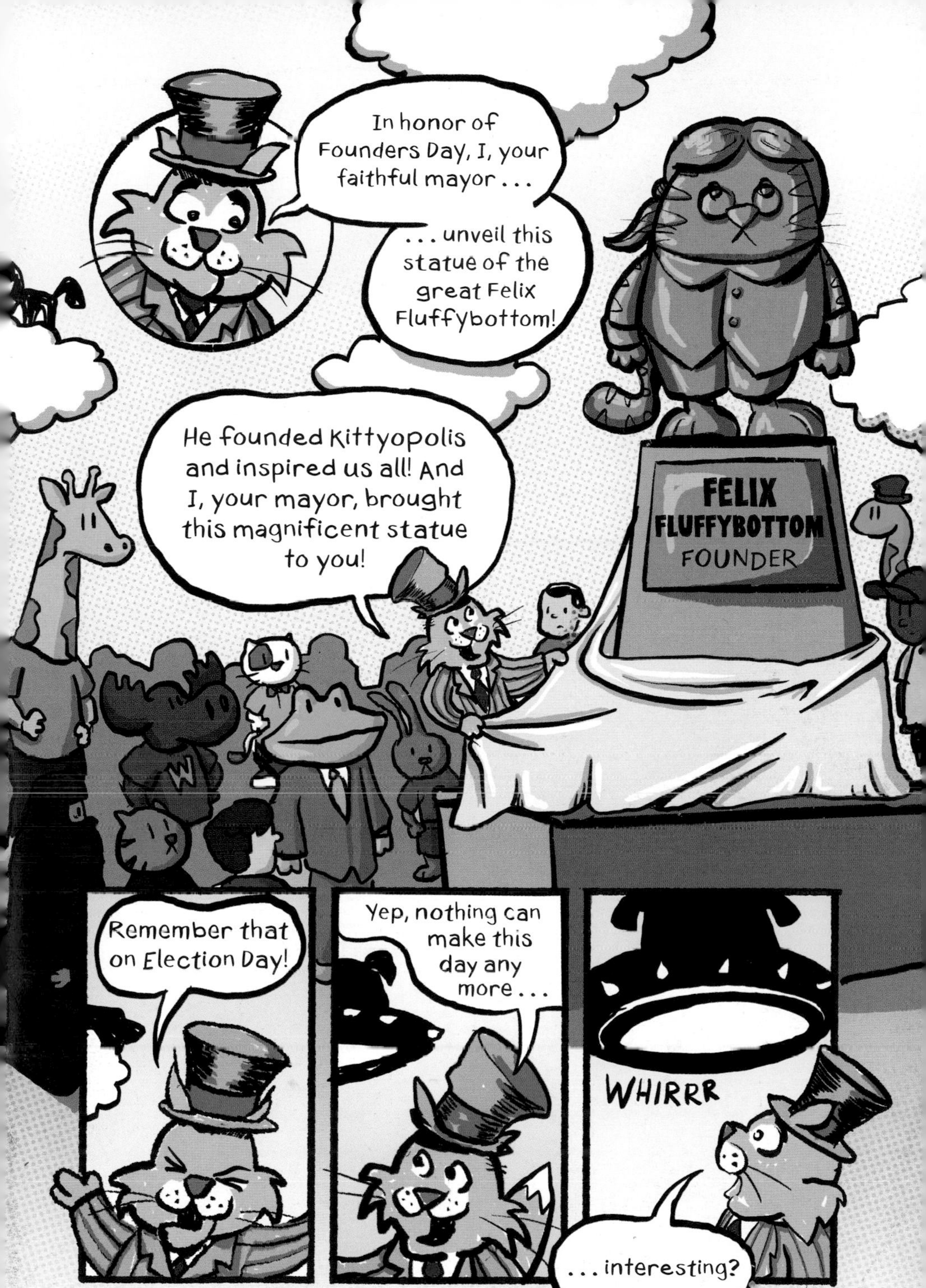
In honor of Founders Day, I, your faithful mayor . . .
. . . unveil this statue of the great Felix Fluffybottom!
He founded Kittyopolis and inspired us all! And I, your mayor, brought this magnificent statue to you!
FELIX FLUFFYBOTTOM FOUNDER
Remember that on Election Day!
Yep, nothing can make this day any more . . .
WHIRRR
. . . interesting?

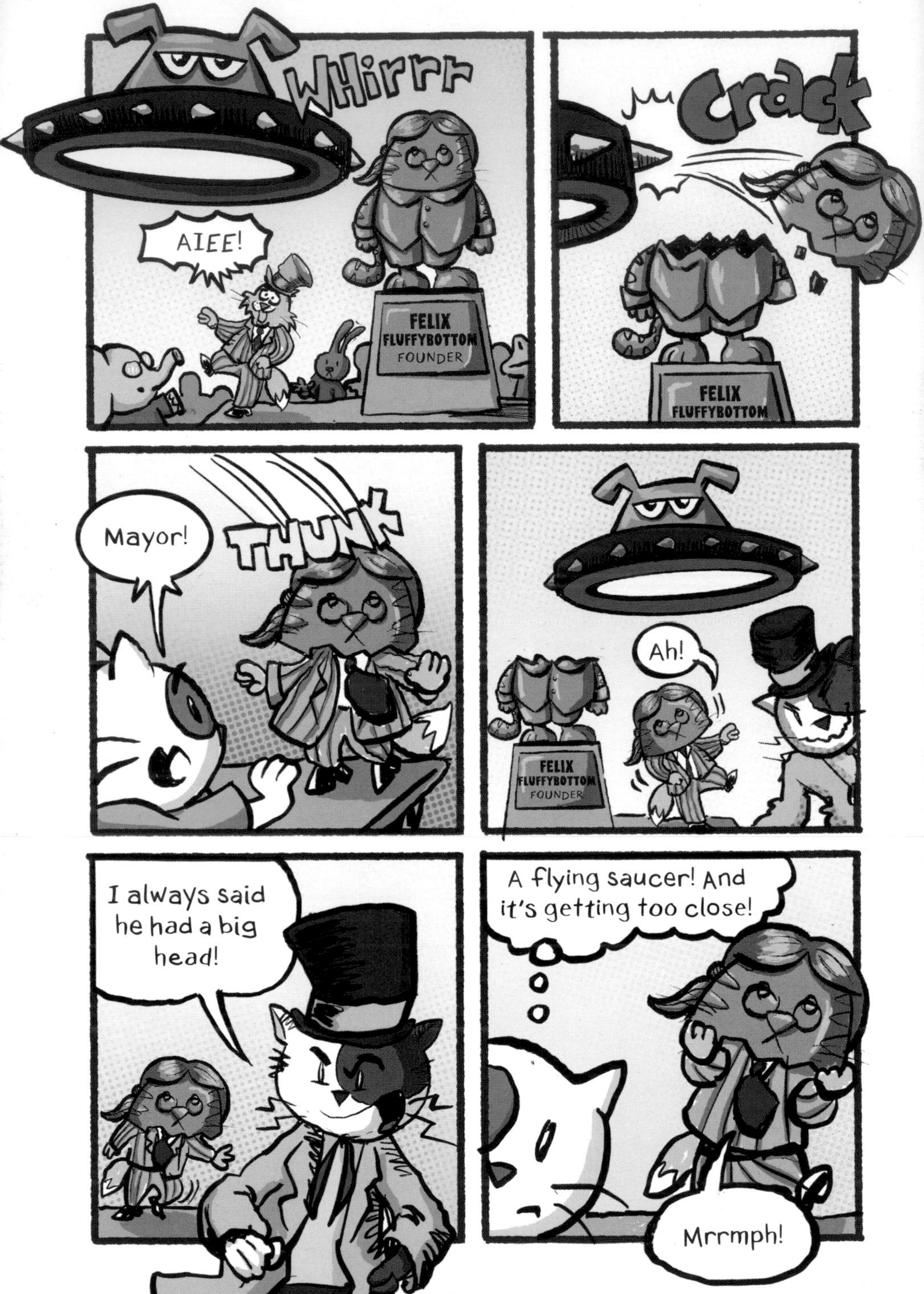
WHirrr
AIEE!
FELIX FLUFFYBOTTOM FOUNDER
Crack
FELIX FLUFFYBOTTOM
Mayor!
THUNK
Ah!
FELIX FLUFFYBOTTOM FOUNDER
I always said he had a big head!
A flying saucer! And it's getting too close!
Mrrmph!

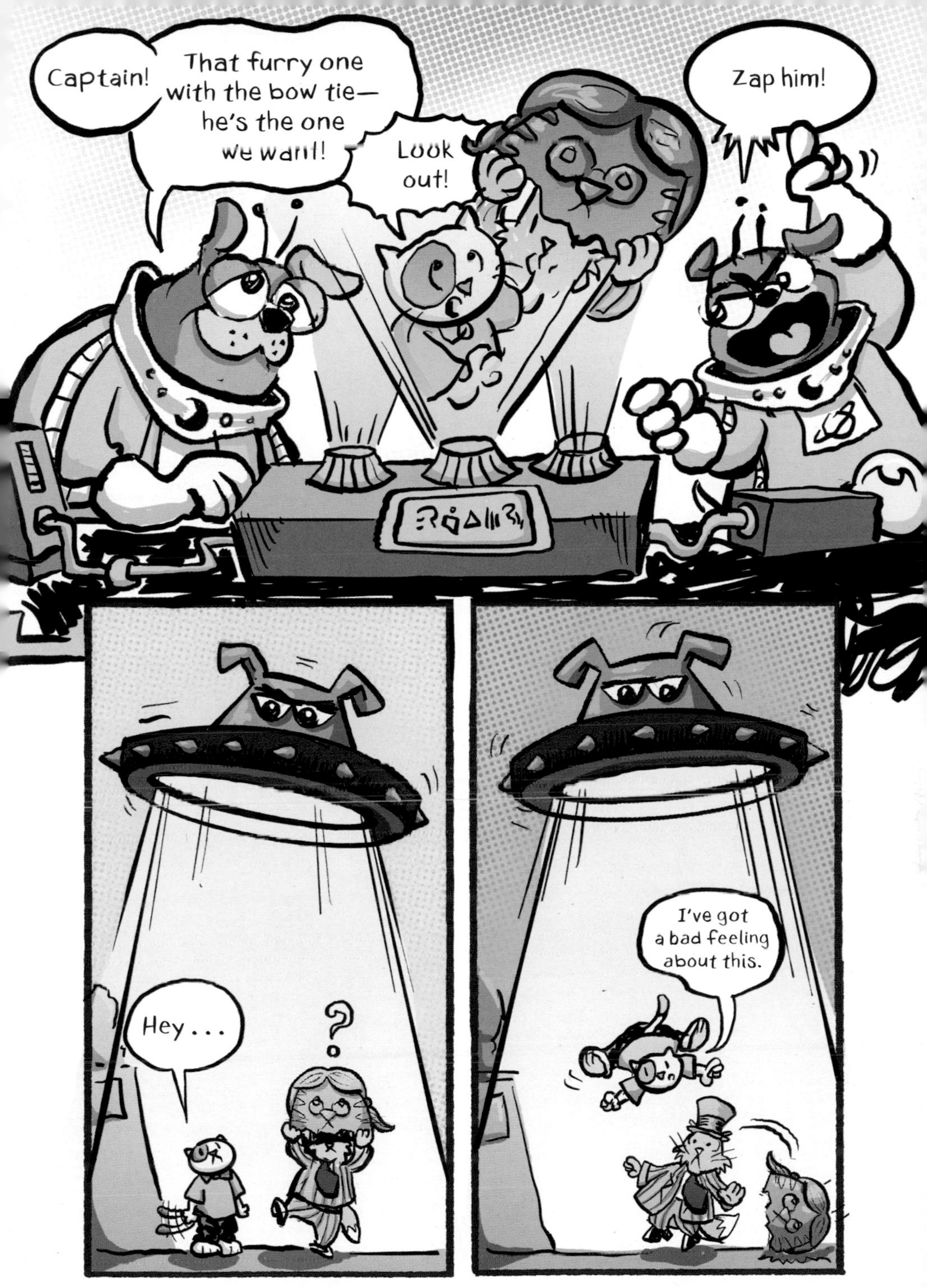

Captain!
That furry one with the bow tie— he's the one we want!
Look out!
Zap him!
Hey . . .
?
I've got a bad feeling about this.

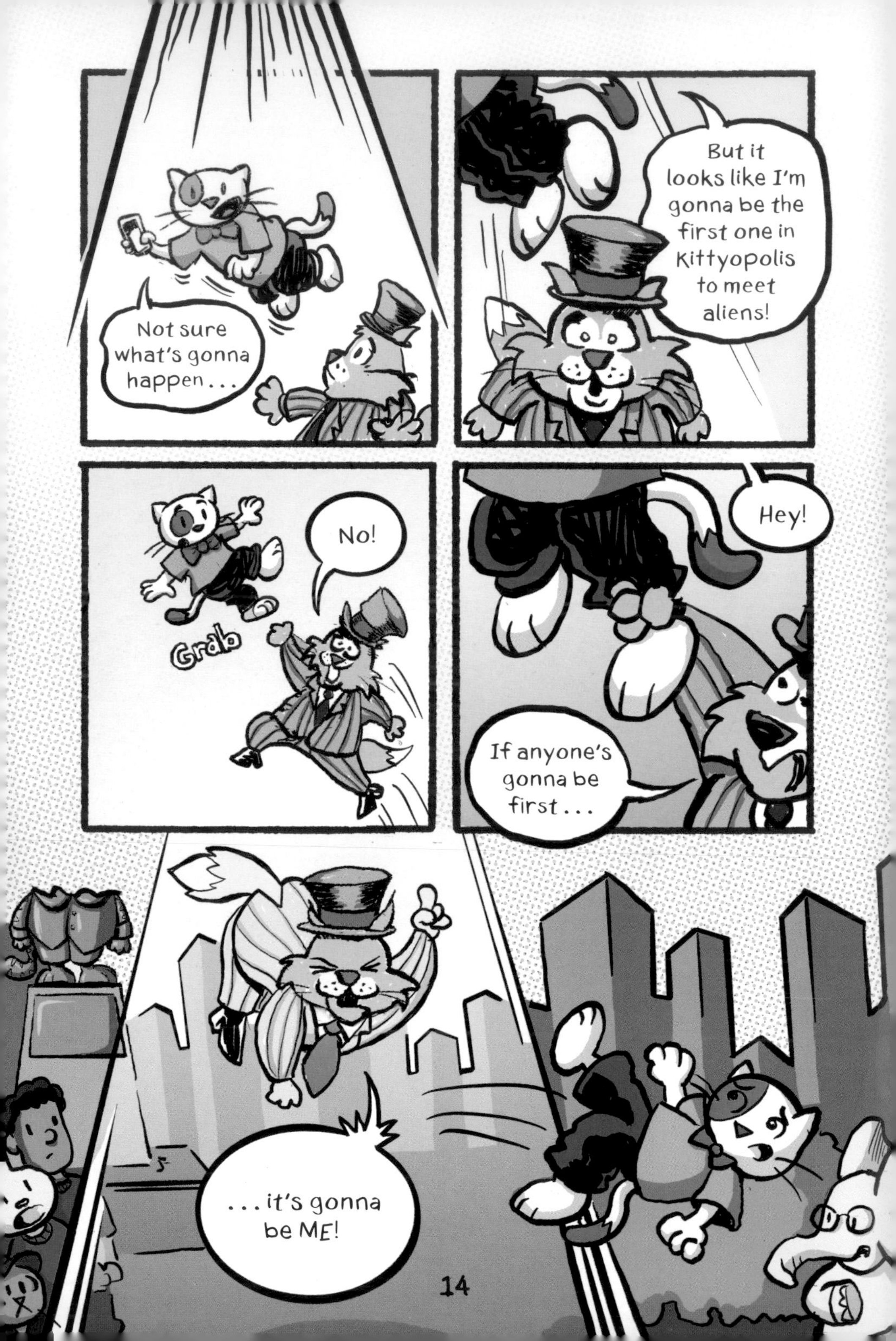
Not sure what's gonna happen . . .
But it looks like I'm gonna be the first one in Kittyopolis to meet aliens!
No!
Grab
Hey!
If anyone's gonna be first . . .
. . . it's gonna be ME!

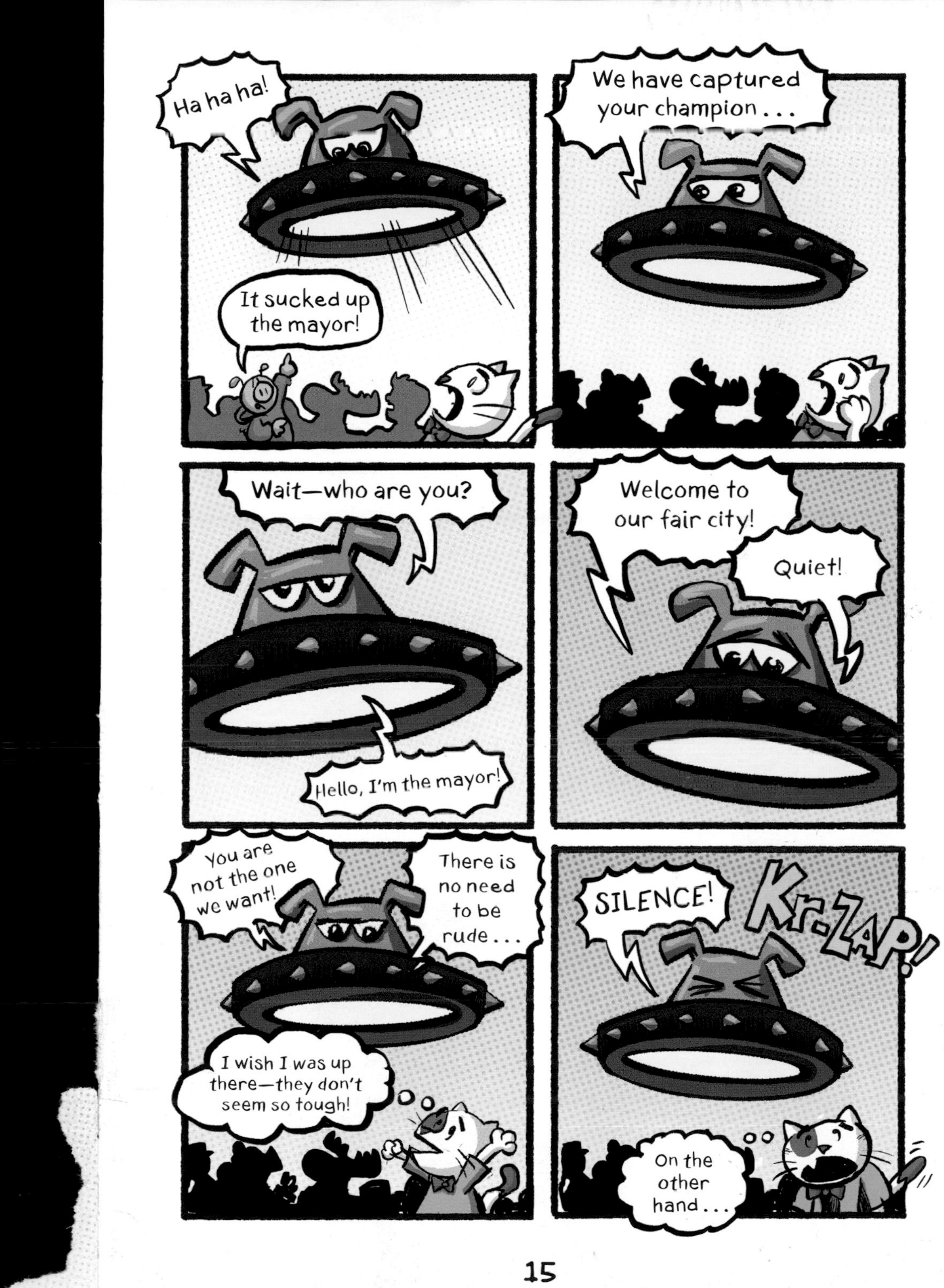
Ha ha ha!
It sucked up the mayor!
We have captured your champion . . .
Wait—who are you?
Hello, I'm the mayor!
Welcome to our fair city!
Quiet!
You are not the one we want!
There is no need to be rude . . .
I wish I was up there—they don't seem so tough!
SILENCE!
Kr-ZAP!
On the other hand . . .

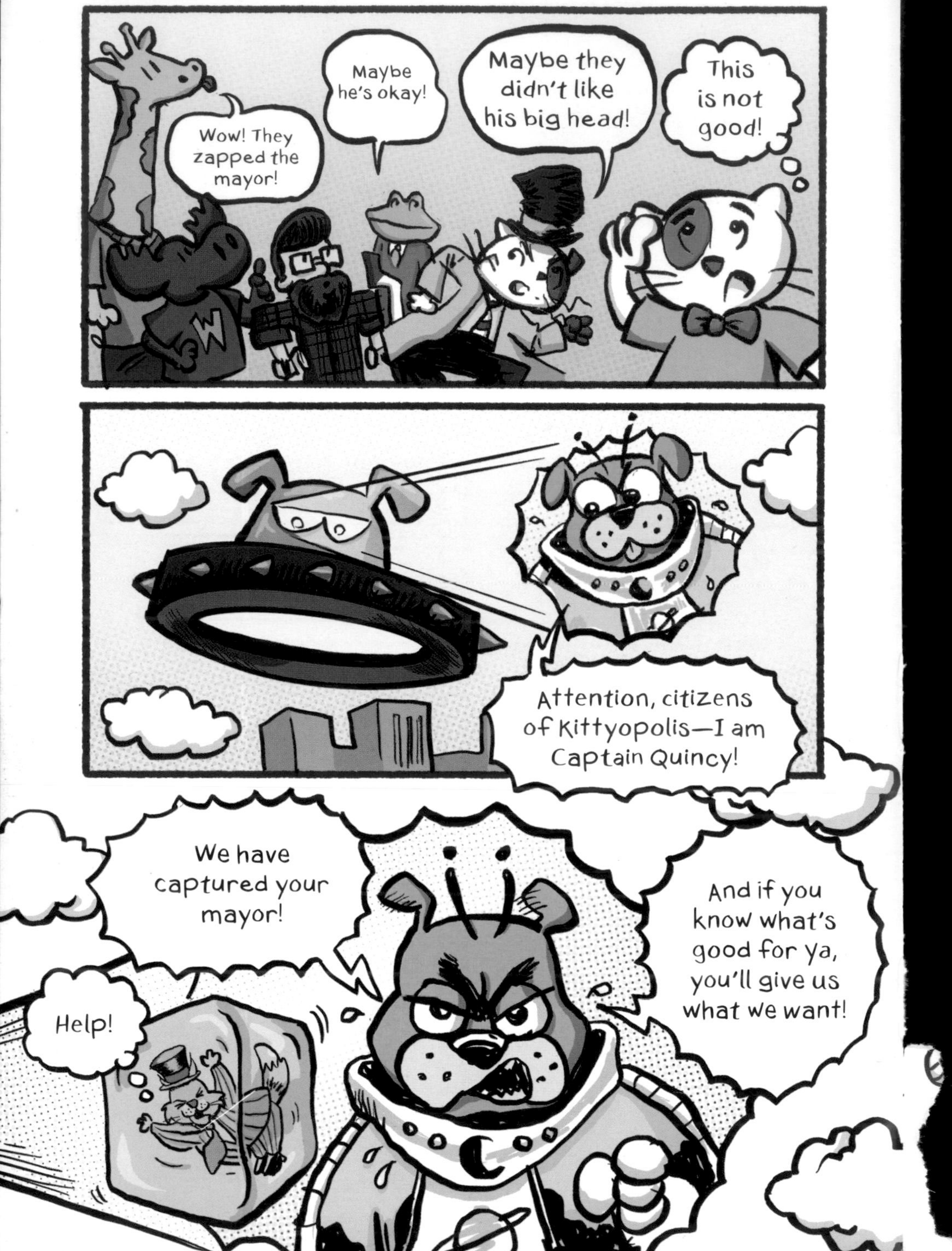
Wow! They zapped the mayor!
Maybe he's okay!
Maybe they didn't like his big head!
This is not good!
Attention, citizens of Kittyopolis—I am Captain Quincy!
We have captured your mayor!
And if you know what's good for ya, you'll give us what we want!
Help!

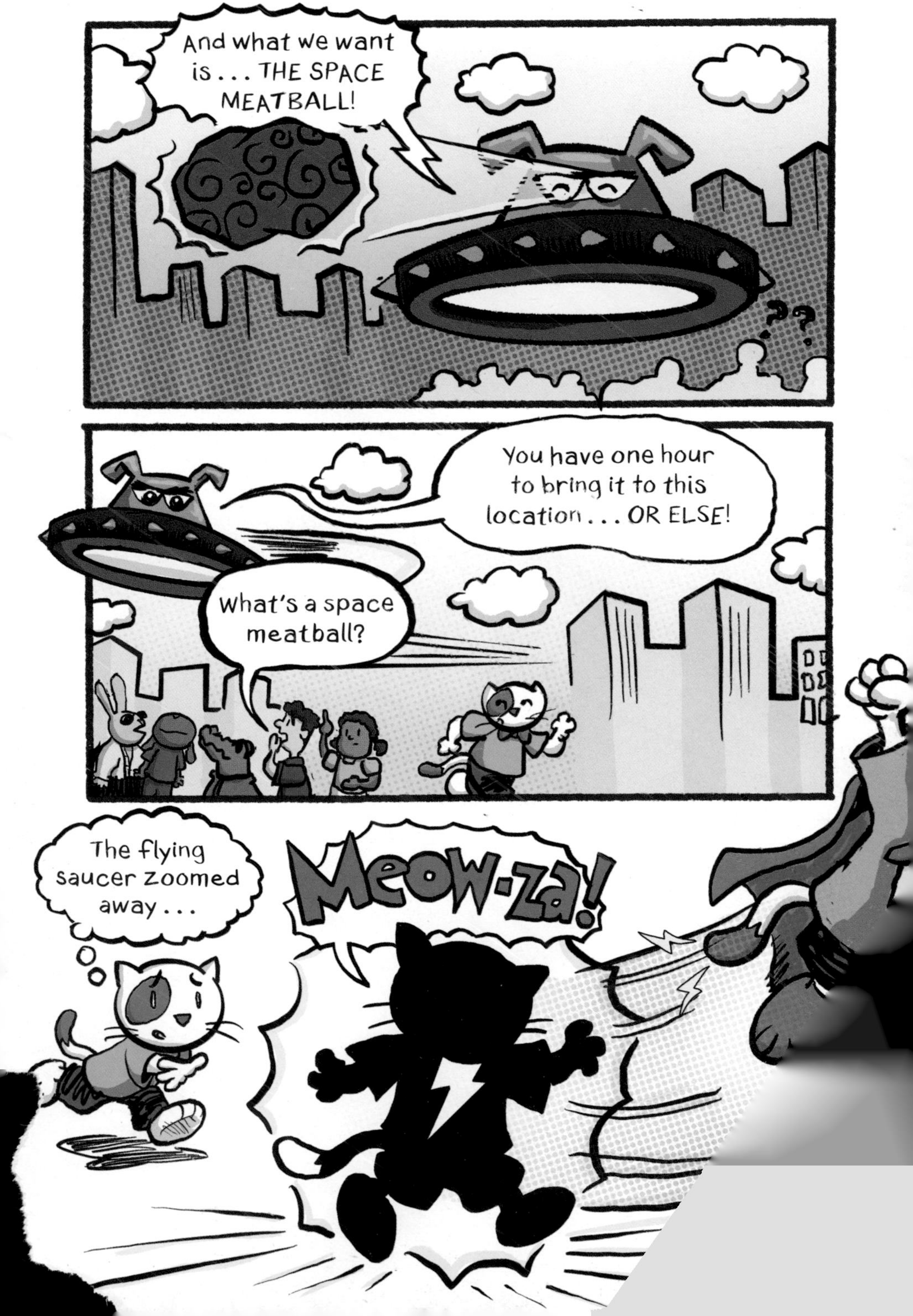
And what we want is . . . THE SPACE MEATBALL!
You have one hour to bring it to this location . . . OR ELSE!
What's a space meatball?
The flying saucer zoomed away . . .
Meow-za!

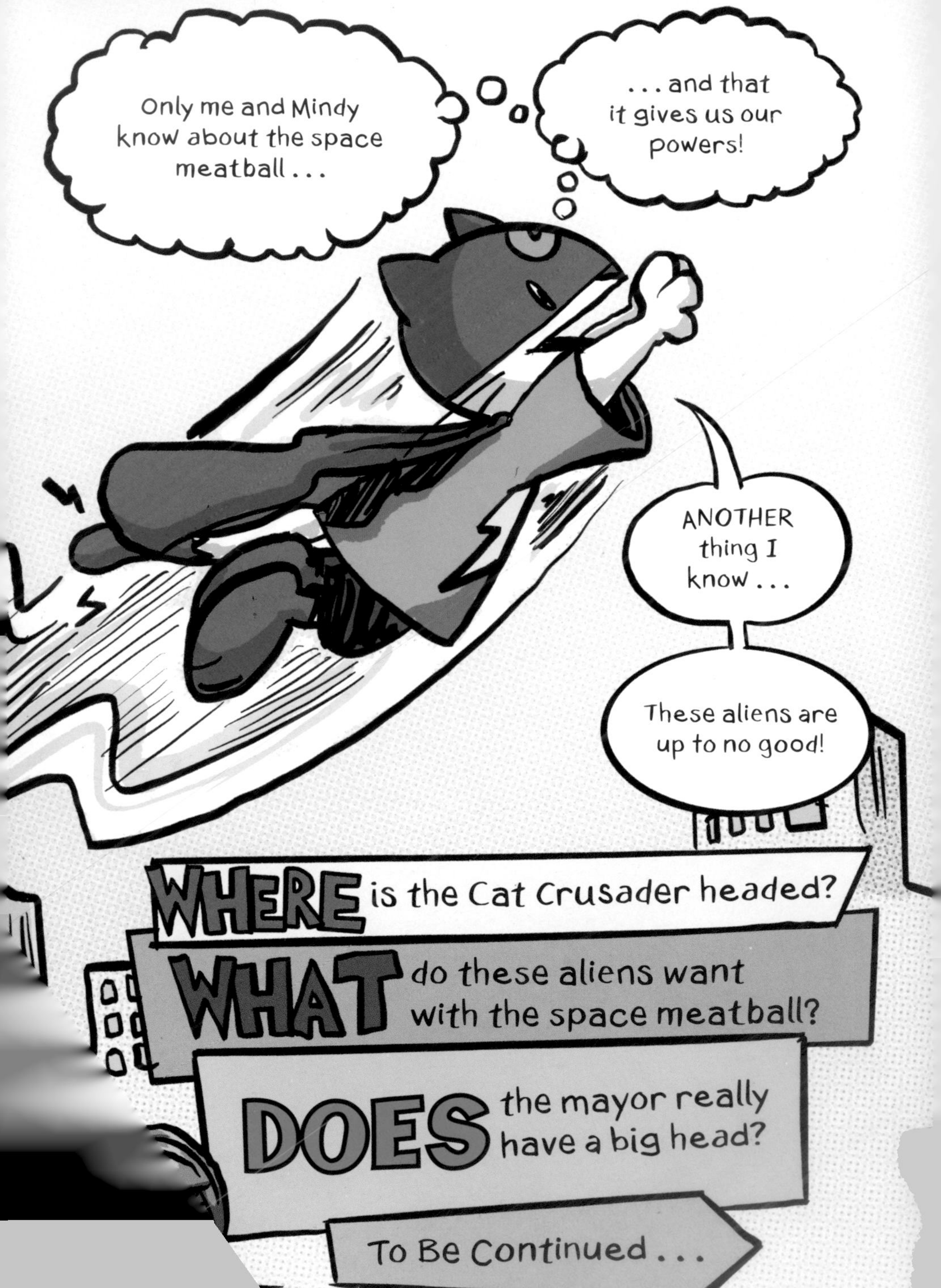

Only me and Mindy know about the space meatball . . .
. . . and that it gives us our powers!
ANOTHER thing I know . . .
These aliens are up to no good!
WHERE is the Cat Crusader headed?
WHAT do these aliens want with the space meatball?
DOES the mayor really have a big head?
To Be Continued . . .

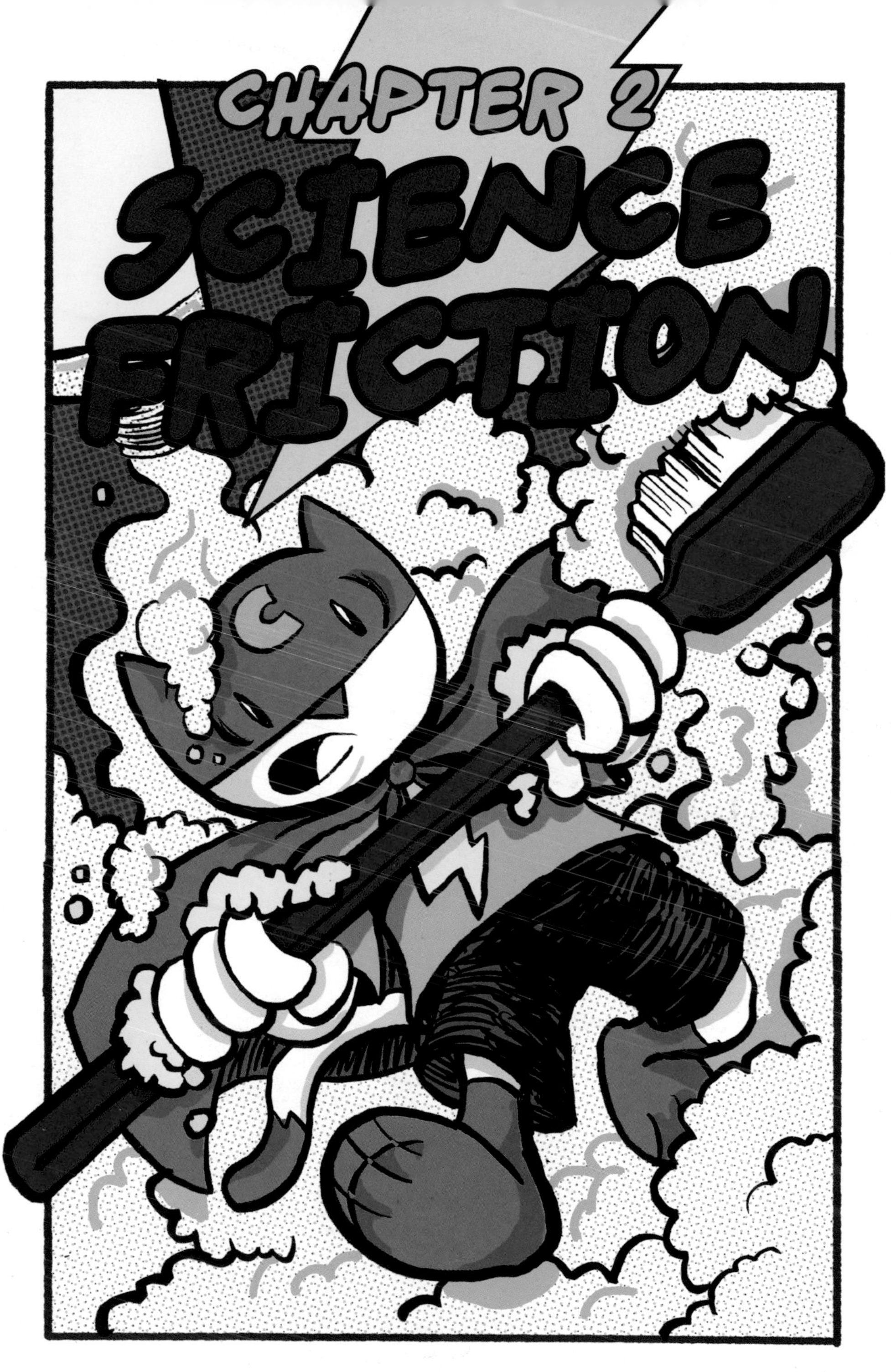
CHAPTER 2
SCIENCE FRICTION

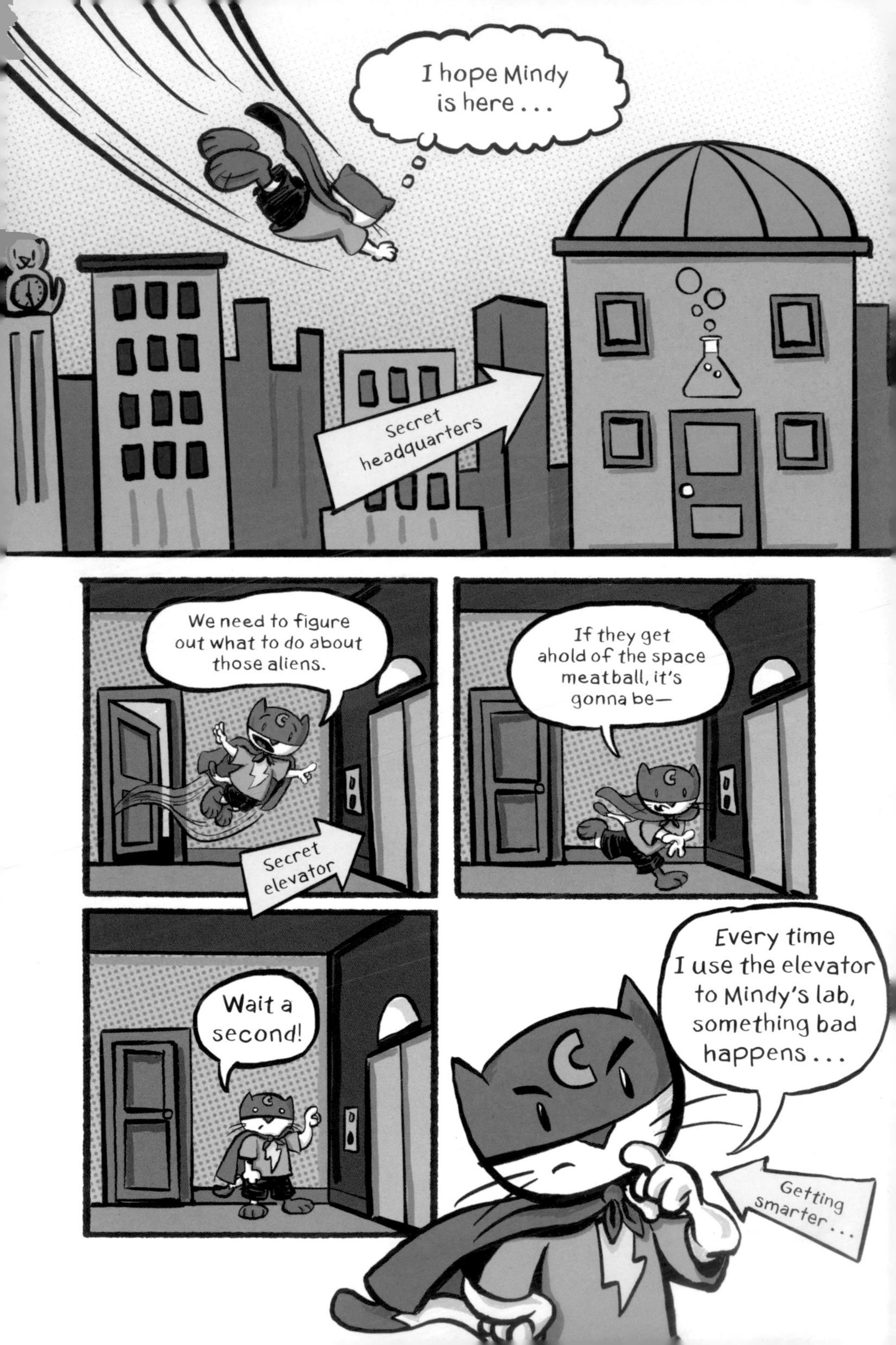
I hope Mindy is here . . .
Secret headquarters
We need to figure out what to do about those aliens.
Secret elevator
If they get ahold of the space meatball, it's gonna be—
Wait a second!
Every time I use the elevator to Mindy's lab, something bad happens . . .
Getting smarter . . .

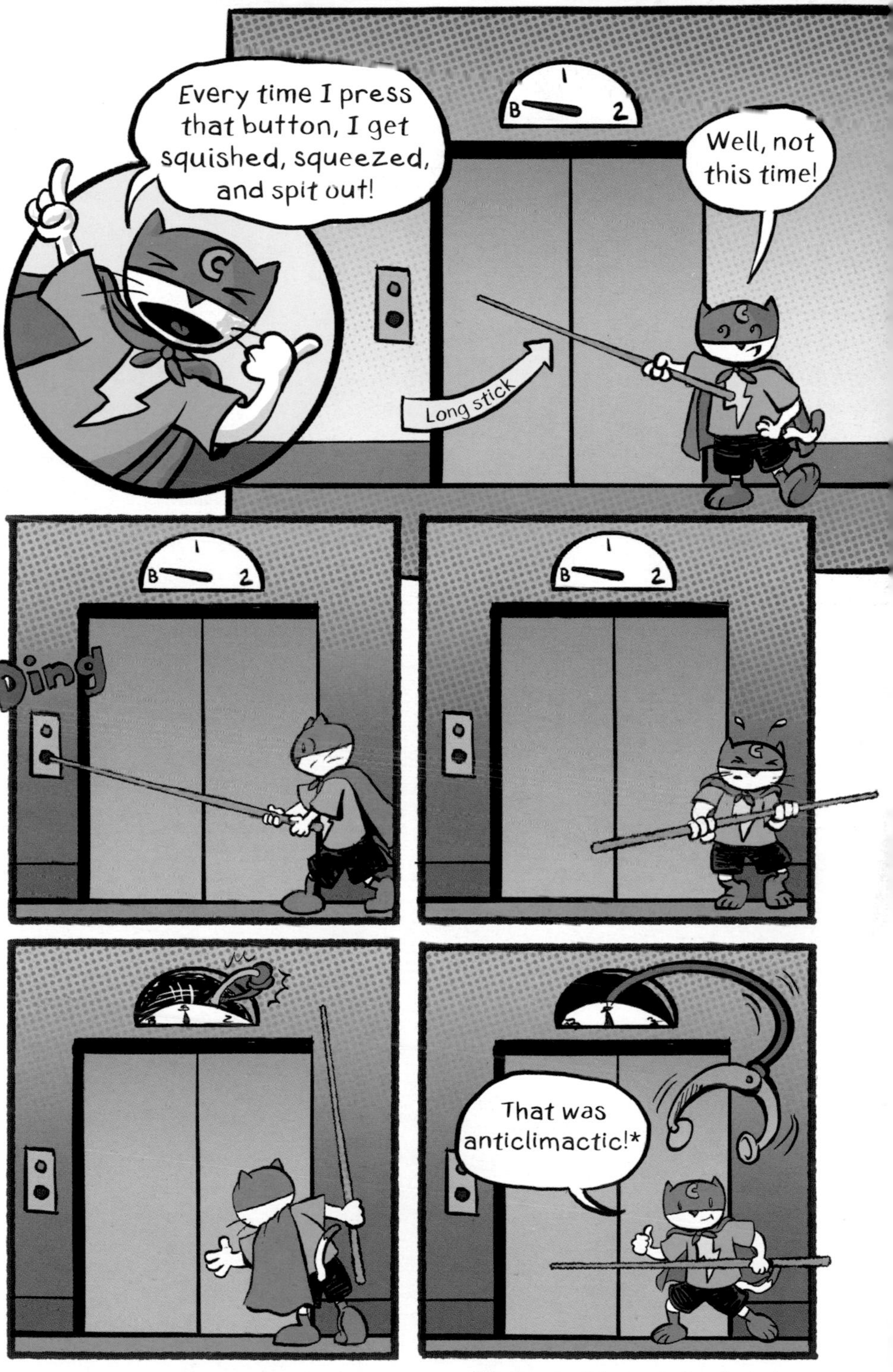
Every time I press that button, I get squished, squeezed, and spit out!
Well, not this time!
Long stick
B
1
2
Ding
That was anticlimactic!*

*Not as exciting as expected.

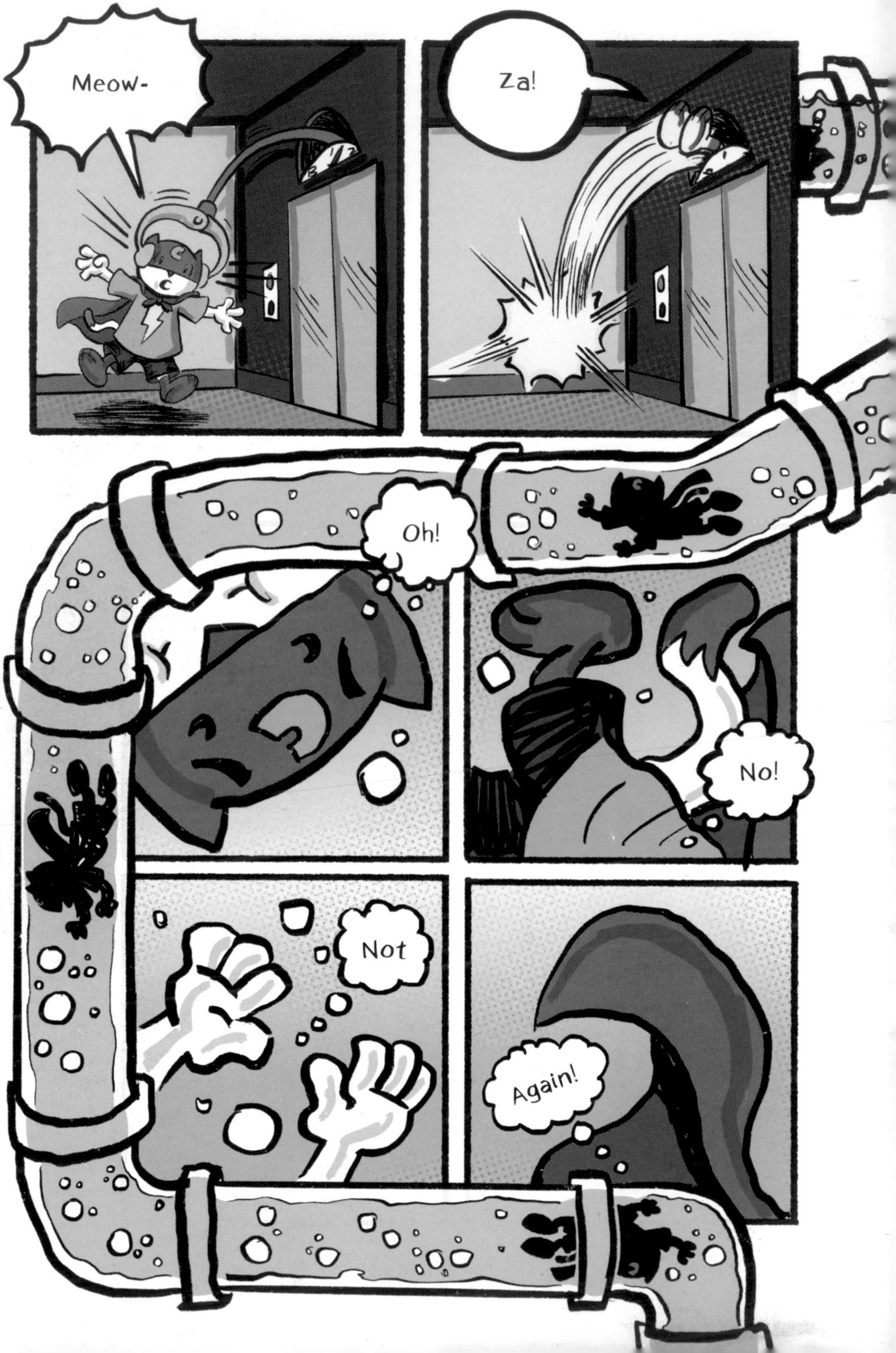
Meow-
Za!
Oh!
No!
Not
Again!

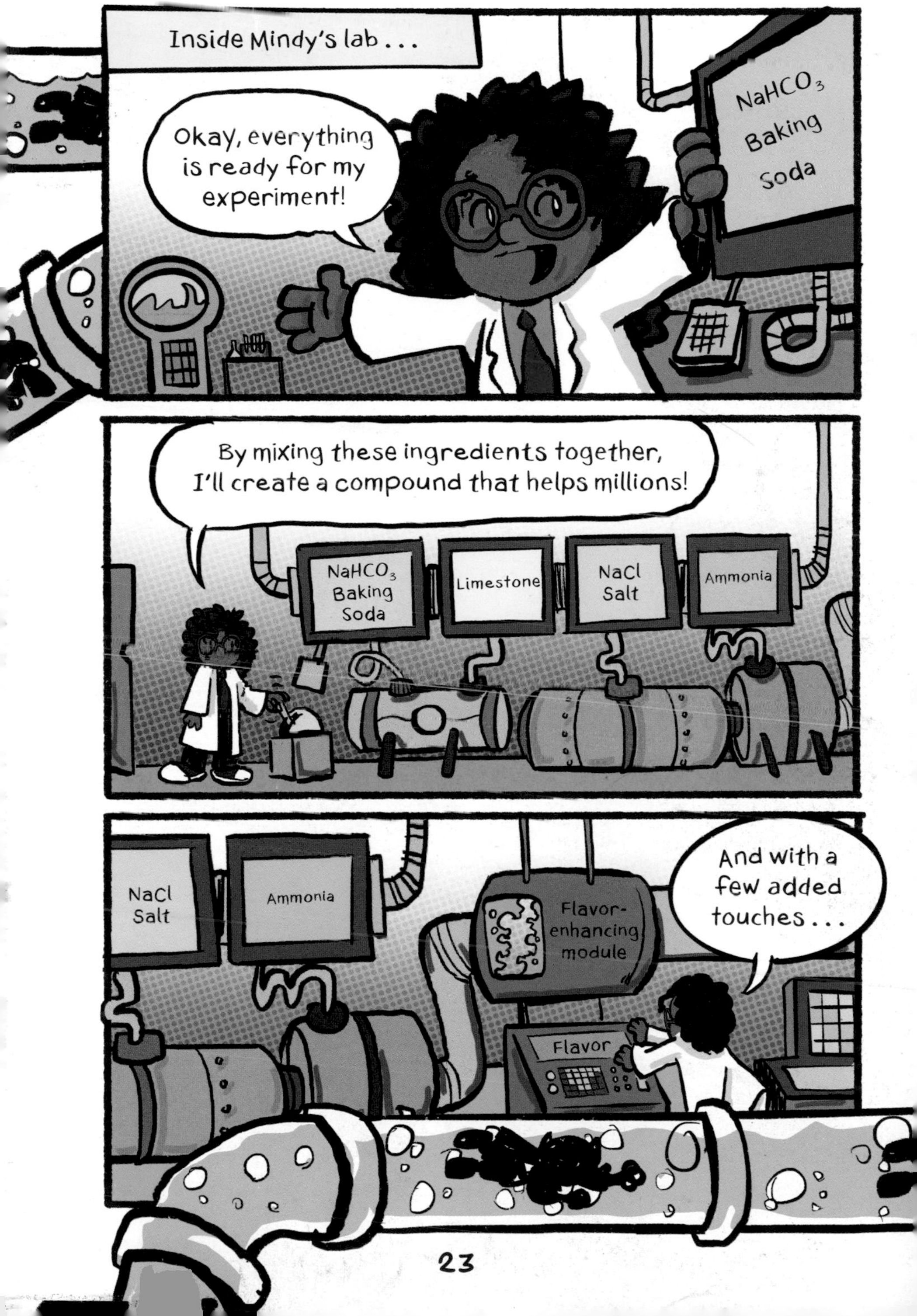

Inside Mindy's lab . . .
Okay, everything is ready for my experiment!
$NaHCO_3$ Baking Soda
By mixing these ingredients together, I'll create a compound that helps millions!
$NaHCO_3$ Baking Soda
Limestone
NaCl Salt
Ammonia
NaCl Salt
Ammonia
Flavor-enhancing module
Flavor
And with a few added touches . . .

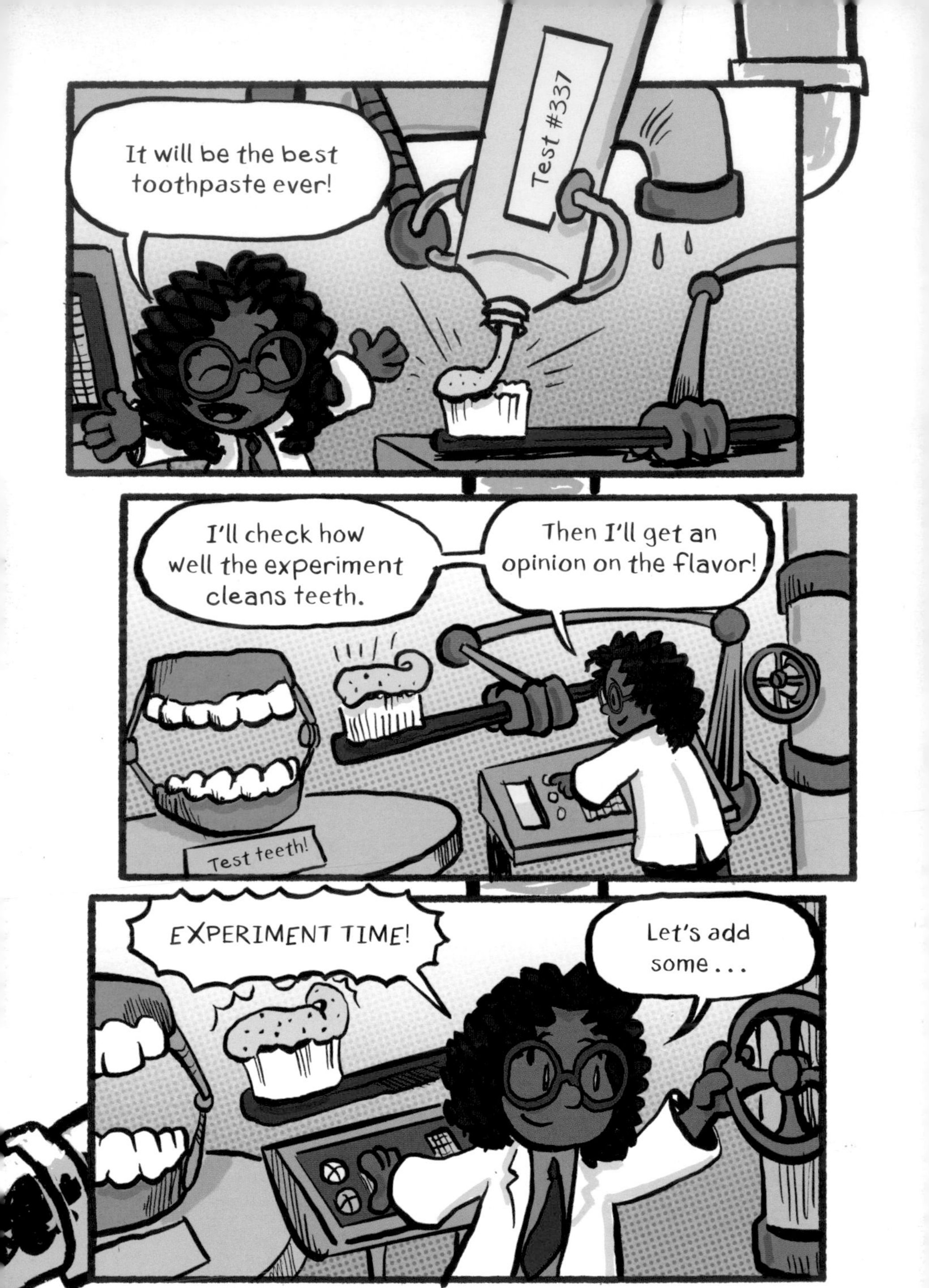
Test #337
It will be the best toothpaste ever!
I'll check how well the experiment cleans teeth.
Then I'll get an opinion on the flavor!
Test teeth!
EXPERIMENT TIME!
Let's add some . . .

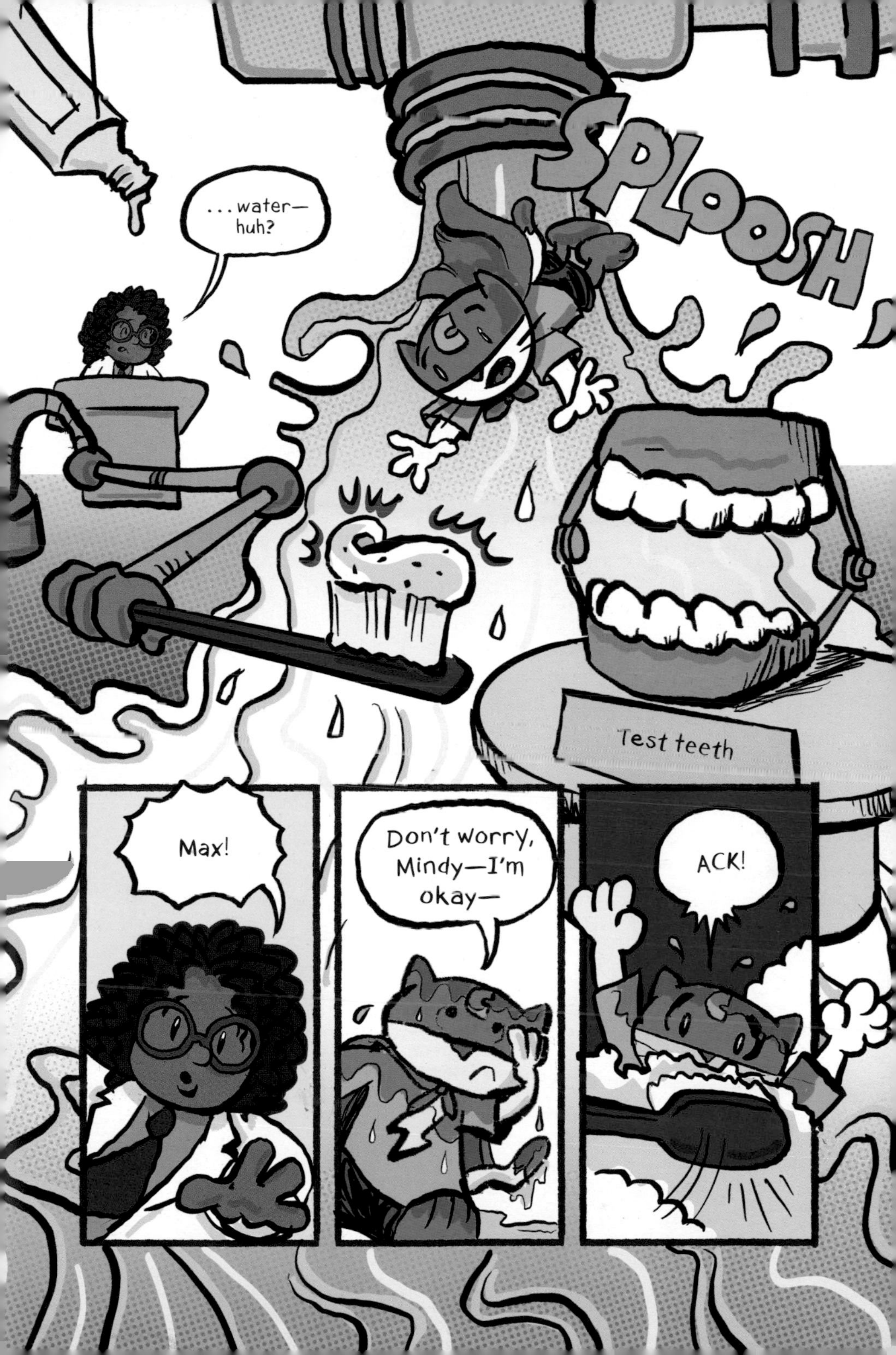

...water—
huh?
SPLOOSH
Test teeth
Max!
Don't worry,
Mindy—I'm
okay—
ACK!

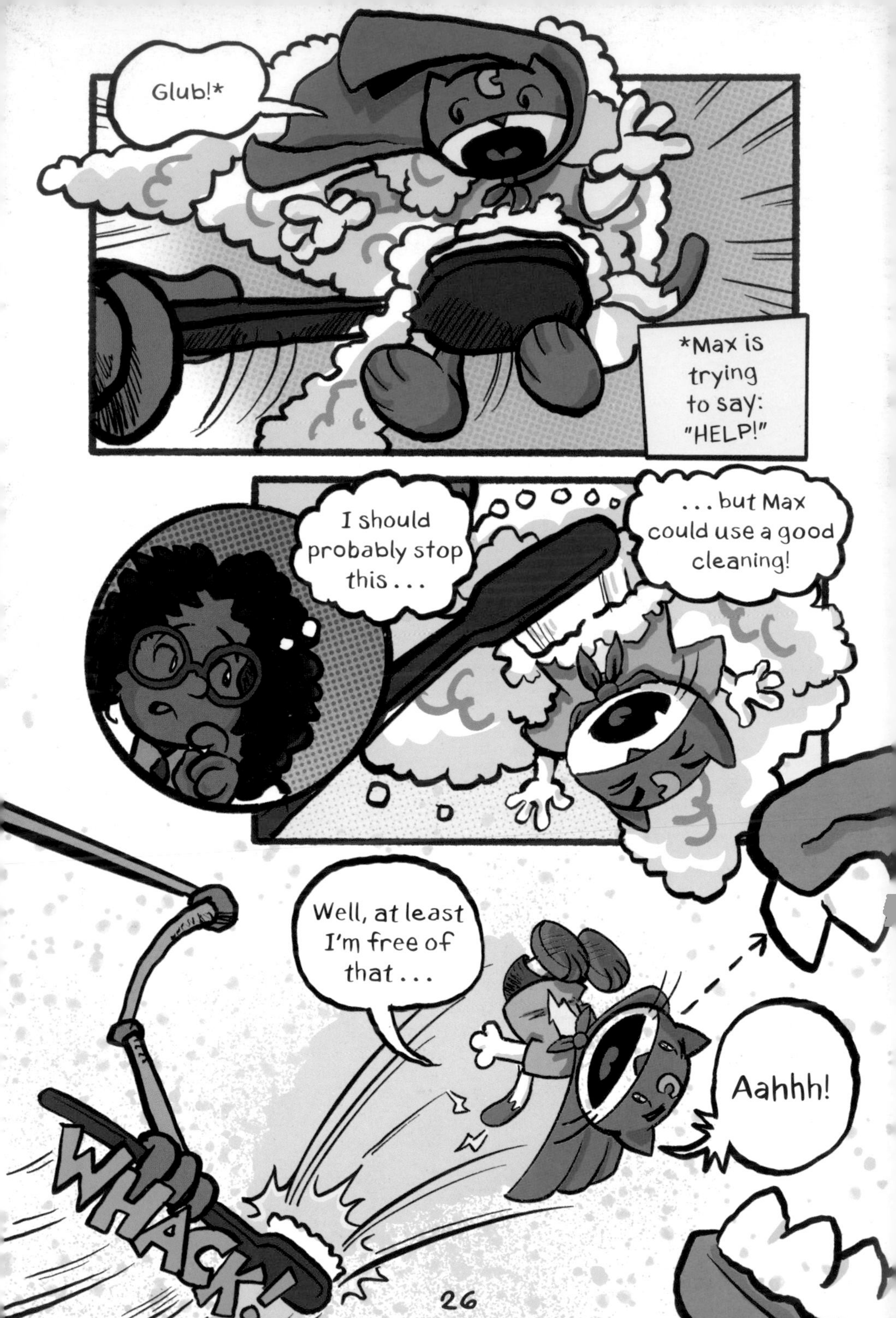
Glub!*
*Max is trying to say: "HELP!"
I should probably stop this . . .
. . . but Max could use a good cleaning!
Well, at least I'm free of that . . .
Aahhh!
WHACK!

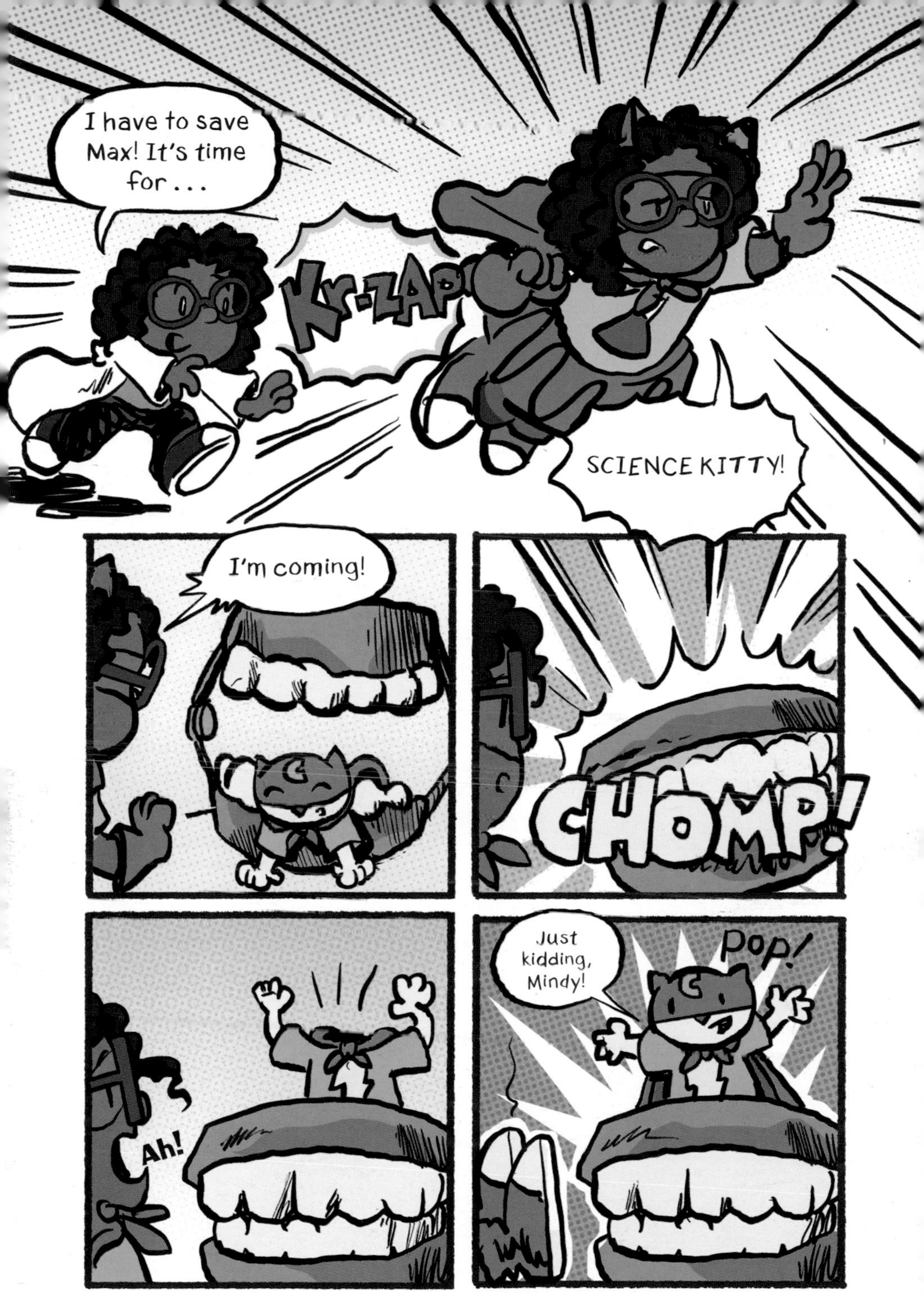
I have to save Max! It's time for . . .
Kr-ZAP!
SCIENCE KITTY!
I'm coming!
CHOMP!
Ah!
Just kidding, Mindy!
Pop!

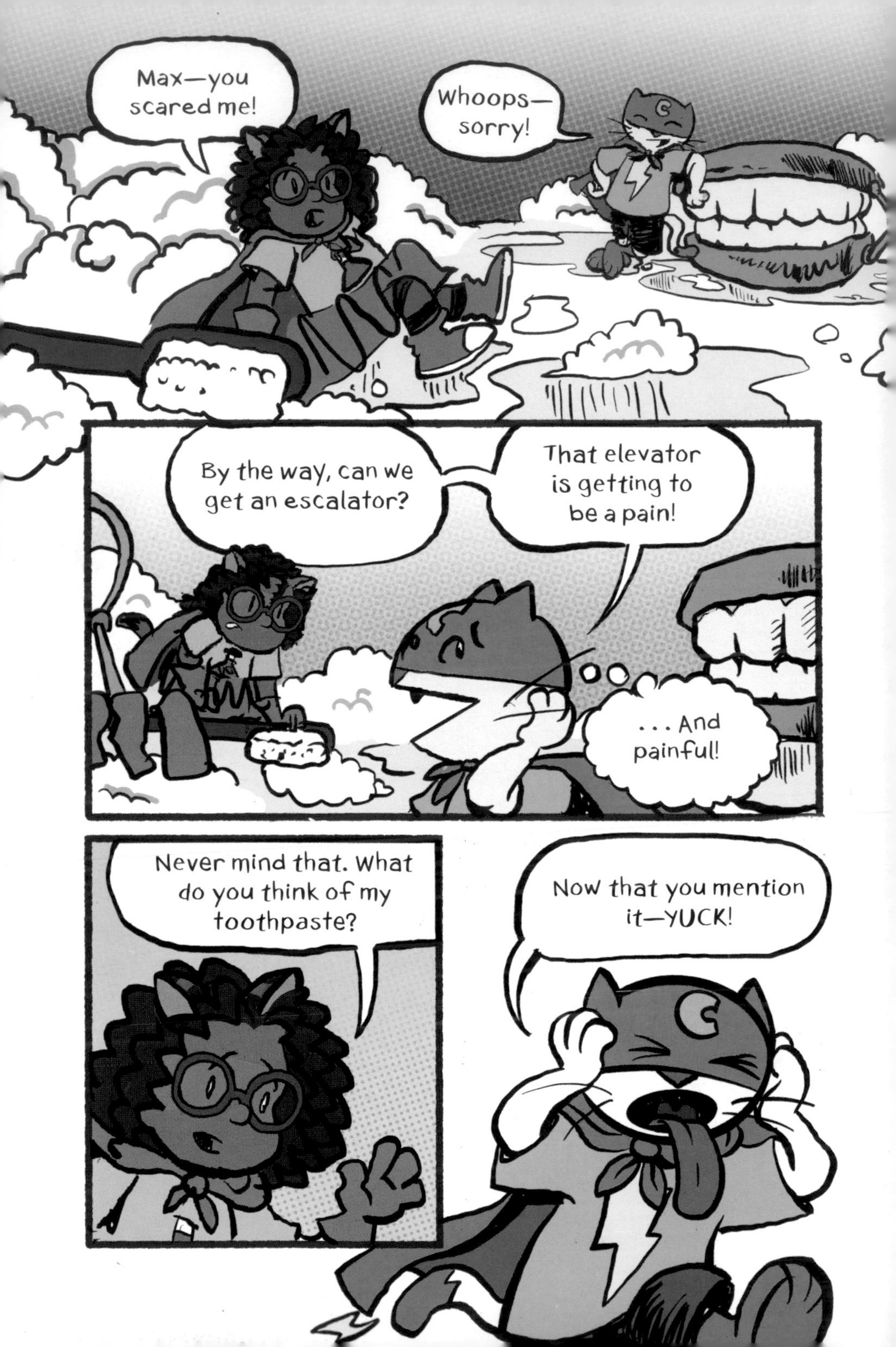
Max—you scared me!
Whoops—sorry!
By the way, can we get an escalator?
That elevator is getting to be a pain!
. . . And painful!
Never mind that. What do you think of my toothpaste?
Now that you mention it—YUCK!

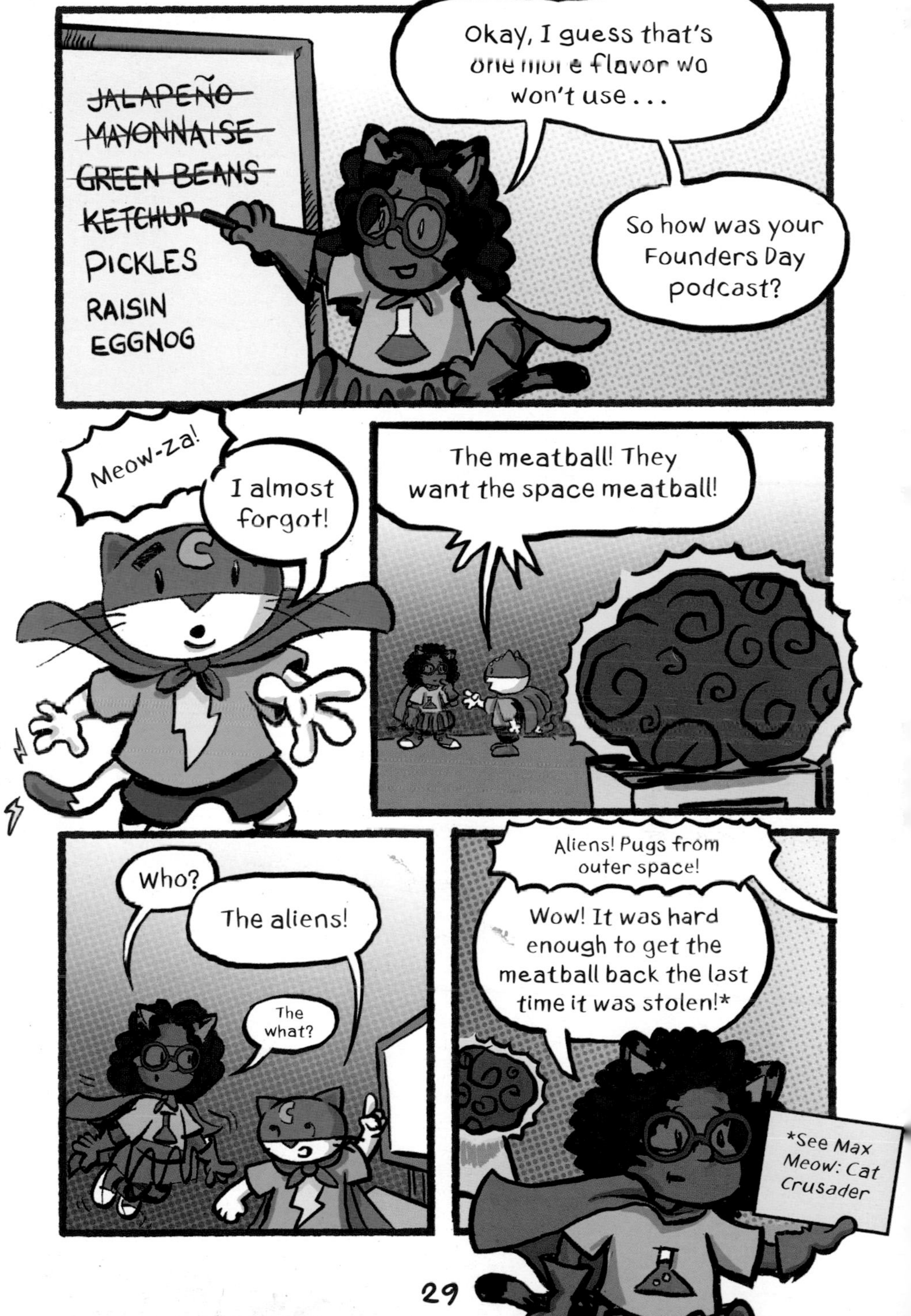
JALAPEÑO
MAYONNAISE
GREEN BEANS
KETCHUP
PICKLES
RAISIN EGGNOG
Okay, I guess that's one more flavor we won't use . . .
So how was your Founders Day podcast?
Meow-za!
I almost forgot!
The meatball! They want the space meatball!
Who?
The aliens!
The what?
Aliens! Pugs from outer space!
Wow! It was hard enough to get the meatball back the last time it was stolen!*
*See Max Meow: Cat Crusader

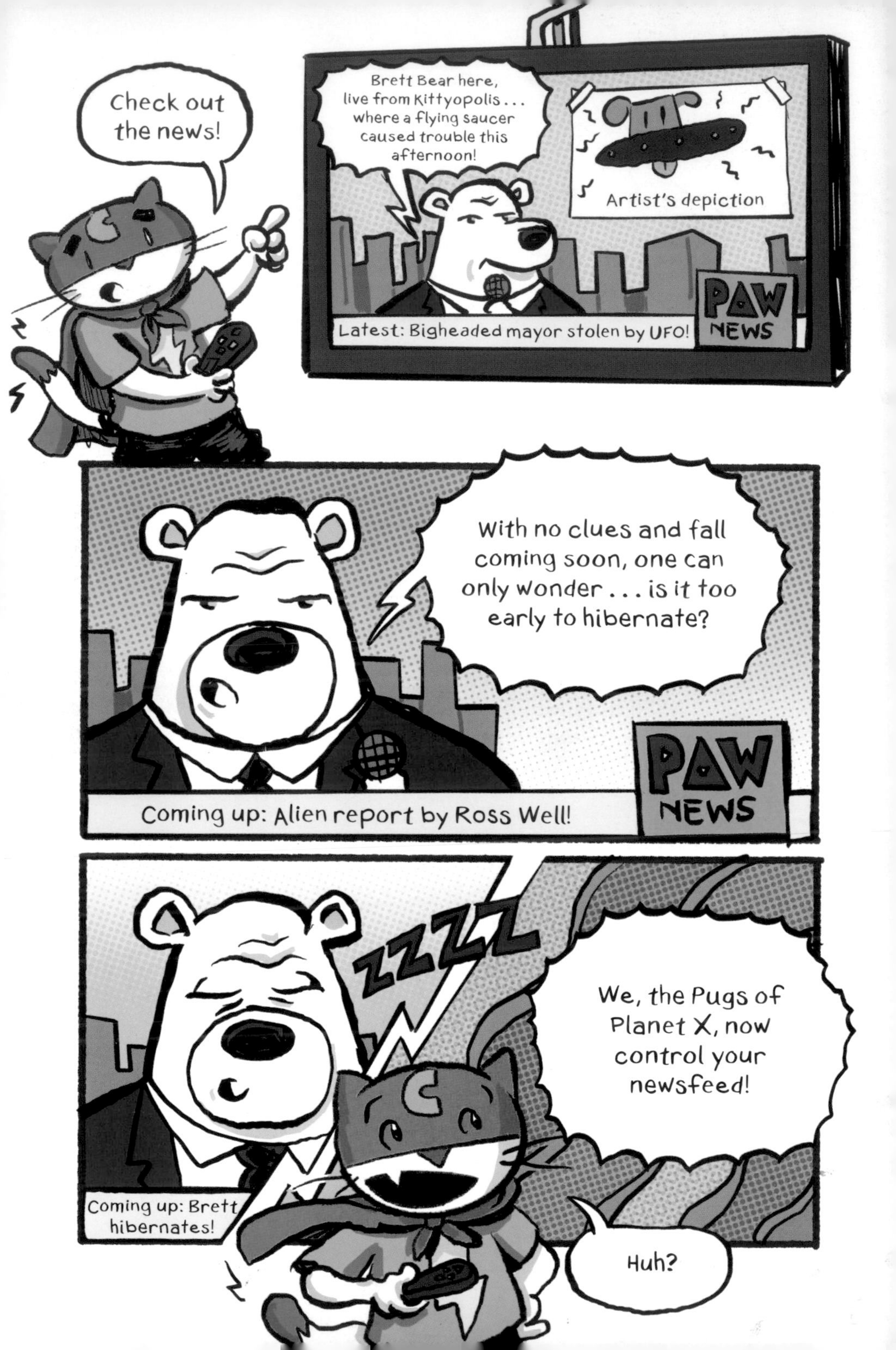
Check out the news!
Brett Bear here, live from Kittyopolis . . . where a flying saucer caused trouble this afternoon!
Artist's depiction
PAW NEWS
Latest: Bigheaded mayor stolen by UFO!
With no clues and fall coming soon, one can only wonder . . . is it too early to hibernate?
PAW NEWS
Coming up: Alien report by Ross Well!
ZZZZ
We, the Pugs of Planet X, now control your newsfeed!
Coming up: Brett hibernates!
Huh?

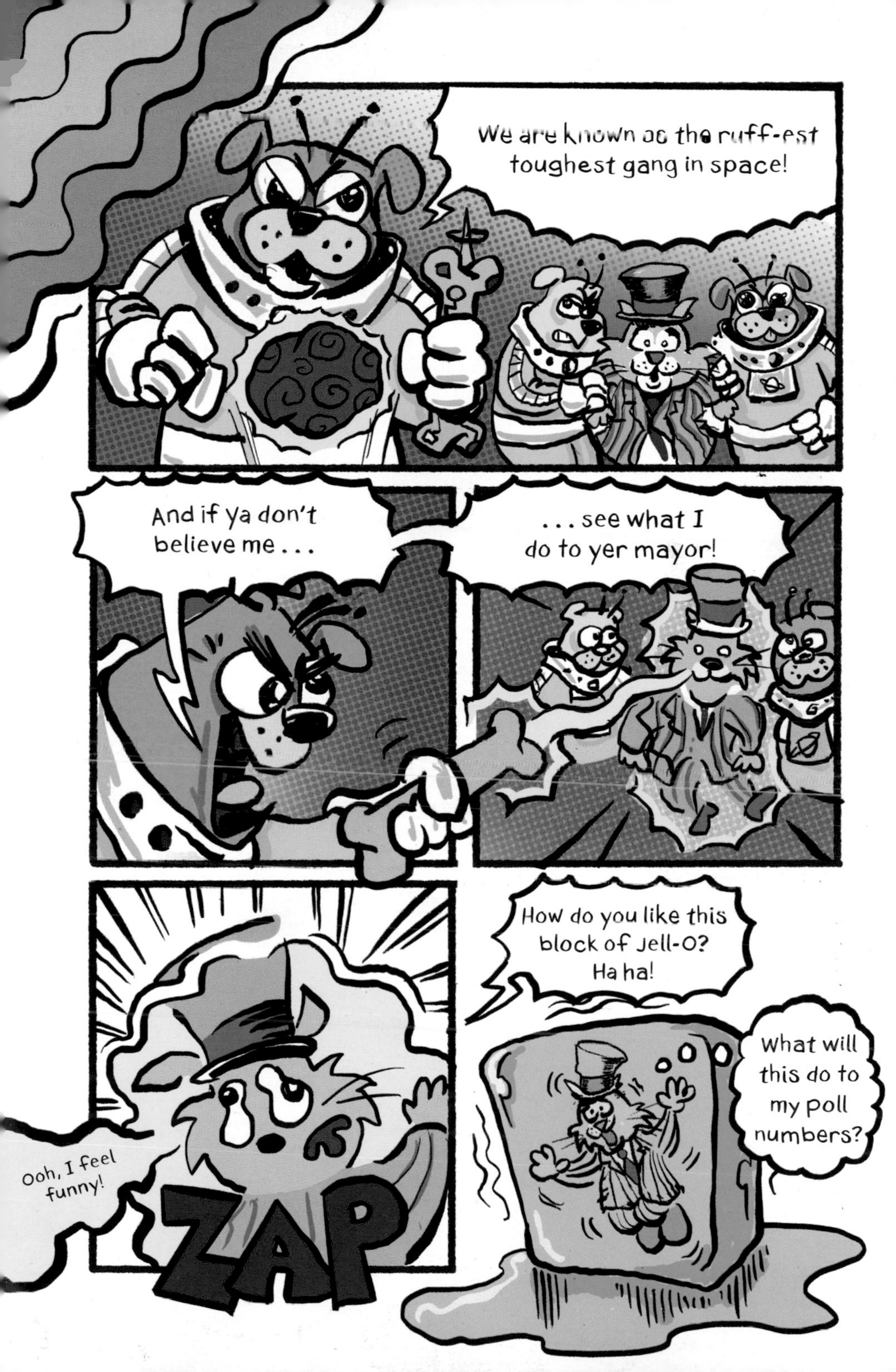
We are known as the ruff-est toughest gang in space!
And if ya don't believe me . . .
. . . see what I do to yer mayor!
Ooh, I feel funny!
ZAP
How do you like this block of Jell-O? Ha ha!
What will this do to my poll numbers?

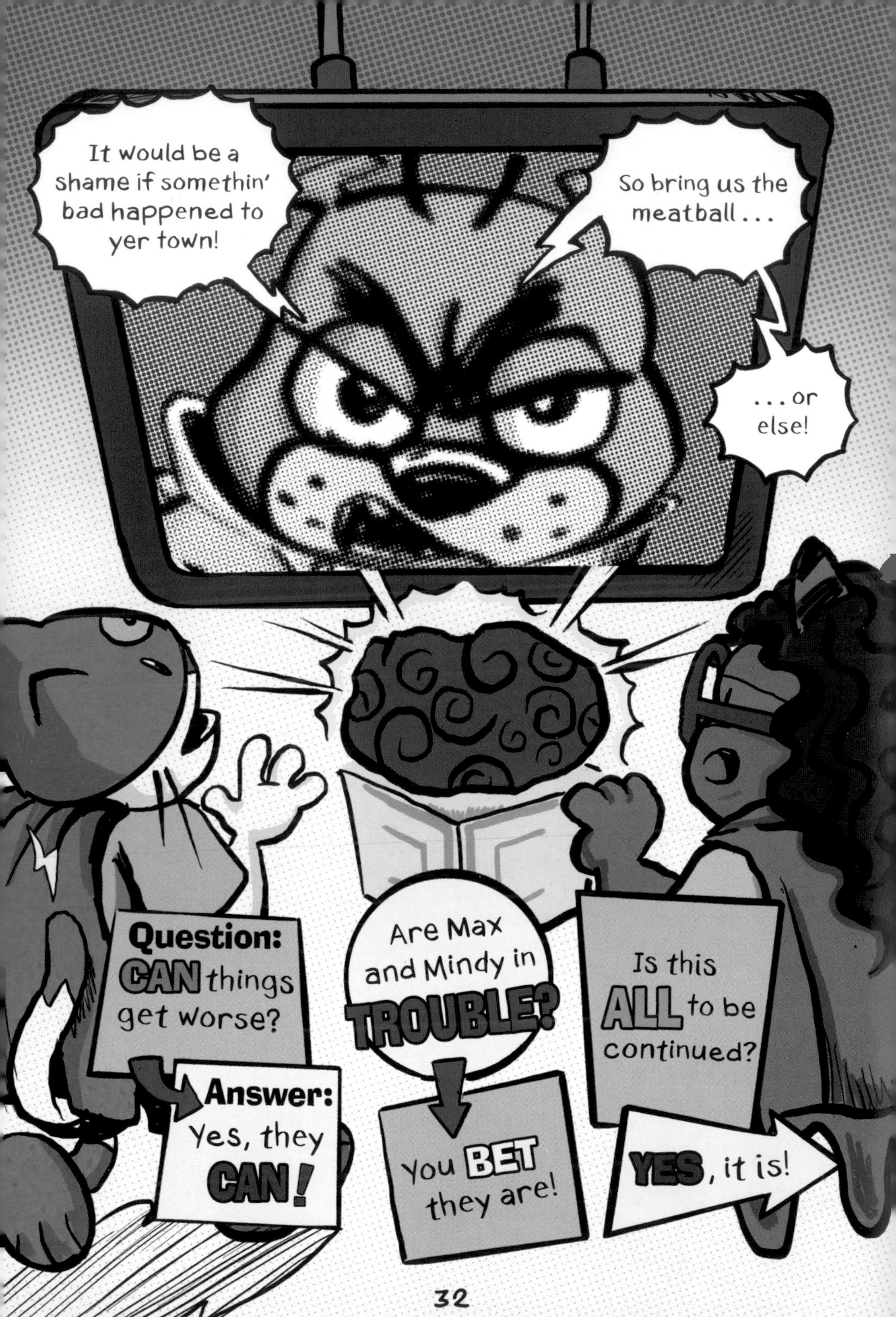
It would be a shame if somethin' bad happened to yer town!
So bring us the meatball . . .
. . . or else!
Question: CAN things get worse?
Answer: Yes, they CAN!
Are Max and Mindy in TROUBLE?
You BET they are!
Is this ALL to be continued?
YES, it is!

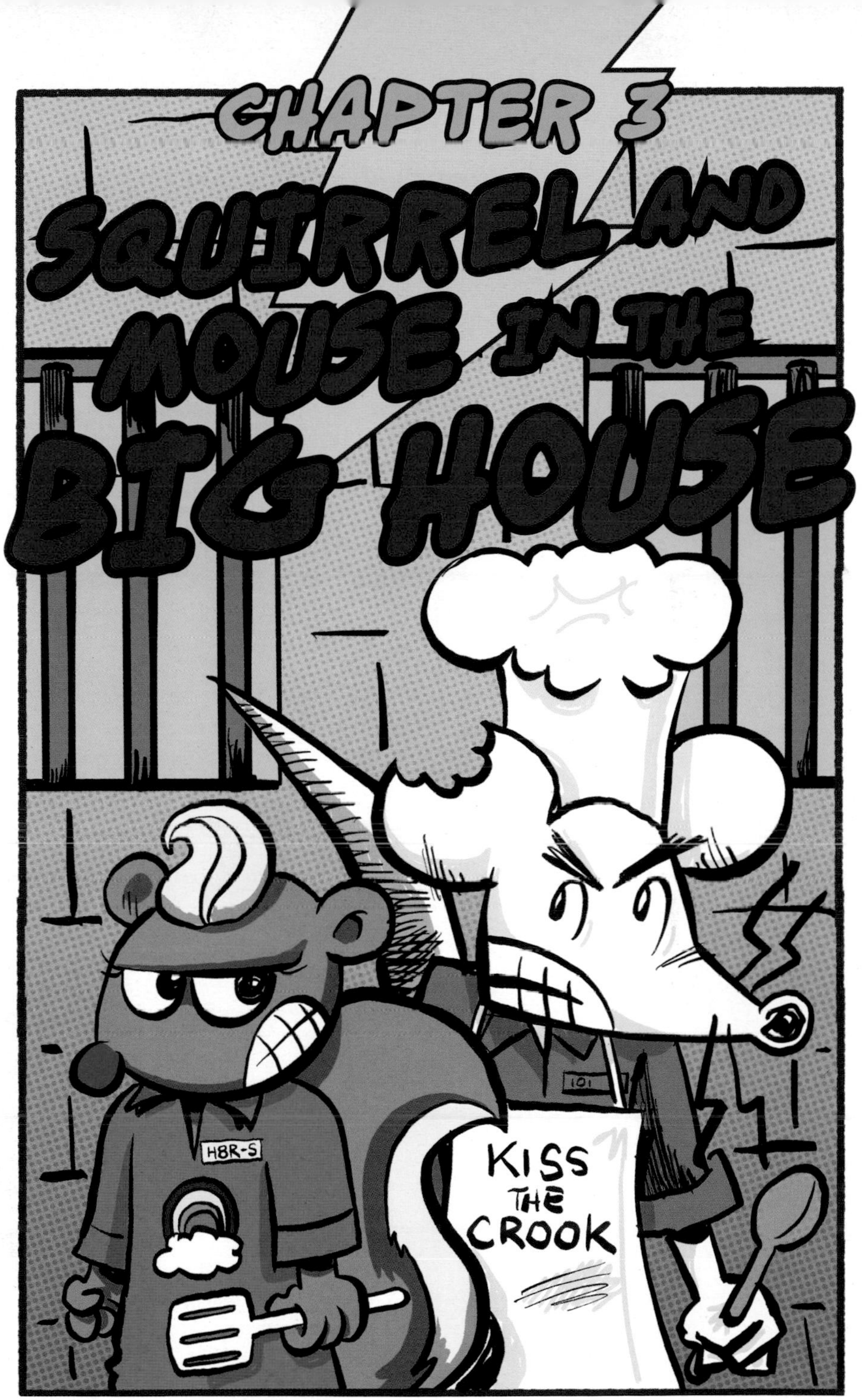
CHAPTER 3
SQUIRREL AND MOUSE IN THE BIG HOUSE
H8R-S
101
KISS THE CROOK

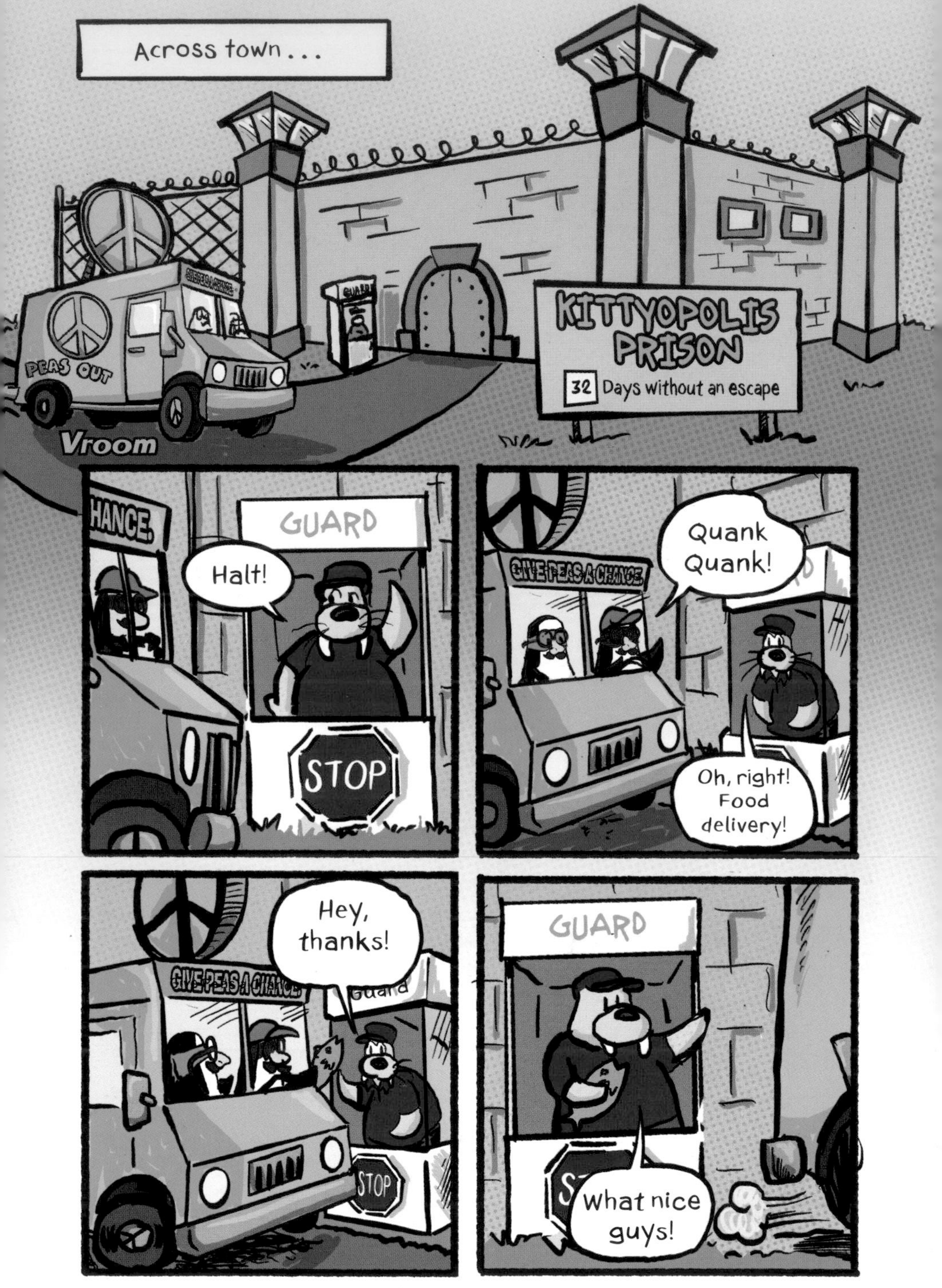
Across town . . .
GIVE PEAS A CHANCE.
PEAS OUT
GUARD
KITTYOPOLIS PRISON
32 Days without an escape
Vroom
HANCE.
GUARD
Halt!
STOP
GIVE PEAS A CHANCE
Quank Quank!
Oh, right! Food delivery!
GIVE PEAS A CHANCE
Hey, thanks!
STOP
GUARD
What nice guys!

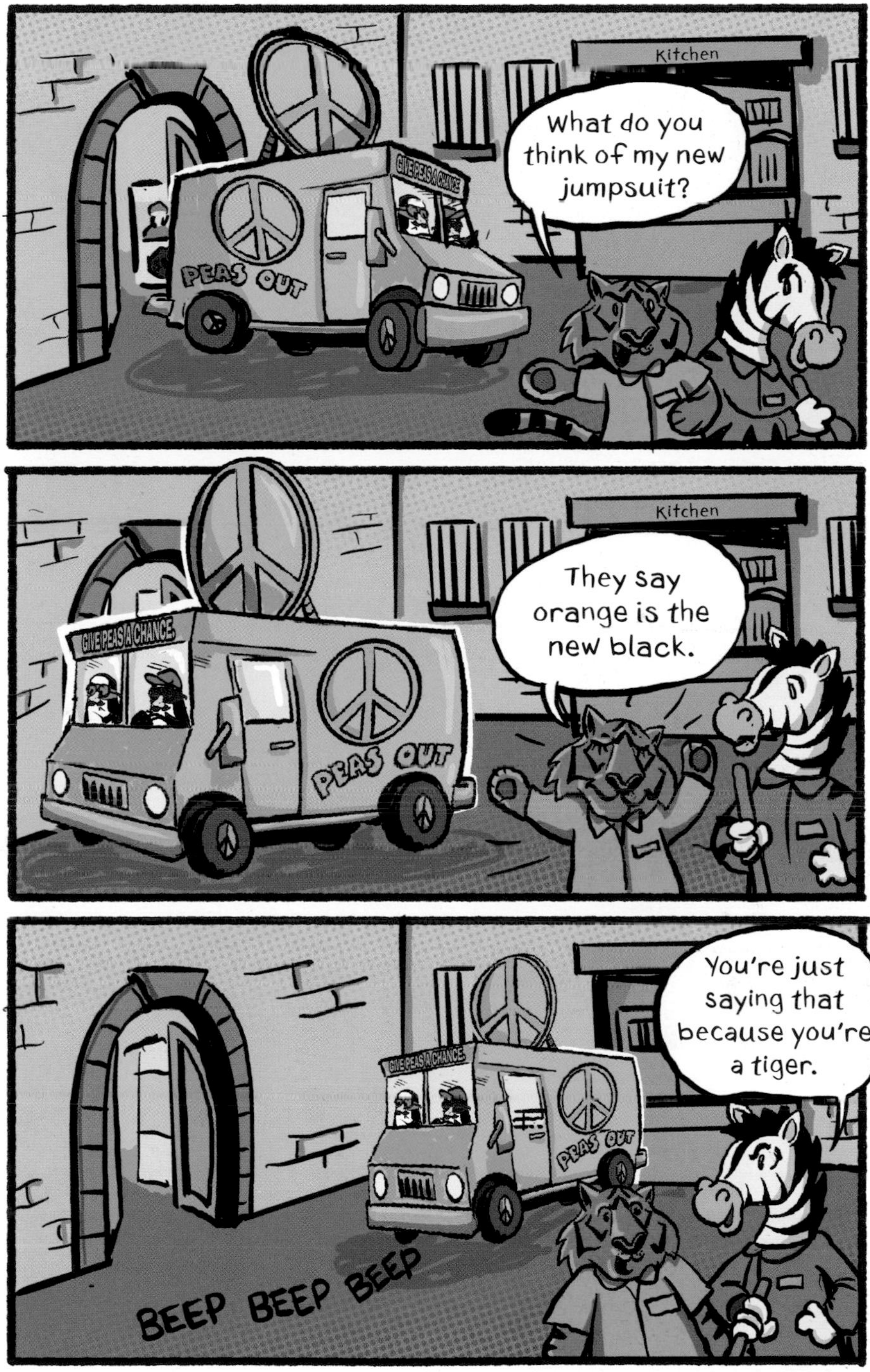
Kitchen
GIVE PEAS A CHANCE
PEAS OUT
What do you think of my new jumpsuit?
Kitchen
GIVE PEAS A CHANCE.
PEAS OUT
They say orange is the new black.
GIVE PEAS A CHANCE.
PEAS OUT
You're just saying that because you're a tiger.
BEEP BEEP BEEP

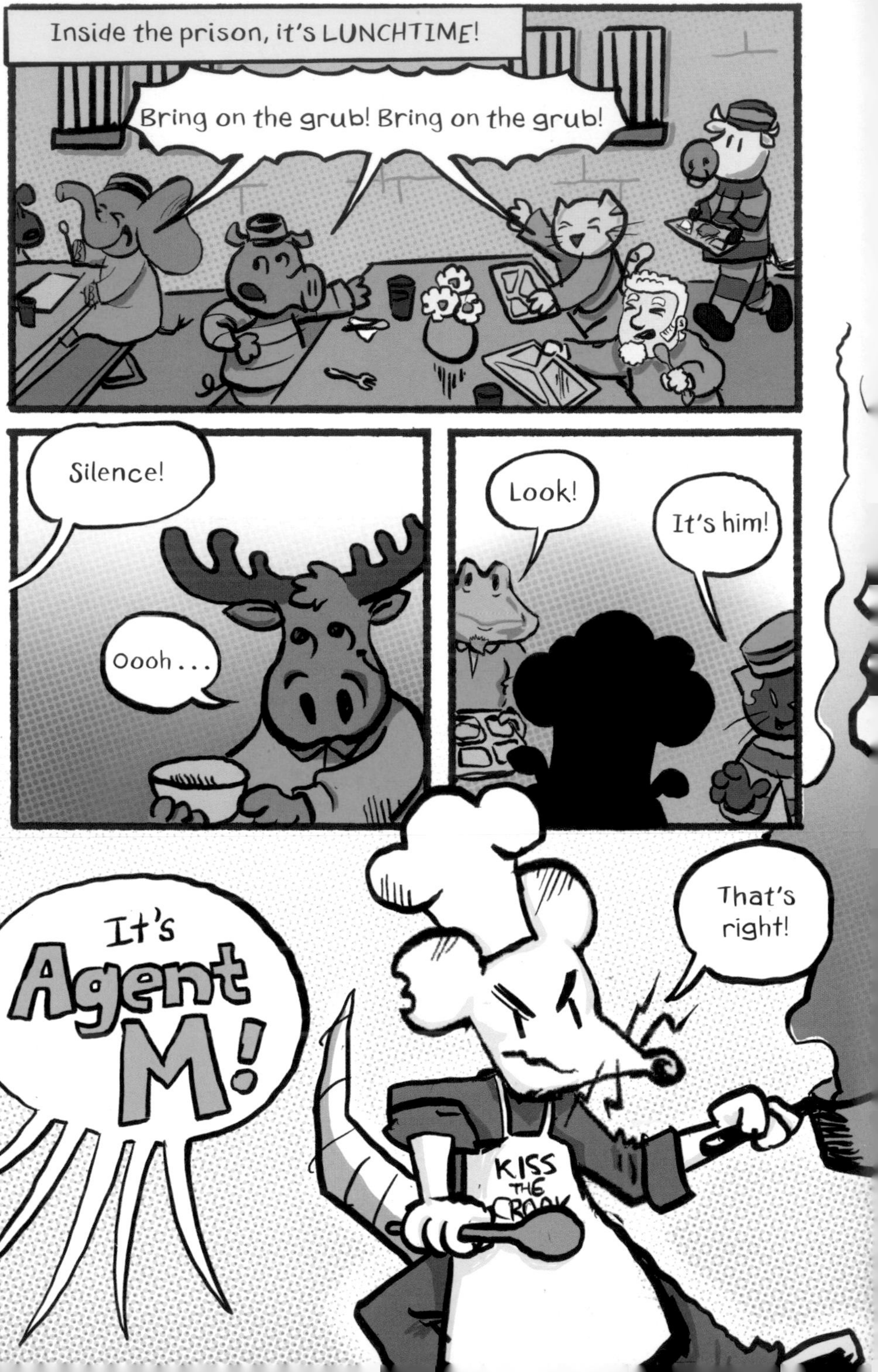
Inside the prison, it's LUNCHTIME!
Bring on the grub! Bring on the grub!
Silence!
Oooh . . .
Look!
It's him!
It's Agent M!
That's right!
KISS THE CROOK

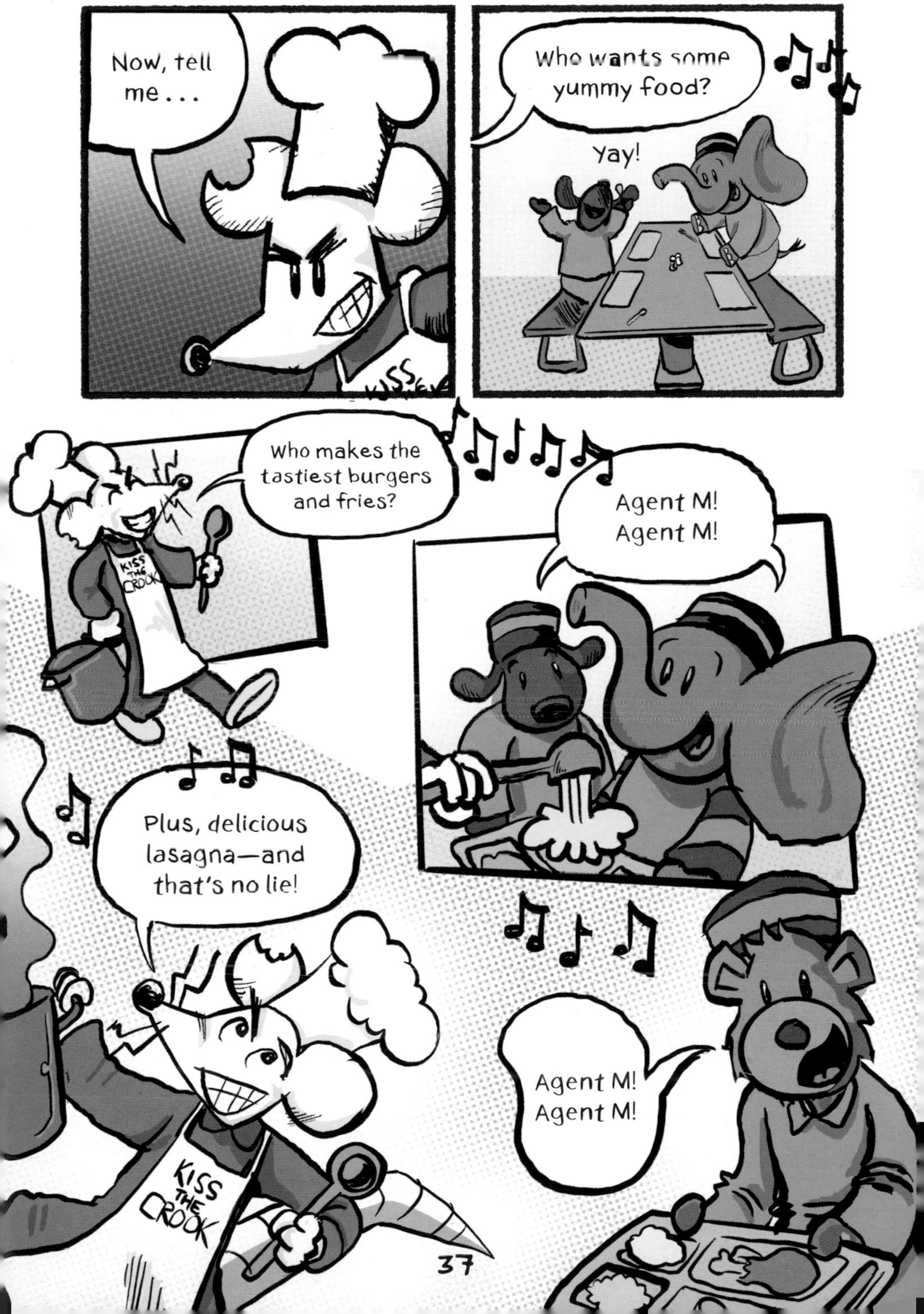
Now, tell me . . .
Who wants some yummy food?
Yay!
Who makes the tastiest burgers and fries?
Agent M! Agent M!
Plus, delicious lasagna—and that's no lie!
Agent M! Agent M!
KISS THE CROOK

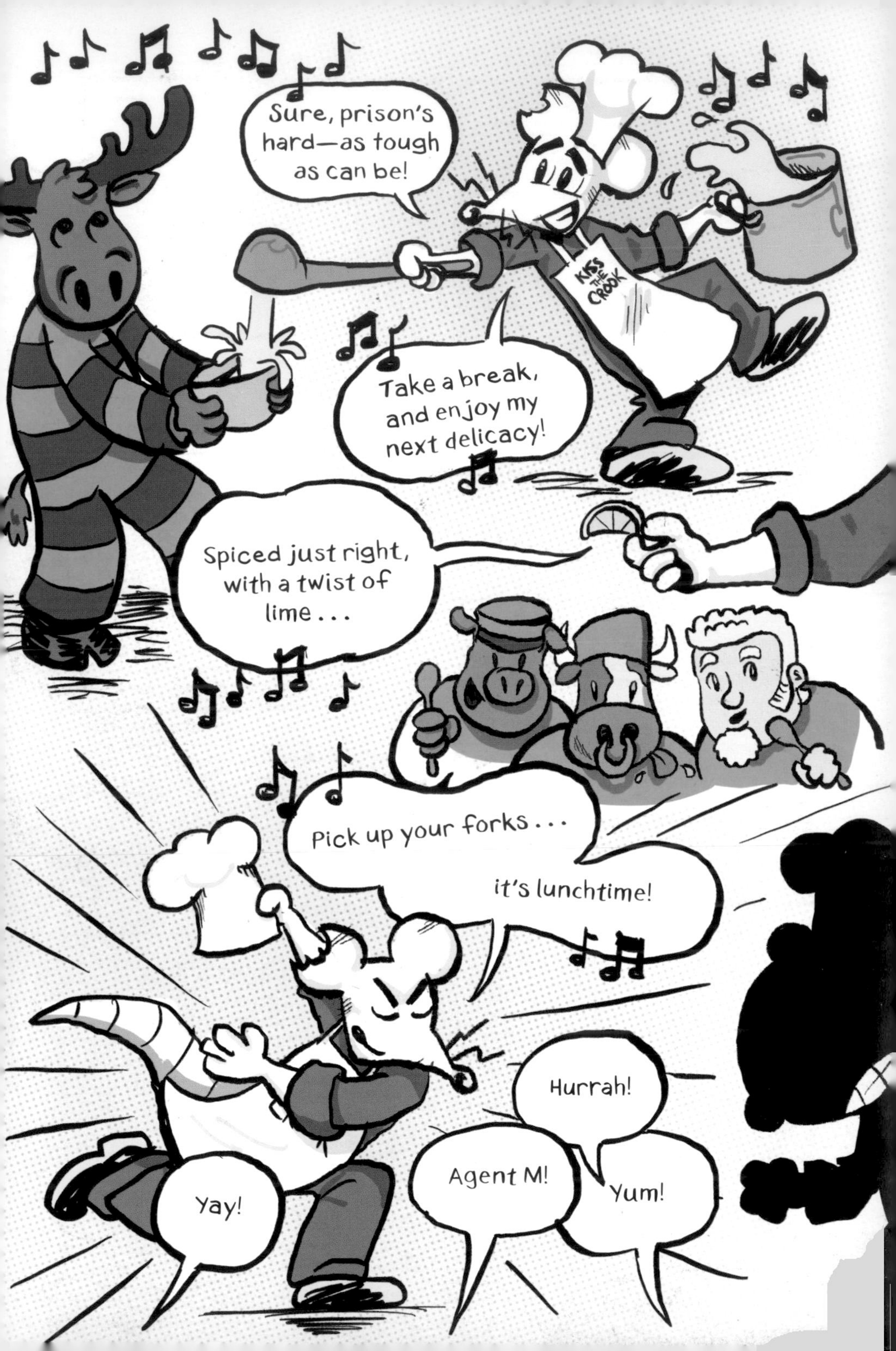
Sure, prison's hard—as tough as can be!
KISS THE CROOK
Take a break, and enjoy my next delicacy!
Spiced just right, with a twist of lime . . .
Pick up your forks . . .
it's lunchtime!
Hurrah!
Agent M!
Yum!
Yay!

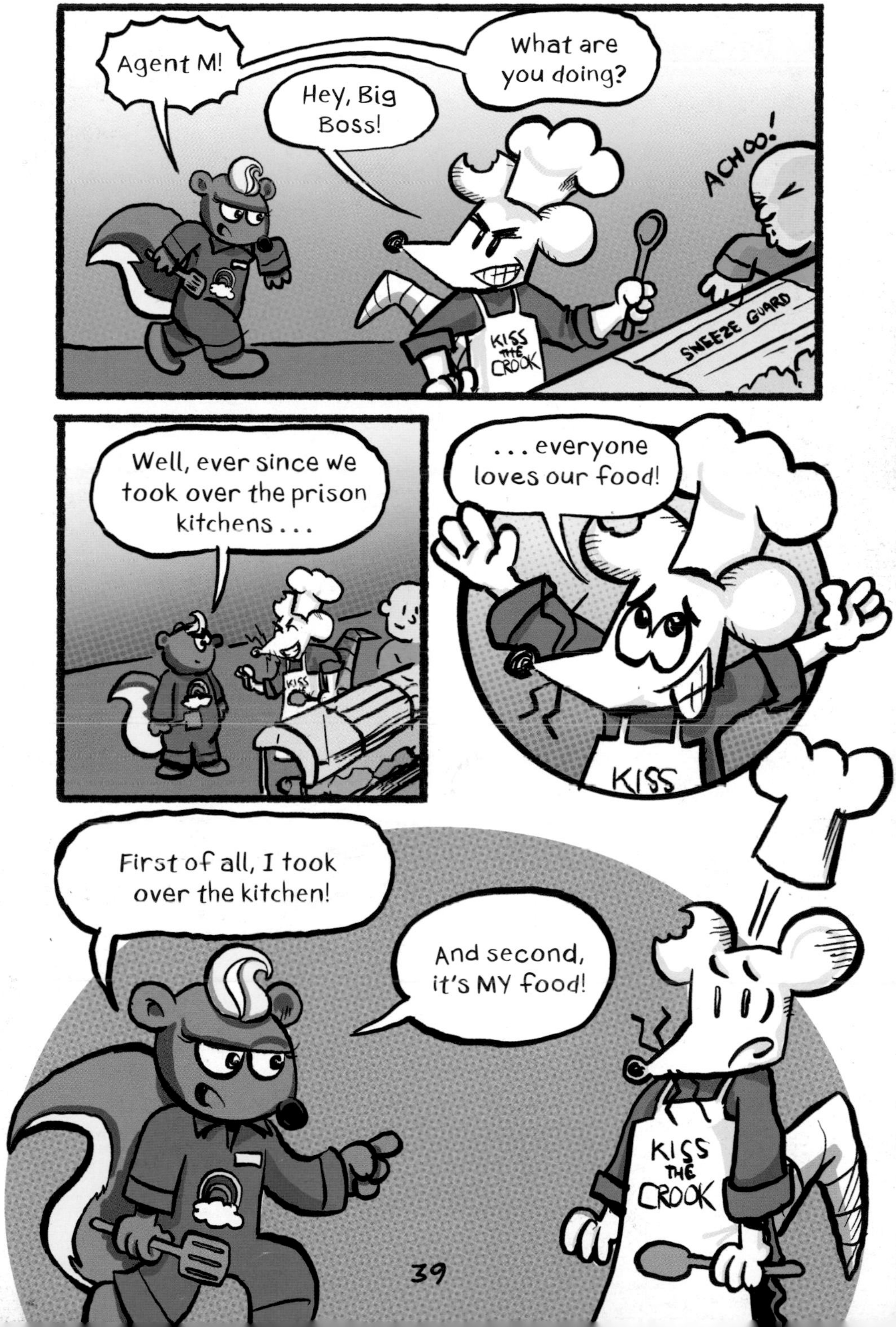
Agent M!
What are you doing?
Hey, Big Boss!
ACHOO!
KISS THE CROOK
SNEEZE GUARD
Well, ever since we took over the prison kitchens . . .
KISS
. . . everyone loves our food!
KISS
First of all, I took over the kitchen!
And second, it's MY food!
KISS THE CROOK

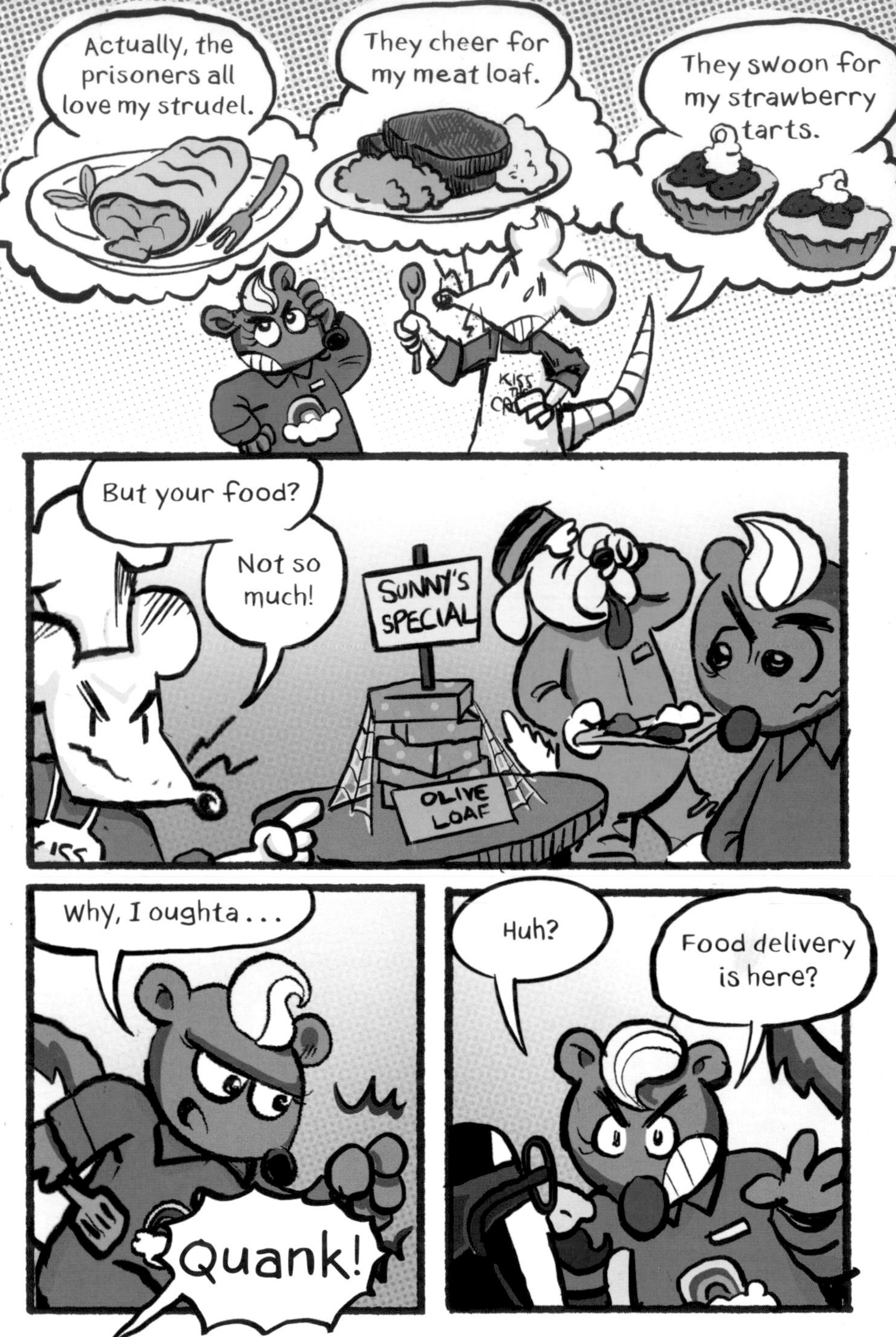
Actually, the prisoners all love my strudel.
They cheer for my meat loaf.
They swoon for my strawberry tarts.
But your food?
Not so much!
SUNNY'S SPECIAL
OLIVE LOAF
Why, I oughta . . .
Quank!
Huh?
Food delivery is here?

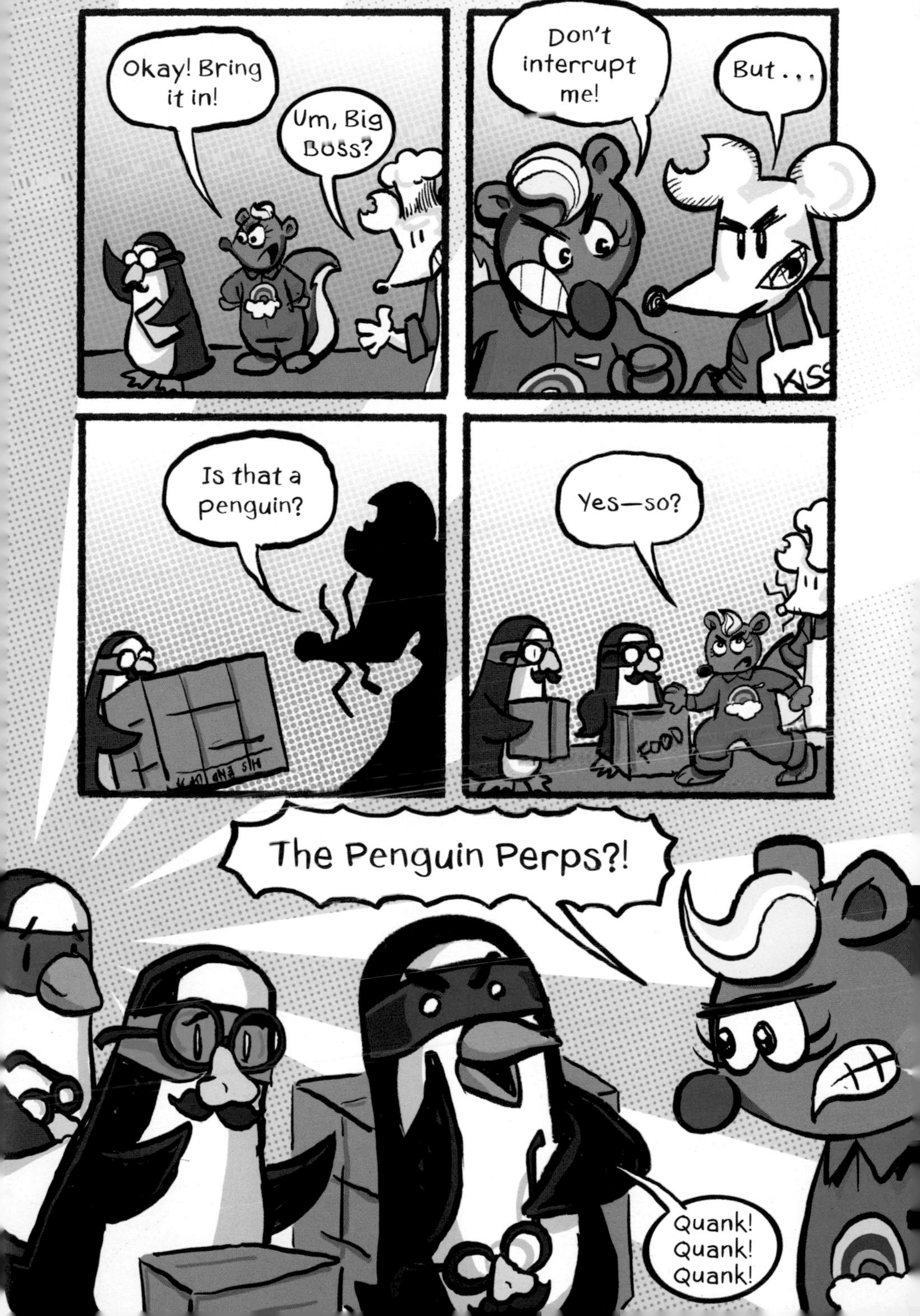
Okay! Bring it in!
Um, Big Boss?
Don't interrupt me!
But . . .
KISS
Is that a penguin?
Yes—so?
FOOD
The Penguin Perps?!
Quank! Quank! Quank!

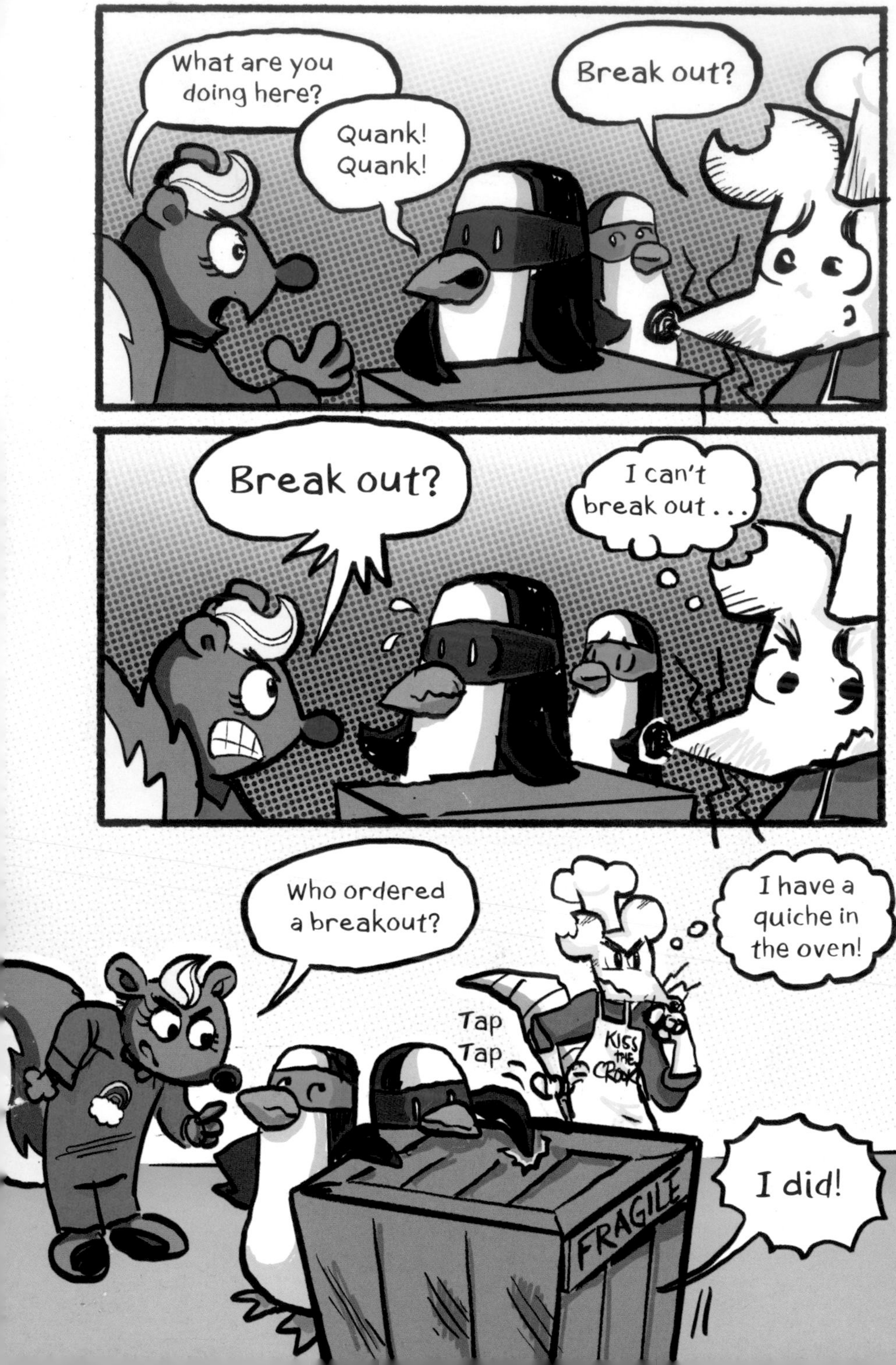
What are you doing here?
Quank! Quank!
Break out?
Break out?
I can't break out . . .
Who ordered a breakout?
I have a quiche in the oven!
Tap Tap
KISS THE CROOK
FRAGILE
I did!

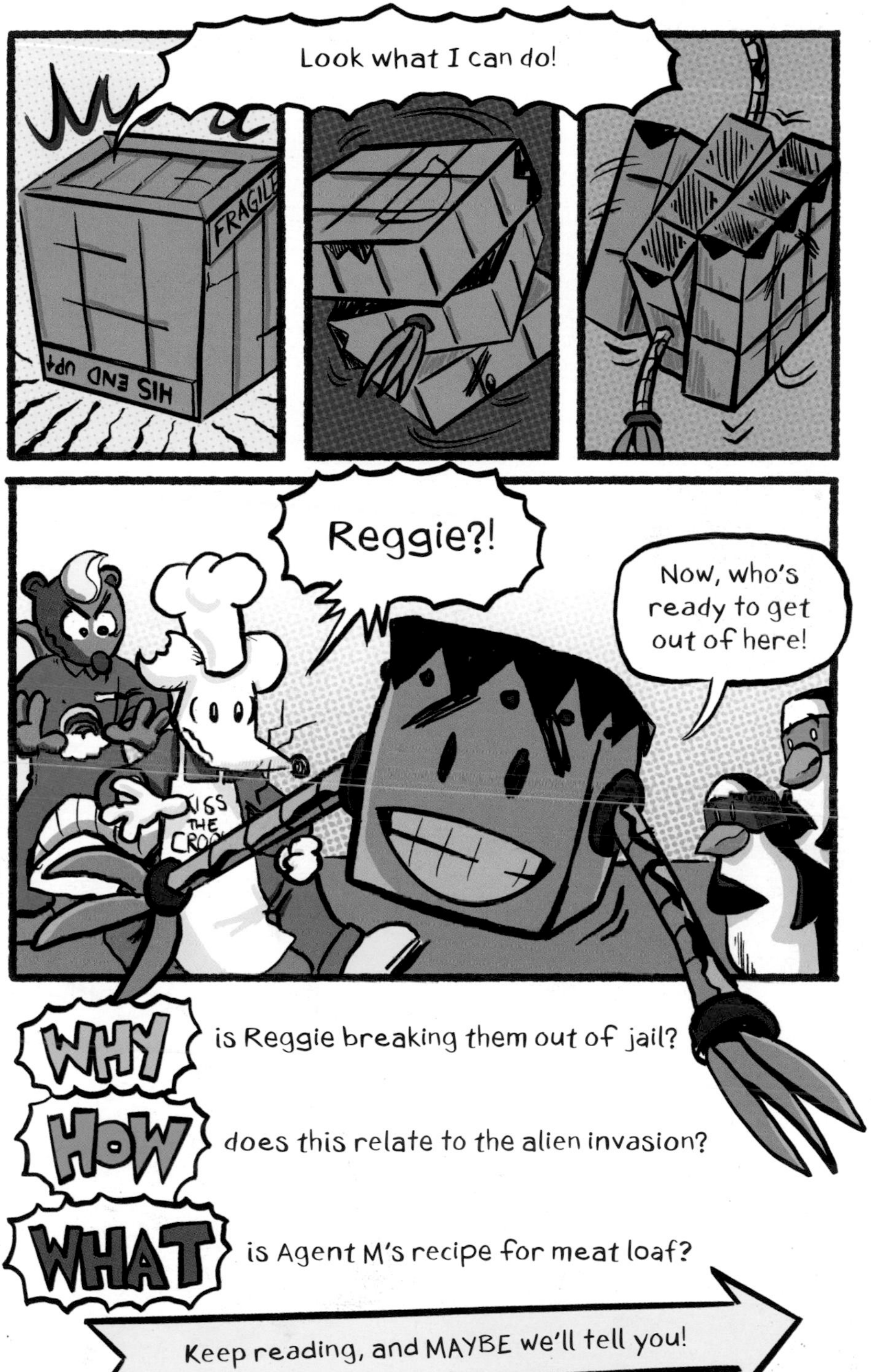
Look what I can do!
Reggie?!
Now, who's ready to get out of here!
WHY is Reggie breaking them out of jail?
HOW does this relate to the alien invasion?
WHAT is Agent M's recipe for meat loaf?
Keep reading, and MAYBE we'll tell you!

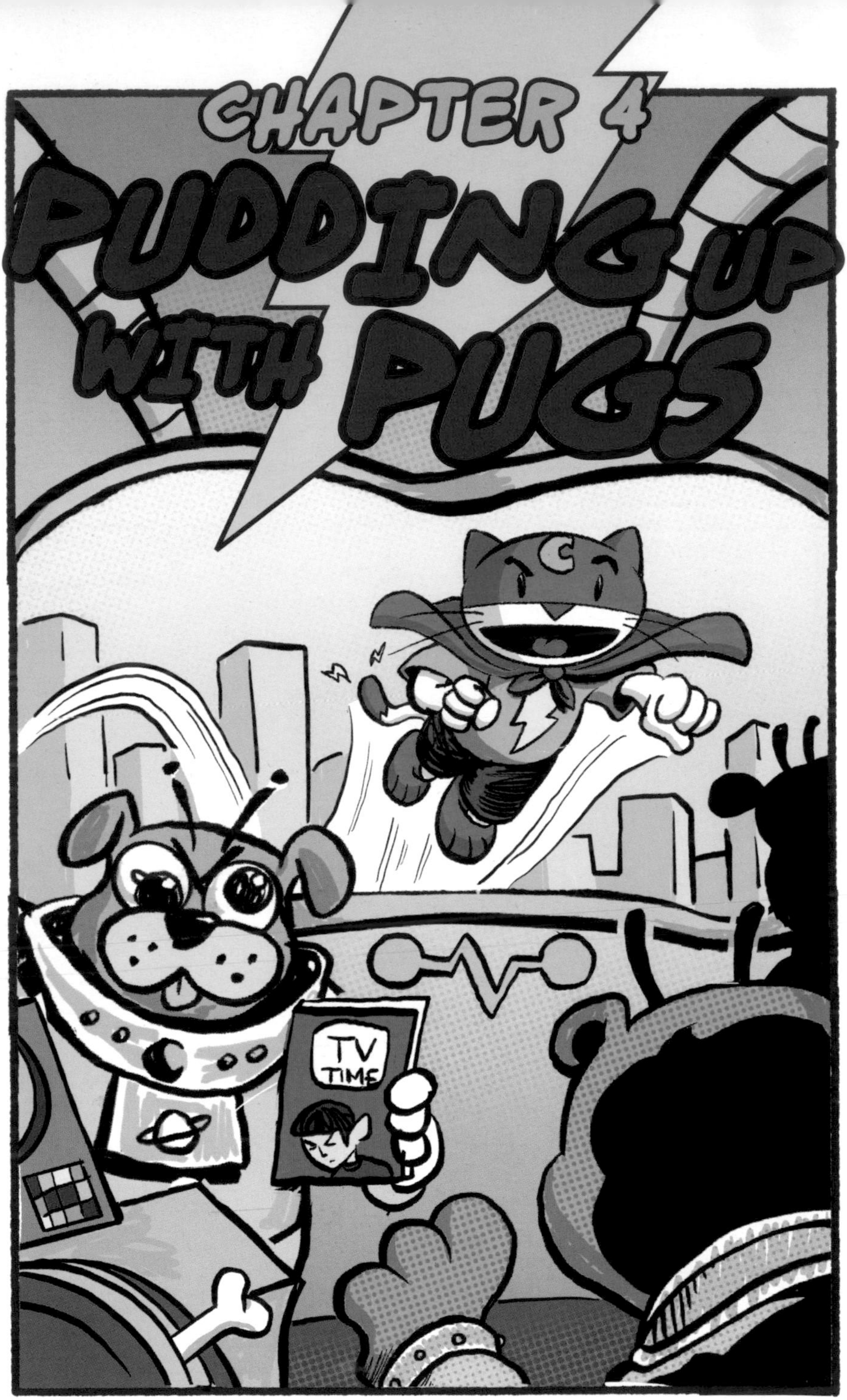
CHAPTER 4
PUDDING UP WITH PUGS
TV TIME

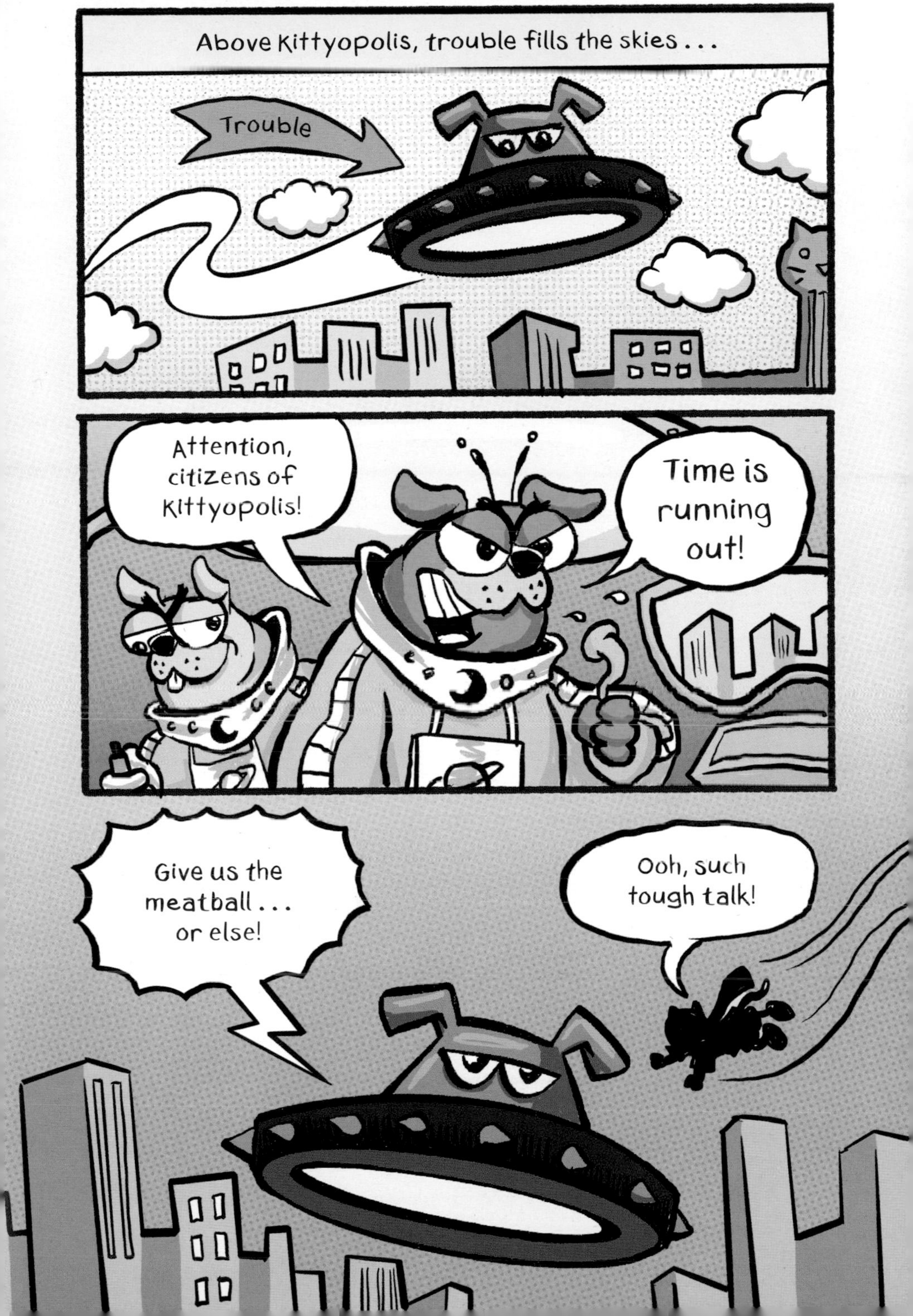
Above Kittyopolis, trouble fills the skies . . .
Trouble
Attention, citizens of Kittyopolis!
Time is running out!
Give us the meatball . . . or else!
Ooh, such tough talk!

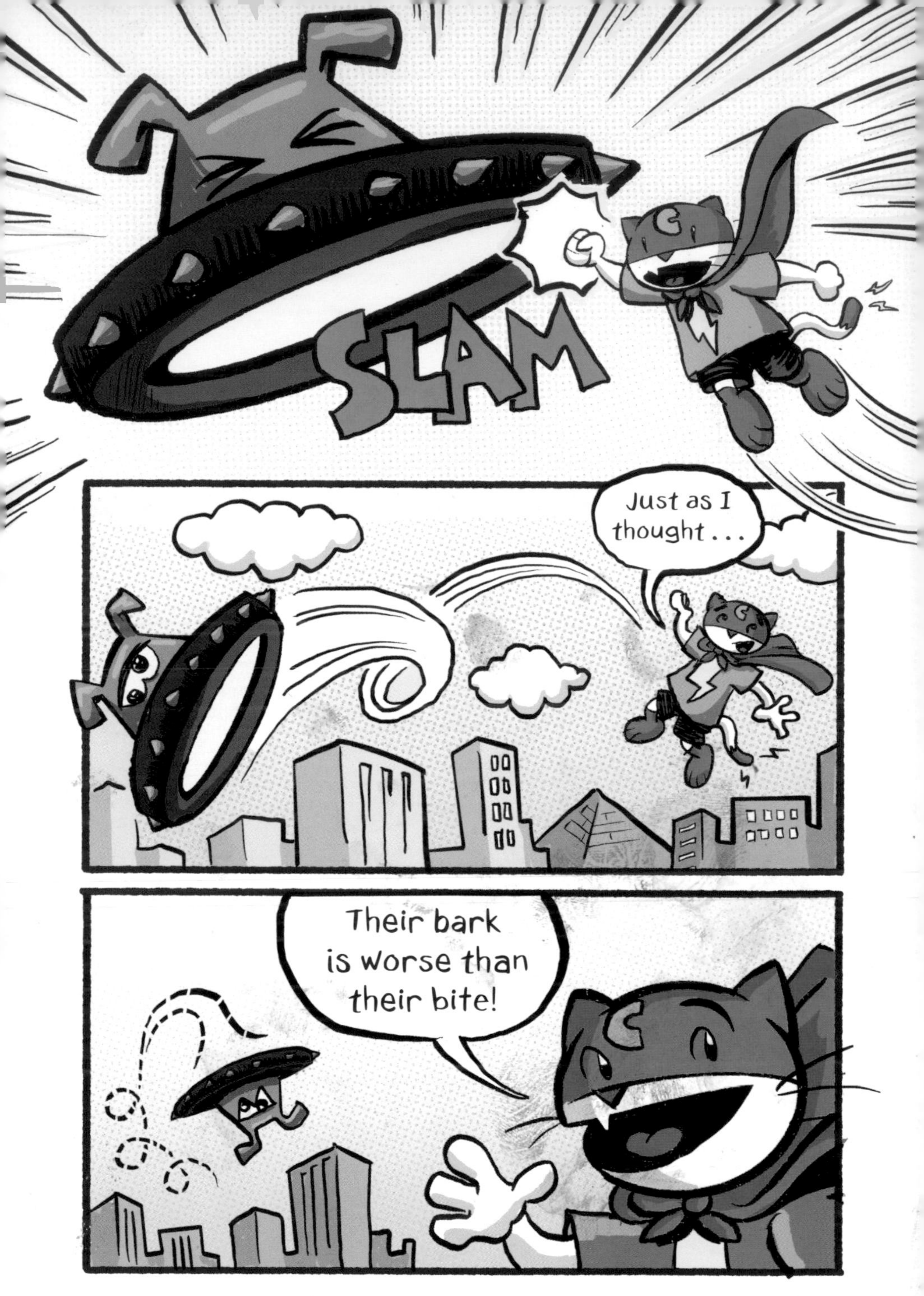
SLAM
Just as I thought . . .
Their bark is worse than their bite!

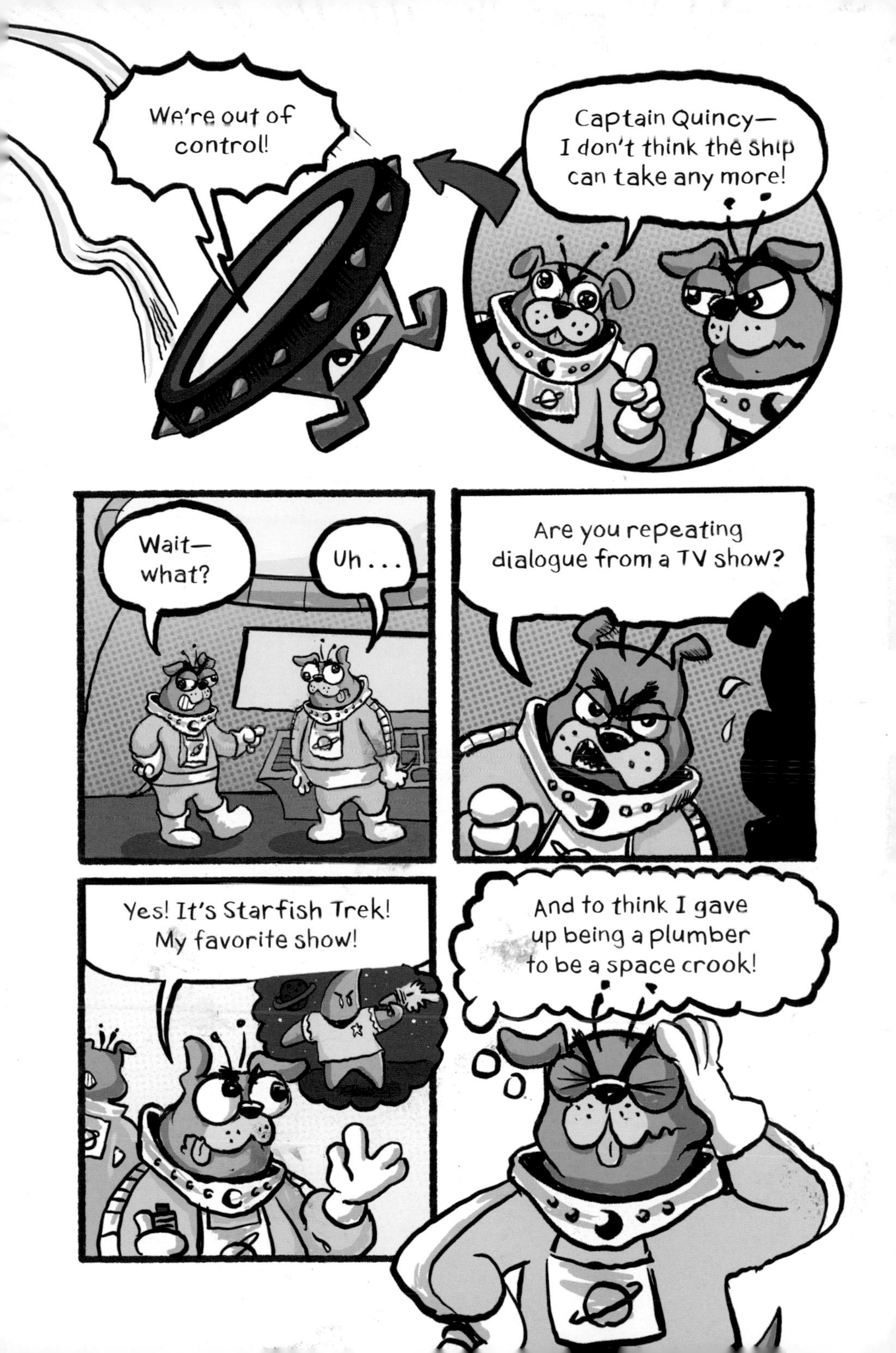
We're out of control!
Captain Quincy—I don't think the ship can take any more!
Wait—what?
Uh . . .
Are you repeating dialogue from a TV show?
Yes! It's Starfish Trek! My favorite show!
And to think I gave up being a plumber to be a space crook!

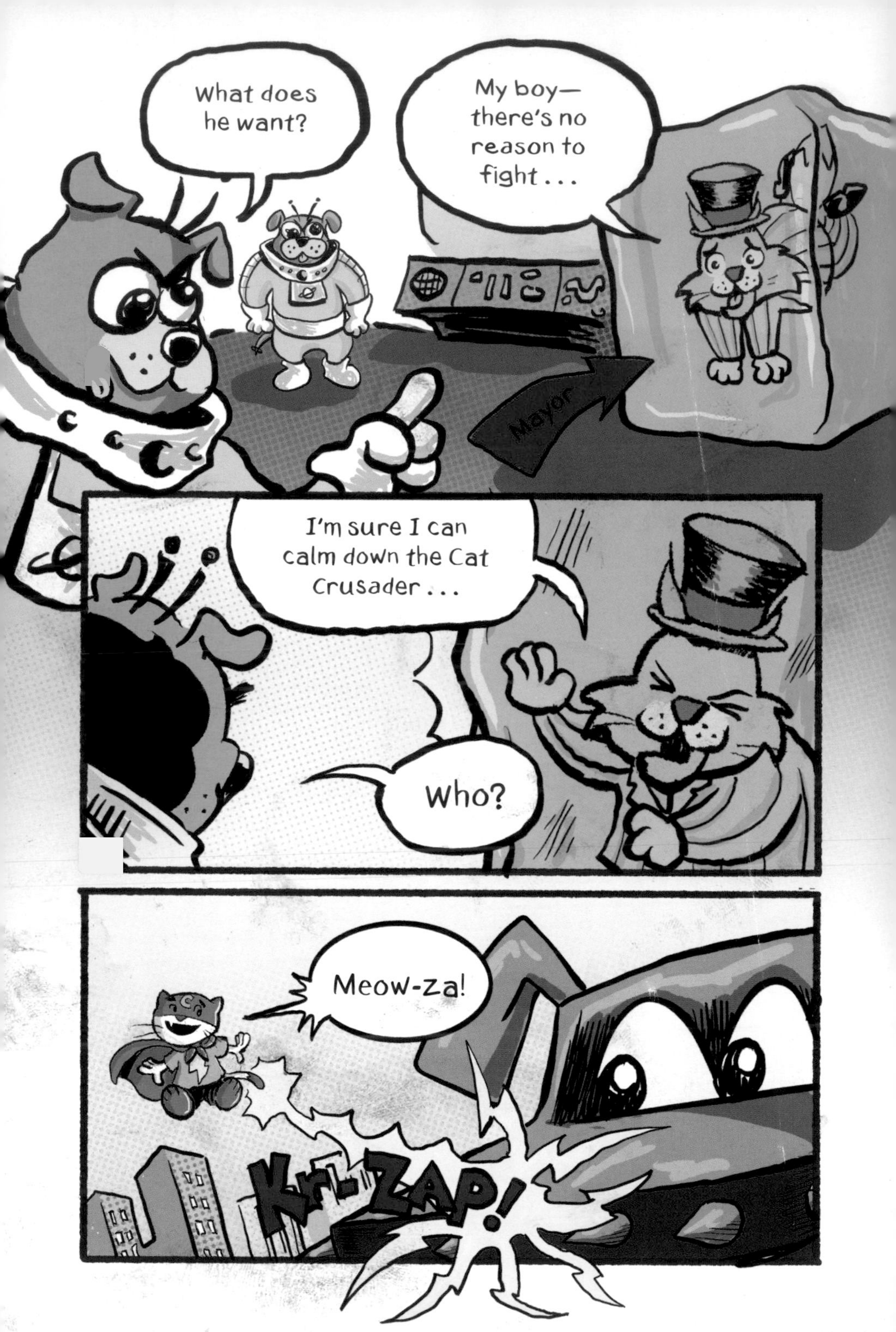
What does he want?
My boy— there's no reason to fight . . .
Mayor
I'm sure I can calm down the Cat Crusader . . .
Who?
Meow-za!
Krr-ZAP!

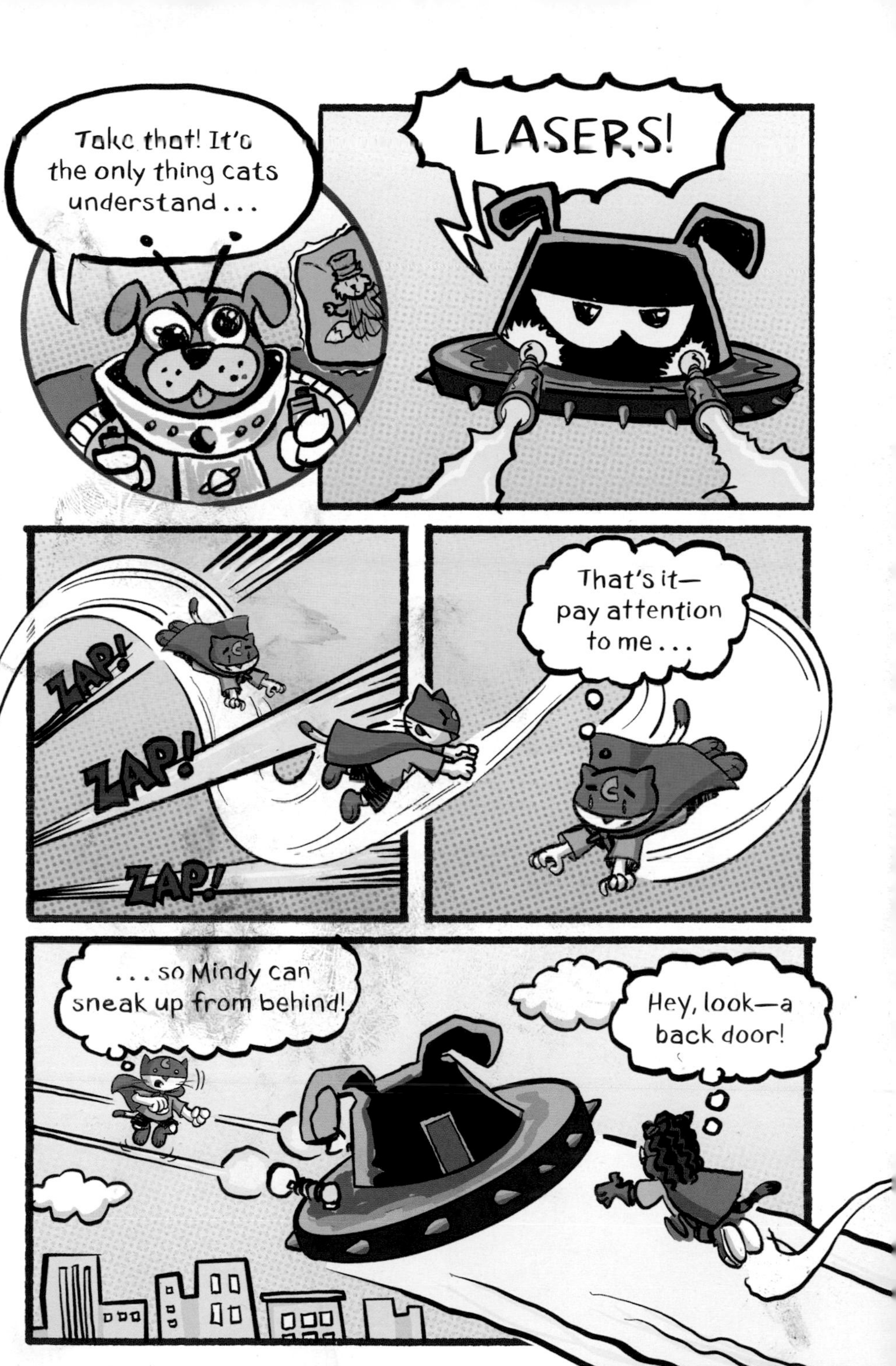
Take that! It's the only thing cats understand . . .
LASERS!
ZAP!
ZAP!
ZAP!
That's it—pay attention to me . . .
. . . so Mindy can sneak up from behind!
Hey, look—a back door!

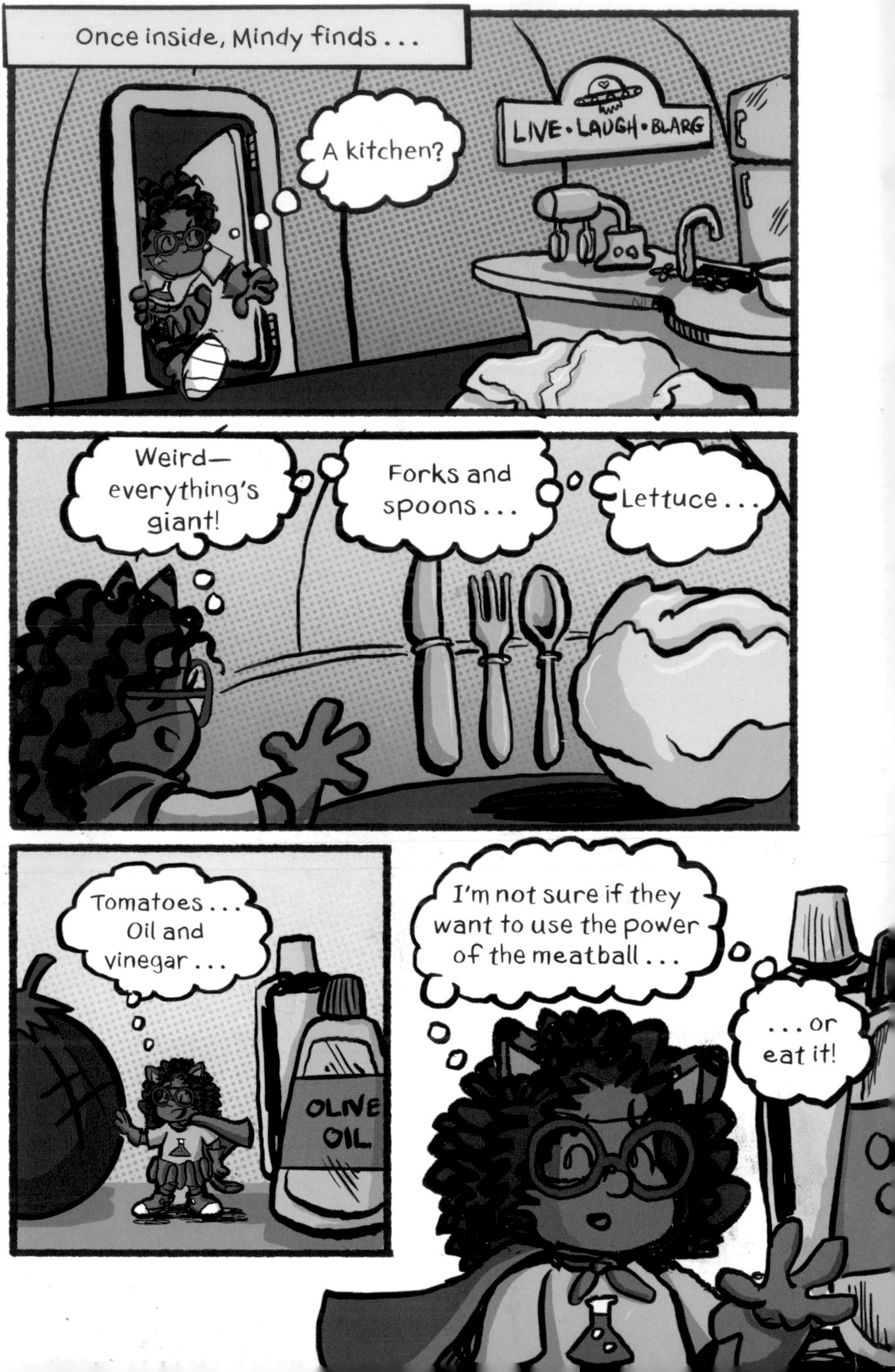
Once inside, Mindy finds . . .
A kitchen?
LIVE • LAUGH • BLARG
Weird—everything's giant!
Forks and spoons . . .
Lettuce . . .
Tomatoes . . . Oil and vinegar . . .
OLIVE OIL
I'm not sure if they want to use the power of the meatball . . .
. . . or eat it!

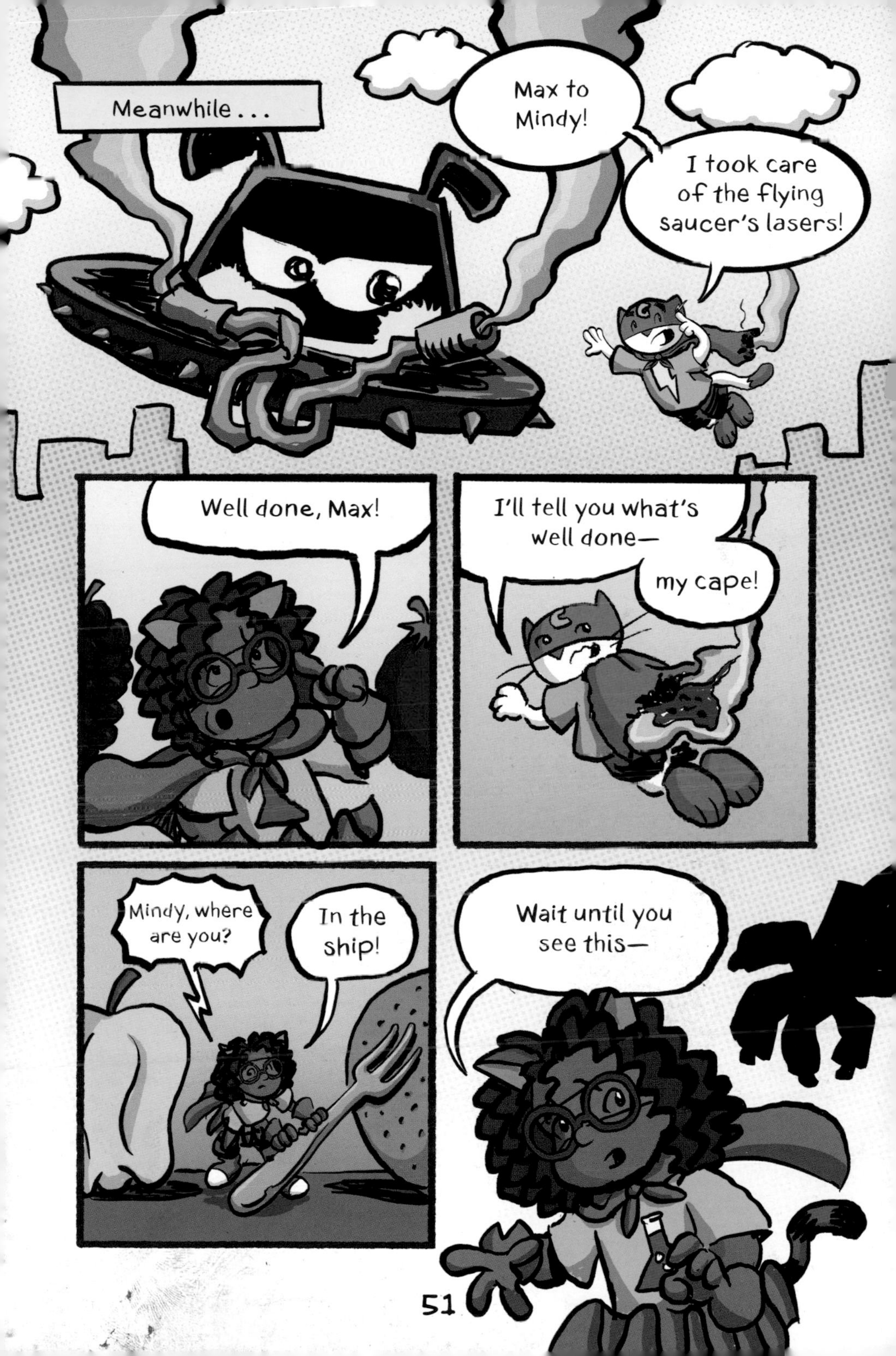
Meanwhile . . .
Max to Mindy!
I took care of the flying saucer's lasers!
Well done, Max!
I'll tell you what's well done—
my cape!
Mindy, where are you?
In the ship!
Wait until you see this—

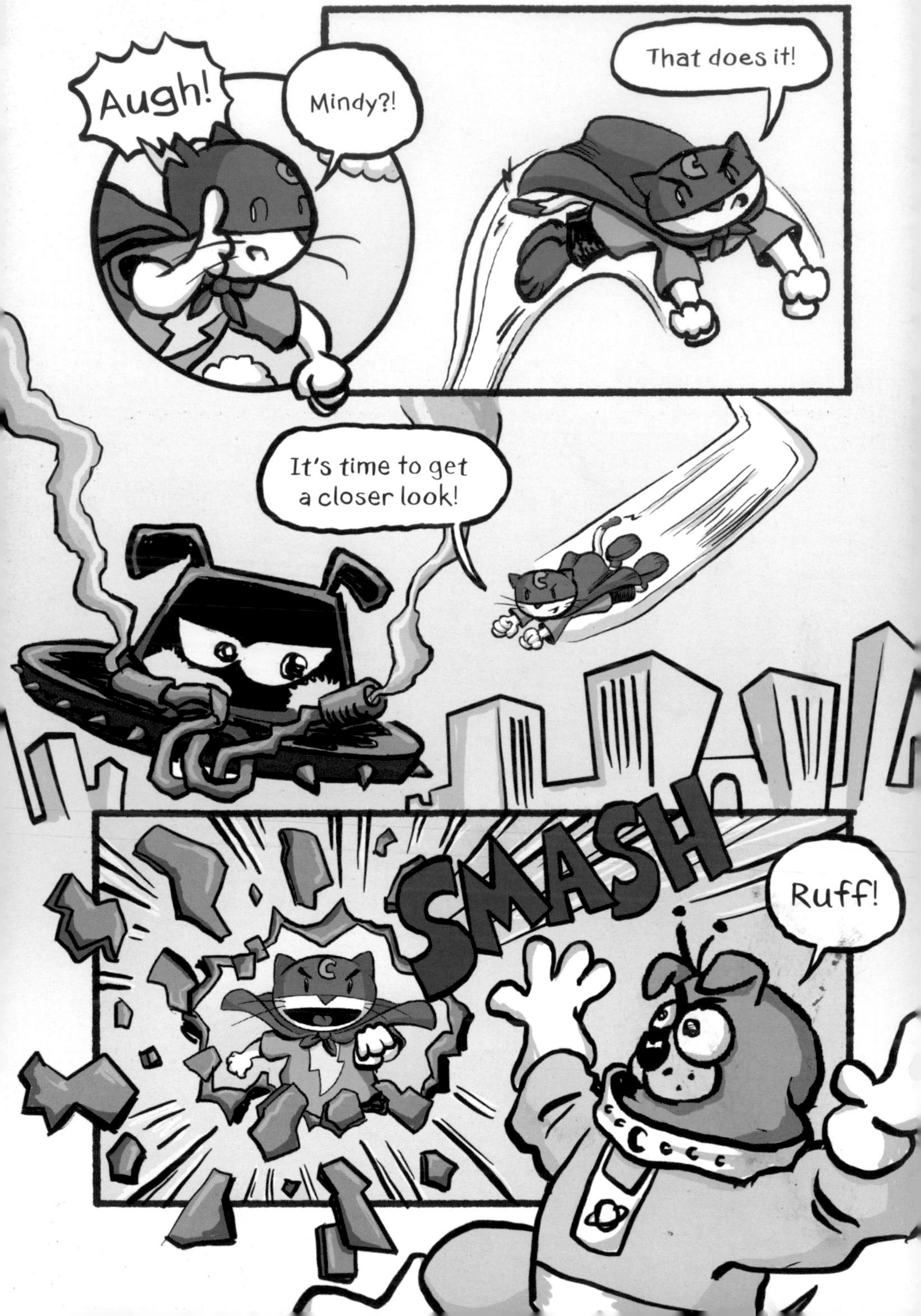
Augh!
Mindy?!
That does it!
It's time to get a closer look!
SMASH
Ruff!

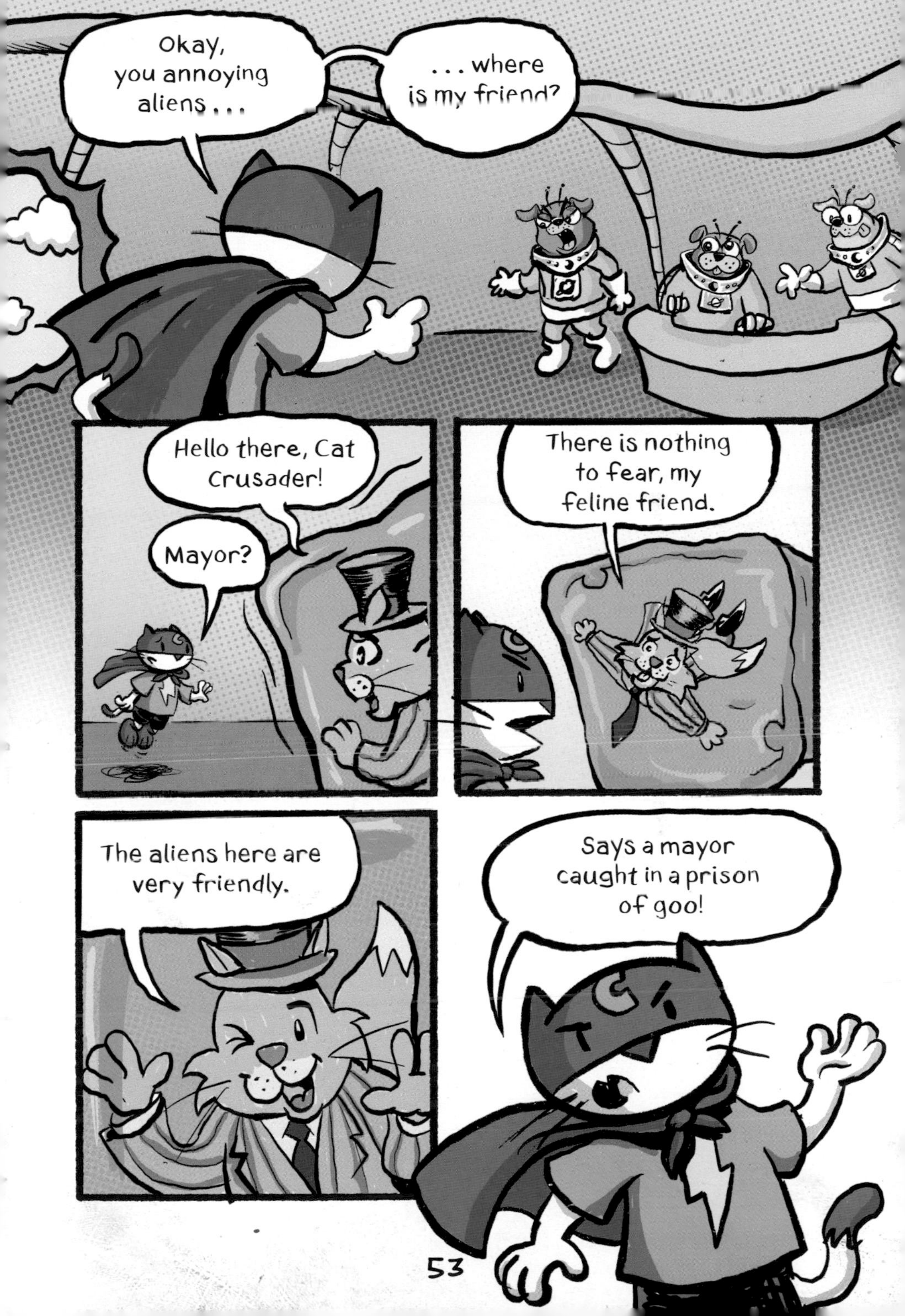
Okay, you annoying aliens . . .
. . . where is my friend?
Hello there, Cat Crusader!
Mayor?
There is nothing to fear, my feline friend.
The aliens here are very friendly.
Says a mayor caught in a prison of goo!

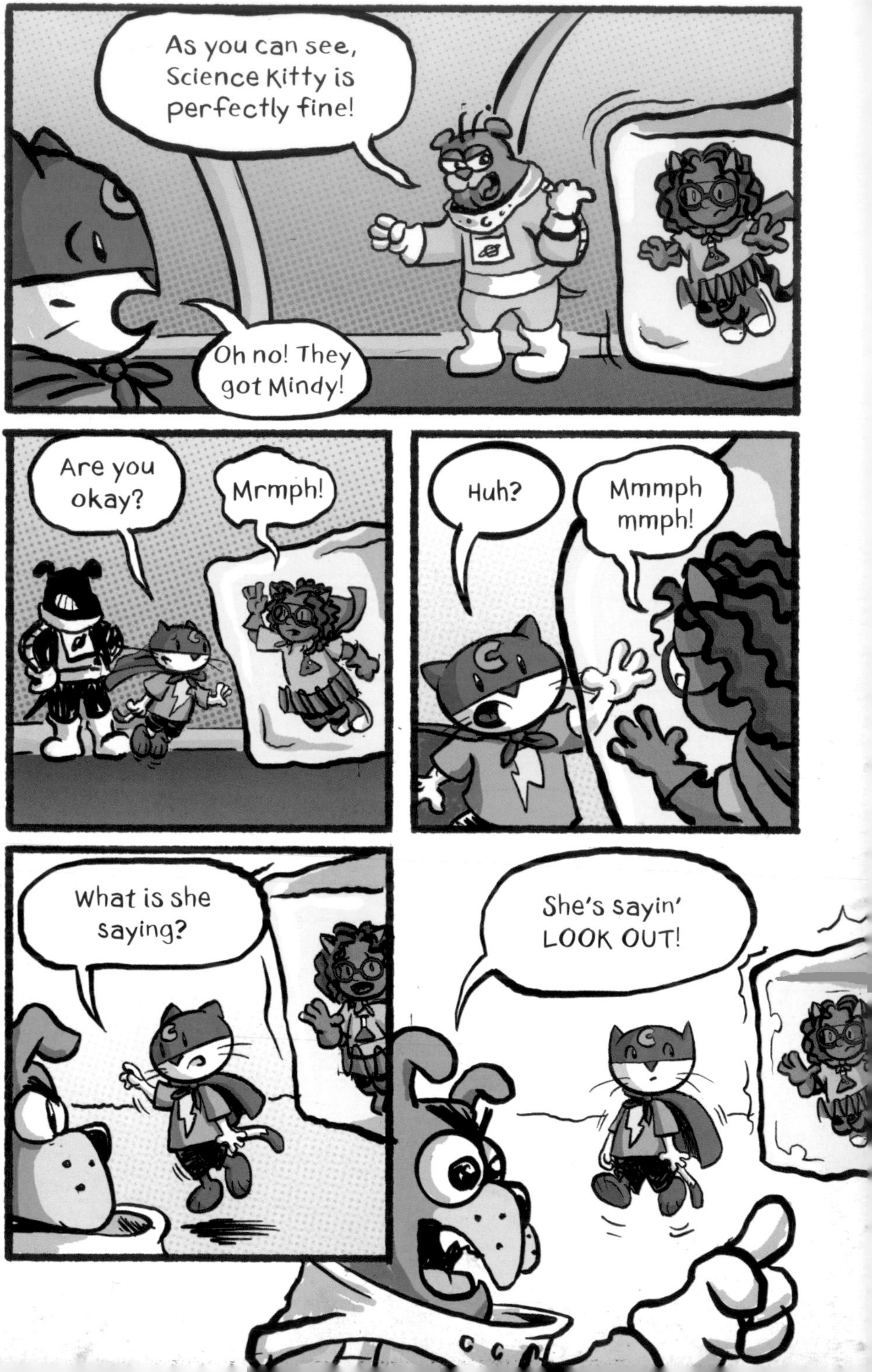
As you can see, Science Kitty is perfectly fine!
Oh no! They got Mindy!
Are you okay?
Mrmph!
Huh?
Mmmph mmph!
What is she saying?
She's sayin' LOOK OUT!

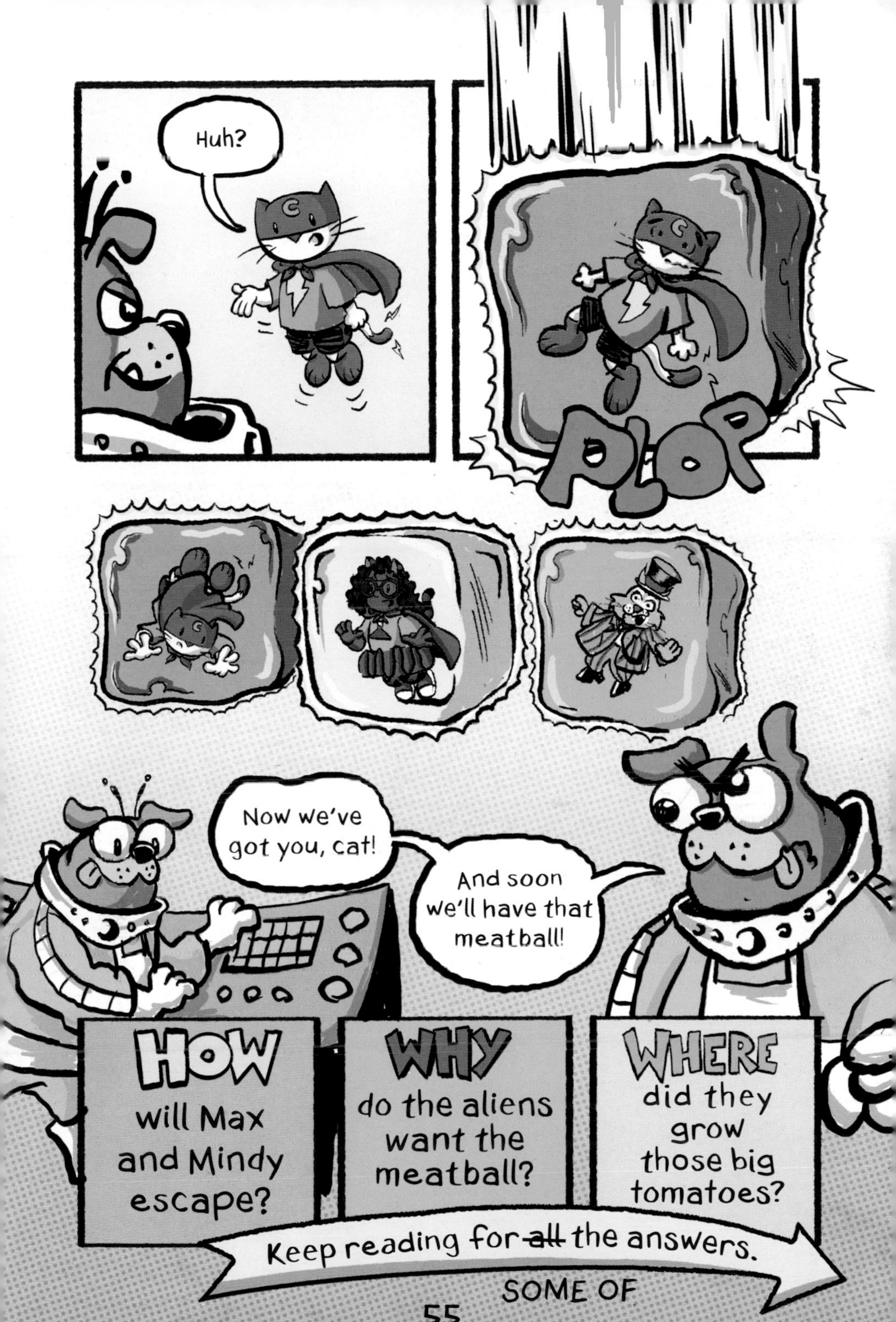
Huh?
PLOP
Now we've got you, cat!
And soon we'll have that meatball!
HOW will Max and Mindy escape?
WHY do the aliens want the meatball?
WHERE did they grow those big tomatoes?
Keep reading for all the answers.
SOME OF

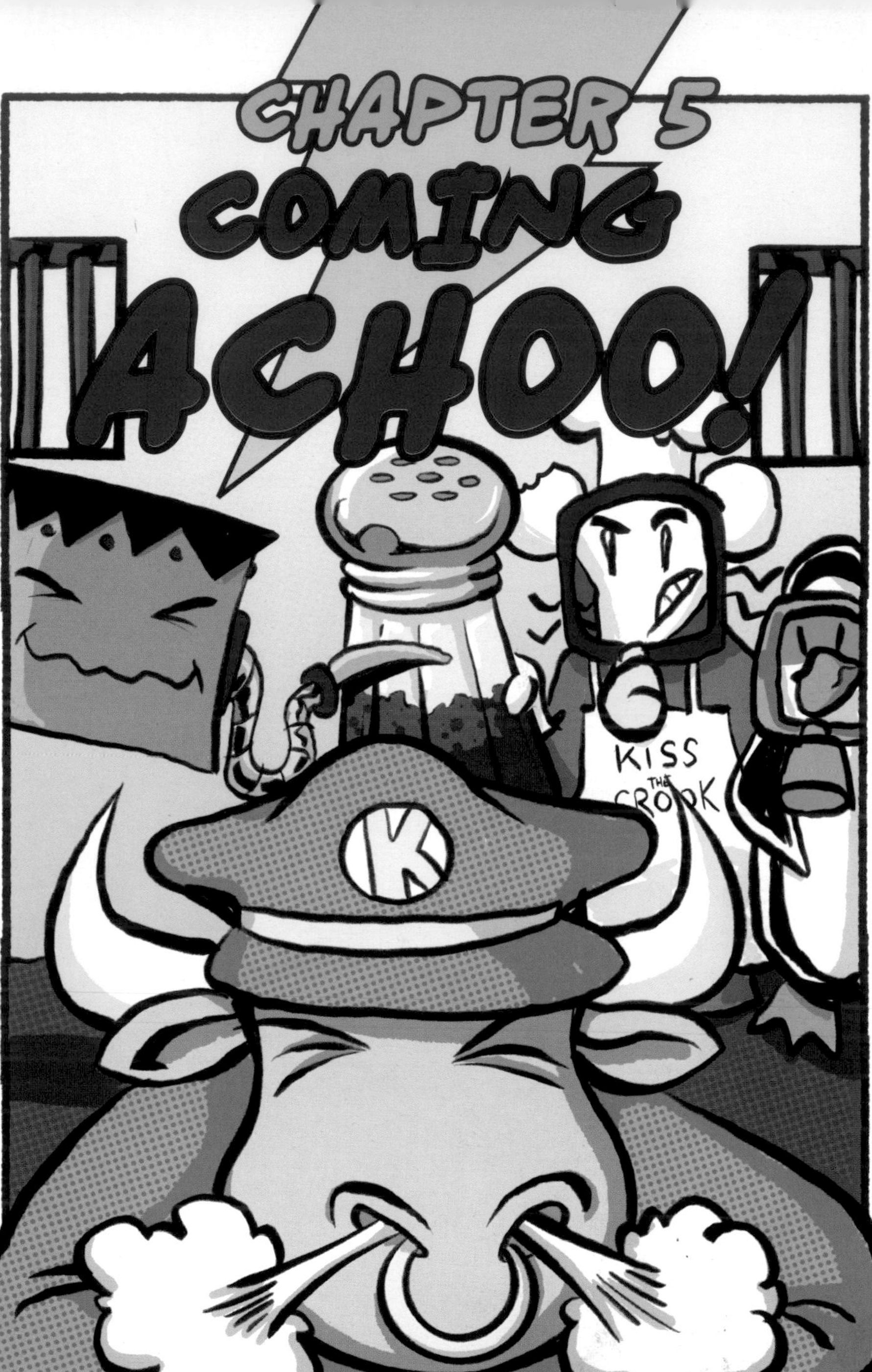
CHAPTER 5
COMING ACHOO!
KISS THE CROOK

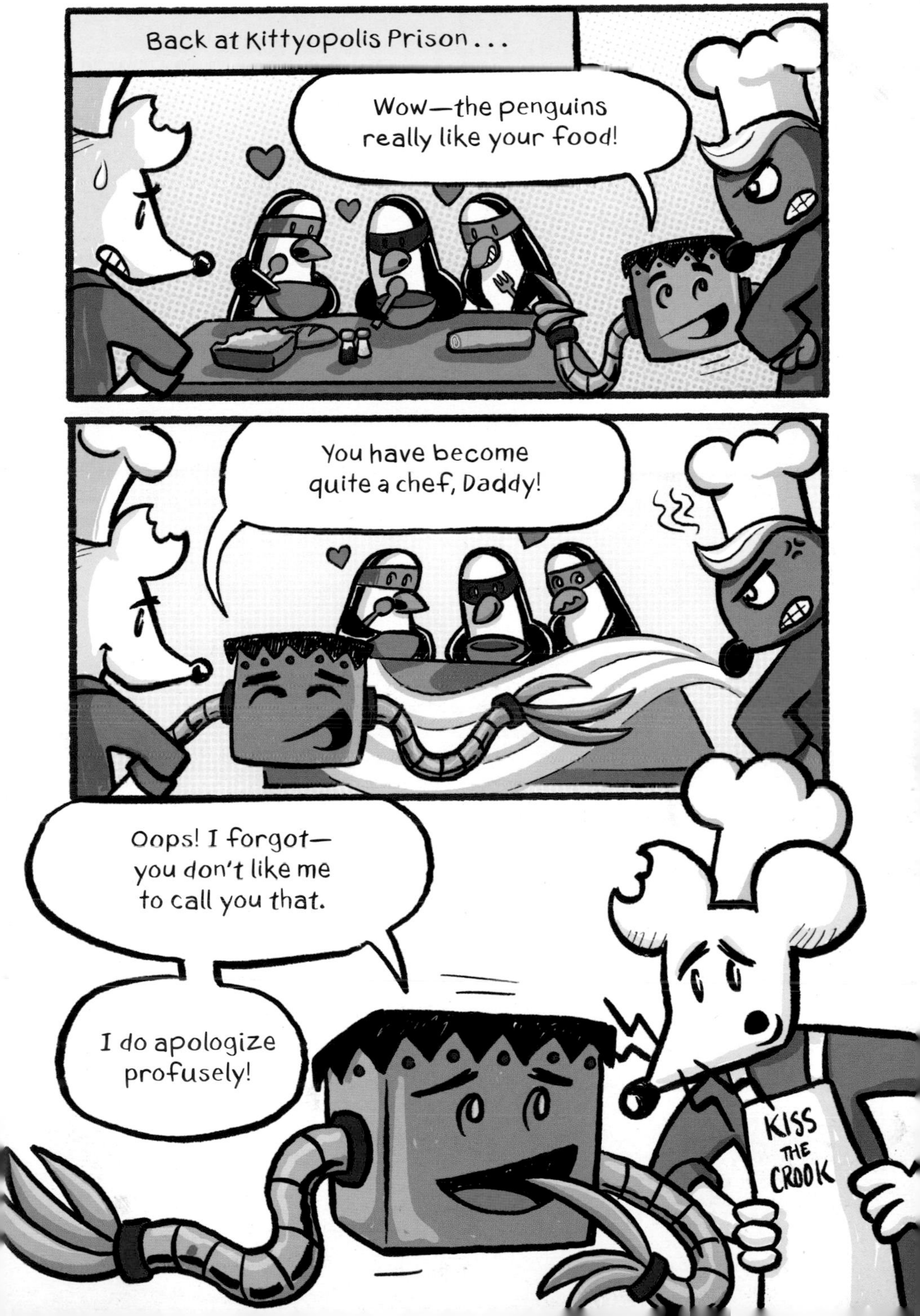
Back at Kittyopolis Prison . . .
Wow—the penguins really like your food!
You have become quite a chef, Daddy!
Oops! I forgot—you don't like me to call you that.
I do apologize profusely!
KISS THE CROOK

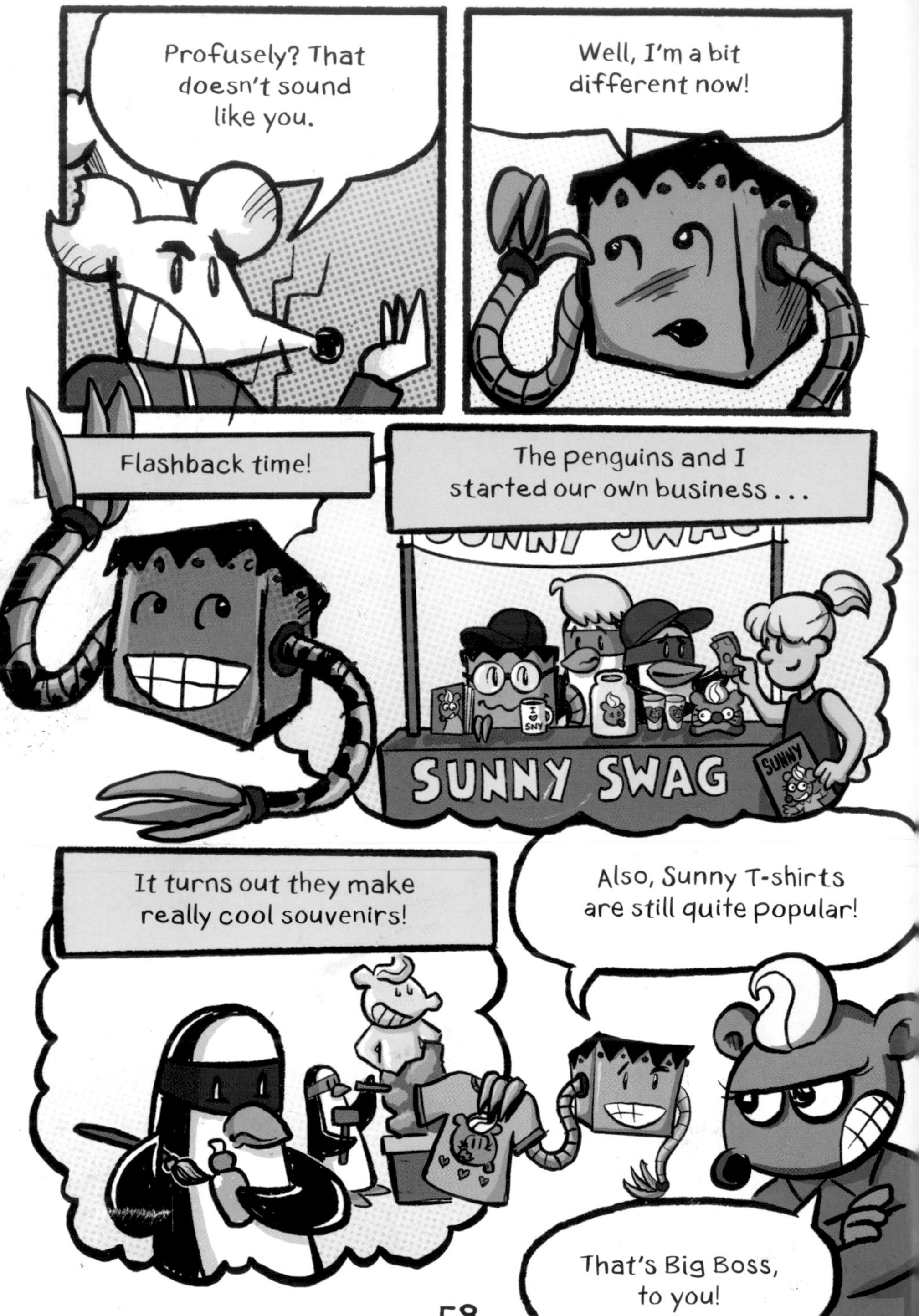

Profusely? That doesn't sound like you.
Well, I'm a bit different now!
Flashback time!
The penguins and I started our own business . . .
SUNNY SWAG
I ♥ SNY
SUNNY SWAG
SUNNY
It turns out they make really cool souvenirs!
Also, Sunny T-shirts are still quite popular!
That's Big Boss, to you!

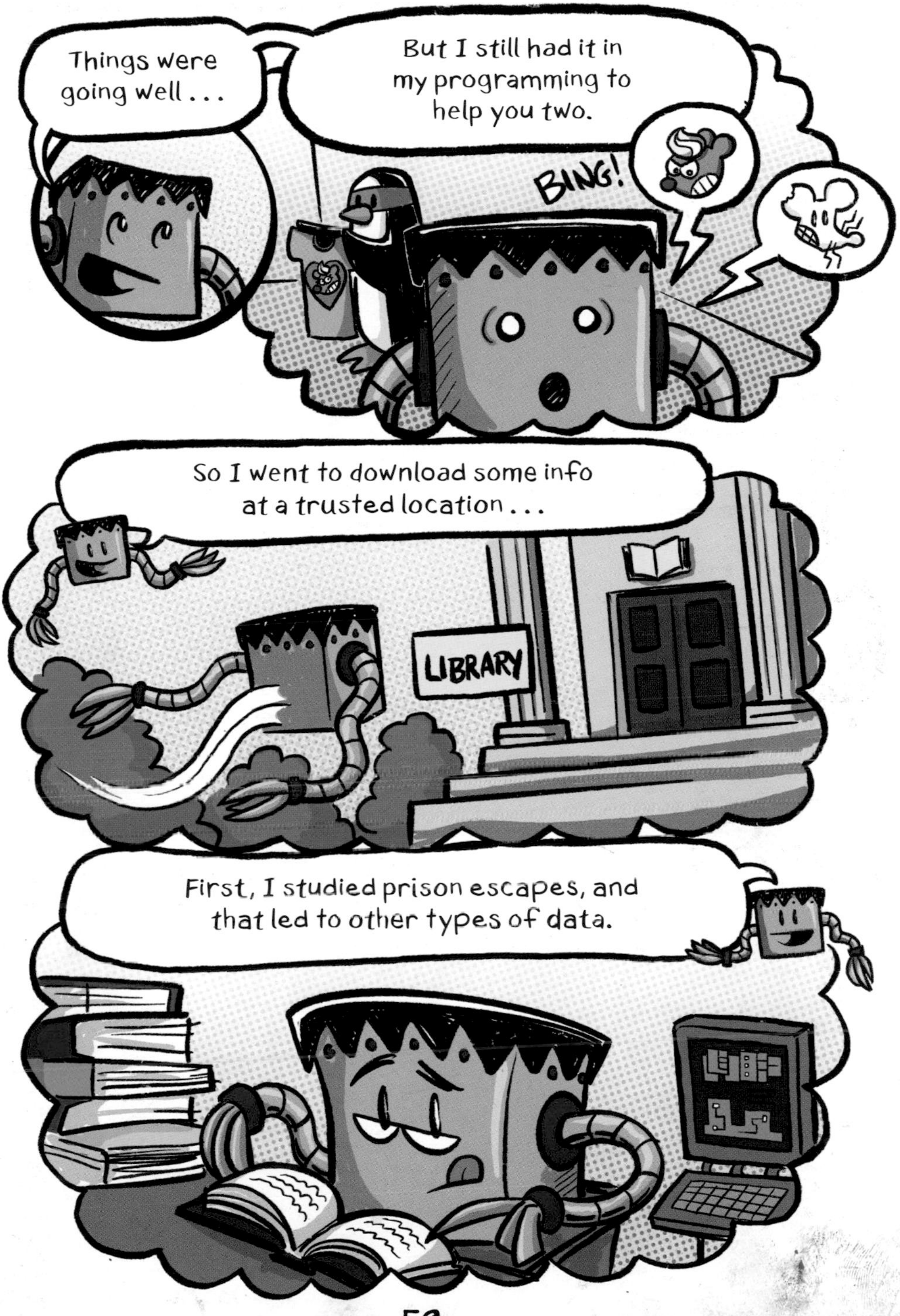

Things were going well . . .
But I still had it in my programming to help you two.
BING!
So I went to download some info at a trusted location . . .
LIBRARY
First, I studied prison escapes, and that led to other types of data.

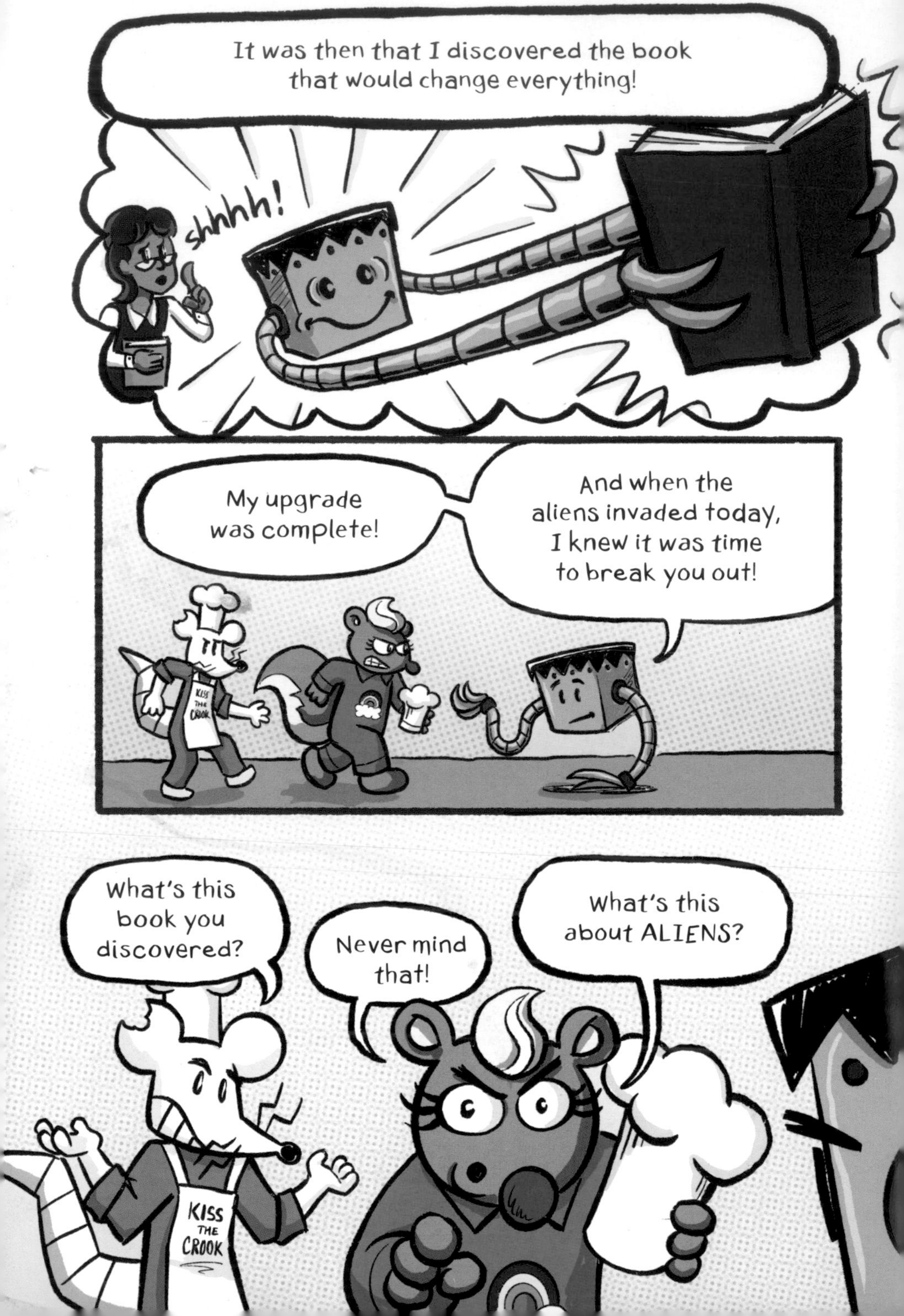
It was then that I discovered the book that would change everything!
shhhh!
My upgrade was complete!
And when the aliens invaded today, I knew it was time to break you out!
KISS THE CROOK
What's this book you discovered?
Never mind that!
What's this about ALIENS?
KISS THE CROOK

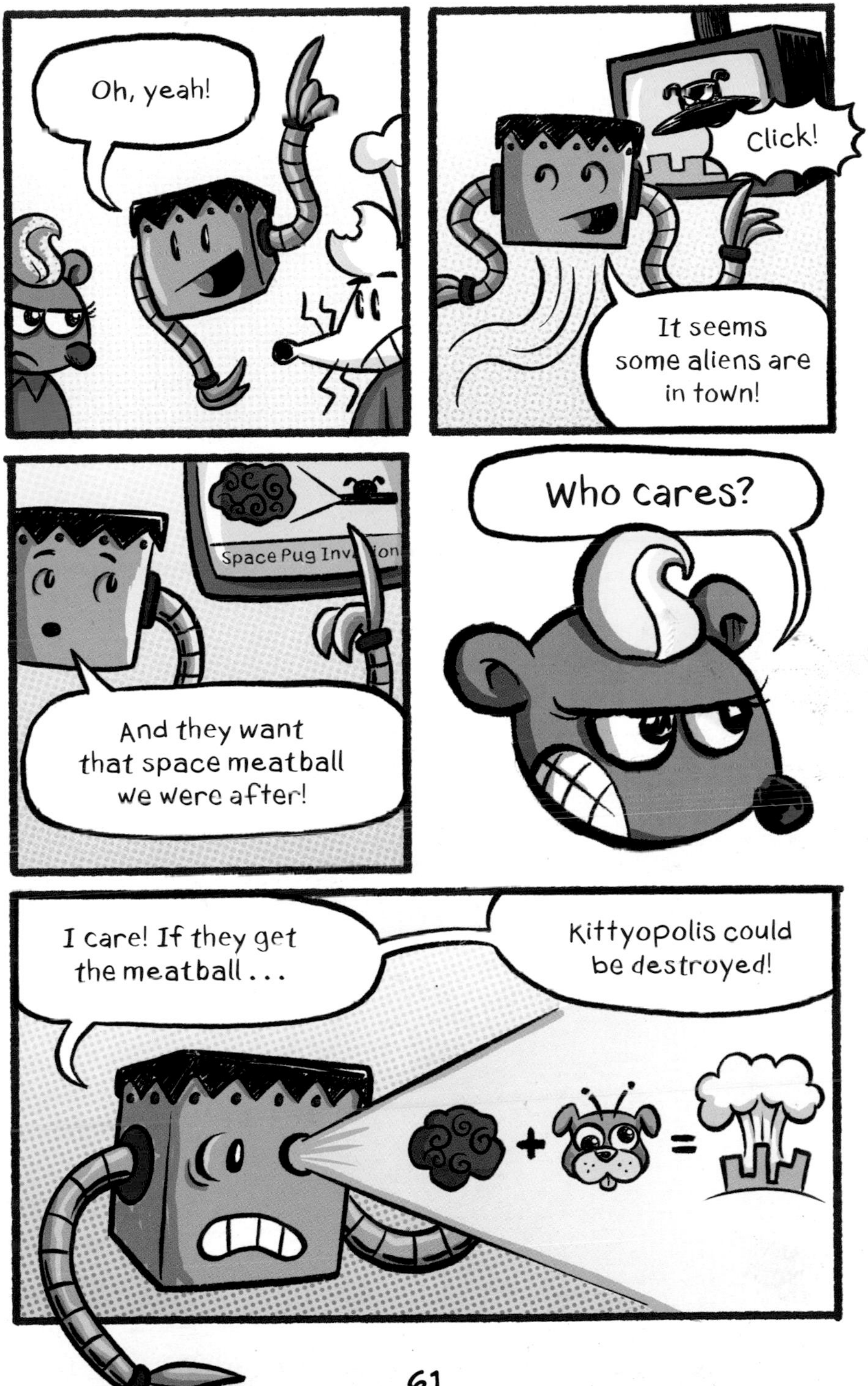
Oh, yeah!
Click!
It seems some aliens are in town!
Space Pug Inv
And they want that space meatball we were after!
Who cares?
I care! If they get the meatball . . .
Kittyopolis could be destroyed!

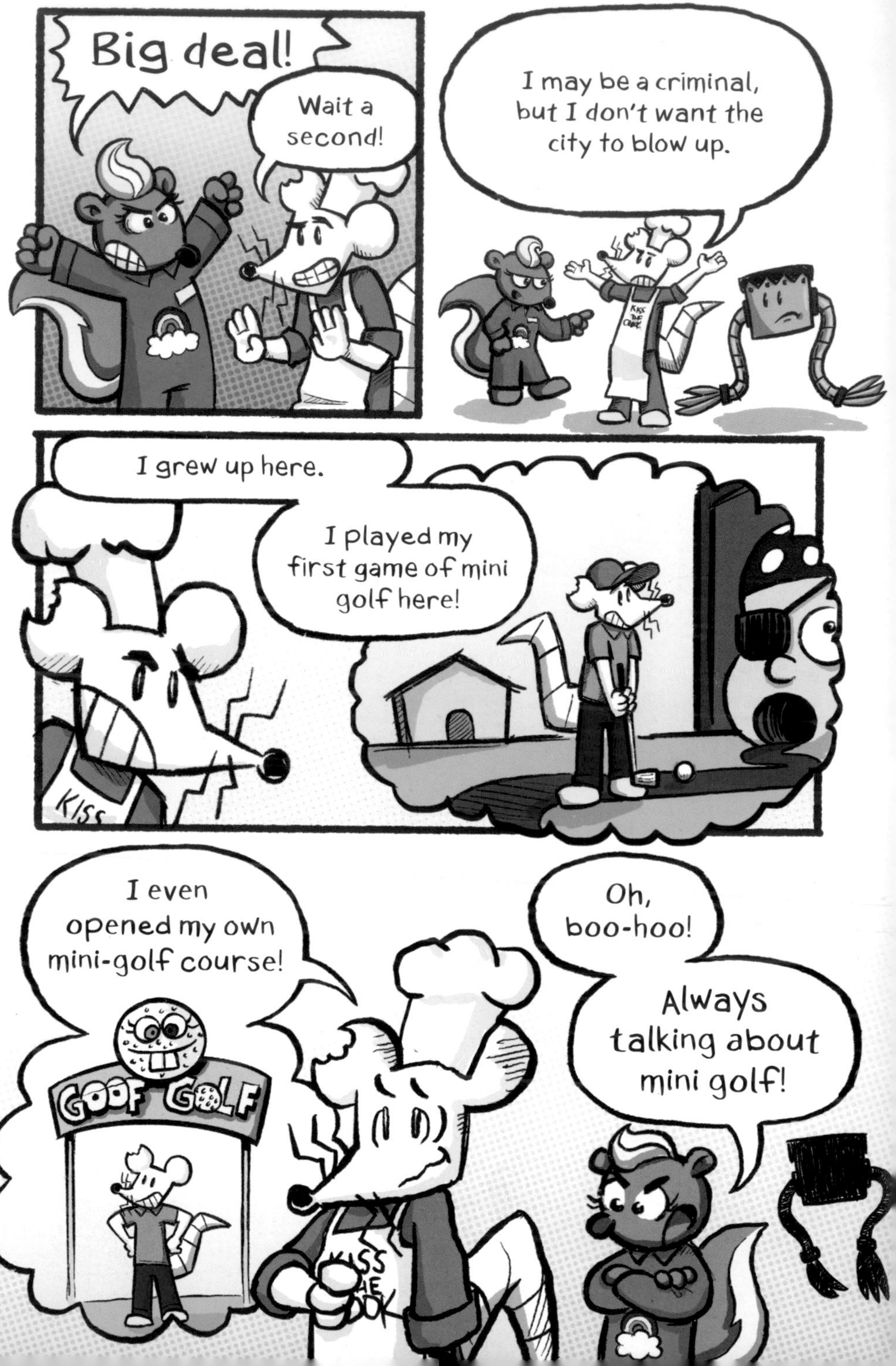
Big deal!
Wait a second!
I may be a criminal, but I don't want the city to blow up.
KISS THE COOK
I grew up here.
I played my first game of mini golf here!
KISS
I even opened my own mini-golf course!
GOOF GOLF
Oh, boo-hoo!
Always talking about mini golf!
KISS THE COOK

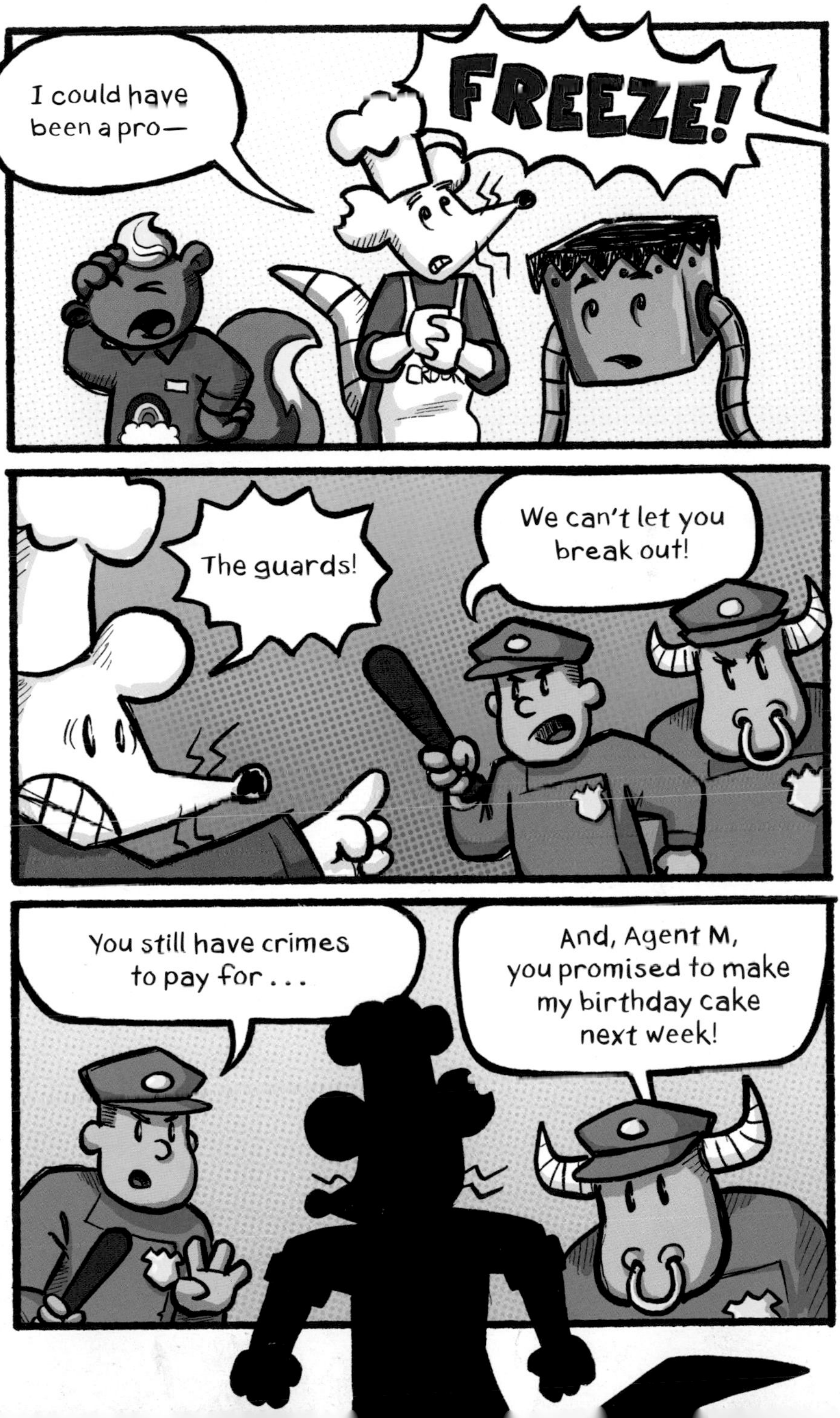
I could have been a pro—
FREEZE!
CROOK
The guards!
We can't let you break out!
You still have crimes to pay for . . .
And, Agent M, you promised to make my birthday cake next week!

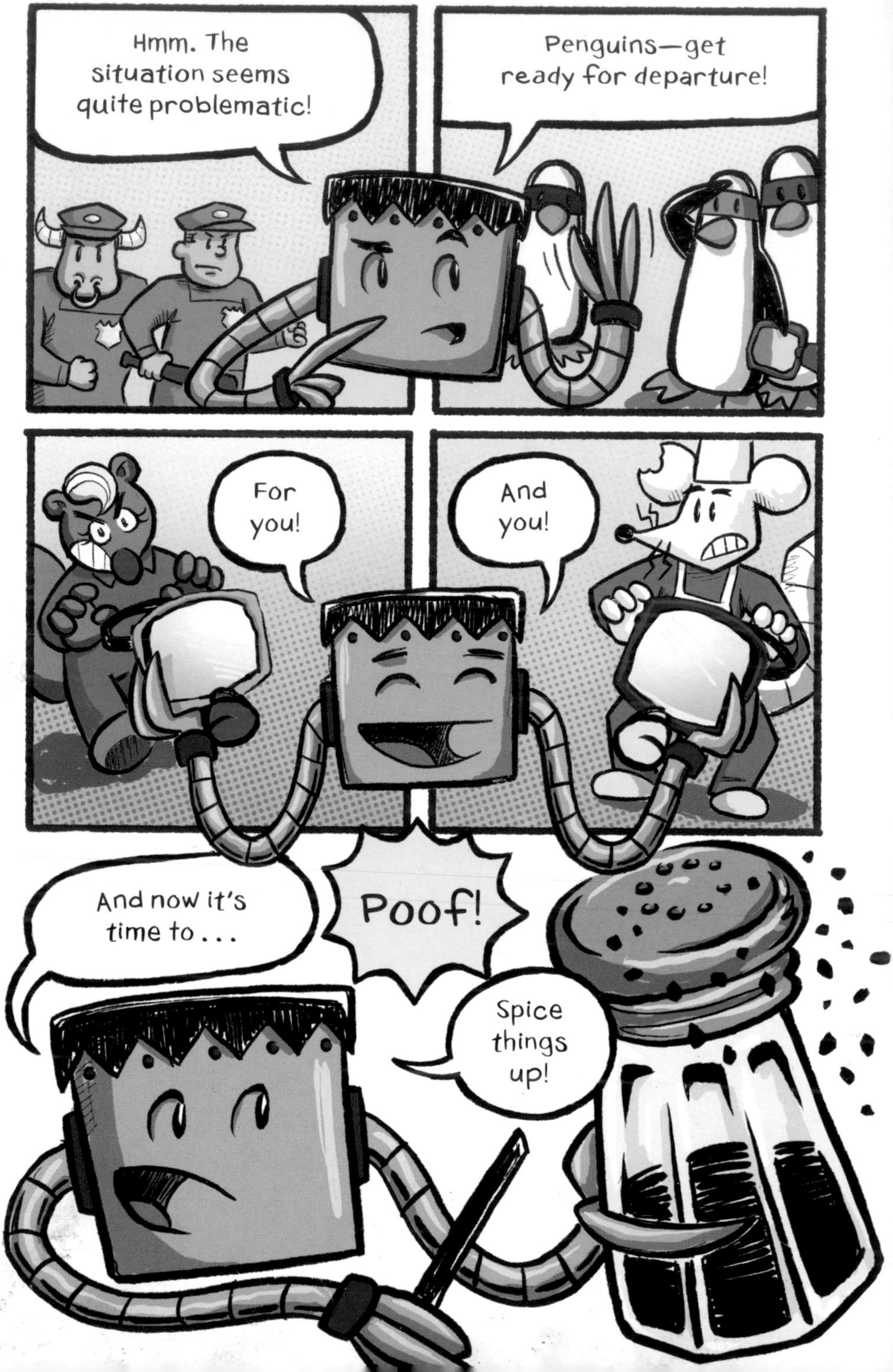
Hmm. The situation seems quite problematic!
Penguins—get ready for departure!
For you!
And you!
And now it's time to . . .
Poof!
Spice things up!

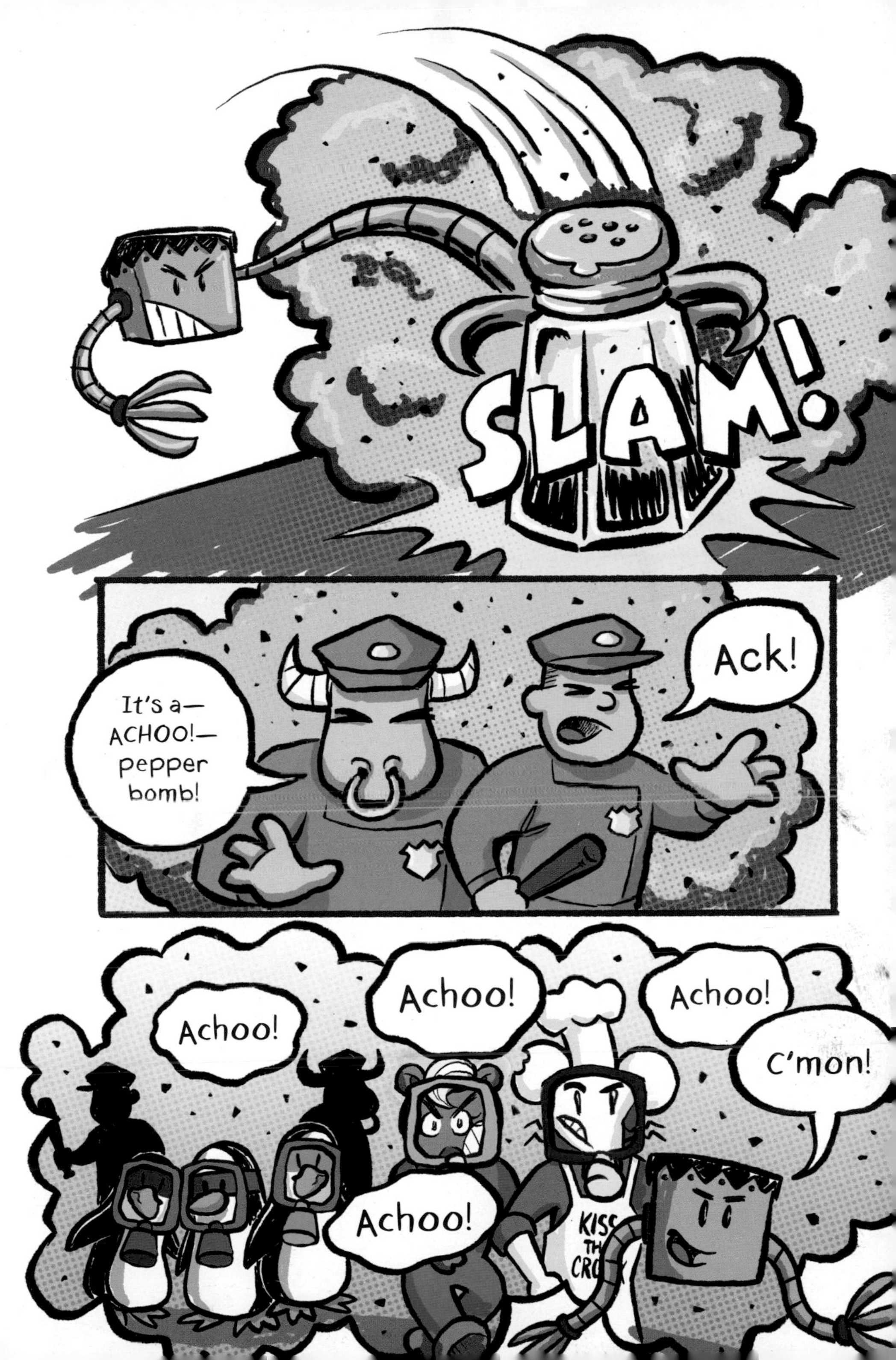
SLAM!
It's a—
ACHOO!—
pepper
bomb!
Ack!
Achoo!
Achoo!
Achoo!
C'mon!
Achoo!
KISS
TH
CRO

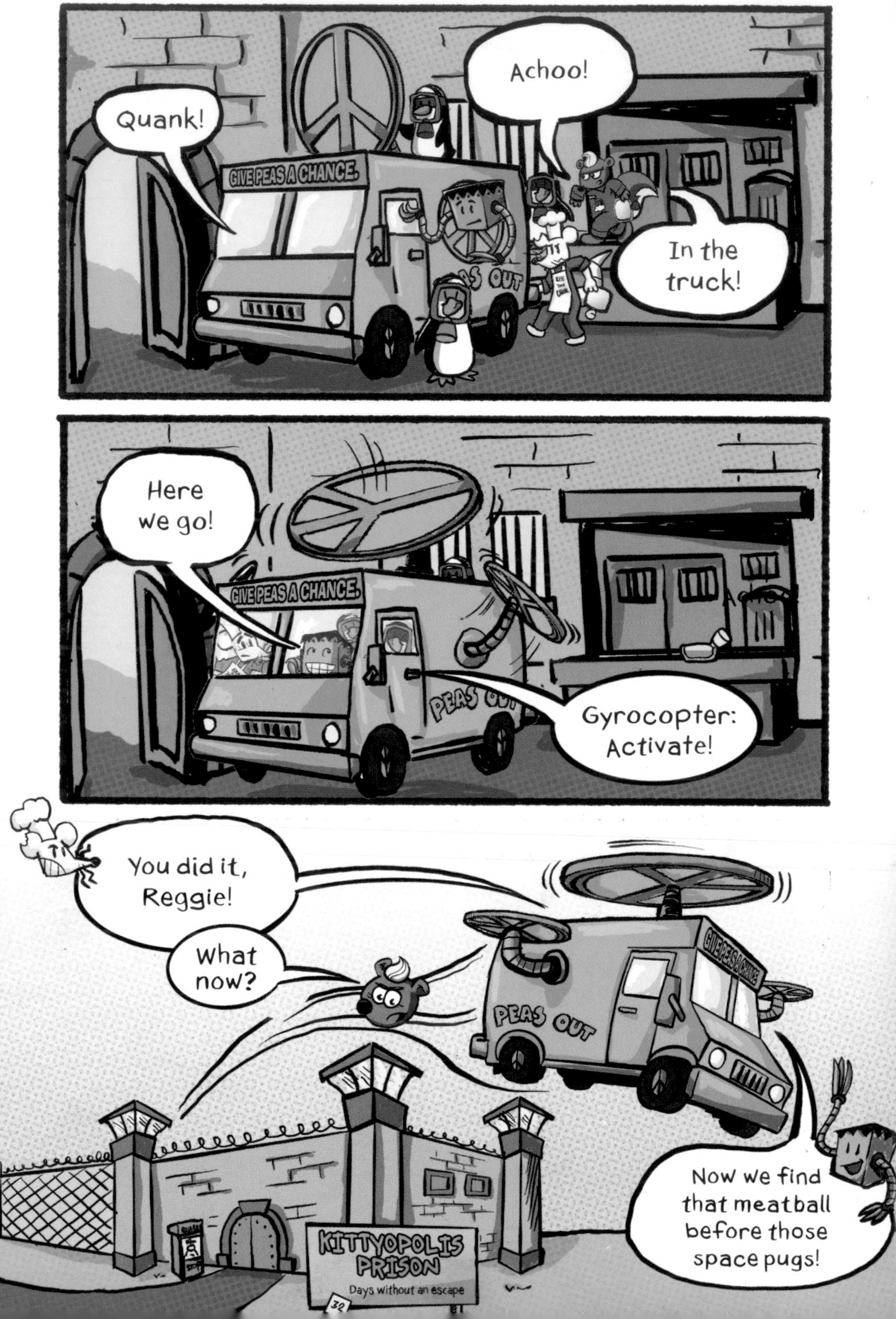
GIVE PEAS A CHANCE.
Quank!
Achoo!
PEAS OUT
In the truck!
Here we go!
GIVE PEAS A CHANCE.
PEAS OUT
Gyrocopter: Activate!
You did it, Reggie!
What now?
GIVE PEAS A CHANCE
PEAS OUT
Now we find that meatball before those space pugs!
KITTYOPOLIS PRISON
Days without an escape
32

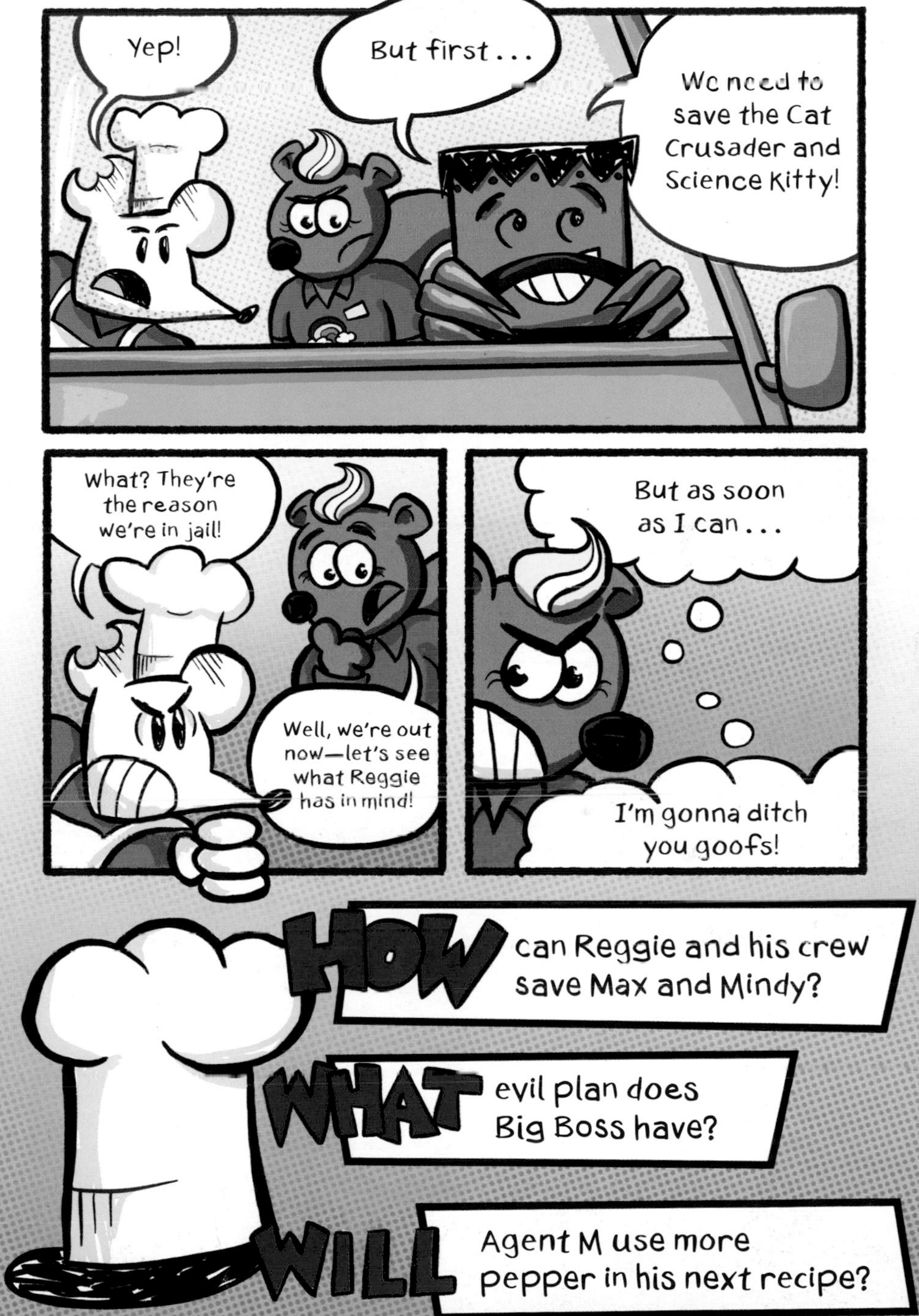

Yep!
But first . . .
We need to save the Cat Crusader and Science Kitty!
What? They're the reason we're in jail!
Well, we're out now—let's see what Reggie has in mind!
But as soon as I can . . .
I'm gonna ditch you goofs!
HOW can Reggie and his crew save Max and Mindy?
WHAT evil plan does Big Boss have?
WILL Agent M use more pepper in his next recipe?

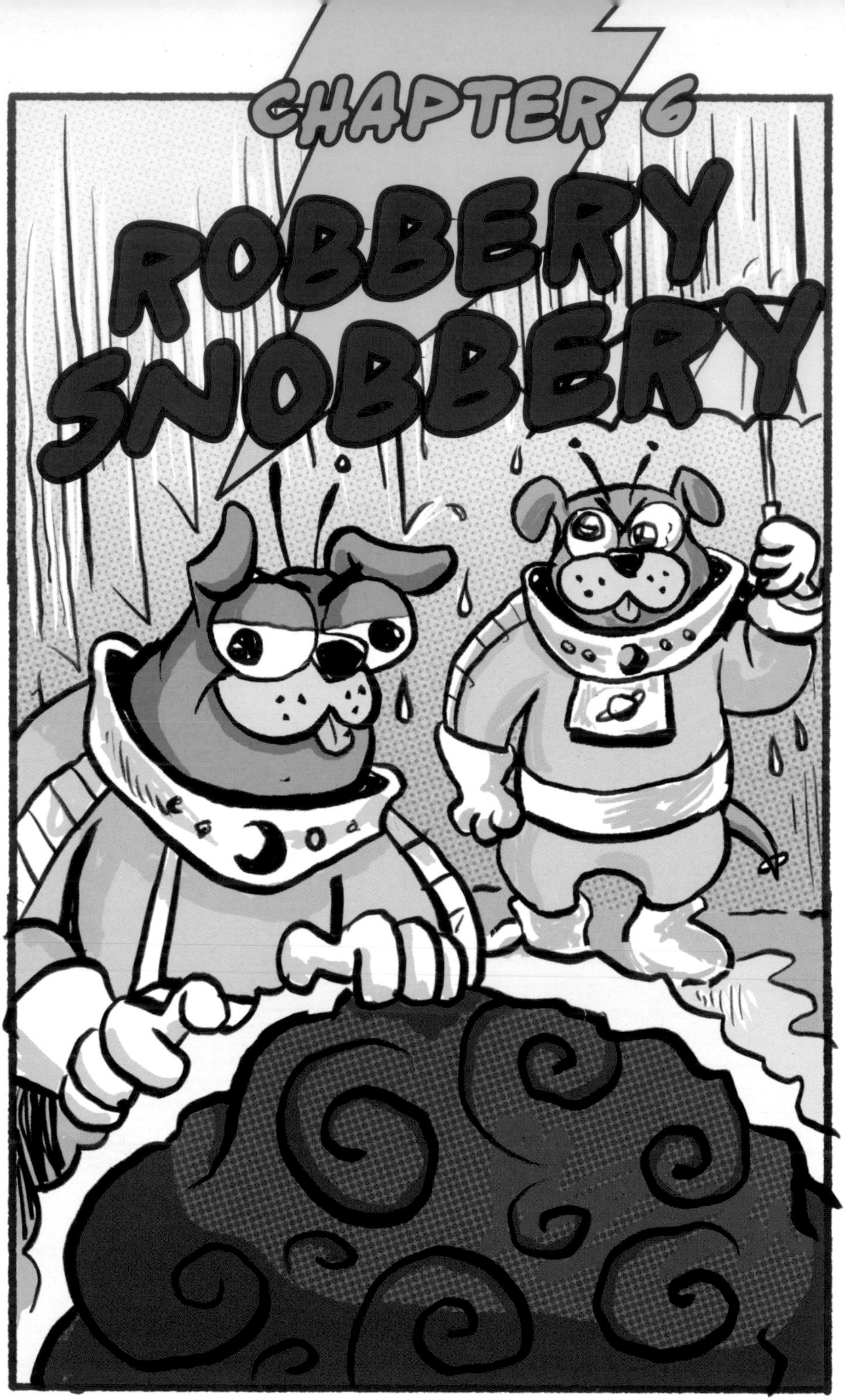
CHAPTER 6
ROBBERY SNOBBERY

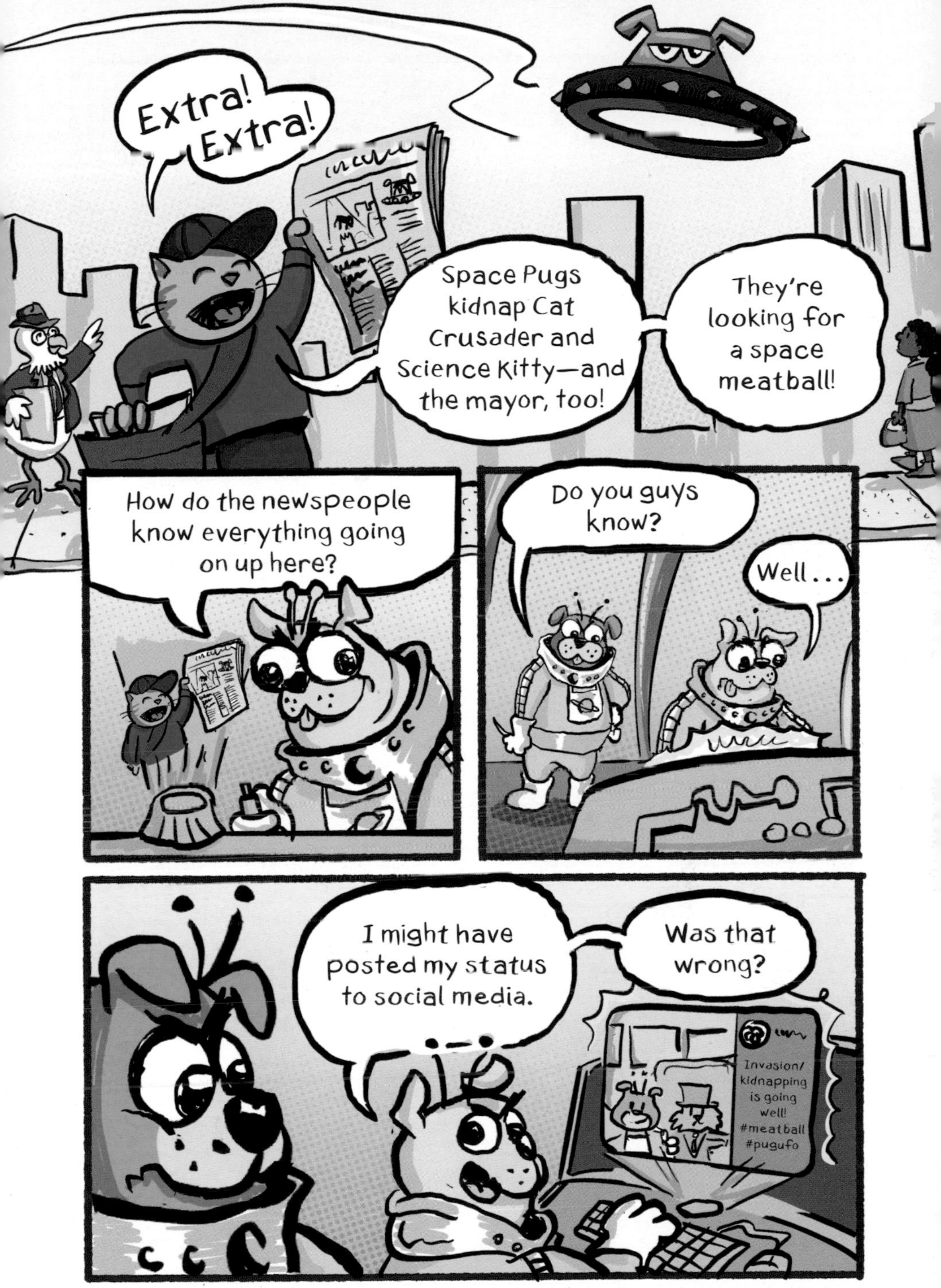
Extra! Extra!
Space Pugs kidnap Cat Crusader and Science Kitty—and the mayor, too!
They're looking for a space meatball!
How do the newspeople know everything going on up here?
Do you guys know?
Well . . .
I might have posted my status to social media.
Was that wrong?
Invasion/ kidnapping is going well! #meatball #pugufo

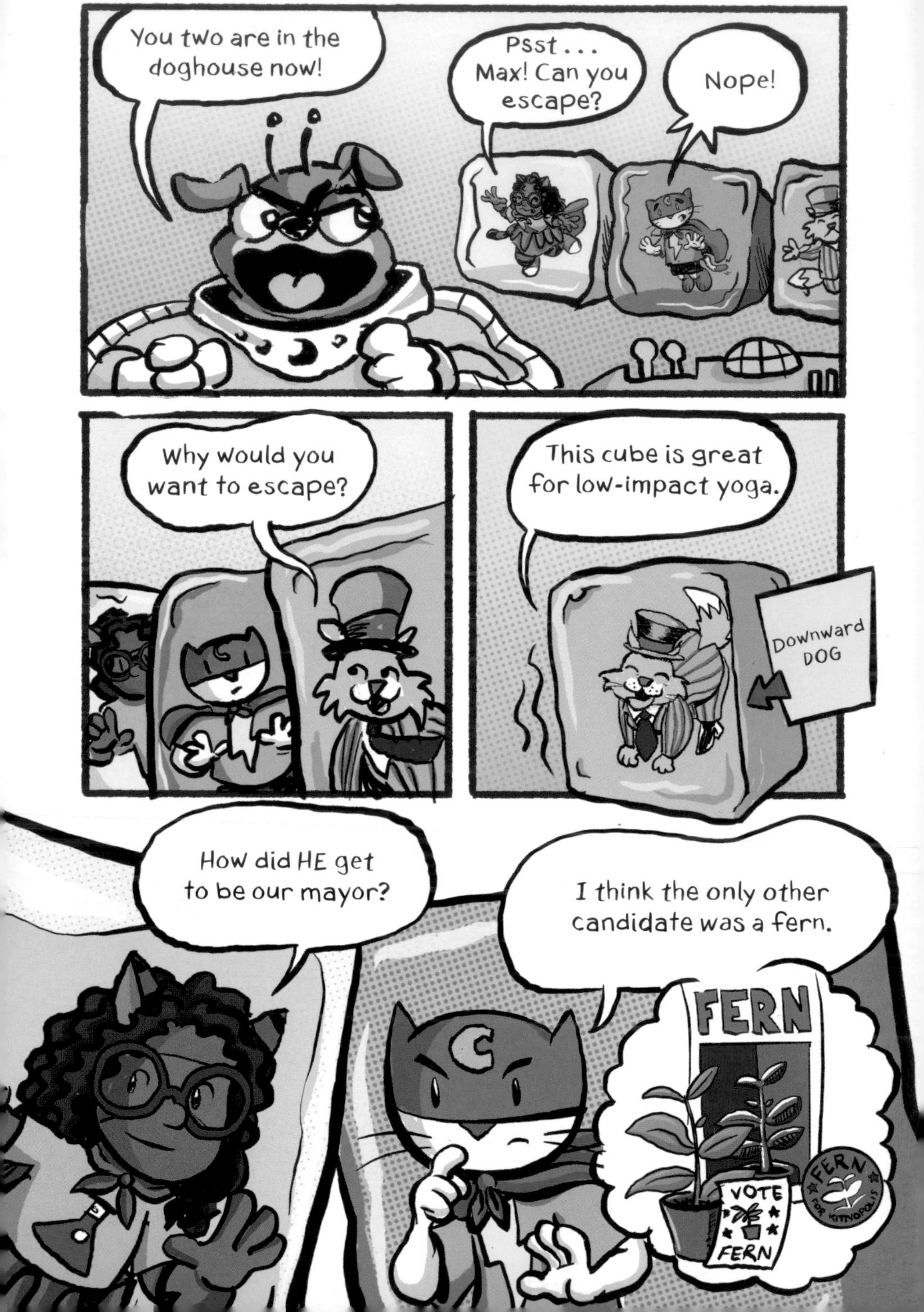
You two are in the doghouse now!
Psst . . . Max! Can you escape?
Nope!
Why would you want to escape?
This cube is great for low-impact yoga.
Downward DOG
How did HE get to be our mayor?
I think the only other candidate was a fern.
FERN
VOTE FERN
FERN FOR KITTYOPOLIS

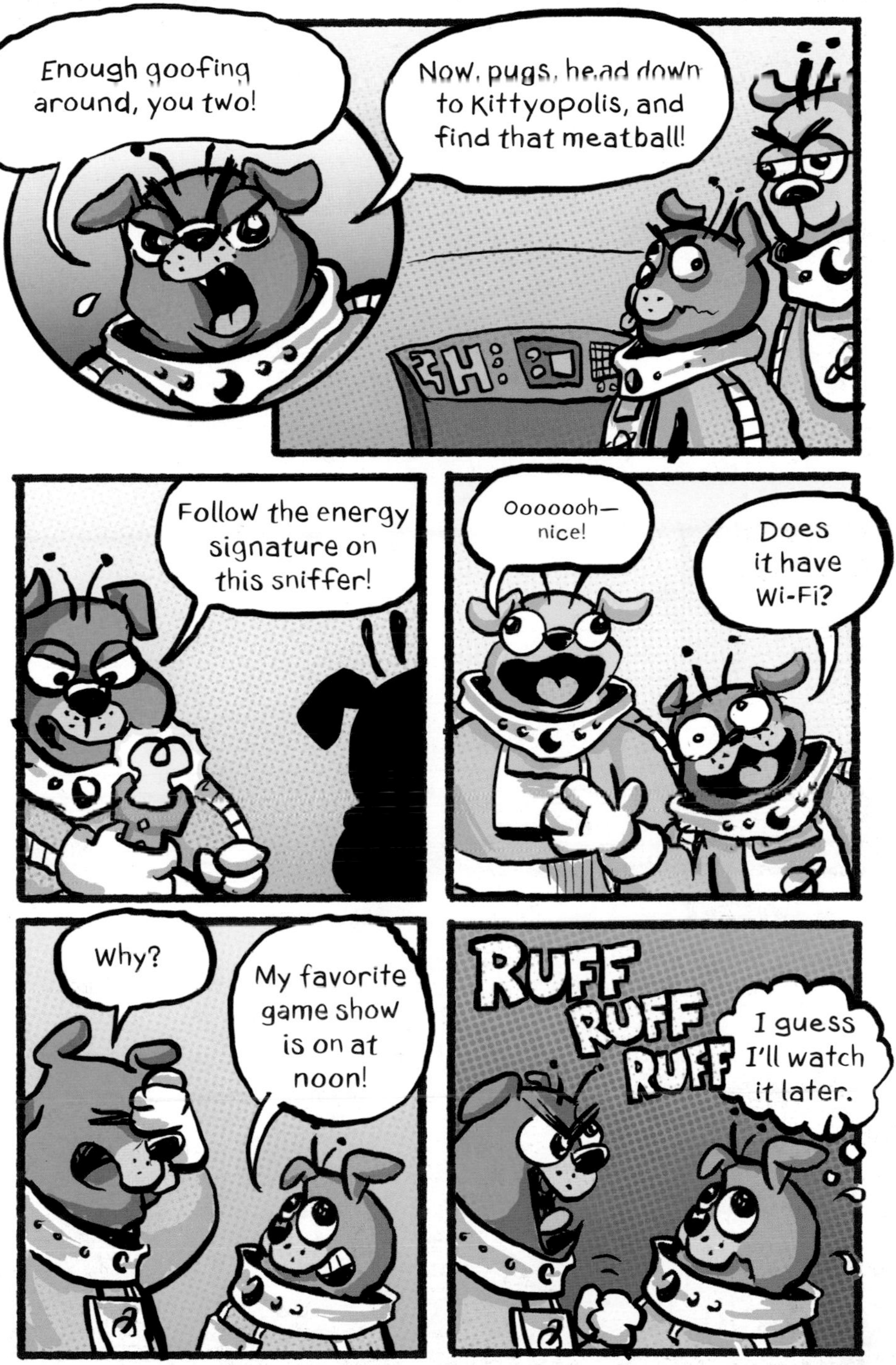
Enough goofing around, you two!
Now, pugs, head down to Kittyopolis, and find that meatball!
Follow the energy signature on this sniffer!
Ooooooh— nice!
Does it have Wi-Fi?
Why?
My favorite game show is on at noon!
RUFF RUFF RUFF
I guess I'll watch it later.

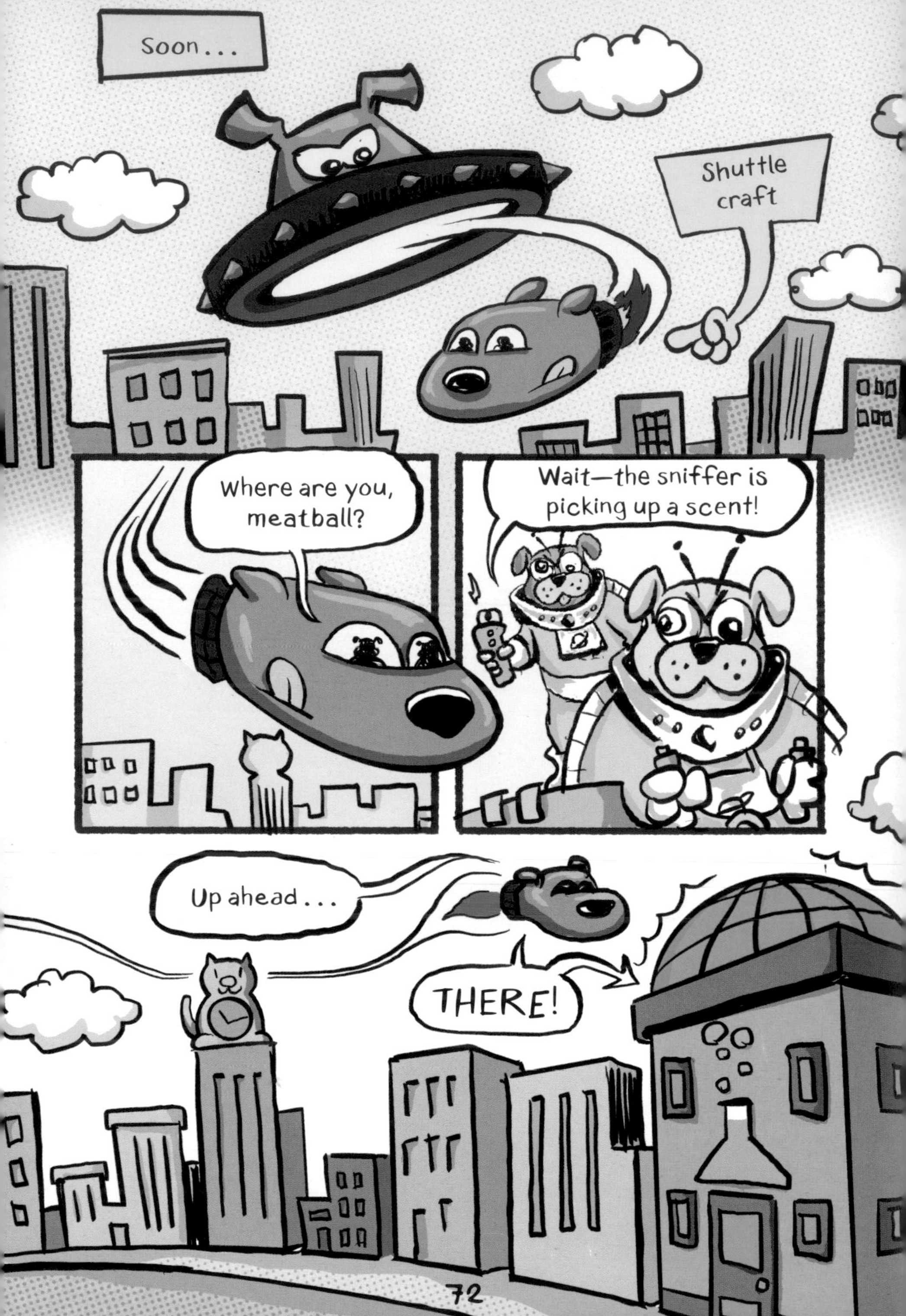
Soon...
Shuttle craft
Where are you, meatball?
Wait—the sniffer is picking up a scent!
Up ahead...
THERE!

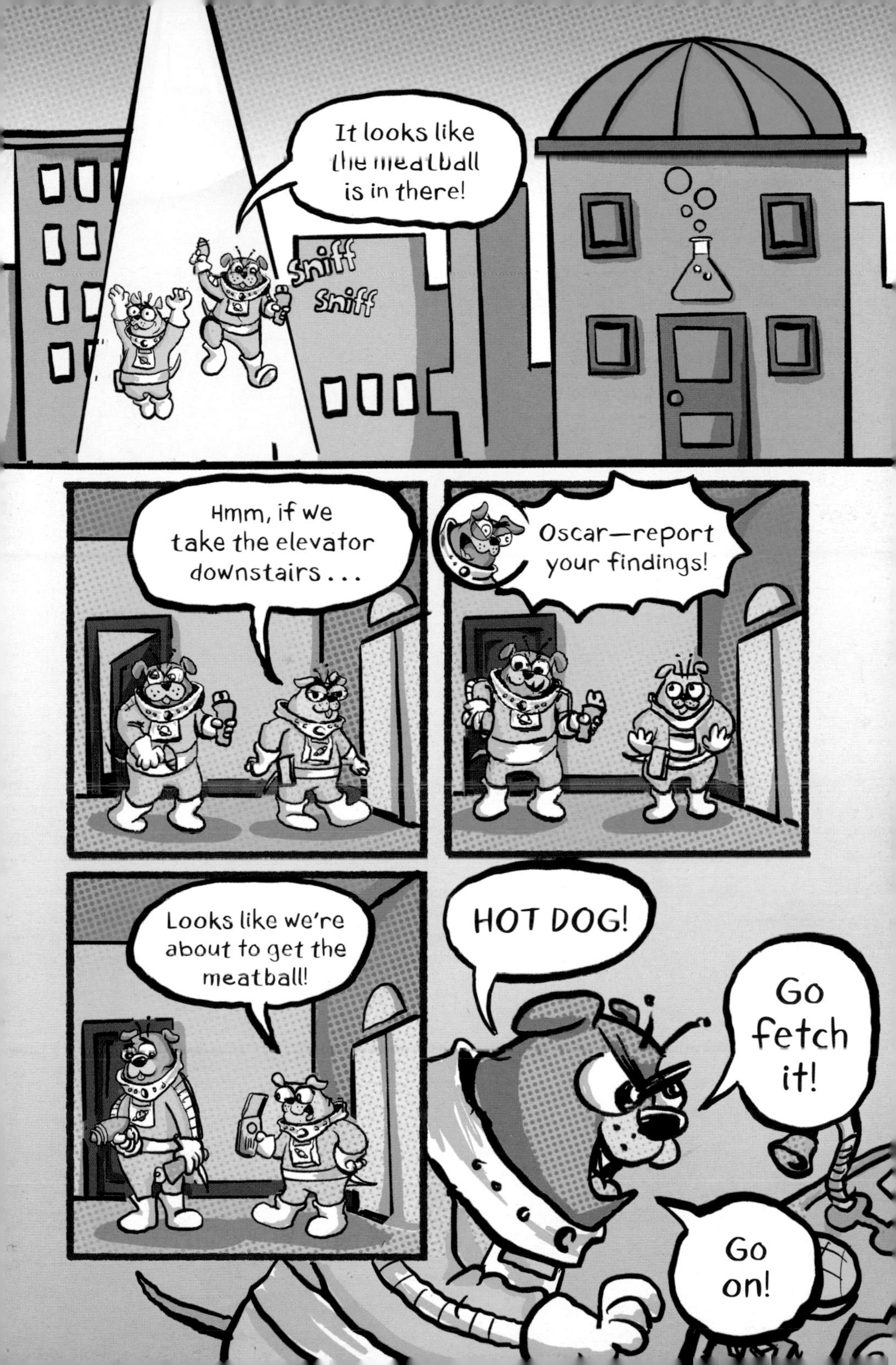
It looks like the meatball is in there!
Sniff
Sniff
Hmm, if we take the elevator downstairs . . .
Oscar—report your findings!
Looks like we're about to get the meatball!
HOT DOG!
Go fetch it!
Go on!

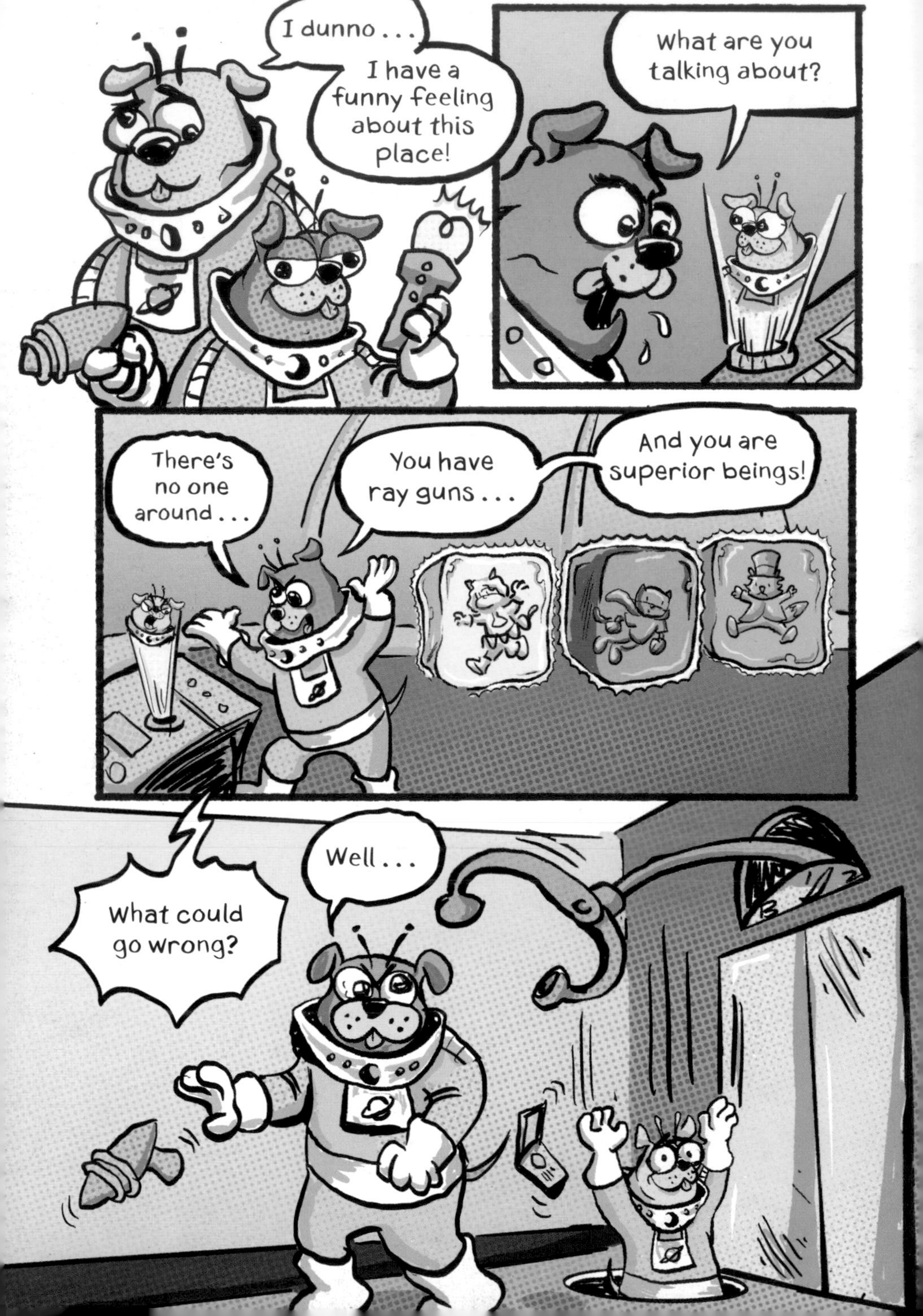
I dunno . . .
I have a funny feeling about this place!
What are you talking about?
There's no one around . . .
You have ray guns . . .
And you are superior beings!
What could go wrong?
Well . . .

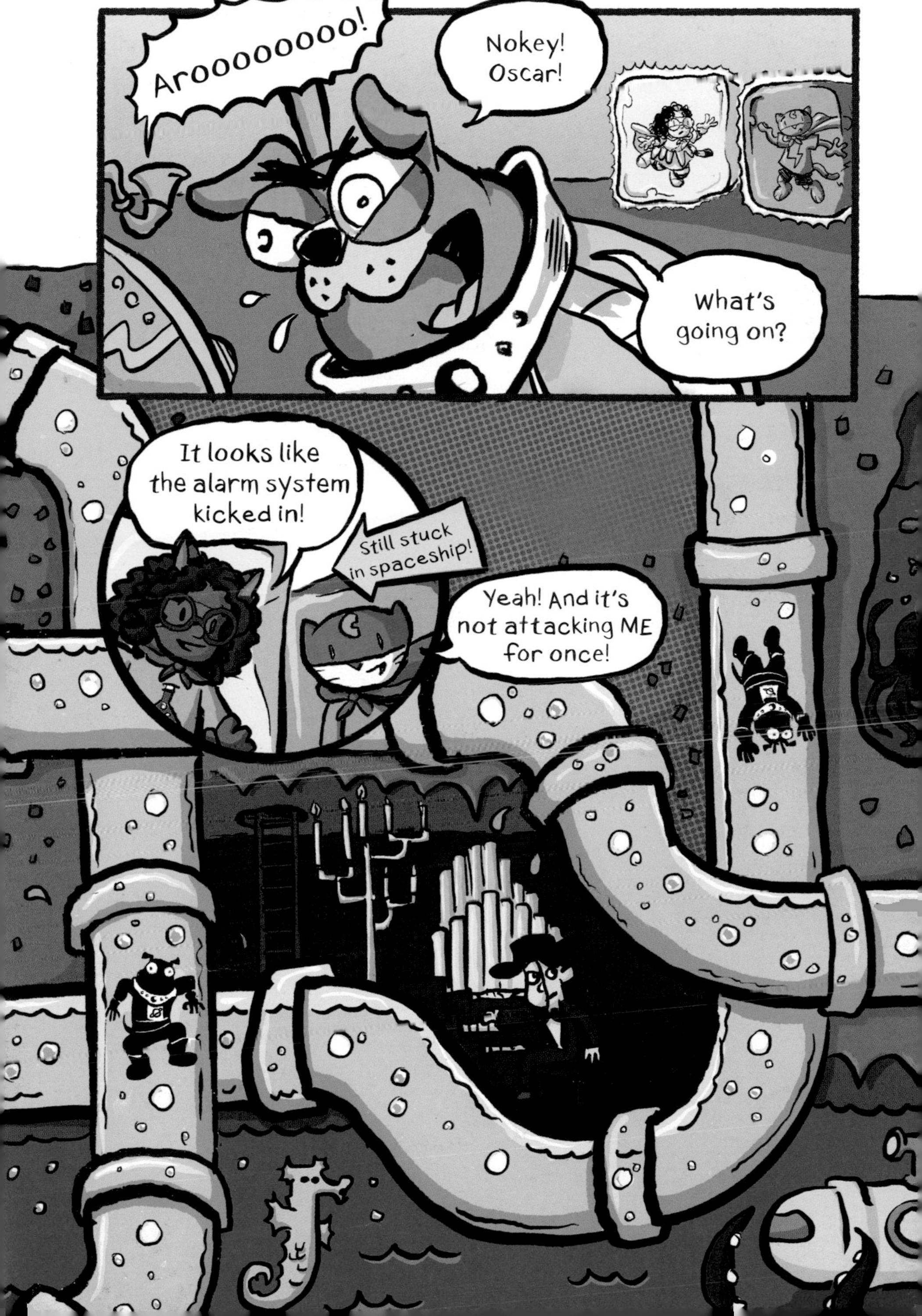
Arooooooooo!
Nokey! Oscar!
What's going on?
It looks like the alarm system kicked in!
Still stuck in spaceship!
Yeah! And it's not attacking ME for once!

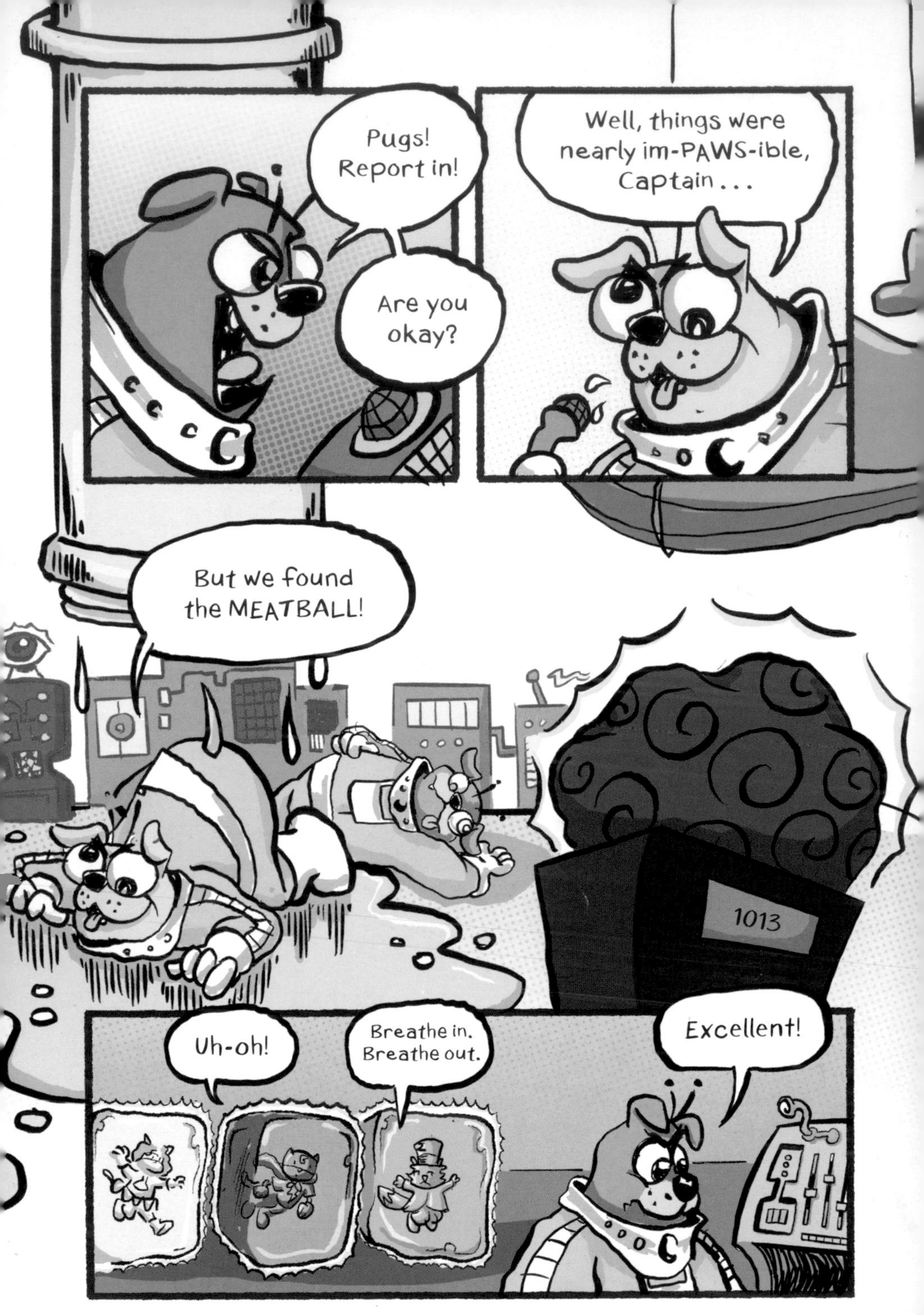
Pugs!
Report in!
Are you okay?
Well, things were nearly im-PAWS-ible, Captain . . .
But we found the MEATBALL!
1013
Uh-oh!
Breathe in. Breathe out.
Excellent!

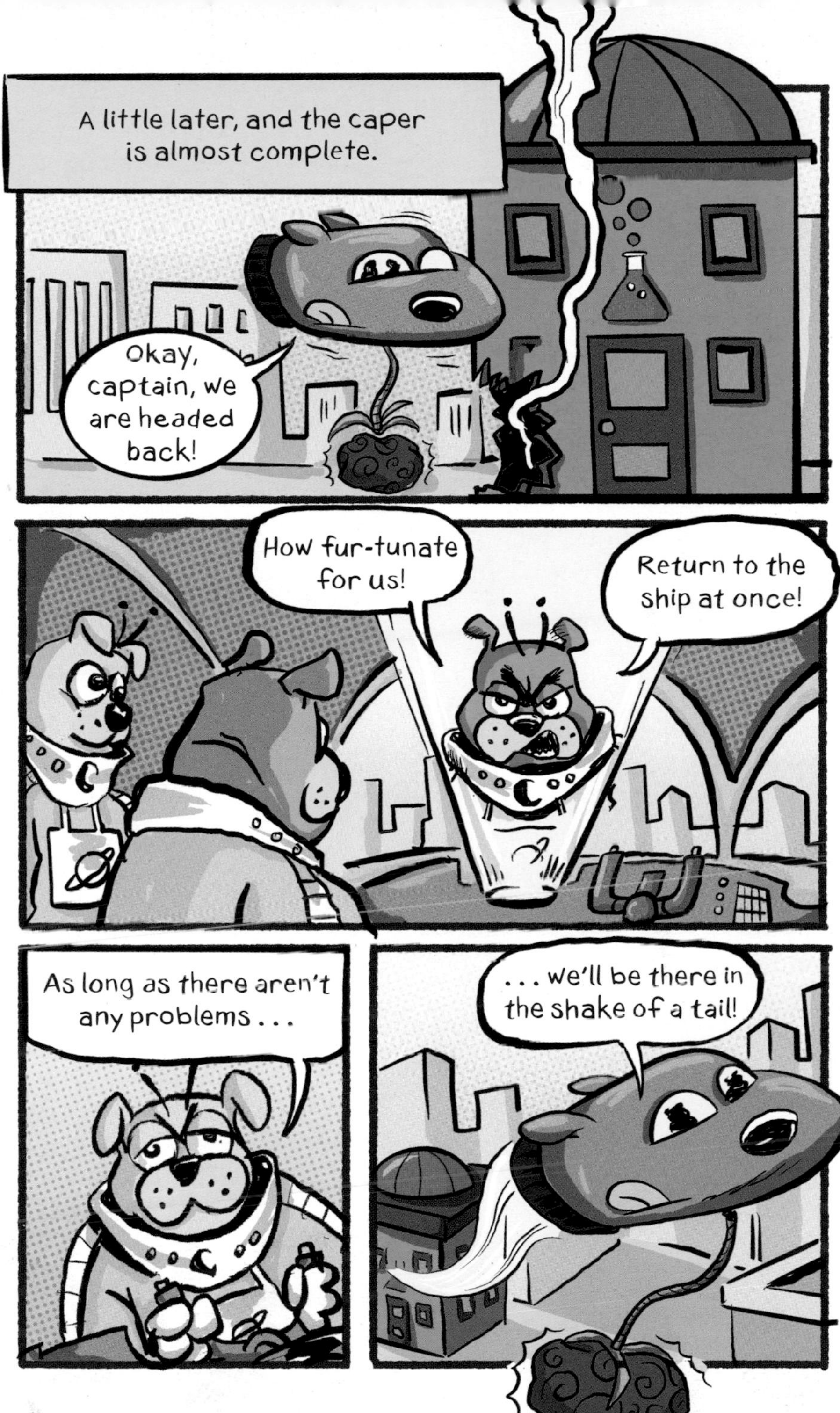
A little later, and the caper is almost complete.
Okay, captain, we are headed back!
How fur-tunate for us!
Return to the ship at once!
As long as there aren't any problems . . .
. . . we'll be there in the shake of a tail!

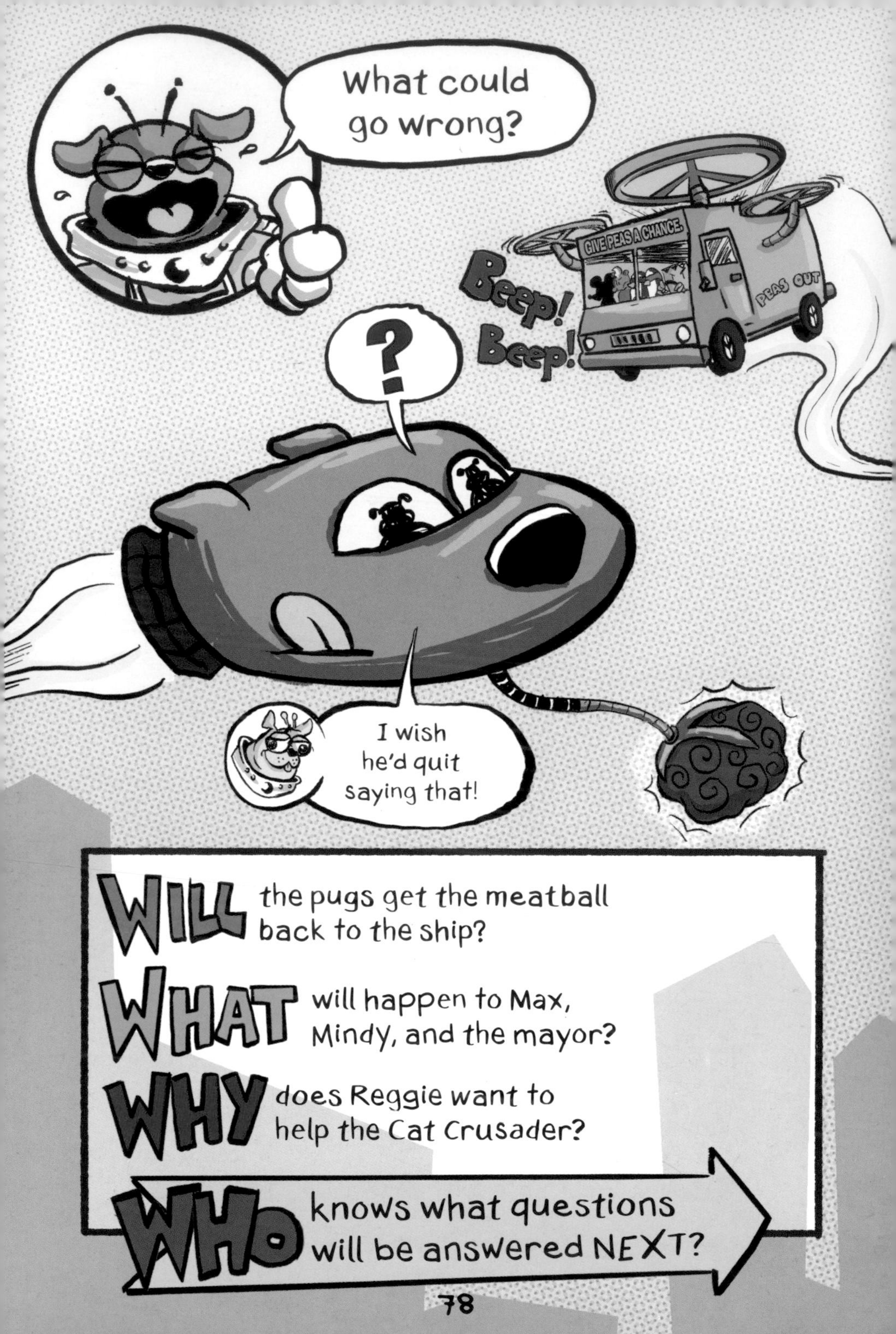
What could go wrong?
GIVE PEAS A CHANCE.
PEAS OUT
Beep! Beep!
?
I wish he'd quit saying that!
WILL the pugs get the meatball back to the ship?
WHAT will happen to Max, Mindy, and the mayor?
WHY does Reggie want to help the Cat Crusader?
WHO knows what questions will be answered NEXT?

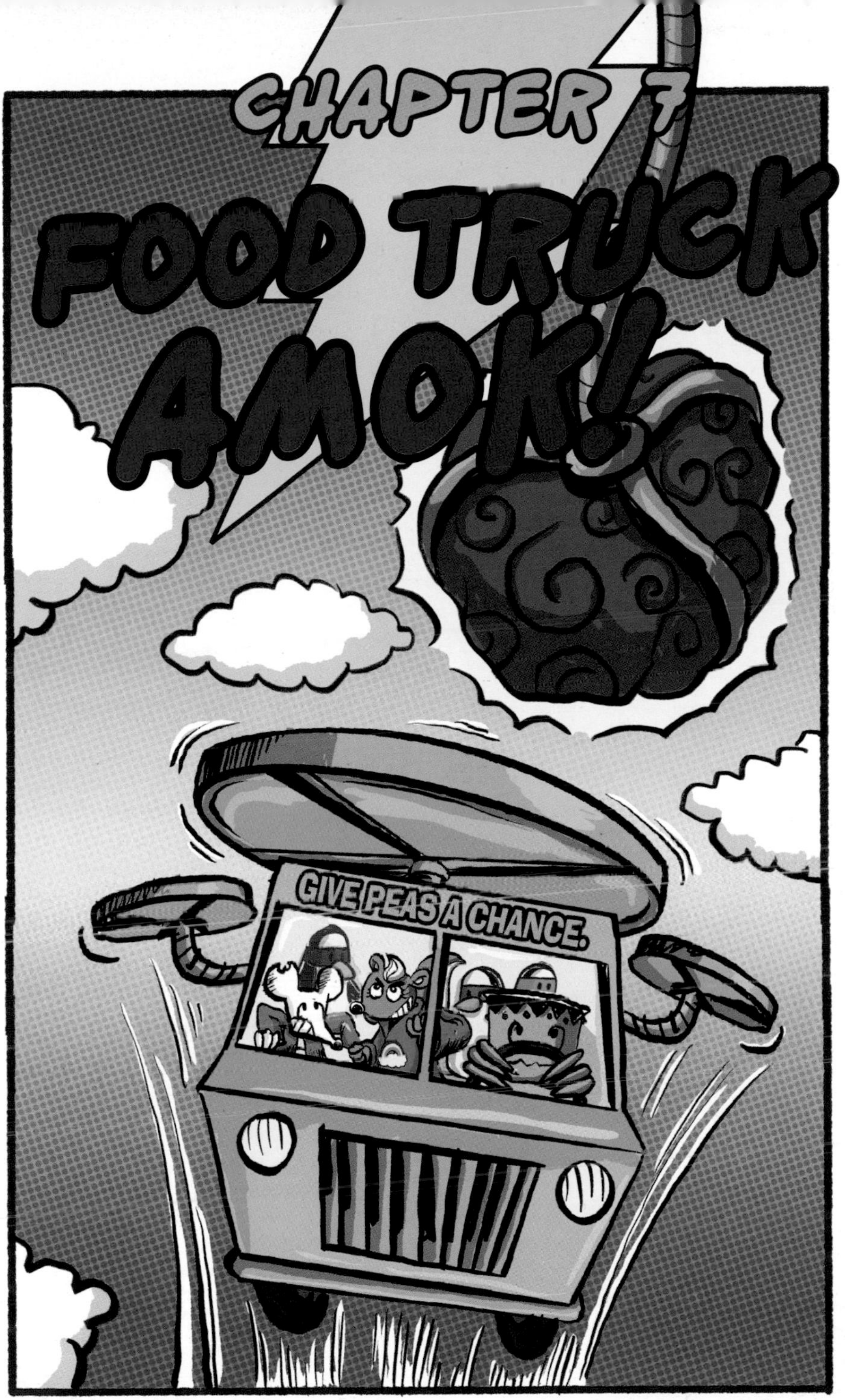
CHAPTER 7
FOOD TRUCK AMOK!
GIVE PEAS A CHANCE.

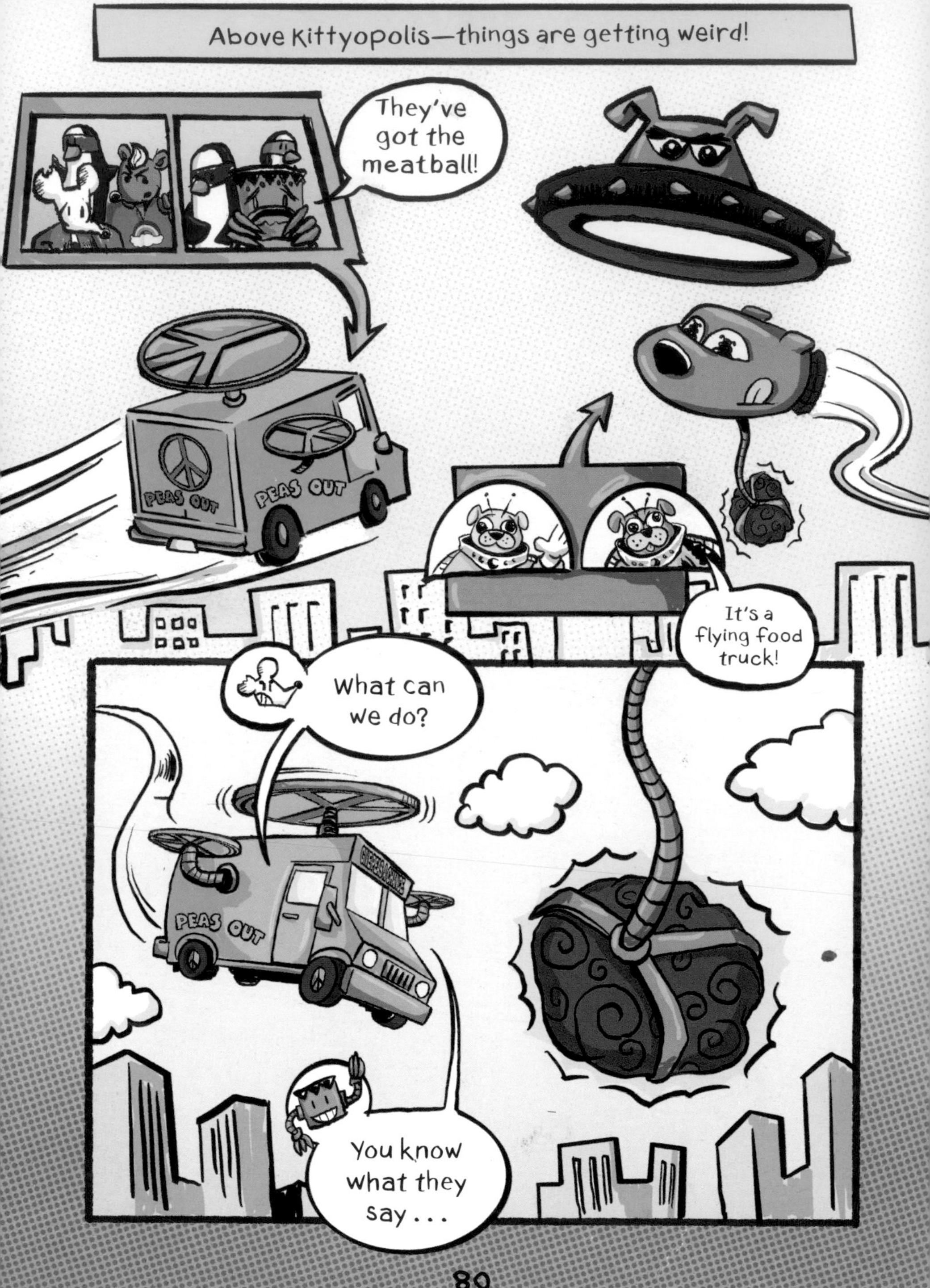
Above Kittyopolis—things are getting weird!
They've got the meatball!
PEAS OUT
PEAS OUT
It's a flying food truck!
What can we do?
PEAS OUT
You know what they say . . .

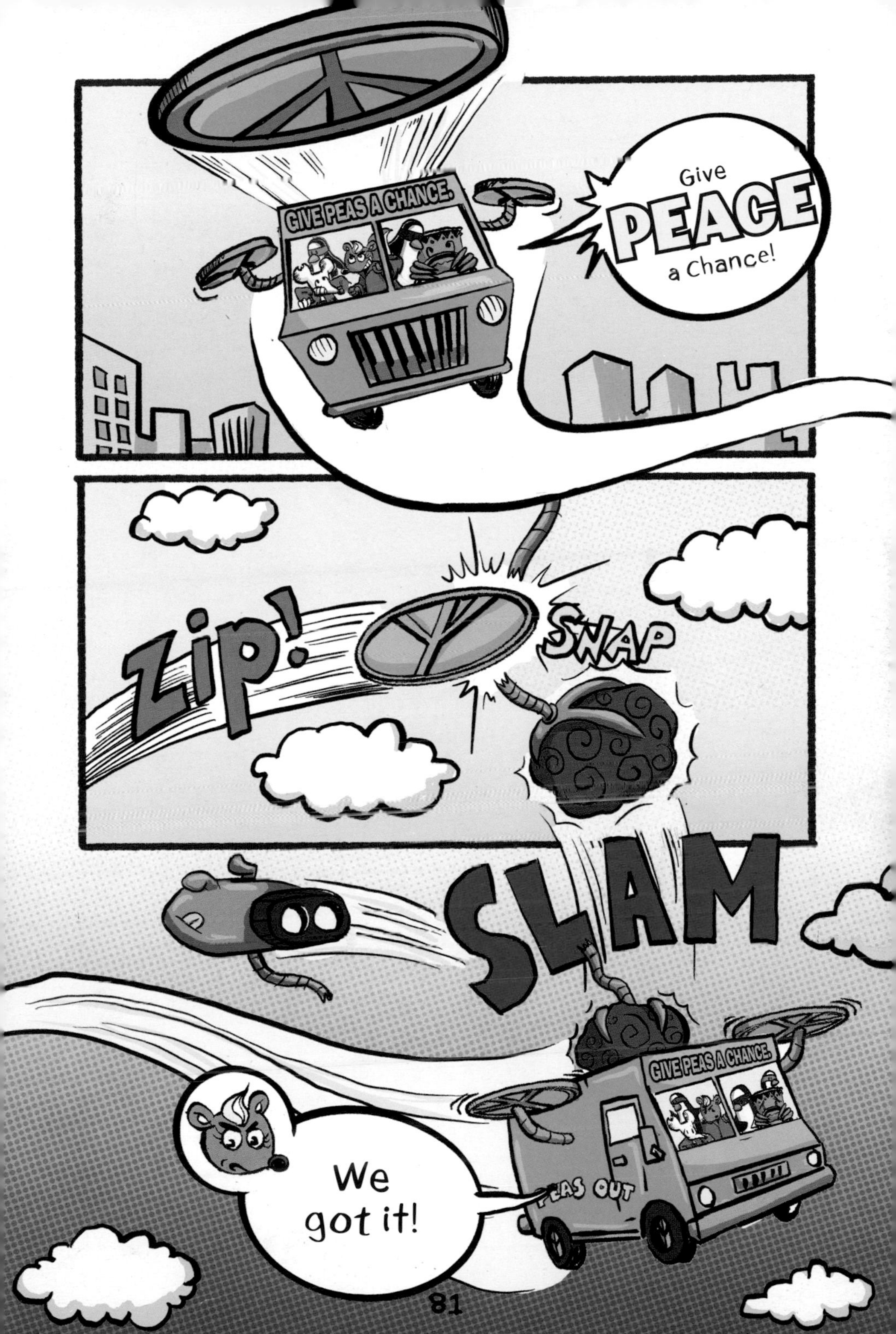
GIVE PEAS A CHANCE.
Give PEACE a Chance!
Zip!
SNAP
SLAM
GIVE PEAS A CHANCE.
PEAS OUT
We got it!

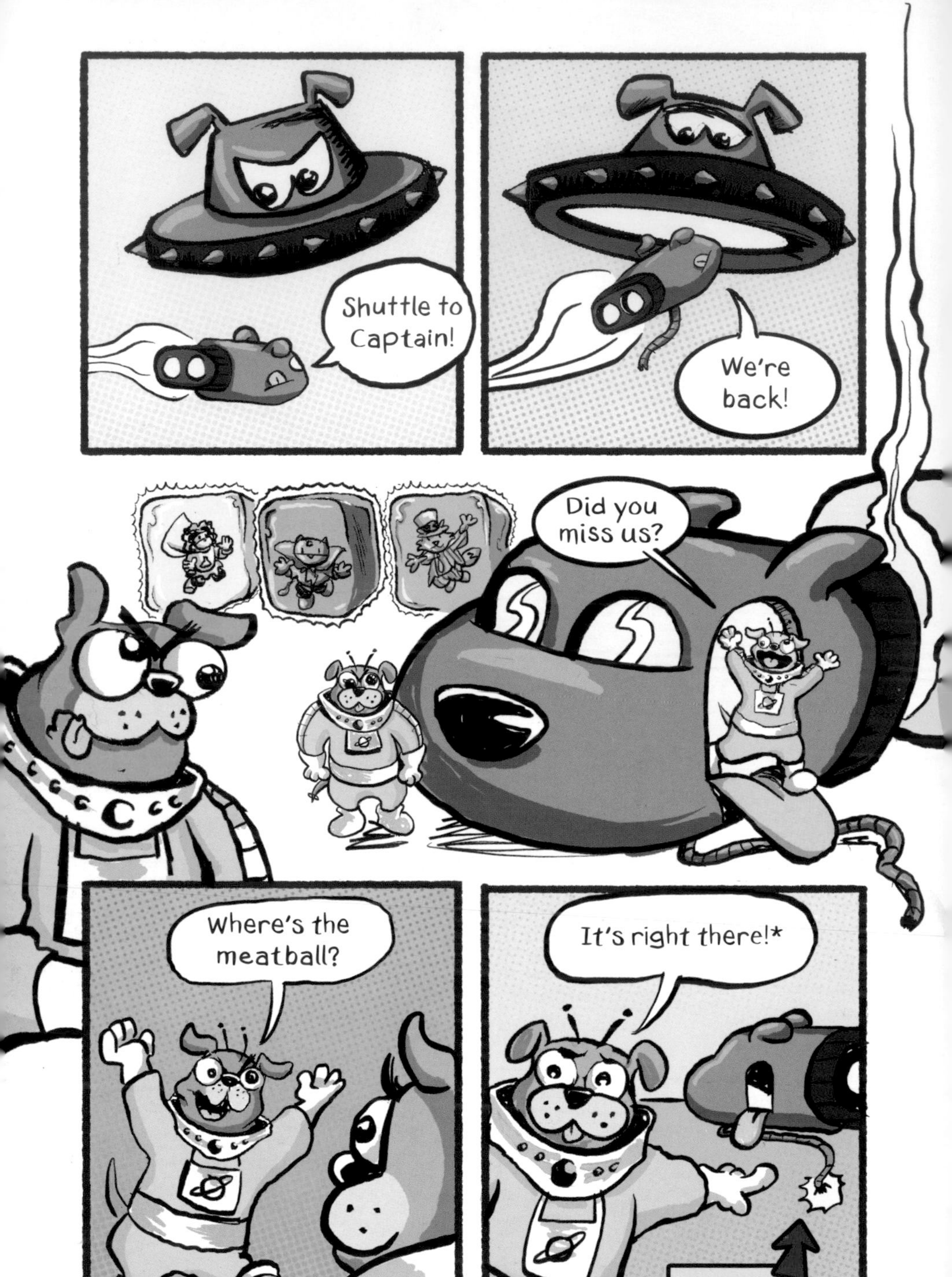
Shuttle to Captain!
We're back!
Did you miss us?
Where's the meatball?
It's right there!*
*It's not!

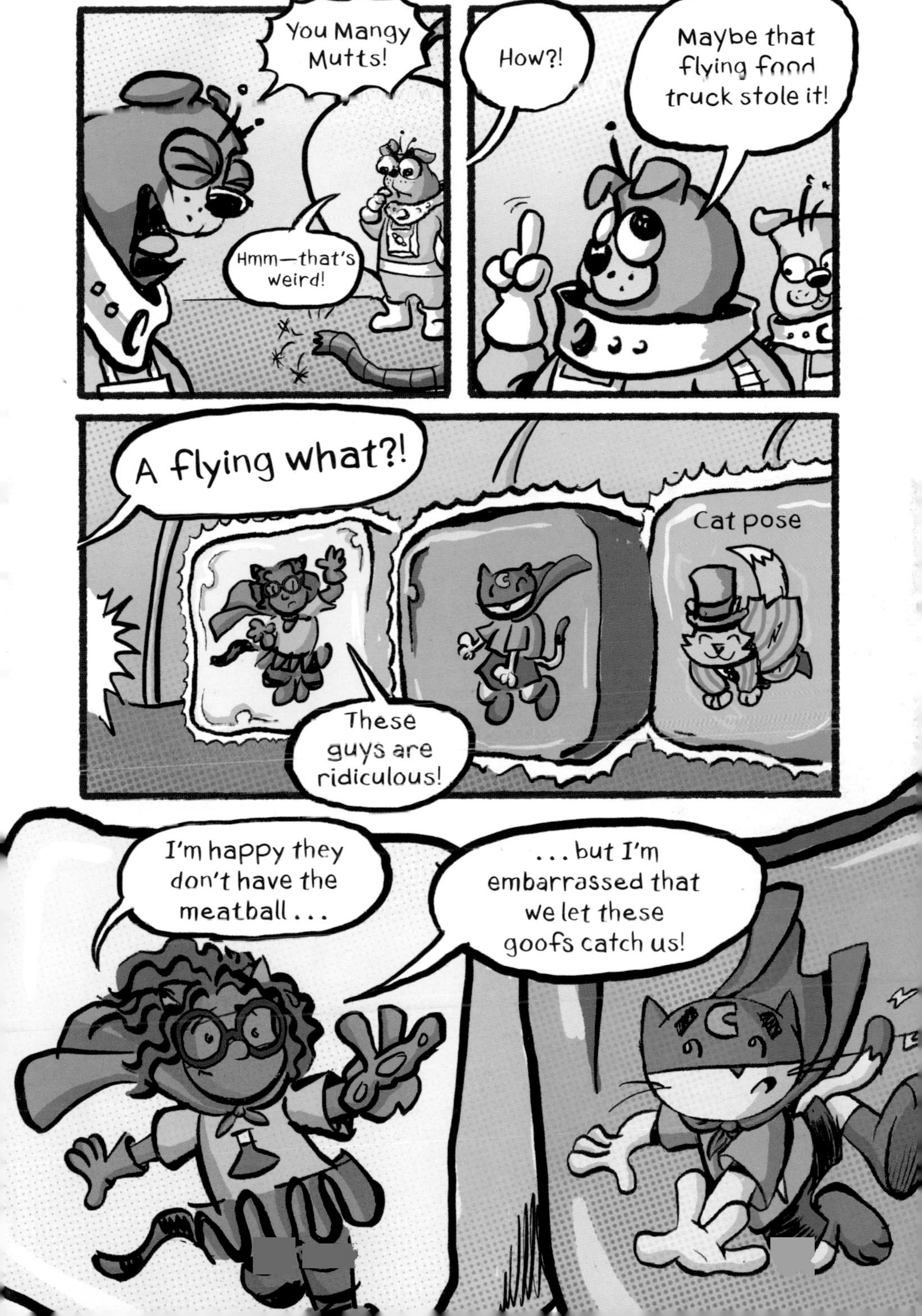

You Mangy Mutts!
Hmm—that's weird!
How?!
Maybe that flying food truck stole it!
A flying what?!
Cat pose
These guys are ridiculous!
I'm happy they don't have the meatball . . .
. . . but I'm embarrassed that we let these goofs catch us!

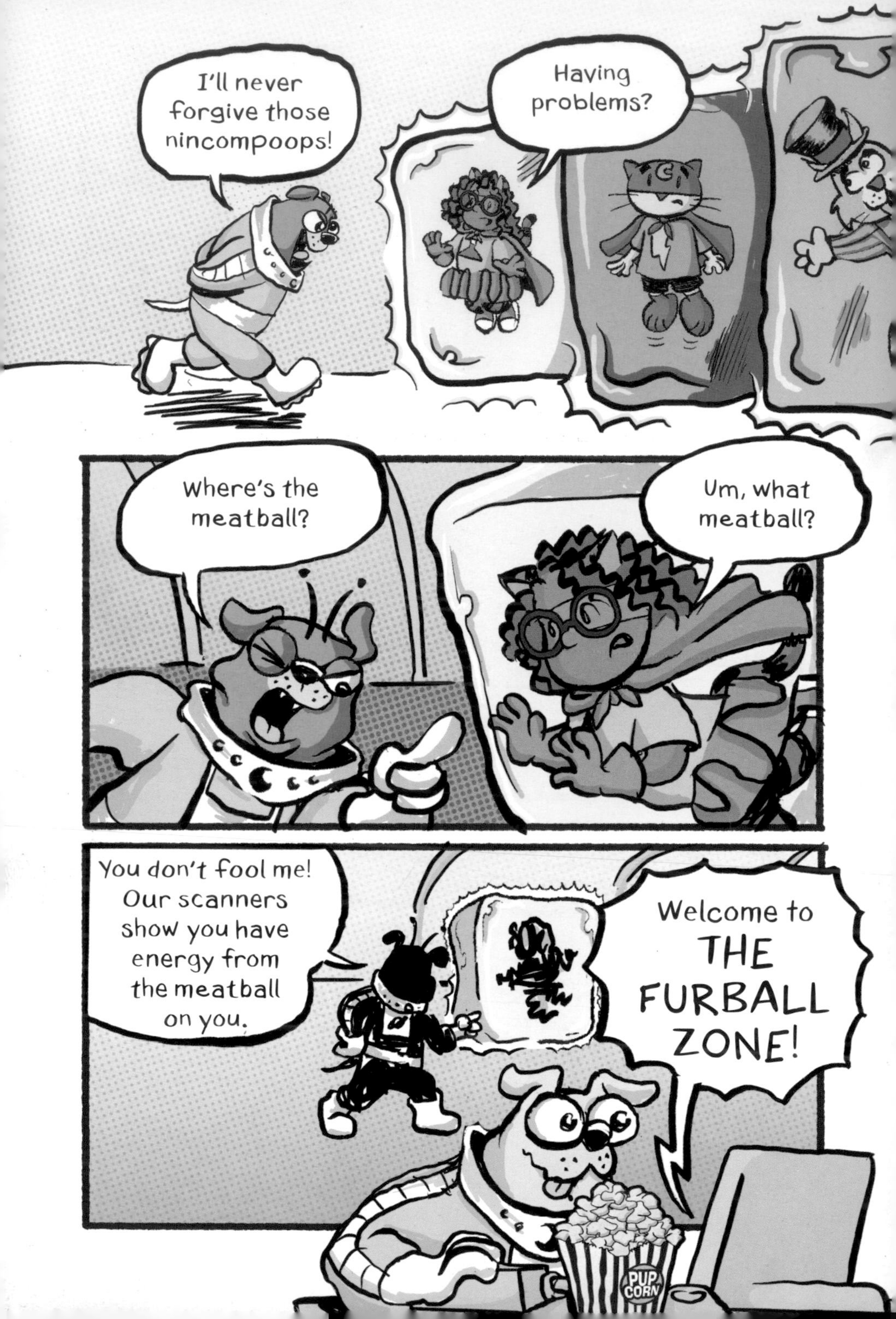
I'll never forgive those nincompoops!
Having problems?
Where's the meatball?
Um, what meatball?
You don't fool me! Our scanners show you have energy from the meatball on you.
Welcome to THE FURBALL ZONE!
PUP CORN

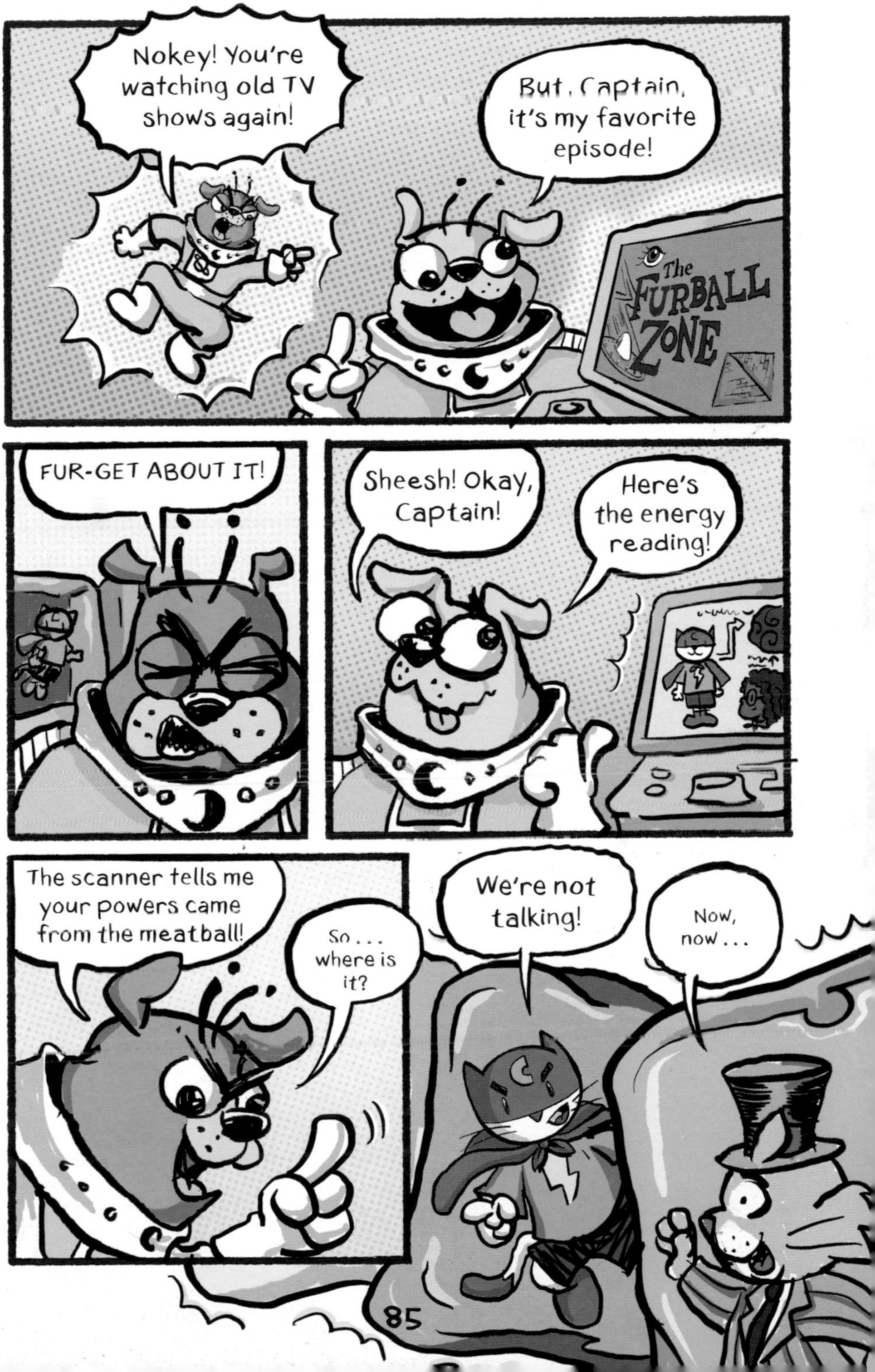
Nokey! You're watching old TV shows again!
But, Captain, it's my favorite episode!
The FURBALL ZONE
FUR-GET ABOUT IT!
Sheesh! Okay, Captain!
Here's the energy reading!
The scanner tells me your powers came from the meatball!
So . . . where is it?
We're not talking!
Now, now . . .

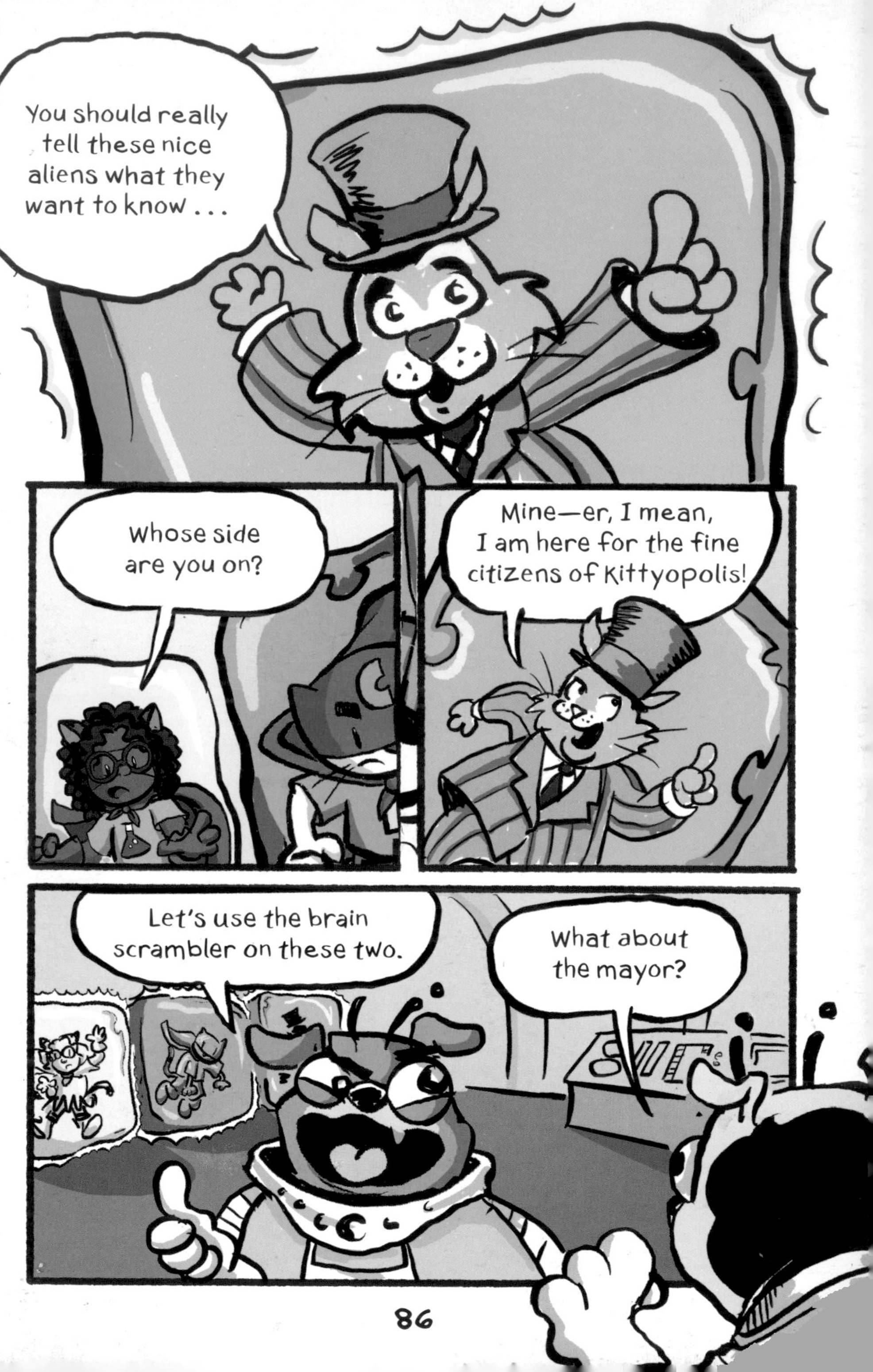
You should really tell these nice aliens what they want to know . . .
Whose side are you on?
Mine—er, I mean, I am here for the fine citizens of Kittyopolis!
Let's use the brain scrambler on these two.
What about the mayor?

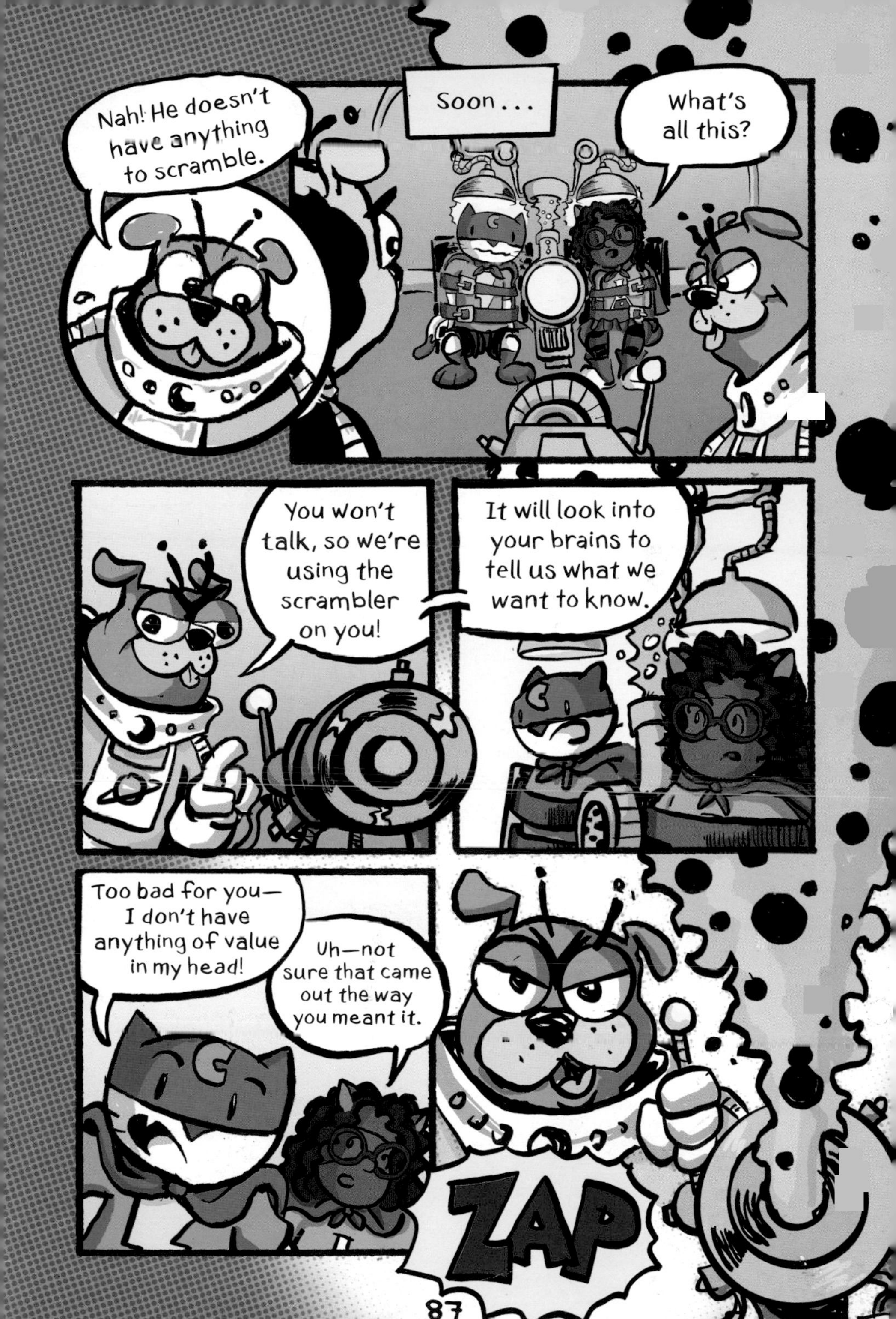
Soon...
Nah! He doesn't have anything to scramble.
What's all this?
You won't talk, so we're using the scrambler on you!
It will look into your brains to tell us what we want to know.
Too bad for you— I don't have anything of value in my head!
Uh—not sure that came out the way you meant it.
ZAP

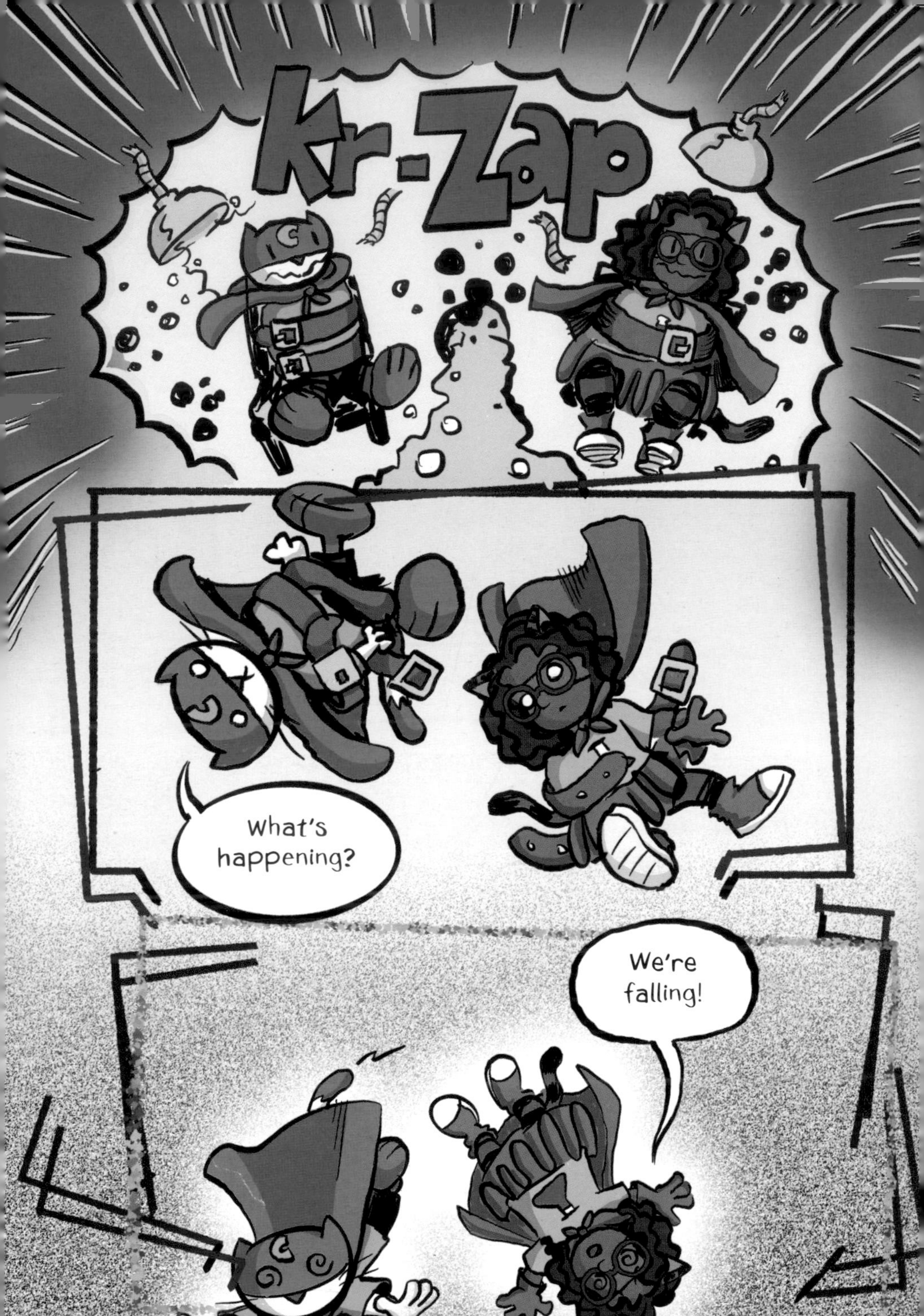
Kr-Zap
What's happening?
We're falling!

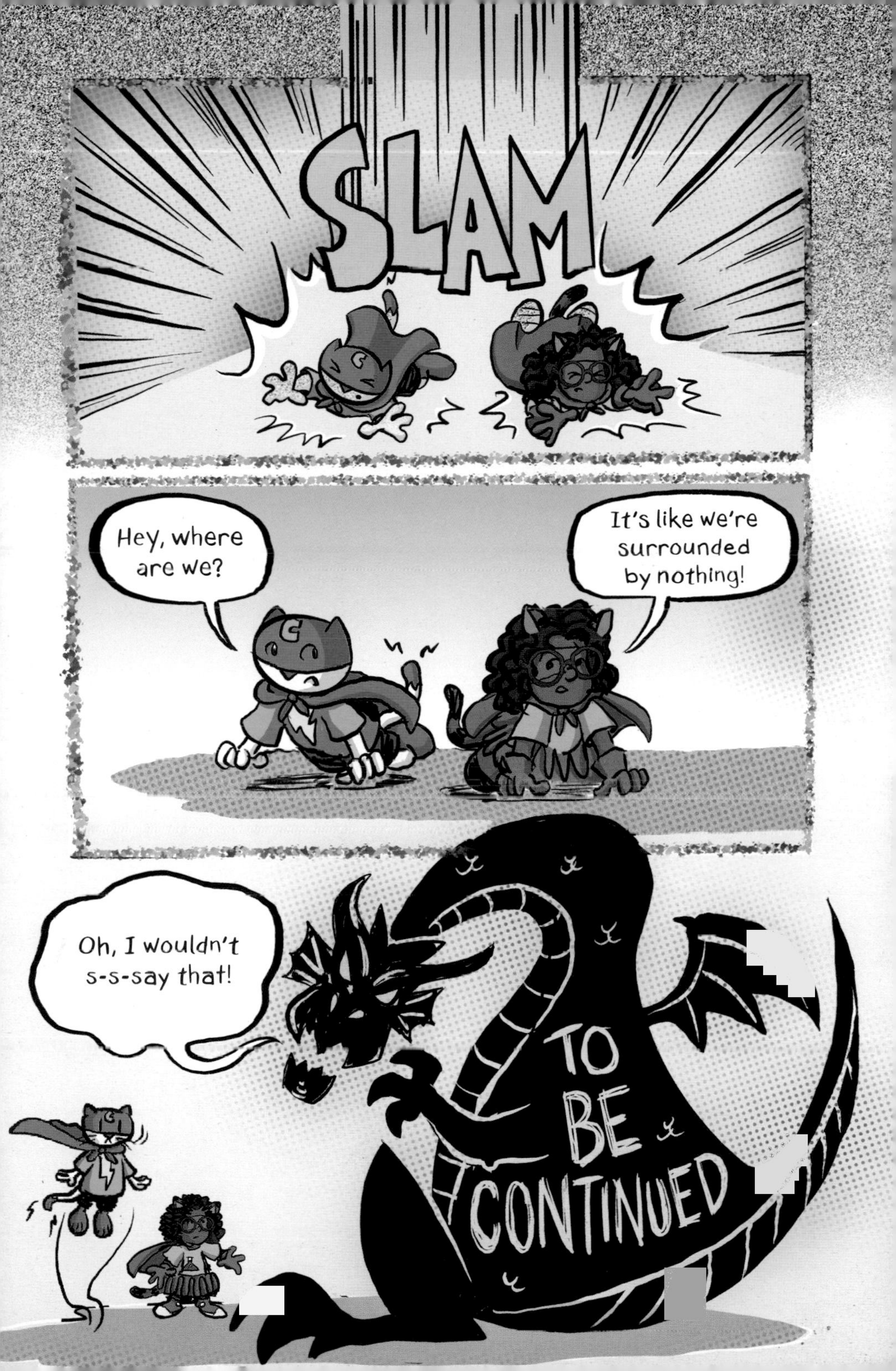
SLAM
Hey, where are we?
It's like we're surrounded by nothing!
Oh, I wouldn't s-s-say that!
TO BE CONTINUED

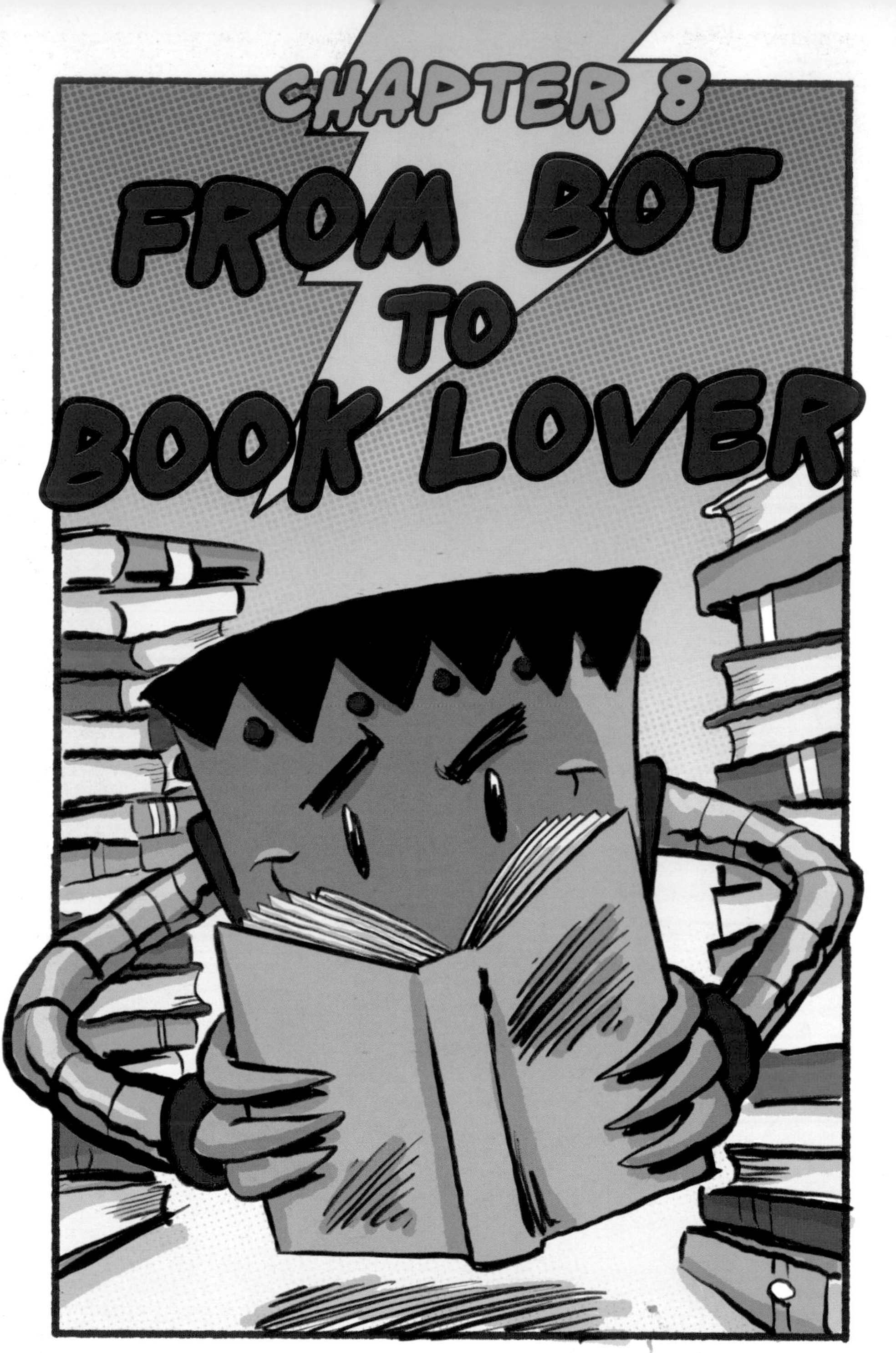
CHAPTER 8
FROM BOT TO BOOK LOVER

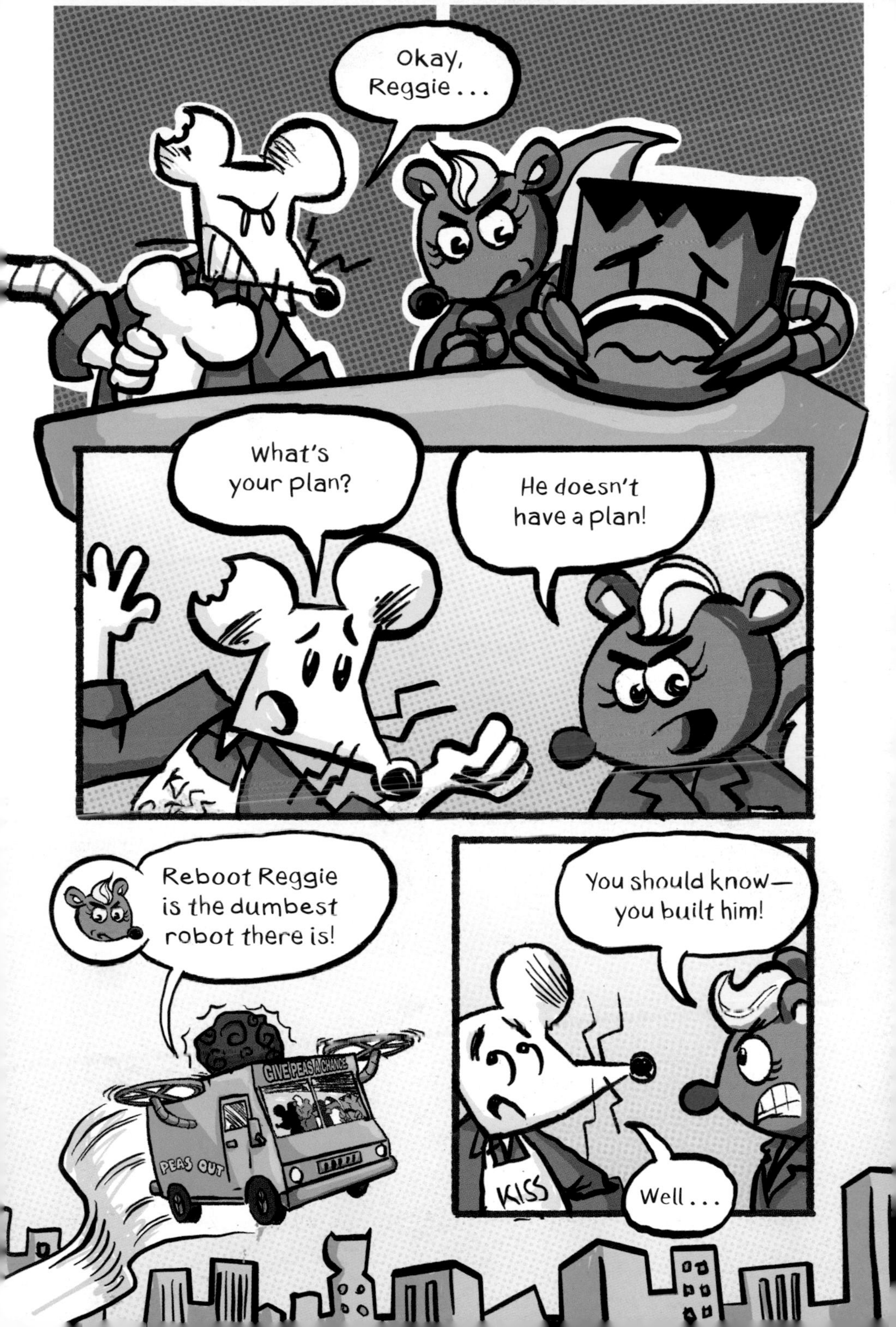
Okay, Reggie . . .
What's your plan?
He doesn't have a plan!
Reboot Reggie is the dumbest robot there is!
GIVE PEAS A CHANCE
PEAS OUT
You should know—you built him!
KISS
Well . . .

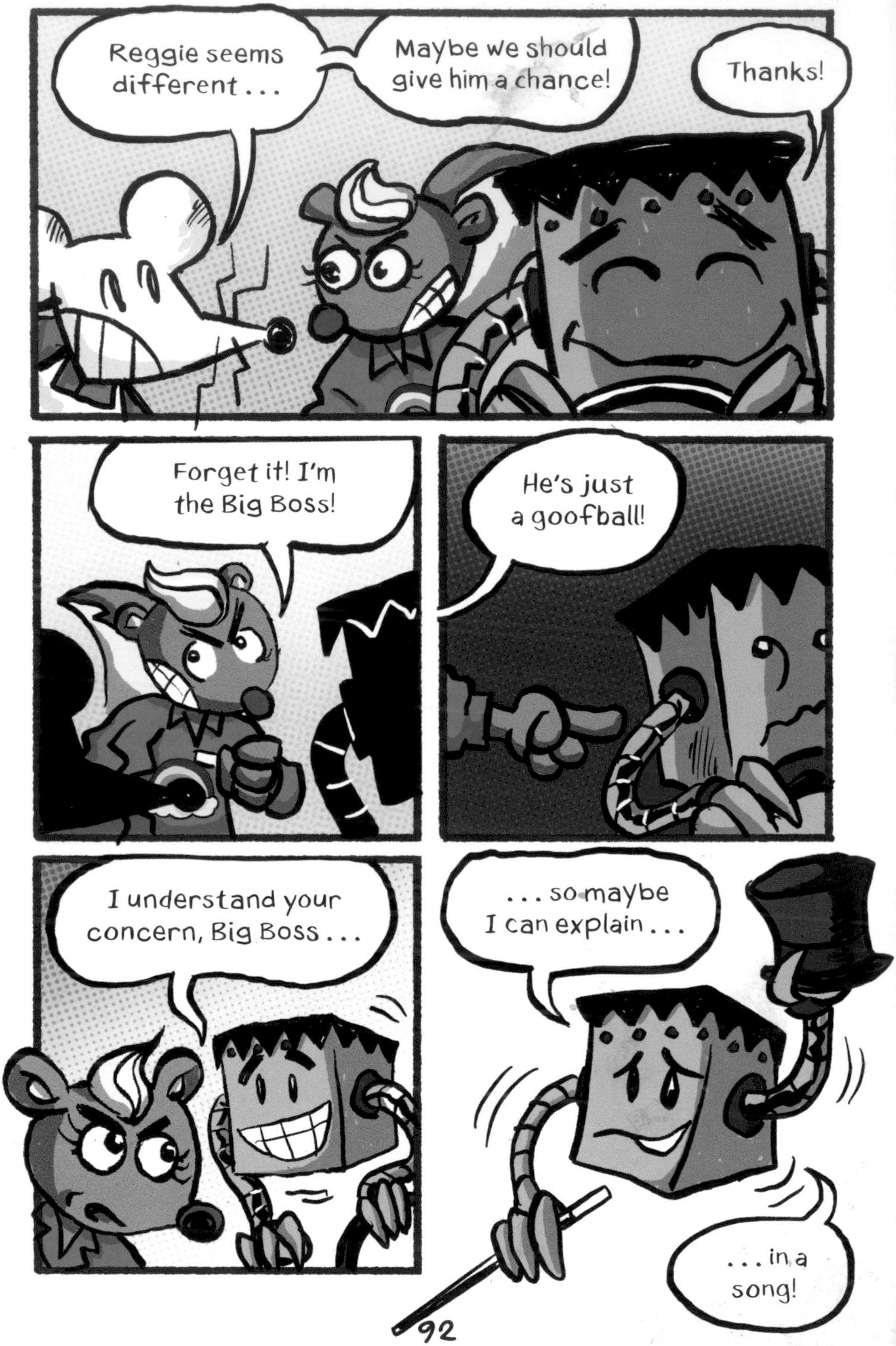
Reggie seems different . . .
Maybe we should give him a chance!
Thanks!
Forget it! I'm the Big Boss!
He's just a goofball!
I understand your concern, Big Boss . . .
. . . so maybe I can explain . . .
. . . in a song!

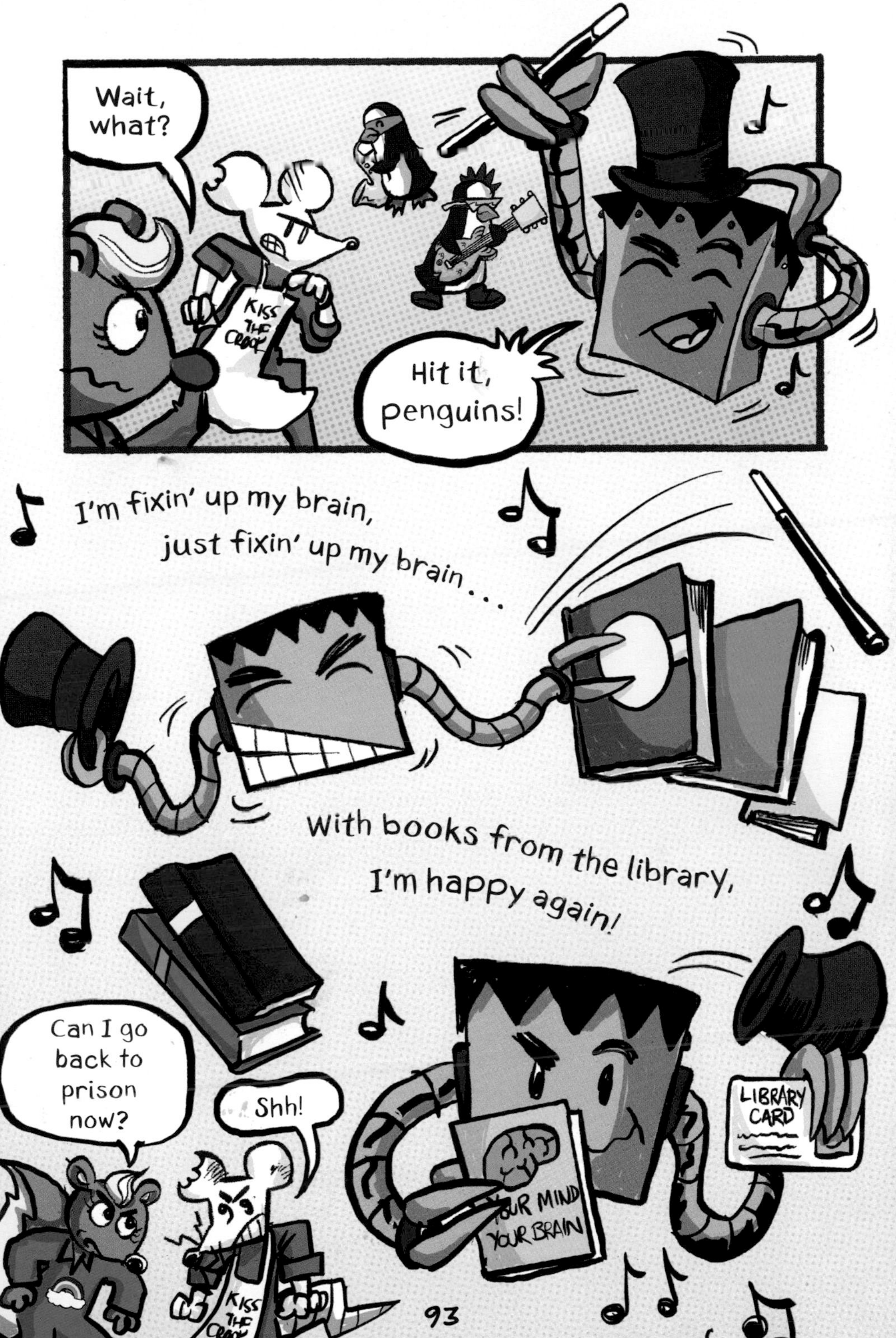
Wait, what?
Hit it, penguins!
KISS THE CROOK
I'm fixin' up my brain,
just fixin' up my brain . . .
With books from the library,
I'm happy again!
Can I go back to prison now?
Shh!
LIBRARY CARD
YOUR MIND YOUR BRAIN
KISS THE CROOK

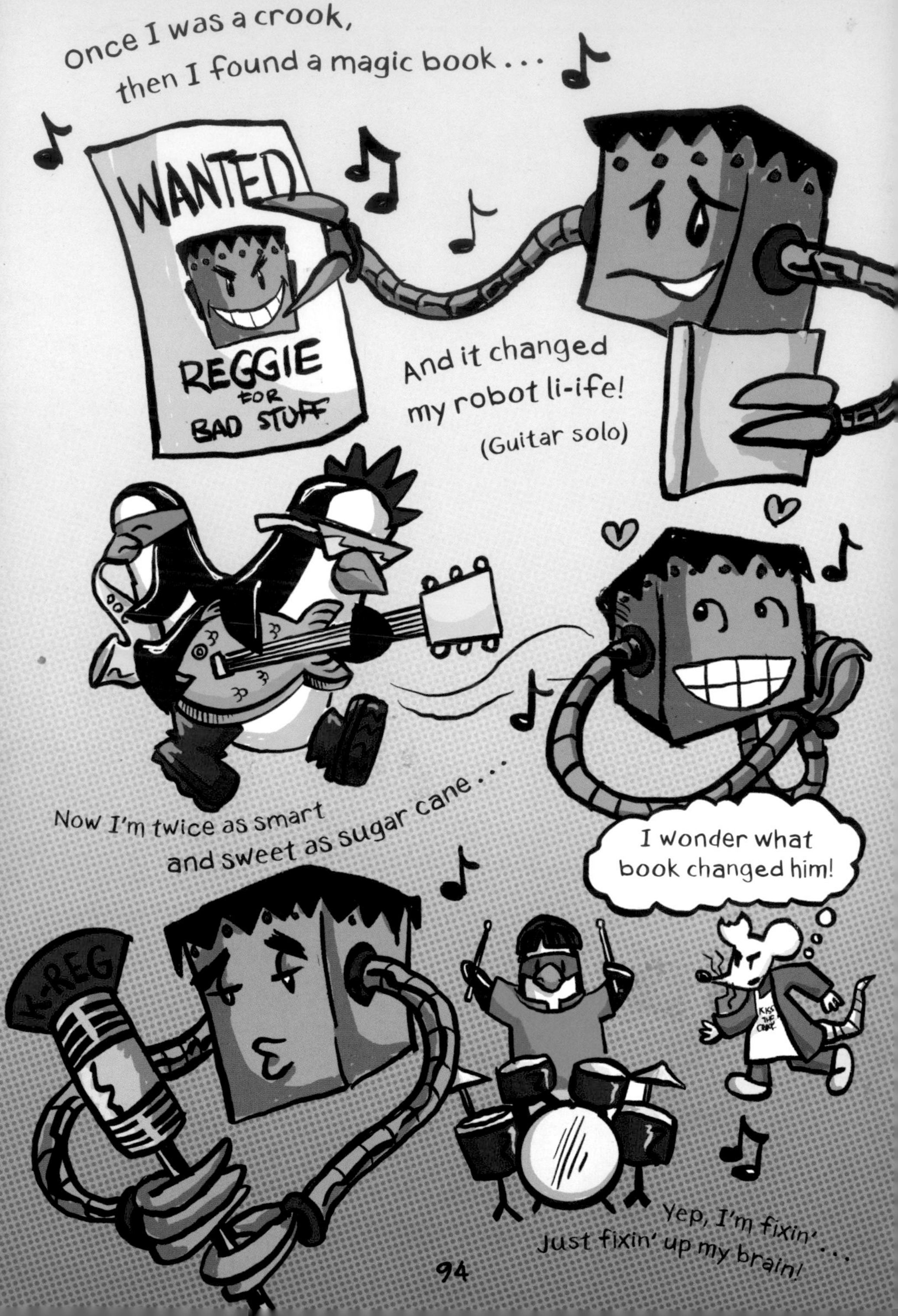
Once I was a crook,
then I found a magic book . . .
WANTED
REGGIE
FOR
BAD STUFF
And it changed
my robot li-ife!
(Guitar solo)
Now I'm twice as smart
and sweet as sugar cane . . .
I wonder what
book changed him!
K-REG
Yep, I'm fixin' . . .
Just fixin' up my brain!

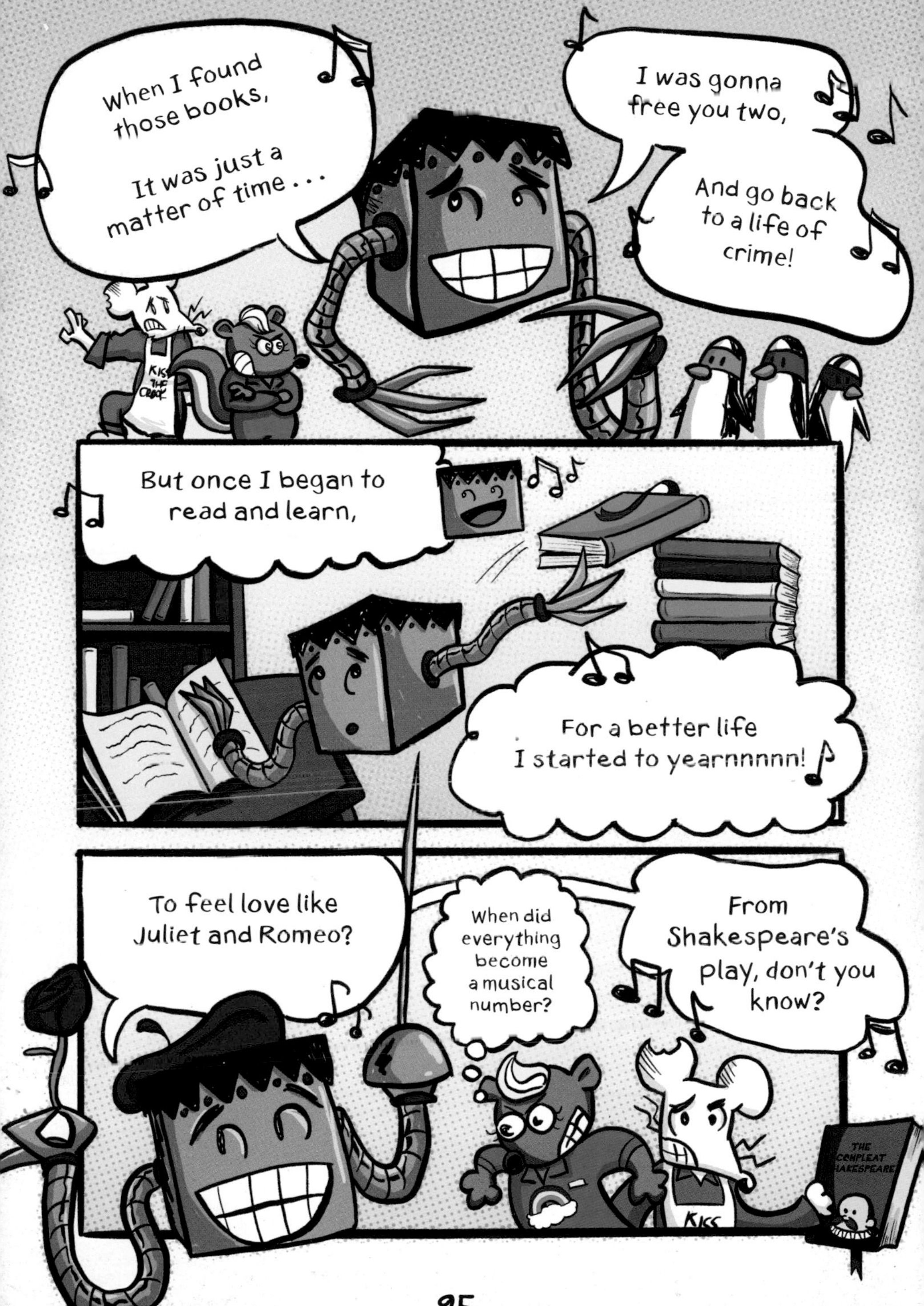
When I found those books, It was just a matter of time . . .
I was gonna free you two, And go back to a life of crime!
KISS THE CROOK
But once I began to read and learn,
For a better life I started to yearnnnnn!
To feel love like Juliet and Romeo?
When did everything become a musical number?
From Shakespeare's play, don't you know?
THE COMPLEAT SHAKESPEARE
KISS

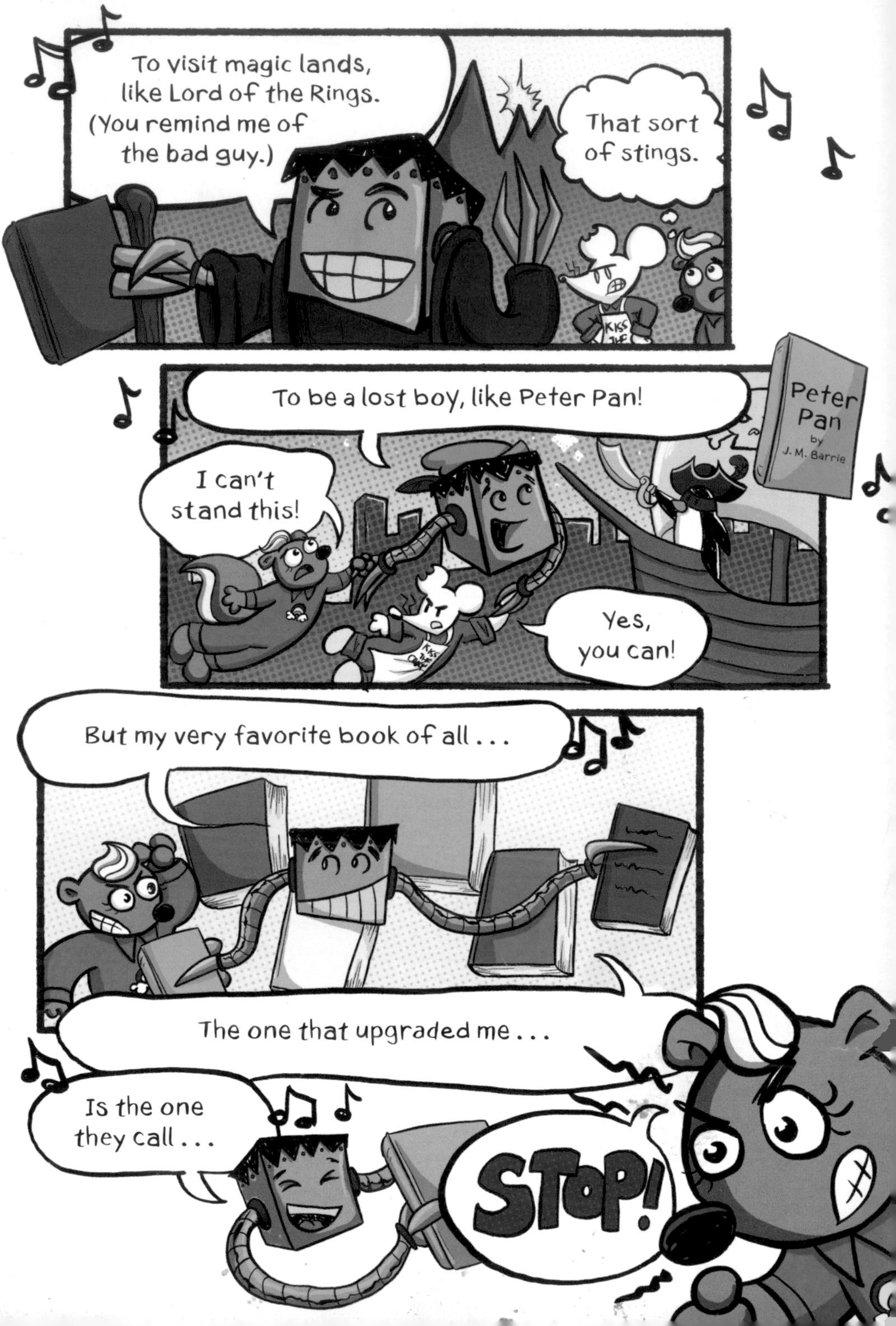

To visit magic lands, like Lord of the Rings. (You remind me of the bad guy.)
That sort of stings.
To be a lost boy, like Peter Pan!
Peter Pan by J. M. Barrie
I can't stand this!
Yes, you can!
But my very favorite book of all . . .
The one that upgraded me . . .
Is the one they call . . .
STOP!

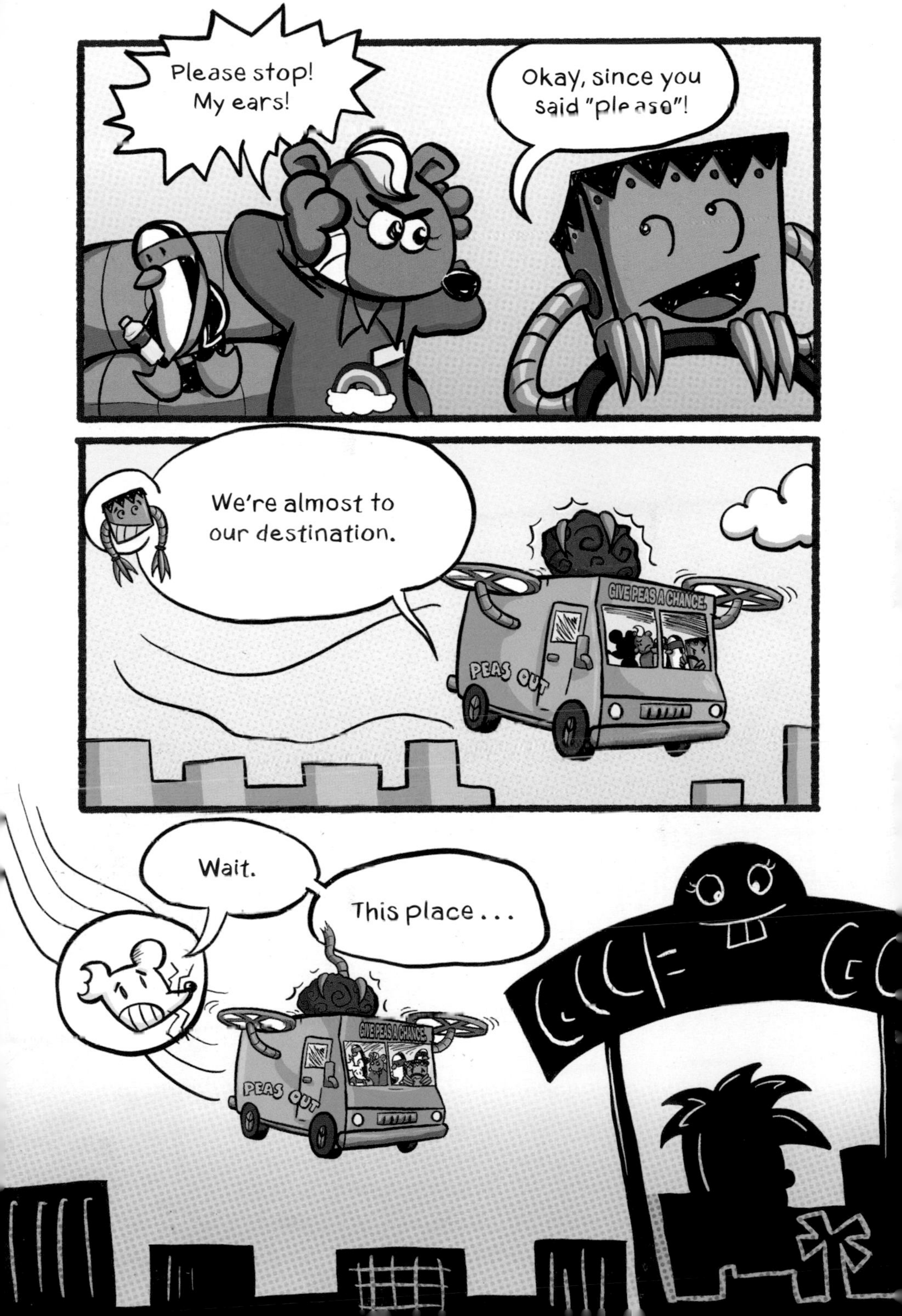
Please stop! My ears!
Okay, since you said "please"!
We're almost to our destination.
GIVE PEAS A CHANCE.
PEAS OUT
Wait.
This place . . .
GIVE PEAS A CHANCE.
PEAS OUT

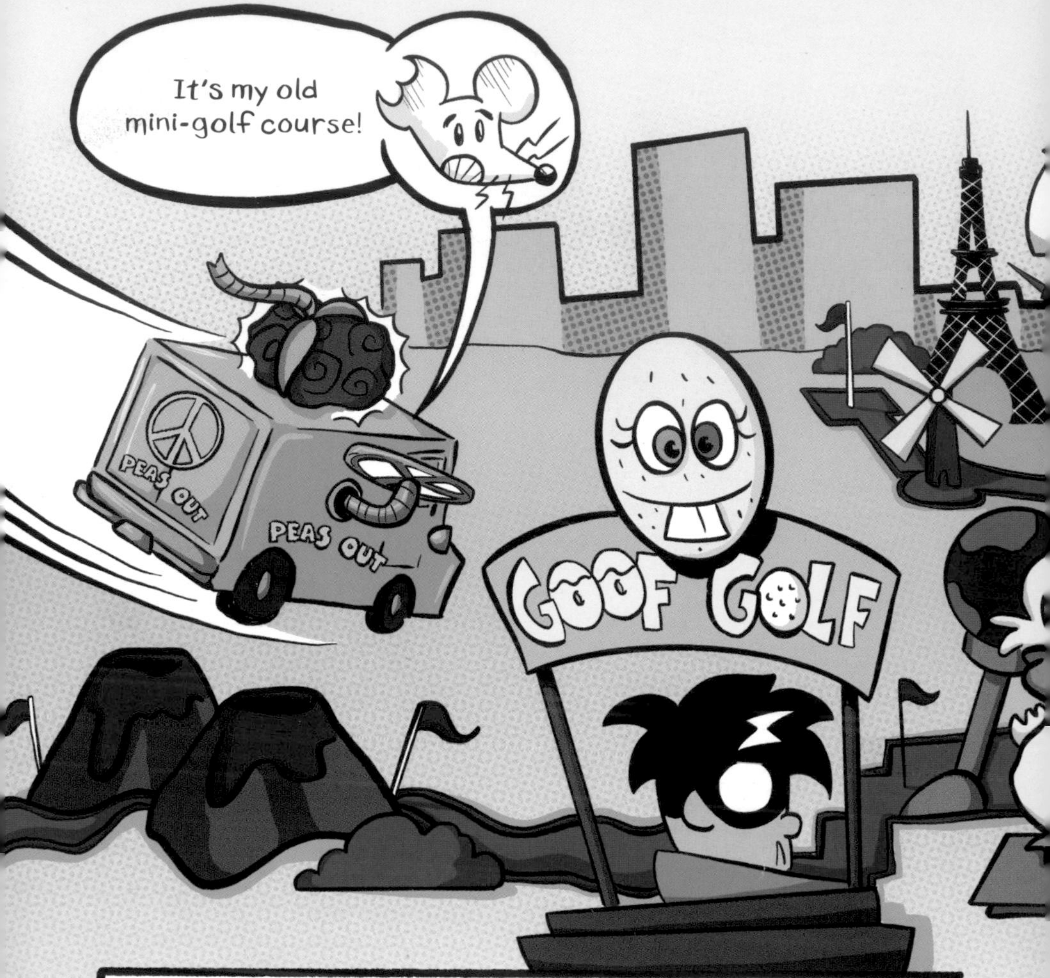
It's my old mini-golf course!
PEAS OUT
PEAS OUT
GOOF GOLF

WHY has Reggie brought everyone here?

WHAT will they do with the meatball?

WHO is the new owner of Goof Golf?

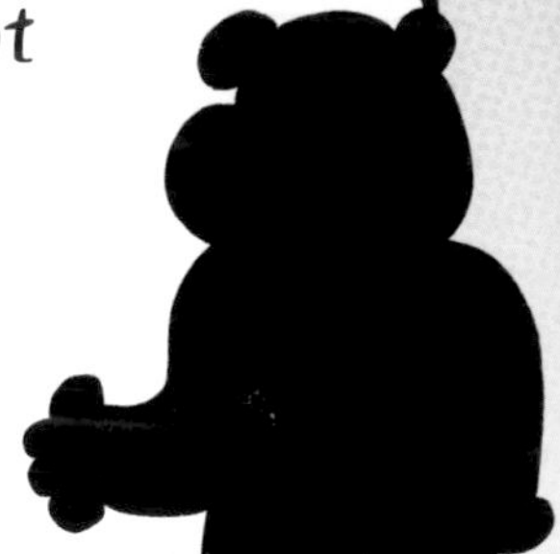

Find out in the next chapter!

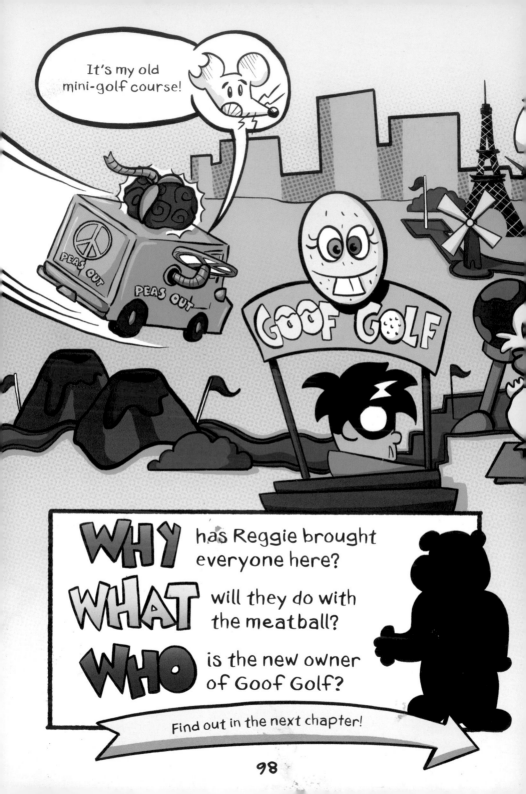

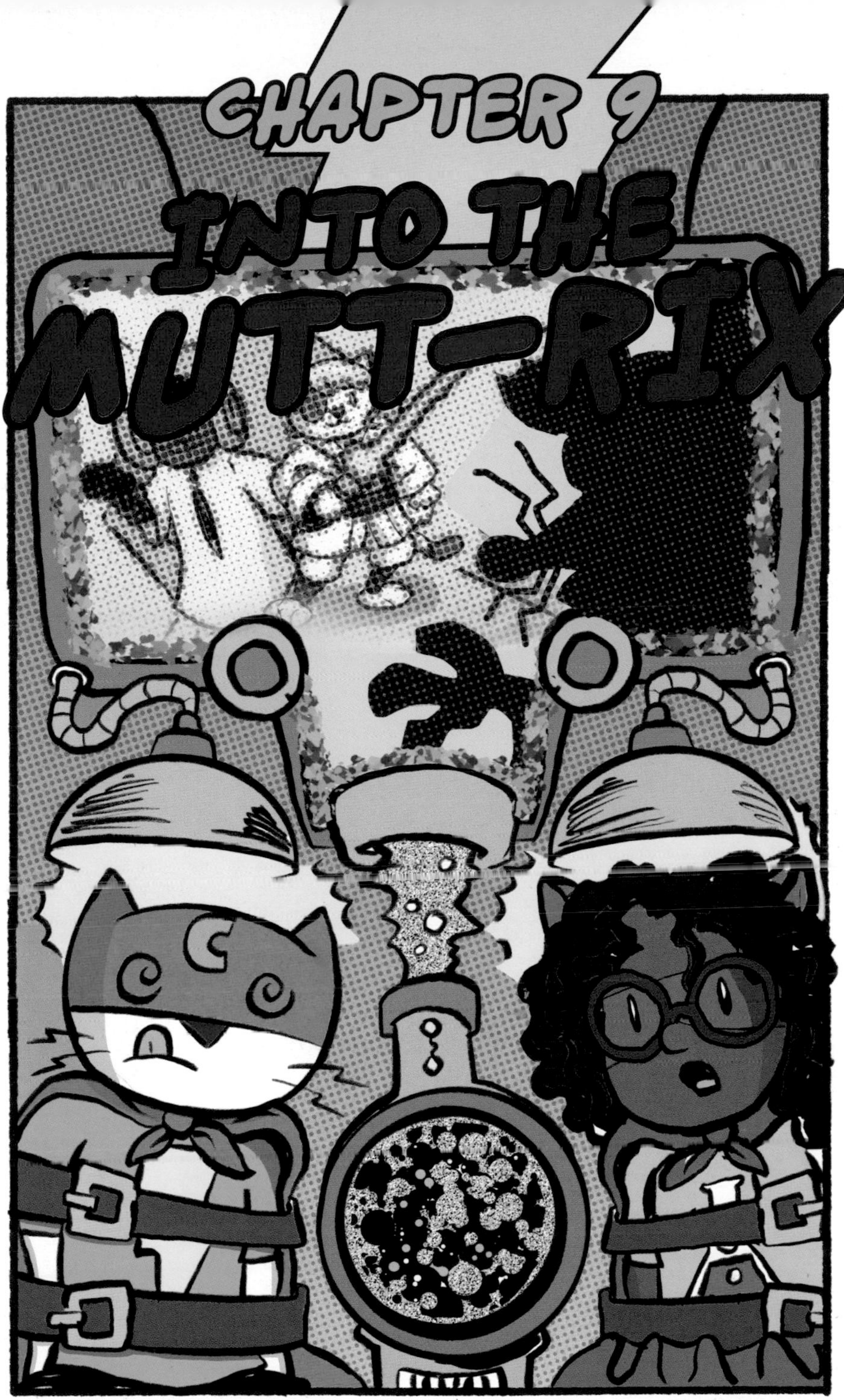
CHAPTER 9
INTO THE
MUTT-RIX

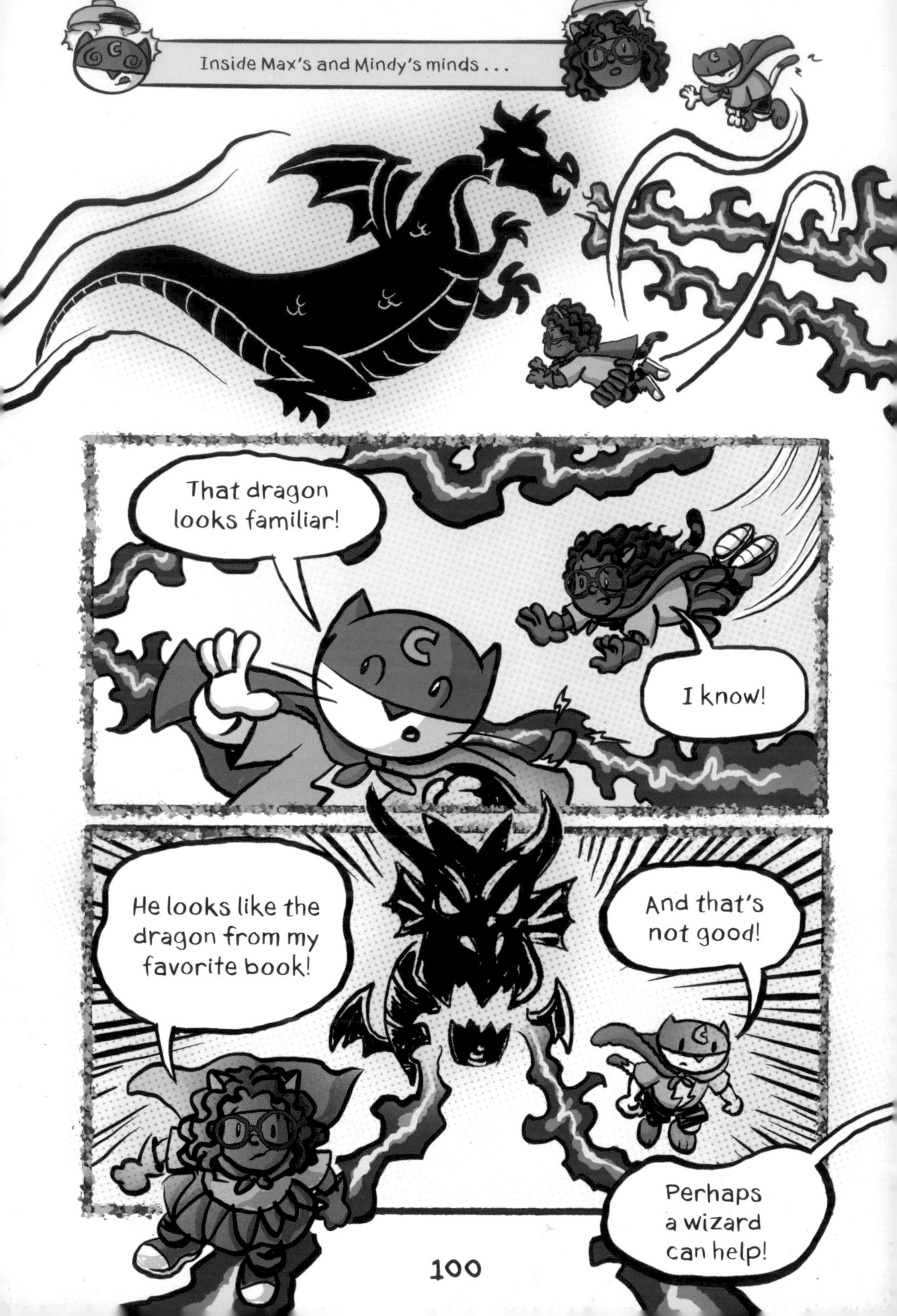
Inside Max's and Mindy's minds . . .
That dragon looks familiar!
I know!
He looks like the dragon from my favorite book!
And that's not good!
Perhaps a wizard can help!

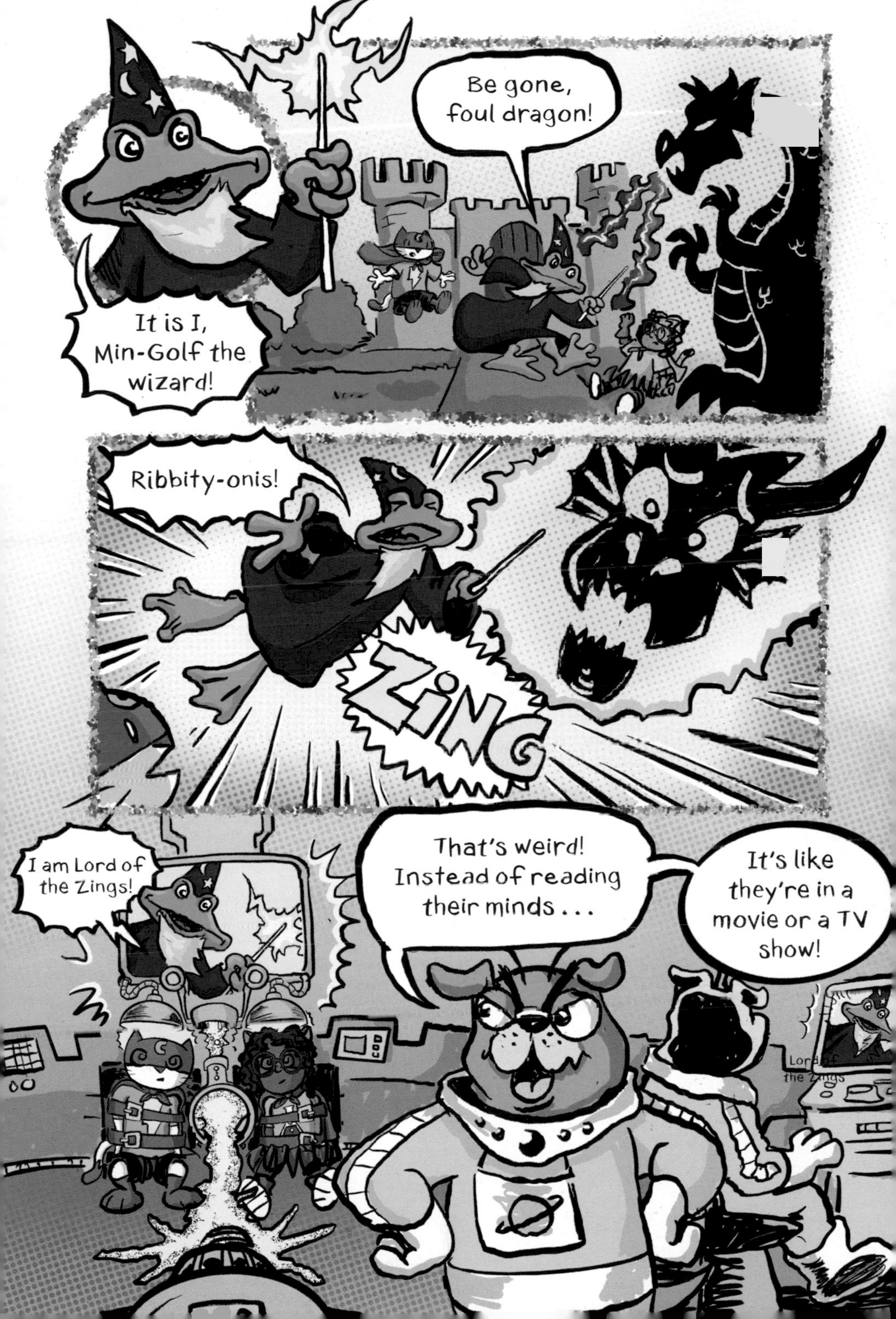

It is I, Min-Golf the wizard!
Be gone, foul dragon!
Ribbity-onis!
ZING
I am Lord of the Zings!
That's weird! Instead of reading their minds . . .
It's like they're in a movie or a TV show!
Lord of the Zings

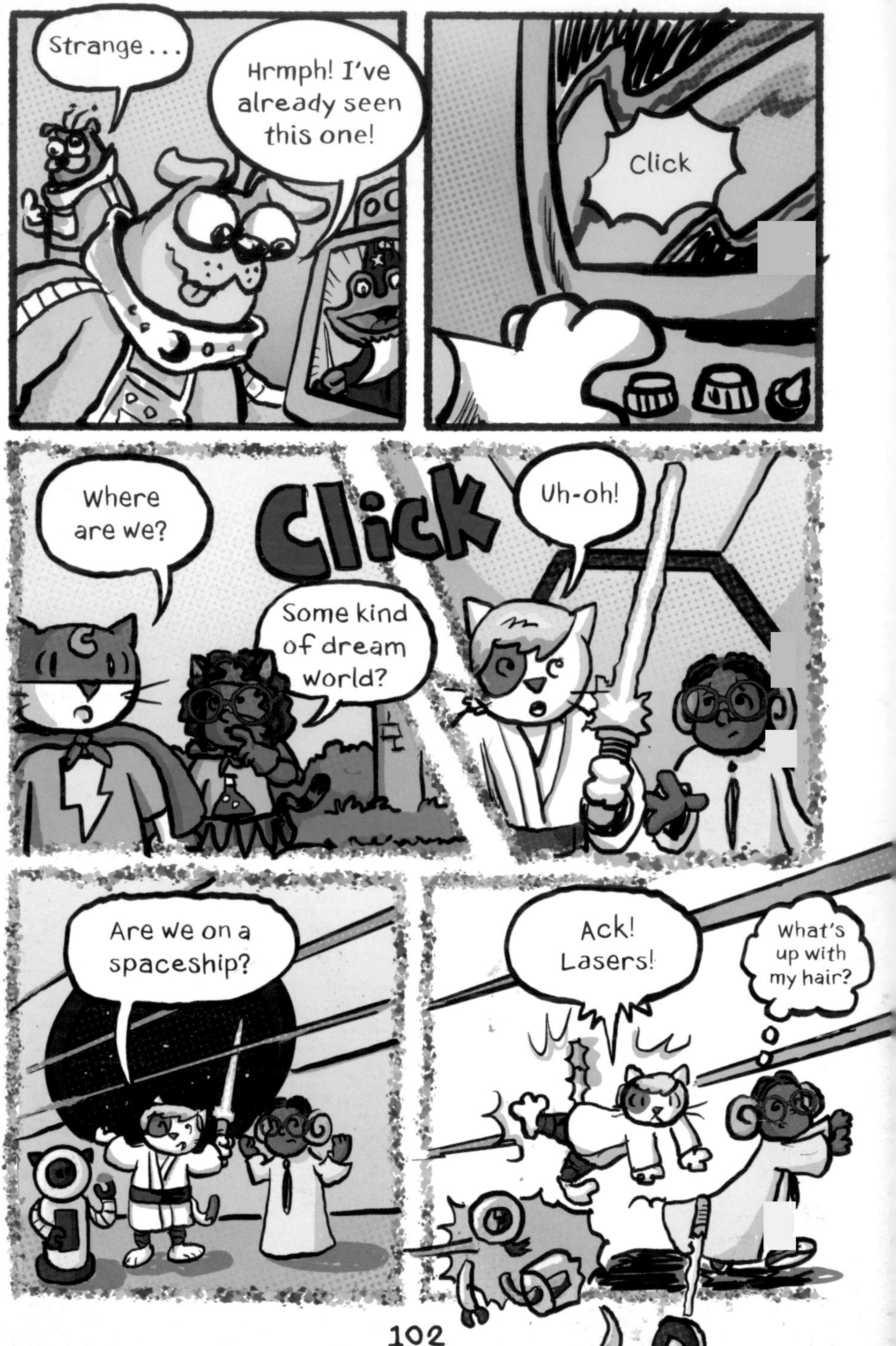
Strange . . .
Hrmph! I've already seen this one!
Click
Where are we?
Click
Uh-oh!
Some kind of dream world?
Are we on a spaceship?
Ack! Lasers!
What's up with my hair?

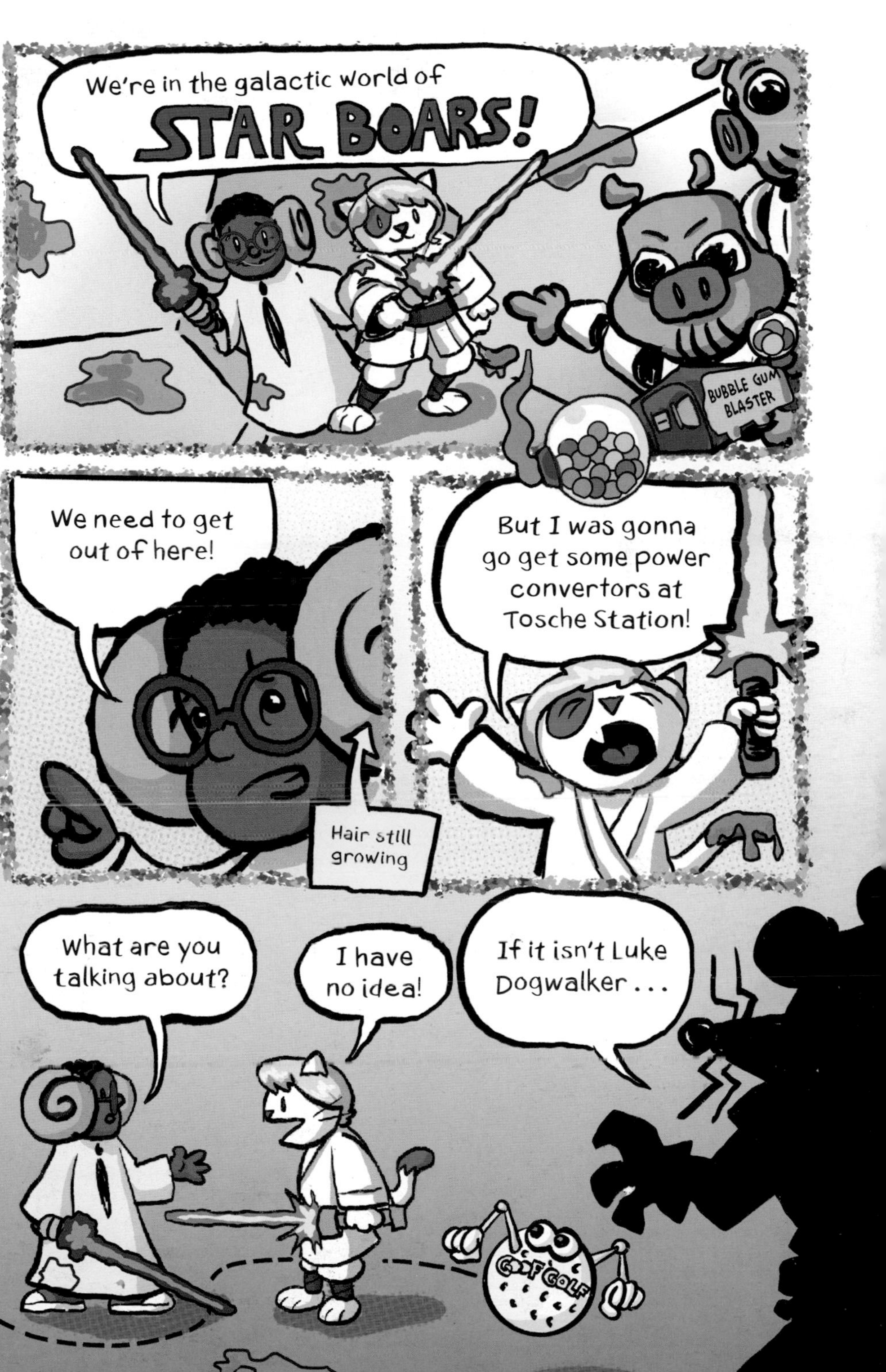
We're in the galactic world of STAR BOARS!
BUBBLE GUM BLASTER
We need to get out of here!
Hair still growing
But I was gonna go get some power convertors at Tosche Station!
What are you talking about?
I have no idea!
If it isn't Luke Dogwalker . . .
GOOF GOLF

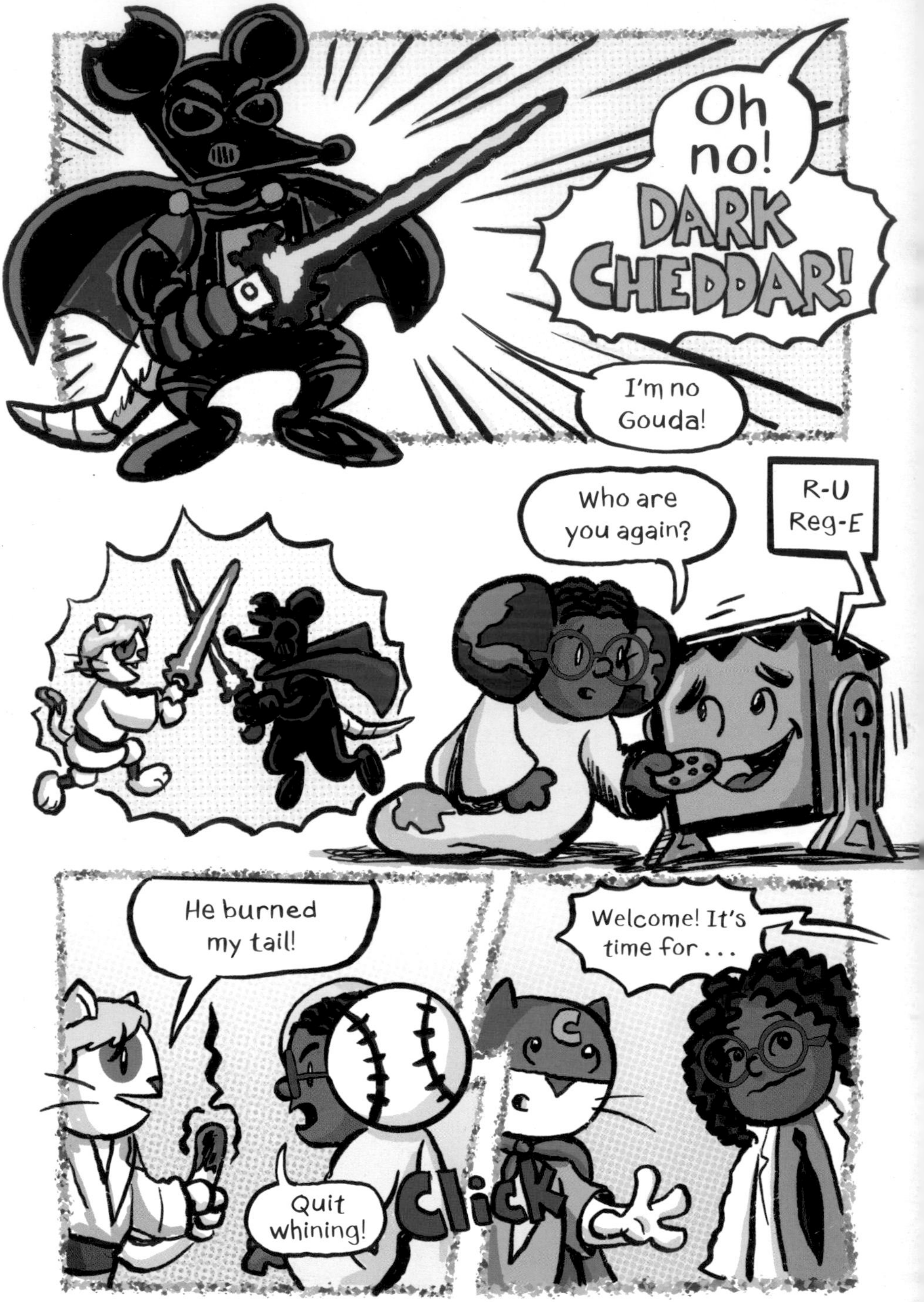
Oh no! DARK CHEDDAR!
I'm no Gouda!
Who are you again?
R-U Reg-E
He burned my tail!
Quit whining!
Click
Welcome! It's time for . . .

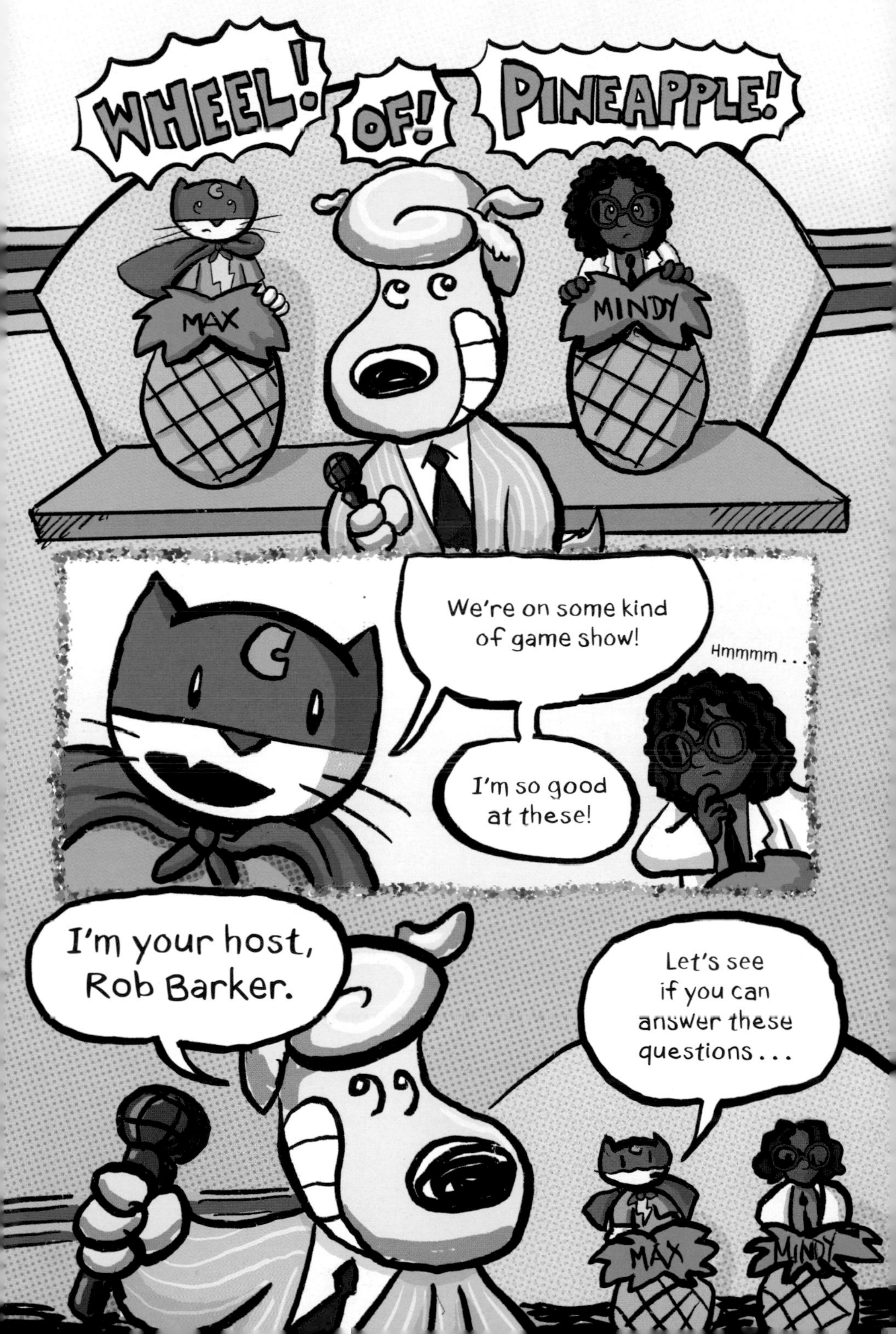
WHEEL! OF! PINEAPPLE!
MAX
MINDY
We're on some kind of game show!
I'm so good at these!
Hmmmm . . .
I'm your host, Rob Barker.
Let's see if you can answer these questions . . .
MAX
MINDY

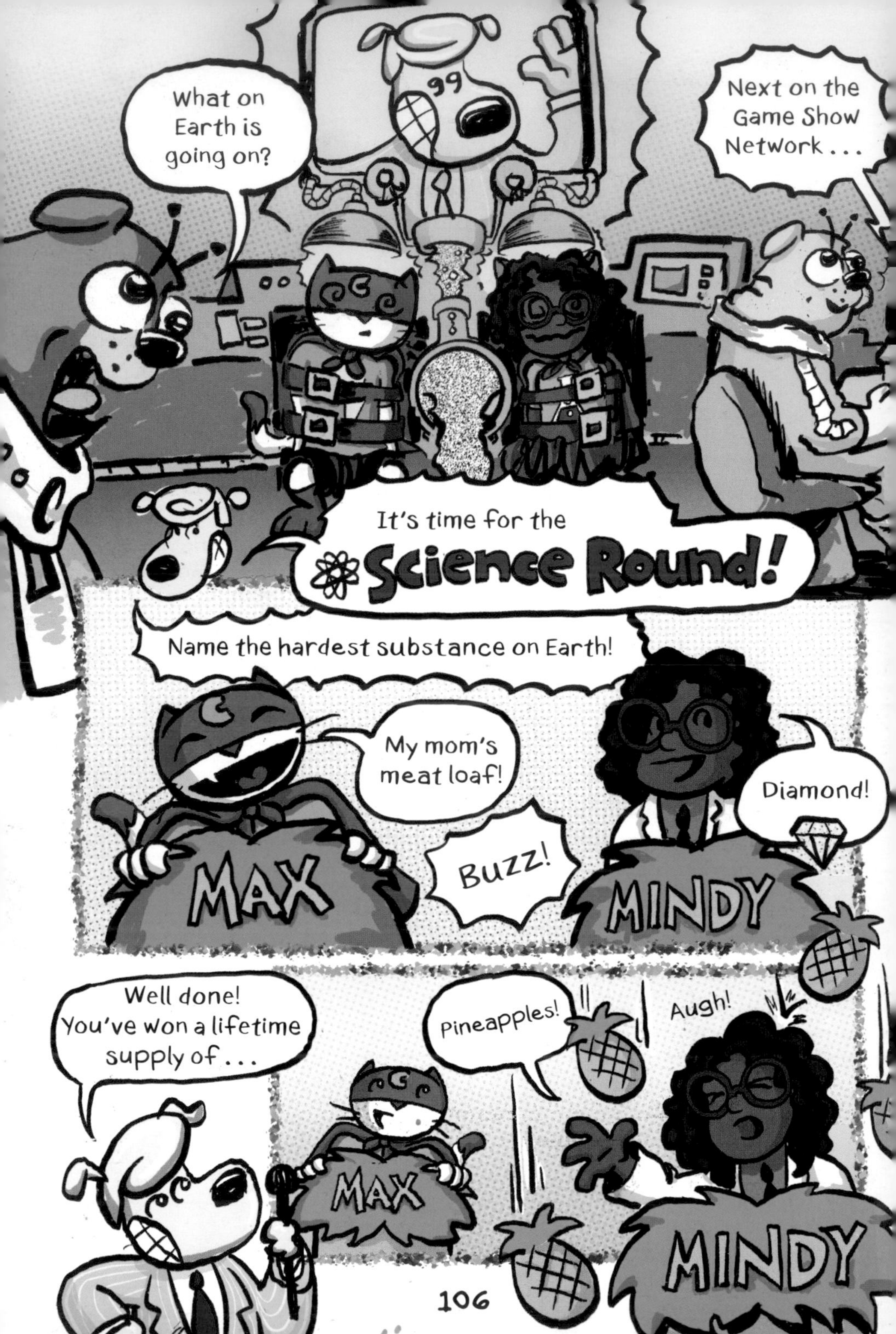
What on Earth is going on?
Next on the Game Show Network . . .
It's time for the Science Round!
Name the hardest substance on Earth!
My mom's meat loaf!
Buzz!
Diamond!
MAX
MINDY
Well done! You've won a lifetime supply of . . .
Pineapples!
Augh!
MAX
MINDY

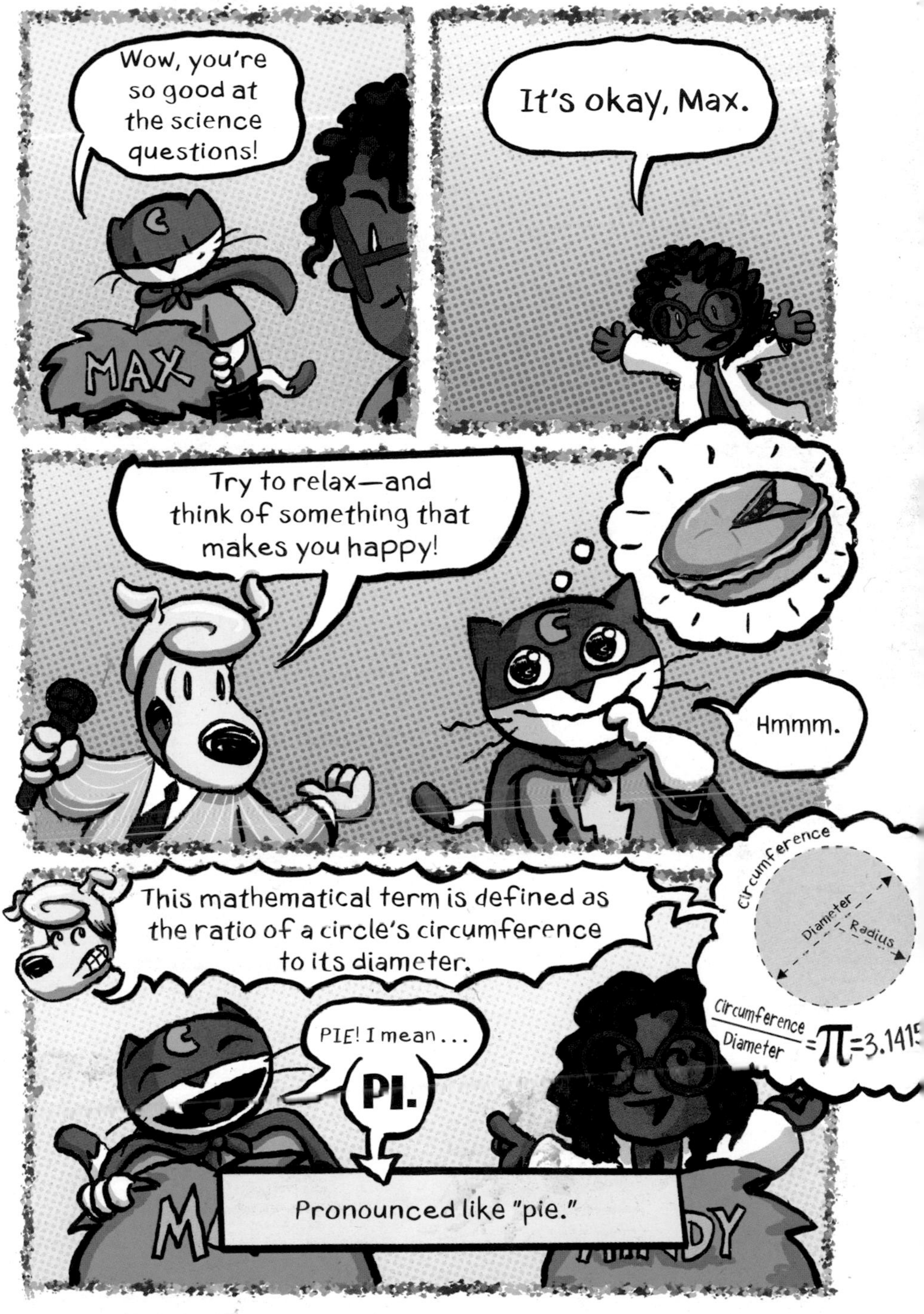
Wow, you're so good at the science questions!
MAX
It's okay, Max.
Try to relax—and think of something that makes you happy!
Hmmm.
This mathematical term is defined as the ratio of a circle's circumference to its diameter.
Circumference
Diameter
Radius
Circumference / Diameter = π = 3.1415
PIE! I mean . . .
PI.
Pronounced like "pie."

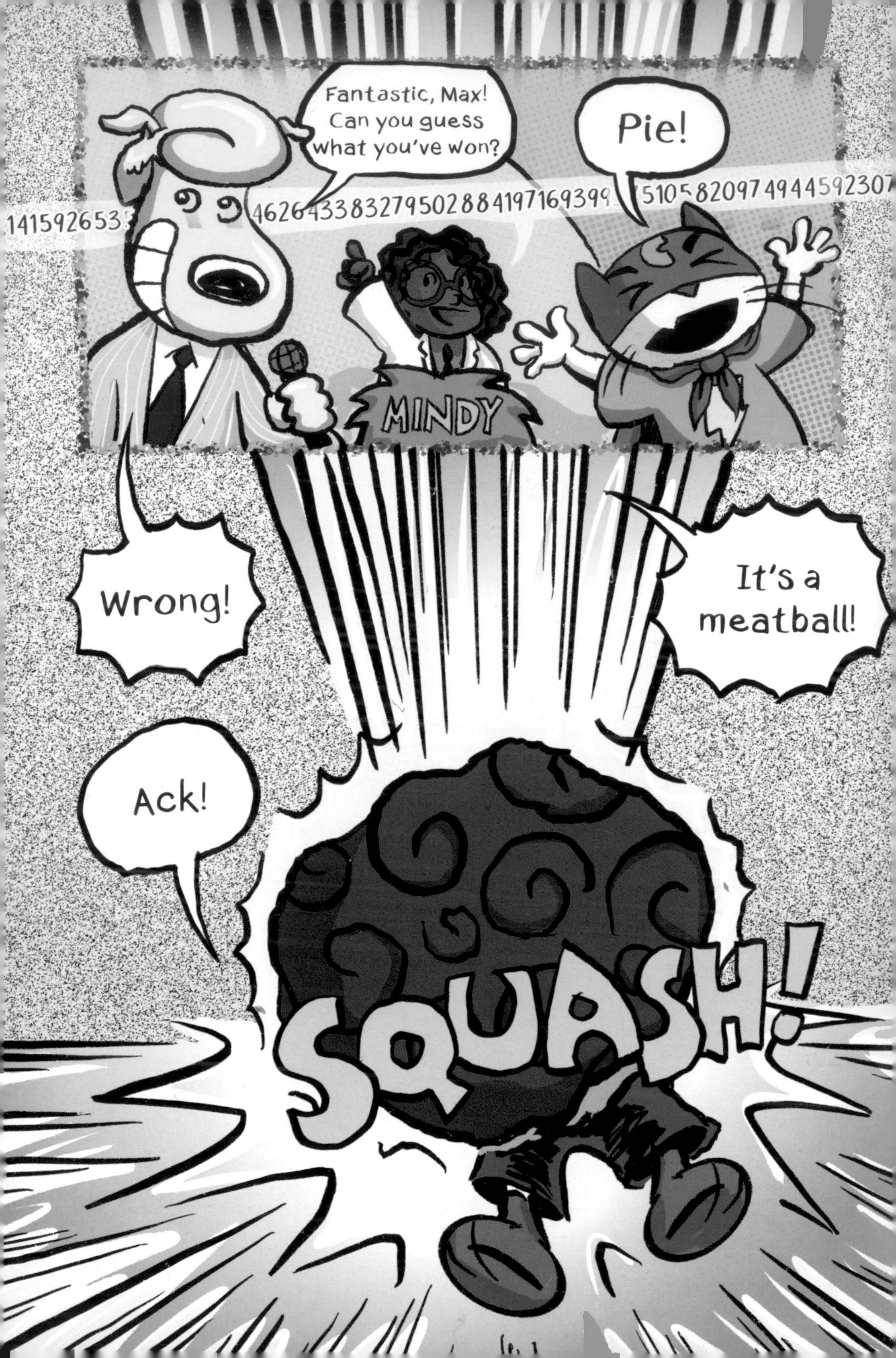
Fantastic, Max! Can you guess what you've won?
Pie!
141592653
4626433832795028841971693
5105820974944592307
MINDY
Wrong!
It's a meatball!
Ack!
SQUASH!

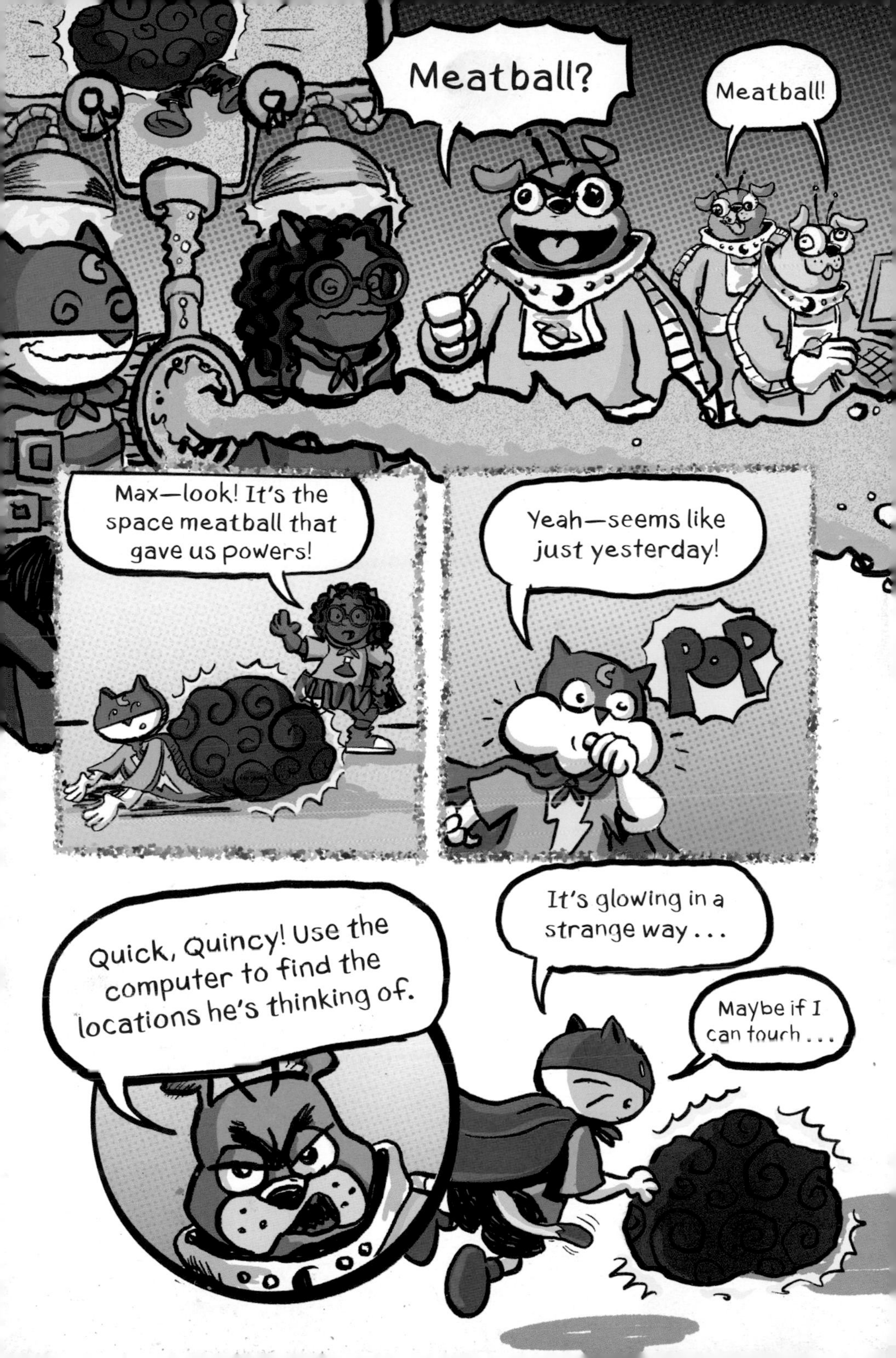

Meatball?
Meatball!
Max—look! It's the space meatball that gave us powers!
Yeah—seems like just yesterday!
POP
Quick, Quincy! Use the computer to find the locations he's thinking of.
It's glowing in a strange way . . .
Maybe if I can touch . . .

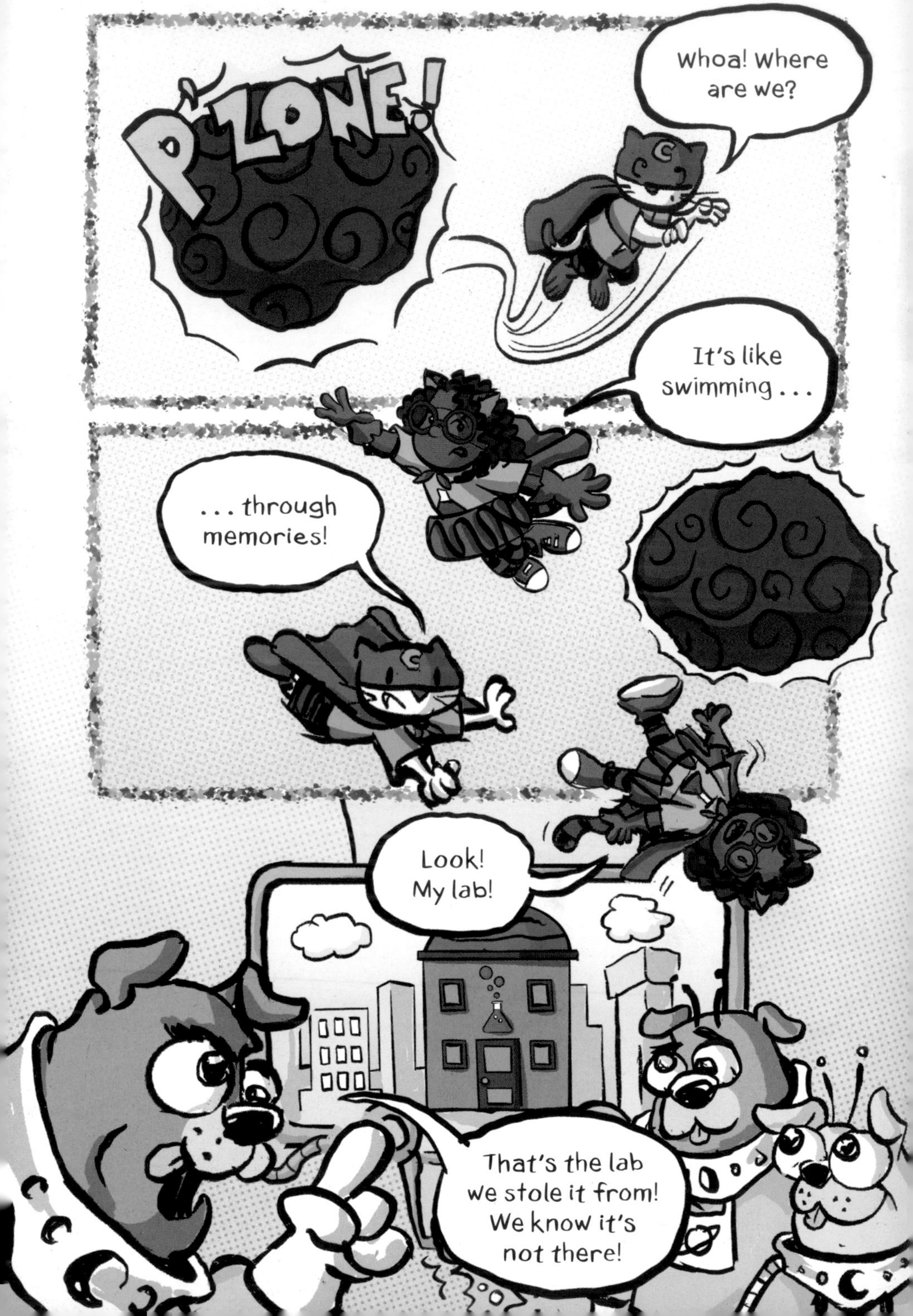
P'ZONE!
Whoa! Where are we?
It's like swimming . . .
. . . through memories!
Look! My lab!
That's the lab we stole it from! We know it's not there!

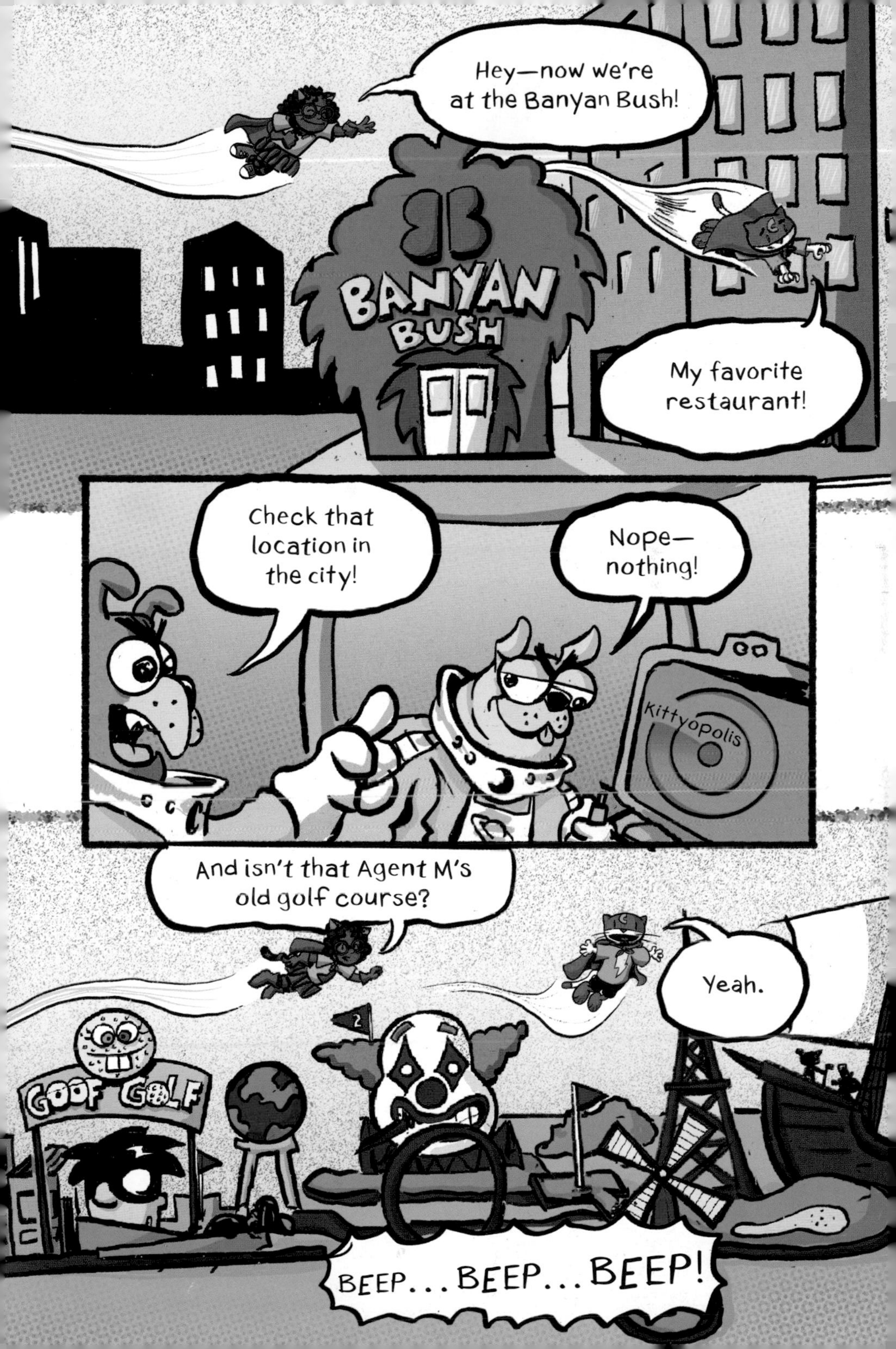
Hey—now we're at the Banyan Bush!
BB
BANYAN BUSH
My favorite restaurant!
Check that location in the city!
Nope—nothing!
Kittyopolis
And isn't that Agent M's old golf course?
Yeah.
GOOF GOLF
2
BEEP... BEEP... BEEP!

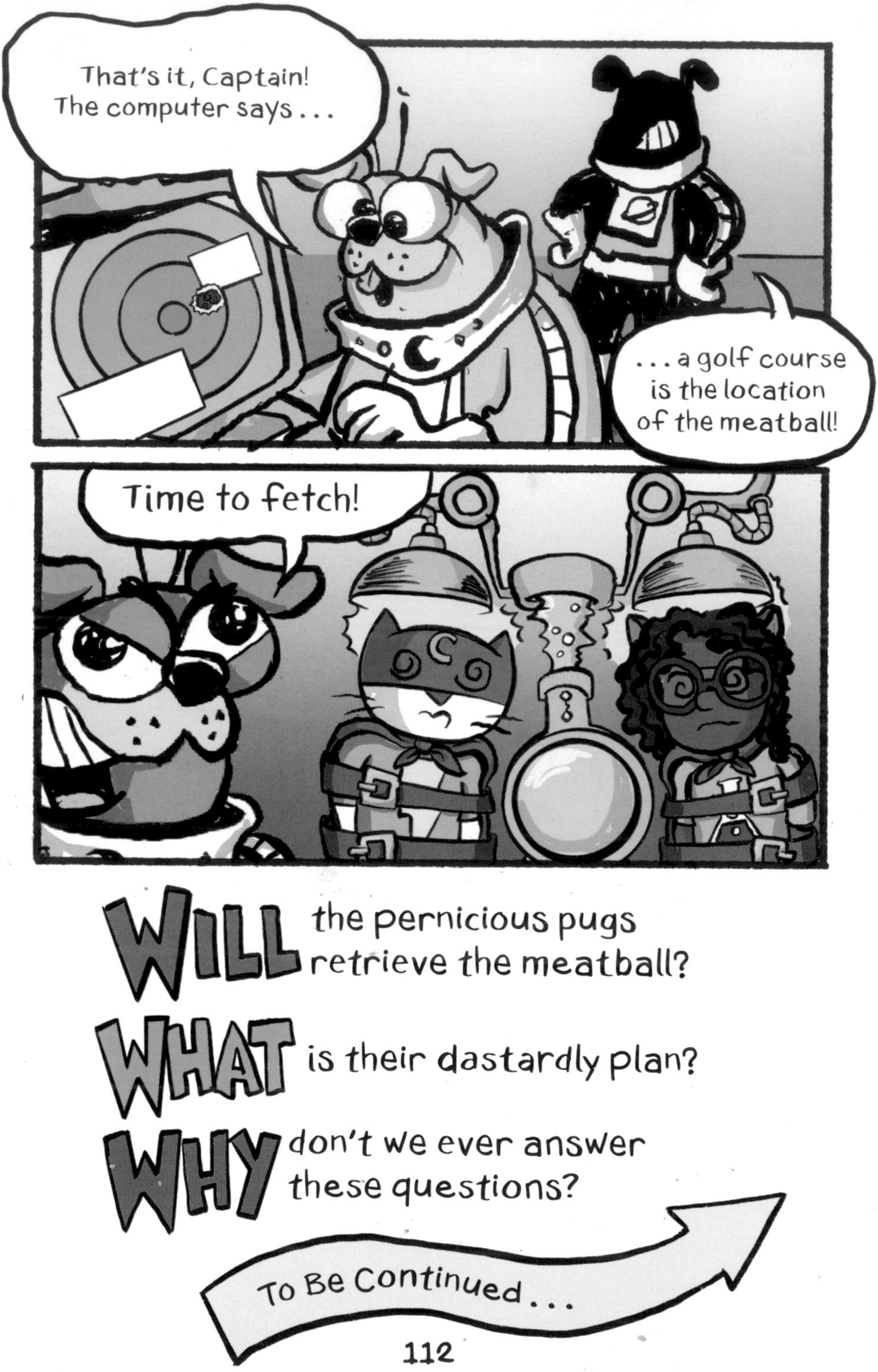
That's it, Captain! The computer says . . .
. . . a golf course is the location of the meatball!
Time to fetch!

WILL the pernicious pugs retrieve the meatball?

WHAT is their dastardly plan?

WHY don't we ever answer these questions?

To Be Continued . . .

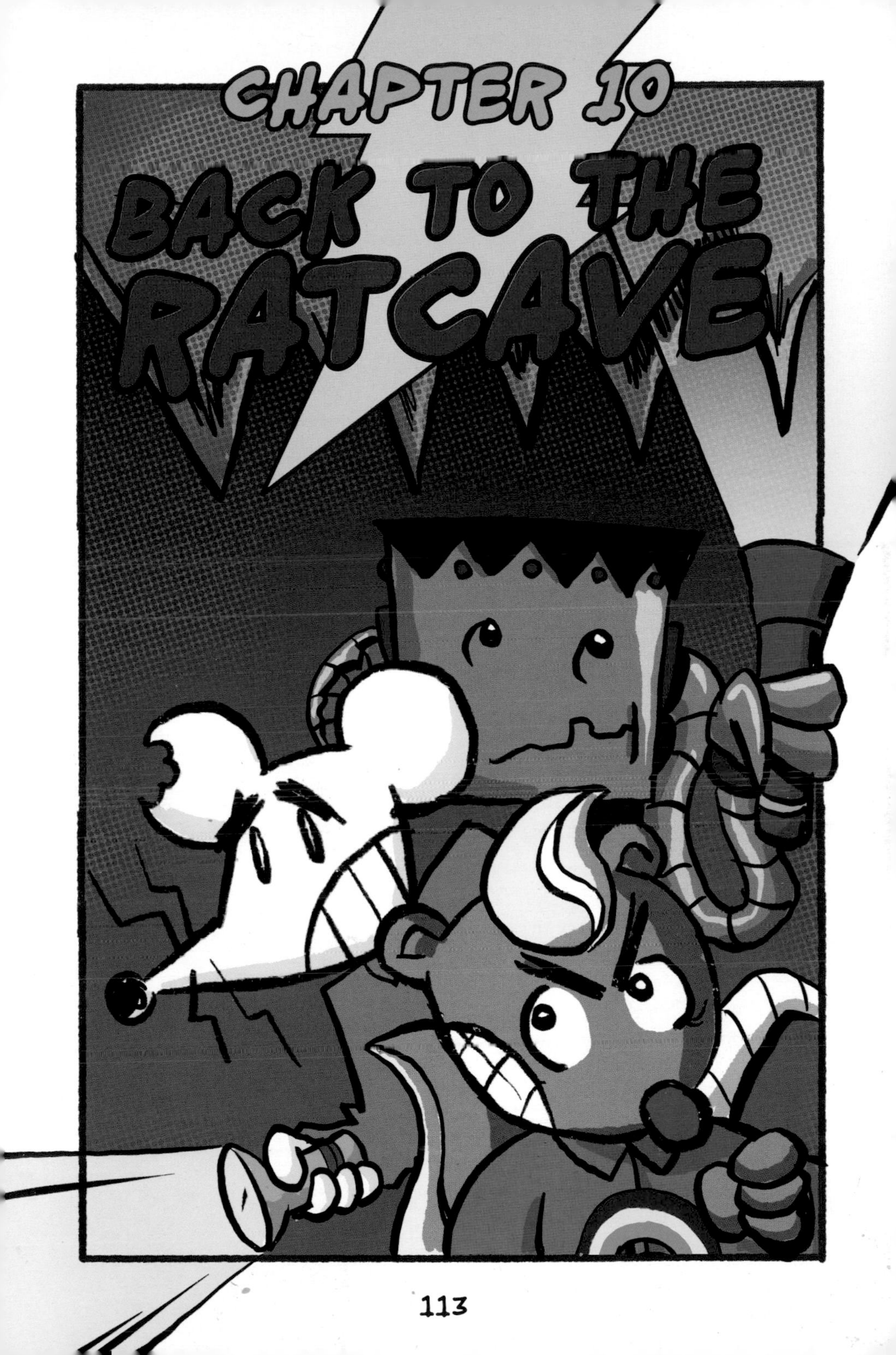
CHAPTER 10
BACK TO THE RATCAVE

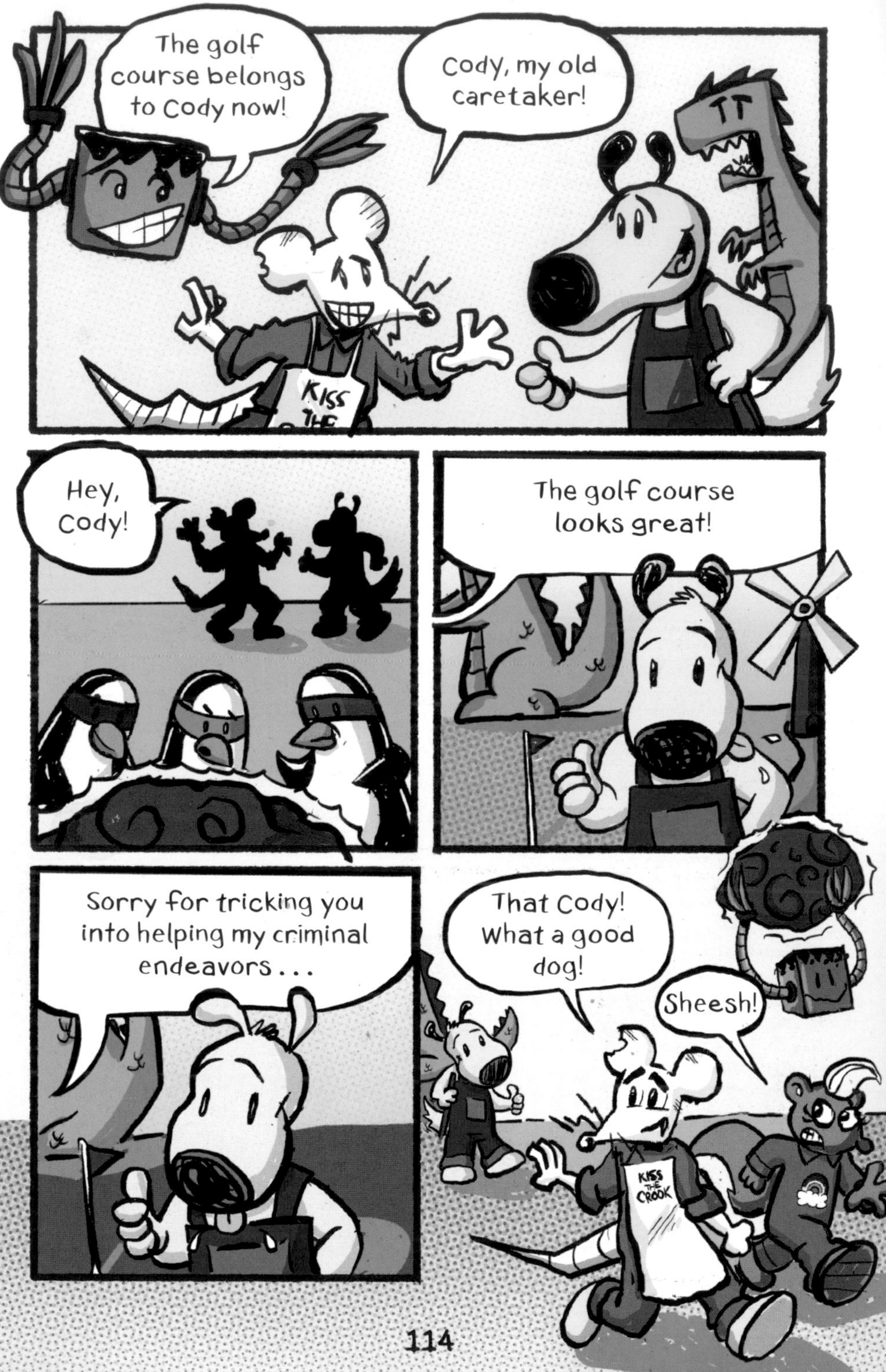
The golf course belongs to Cody now!
Cody, my old caretaker!
KISS THE
Hey, Cody!
The golf course looks great!
Sorry for tricking you into helping my criminal endeavors . . .
That Cody! What a good dog!
Sheesh!
KISS THE CROOK

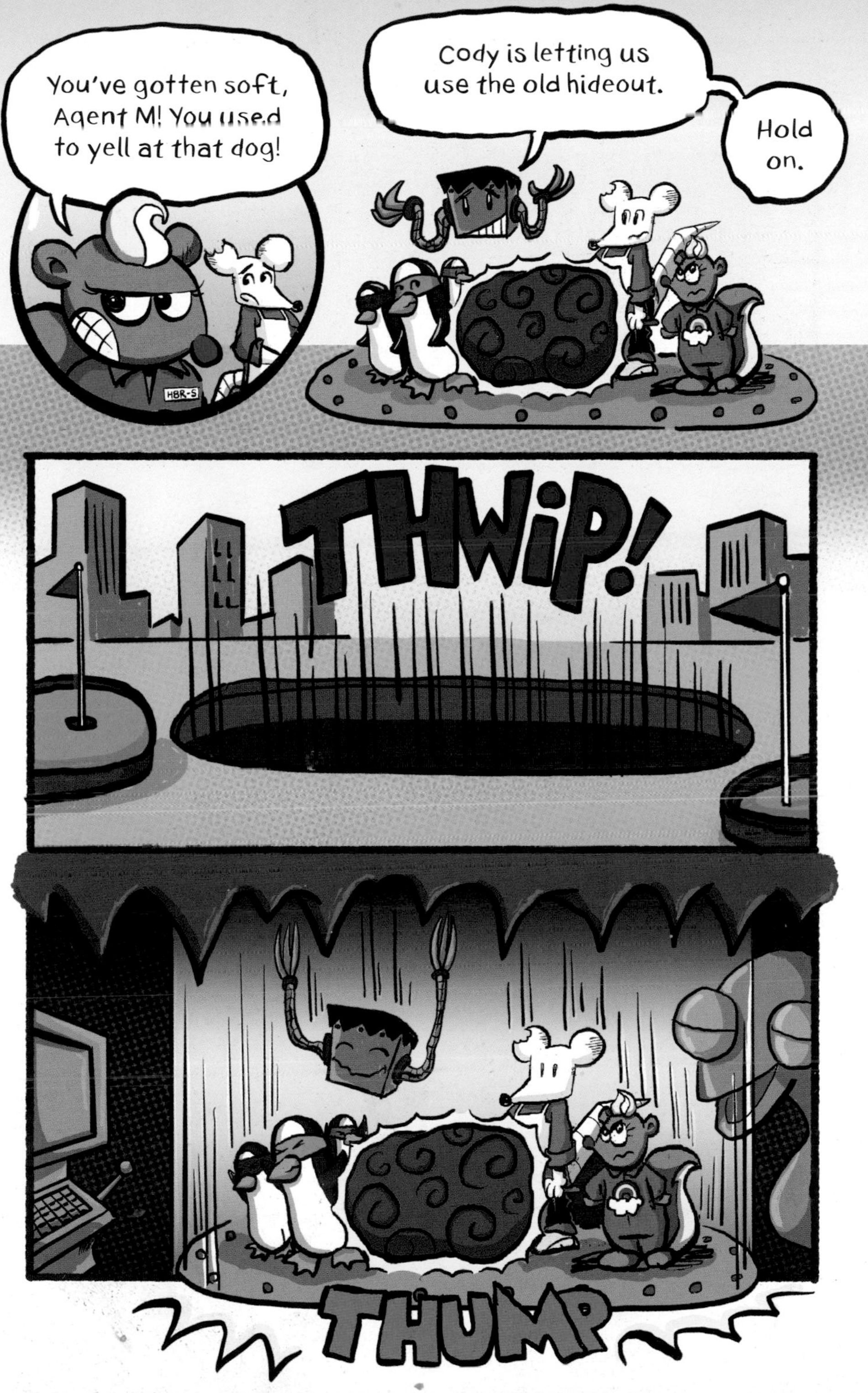
You've gotten soft, Agent M! You used to yell at that dog!
Cody is letting us use the old hideout.
Hold on.
THWIP!
THUMP

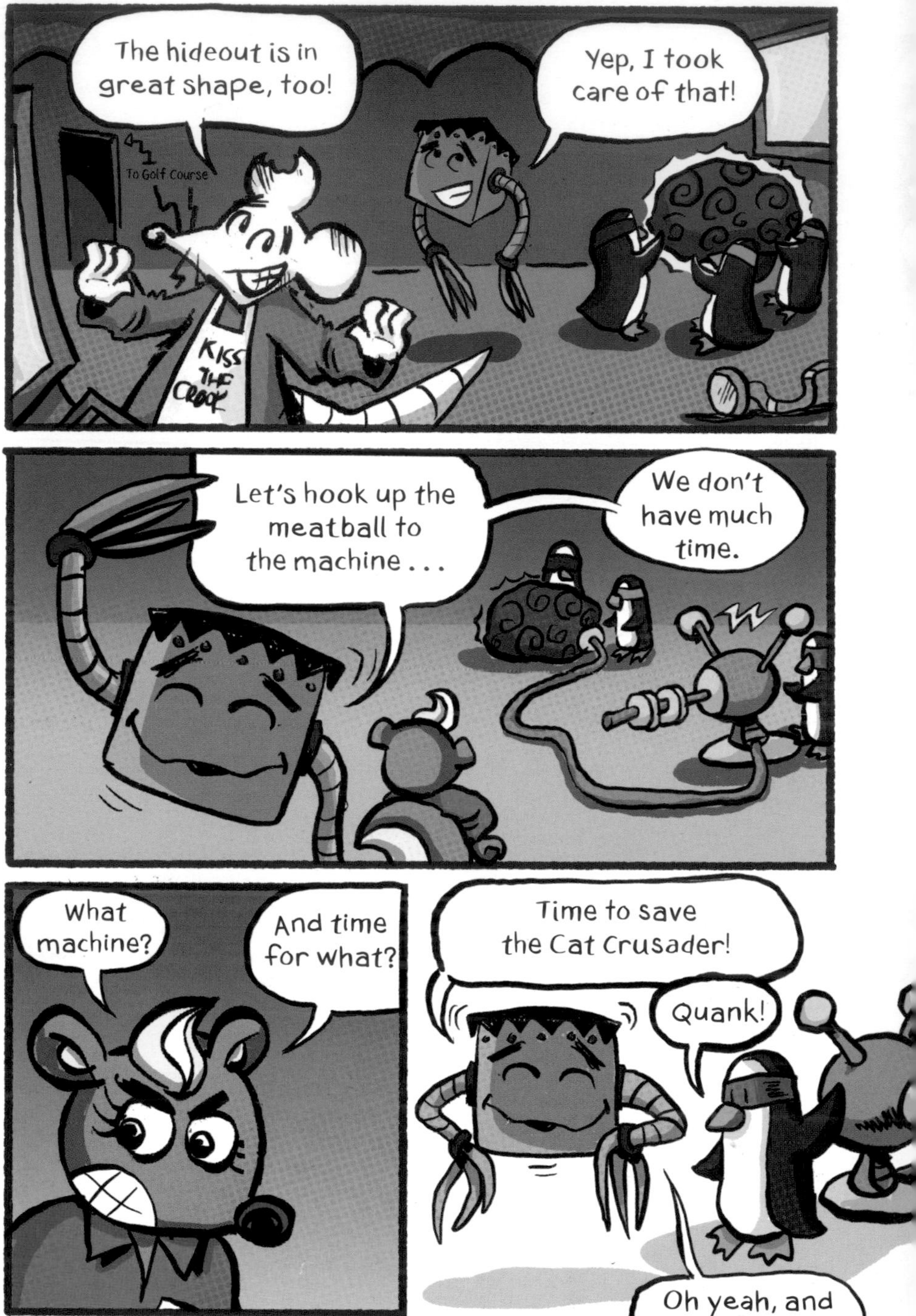
The hideout is in great shape, too!
To Golf Course
KISS THE CROOK
Yep, I took care of that!
Let's hook up the meatball to the machine . . .
We don't have much time.
What machine?
And time for what?
Time to save the Cat Crusader!
Quank!
Oh yeah, and Science Kitty!

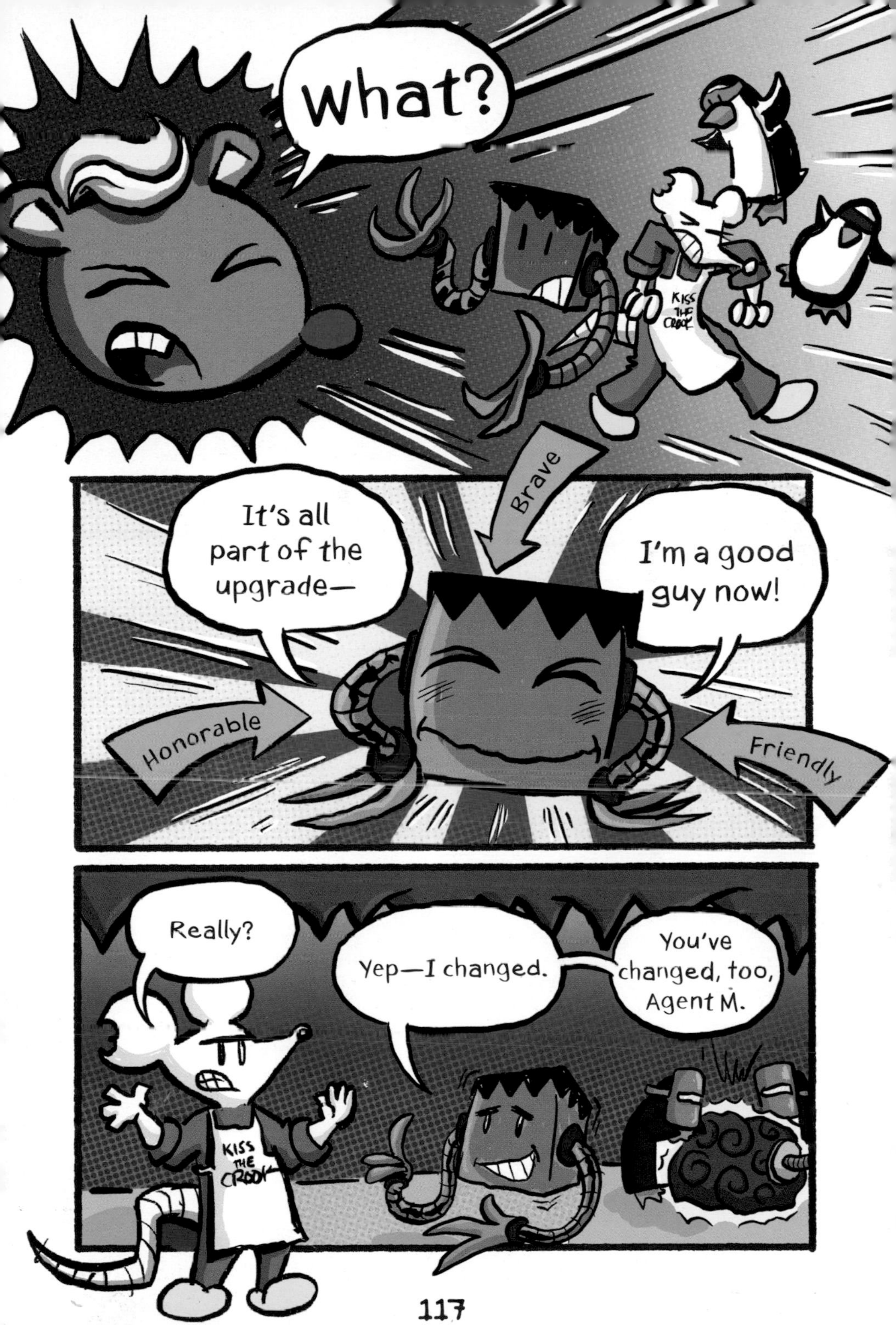
What?
KISS THE CROOK
It's all part of the upgrade—
Brave
I'm a good guy now!
Honorable
Friendly
Really?
Yep—I changed.
You've changed, too, Agent M.
KISS THE CROOK

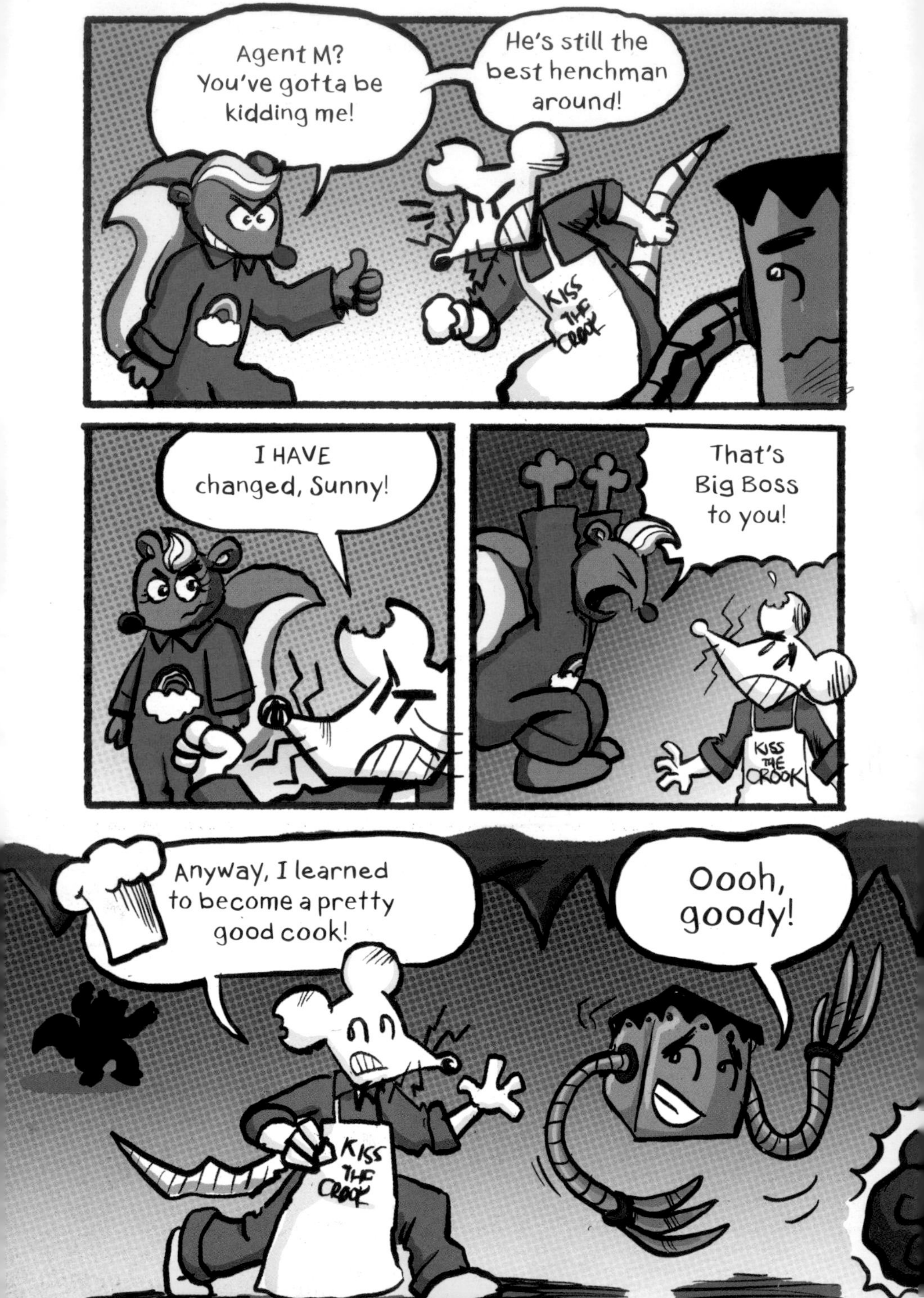
Agent M? You've gotta be kidding me!
He's still the best henchman around!
KISS THE CROOK
I HAVE changed, Sunny!
That's Big Boss to you!
KISS THE CROOK
Anyway, I learned to become a pretty good cook!
Oooh, goody!
KISS THE CROOK

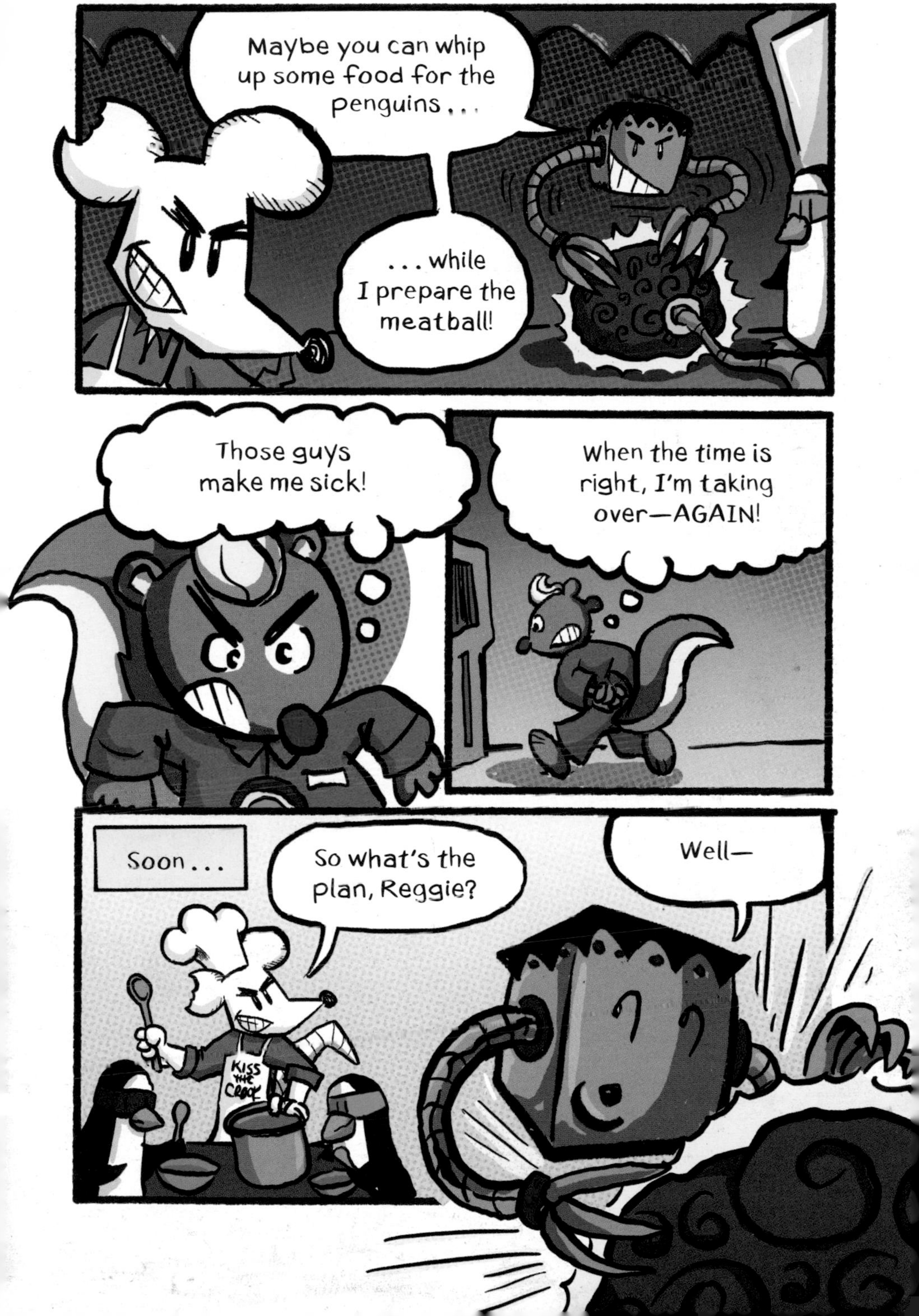

Maybe you can whip up some food for the penguins . . .
. . . while I prepare the meatball!
Those guys make me sick!
When the time is right, I'm taking over—AGAIN!
Soon . . .
So what's the plan, Reggie?
Well—
KISS THE CROOK

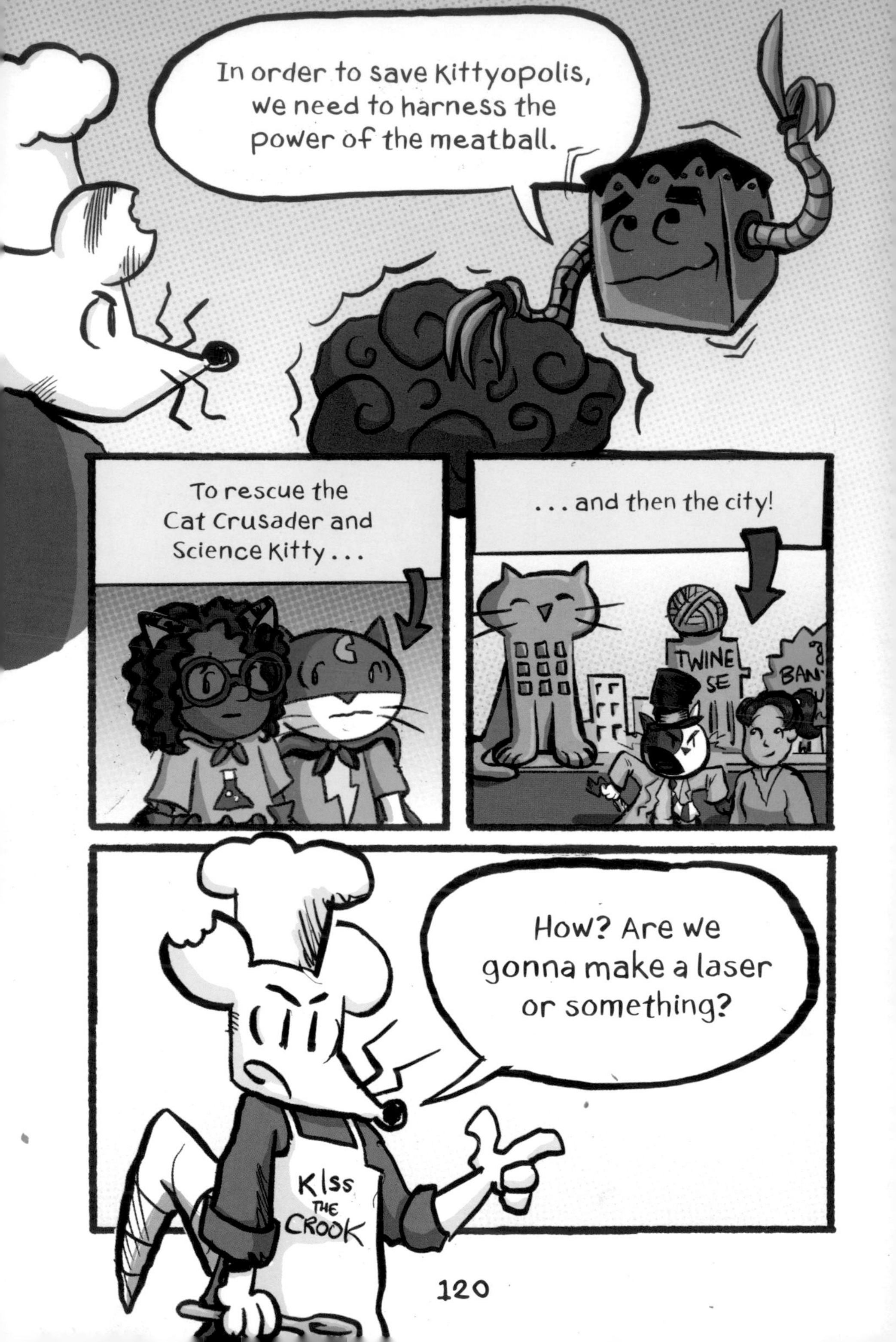
In order to save Kittyopolis, we need to harness the power of the meatball.
To rescue the Cat Crusader and Science Kitty . . .
. . . and then the city!
TWINE
SE
BAN-
How? Are we gonna make a laser or something?
KISS THE CROOK

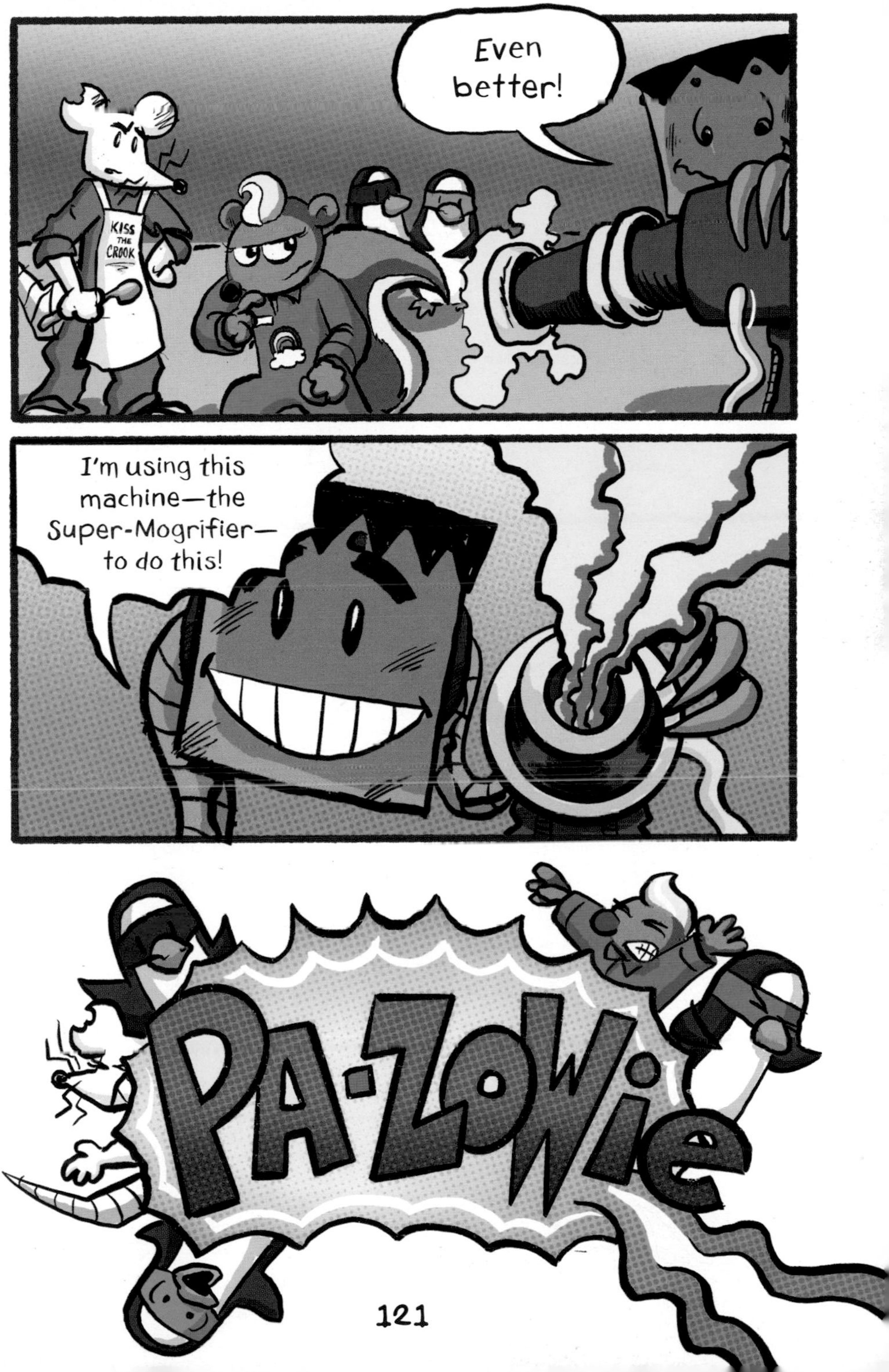
Even better!
KISS THE CROOK
I'm using this machine—the Super-Mogrifier—to do this!
PA-ZOWIE

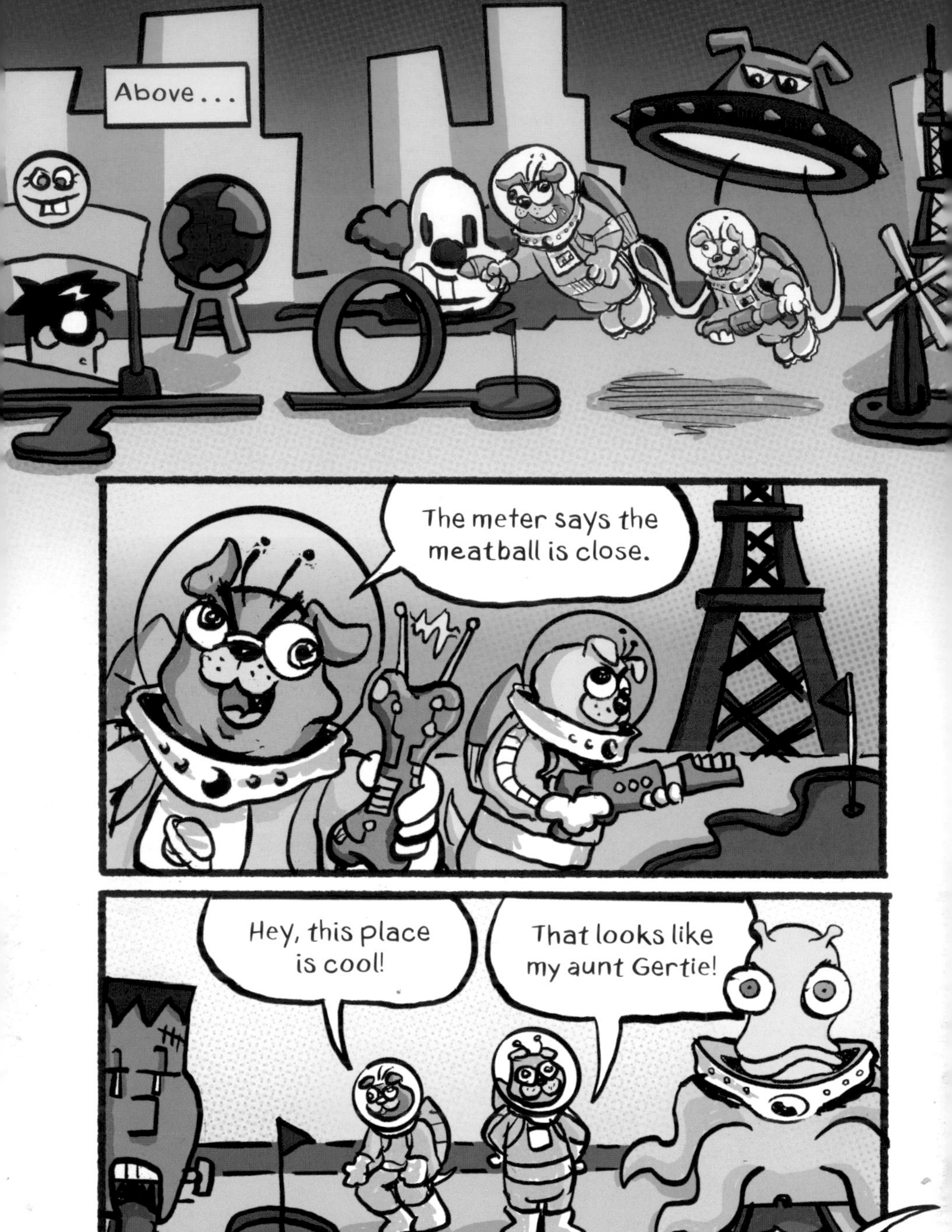
Above...
The meter says the meatball is close.
Hey, this place is cool!
That looks like my aunt Gertie!
WOOF!

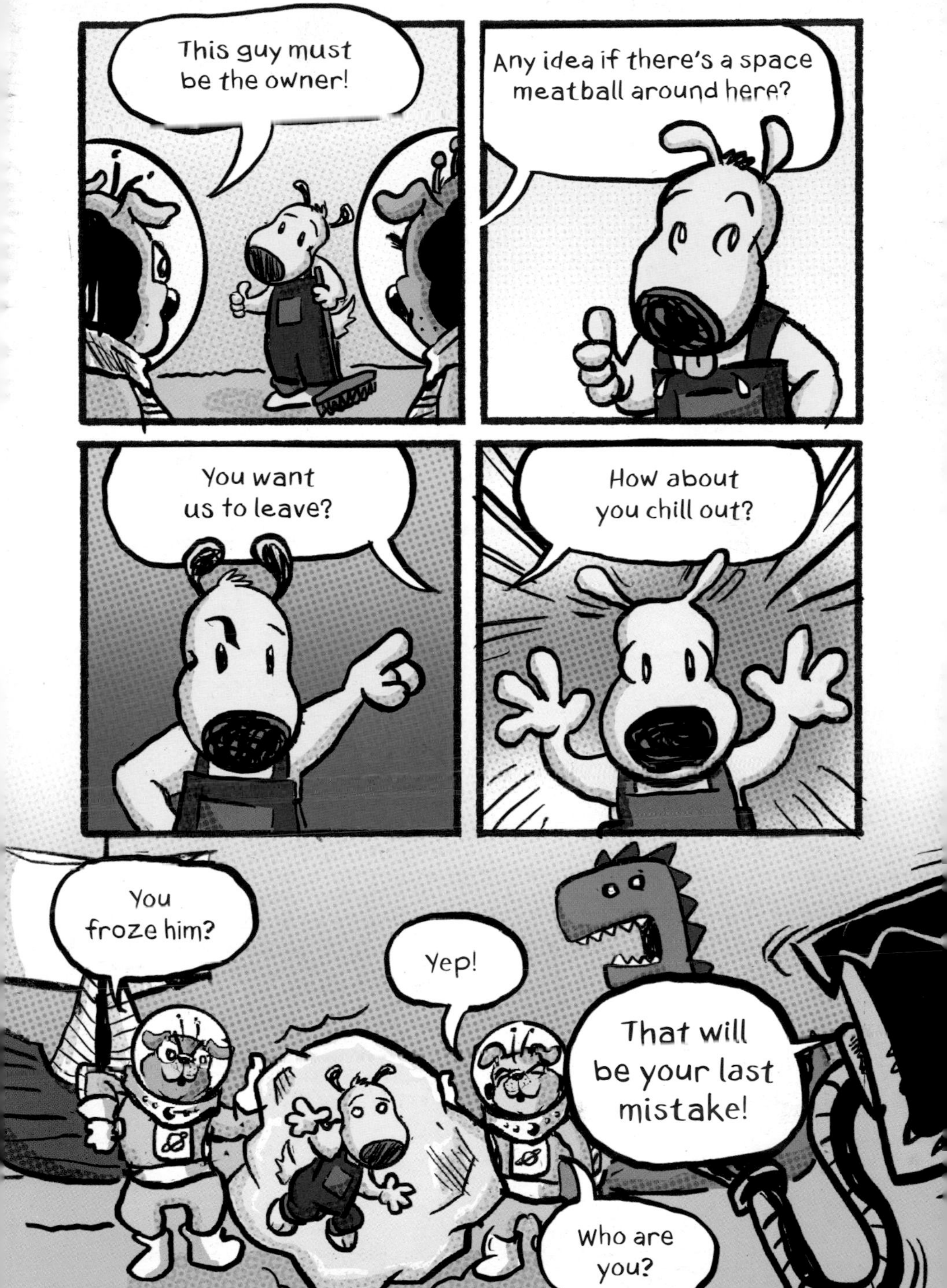
This guy must be the owner!
Any idea if there's a space meatball around here?
You want us to leave?
How about you chill out?
You froze him?
Yep!
That will be your last mistake!
Who are you?

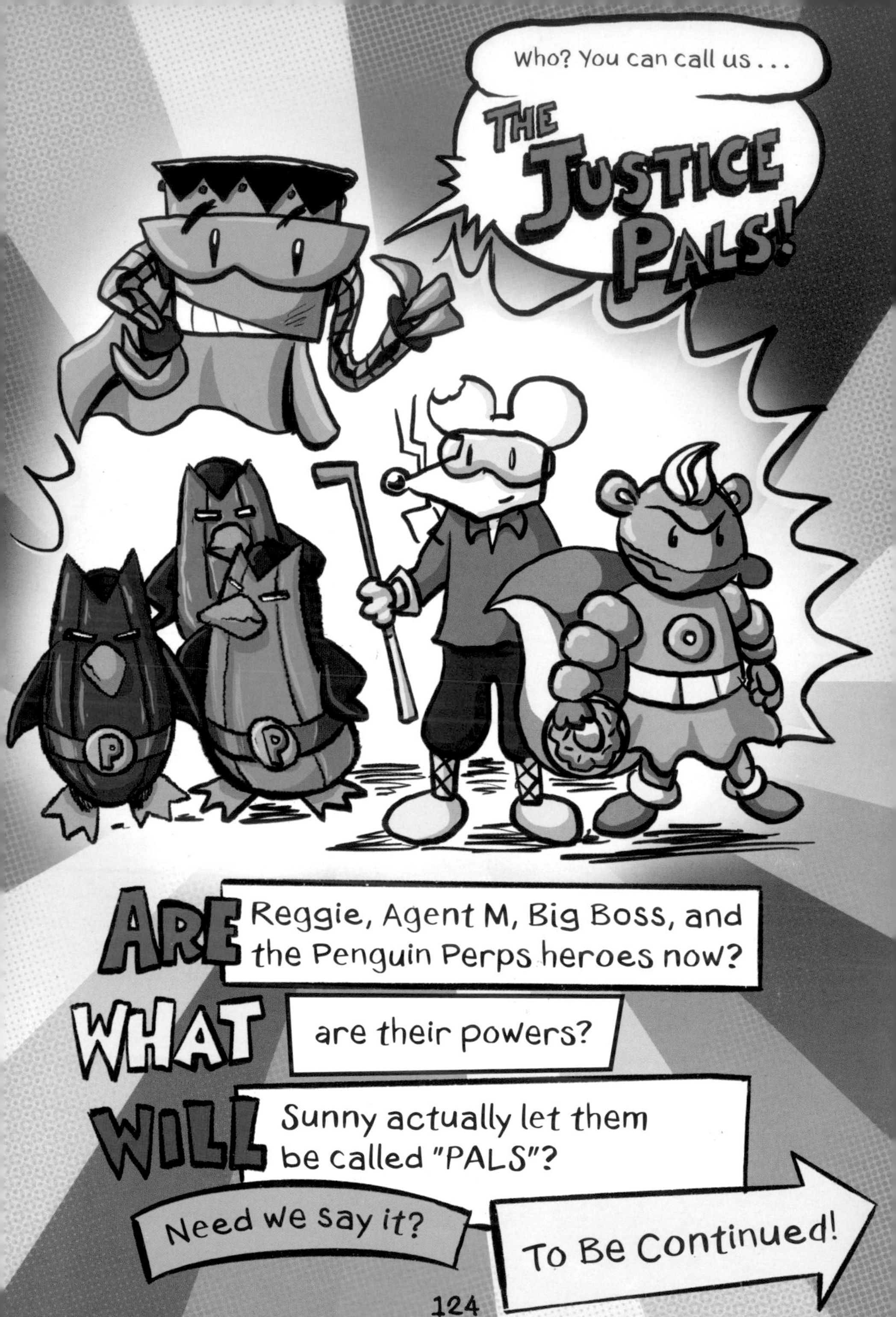
Who? You can call us . . .
THE JUSTICE PALS!
ARE Reggie, Agent M, Big Boss, and the Penguin Perps heroes now?
WHAT are their powers?
WILL Sunny actually let them be called "PALS"?
Need we say it?
To Be Continued!

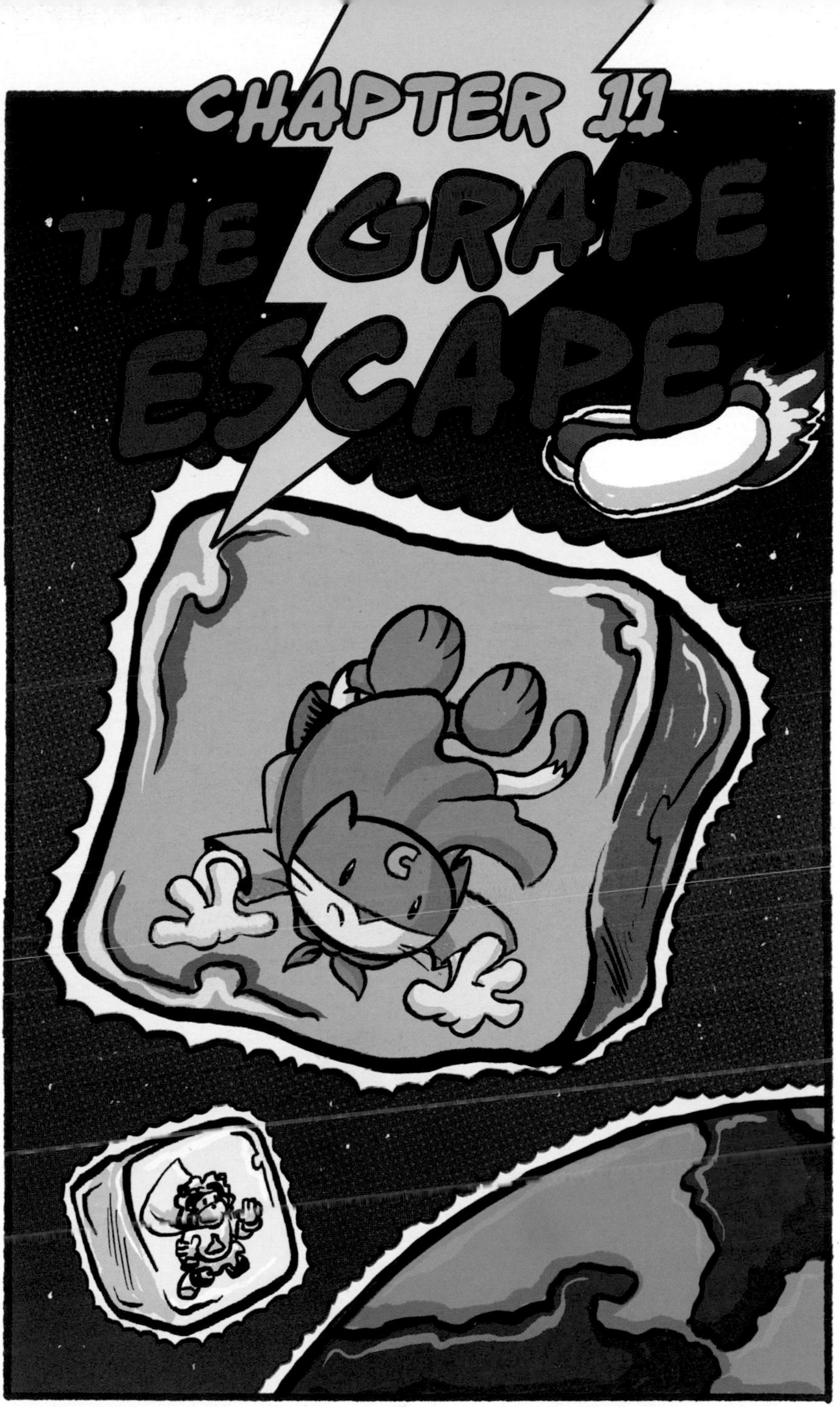
CHAPTER 11
THE GRAPE ESCAPE

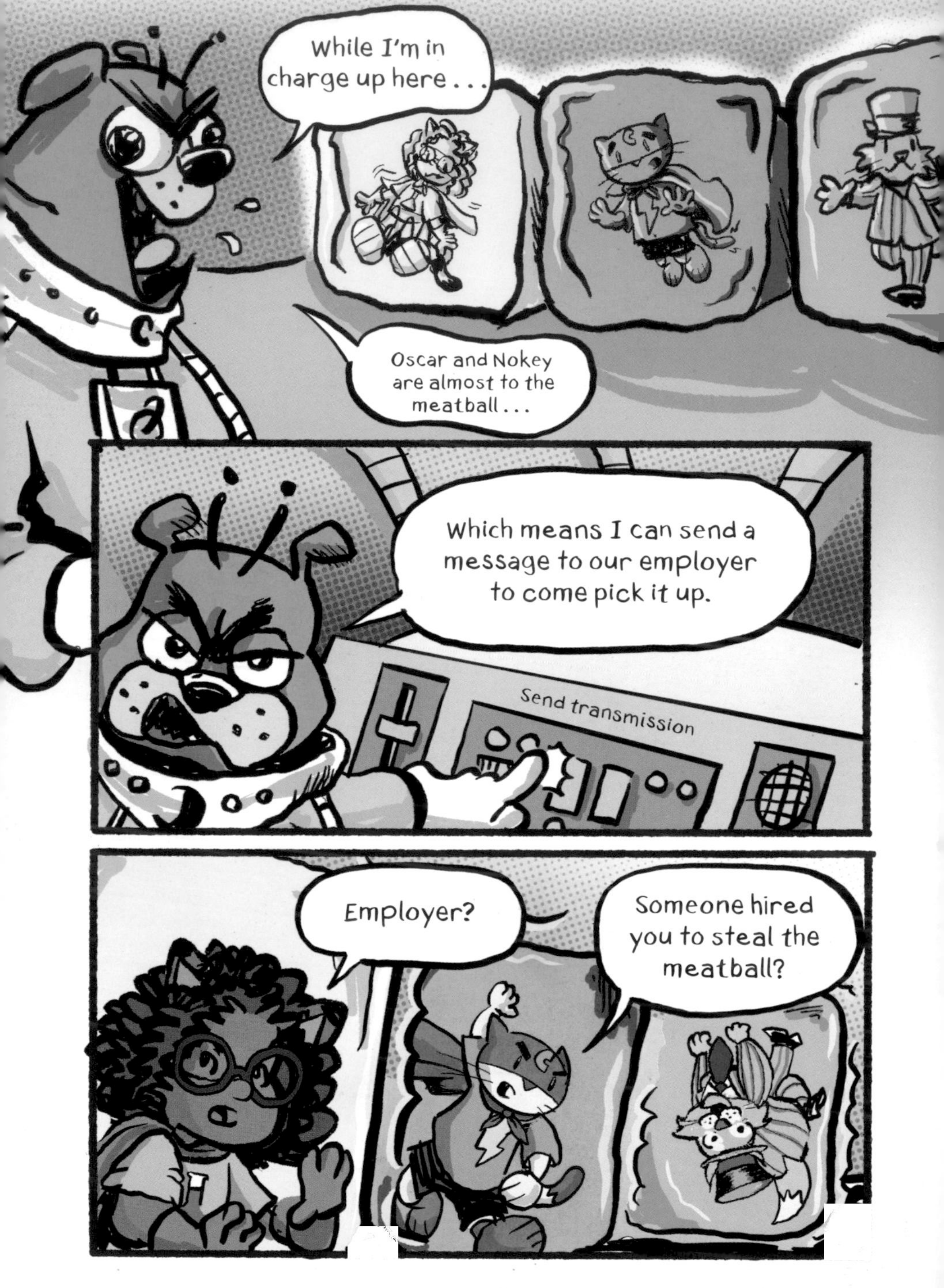
While I'm in charge up here . . .
Oscar and Nokey are almost to the meatball . . .
Which means I can send a message to our employer to come pick it up.
Send transmission
Employer?
Someone hired you to steal the meatball?

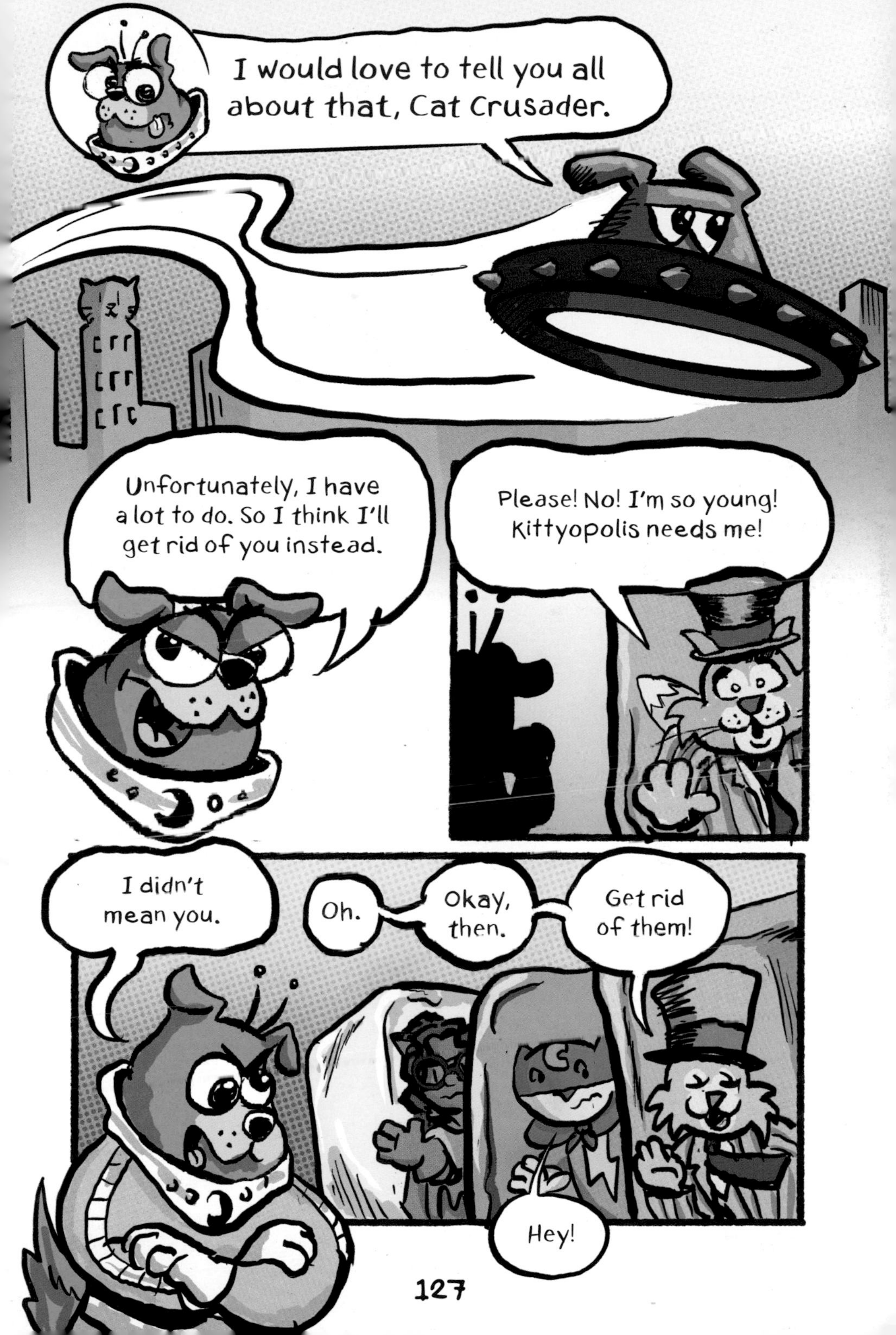
I would love to tell you all about that, Cat Crusader.
Unfortunately, I have a lot to do. So I think I'll get rid of you instead.
Please! No! I'm so young! Kittyopolis needs me!
I didn't mean you.
Oh.
Okay, then.
Get rid of them!
Hey!

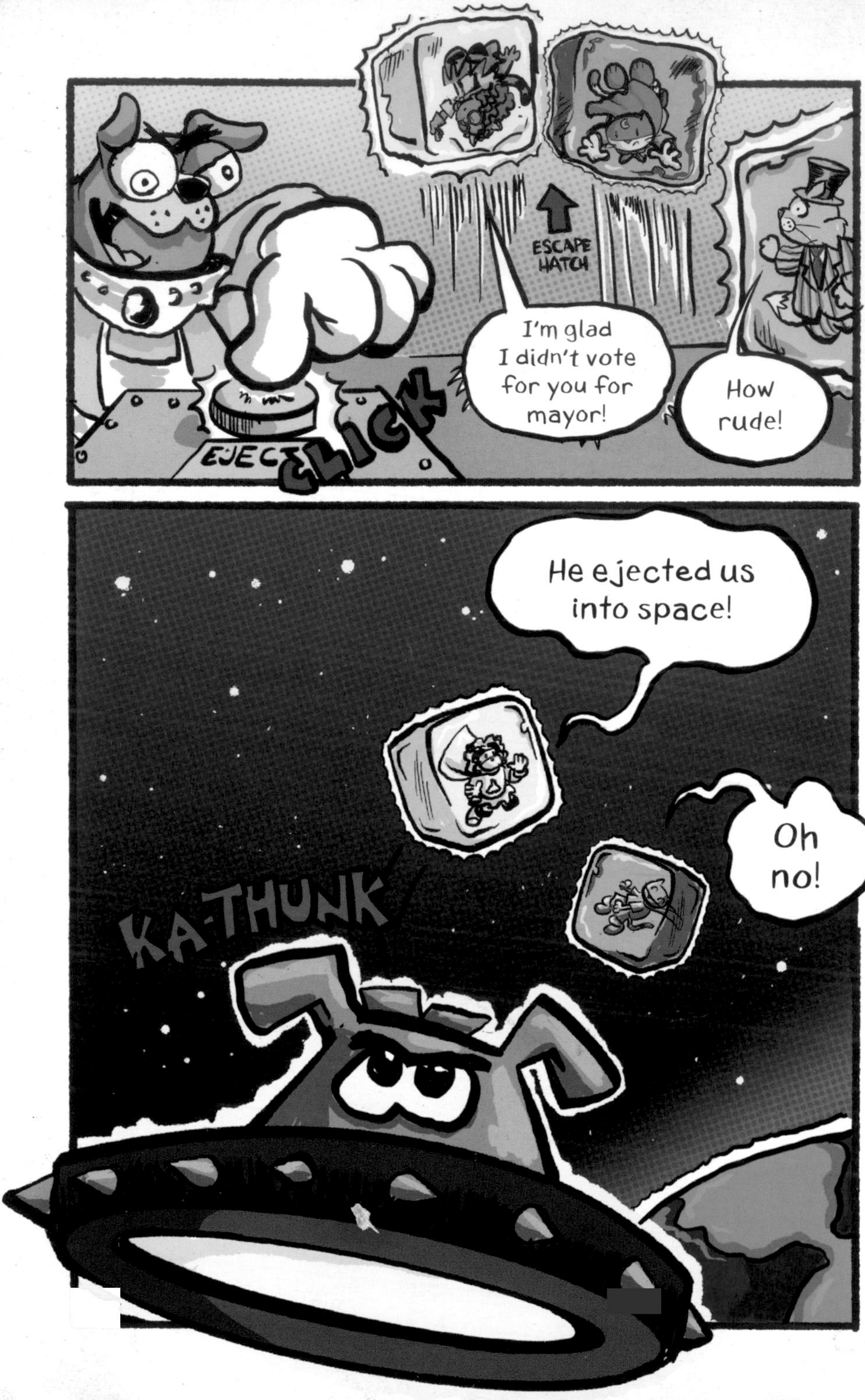
ESCAPE HATCH
EJECT
CLICK
I'm glad I didn't vote for you for mayor!
How rude!
He ejected us into space!
Oh no!
KA-THUNK

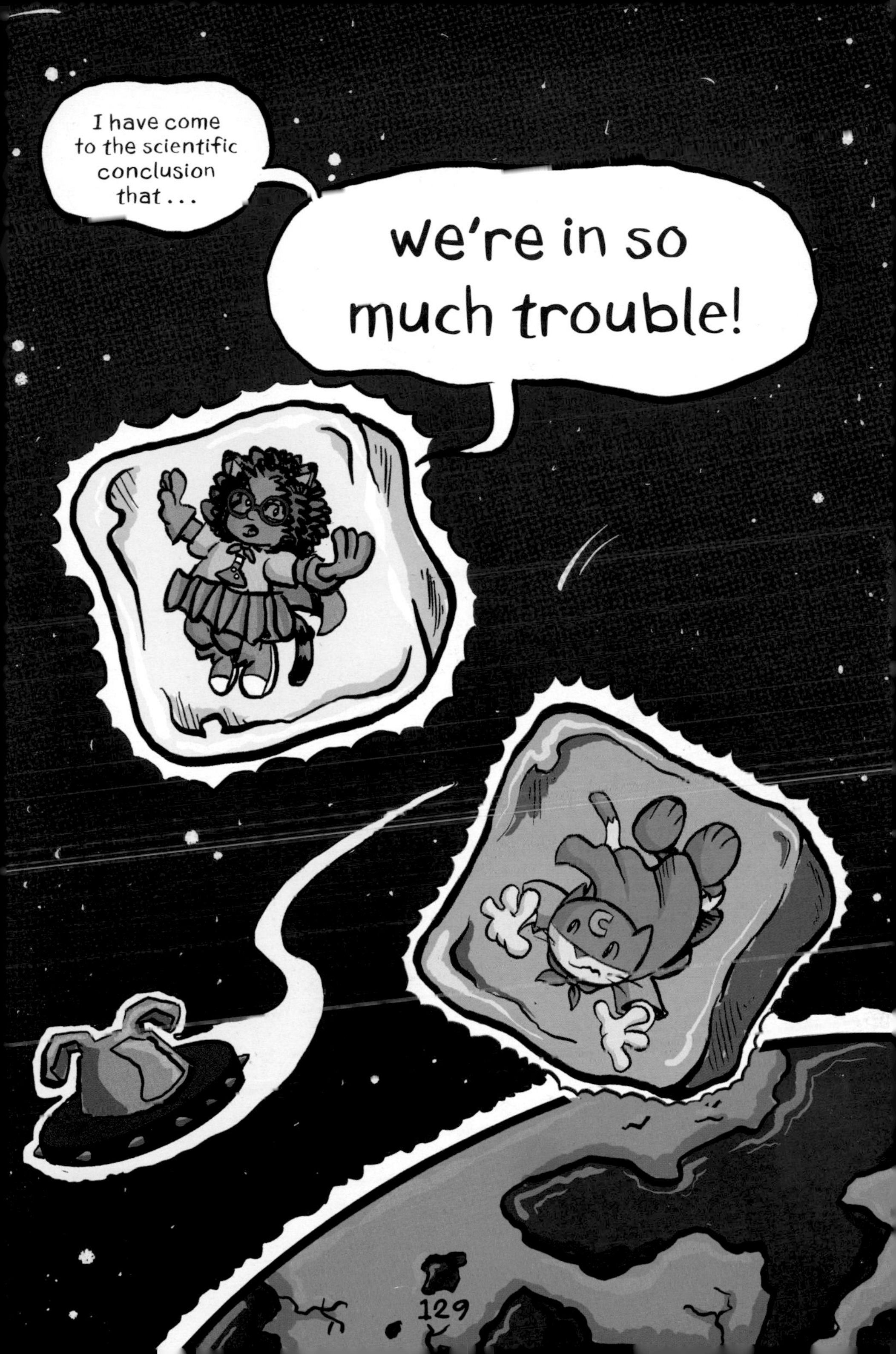
I have come to the scientific conclusion that . . .
we're in so much trouble!

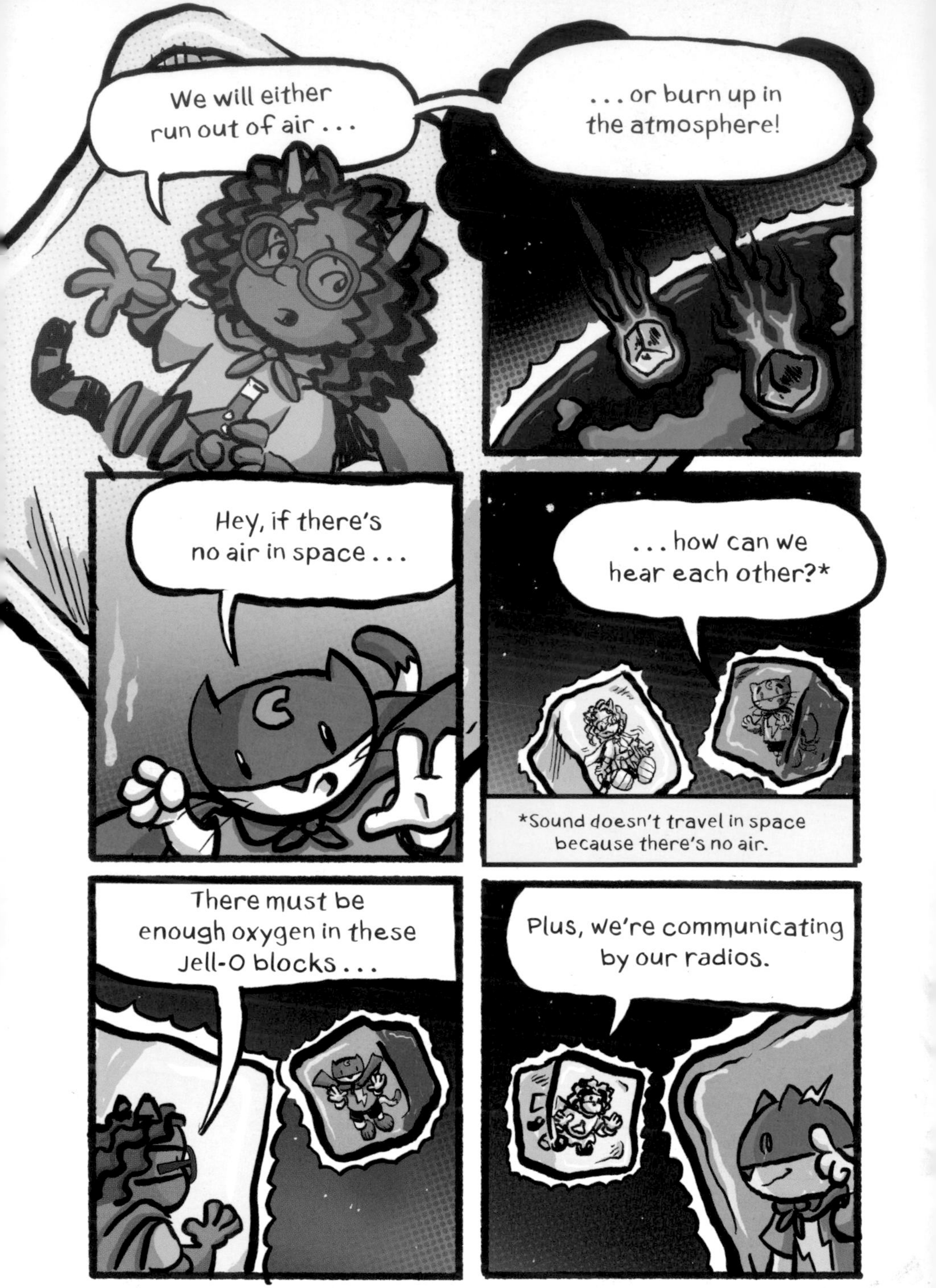
We will either run out of air . . .
. . . or burn up in the atmosphere!
Hey, if there's no air in space . . .
. . . how can we hear each other?*
*Sound doesn't travel in space because there's no air.
There must be enough oxygen in these Jell-O blocks . . .
Plus, we're communicating by our radios.

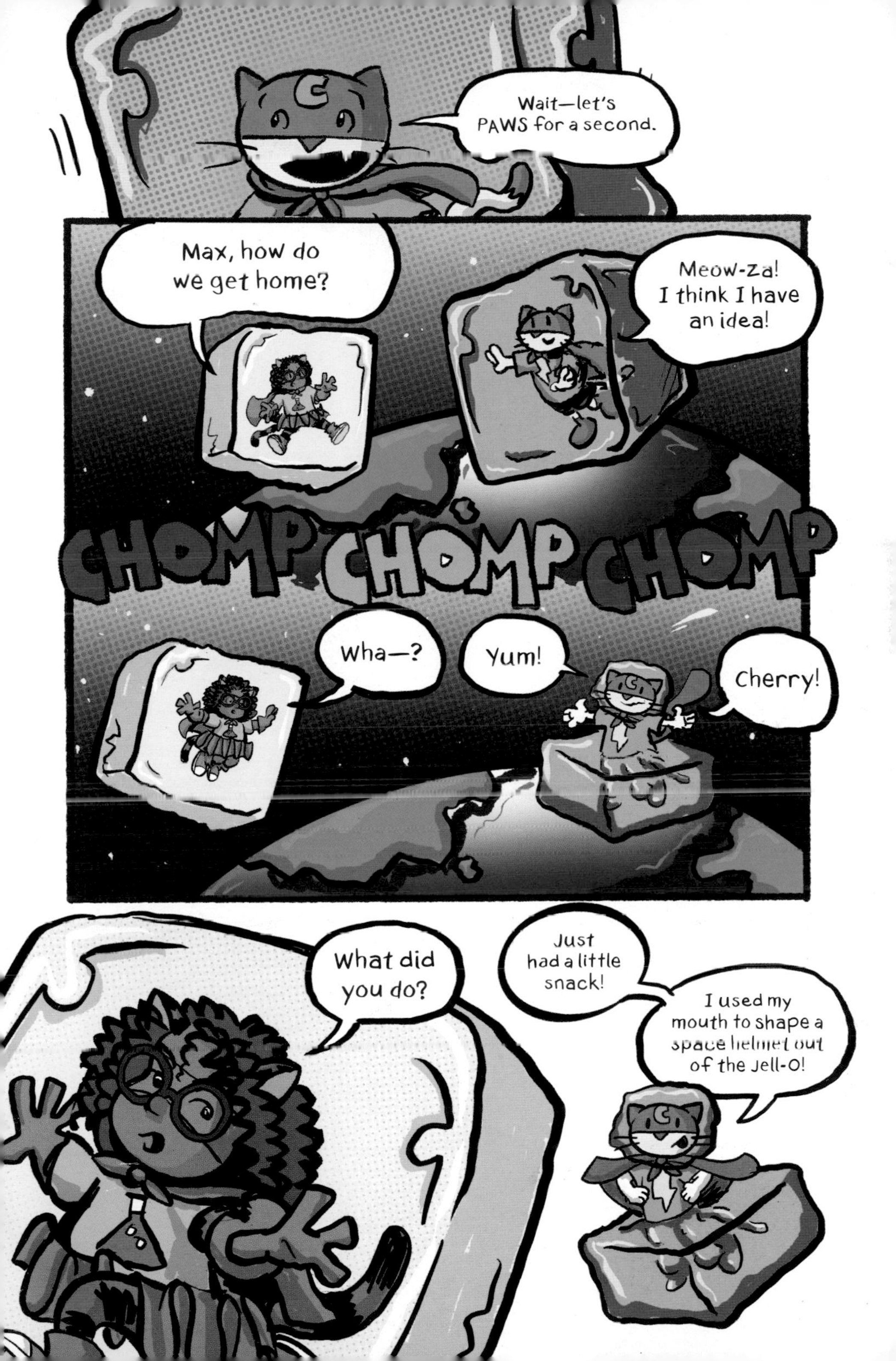
Wait—let's PAWS for a second.
Max, how do we get home?
Meow-za! I think I have an idea!
CHOMP CHOMP CHOMP
Wha—?
Yum!
Cherry!
What did you do?
Just had a little snack!
I used my mouth to shape a space helmet out of the Jell-O!

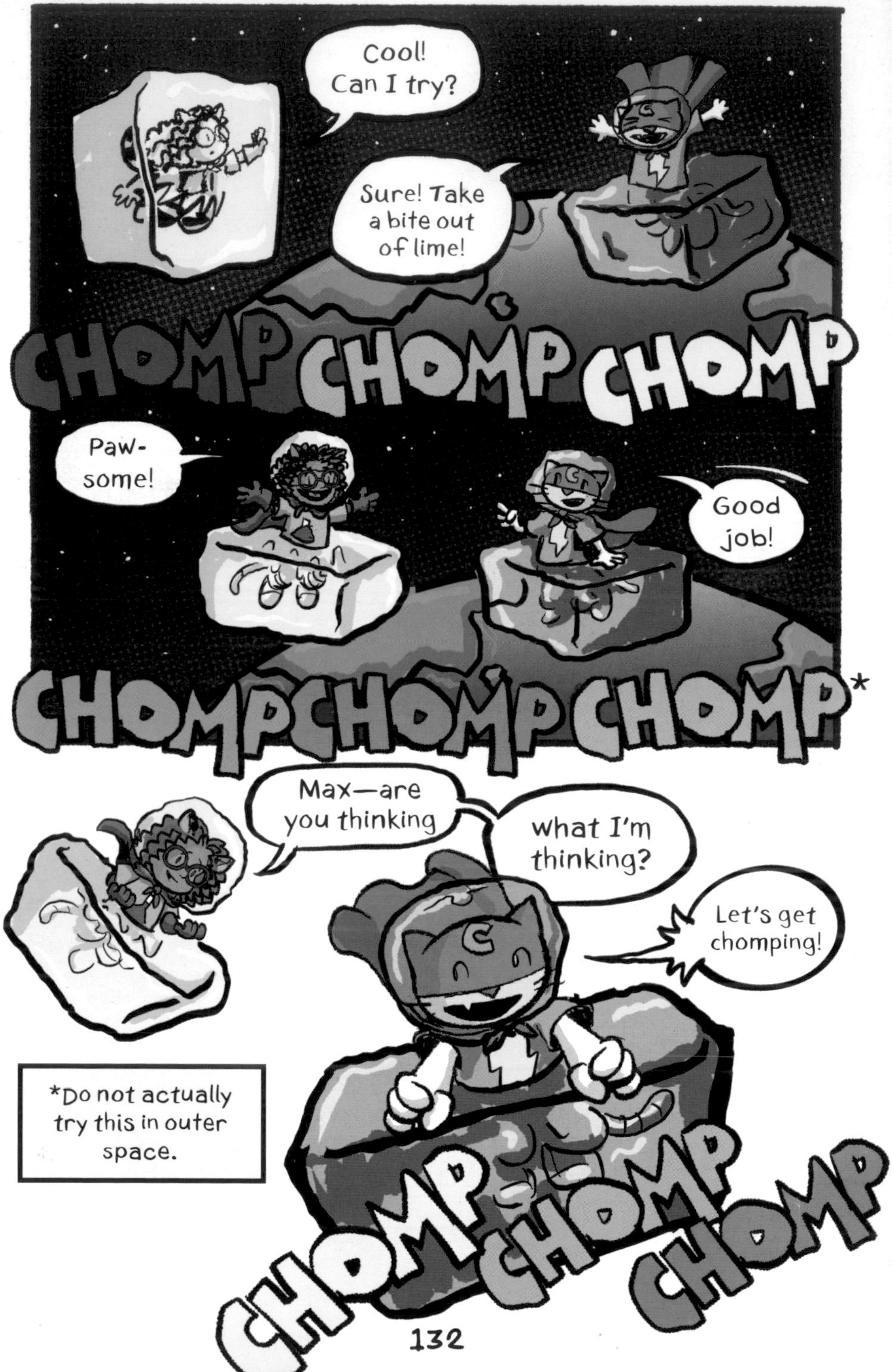
Cool! Can I try?
Sure! Take a bite out of lime!
CHOMP CHOMP CHOMP
Paw-some!
Good job!
CHOMP CHOMP CHOMP*
Max—are you thinking
what I'm thinking?
Let's get chomping!
CHOMP CHOMP CHOMP

*Do not actually try this in outer space.

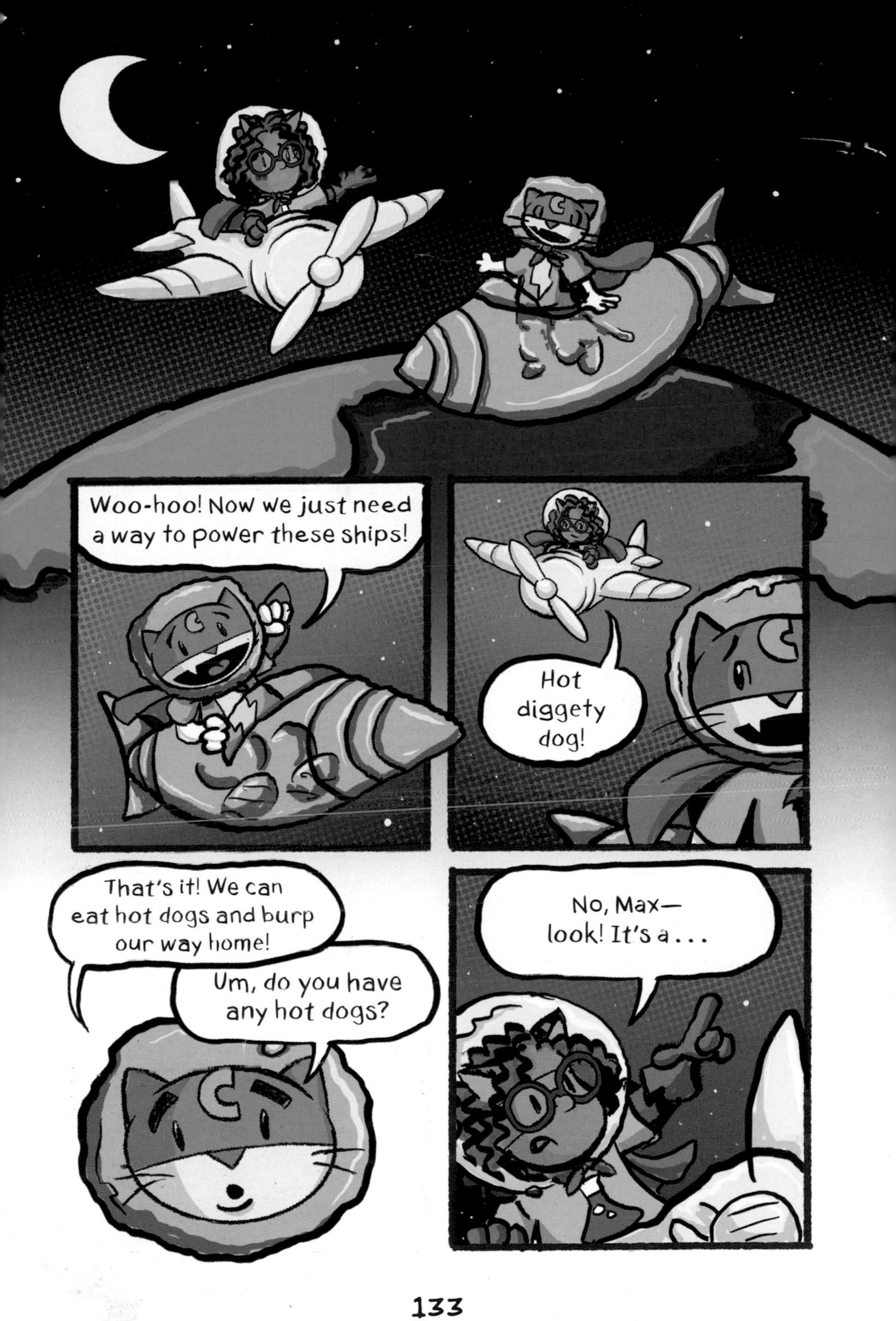
Woo-hoo! Now we just need a way to power these ships!
Hot diggety dog!
That's it! We can eat hot dogs and burp our way home!
Um, do you have any hot dogs?
No, Max— look! It's a . . .

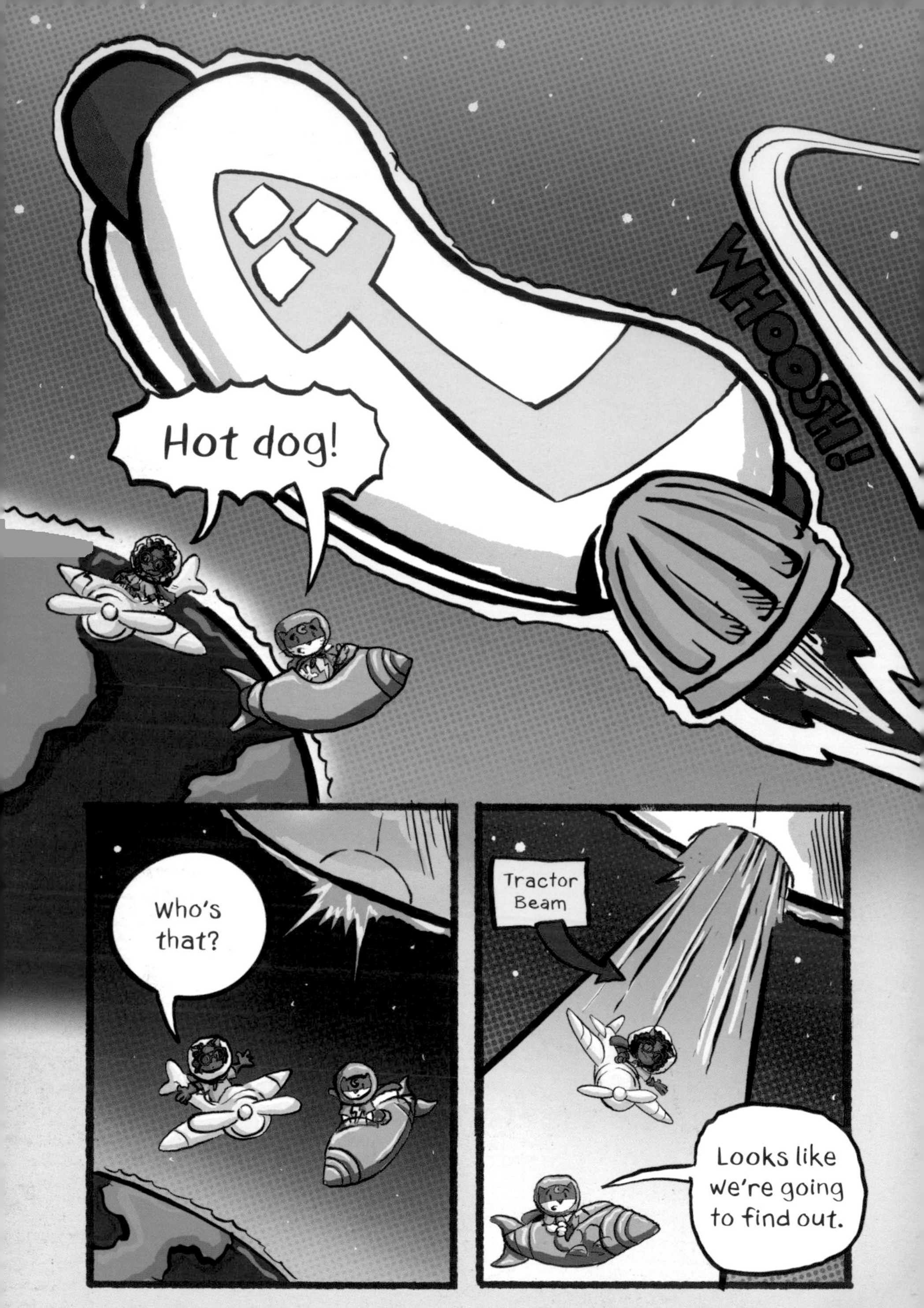
WHOOSH!
Hot dog!
Who's that?
Tractor Beam
Looks like we're going to find out.

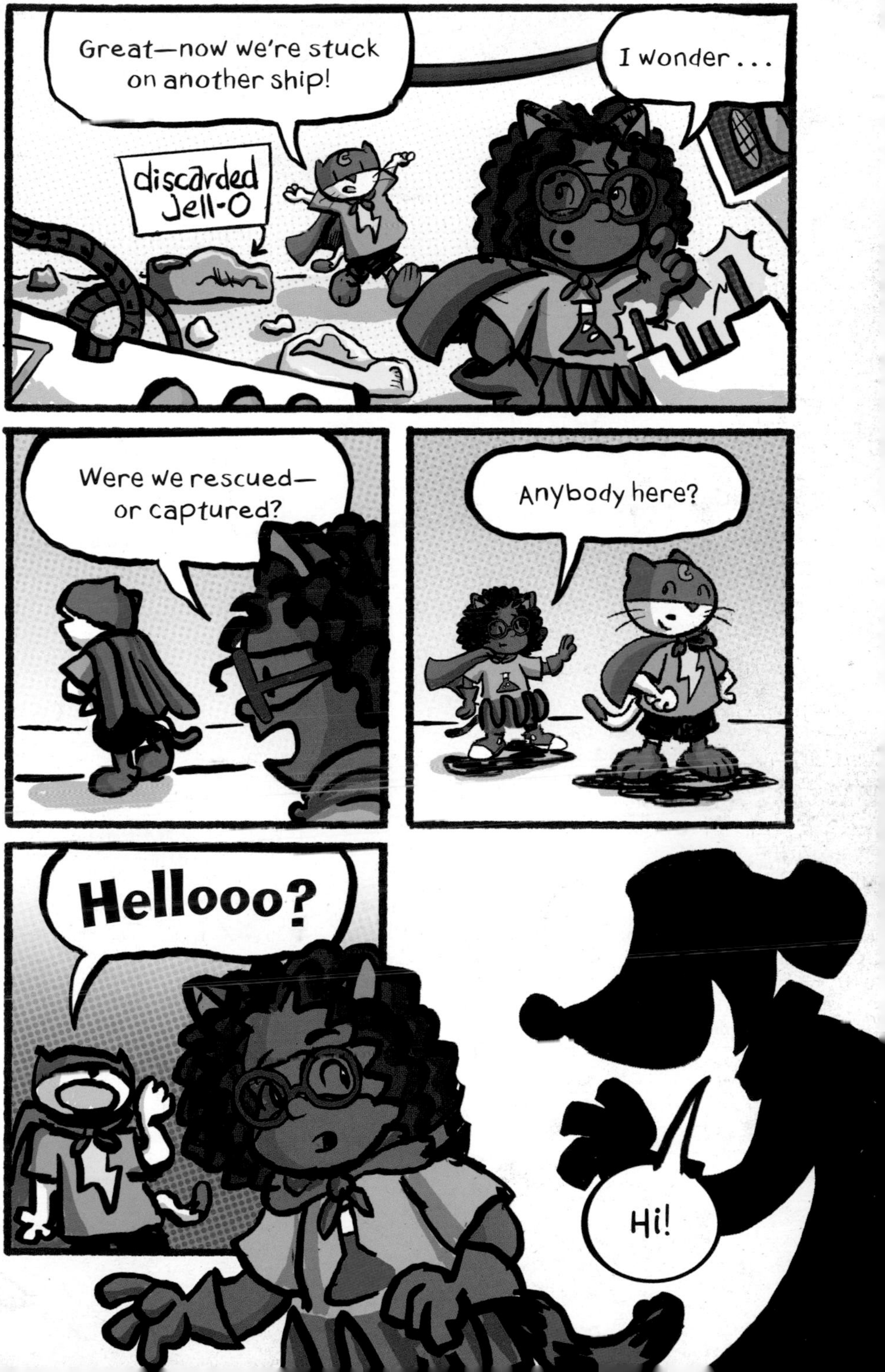
Great—now we're stuck on another ship!
I wonder . . .
discarded Jell-O
Were we rescued— or captured?
Anybody here?
Hellooo?
Hi!

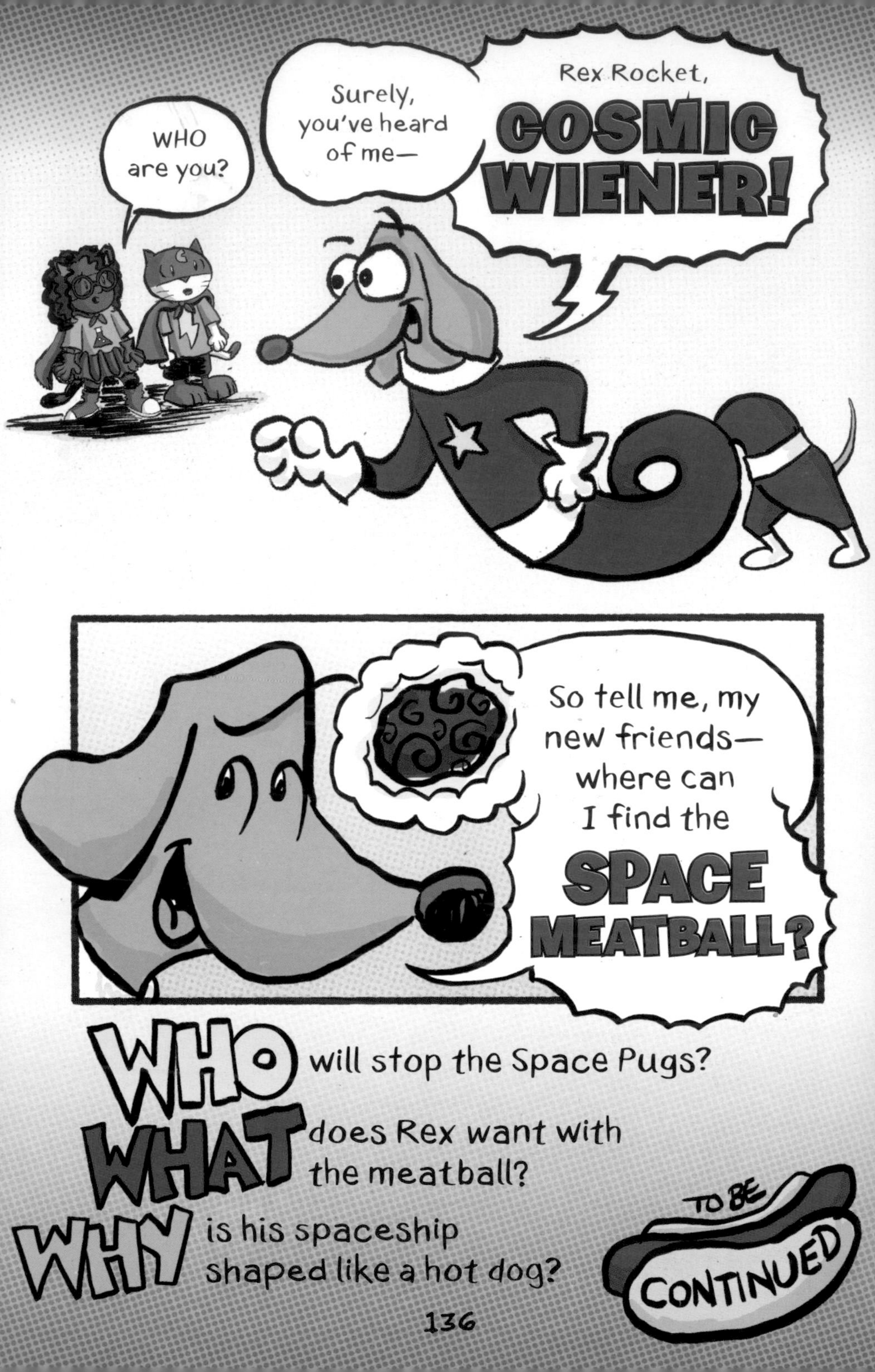
WHO are you?
Surely, you've heard of me—
Rex Rocket, COSMIC WIENER!
So tell me, my new friends— where can I find the SPACE MEATBALL?
WHO will stop the Space Pugs?
WHAT does Rex want with the meatball?
WHY is his spaceship shaped like a hot dog?
TO BE CONTINUED

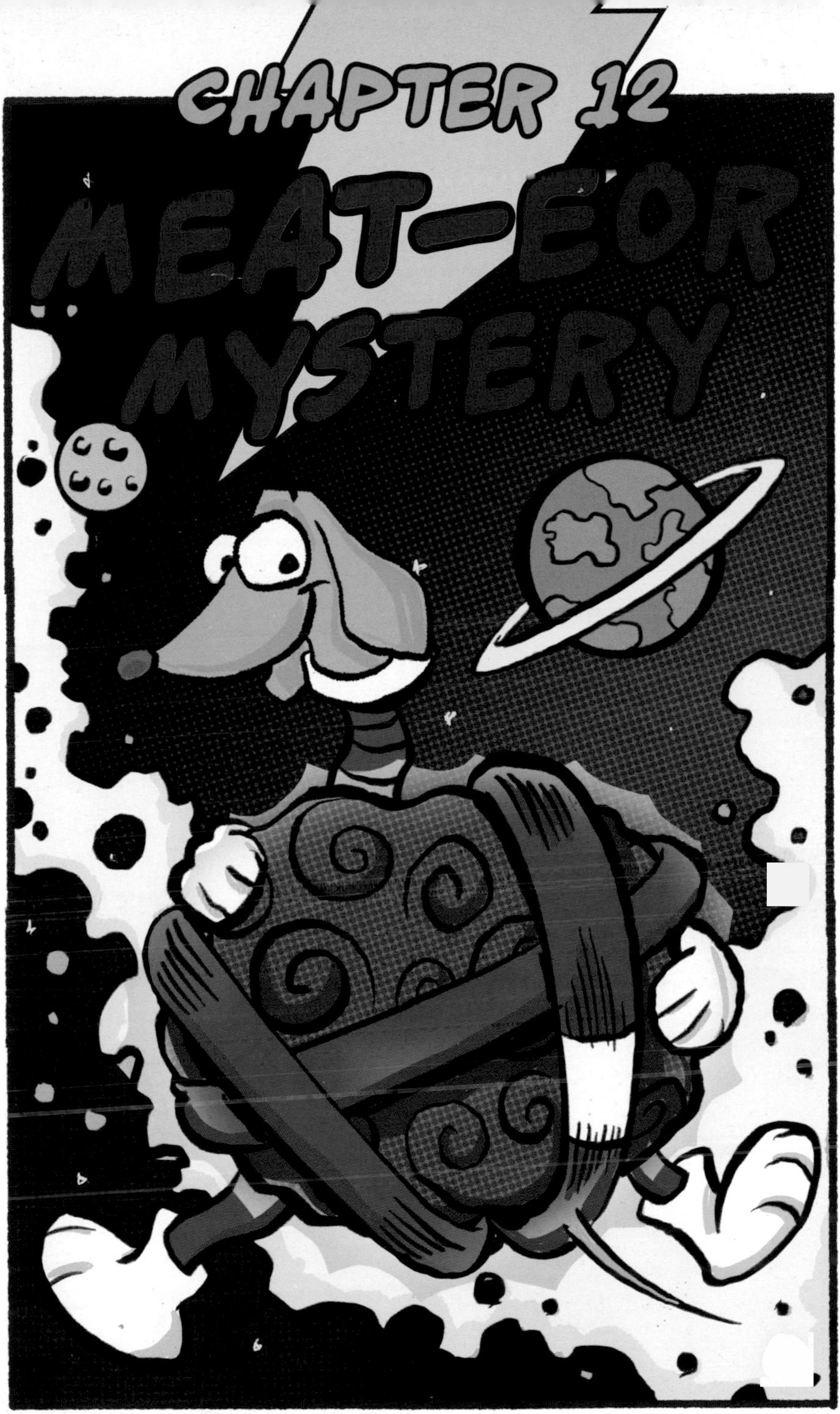
CHAPTER 12
MEAT-EOR MYSTERY

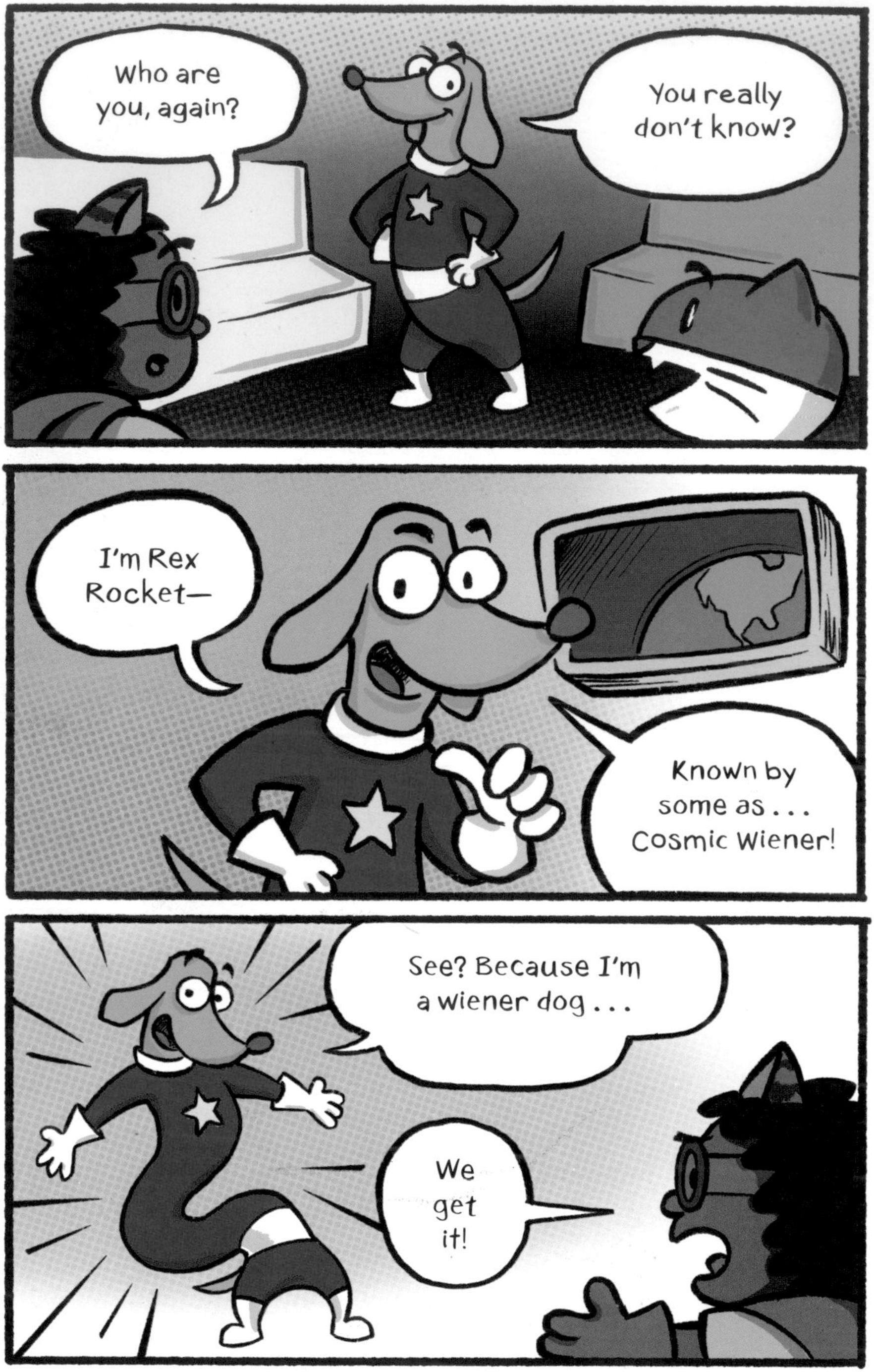
Who are you, again?
You really don't know?
I'm Rex Rocket—
Known by some as . . . Cosmic Wiener!
See? Because I'm a wiener dog . . .
We get it!

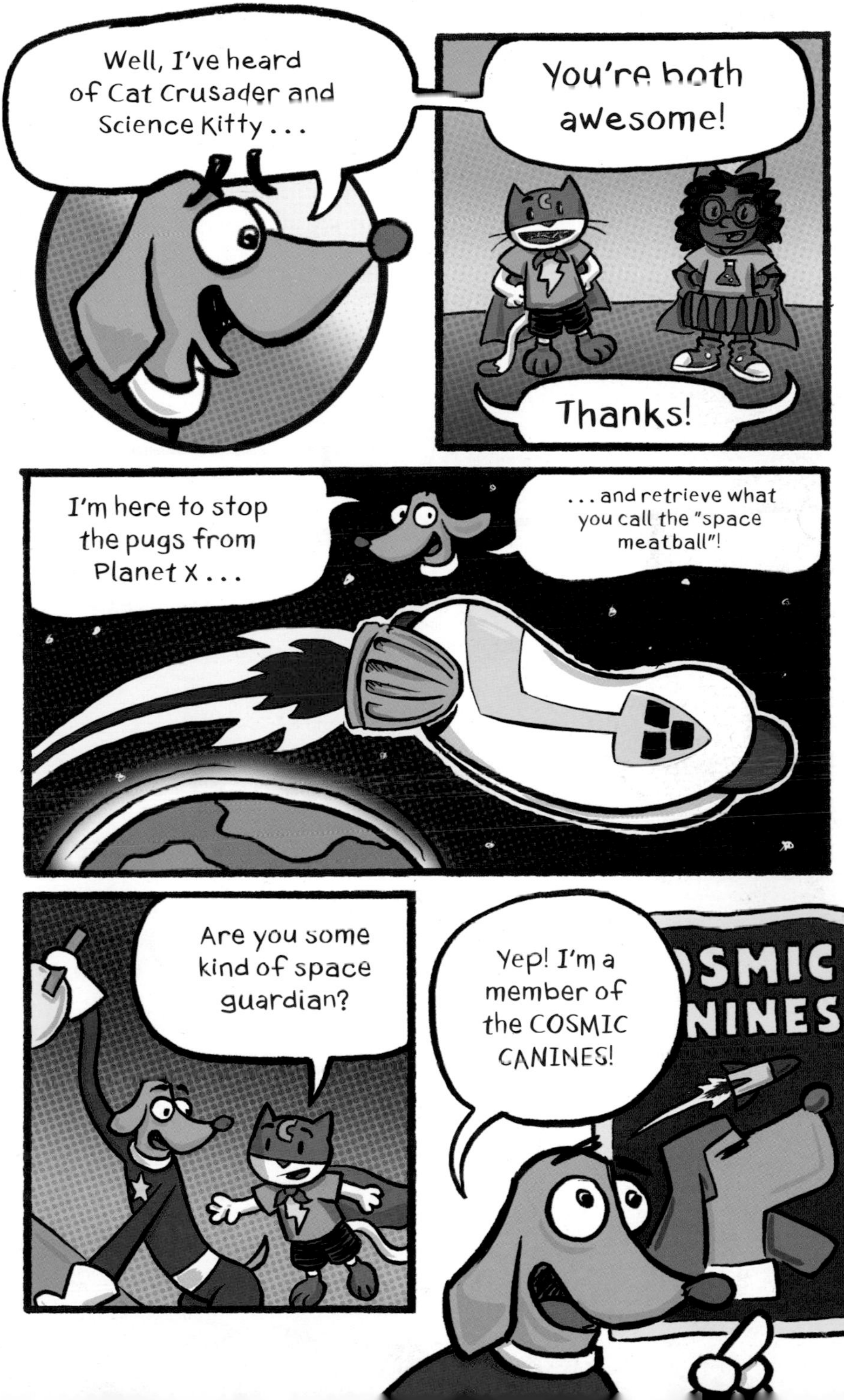

Well, I've heard of Cat Crusader and Science Kitty . . .
You're both awesome!
Thanks!
I'm here to stop the pugs from Planet X . . .
. . . and retrieve what you call the "space meatball"!
Are you some kind of space guardian?
Yep! I'm a member of the COSMIC CANINES!

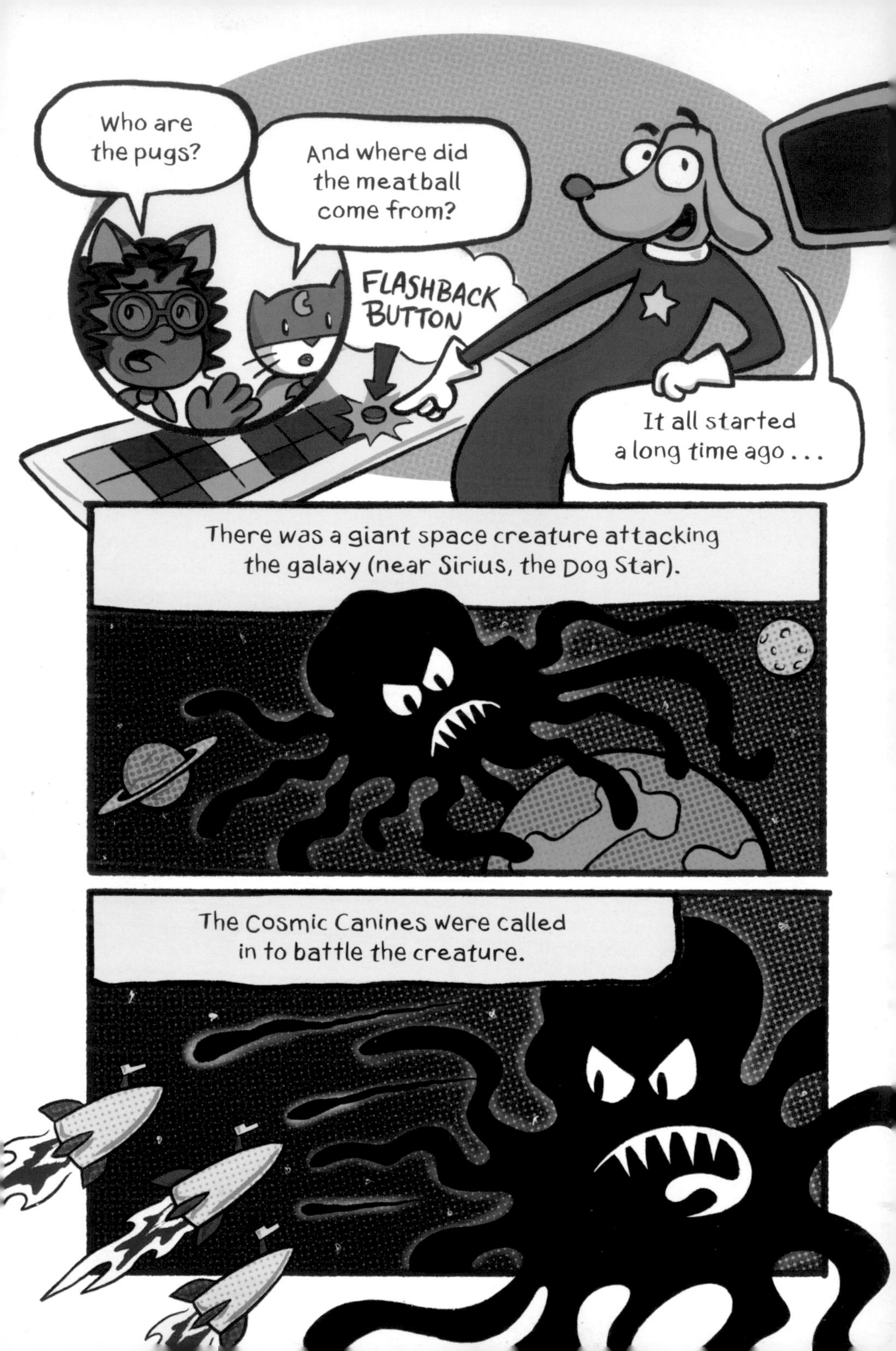
Who are the pugs?
And where did the meatball come from?
FLASHBACK BUTTON
It all started a long time ago . . .
There was a giant space creature attacking the galaxy (near Sirius, the Dog Star).
The Cosmic Canines were called in to battle the creature.

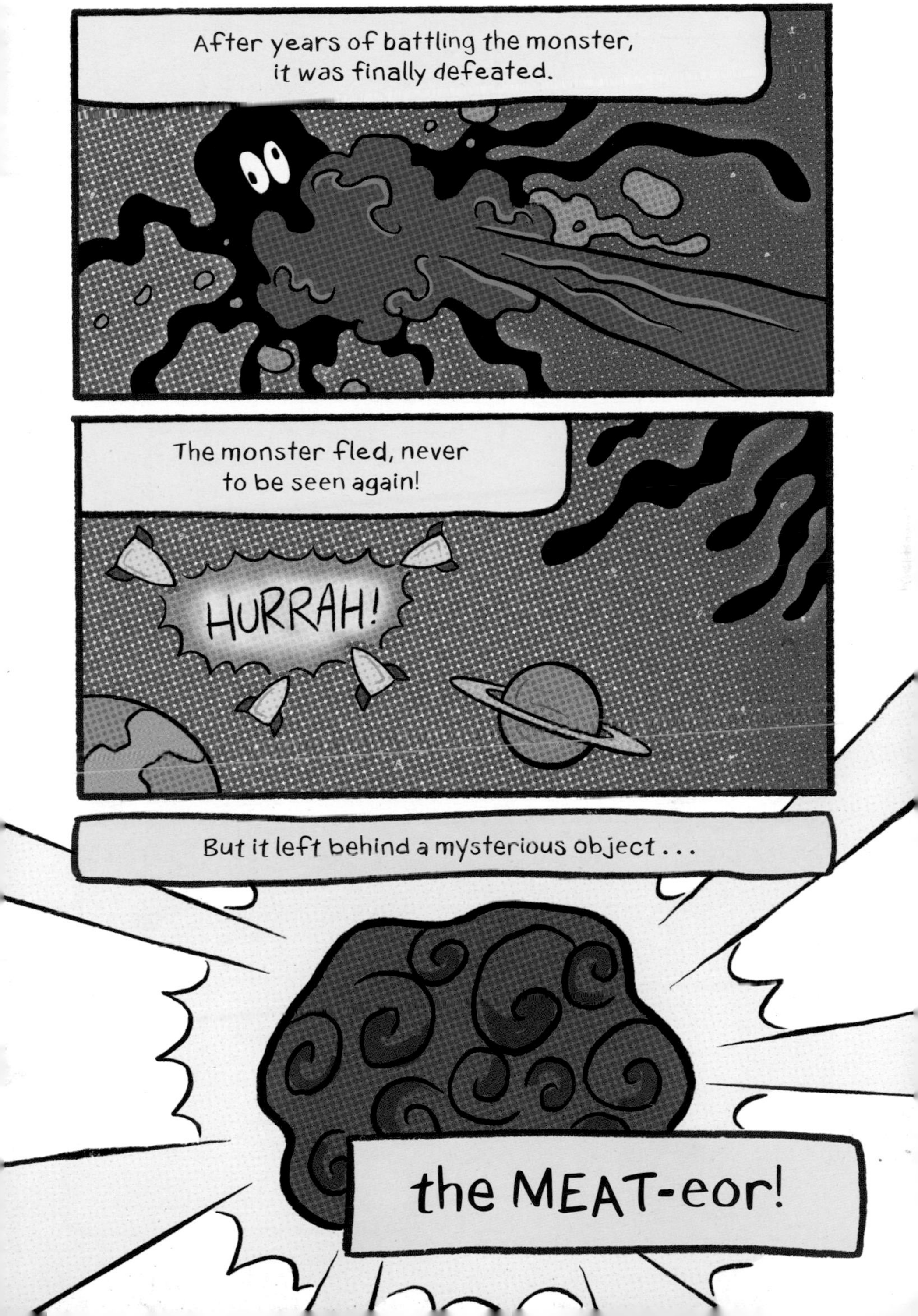
After years of battling the monster, it was finally defeated.
The monster fled, never to be seen again!
HURRAH!
But it left behind a mysterious object . . .
the MEAT-eor!

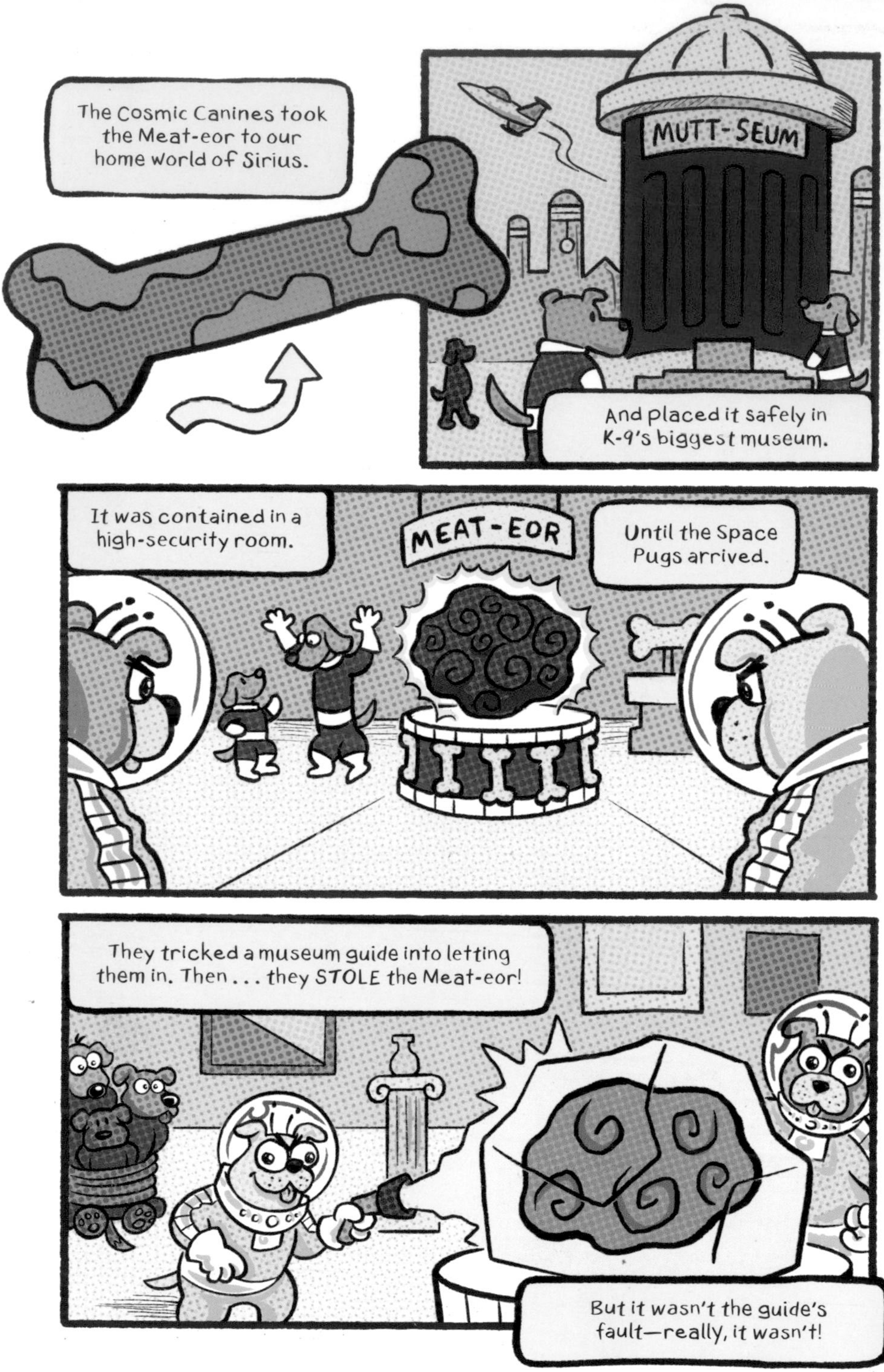
The Cosmic Canines took the Meat-eor to our home world of Sirius.
MUTT-SEUM
And placed it safely in K-9's biggest museum.
It was contained in a high-security room.
MEAT-EOR
Until the Space Pugs arrived.
They tricked a museum guide into letting them in. Then . . . they STOLE the Meat-eor!
But it wasn't the guide's fault—really, it wasn't!

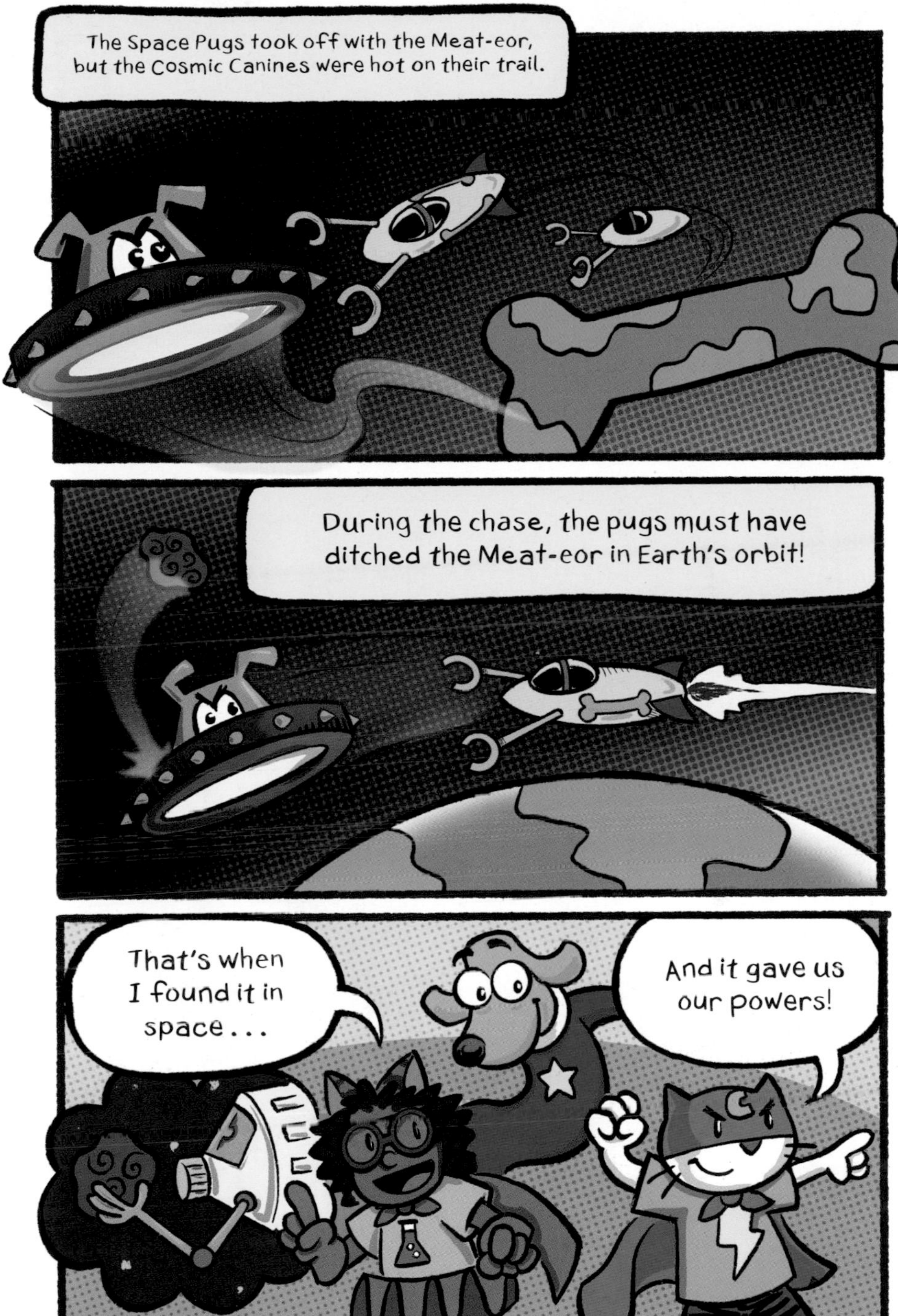
The Space Pugs took off with the Meat-eor, but the Cosmic Canines were hot on their trail.
During the chase, the pugs must have ditched the Meat-eor in Earth's orbit!
That's when I found it in space . . .
And it gave us our powers!

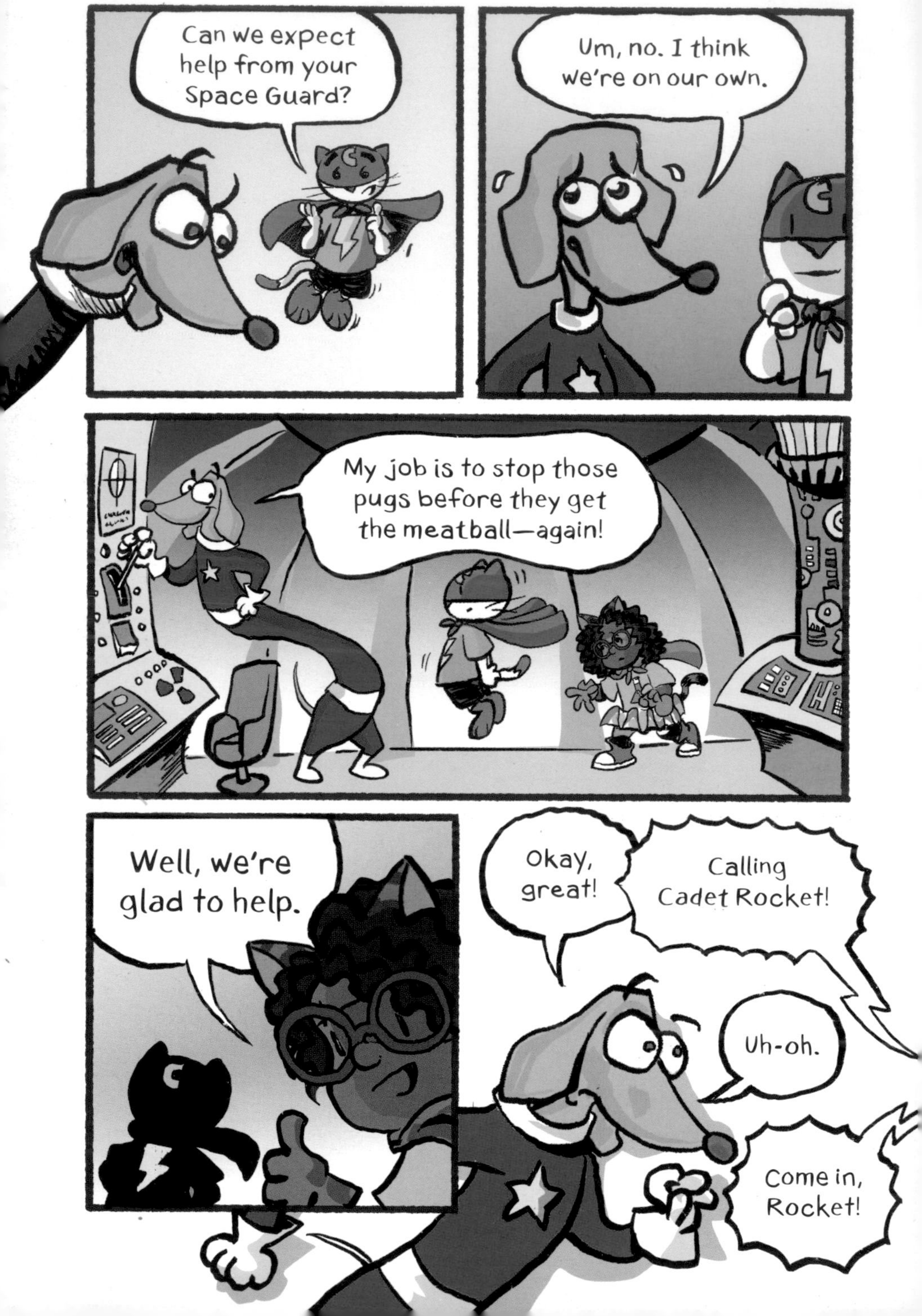
Can we expect help from your Space Guard?
Um, no. I think we're on our own.
My job is to stop those pugs before they get the meatball—again!
Well, we're glad to help.
Okay, great!
Calling Cadet Rocket!
Uh-oh.
Come in, Rocket!

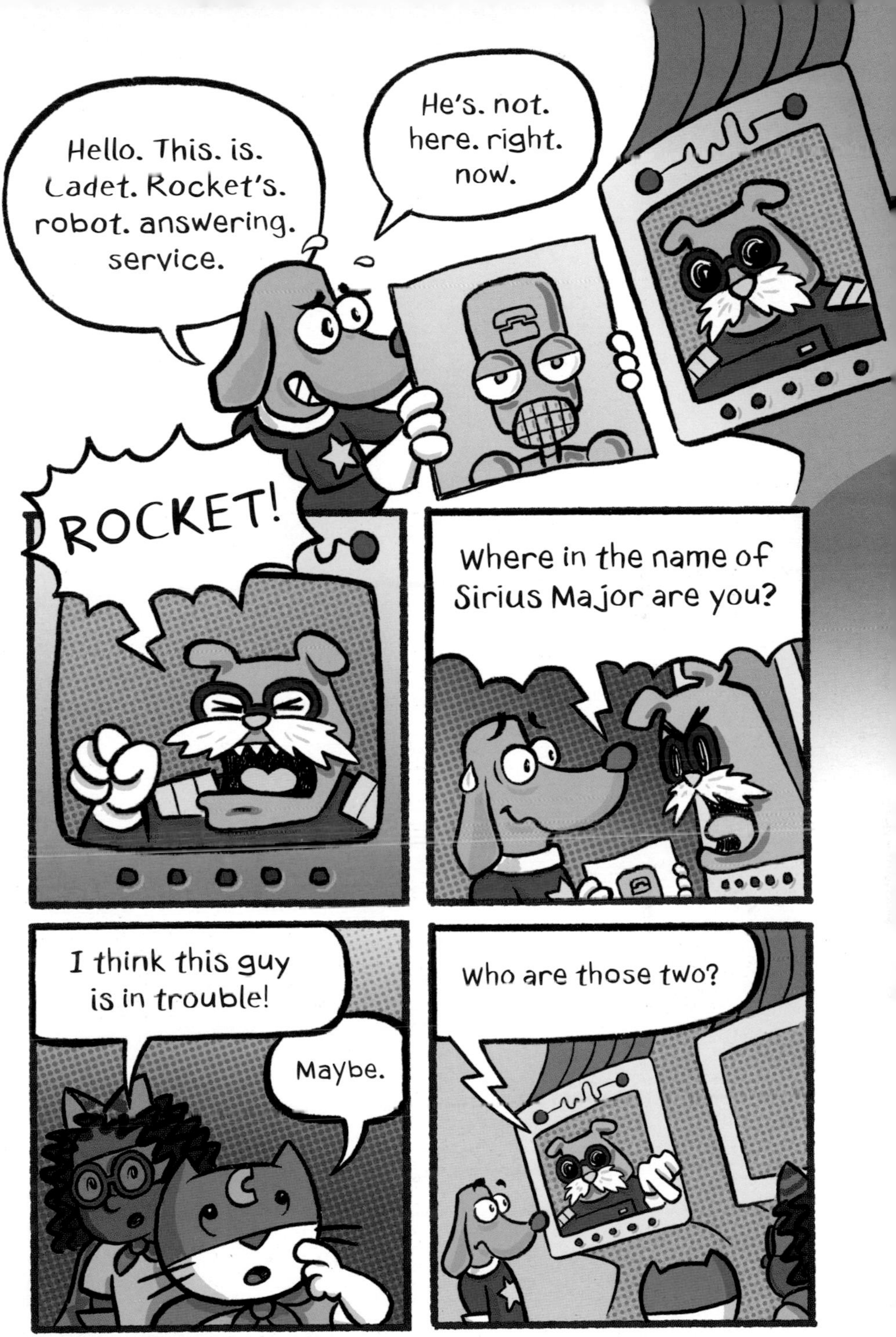
Hello. This. is. Cadet. Rocket's. robot. answering. service.
He's. not. here. right. now.
ROCKET!
Where in the name of Sirius Major are you?
I think this guy is in trouble!
Maybe.
Who are those two?

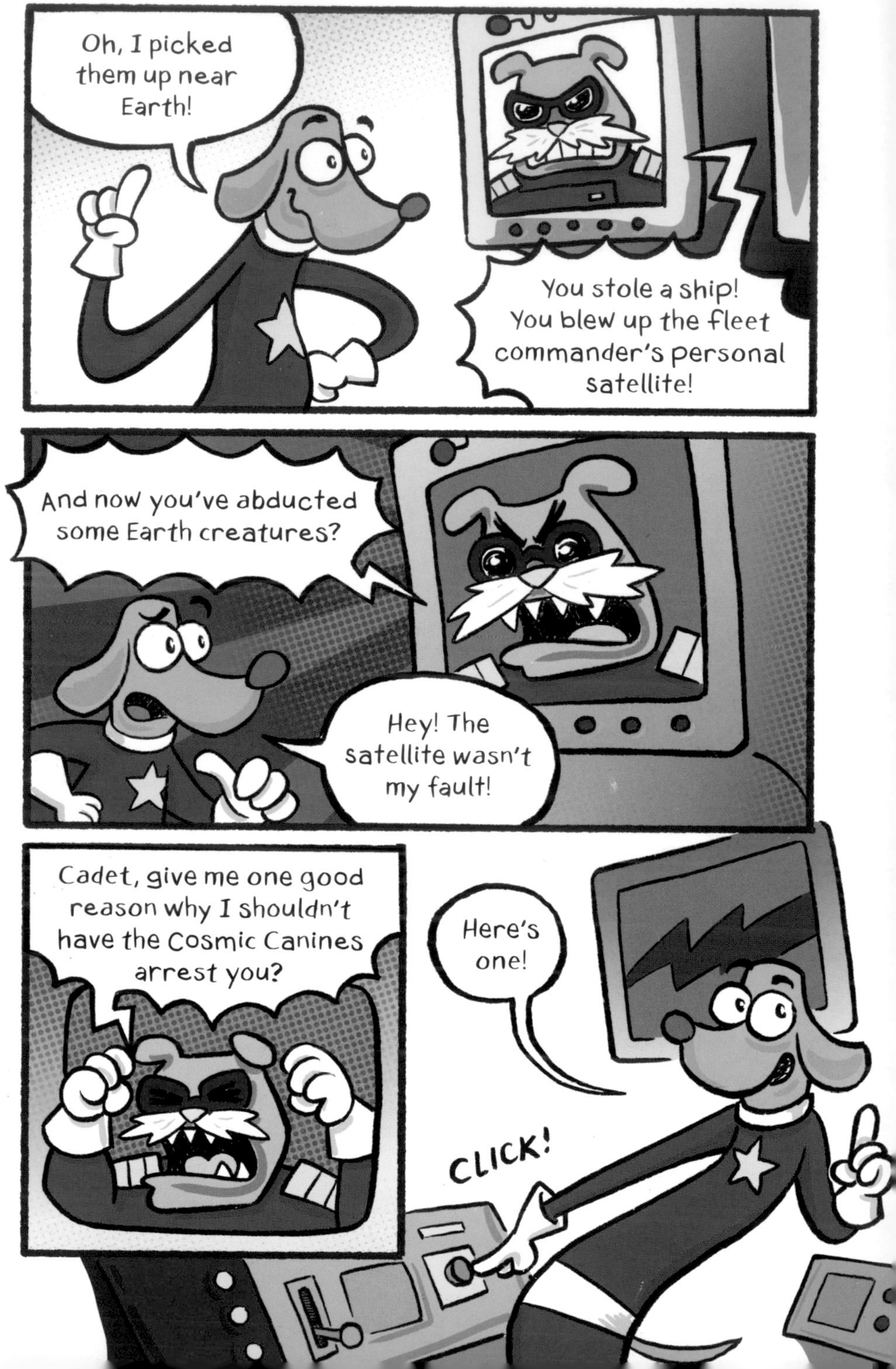
Oh, I picked them up near Earth!
You stole a ship! You blew up the fleet commander's personal satellite!
And now you've abducted some Earth creatures?
Hey! The satellite wasn't my fault!
Cadet, give me one good reason why I shouldn't have the Cosmic Canines arrest you?
Here's one!
CLICK!

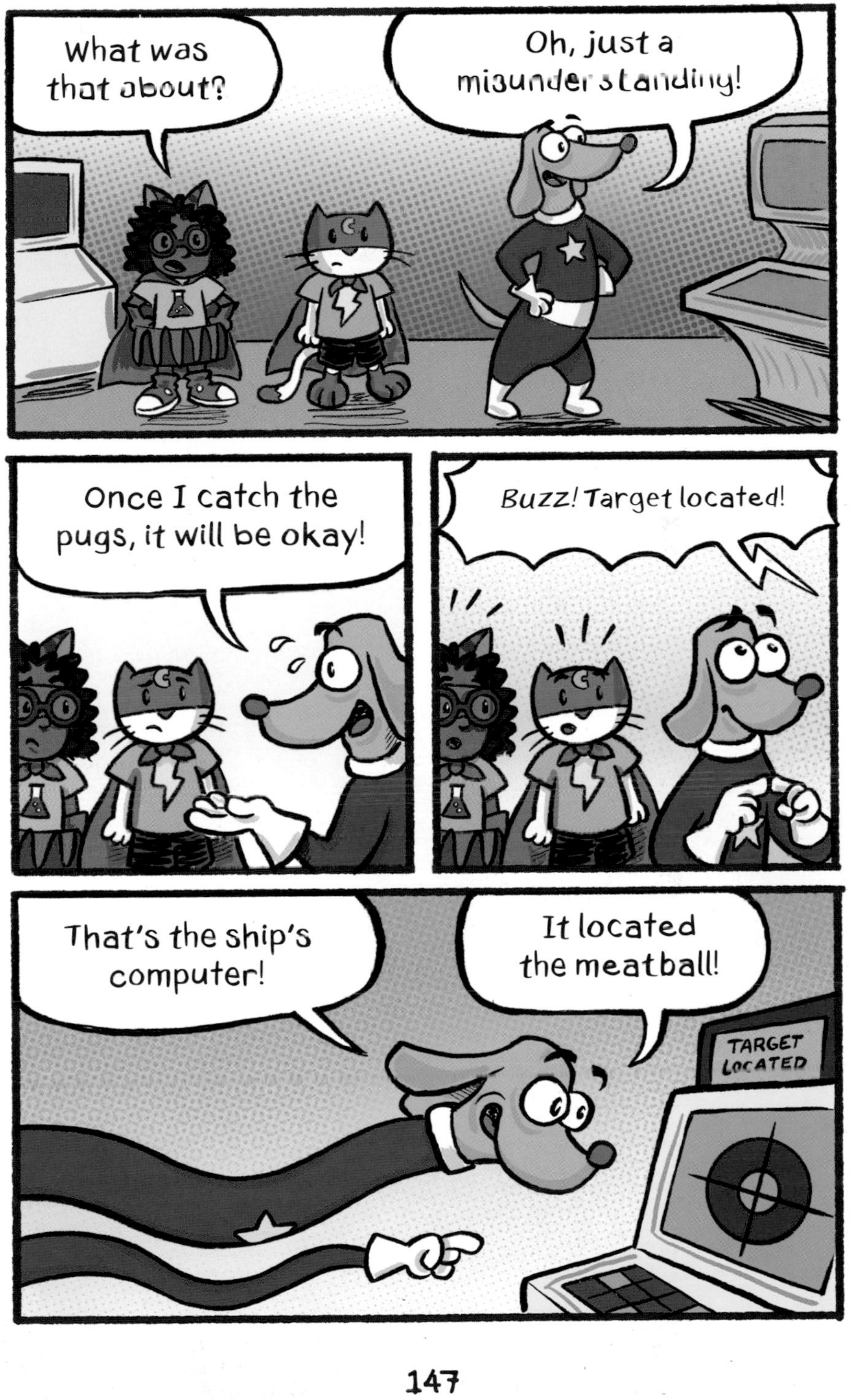
What was that about?
Oh, just a misunderstanding!
Once I catch the pugs, it will be okay!
Buzz! Target located!
That's the ship's computer!
It located the meatball!
TARGET LOCATED

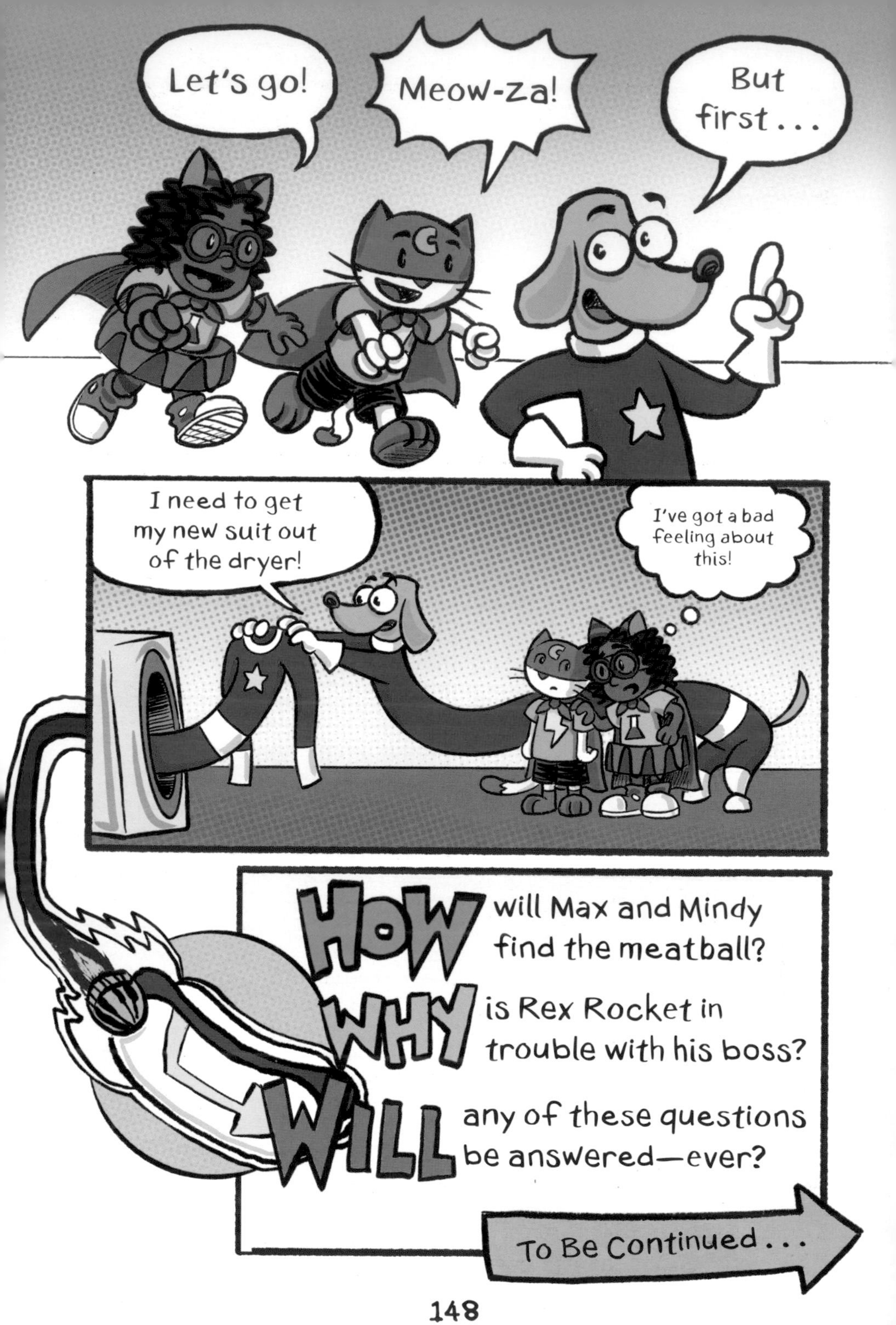
Let's go!
Meow-za!
But first . . .
I need to get my new suit out of the dryer!
I've got a bad feeling about this!
HOW will Max and Mindy find the meatball?
WHY is Rex Rocket in trouble with his boss?
WILL any of these questions be answered—ever?
To Be Continued . . .

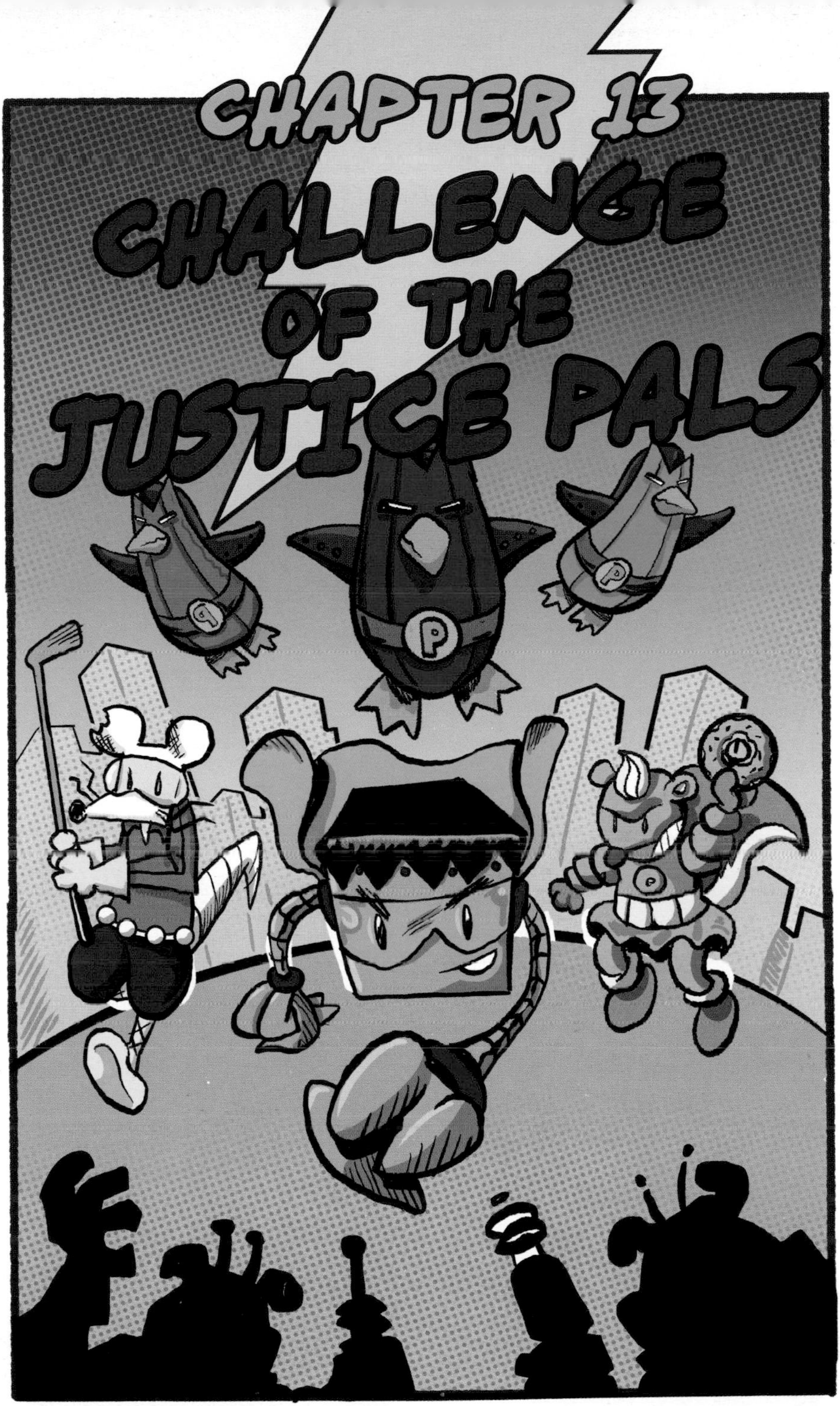
CHAPTER 13
CHALLENGE OF THE JUSTICE PALS

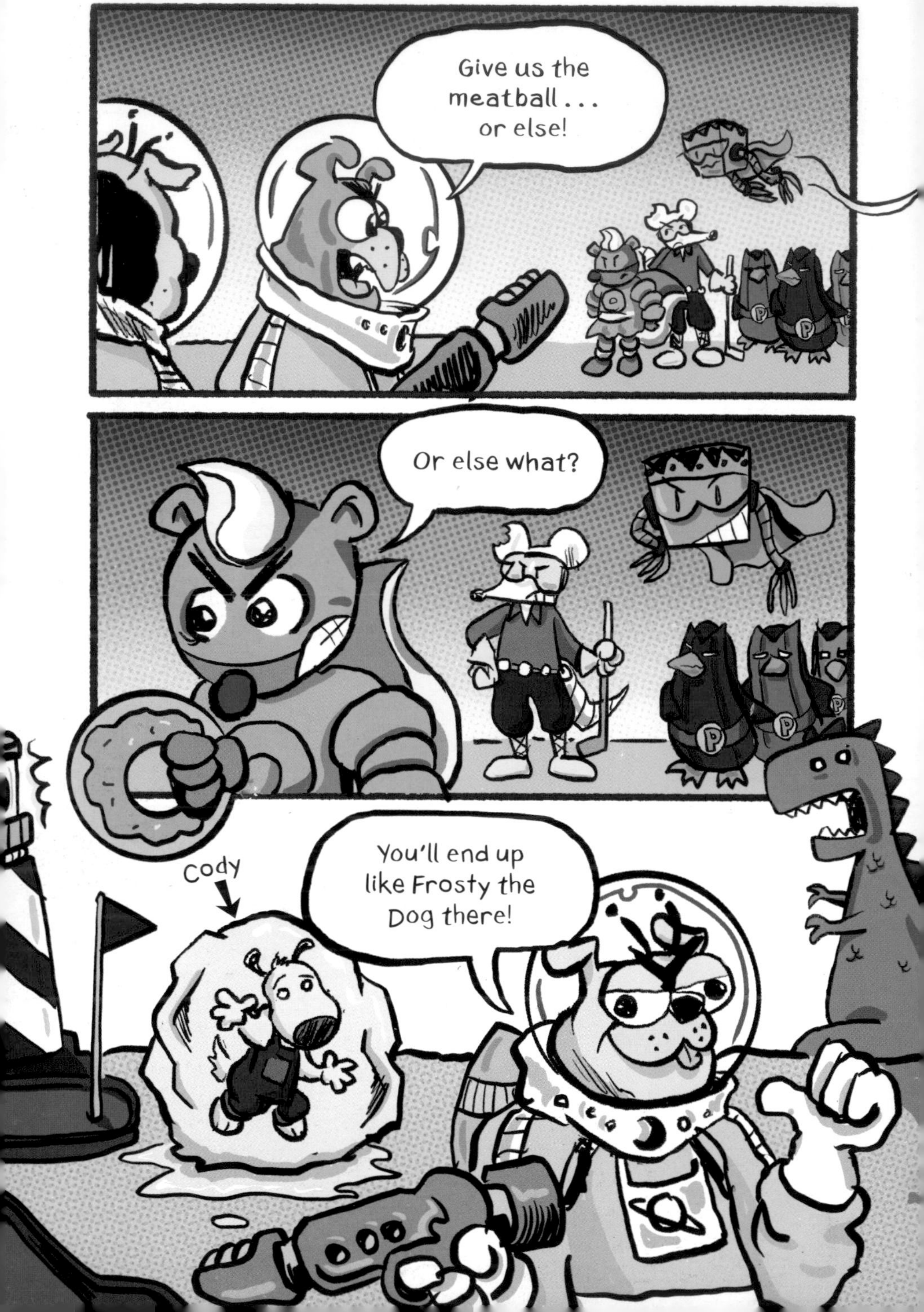
Give us the meatball . . . or else!
Or else what?
Cody
You'll end up like Frosty the Dog there!

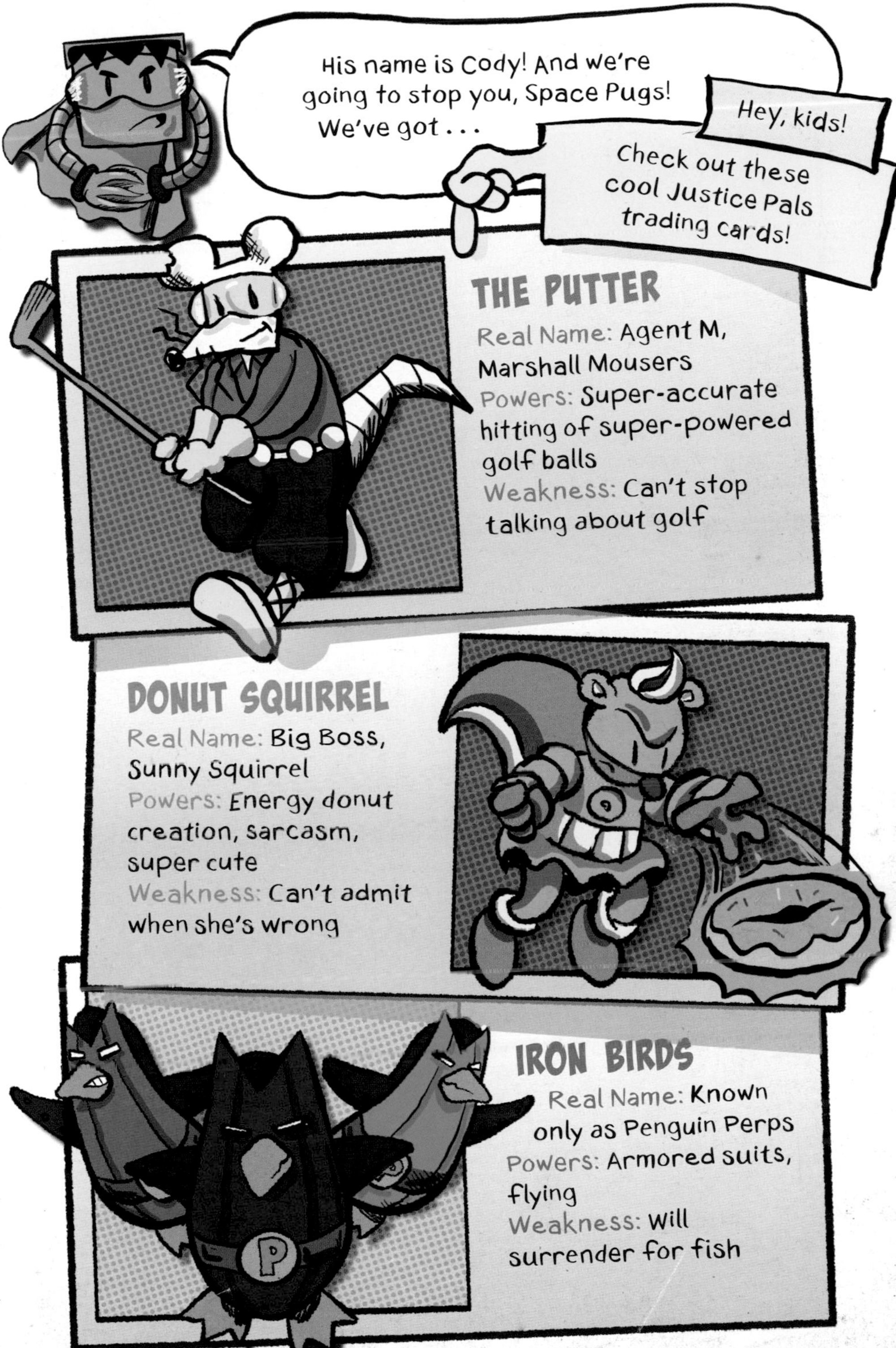

His name is Cody! And we're going to stop you, Space Pugs! We've got . . .
Hey, kids!
Check out these cool Justice Pals trading cards!
THE PUTTER
Real Name: Agent M, Marshall Mousers
Powers: Super-accurate hitting of super-powered golf balls
Weakness: Can't stop talking about golf
DONUT SQUIRREL
Real Name: Big Boss, Sunny Squirrel
Powers: Energy donut creation, sarcasm, super cute
Weakness: Can't admit when she's wrong
IRON BIRDS
Real Name: Known only as Penguin Perps
Powers: Armored suits, flying
Weakness: Will surrender for fish

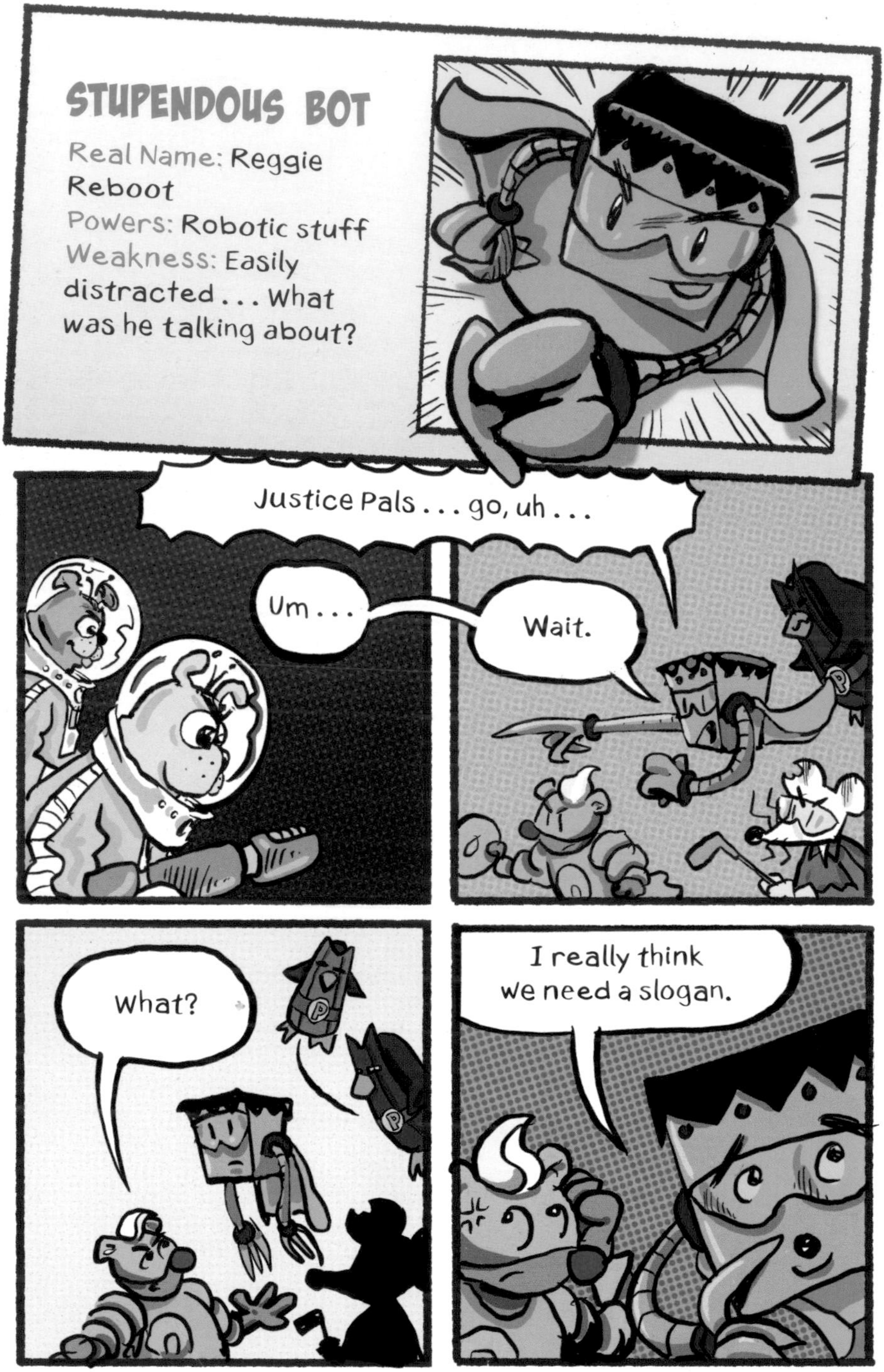
STUPENDOUS BOT
Real Name: Reggie Reboot
Powers: Robotic stuff
Weakness: Easily distracted . . . What was he talking about?
Justice Pals . . . go, uh . . .
Um . . .
Wait.
What?
I really think we need a slogan.

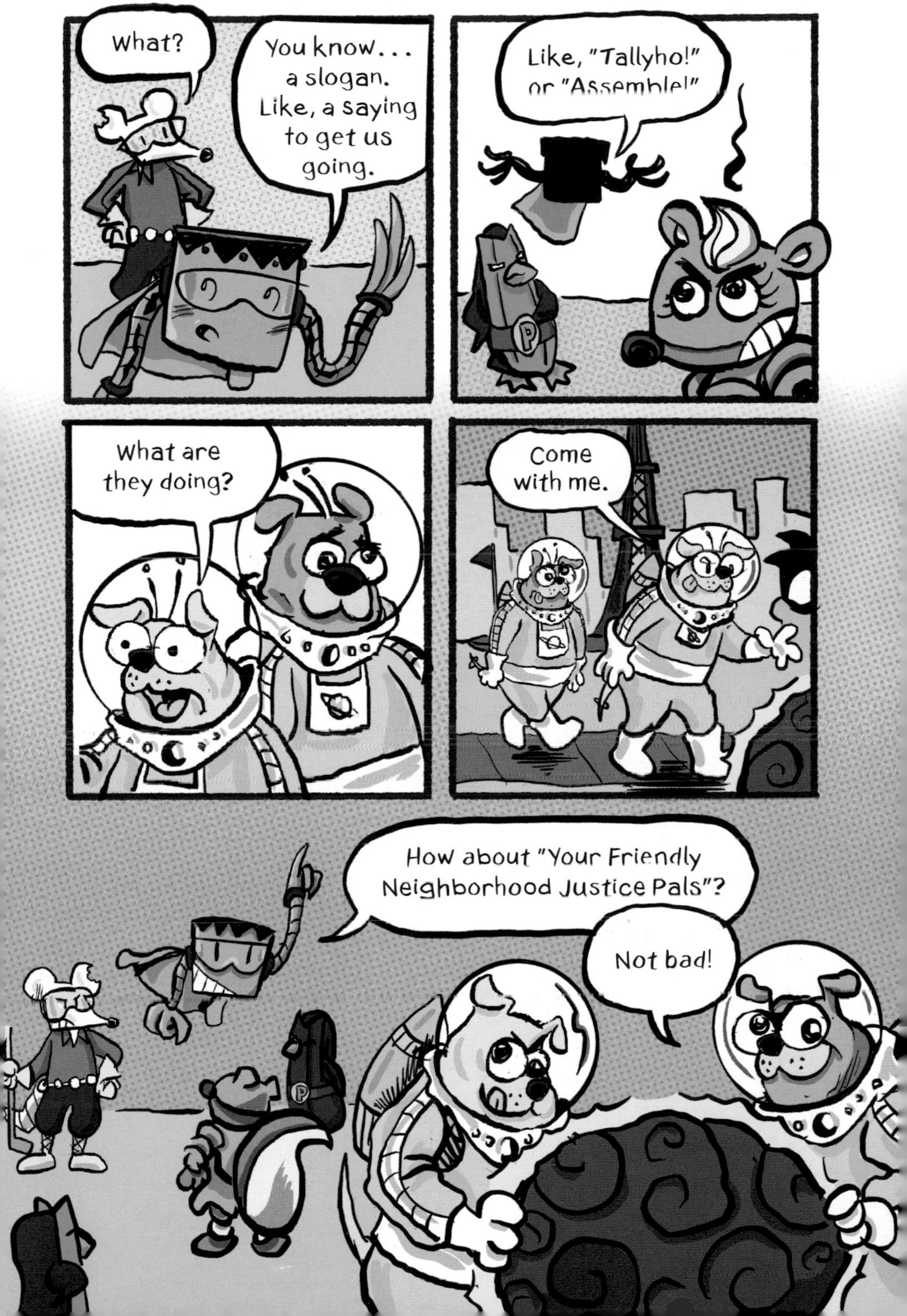
What?
You know... a slogan. Like, a saying to get us going.
Like, "Tallyho!" or "Assemble!"
What are they doing?
Come with me.
How about "Your Friendly Neighborhood Justice Pals"?
Not bad!

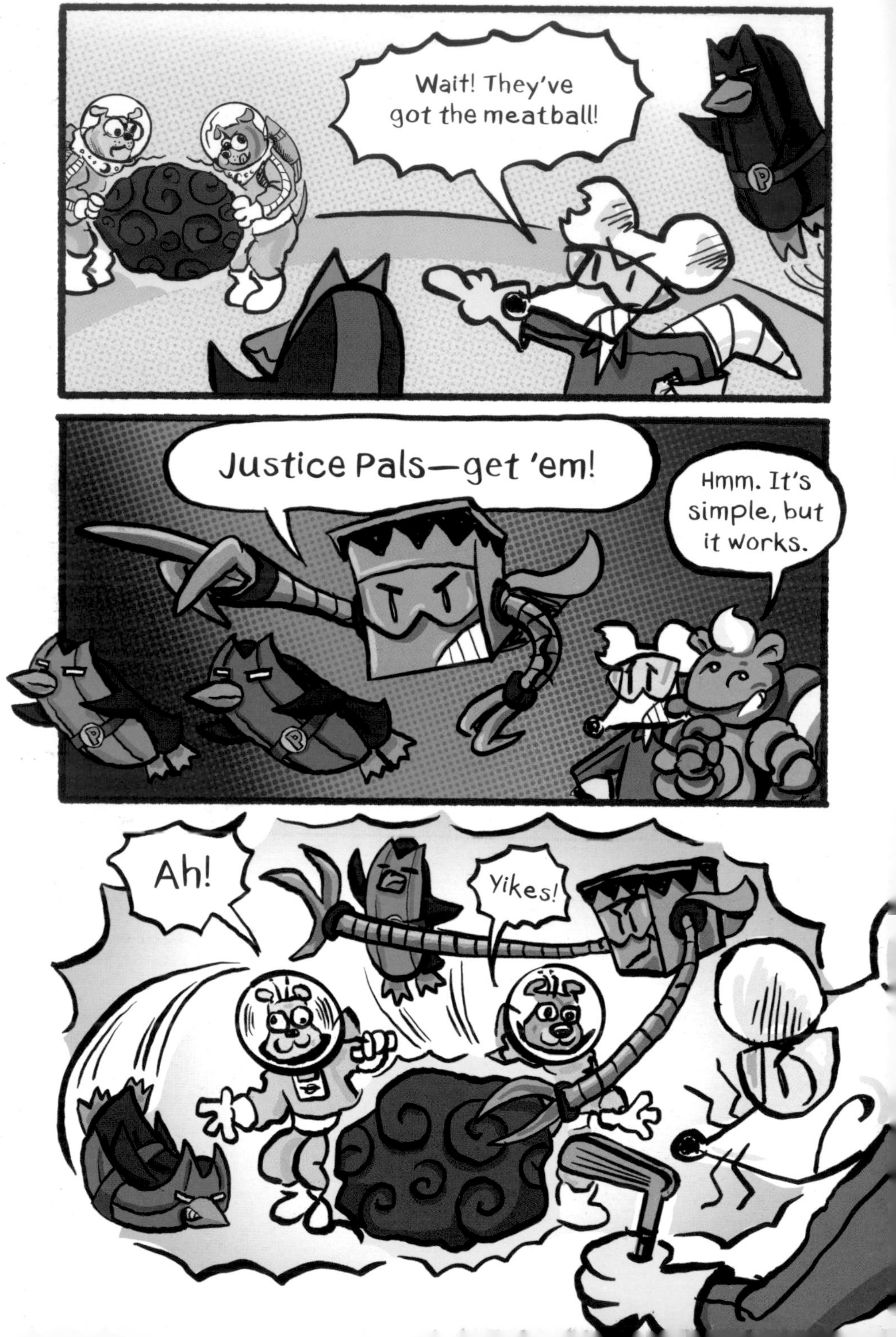
Wait! They've got the meatball!
Justice Pals—get 'em!
Hmm. It's simple, but it works.
Ah!
Yikes!

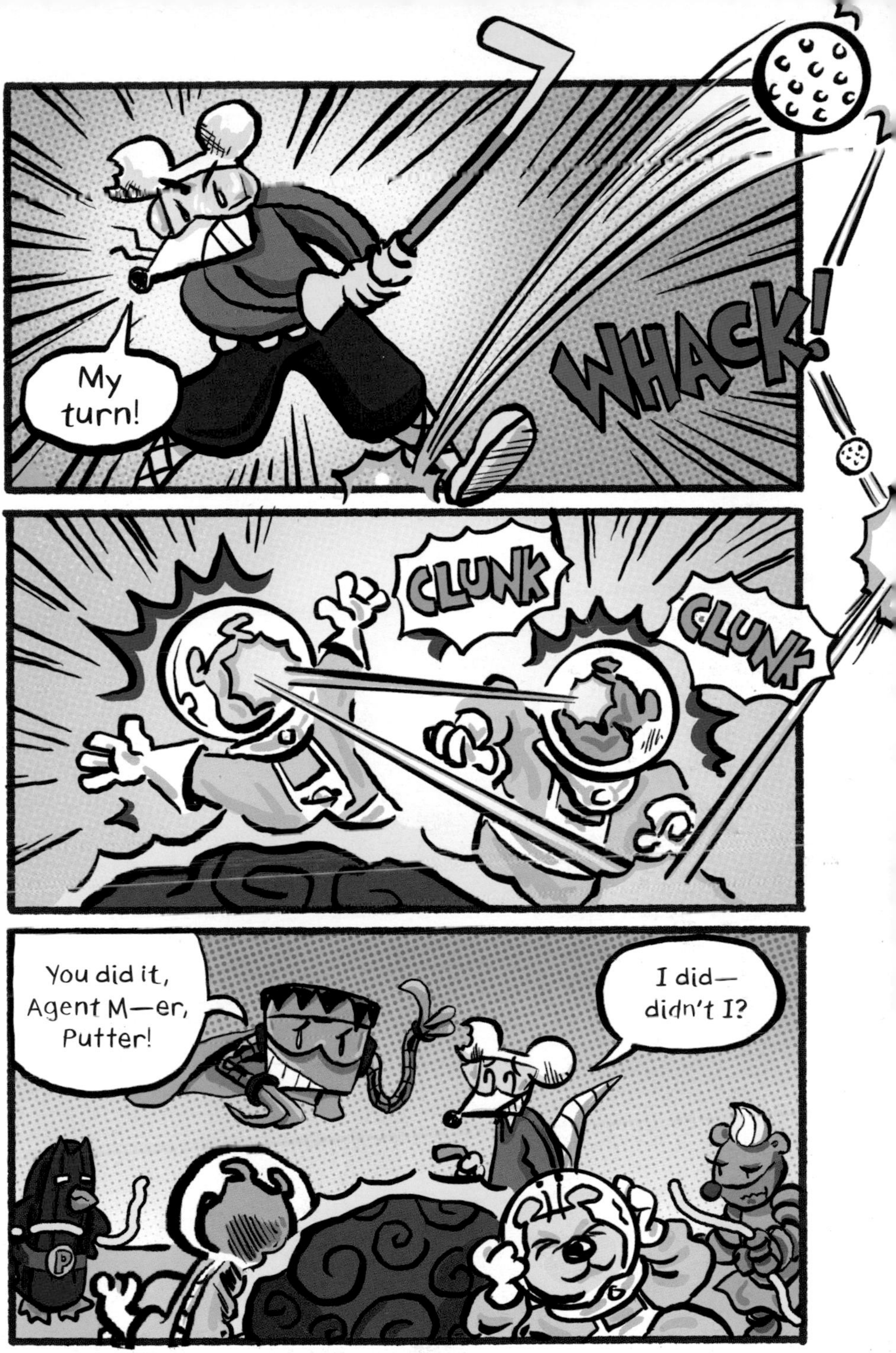
My turn!
WHACK!
CLUNK
CLUNK
You did it, Agent M—er, Putter!
I did—didn't I?

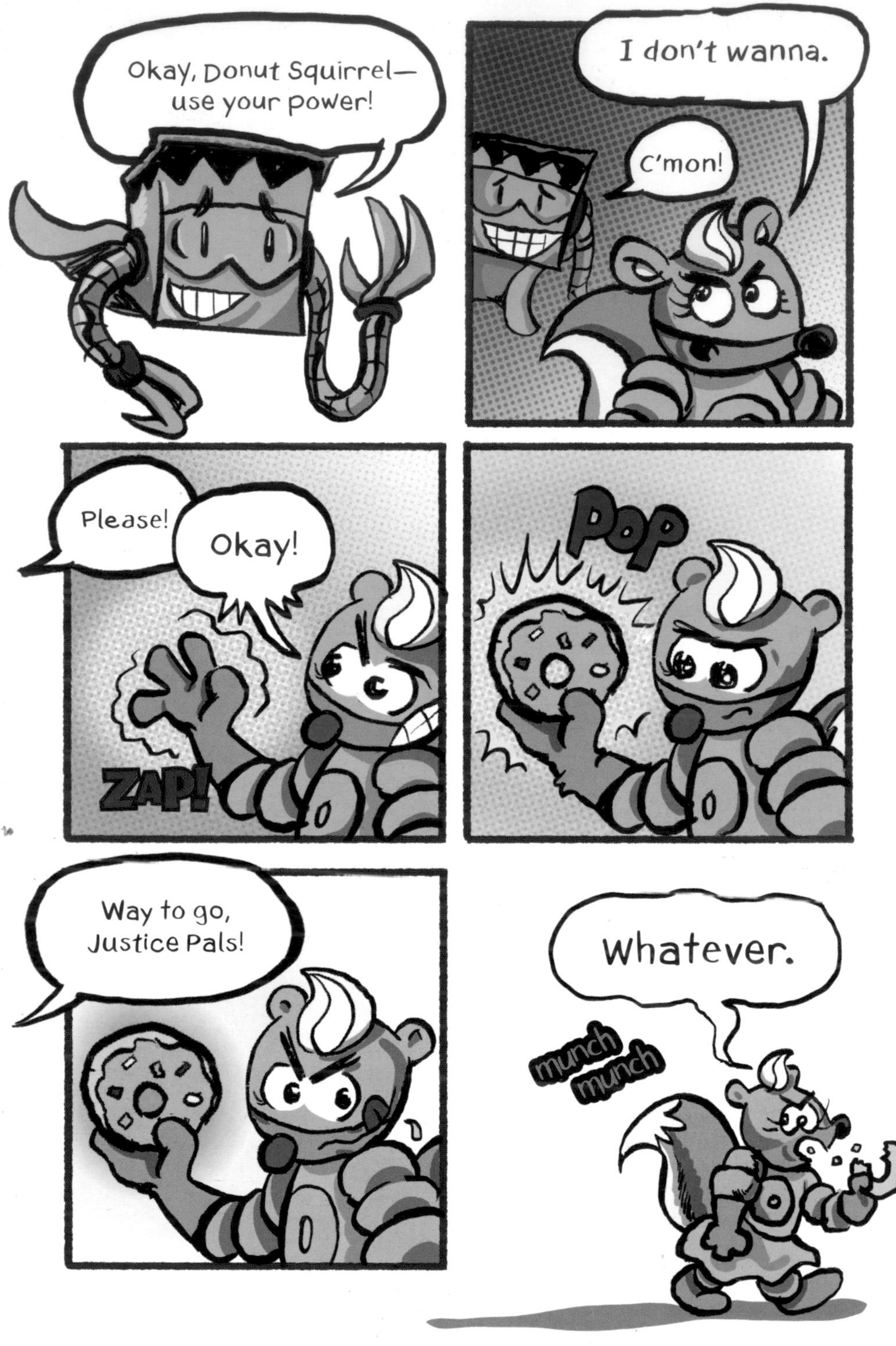
Okay, Donut Squirrel—
use your power!
I don't wanna.
C'mon!
Please!
Okay!
ZAP!
POP
Way to go,
Justice Pals!
Whatever.
munch
munch

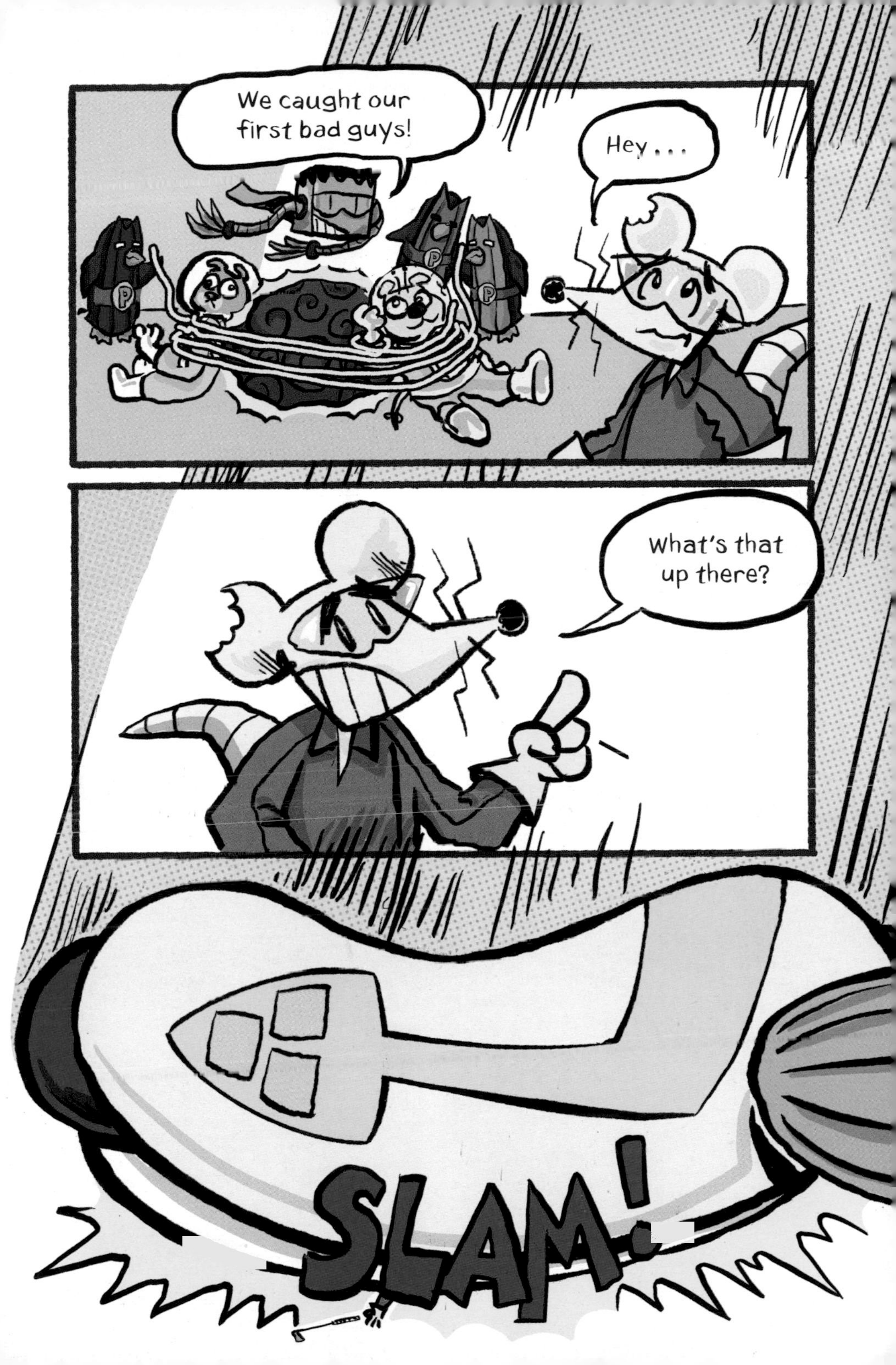
We caught our first bad guys!
Hey . . .
What's that up there?
SLAM!

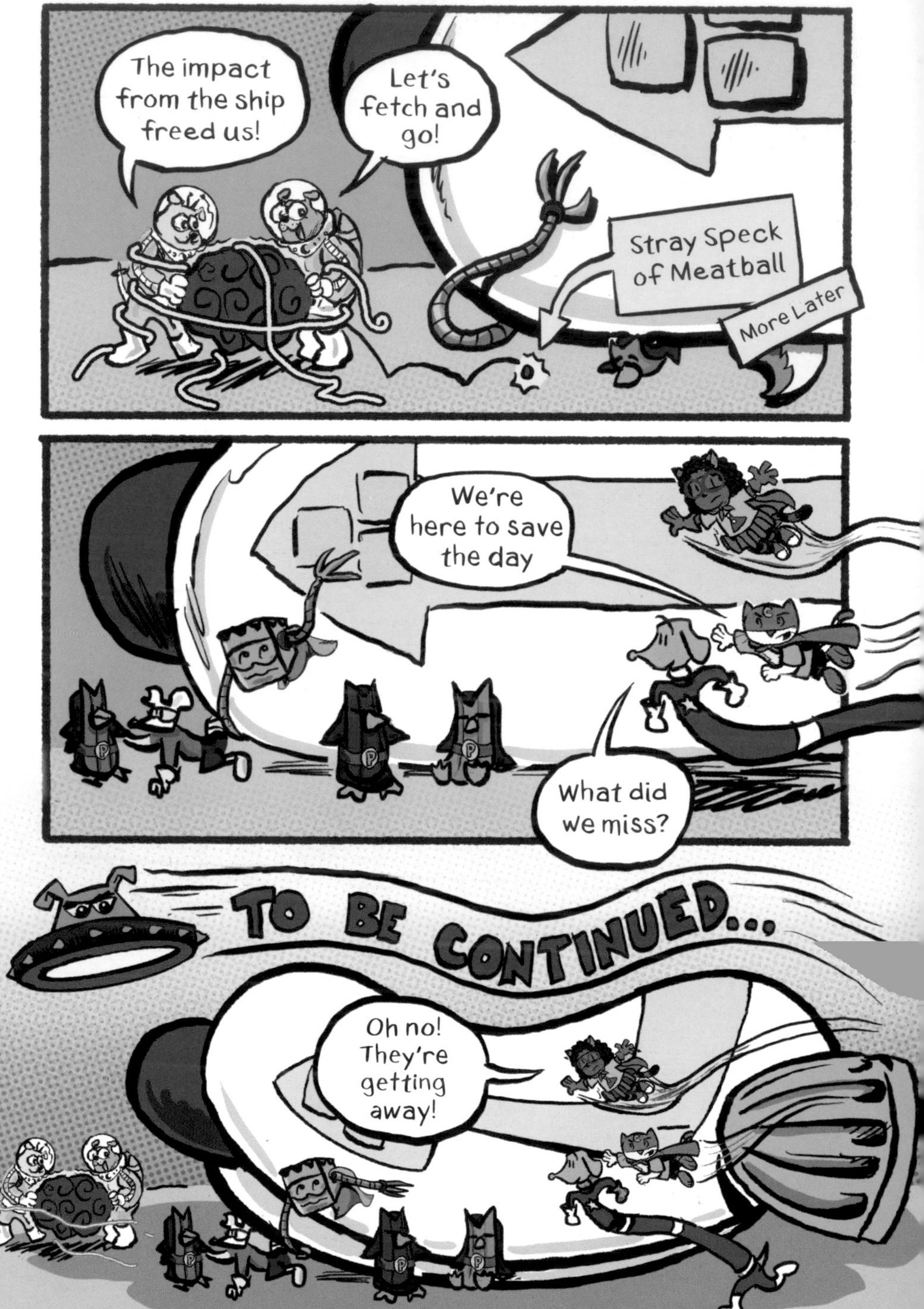
The impact from the ship freed us!
Let's fetch and go!
Stray Speck of Meatball
More Later
We're here to save the day
What did we miss?
TO BE CONTINUED...
Oh no! They're getting away!

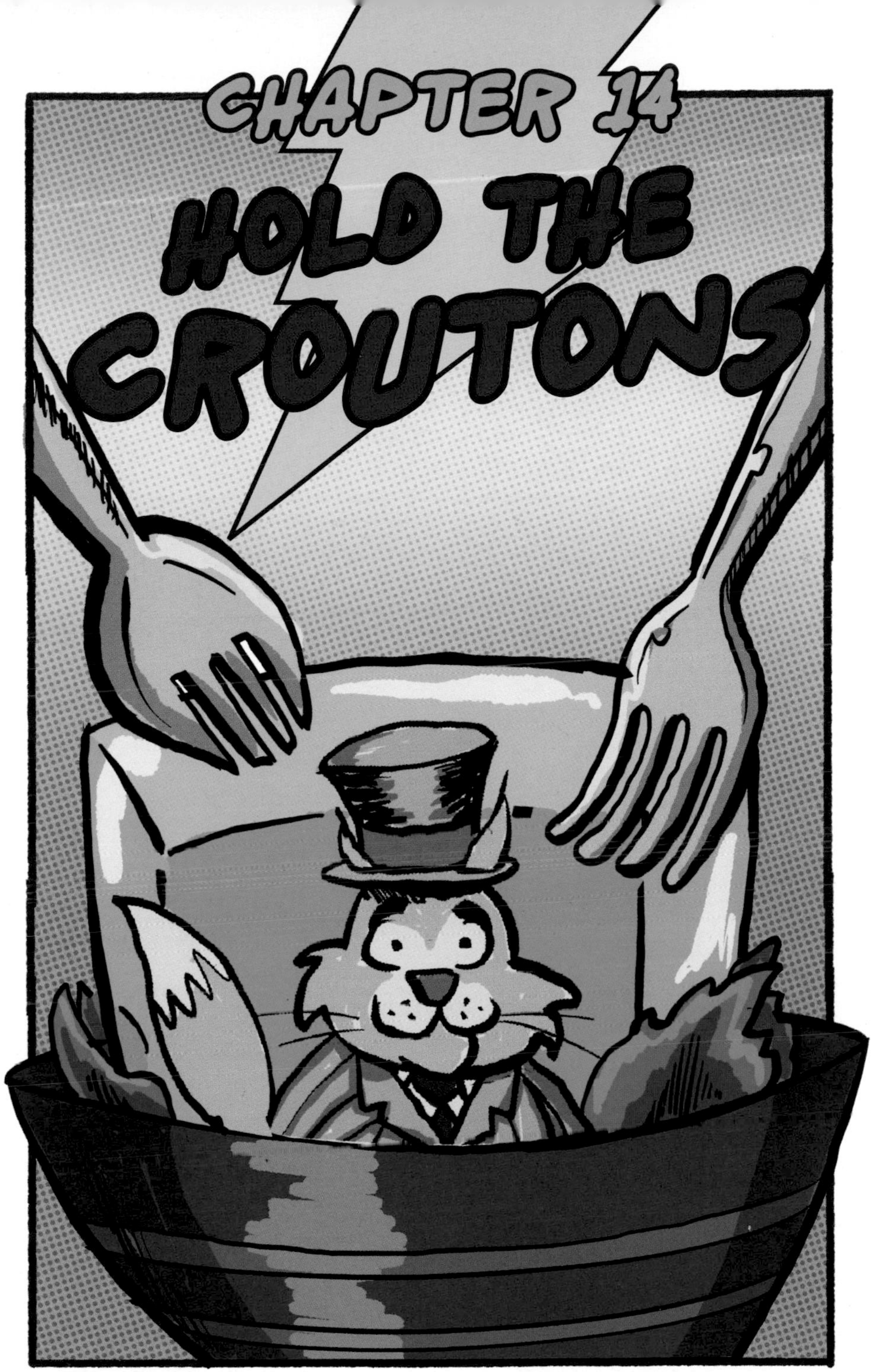
CHAPTER 14
HOLD THE CROUTONS

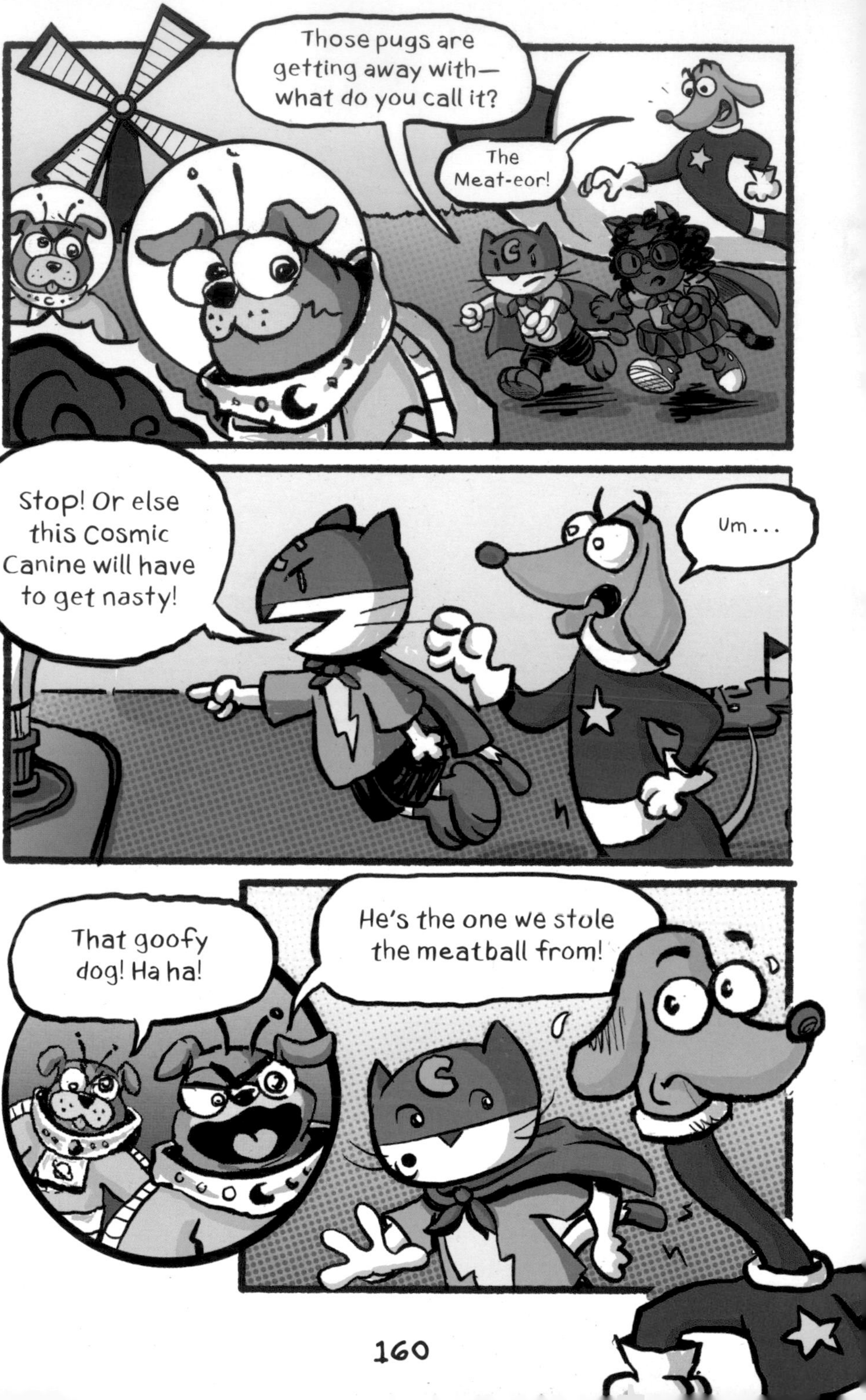
Those pugs are getting away with— what do you call it?
The Meat-eor!
Stop! Or else this Cosmic Canine will have to get nasty!
Um . . .
That goofy dog! Ha ha!
He's the one we stole the meatball from!

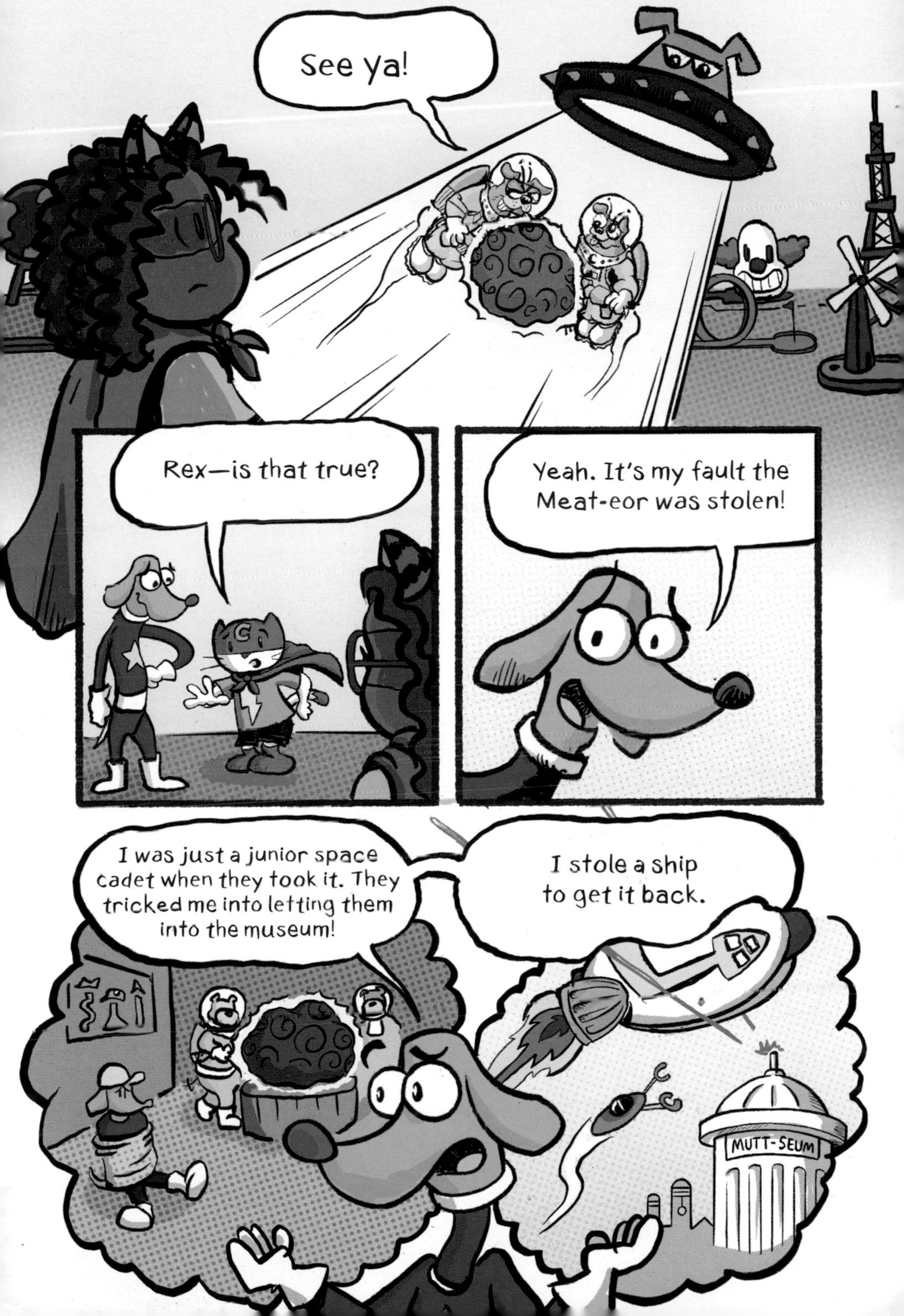
See ya!
Rex—is that true?
Yeah. It's my fault the Meat-eor was stolen!
I was just a junior space cadet when they took it. They tricked me into letting them into the museum!
I stole a ship to get it back.
MUTT-SEUM

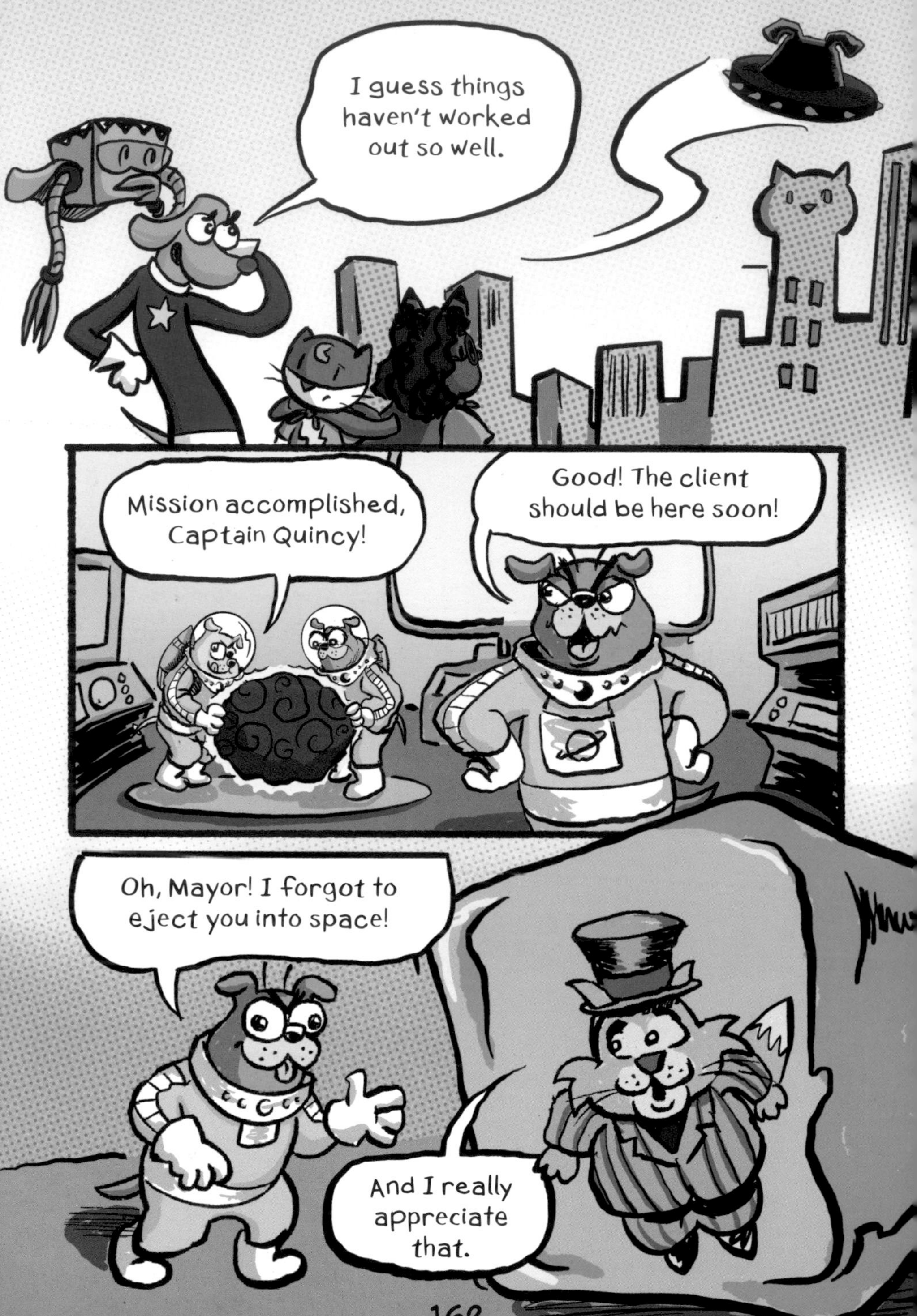
I guess things haven't worked out so well.
Mission accomplished, Captain Quincy!
Good! The client should be here soon!
Oh, Mayor! I forgot to eject you into space!
And I really appreciate that.

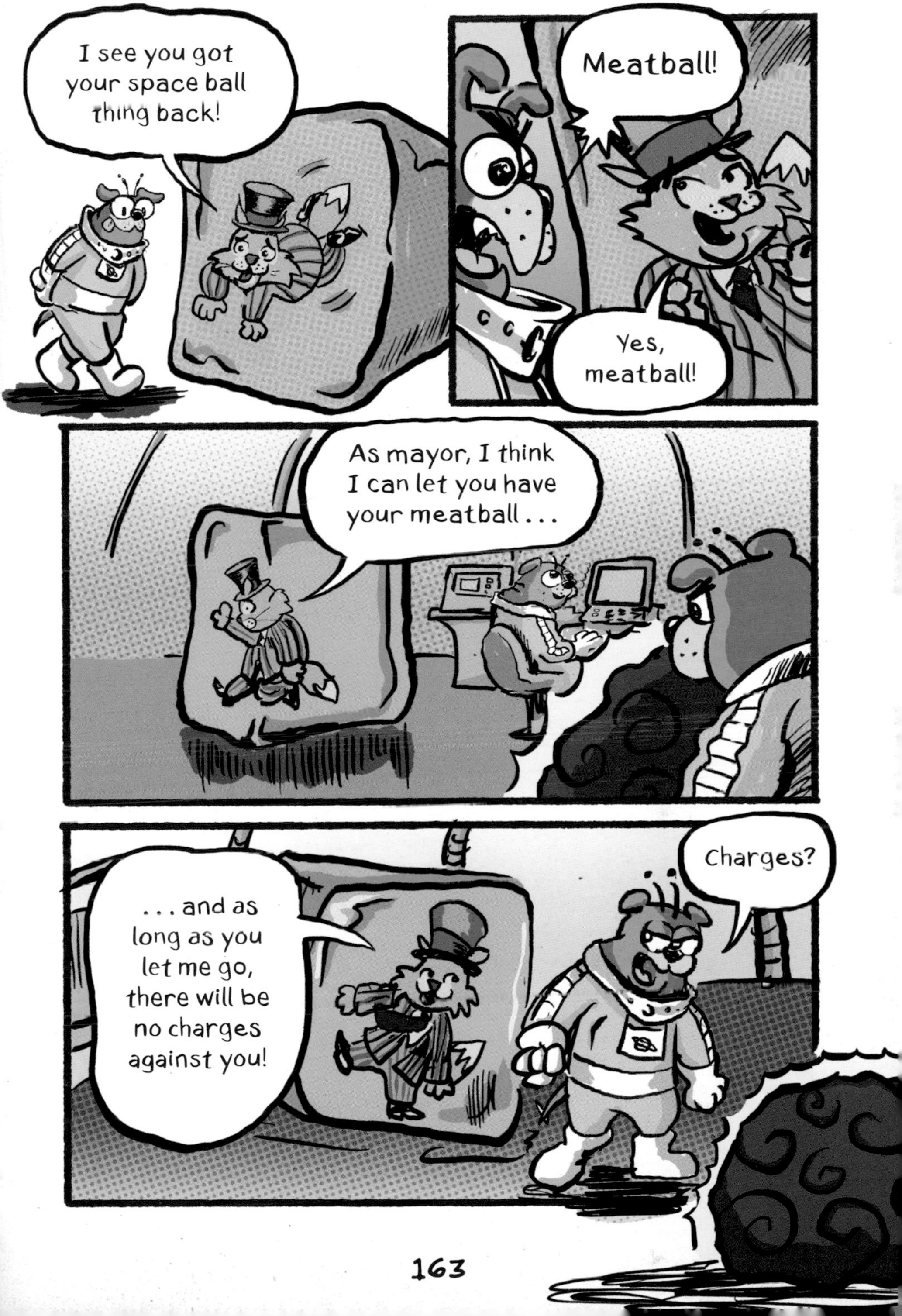
I see you got your space ball thing back!
Meatball!
Yes, meatball!
As mayor, I think I can let you have your meatball . . .
. . . and as long as you let me go, there will be no charges against you!
Charges?

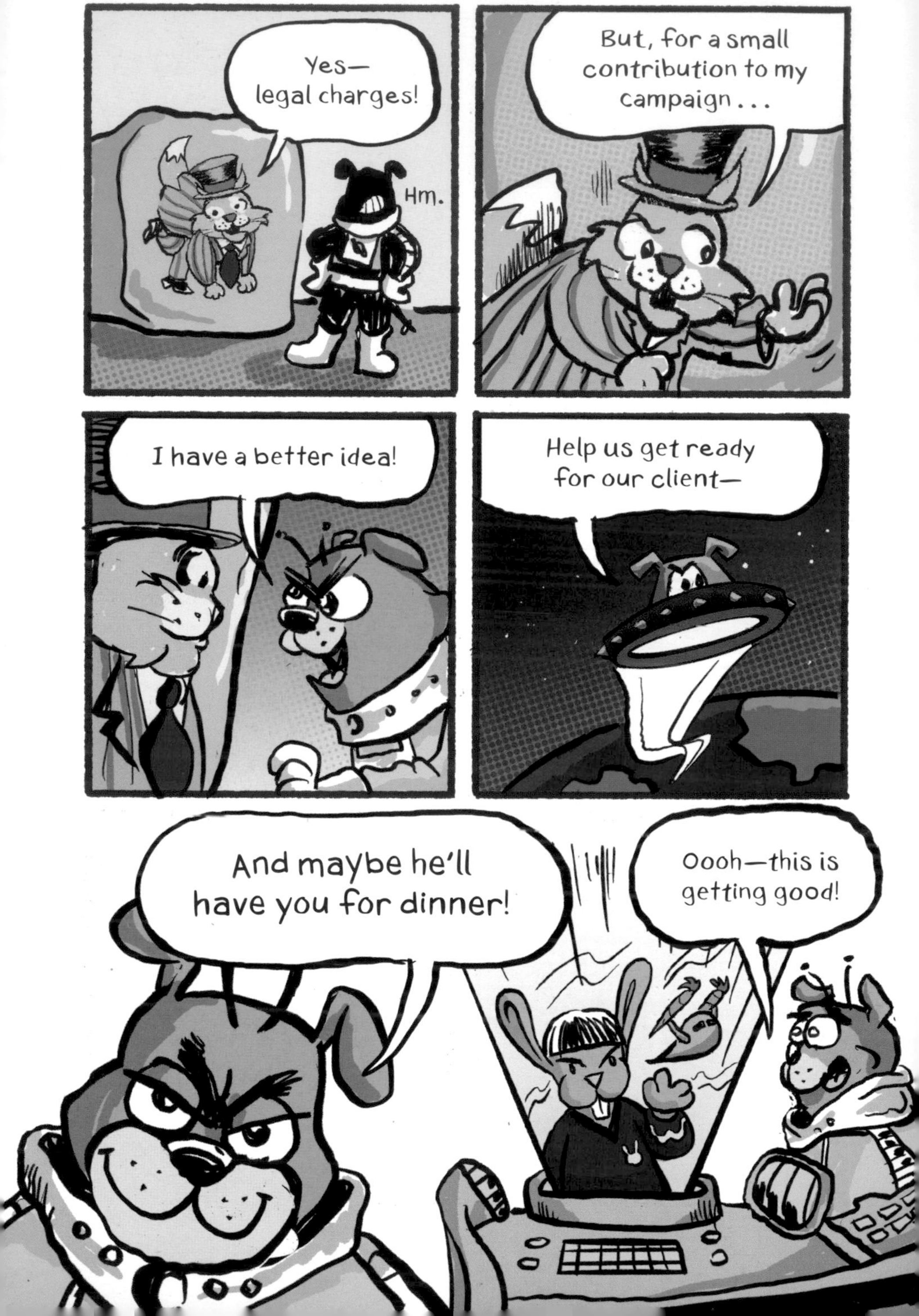
Yes—
legal charges!
Hm.
But, for a small contribution to my campaign . . .
I have a better idea!
Help us get ready for our client—
And maybe he'll have you for dinner!
Oooh—this is getting good!

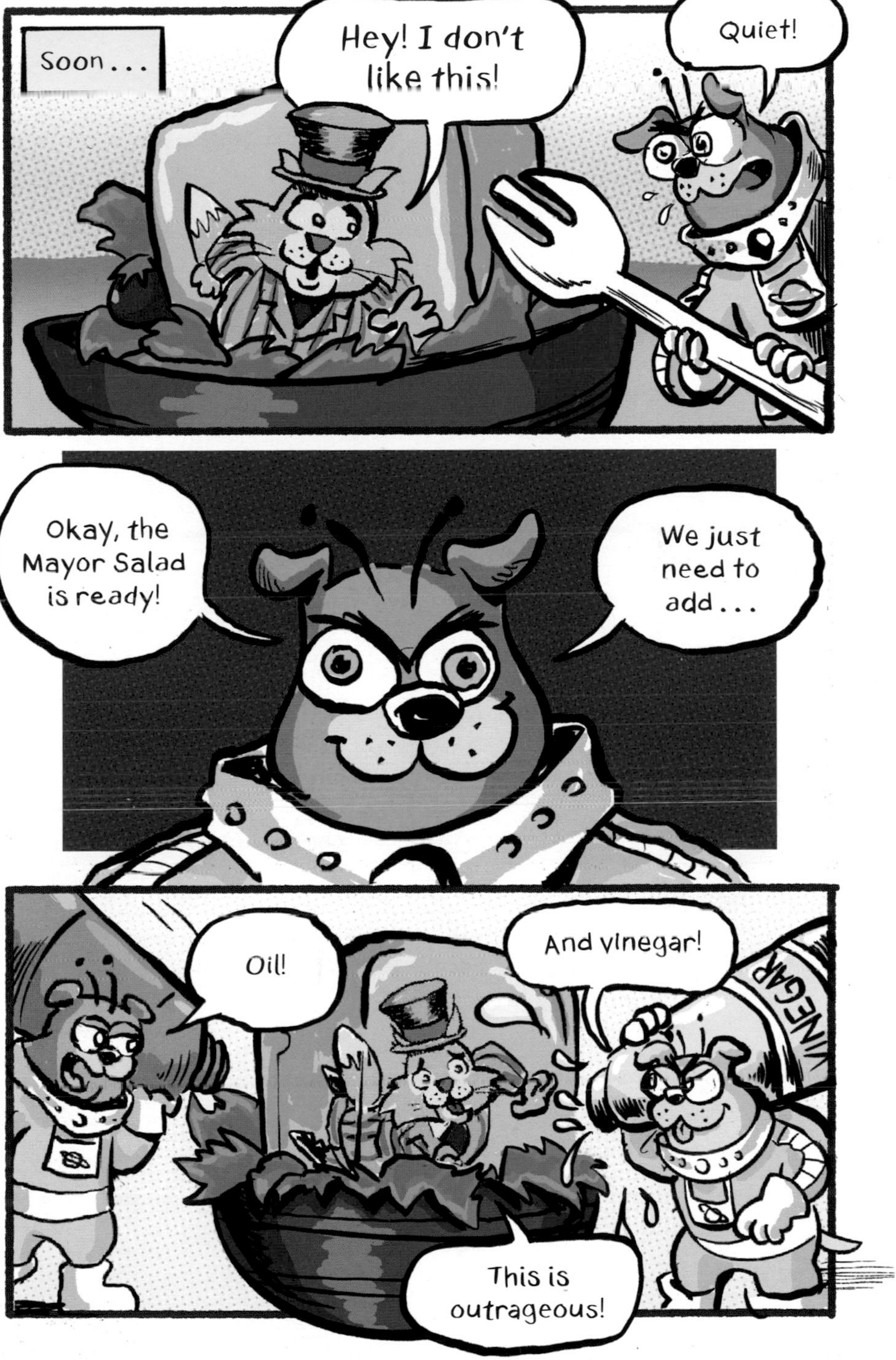
Soon . . .
Hey! I don't like this!
Quiet!
Okay, the Mayor Salad is ready!
We just need to add . . .
Oil!
And vinegar!
VINEGAR
This is outrageous!

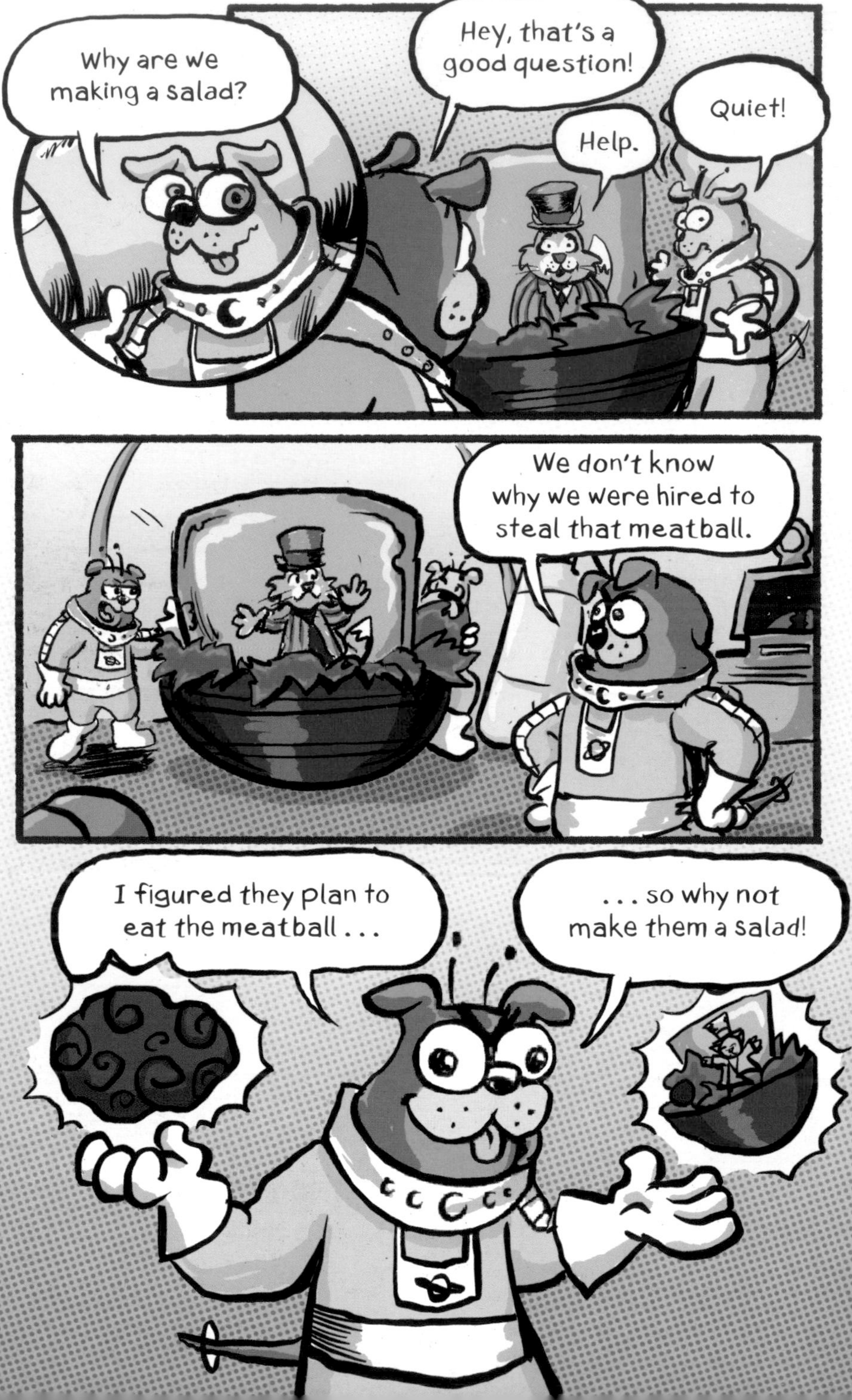
Why are we making a salad?
Hey, that's a good question!
Help.
Quiet!
We don't know why we were hired to steal that meatball.
I figured they plan to eat the meatball . . .
. . . so why not make them a salad!

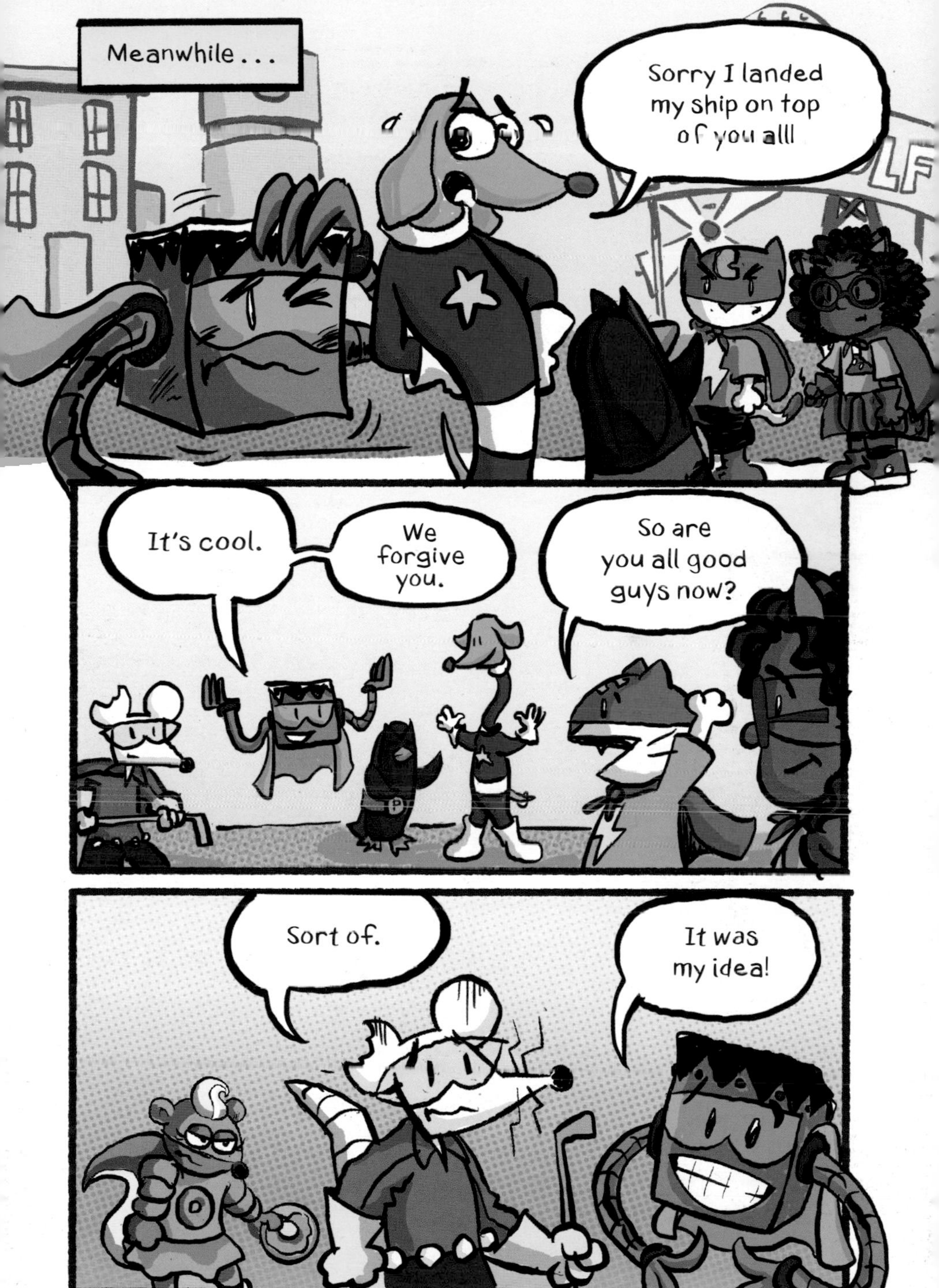
Meanwhile...
Sorry I landed my ship on top of you all!
It's cool.
We forgive you.
So are you all good guys now?
Sort of.
It was my idea!

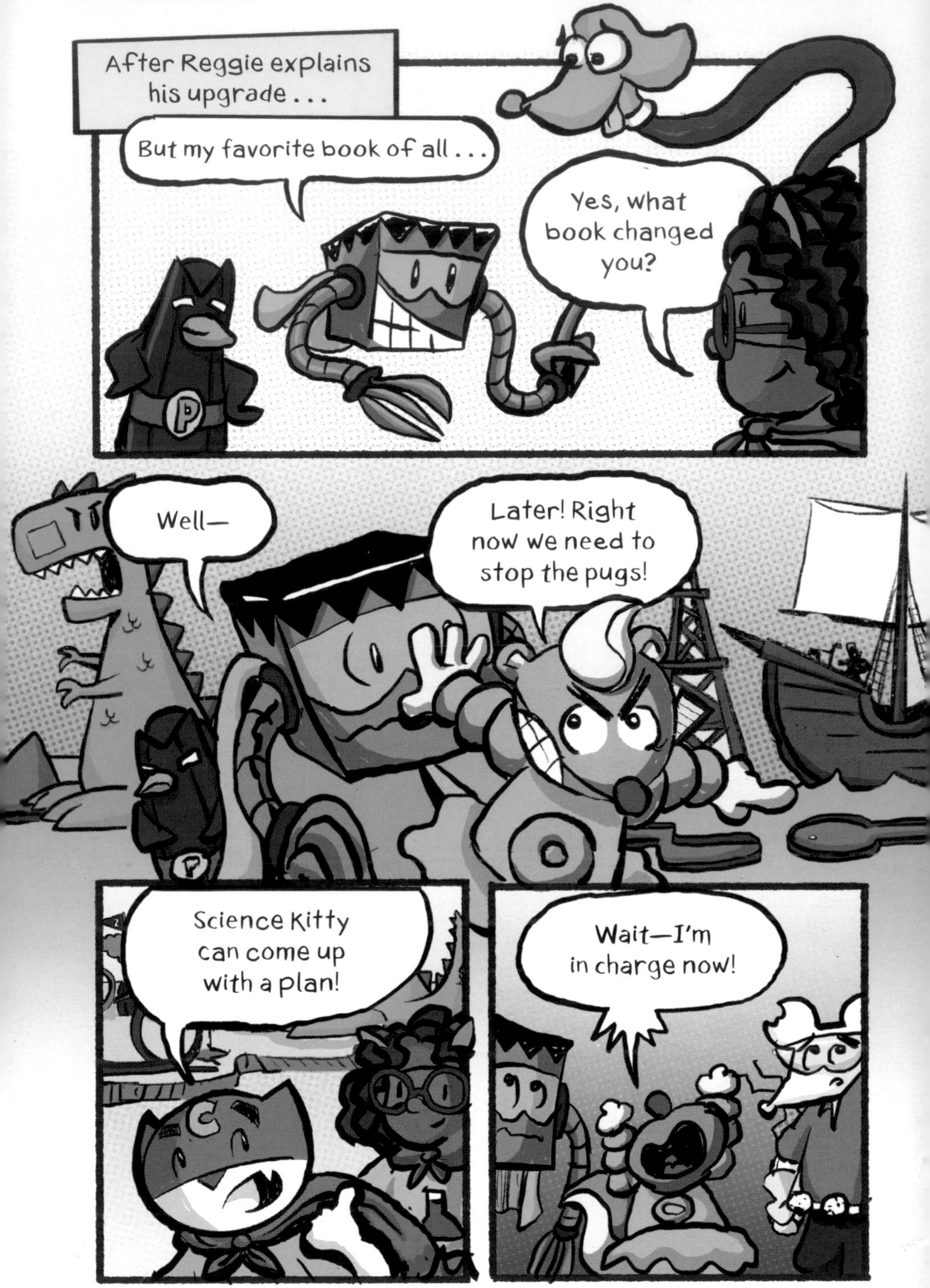
After Reggie explains his upgrade . . .
But my favorite book of all . . .
Yes, what book changed you?
Well—
Later! Right now we need to stop the pugs!
Science Kitty can come up with a plan!
Wait—I'm in charge now!

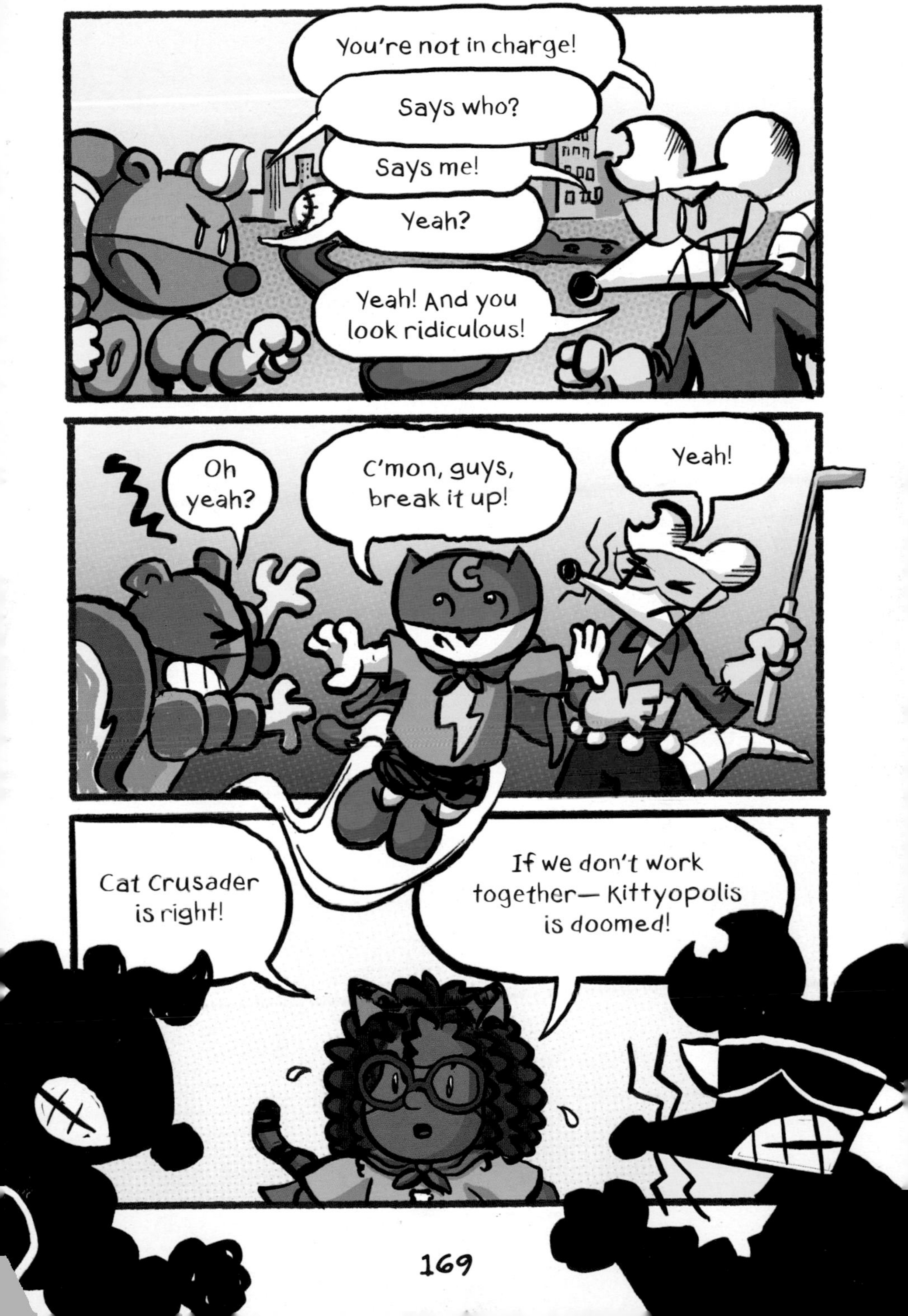
You're not in charge!
Says who?
Says me!
Yeah?
Yeah! And you look ridiculous!
Oh yeah?
C'mon, guys, break it up!
Yeah!
Cat Crusader is right!
If we don't work together— Kittyopolis is doomed!

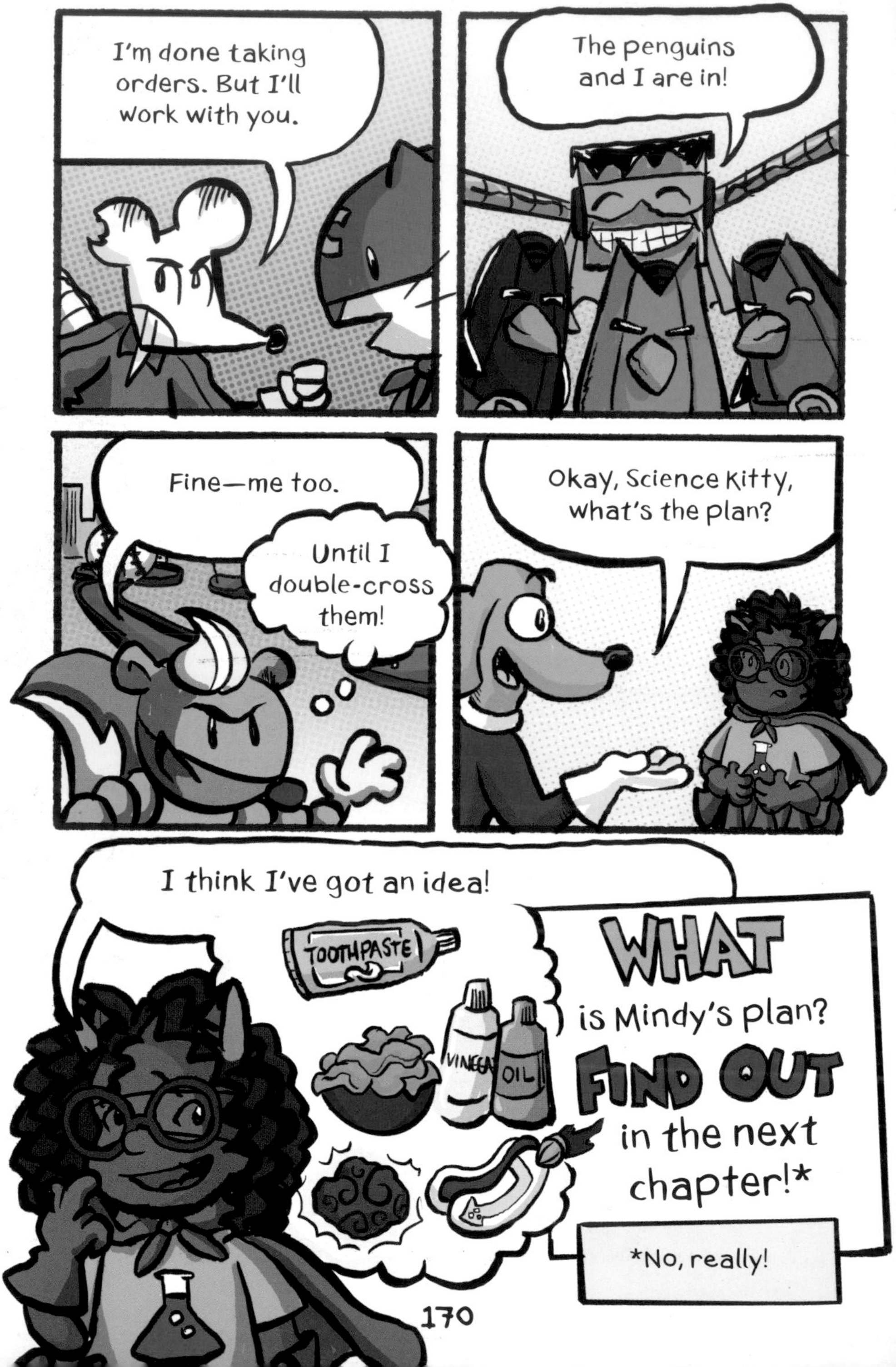
I'm done taking orders. But I'll work with you.
The penguins and I are in!
Fine—me too.
Until I double-cross them!
Okay, Science Kitty, what's the plan?
I think I've got an idea!
TOOTHPASTE
VINEGAR
OIL
WHAT is Mindy's plan? FIND OUT in the next chapter!*
*No, really!

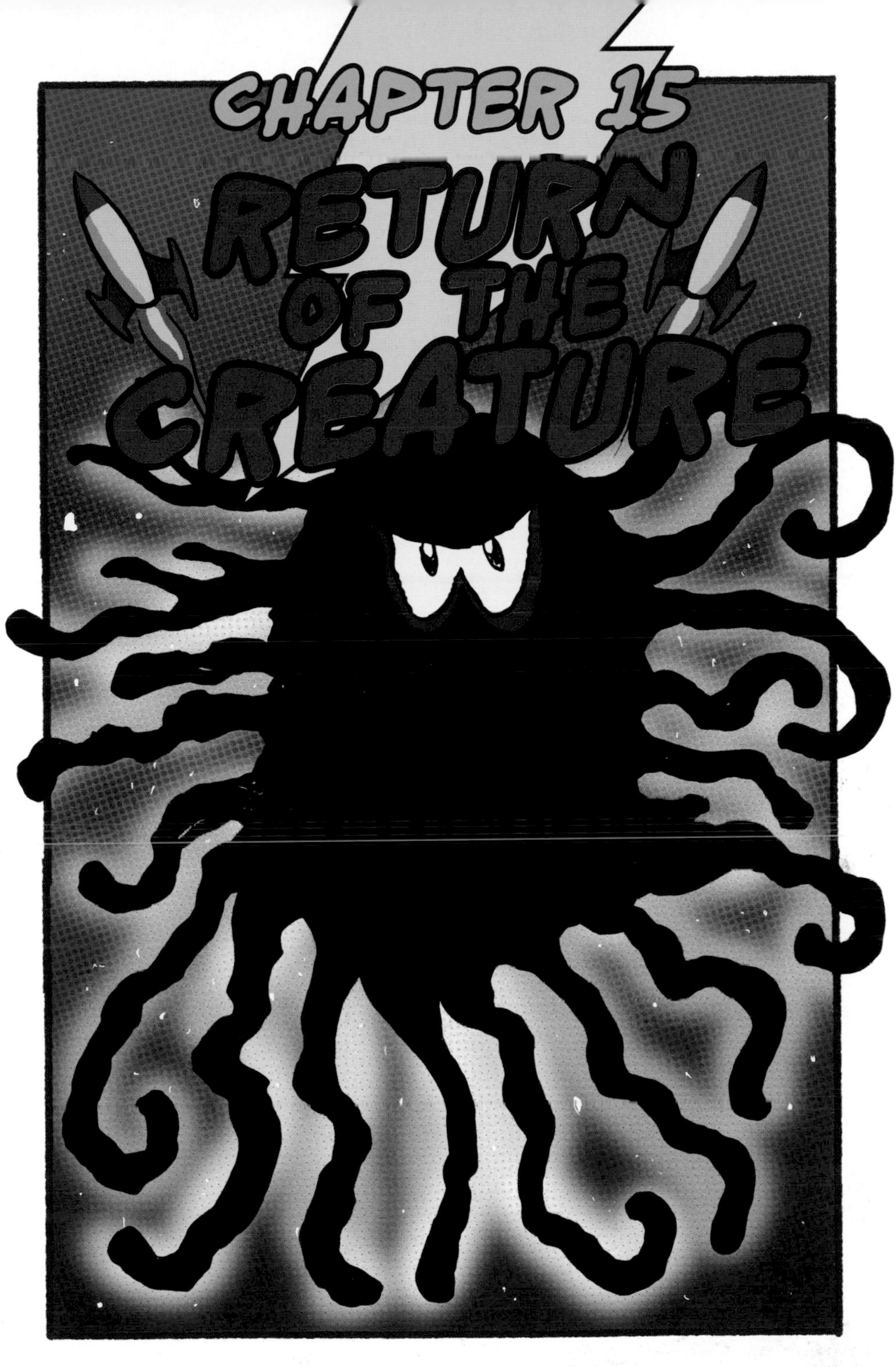
CHAPTER 15
RETURN OF THE CREATURE

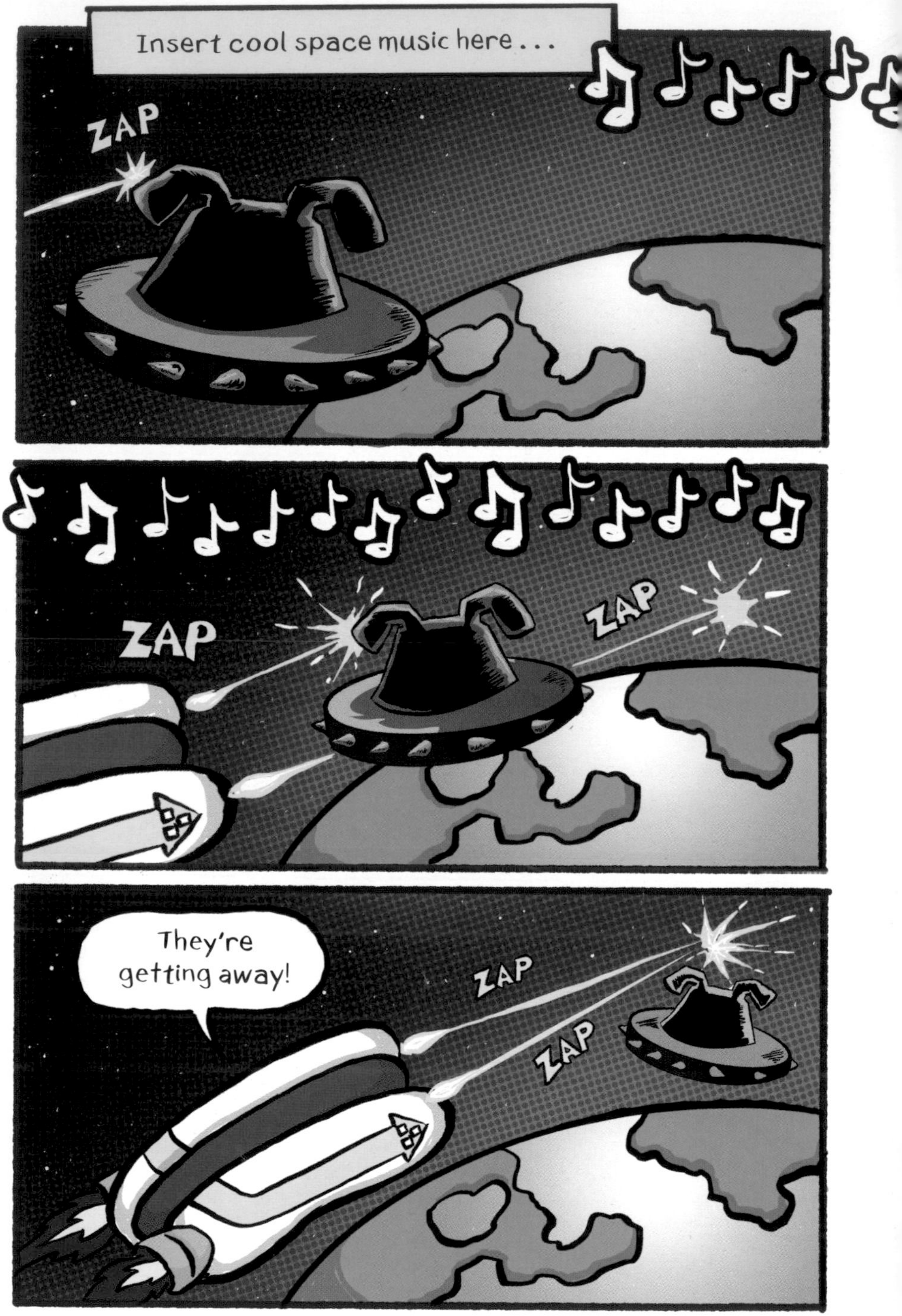
Insert cool space music here . . .
ZAP
ZAP
ZAP
They're getting away!
ZAP
ZAP

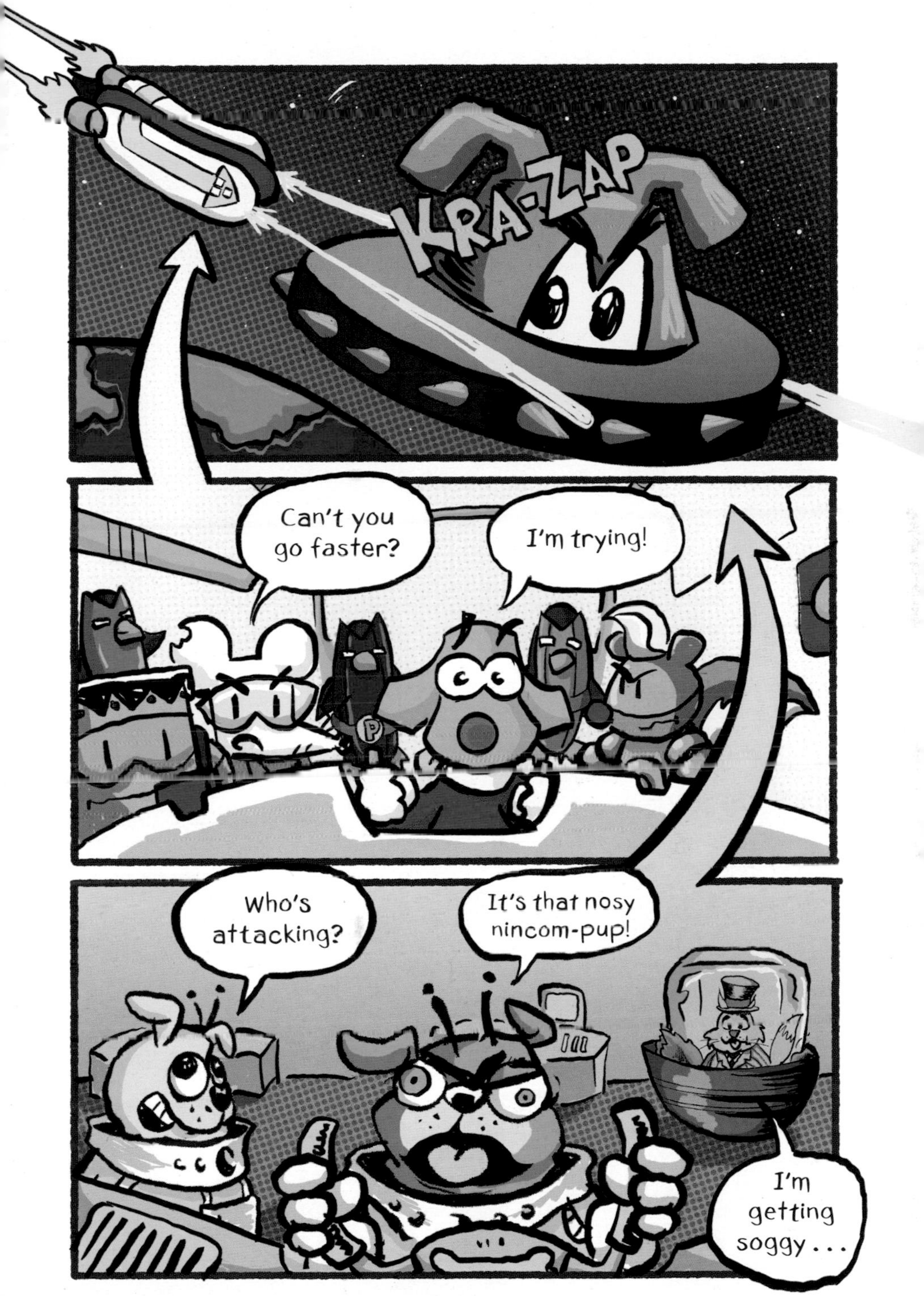
KRA-ZAP
Can't you go faster?
I'm trying!
Who's attacking?
It's that nosy nincom-pup!
I'm getting soggy . . .

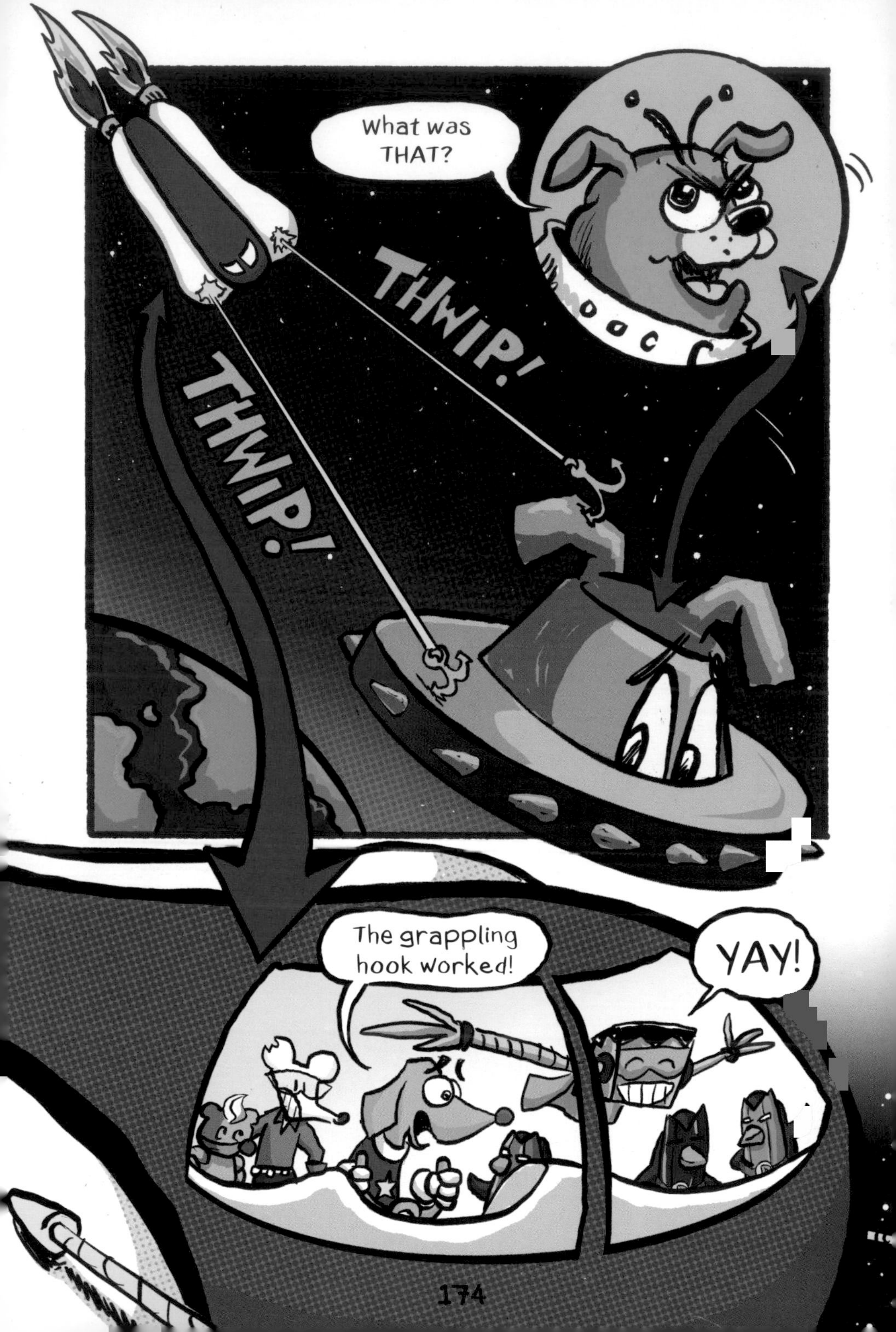
What was THAT?
THWIP!
THWIP!
The grappling hook worked!
YAY!

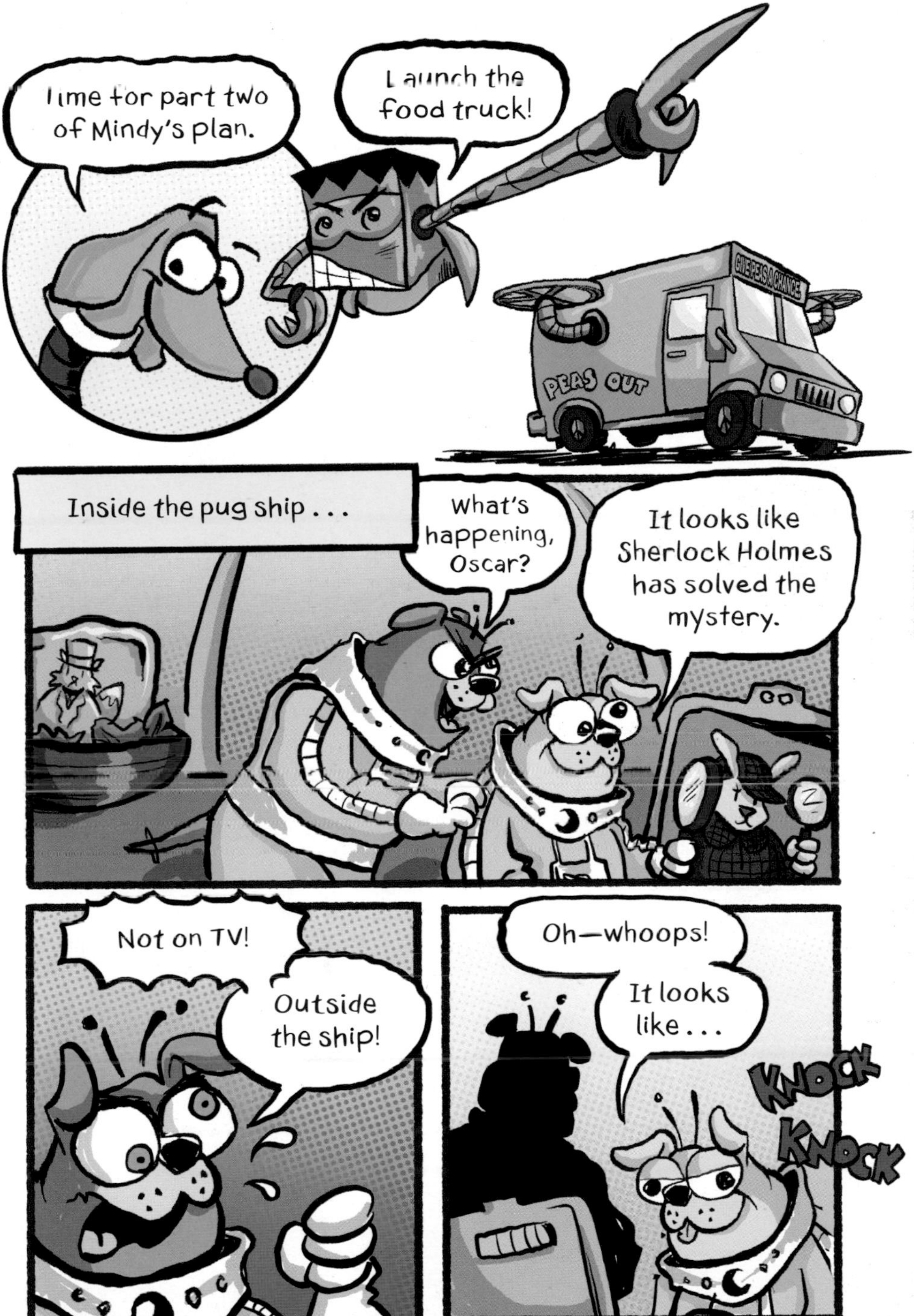
Time for part two of Mindy's plan.
Launch the food truck!
GIVE PEAS A CHANCE
PEAS OUT
Inside the pug ship . . .
What's happening, Oscar?
It looks like Sherlock Holmes has solved the mystery.
Not on TV!
Outside the ship!
Oh—whoops!
It looks like . . .
KNOCK
KNOCK

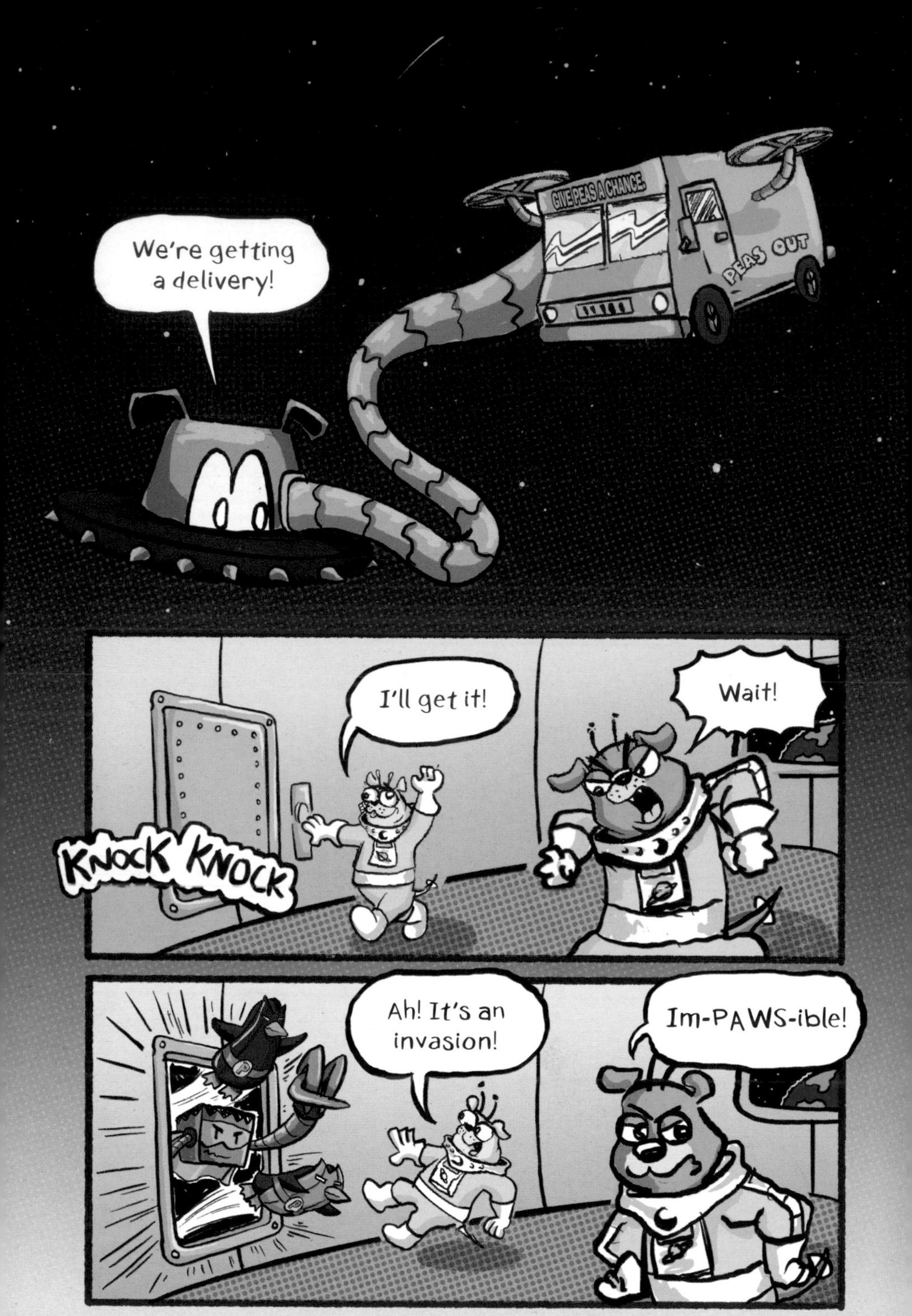

GIVE PEAS A CHANCE.
PEAS OUT
We're getting a delivery!
I'll get it!
Wait!
KNOCK KNOCK
Ah! It's an invasion!
Im-PAWS-ible!

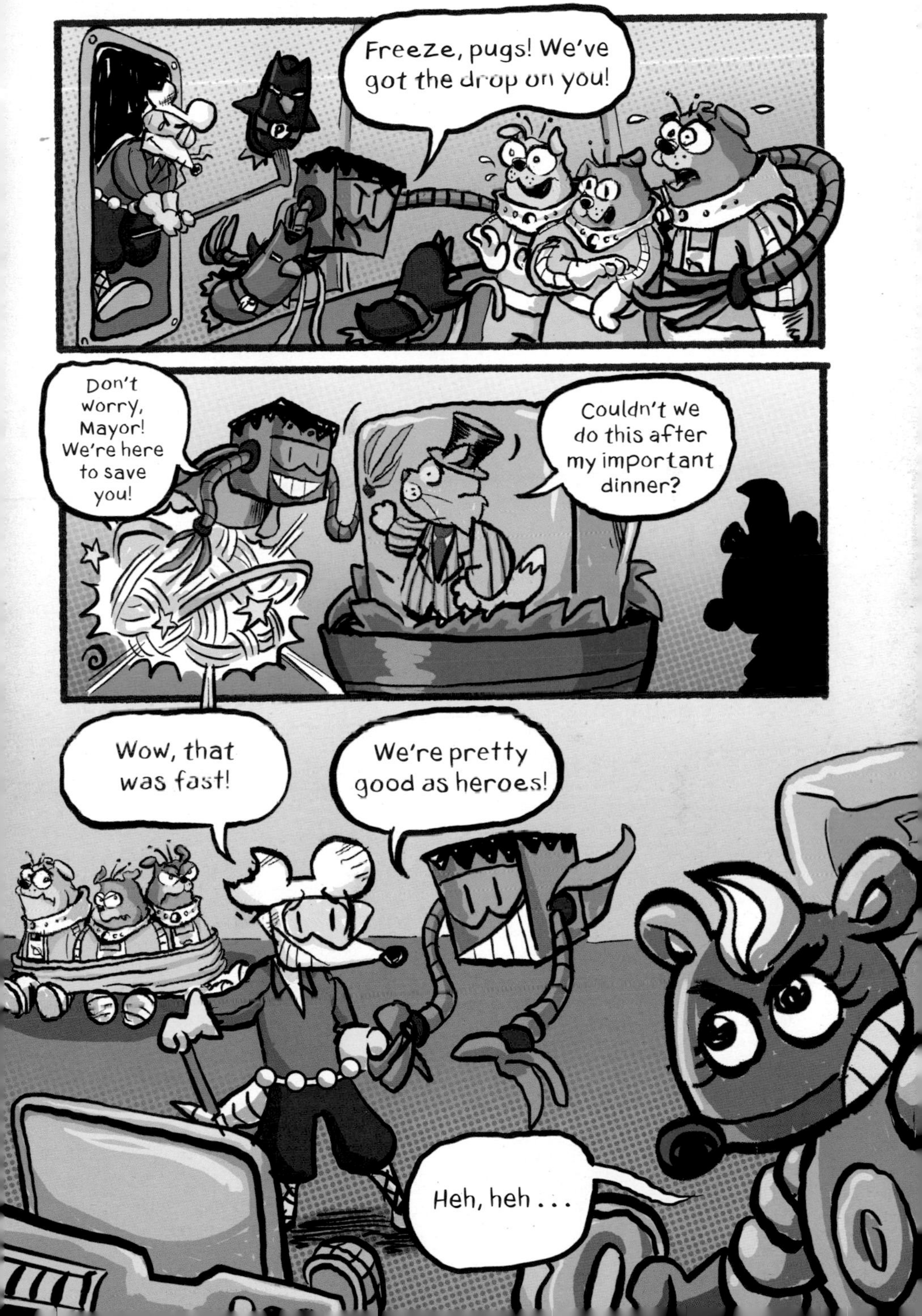
Freeze, pugs! We've got the drop on you!
Don't worry, Mayor! We're here to save you!
Couldn't we do this after my important dinner?
Wow, that was fast!
We're pretty good as heroes!
Heh, heh . . .

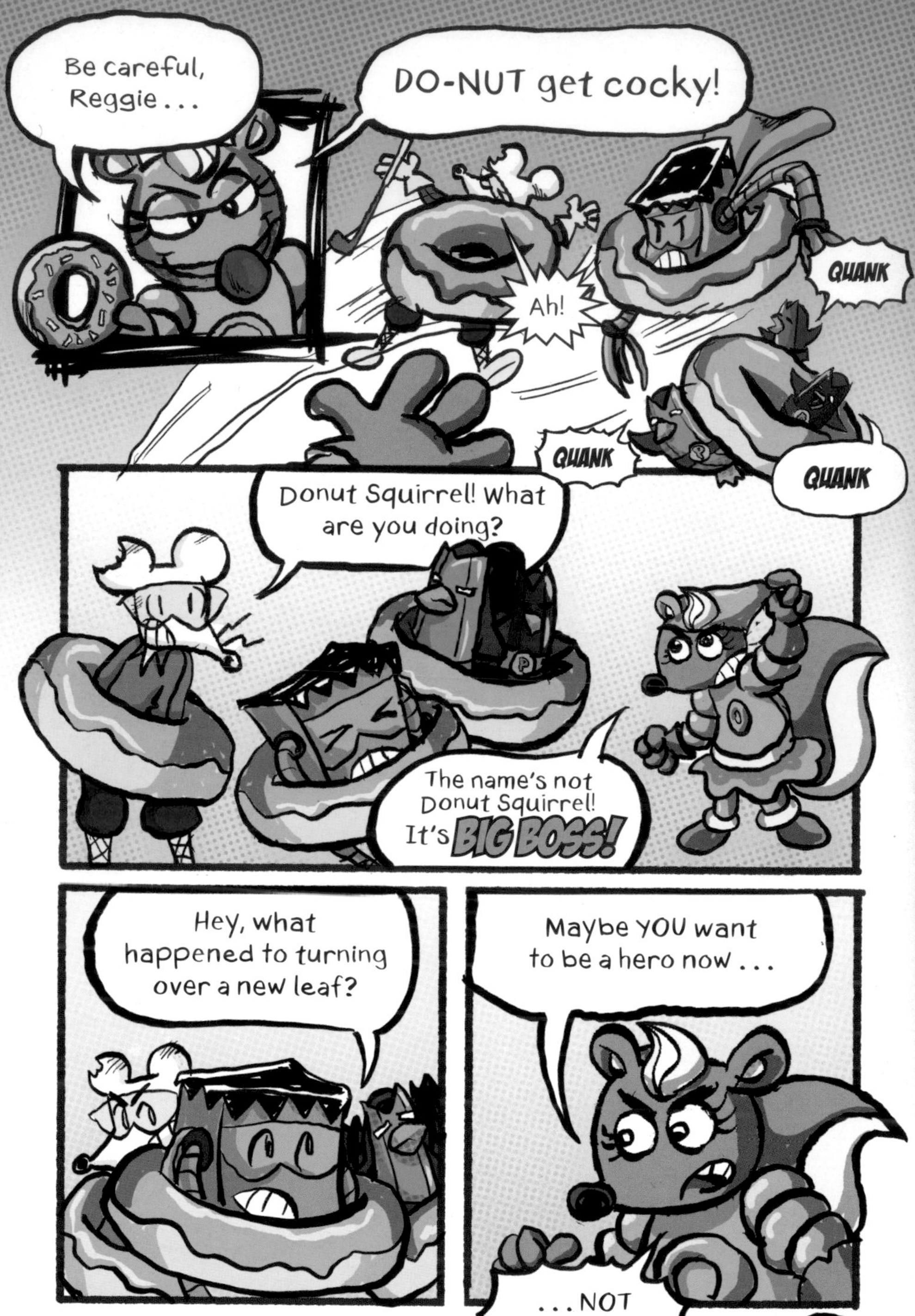
Be careful, Reggie . . .
DO-NUT get cocky!
Ah!
QUANK
QUANK
QUANK
Donut Squirrel! What are you doing?
The name's not Donut Squirrel! It's BIG BOSS!
Hey, what happened to turning over a new leaf?
Maybe YOU want to be a hero now . . .
. . . NOT me!

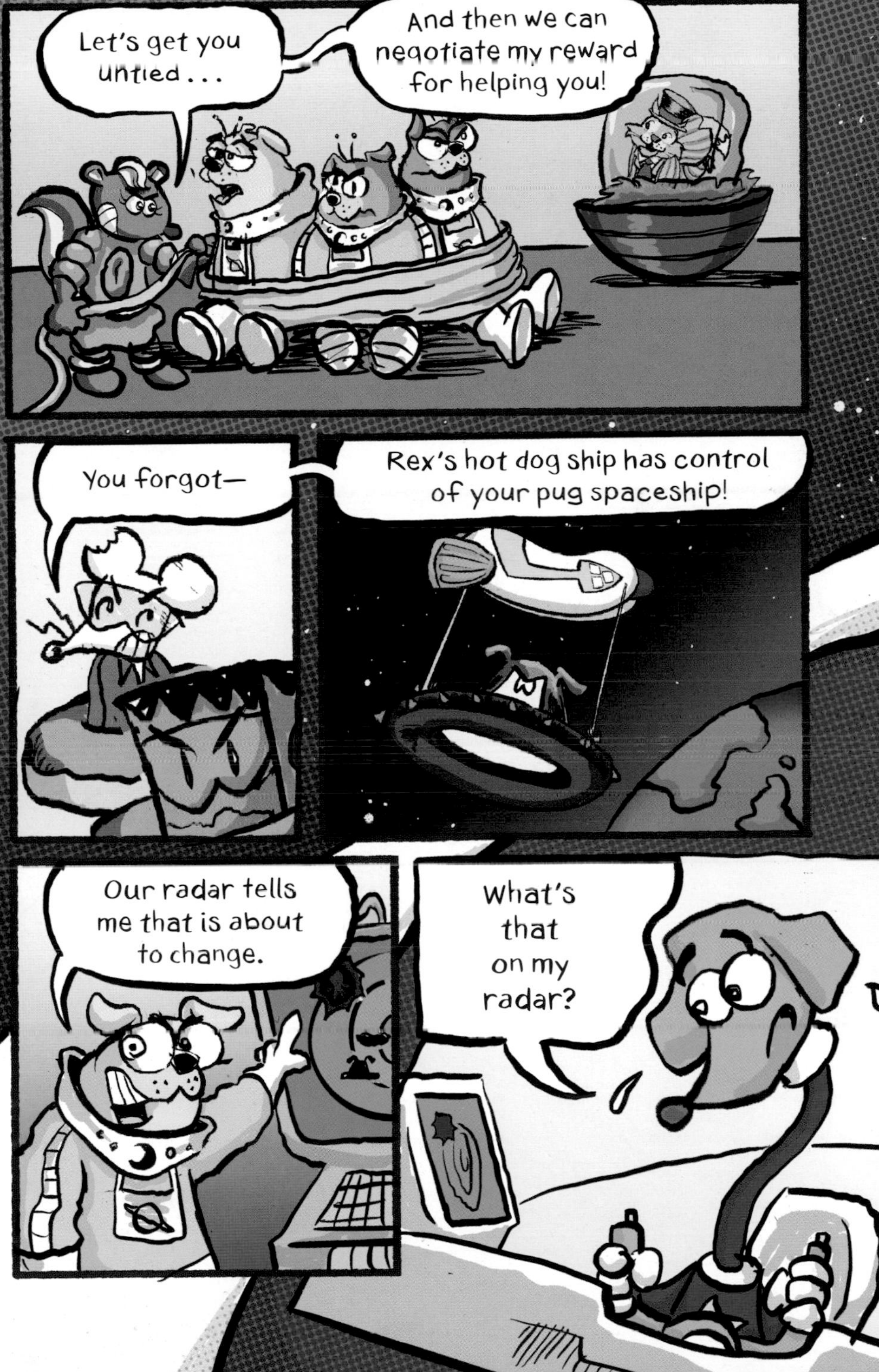
Let's get you untied . . .
And then we can negotiate my reward for helping you!
You forgot—
Rex's hot dog ship has control of your pug spaceship!
Our radar tells me that is about to change.
What's that on my radar?

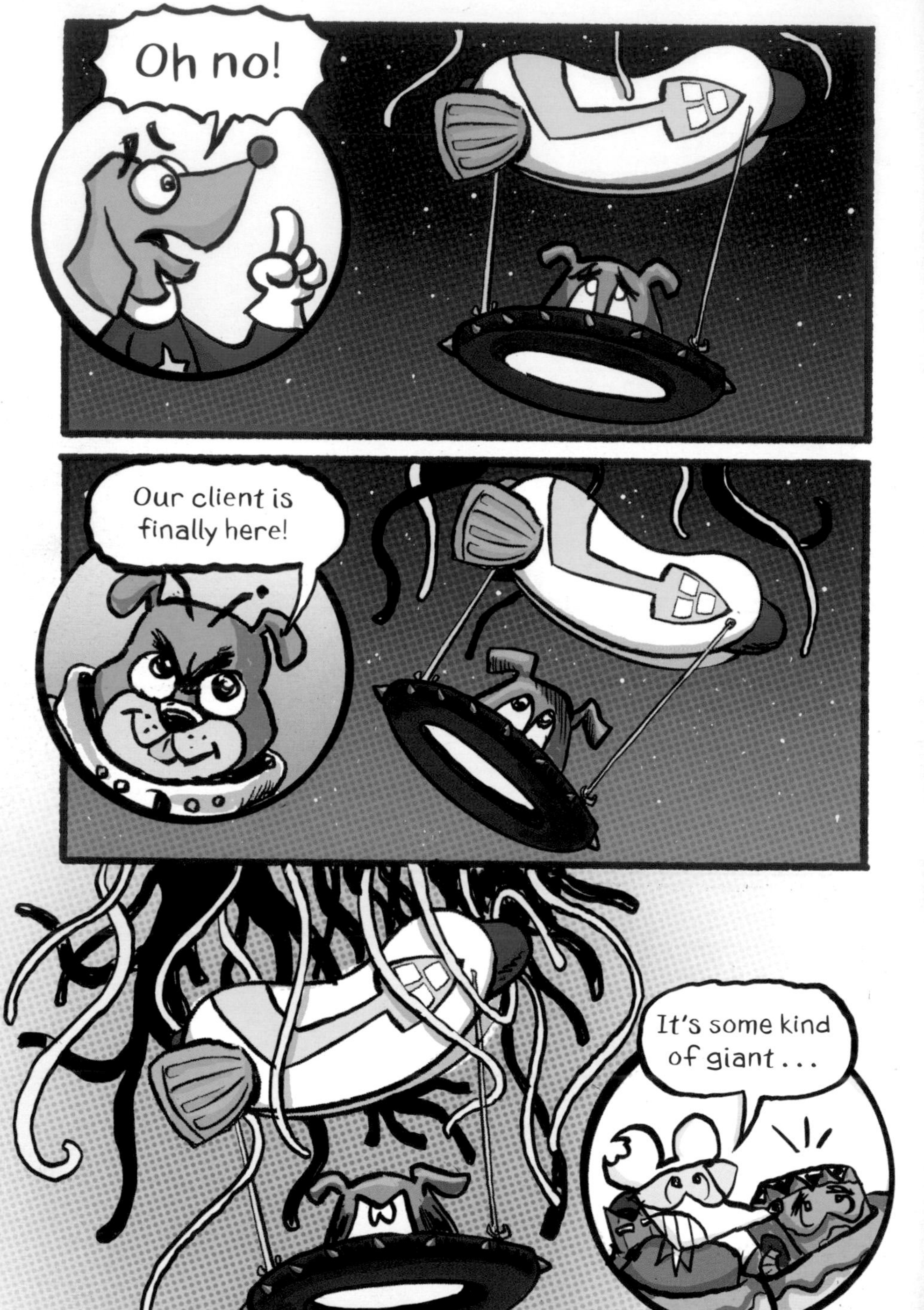
Oh no!
Our client is finally here!
It's some kind of giant . . .

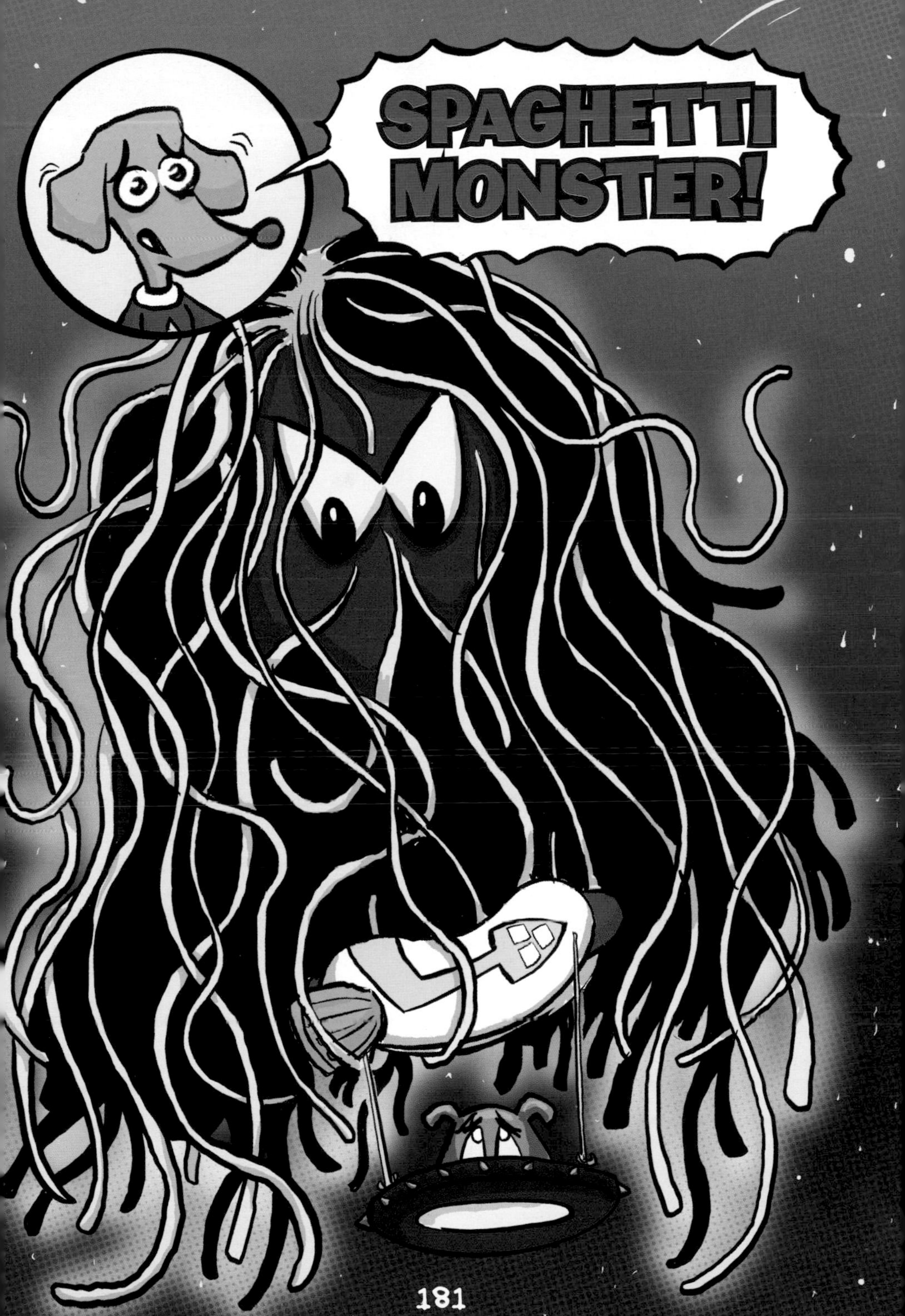
SPAGHETTI MONSTER!

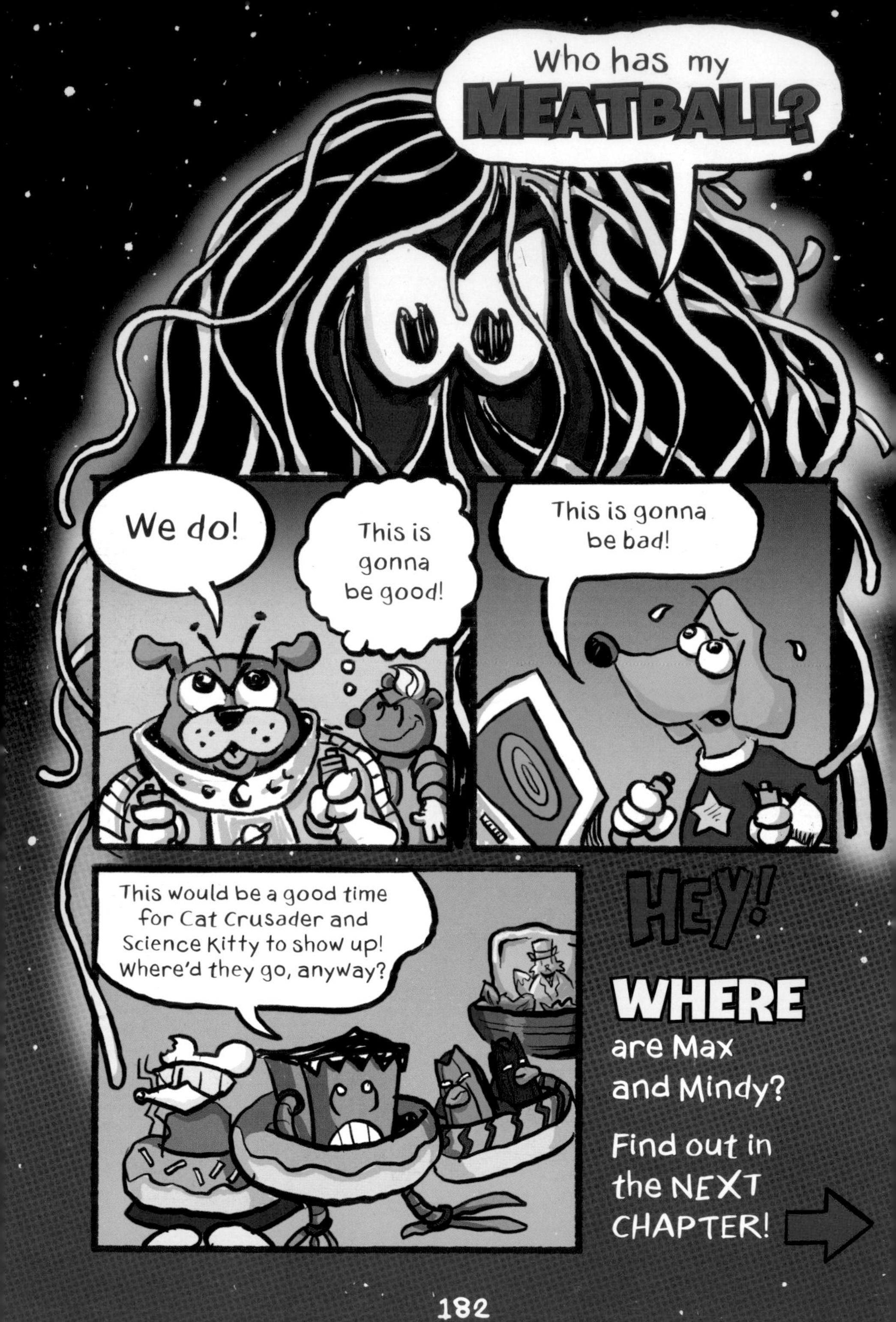
Who has my MEATBALL?
We do!
This is gonna be good!
This is gonna be bad!
This would be a good time for Cat Crusader and Science Kitty to show up! Where'd they go, anyway?
HEY!
WHERE are Max and Mindy?
Find out in the NEXT CHAPTER!

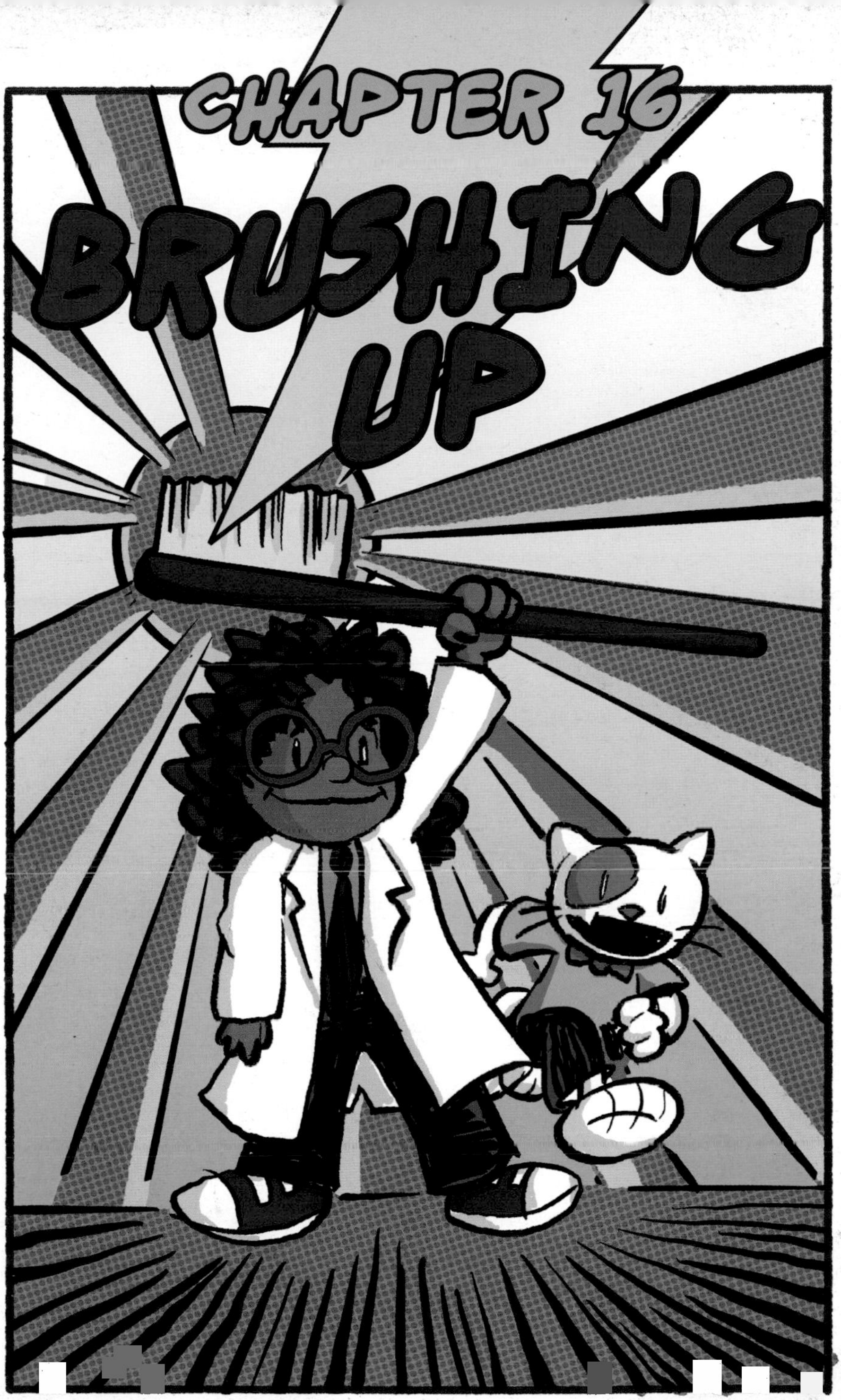
CHAPTER 16
BRUSHING UP

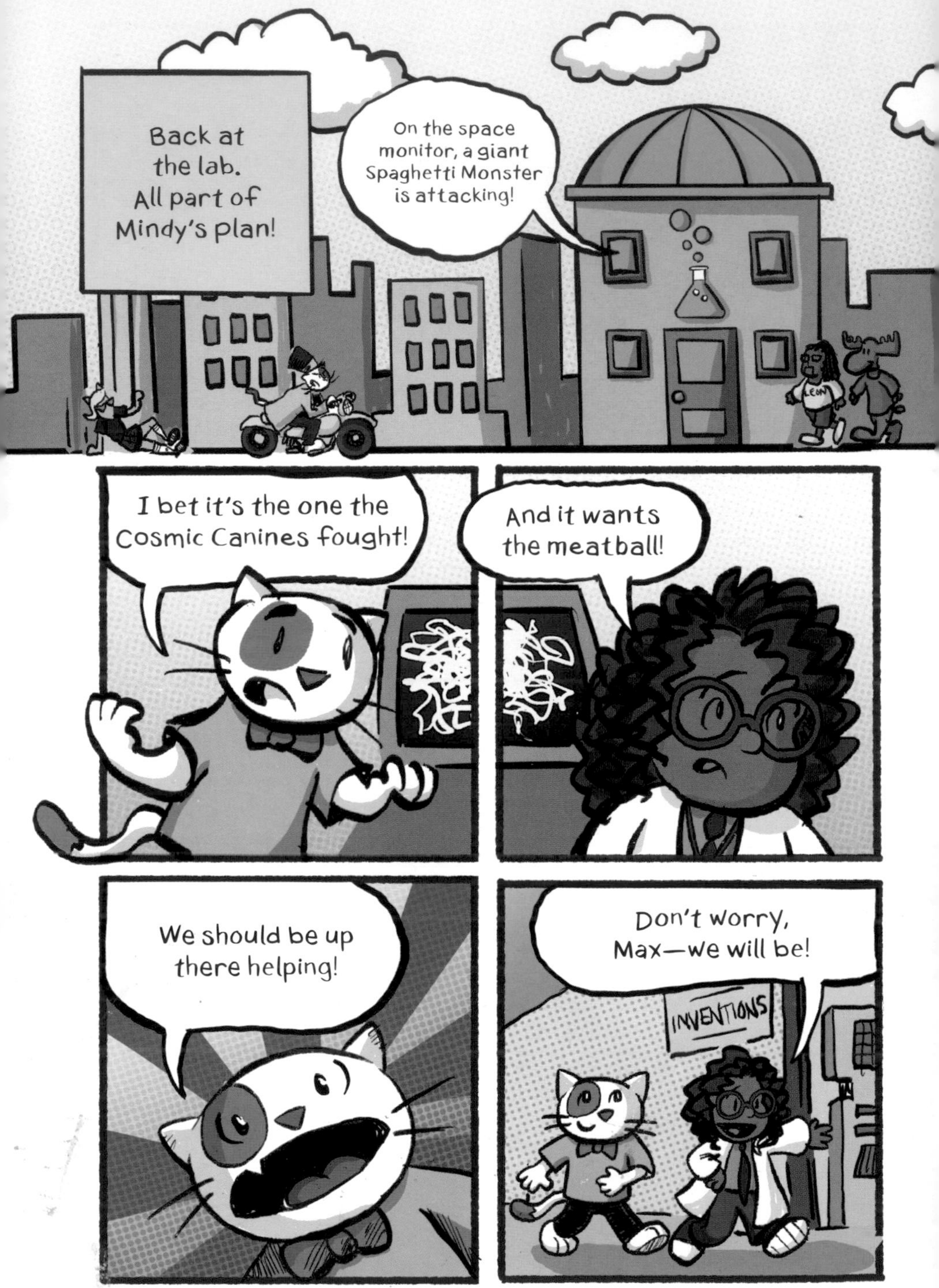
Back at
the lab.
All part of
Mindy's plan!
On the space
monitor, a giant
Spaghetti Monster
is attacking!
LEON
I bet it's the one the
Cosmic Canines fought!
And it wants
the meatball!
We should be up
there helping!
Don't worry,
Max—we will be!
INVENTIONS

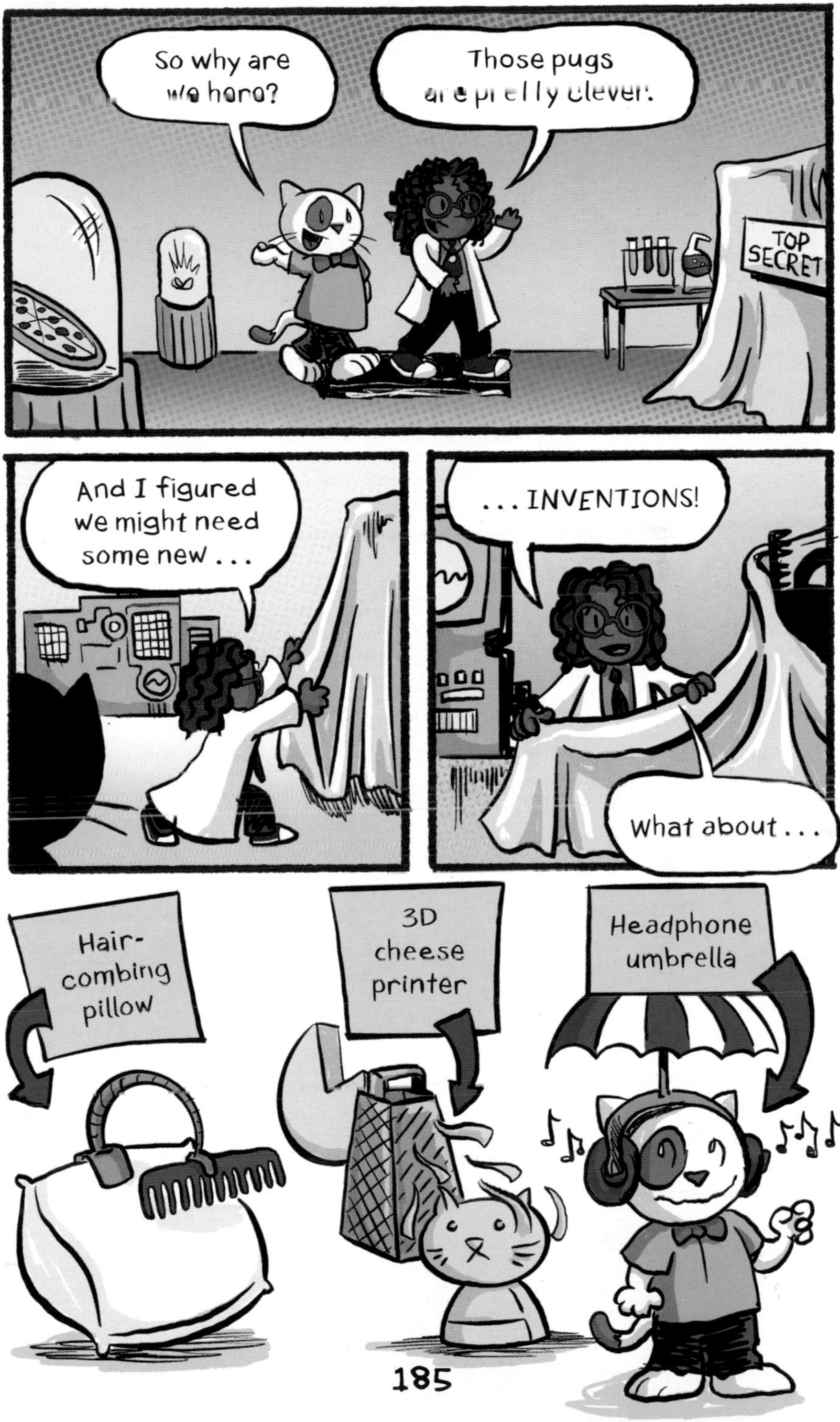
So why are we here?
Those pugs are pretty clever.
TOP SECRET
And I figured we might need some new . . .
. . . INVENTIONS!
What about . . .
Hair-combing pillow
3D cheese printer
Headphone umbrella

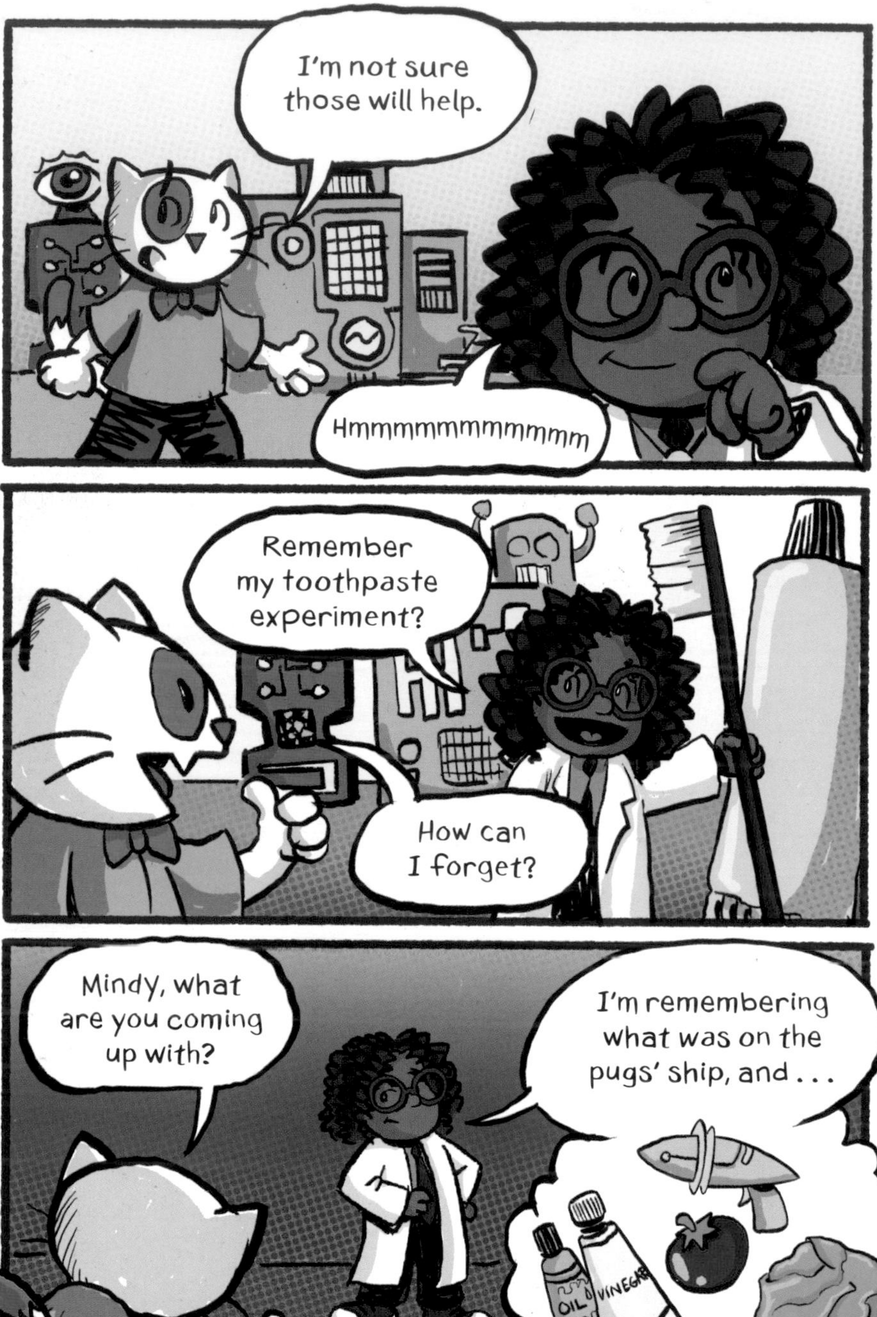
I'm not sure those will help.
Hmmmmmmmmmmm
Remember my toothpaste experiment?
How can I forget?
Mindy, what are you coming up with?
I'm remembering what was on the pugs' ship, and . . .
OIL
VINEGAR

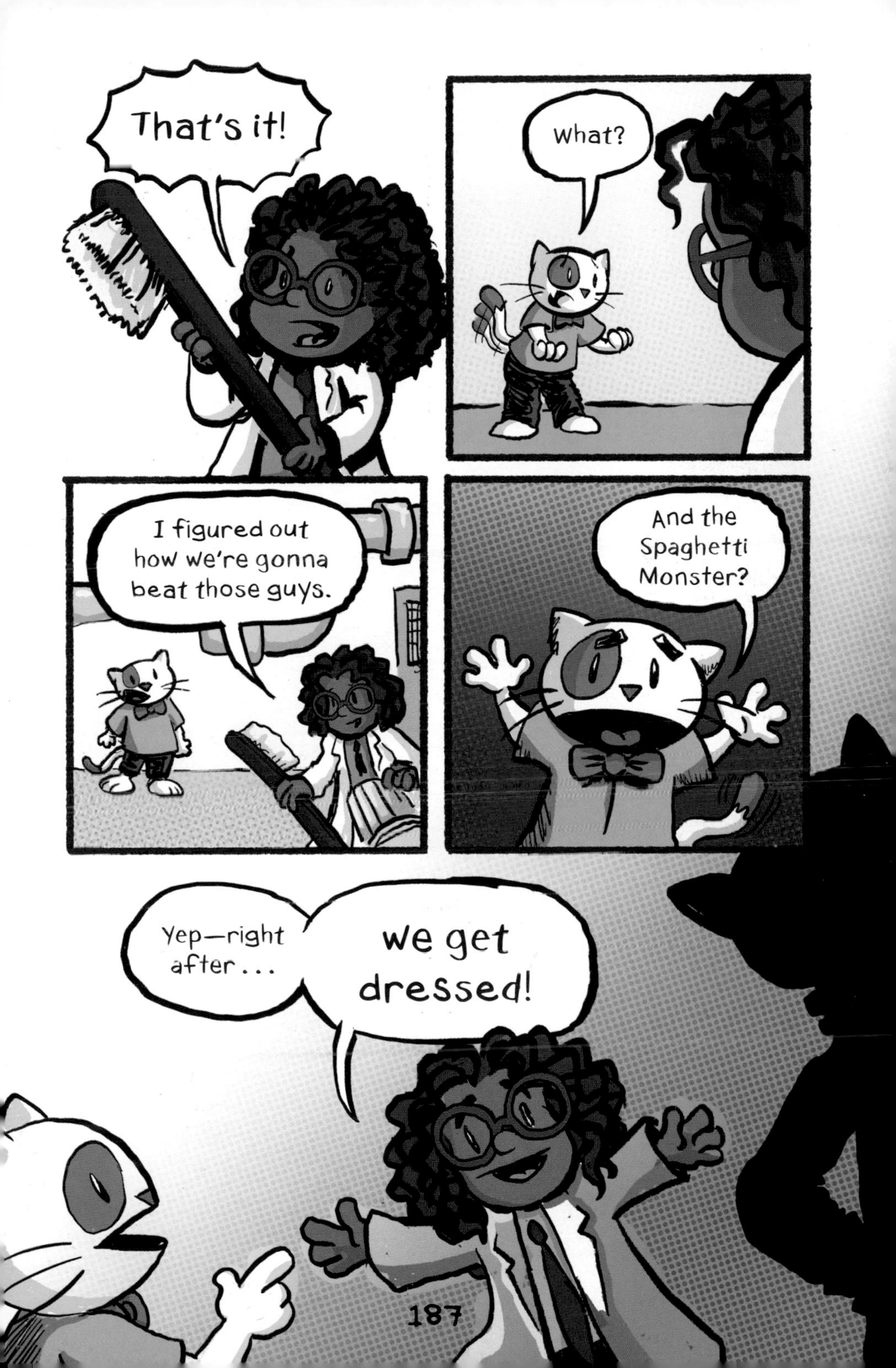
That's it!
What?
I figured out how we're gonna beat those guys.
And the Spaghetti Monster?
Yep—right after . . .
we get dressed!

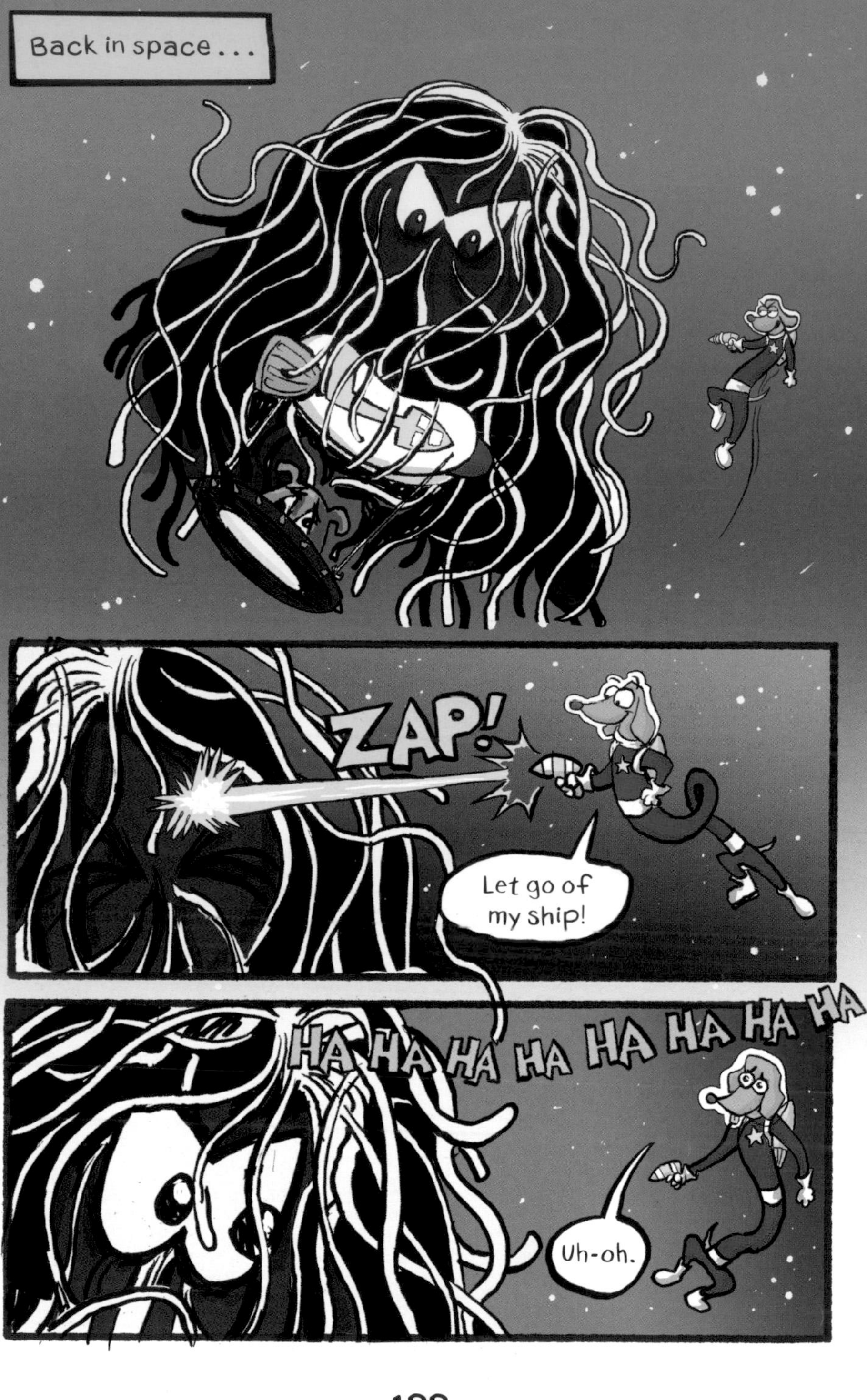
Back in space . . .
ZAP!
Let go of my ship!
HA HA HA HA HA HA HA HA
Uh-oh.

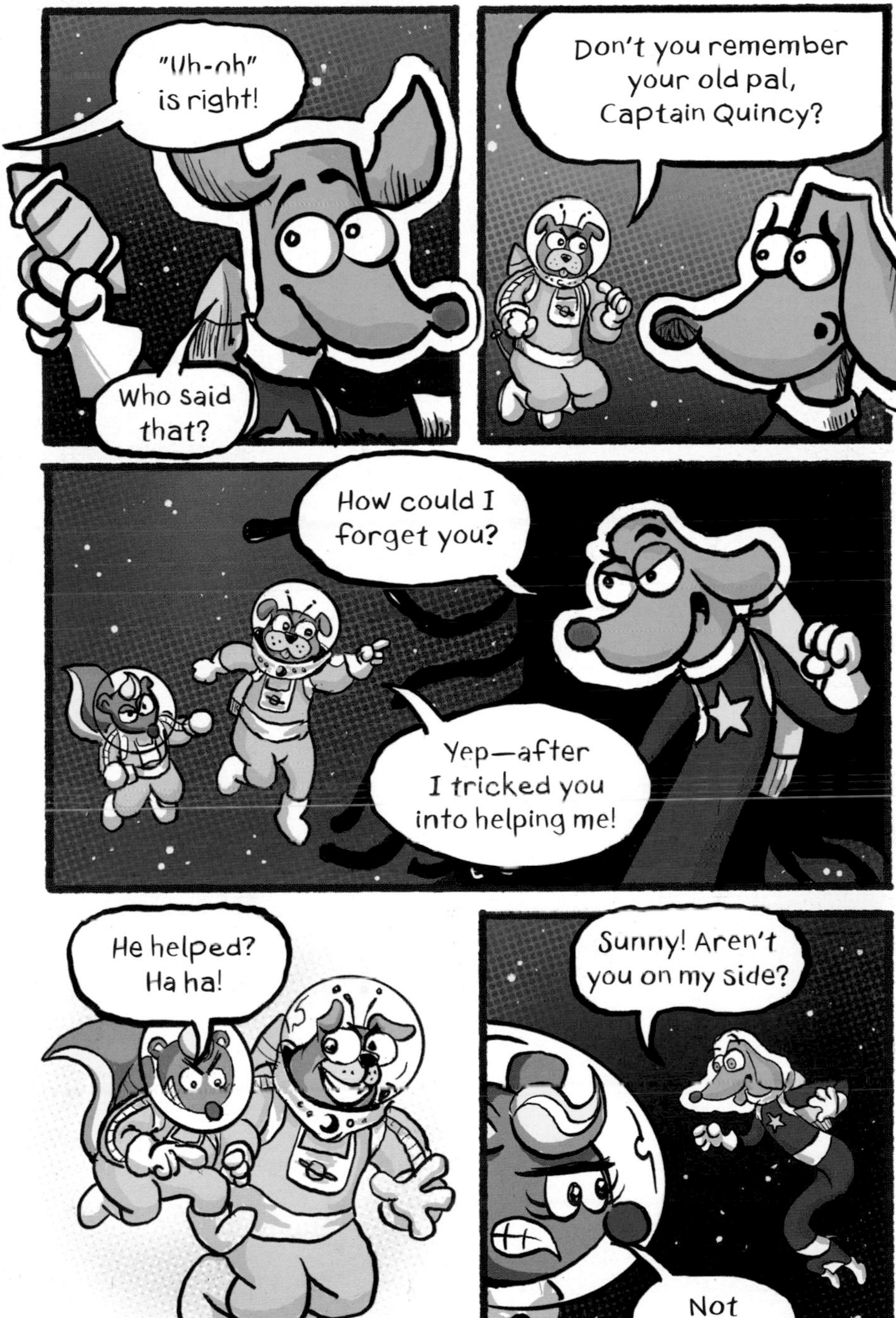
"Uh-oh" is right!
Who said that?
Don't you remember your old pal, Captain Quincy?
How could I forget you?
Yep—after I tricked you into helping me!
He helped? Ha ha!
Sunny! Aren't you on my side?
Not anymore!

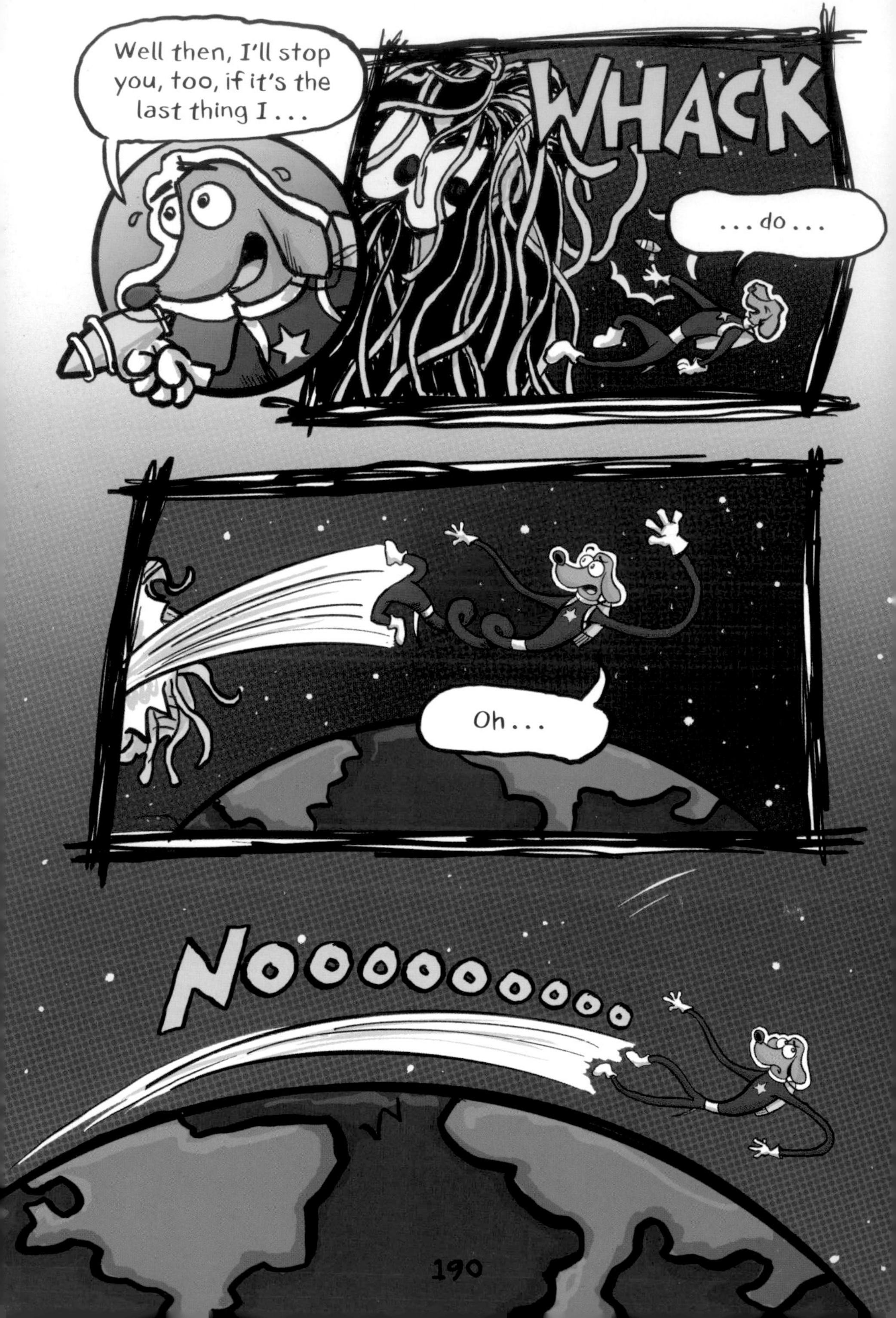

Well then, I'll stop you, too, if it's the last thing I . . .
WHACK
. . . do . . .
Oh . . .
NOOOOOOOOOO

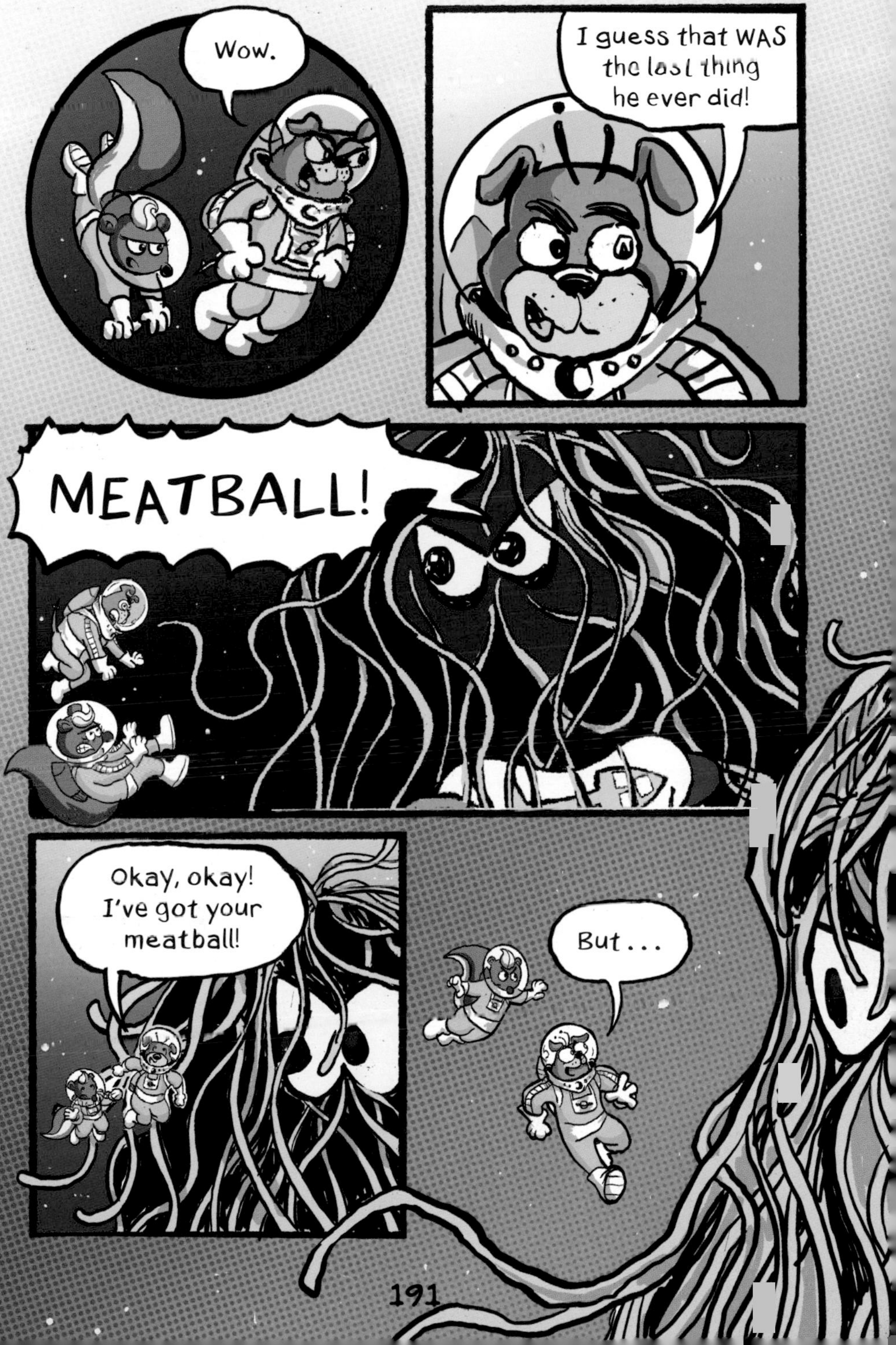
Wow.
I guess that WAS the last thing he ever did!
MEATBALL!
Okay, okay! I've got your meatball!
But . . .

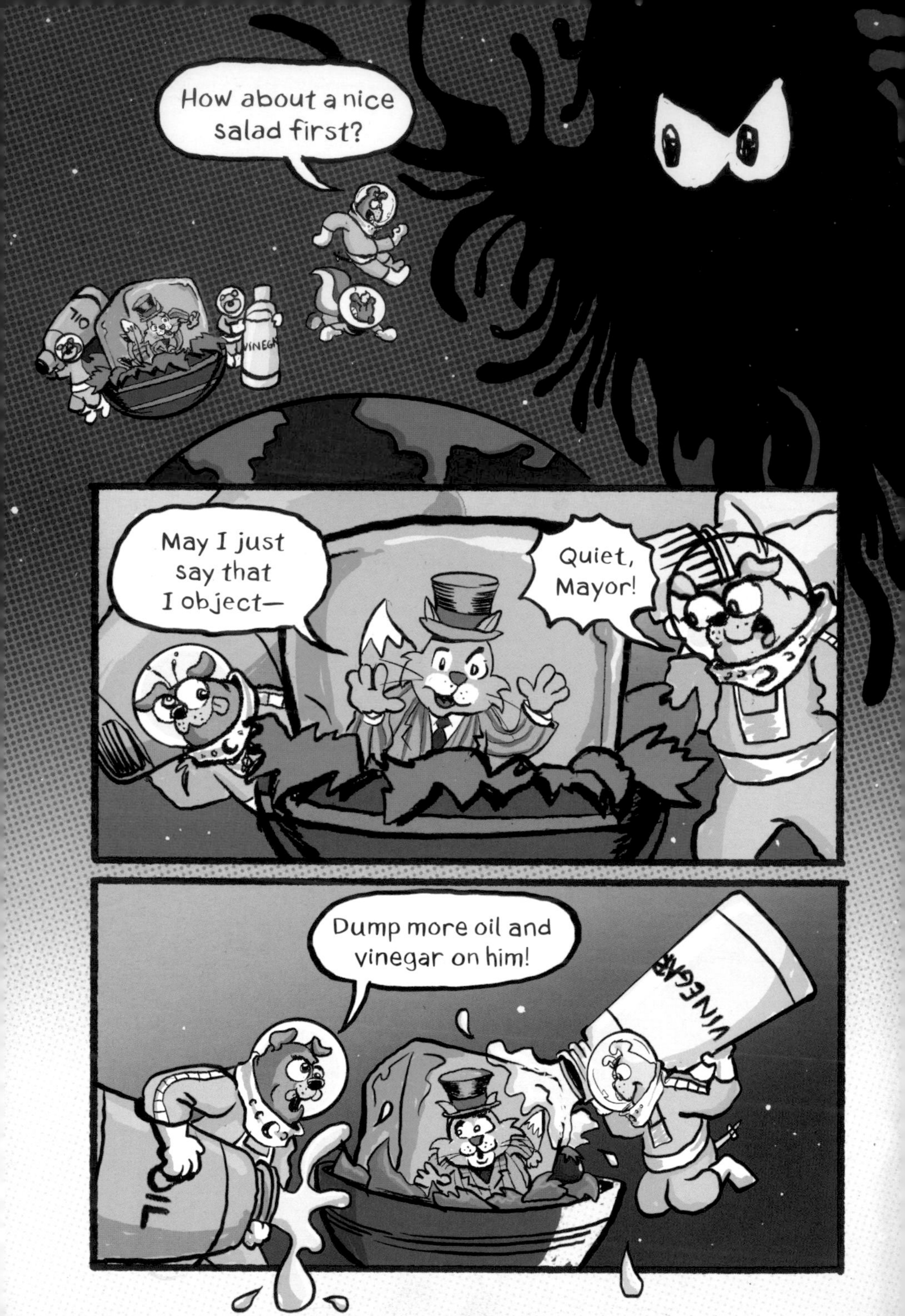
How about a nice salad first?
OIL
VINEGAR
May I just say that I object—
Quiet, Mayor!
Dump more oil and vinegar on him!
VINEGAR
OIL

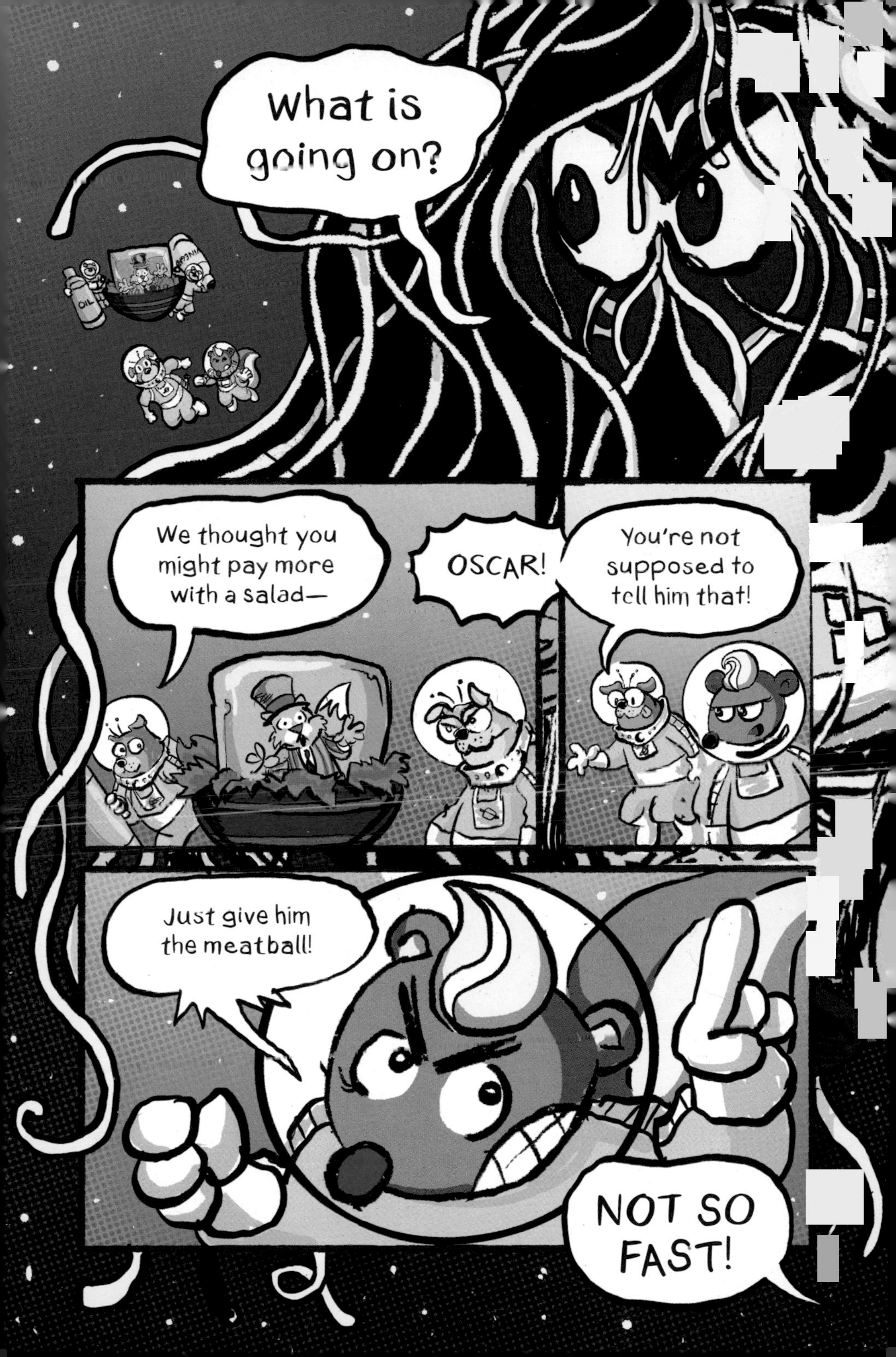
What is going on?
OIL
VINEGAR
We thought you might pay more with a salad—
OSCAR!
You're not supposed to tell him that!
Just give him the meatball!
NOT SO FAST!

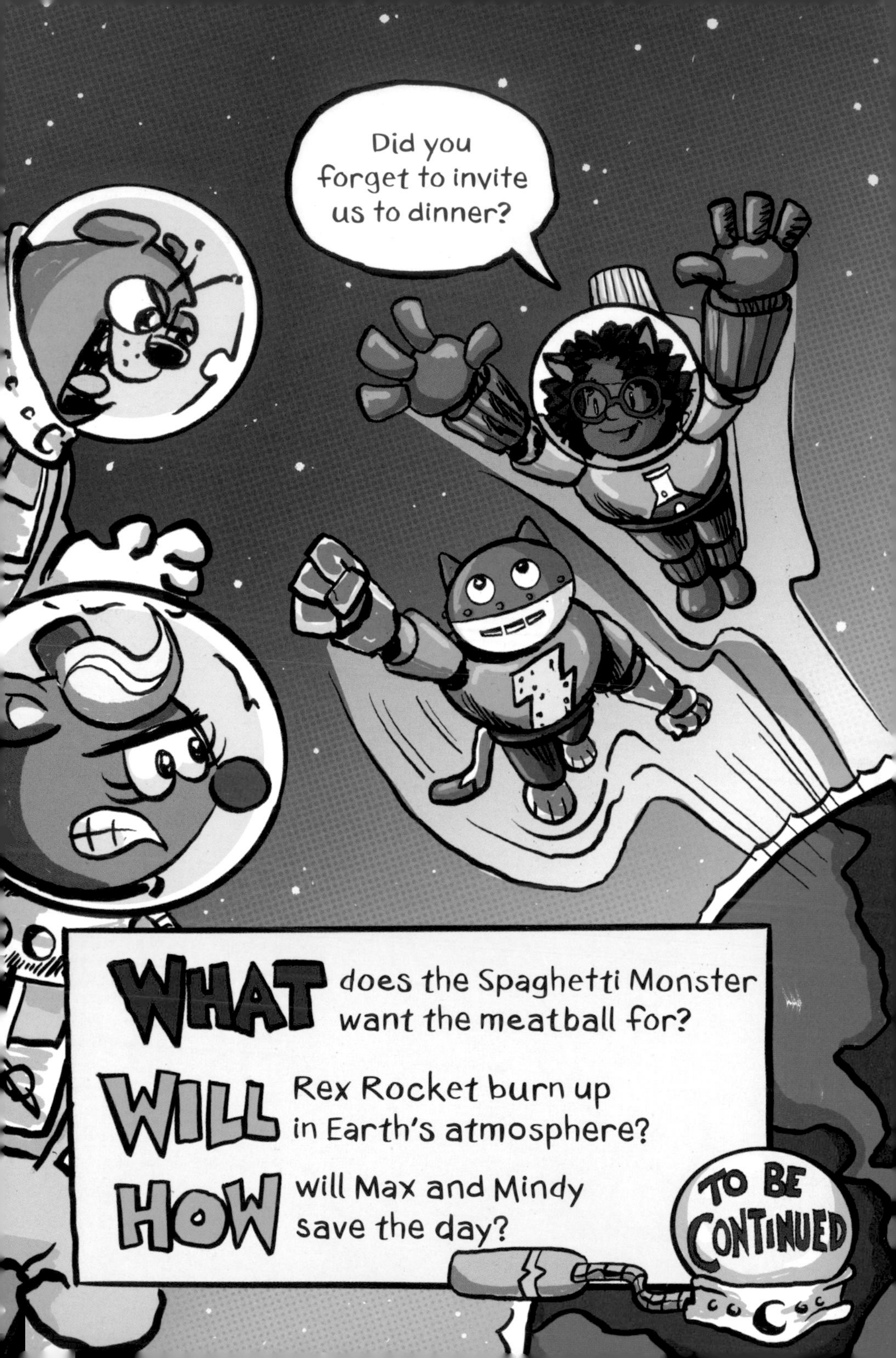
Did you forget to invite us to dinner?
WHAT does the Spaghetti Monster want the meatball for?
WILL Rex Rocket burn up in Earth's atmosphere?
HOW will Max and Mindy save the day?
TO BE CONTINUED

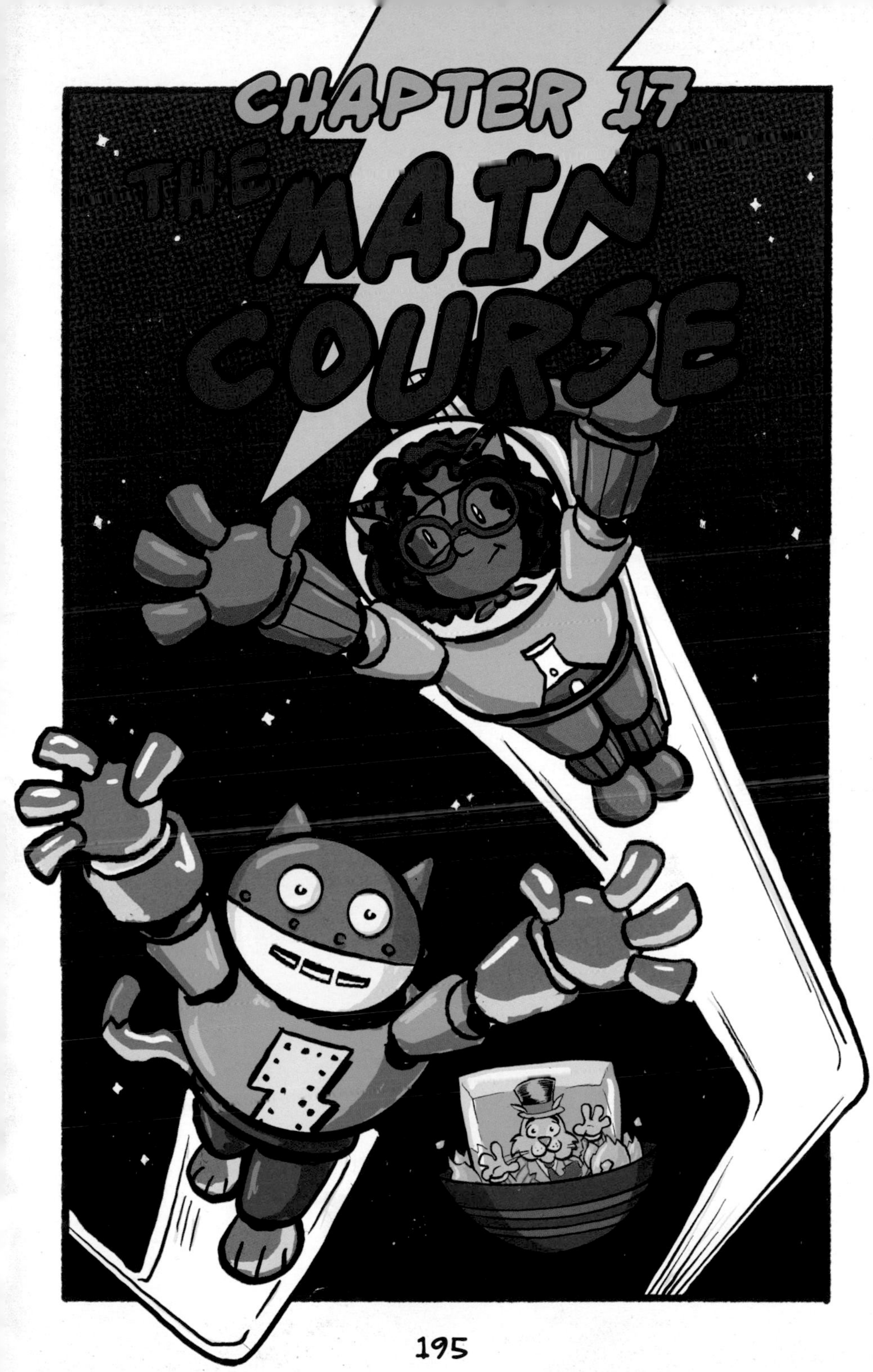
CHAPTER 17
THE MAIN COURSE

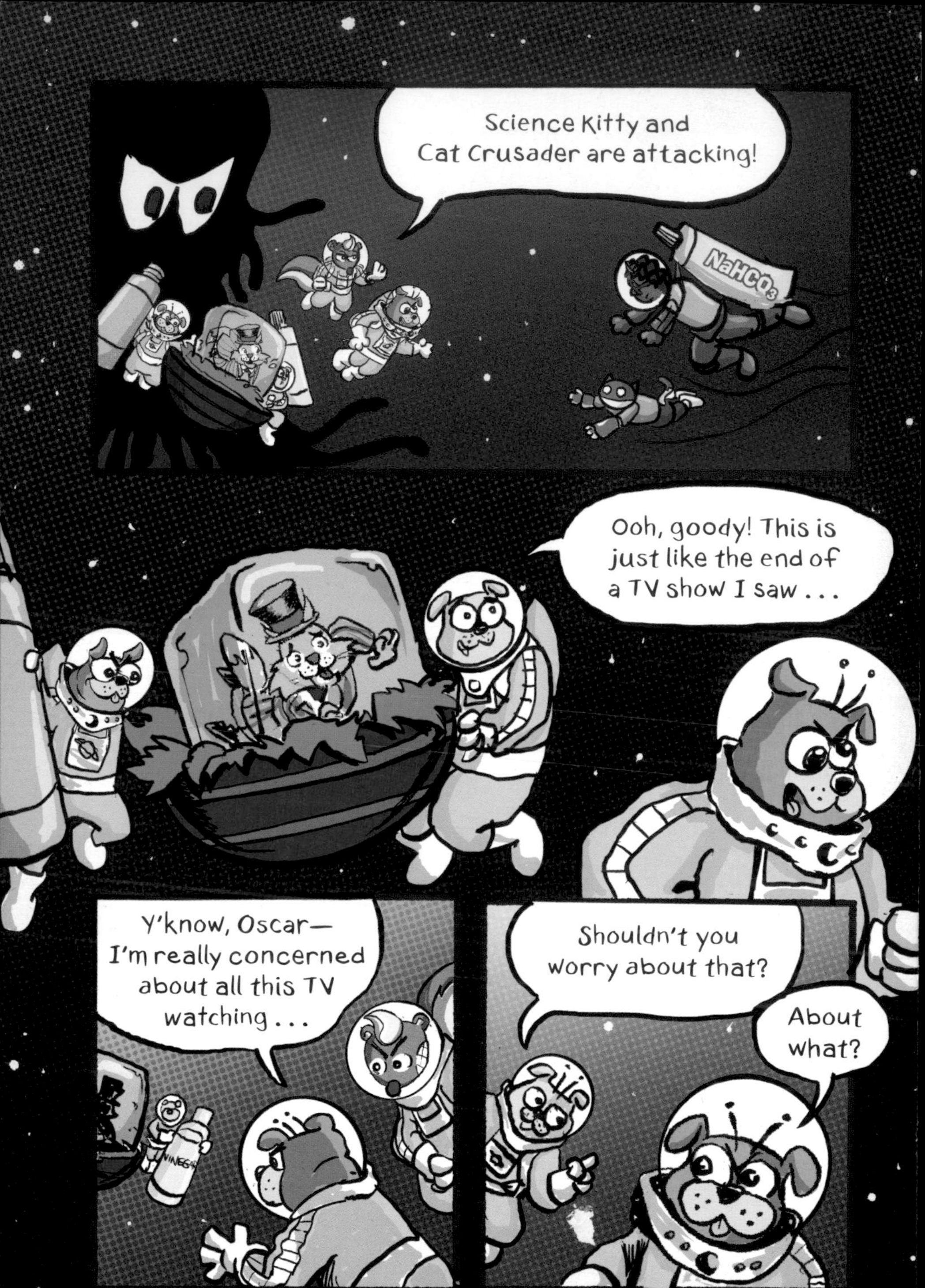

Science Kitty and Cat Crusader are attacking!
NaHCO3
Ooh, goody! This is just like the end of a TV show I saw . . .
Y'know, Oscar— I'm really concerned about all this TV watching . . .
VINEGAR
Shouldn't you worry about that?
About what?

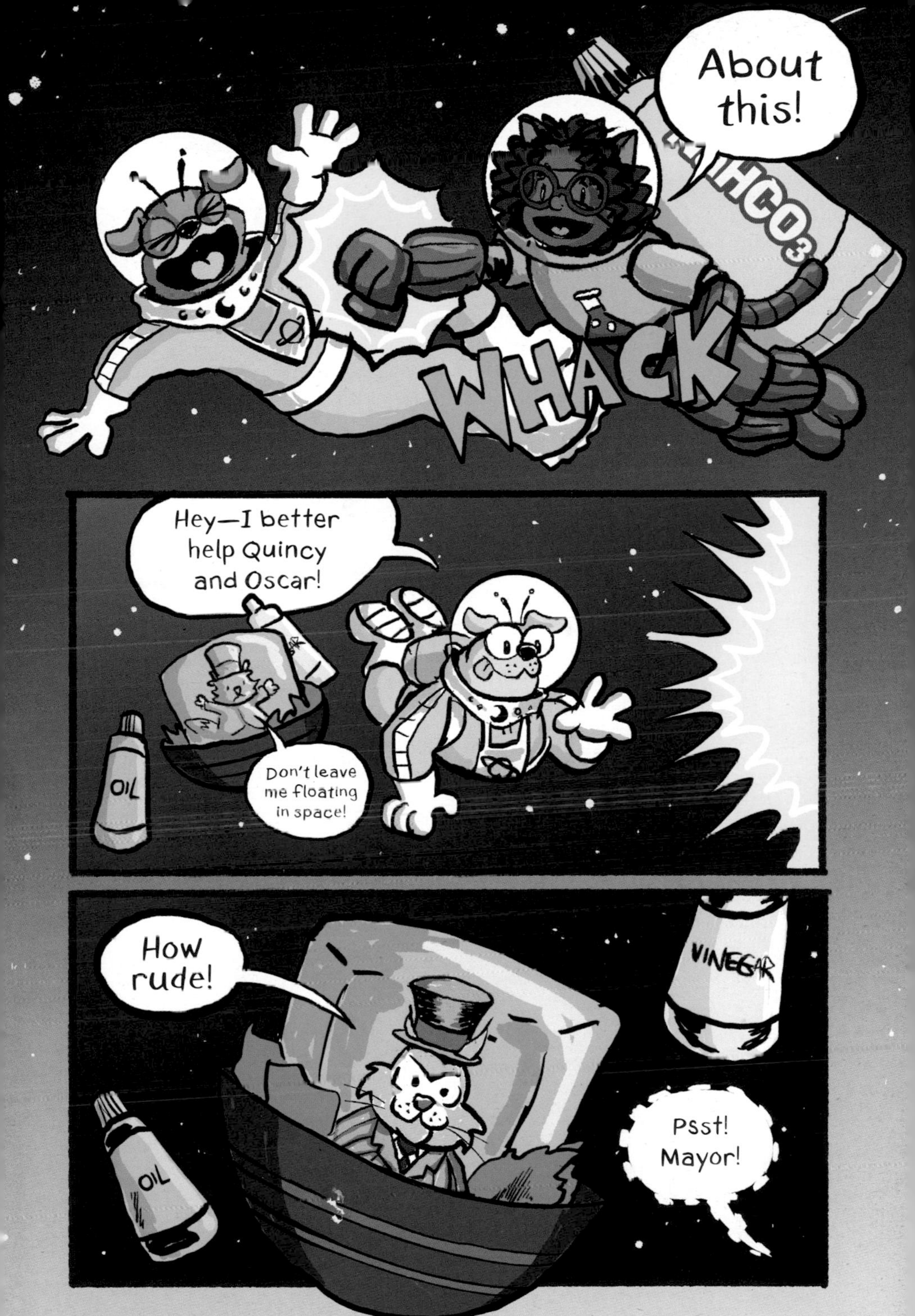
About this!
HCO3
WHACK
Hey—I better help Quincy and Oscar!
Don't leave me floating in space!
OIL
How rude!
VINEGAR
OIL
Psst! Mayor!

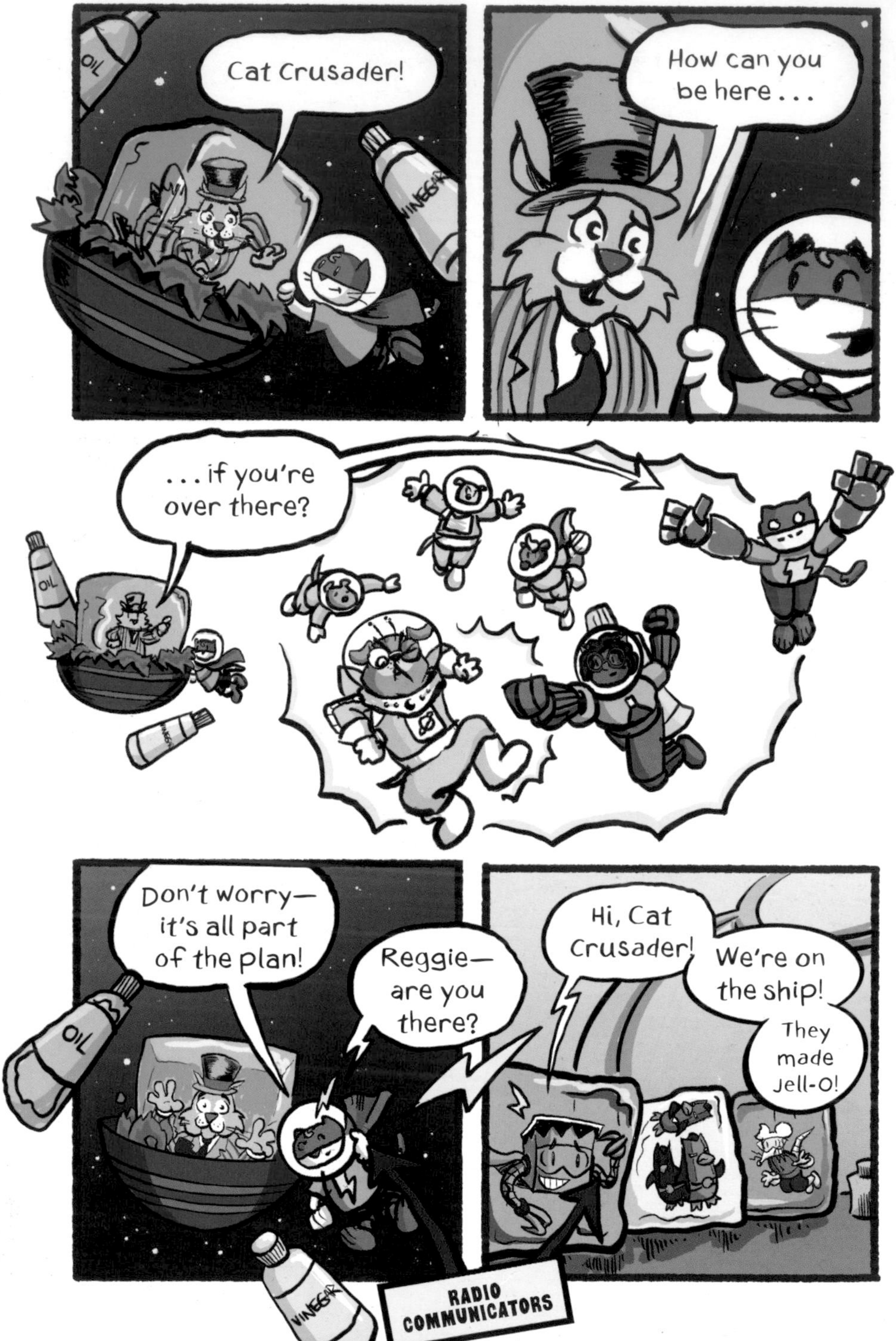
OIL
Cat Crusader!
VINEGAR
How can you be here . . .
. . . if you're over there?
OIL
VINEGAR
Don't worry— it's all part of the plan!
OIL
Reggie— are you there?
Hi, Cat Crusader!
We're on the ship!
They made Jell-O!
VINEGAR
RADIO COMMUNICATORS

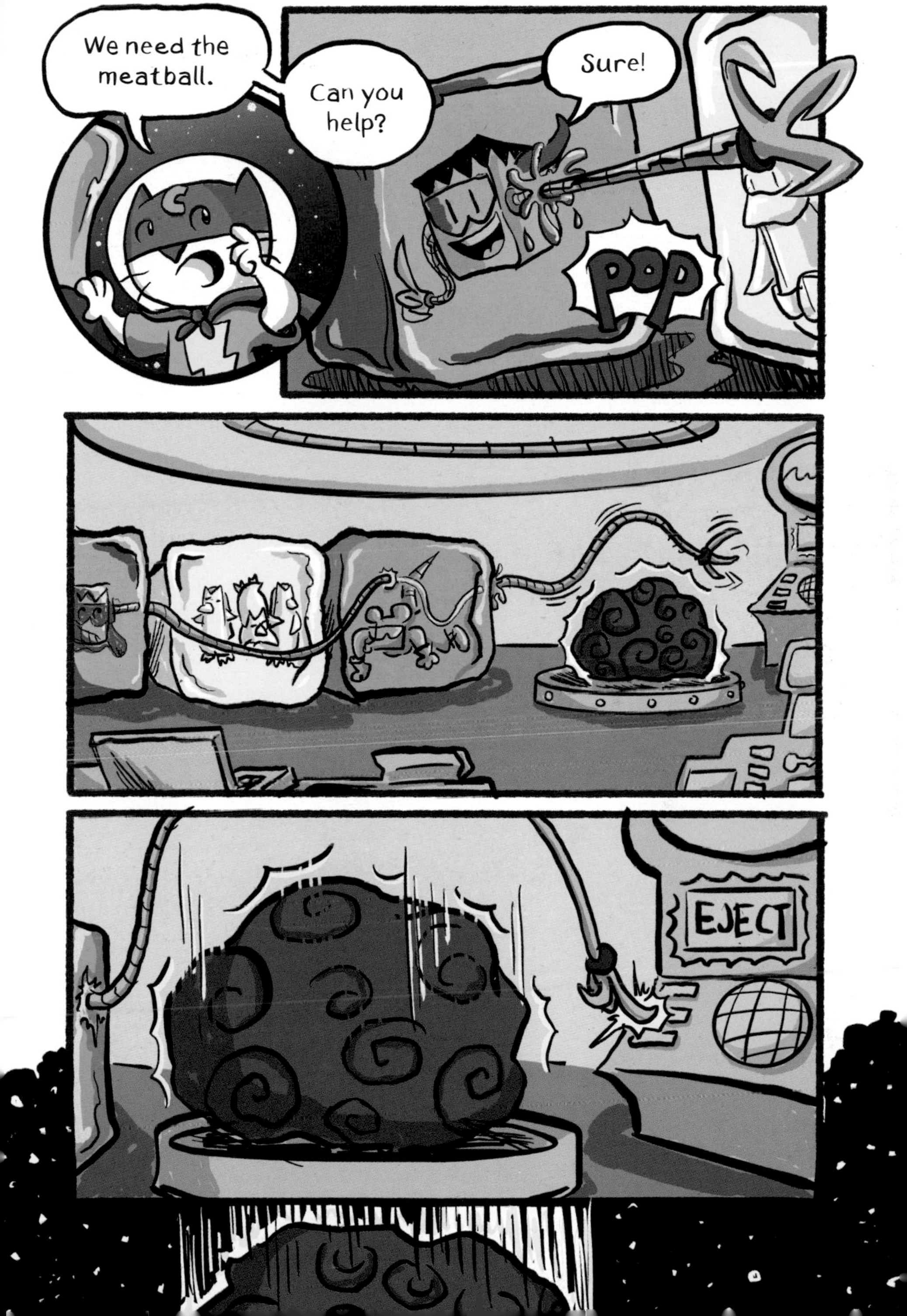
We need the meatball.
Can you help?
Sure!
POP
EJECT

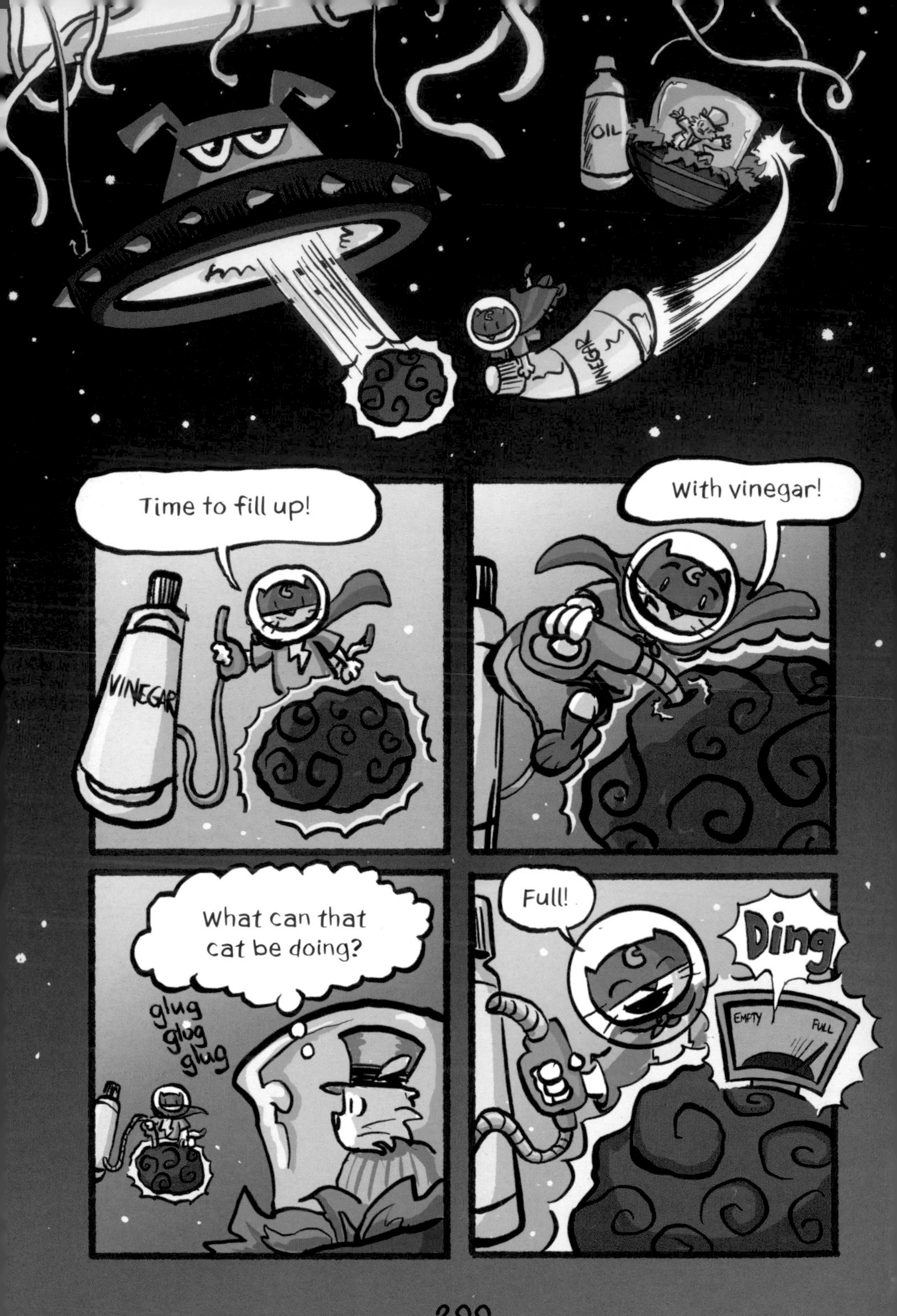
OIL
VINEGAR
Time to fill up!
With vinegar!
VINEGAR
What can that cat be doing?
glug
glug
glug
Full!
Ding
EMPTY
FULL

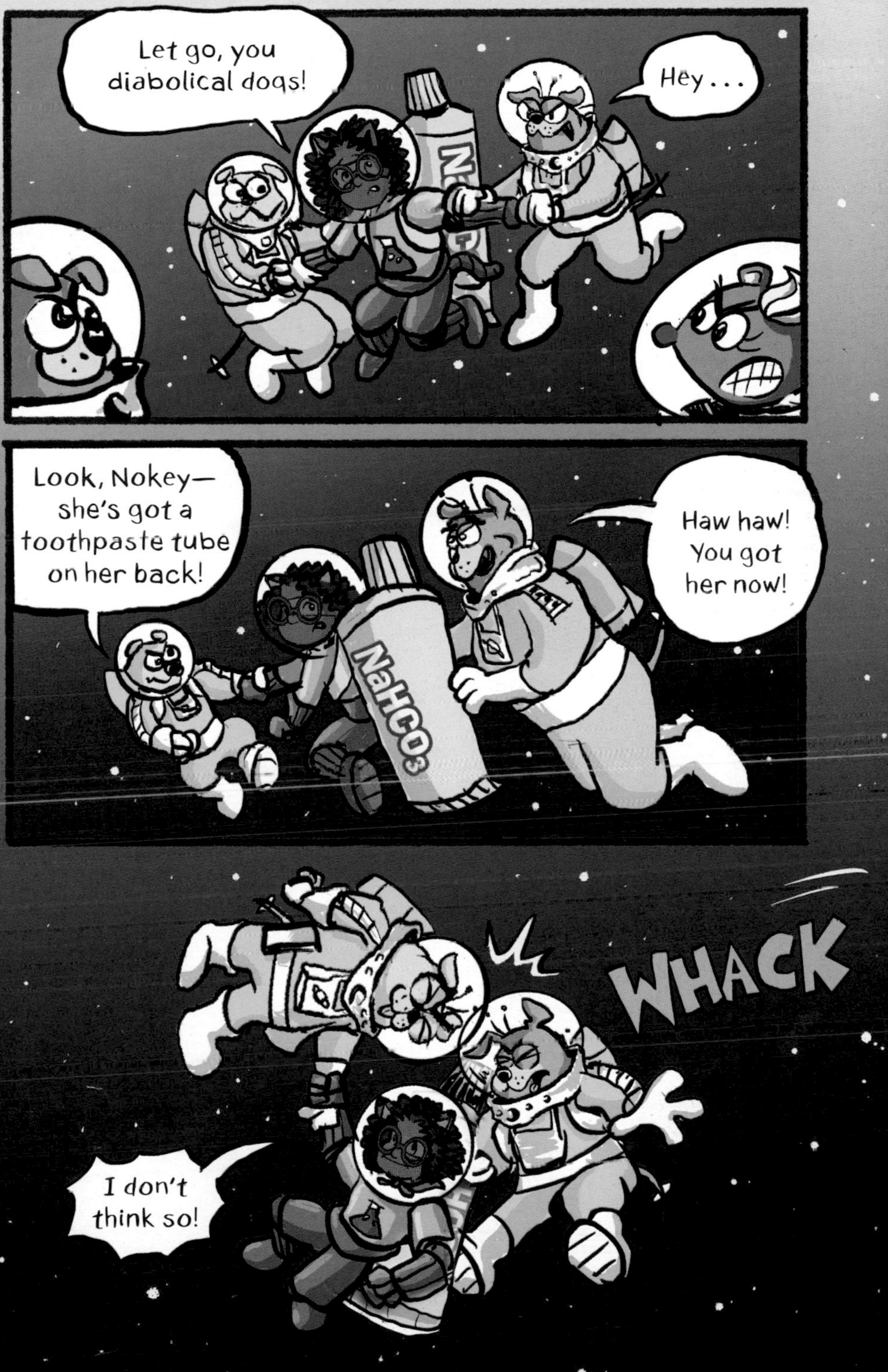

Let go, you diabolical dogs!
Hey . . .
NaHCO3
Look, Nokey—she's got a toothpaste tube on her back!
Haw haw! You got her now!
NaHCO3
WHACK
I don't think so!

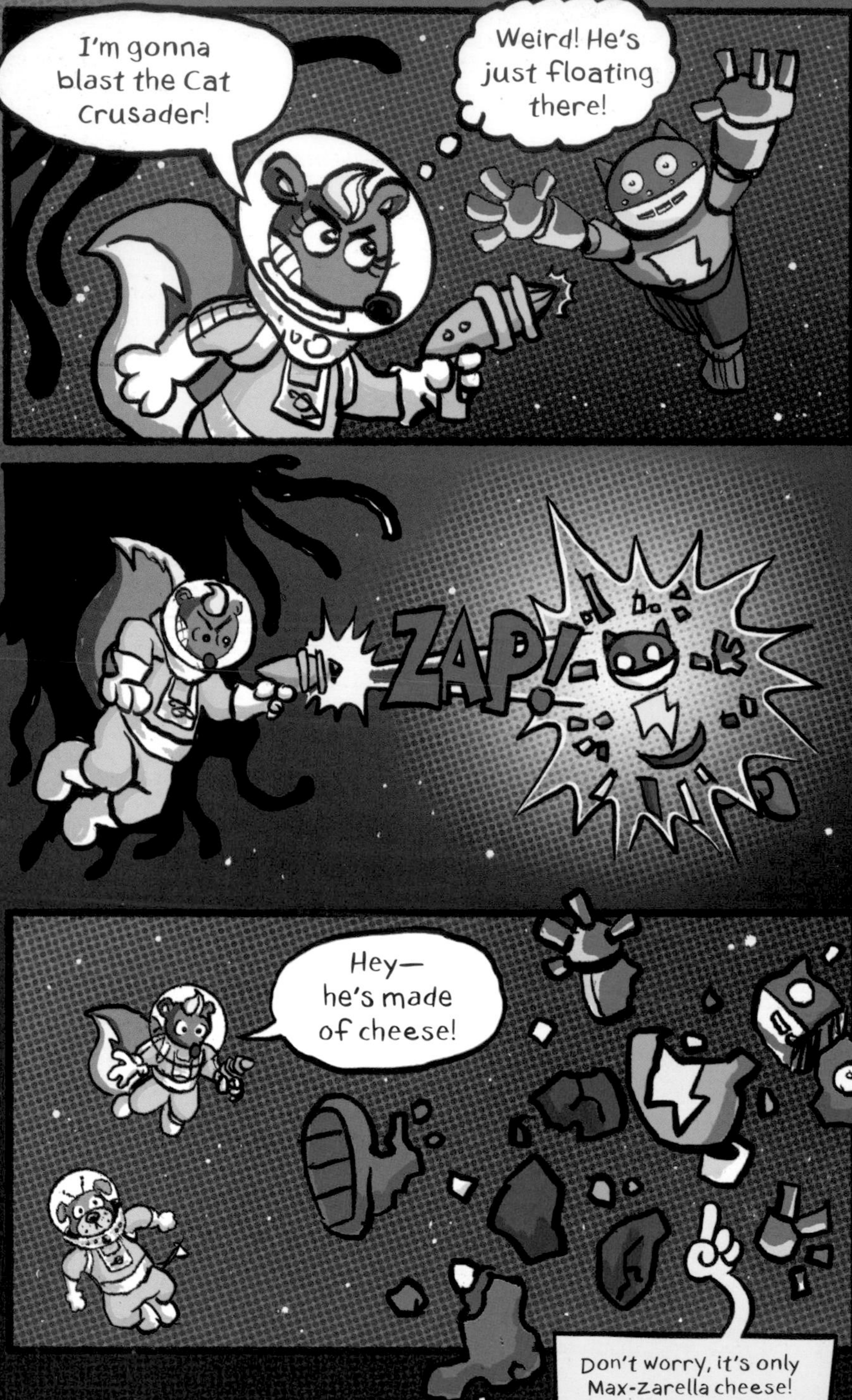
I'm gonna blast the Cat Crusader!
Weird! He's just floating there!
ZAP!
Hey— he's made of cheese!
Don't worry, it's only Max-Zarella cheese!

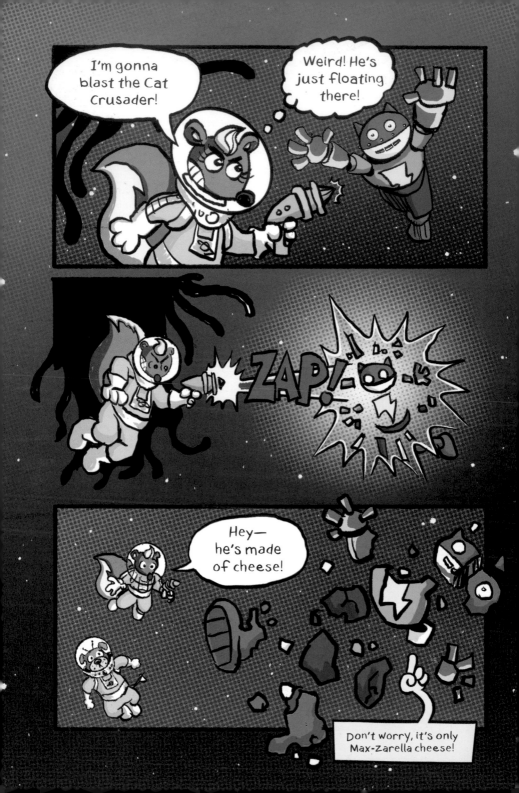

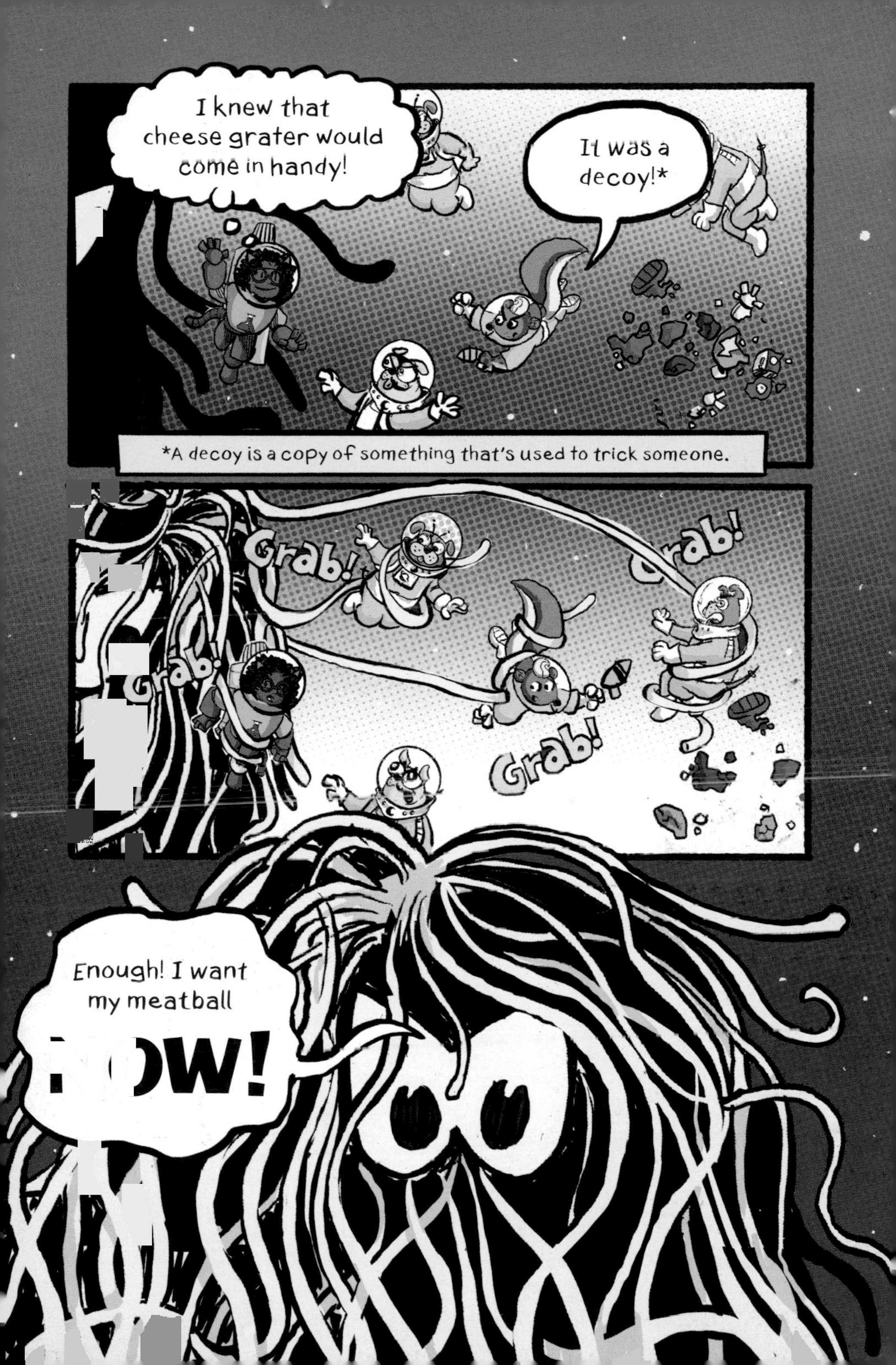
I knew that cheese grater would come in handy!
It was a decoy!*
*A decoy is a copy of something that's used to trick someone.
Grab!
Grab!
Grab!
Grab!
Enough! I want my meatball
NOW!

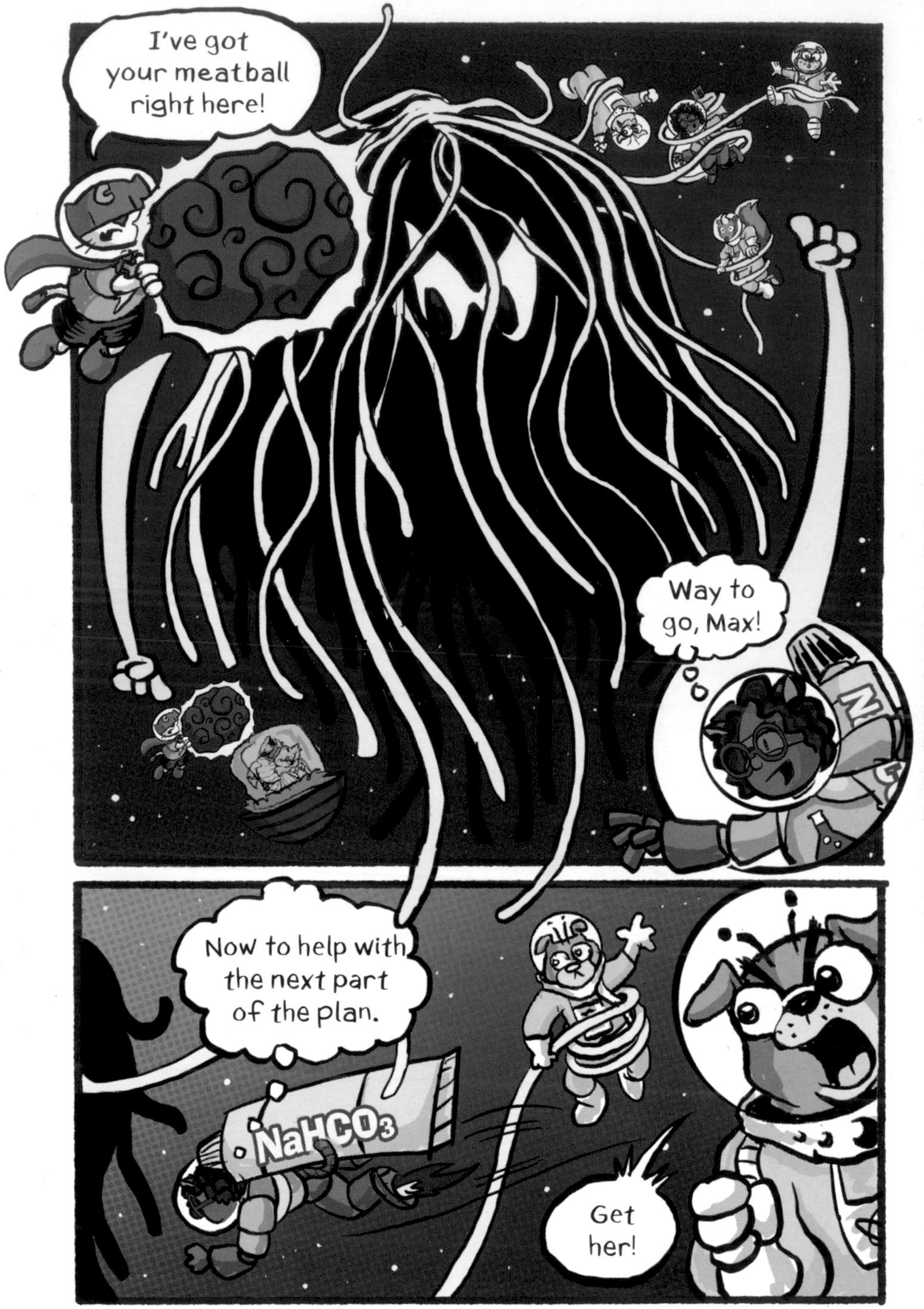
I've got your meatball right here!
Way to go, Max!
Now to help with the next part of the plan.
NaHCO3
Get her!

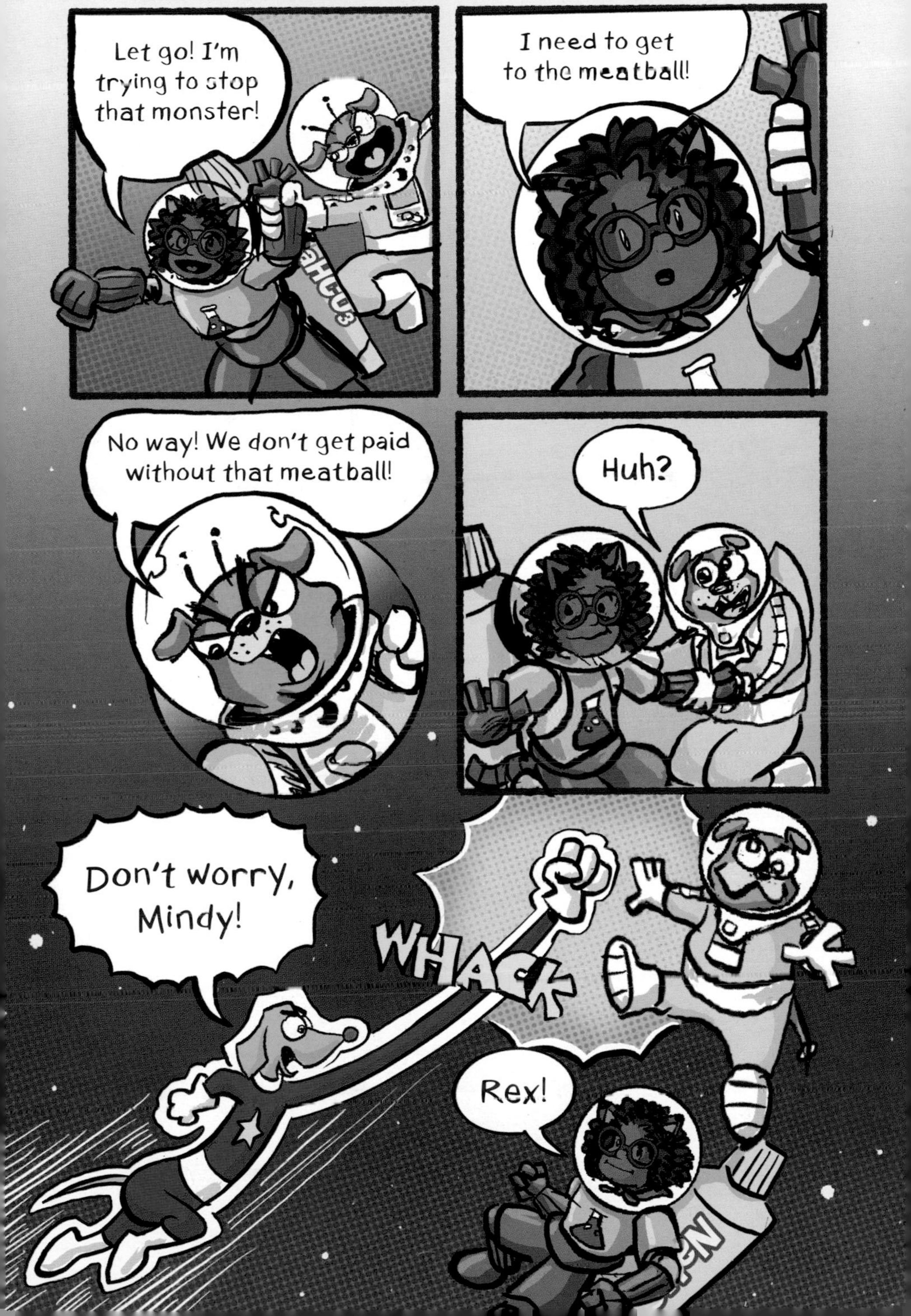
Let go! I'm trying to stop that monster!
I need to get to the meatball!
No way! We don't get paid without that meatball!
Huh?
Don't worry, Mindy!
WHACK
Rex!

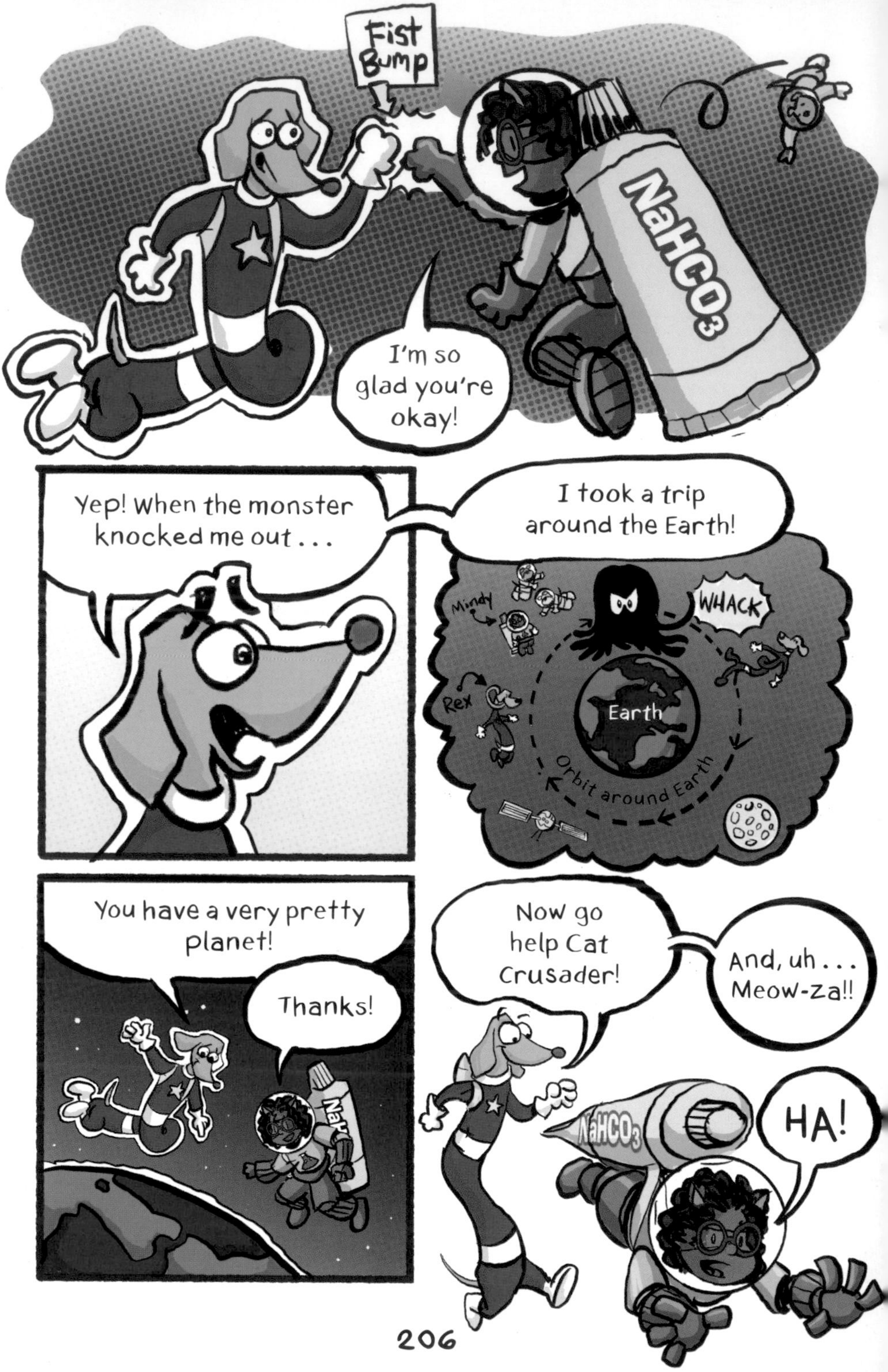
Fist Bump
NaHCO3
I'm so glad you're okay!
Yep! When the monster knocked me out . . .
I took a trip around the Earth!
Mindy
WHACK
Rex
Earth
Orbit around Earth
You have a very pretty planet!
Thanks!
NaH
Now go help Cat Crusader!
And, uh . . . Meow-za!!
NaHCO3
HA!

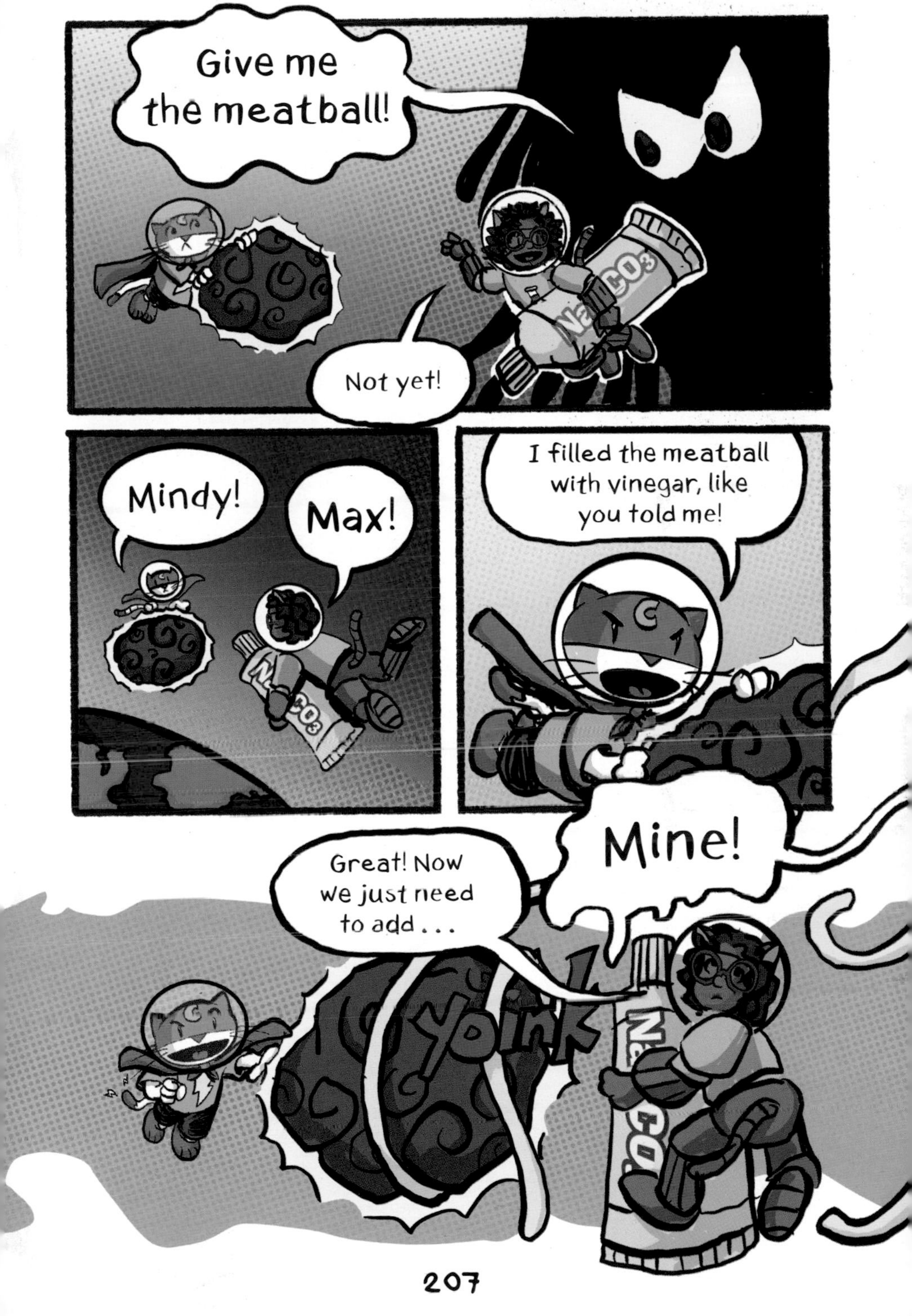

Give me the meatball!
Not yet!
Mindy!
Max!
I filled the meatball with vinegar, like you told me!
Great! Now we just need to add . . .
Mine!
Yoink

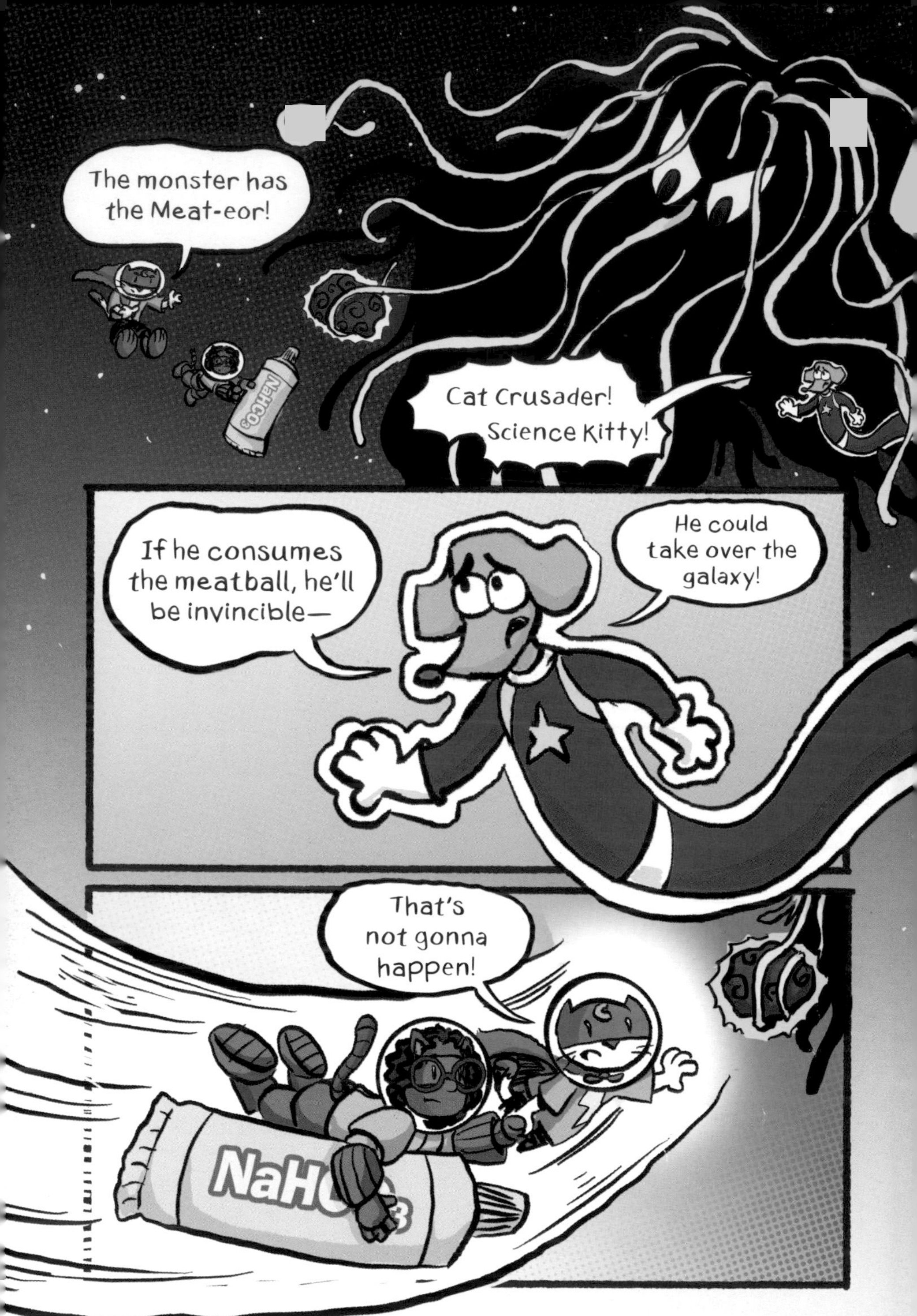
The monster has the Meat-eor!
NaHCO3
Cat Crusader! Science Kitty!
If he consumes the meatball, he'll be invincible—
He could take over the galaxy!
That's not gonna happen!

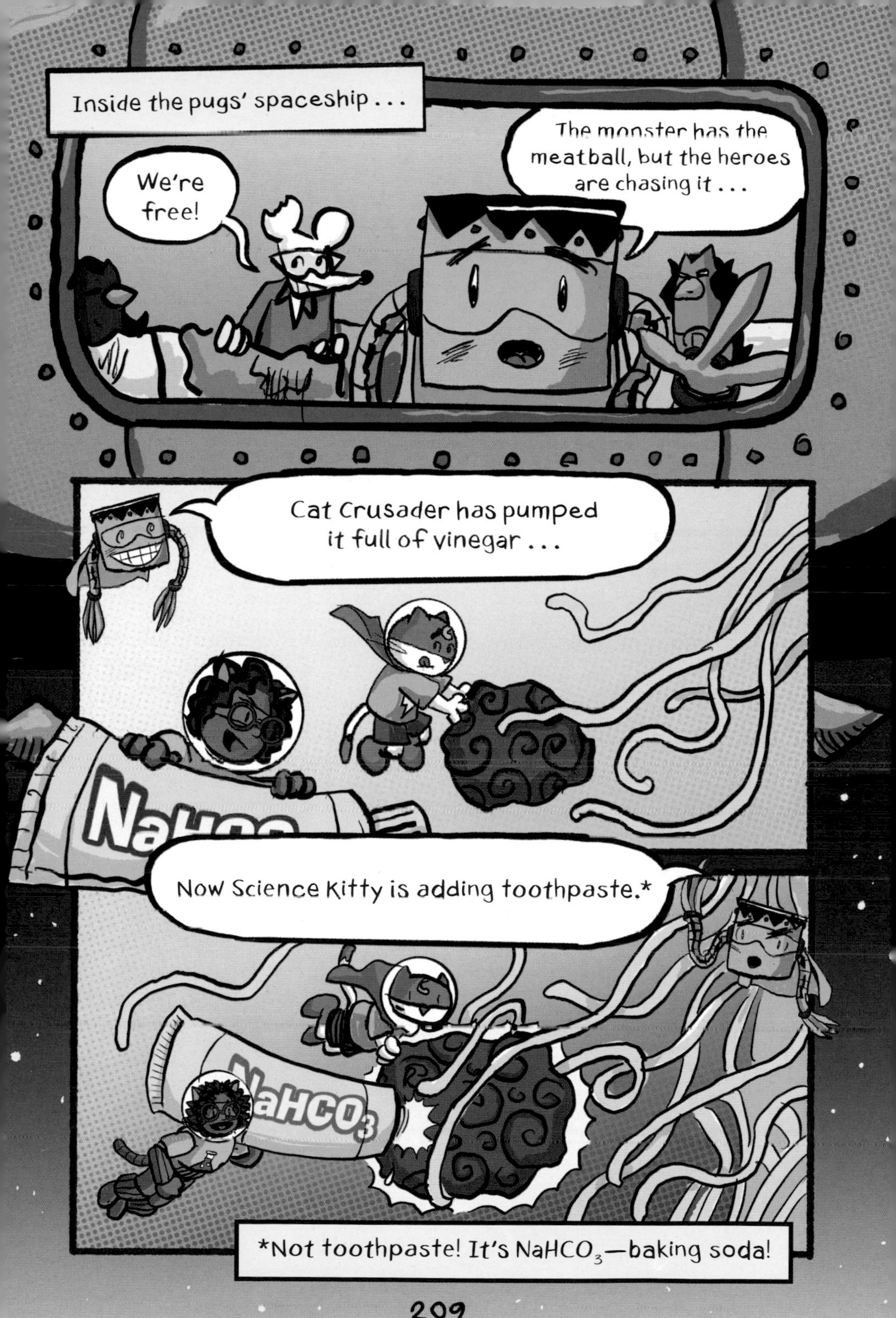
Inside the pugs' spaceship . . .
We're free!
The monster has the meatball, but the heroes are chasing it . . .
Cat Crusader has pumped it full of vinegar . . .
NaHCO
Now Science Kitty is adding toothpaste.*
$NaHCO_3$
*Not toothpaste! It's $NaHCO_3$—baking soda!

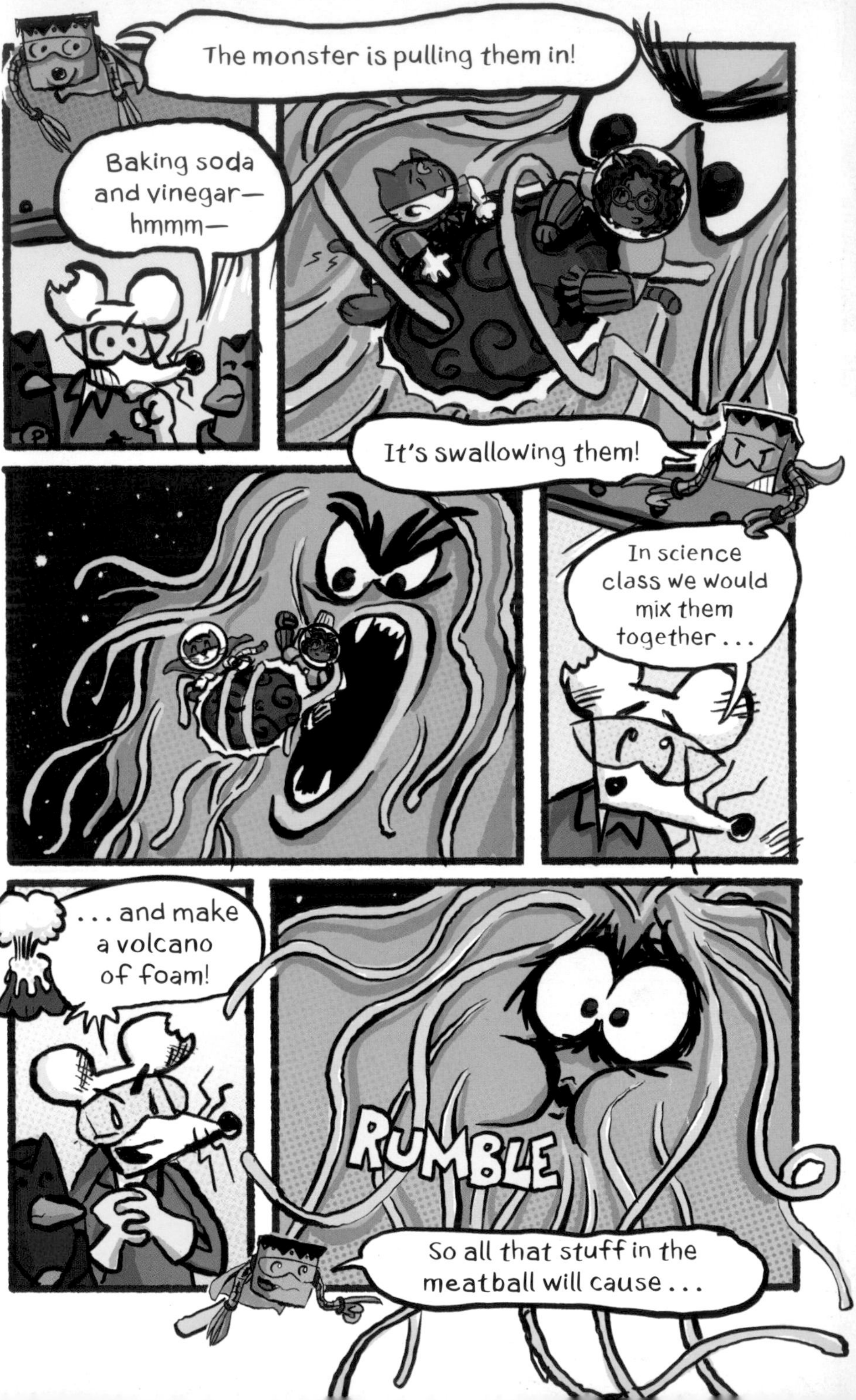
The monster is pulling them in!
Baking soda and vinegar—hmmm—
It's swallowing them!
In science class we would mix them together . . .
. . . and make a volcano of foam!
RUMBLE
So all that stuff in the meatball will cause . . .

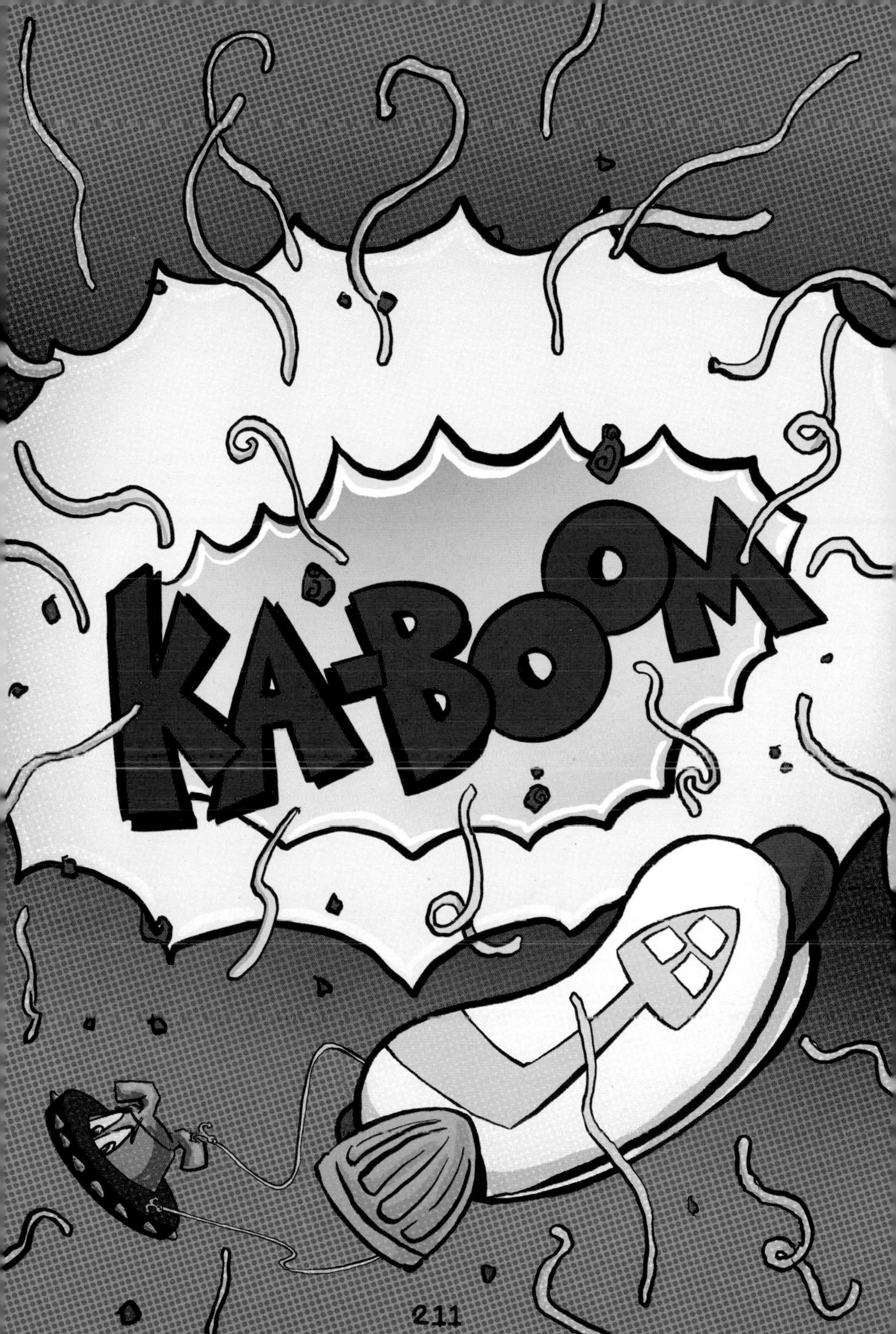
KA-BOOM

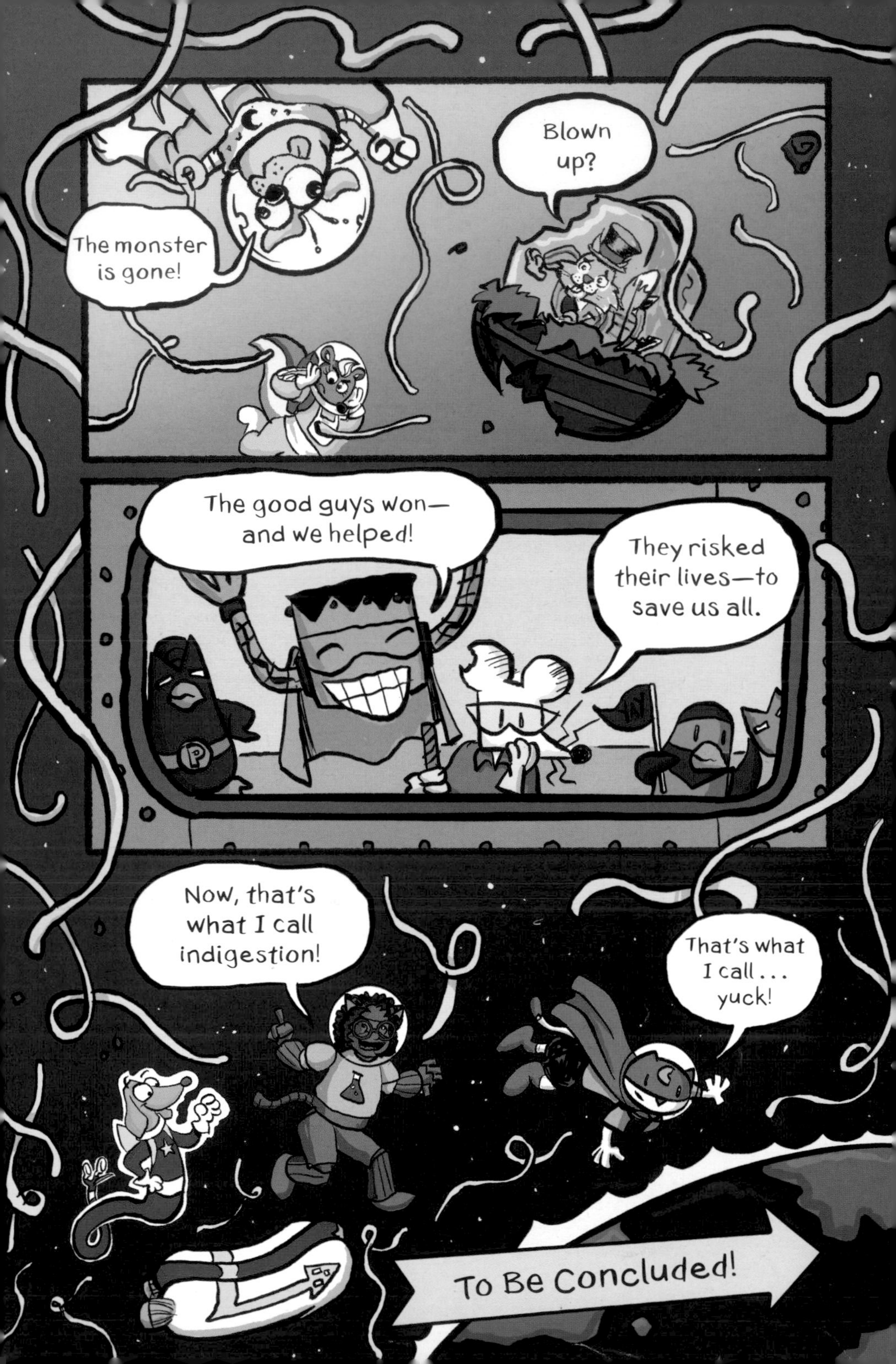

The monster is gone!
Blown up?
The good guys won— and we helped!
They risked their lives—to save us all.
Now, that's what I call indigestion!
That's what I call . . . yuck!
To Be Concluded!

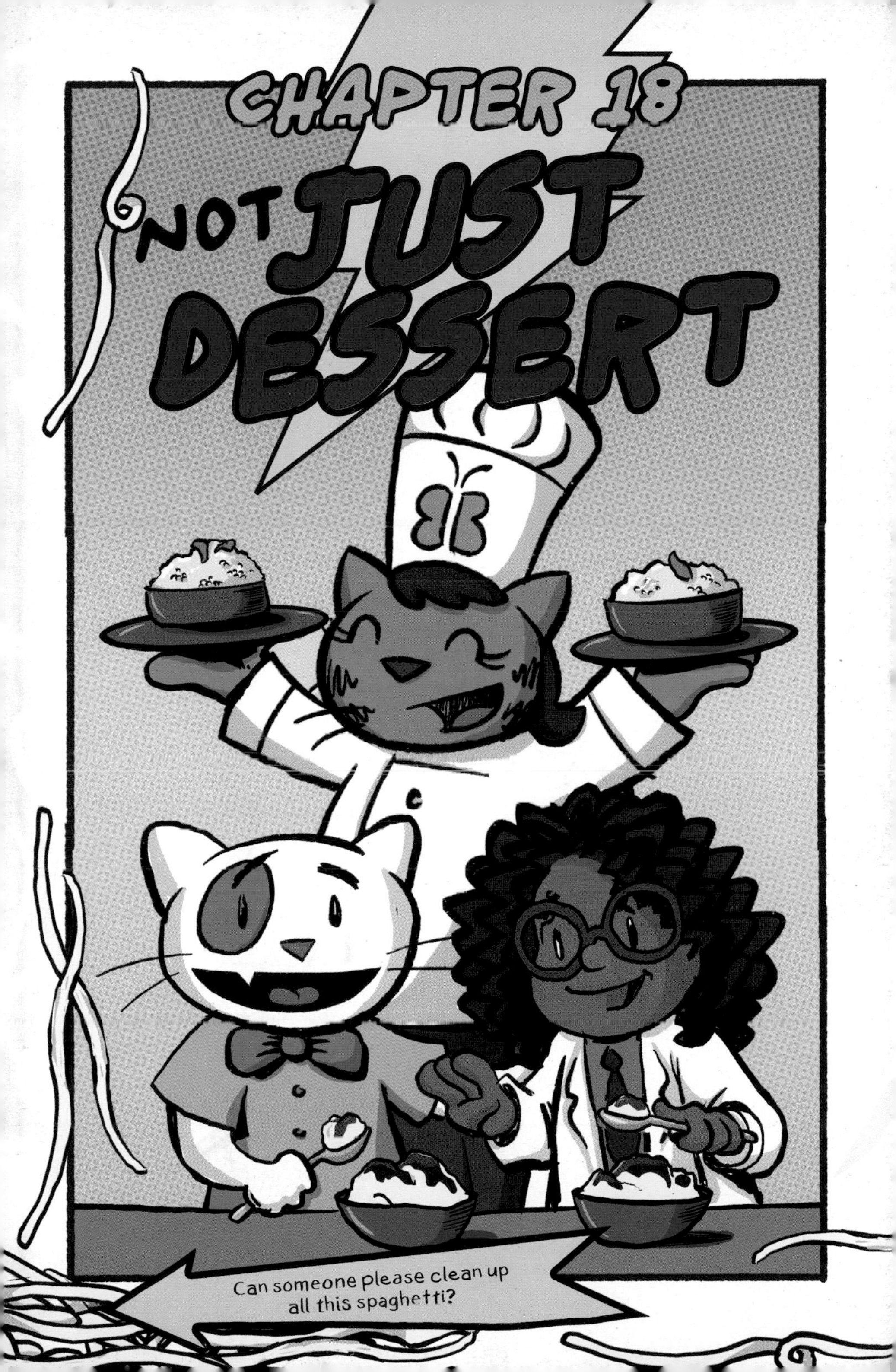

CHAPTER 18
NOT JUST DESSERT
Can someone please clean up all this spaghetti?

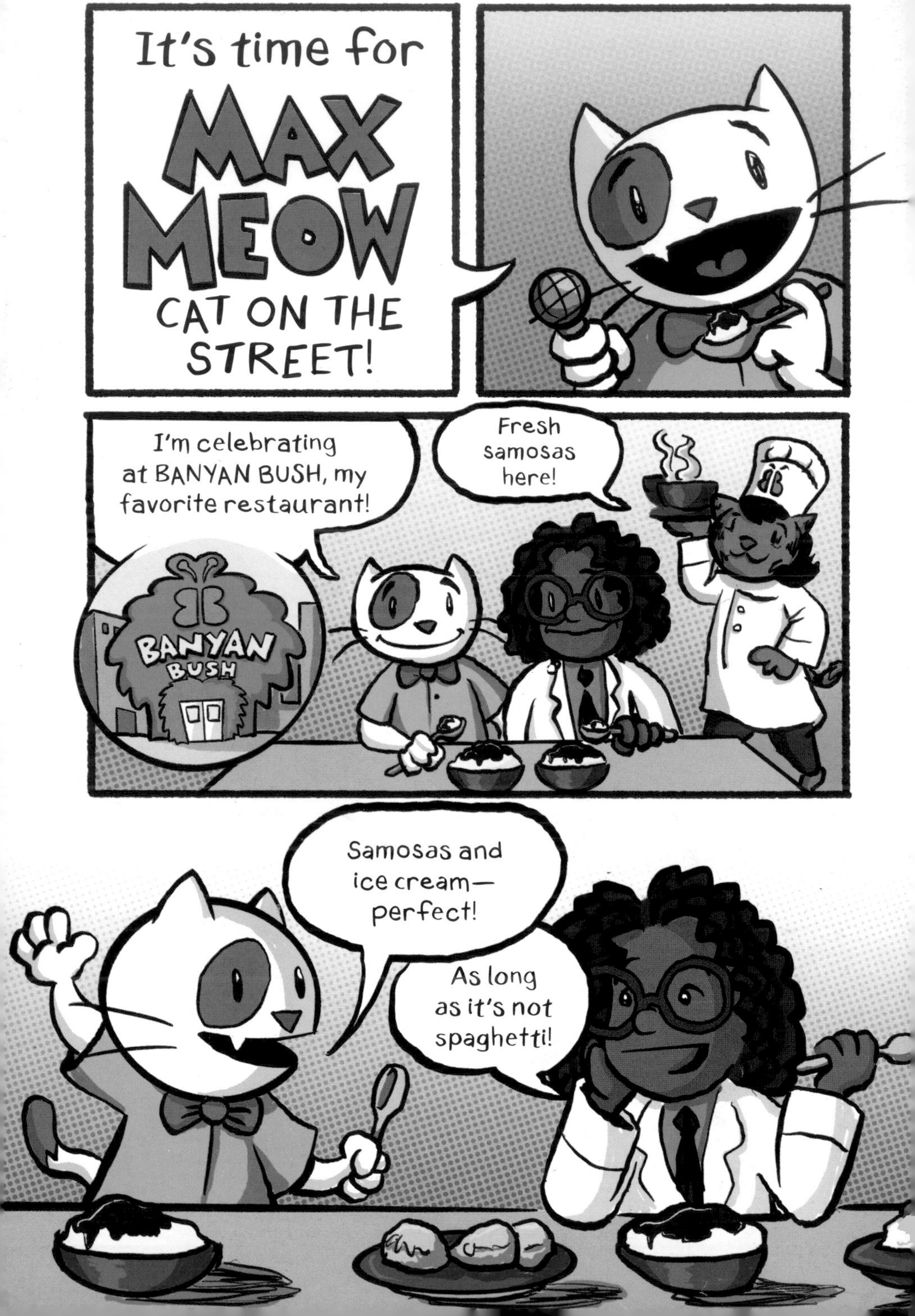
It's time for
MAX MEOW
CAT ON THE STREET!
I'm celebrating at BANYAN BUSH, my favorite restaurant!
Fresh samosas here!
BANYAN BUSH
Samosas and ice cream— perfect!
As long as it's not spaghetti!

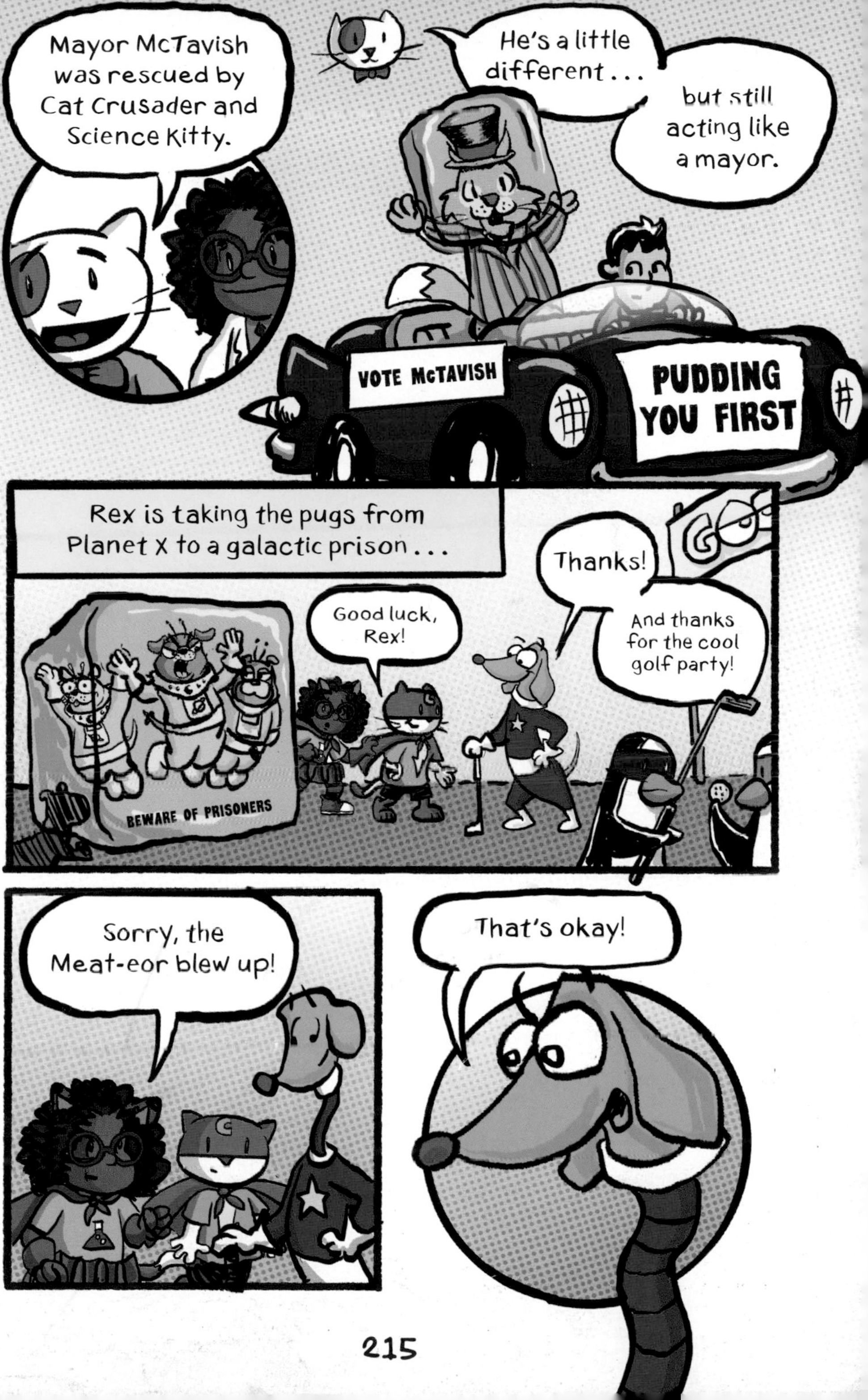
Mayor McTavish was rescued by Cat Crusader and Science Kitty.
He's a little different . . .
but still acting like a mayor.
VOTE McTAVISH
PUDDING YOU FIRST
Rex is taking the pugs from Planet X to a galactic prison . . .
BEWARE OF PRISONERS
Good luck, Rex!
Thanks!
And thanks for the cool golf party!
Sorry, the Meat-eor blew up!
That's okay!

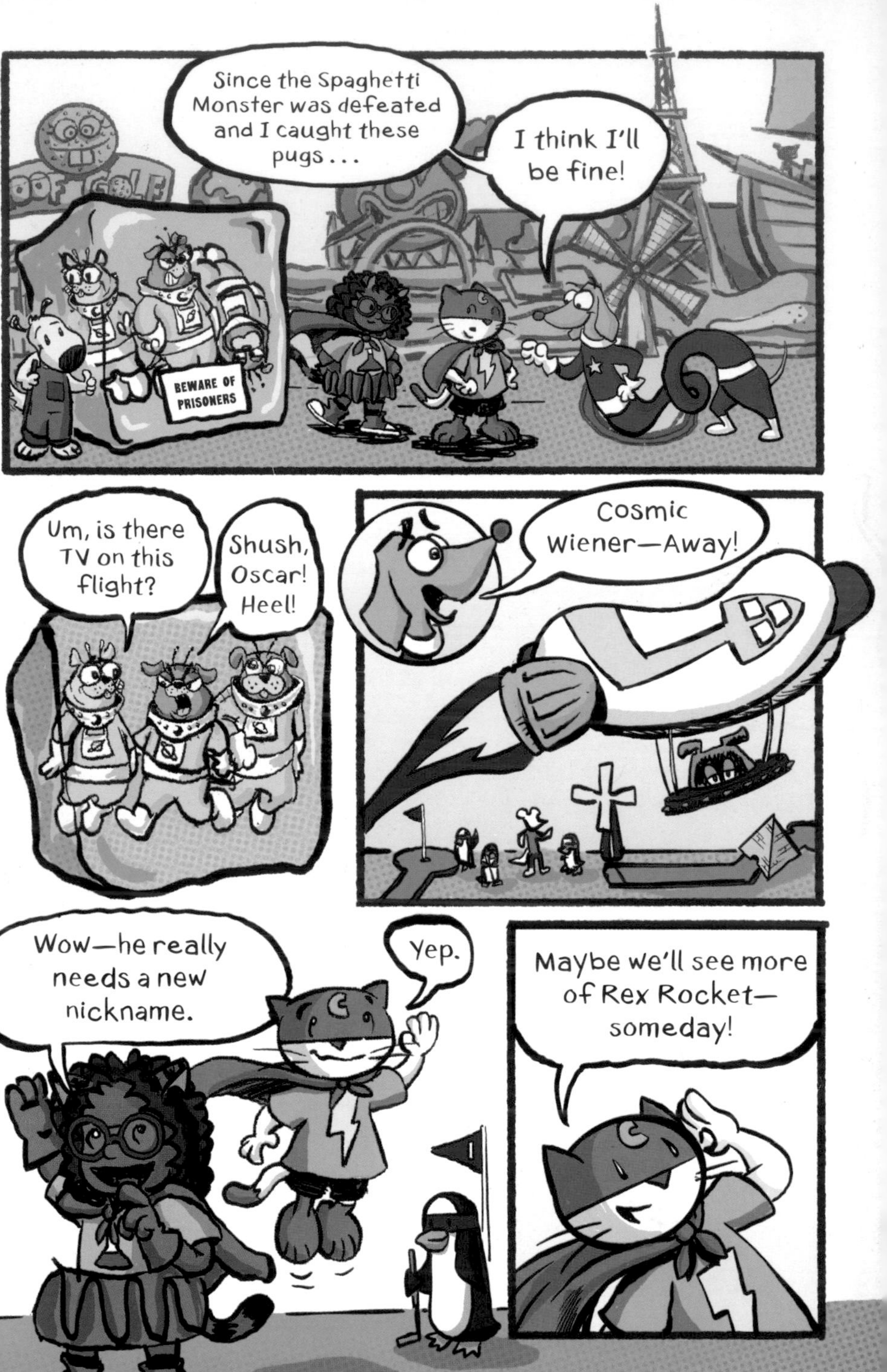
OOF GOLF
BEWARE OF PRISONERS
Since the Spaghetti Monster was defeated and I caught these pugs . . .
I think I'll be fine!
Um, is there TV on this flight?
Shush, Oscar! Heel!
Cosmic Wiener—Away!
Wow—he really needs a new nickname.
Yep.
Maybe we'll see more of Rex Rocket—someday!

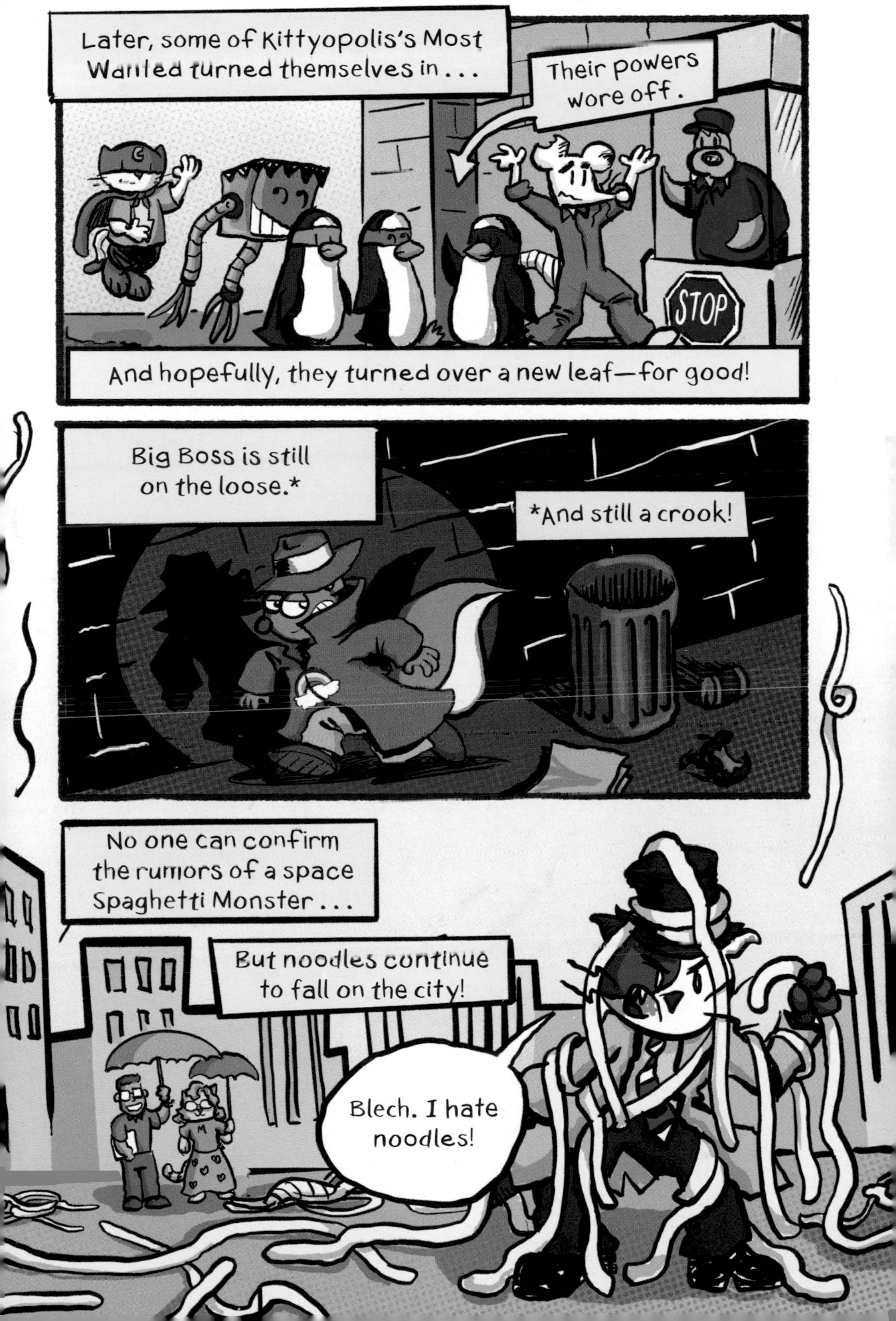
Later, some of Kittyopolis's Most Wanted turned themselves in . . .
Their powers wore off .
STOP
And hopefully, they turned over a new leaf—for good!
Big Boss is still on the loose.*
*And still a crook!
No one can confirm the rumors of a space Spaghetti Monster . . .
But noodles continue to fall on the city!
Blech. I hate noodles!

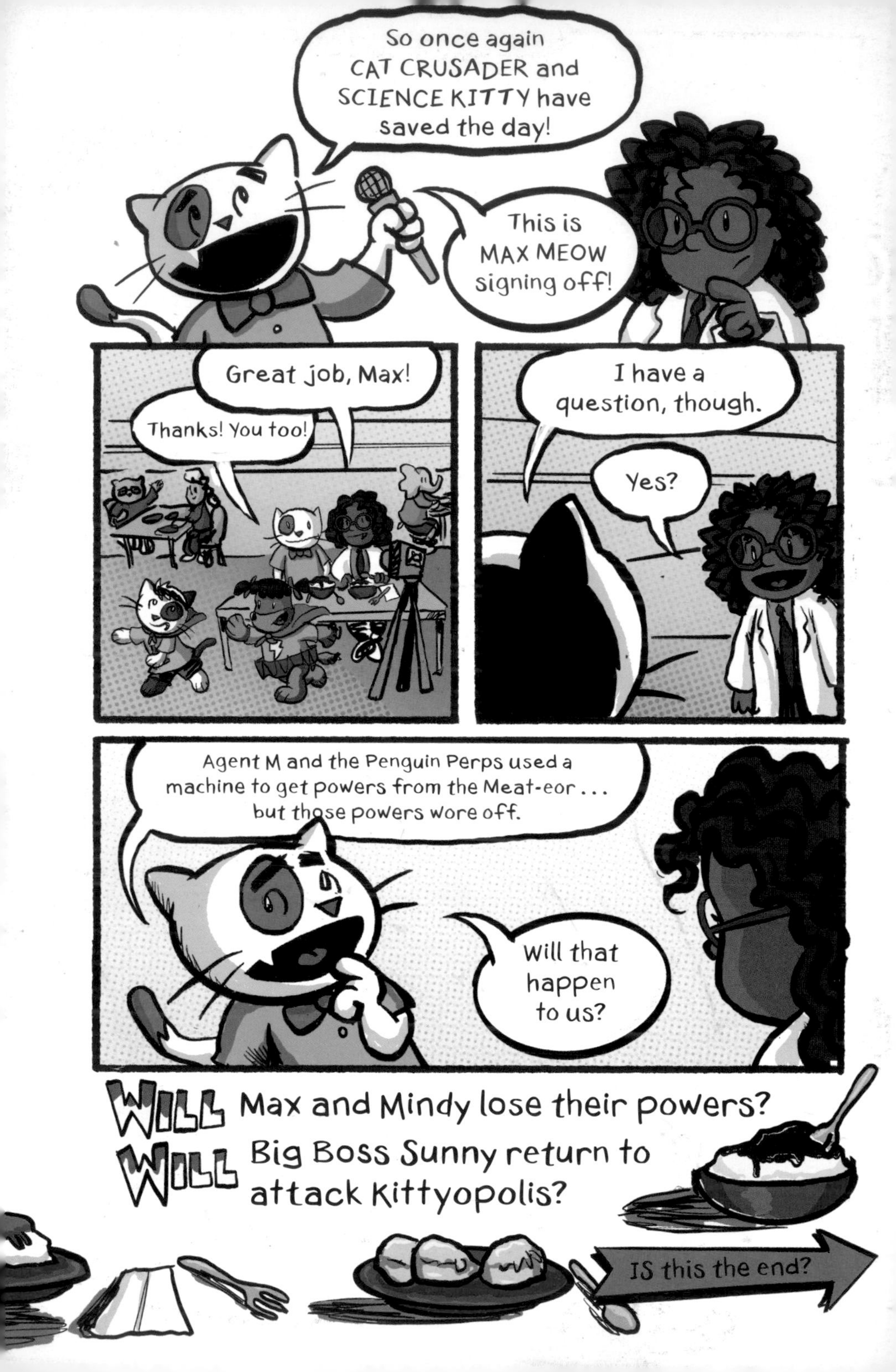
So once again CAT CRUSADER and SCIENCE KITTY have saved the day!
This is MAX MEOW signing off!
Great job, Max!
Thanks! You too!
I have a question, though.
Yes?
Agent M and the Penguin Perps used a machine to get powers from the Meat-eor . . . but those powers wore off.
Will that happen to us?
WILL Max and Mindy lose their powers?
WILL Big Boss Sunny return to attack Kittyopolis?
IS this the end?

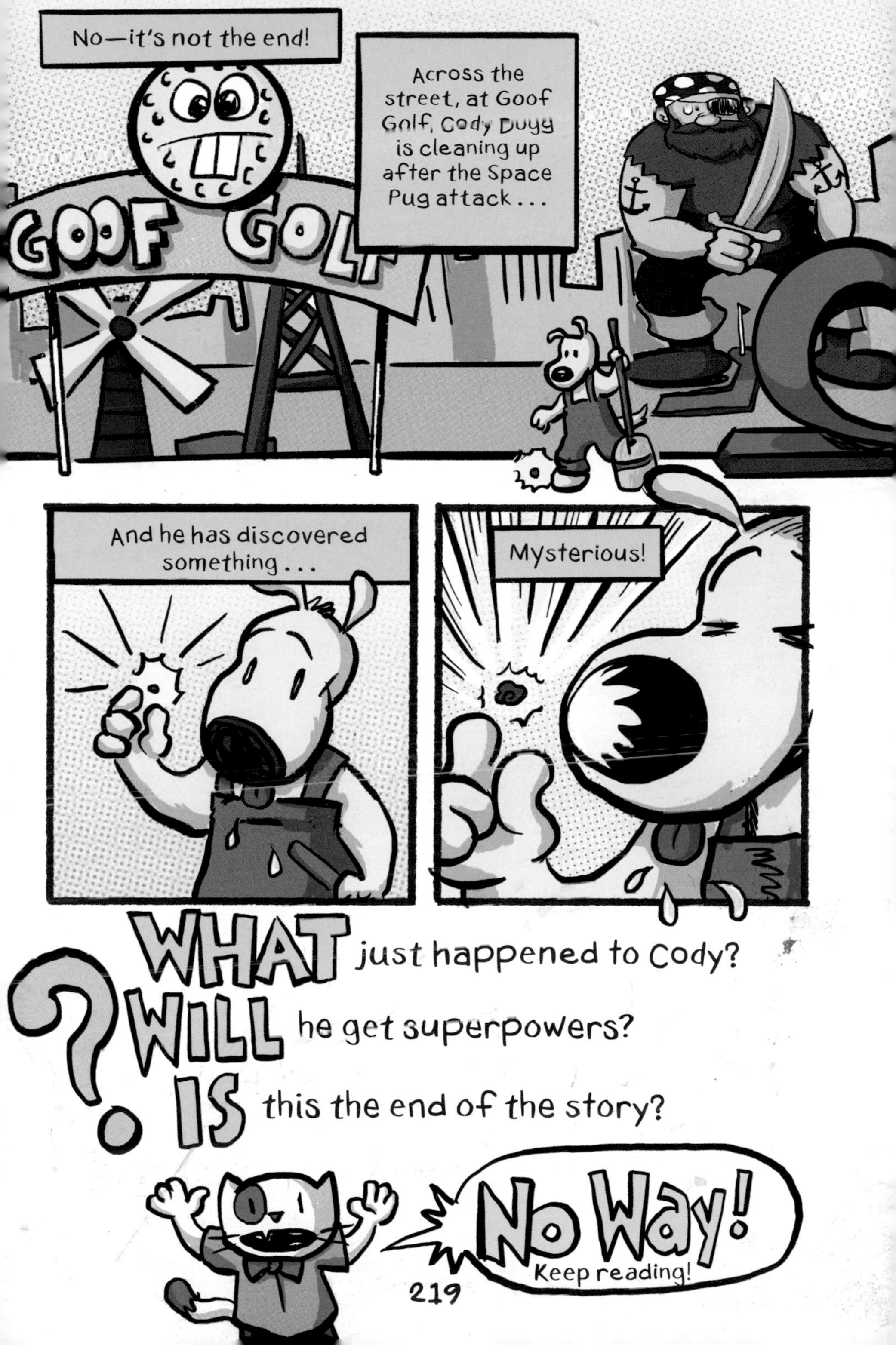
No—it's not the end!
GOOF GOLF
Across the street, at Goof Golf, Cody Dugg is cleaning up after the Space Pug attack . . .
And he has discovered something . . .
Mysterious!
WHAT just happened to Cody?
WILL he get superpowers?
IS this the end of the story?
No Way!
Keep reading!

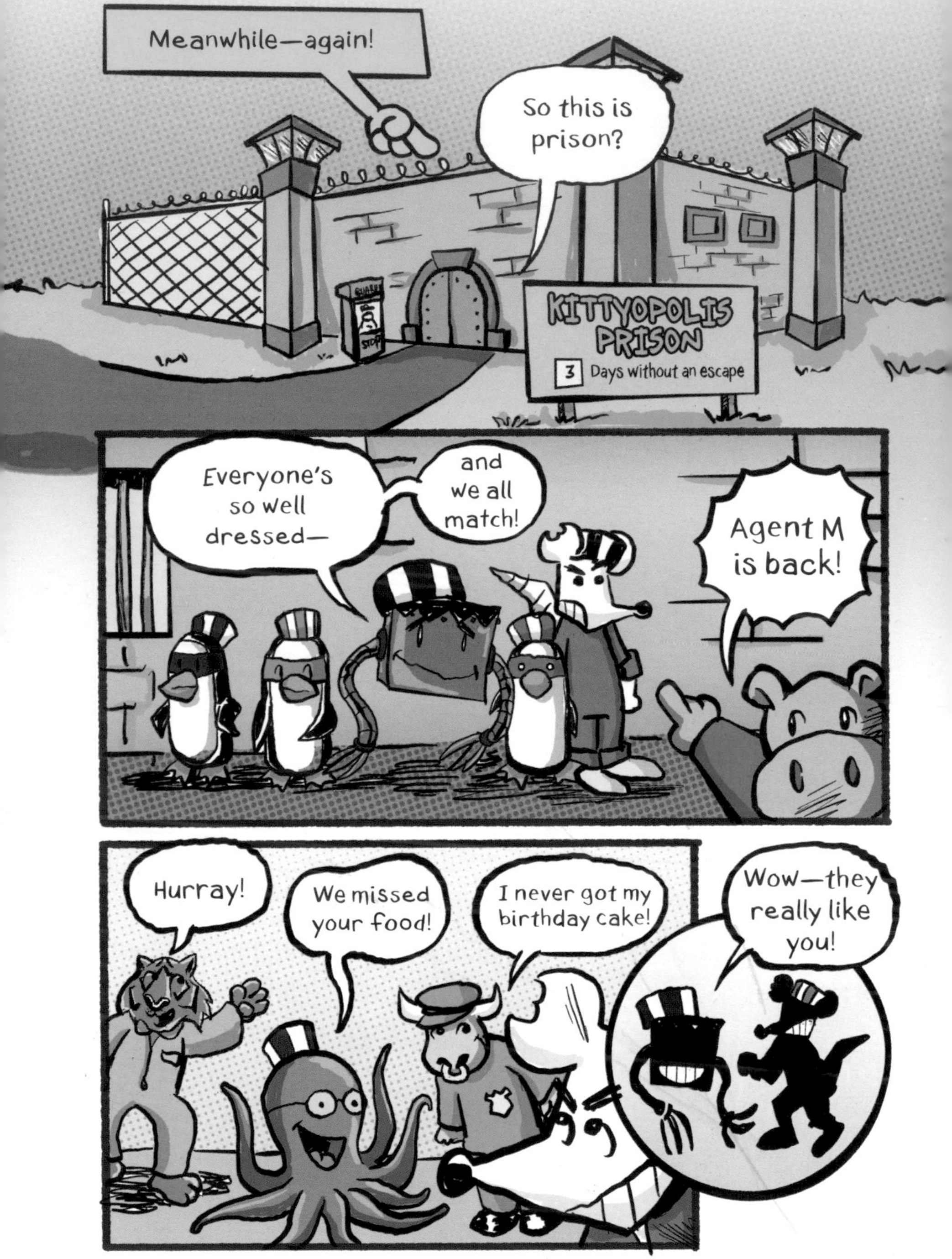

Meanwhile—again!
So this is prison?
KITTYOPOLIS PRISON
3 Days without an escape
Everyone's so well dressed—
and we all match!
Agent M is back!
Hurray!
We missed your food!
I never got my birthday cake!
Wow—they really like you!

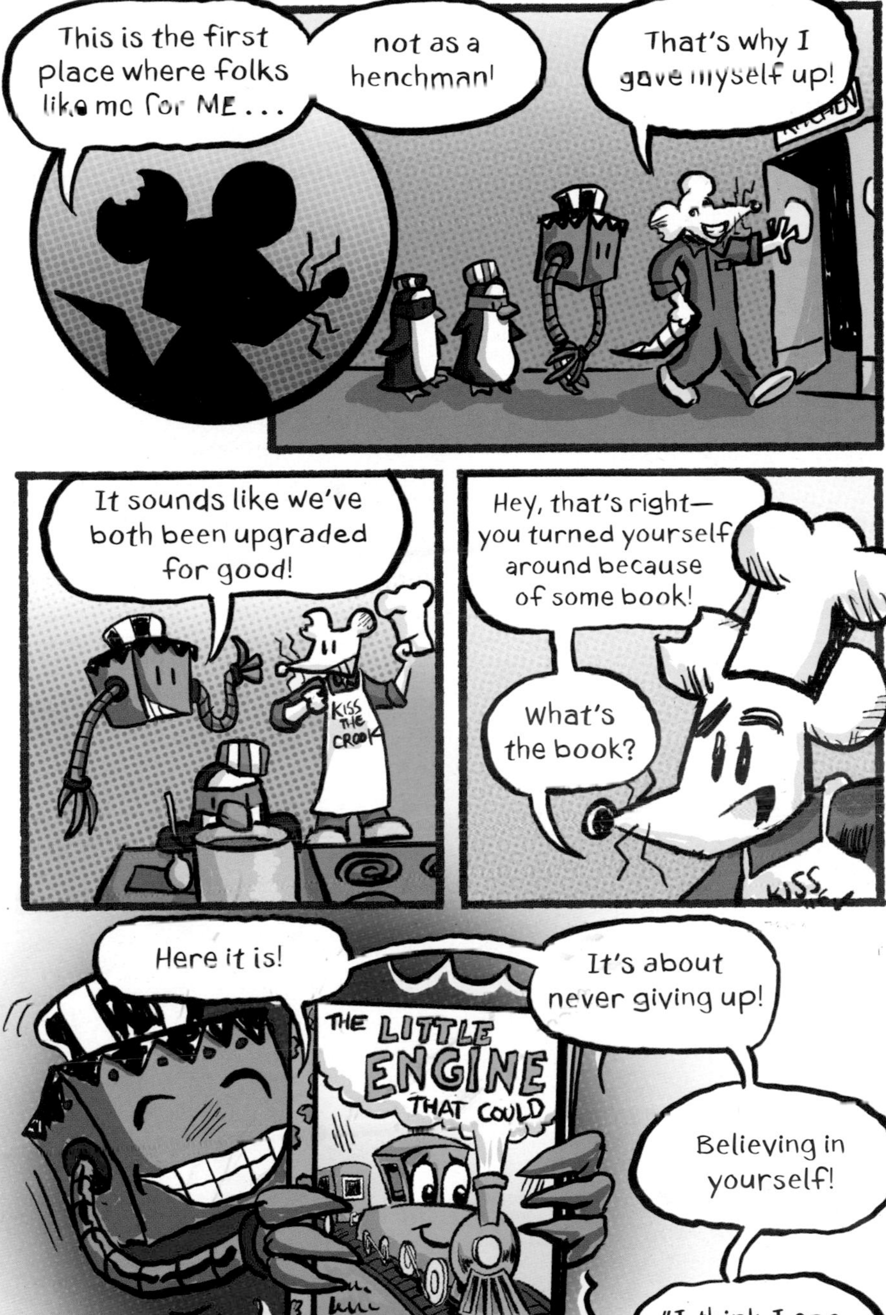
This is the first place where folks like me for ME . . .
not as a henchman!
That's why I gave myself up!
KITCHEN
It sounds like we've both been upgraded for good!
KISS THE CROOK
Hey, that's right—you turned yourself around because of some book!
What's the book?
KISS
Here it is!
It's about never giving up!
THE LITTLE ENGINE THAT COULD
Believing in yourself!
"I think I can, I think I can."

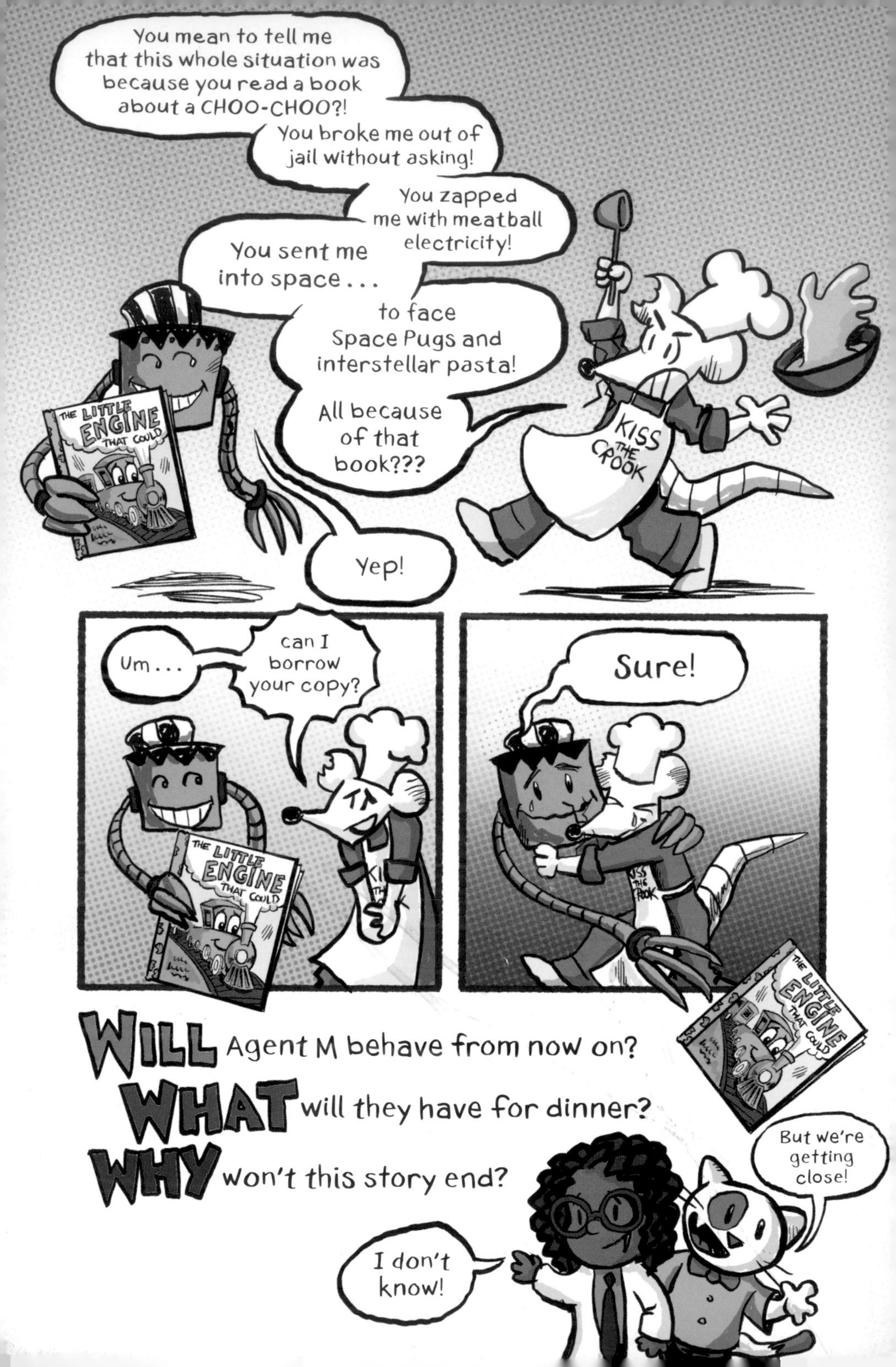
You mean to tell me that this whole situation was because you read a book about a CHOO-CHOO?!
You broke me out of jail without asking!
You zapped me with meatball electricity!
You sent me into space . . .
to face Space Pugs and interstellar pasta!
All because of that book???
Yep!
THE LITTLE ENGINE THAT COULD
KISS THE CROOK
Um . . .
can I borrow your copy?
Sure!
WILL Agent M behave from now on?
WHAT will they have for dinner?
WHY won't this story end?
But we're getting close!
I don't know!

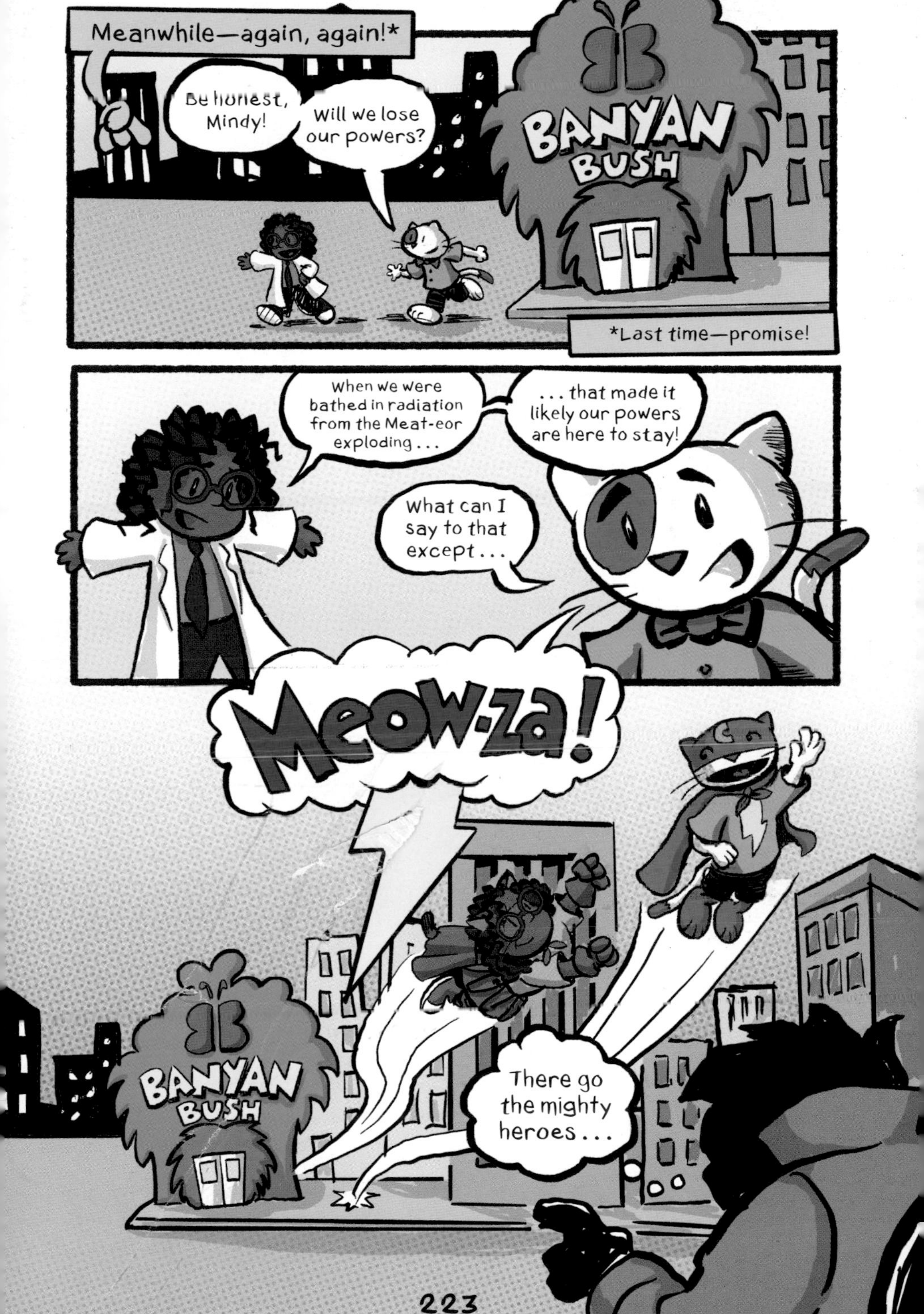
Meanwhile—again, again!*
Be honest, Mindy!
Will we lose our powers?
BANYAN BUSH
*Last time—promise!
When we were bathed in radiation from the Meat-eor exploding . . .
. . . that made it likely our powers are here to stay!
What can I say to that except . . .
Meow-za!
BANYAN BUSH
There go the mighty heroes . . .

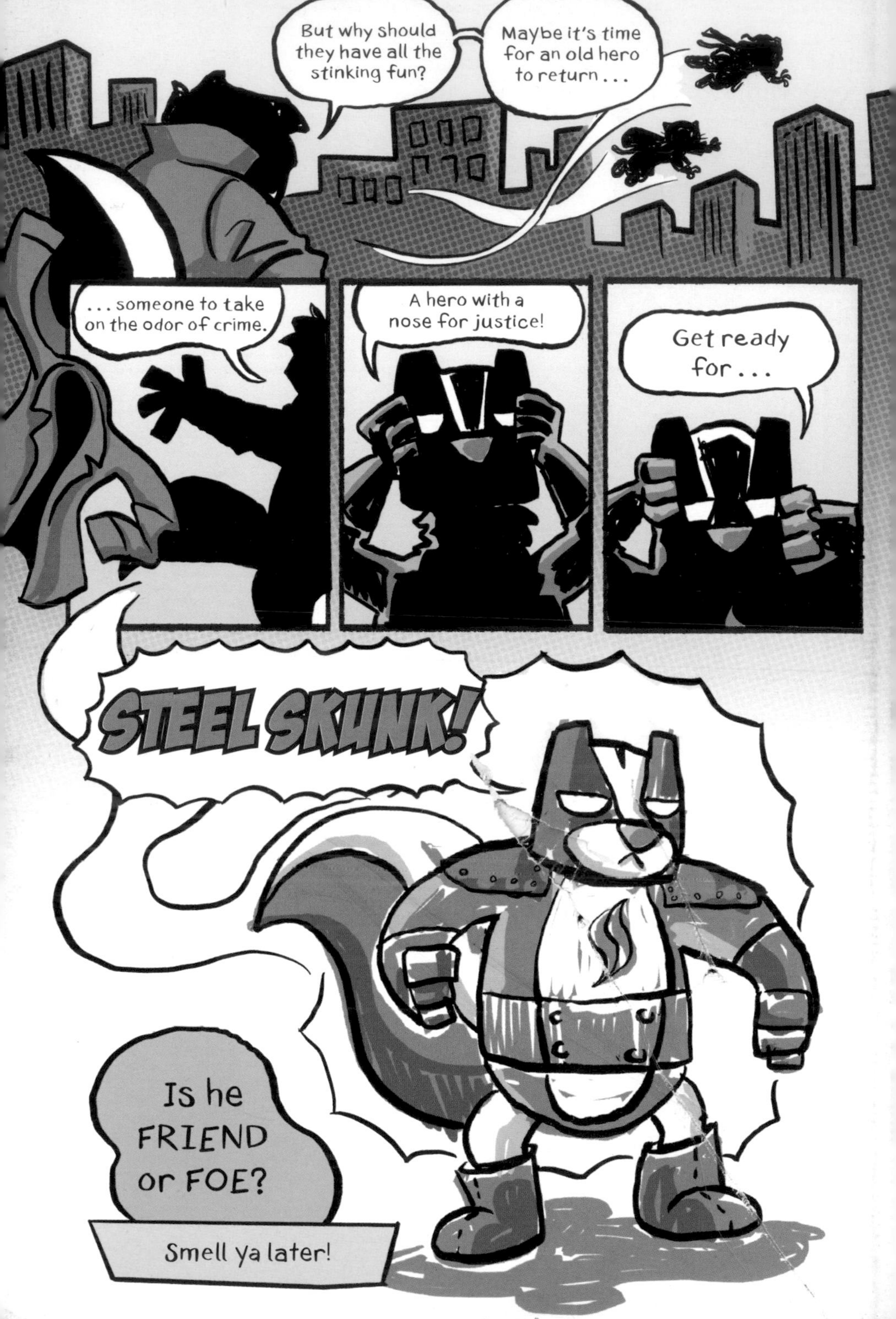

But why should they have all the stinking fun?
Maybe it's time for an old hero to return . . .
. . . someone to take on the odor of crime.
A hero with a nose for justice!
Get ready for . . .
STEEL SKUNK!
Is he FRIEND or FOE?
Smell ya later!

MAX MEOW

Learn to draw Reggie Reboot!

1
2
3
4
5
6
7
8
9
10
11

Now it's your turn!

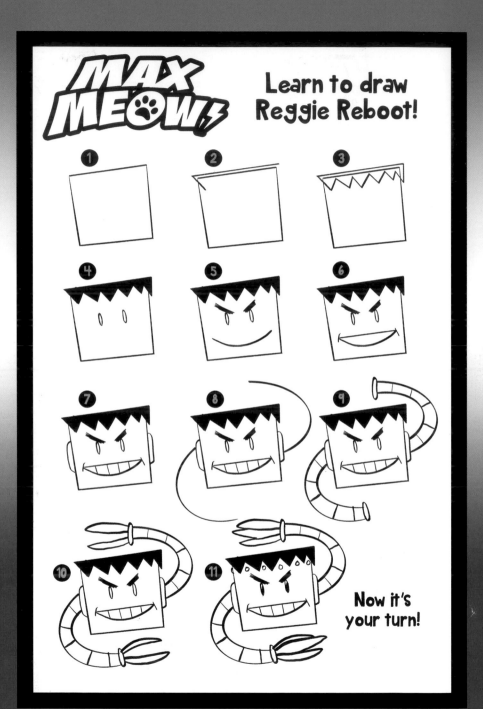

MAX MEOW!

Learn to draw Rex Rocket!

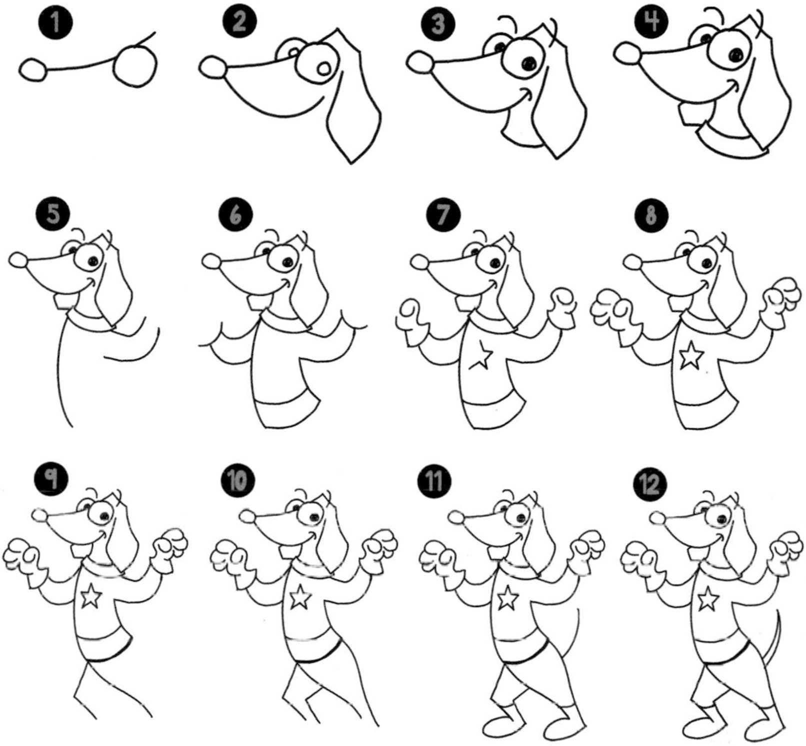
1
2
3
4
5
6
7
8
9
10
11
12

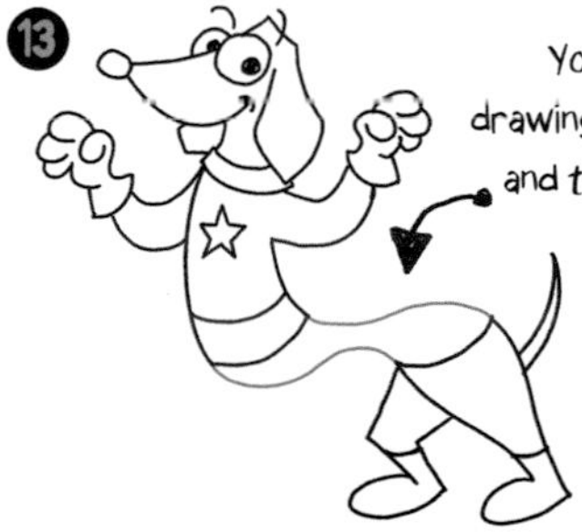
13

You can make Rex stretch by drawing his bottom half farther away and then drawing connecting lines.

Now it's your turn!

ACKNOWLEDGMENTS

PRODUCTION ASSISTANT
J. Robert Deans

ART ASSISTANTS
Sydney Cluff
Chayton Koehler

COLOR AND FLATTING ASSISTANTS
Sydney Cluff
J. Robert Deans
Ryn Gallagher
Giovanni Lucca

SPECIAL THANKS

My wife, Beth, and kids, Katie Ryn, Jack, and Will; my sisters, Ellen and Karen, and brothers, Joe and Robin; the Luccas: Jan, Bill, Rob, Jennie, Blake, and Hayden; my agent, Judith Hansen; my editor, Shana Corey; my art director, April Ward; Max's authenticity reader, Shasta Clinch; and Joel Gori, Jane Magnus, the Beldon Family, the Pinecrest School, Oak View Elementary Comic Class students, and the *Ranger Rick* magazine team. And a tip of the cat ears to John Patrick Green, for coming up with "meat-eor."

And sincere thanks to the teachers, librarians, and booksellers who spark the flames of reading and creativity, and the readers for whom this book was made.

JOHN GALLAGHER has loved comics since he was five. He learned to read through comics and went on to read every book in his elementary school library. When he told his mom there was nothing left to read, she said, "Just because a book's over doesn't mean the *stories* end. Why don't *you* tell me what happens next?" And so John began creating comics to continue his favorite stories. John never stopped drawing comics. He's now the art director of the National Wildlife Federation's *Ranger Rick* magazine and the cofounder of Kids Love Comics, an organization that uses comics and graphic novels to promote literacy. He also leads workshops teaching kids how to create their own comics. John lives in Virginia with his wife and their three kids. Visit him at MaxMeow.com and on social media.

@JohnBGallagher @MaxMeowCatCrusader
@johngallagher_cartoonist

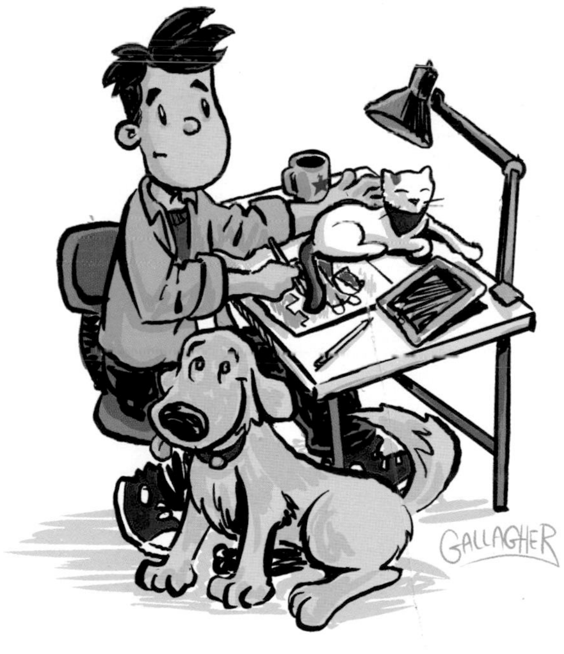
GALLAGHER